THE WIMBLEDON TRILOGY

NIGEL WILLIAMS

The Wimbledon Trilogy

The Wimbledon Poisoner
They Came from SW19
East of Wimbledon

faber and faber

LONDON BOSTON

This open market paperback edition first published in 1995
by Faber and Faber Limited
3 Queen Square London WC1N 3AU

The Wimbledon Poisoner first published in 1990
by Faber and Faber Limited
They Came from SW19 first published in 1992
by Faber and Faber Limited
East of Wimbledon first published in 1993
by Faber and Faber Limited

Phototypeset by Intype, London
Printed in England by Clays Ltd, St Ives plc

A CIP record for this book is
available from the British Library

ISBN 0–571–17633–X

2 4 6 8 10 9 7 5 3 1

Contents

The Wimbledon Poisoner

For Suzan

'It is forbidden to kill; therefore all murderers are punished who kill not in large companies, and to the sound of trumpets.'

Voltaire, *Philosophical Dictionary*

PART ONE

Innocent Enjoyment

'When a felon's not engaged in his employment
Or maturing his felonious little plans,
His capacity for innocent enjoyment,
Is just as great as any honest man's!'

W. S. Gilbert, *Pirates of Penzance*

Henry Farr did not, precisely, decide to murder his wife. It was simply that he could think of no other way of prolonging her absence from him indefinitely.

He had quite often, in the past, when she was being more than usually irritating, had fantasies about her death. She hurtled over cliffs in flaming cars or was brutally murdered on her way to the dry cleaners. But Henry was never actually responsible for the event. He was at the graveside looking mournful and interesting. Or he was coping with his daughter as she roamed the now deserted house, trying not to look as if he was glad to have the extra space. But he was never actually the instigator.

Once he had got the idea of killing her (and at first this fantasy did not seem very different from the reveries in which he wept by her open grave, comforted by young, fashionably dressed women) it took some time to appreciate that this scenario was of quite a different type from the others. It was a dream that could, if he so wished, become reality.

One Friday afternoon in September, he thought about strangling her. The Wimbledon Strangler. He liked that idea. He could see Edgar Lustgarten narrowing his eyes threateningly at the camera, as he paced out the length of Maple Drive. 'But Henry Farr,' Lustgarten was saying, 'with the folly of the criminal, the supreme arrogance of the murderer, had forgotten one vital thing. The shred of fibre that was to send Henry Farr to the gallows was – '

What was he thinking of? They didn't hang people any more. They wrote long, bestselling paperback books about them. Convicted murderers, especially brutal and disgusting ones, were followed around by as many *paparazzi* as the royal family. Their thoughts on life and love and literature were published in Sunday newspapers.

Television documentary-makers asked them, respectfully, about exactly how they felt when they hacked their aged mothers to death or disembowelled a neighbour's child. This was the age of the murderer. And wasn't Edgar Lustgarten dead?

He wouldn't, anyway, be known as the Wimbledon Strangler, but as Henry Farr, cold-blooded psychopath. Or, better still, just Farr, cold-blooded psychopath. Henry liked the idea of being a cold-blooded psychopath. He pictured himself in a cell, as the television cameras rolled. He wouldn't moan and stutter and twitch the way most of these murderers did. He would give a clear, coherent account of how and why he had stabbed, shot, strangled, gassed or electrocuted her. 'Basically,' he would say to the camera, his gestures as urgent and incisive as those of any other citizen laying down the law on television, 'basically I'm a very passionate man. I love and I hate. And when love turns to hate, for me, you know, that's it. I simply had no wish for her to live. I stand by that decision.' Here he would suddenly stare straight into the camera lens in the way he had seen so many politicians do, and say, 'I challenge any red-blooded Englishman who really feels. Who has passion. Not to do the same. When love dies, it dies.'

Hang on. Was he a red-blooded Englishman or a cold-blooded psychopath? Or was he a bit of both? Was it possible to combine the two roles?

Either way, however he did it (and he was becoming increasingly sure that it was a good idea), his life was going to be a lot more fun. Being a convicted murderer had the edge on being a solicitor for Harris, Harris and Overdene of Blackfriars, London. Even Wormwood Scrubs must have more to offer, thought Henry as he rattled the coffee machine on the third floor, than Harris, Harris and Overdene. It wouldn't be so bad, somehow, if he was any good at being a solicitor. But, as Elinor was always telling him, Henry did not inspire confidence as a representative of the legal profession. He had, she maintained, a shifty look about him. 'How could you expect anyone to trust you with their conveyancing?' she had said to him, only last week. 'You look as if you've only just been let out on parole!'

Glumly, Henry carried his coffee along the dark corridor towards the stairs that led to his office. 'Office' was a grandiose term for it really. 'Cupboard' would have been a better description. It was a room about eight to ten feet square, offering, as an estate agent with whom Henry was dealing had put it, 'a superb prospect of a ventilator shaft'. It was, like so many other things in Henry's life, more like a carefully calculated insult from the Almighty than anything else.

He would give himself a treat today. He would go up in the lift. He stabbed angrily at the button. Mr Dent from the third floor, who was waiting by the lift doors, looked at him narrowly. 'Can't you tell – ' his eyes seemed to say, 'that I have already pressed it? Surely you realize that when the button is illuminated someone has pressed it?' Henry, before Dent was able to start talking to him about lifts, weather, the Law Society or any of the other things that Dent usually talked about, headed for the stairs. He pushed open the door and, as he put his foot on the first step, experienced a revelation comparable to that undergone by Newton in the orchard or Archimedes in his bath.

He could kill Elinor, very easily and *no one need know*. The implications of this were absolutely breathtaking. No one need know. He said it aloud to himself as he trudged up the stairs. No one need know. Of course. No one need know. Every minute of every day people were being murdered. Hundreds of people disappeared without trace every year. No one ever found them. The police were all, as far as Henry could see, totally incompetent. They spent their time hiding behind low stone walls and leaping out at motorists travelling in bus lanes. They liked people like Henry. People like Henry, white middle-aged men who lived in Wimbledon and had one daughter, were their idea of what British citizens should be. One young constable had come to the house last year when they had been burgled and, very laboriously, had written the details of the crime into a book. He had looked, Henry thought, like a gigantic blue infant, a curious cross between cunning and *naïveté*, a representative of an England that was as dead as the gold standard. Henry had tried to tempt him into making a racist statement by announcing that he had seen a black person outside the window two weeks ago, but all the constable had said was 'You don't see many coloureds in this part of Wimbledon.' He said this almost with regret, in the tones of a disappointed birdwatcher searching for the great crested grebe.

Nobody would ever suspect Henry. Because – he was well aware – most people thought he was something called a Nice Bloke. Henry was never quite sure what being a nice bloke entailed – it certainly wasn't much to do with behaving scrupulously well towards one's fellow man. If it meant anything at all it probably meant other people thought you were a bit like them. To most of those who knew him Henry was just eccentric enough to be terrifyingly normal, and even his carefully calculated bitterness, the quality of which, on the whole, he was most proud, had become, in early middle age, a Nice Dry Sense of Humour.

I'll give them nice dry sense of humour, he thought savagely as he came out on to his floor and lumbered towards room 4038, I'll give them nice dry sense of humour and then some. I'll give them the real Henry Farr, and he won't just be making witty little remarks about the London orbital motorway either.

Of all Elinor's friends he was the least likely to be suspected of her murder. She had, even at their wedding, surrounded herself with people, nearly all of whom were interesting enough to warrant the close scrutiny of the police. Many of them, to Henry's horror, openly smoked drugs. One of them wore a kaftan. Two wore sandals. And they still trooped in and out of his house occasionally, looking at him pityingly, as they talked of foreign films, the latest play at the Royal Court and the need for the immediate withdrawal of armed forces from Nicaragua. Sometimes they sat in the front room reading aloud from the work of a man called Ian McEwan, an author who, according to Elinor, had 'a great deal to say' to Henry Farr.

Oh yeah, thought Henry grimly as he passed 4021a, his coffee threshing around dangerously in its plastic beaker, and Henry Farr had a great deal to say to Ian McEwan as well.

The trouble was, of course, that among Henry's sort of person, a rugby-playing surveyor, for example, or the kind of dentist like David Sprott who wasn't afraid to get up on his hind legs at a social gathering and talk, seriously and at length, about teeth, he was considered something of a subversive. At their wedding, all those years ago, his friends, all of them even then in suits and ties, had nudged each other when he rose to answer his best man. 'Go on then,' he could see them thinking, 'be a devil!' But as his eyes travelled across to Elinor's crowd, with their frizzy haloes of hair, their flowered dresses and carefully arranged profiles, he realized that there was nothing he could think of to say that would persuade them he was anything other than a boring little man.

But there were certain advantages in being considered boring. And if they wanted him to be boring then that would be the performance that he would offer. He would be so stunningly boring that even the bankers, account executives, product managers and stockbrokers he counted as his friends would start to back away from him. He would play up to Elinor's friends' idea of what he was. He would play the part of the upright citizen, the dull wounded little man whose horizons were bounded by the daily journey to the office, the suburban garden and the suburban sky, set around with suburban roofs and neat suburban trees. He cut a little caper as he walked along the corridor that led to his office, recovering a quality that had suddenly become important to him – his drabness. He would be drab. Drab drab drab drab. He would be as drab as Crewe railway station. As drab as a not very important mayor. He would blend into Wimbledon until he was indistinguishable from the trees, the homing children, the lollipop ladies, or the gables on the red brick houses.

And they would never, never find out that he had done it.

When he came into the office, past Selinda his secretary, an elderly woman who was constantly asking him to give her 'something interesting to do' (How could he? Henry himself never had anything interesting to do), he squeezed close to the wall and coughed to himself in an extra drab way. He left his office door opened and, for the next hour, treated her to a stunningly drab conversation about the searches on a leasehold flat in Esher. When she put her head round the door and asked in her usual, conspiratorial manner if he wanted tea, Henry said, 'Tea would be a delight, my dear!' He said this in a high-pitched monotone that was intended to convey boringness; he was, however, he could tell from Selinda's expression, trying a little too hard.

He pulled out a correspondence file between a landlord and tenant in Ruislip – nearly eighty pages devoted to conflict over responsibility for a dustbin area – and tried to concentrate. How was he going to do it?

Murder should not, he felt, be unnecessarily complicated. It should have a clean, aesthetic line to it. It should involve as few people as possible. Oneself and the victim. If it was like anything, thought Henry, it was probably like the art of eating out.

His first thought was to do something to the Volkswagen Passat. That would have the advantage of getting rid of both car and wife at the same time. If there was anything that Henry hated as much as his wife, it was the car they had chosen and purchased together. He had hated the little brochure that described it – the pathetic attempt to make it look glamorous, the photographs of it, posed, doors open, doors shut, desperately trying not to look like what it was – a square box with hideous speckled seats. The Volkswagen Passat was about as glamorous as a visit to the supermarket, which was what it was principally used for. The people in the photographs in the brochure – a man, his wife, his two children and his stupid, stupid luggage, his folding chairs, his folding table, his hamper, his sensible suitcase packed for his sensible holiday – were exactly how Henry imagined the advertisers thought of him. A man called Frobisher-Zigtermans – a person who insisted on not remaining anonymous during the transaction – had described it as 'all car'. 'It's all car!' he had said. 'I'll say that for it!' And, as Henry smiled and nodded damply, he thought to himself, Is that all you can find to say about it? 'It's all car.' Can't you talk about its roadholding? Its incredible power over women? You can't, can you? Because you think I wouldn't respond. Because you think I'm as boring as this car. Which is why I'm buying it.

Just thinking about his car made Henry want to hire an electric hammer and run with all convenient speed to Wimbledon, to fall upon its bodywork with screams of rage.

He would saw through the brake cable. Not right through. Almost through. He would do it tonight, Friday, just in time for the weekly trip to the supermarket. Elinor would turn left up Maple Drive, left again into Belvedere Road, left again on to the hill . . . and then . . . oh then . . .

Except she didn't go to the supermarket, did she? He did. Which was one of the many reasons, now he thought about it, why he was planning to kill her. How did one saw through a brake cable anyway? It was no good chopping the thing in half, was it? Your victim would catch on before accelerating to a speed likely to be fatal. You had to saw it halfway through, didn't you? Henry wondered where the brake cable was, what it looked like, whether it was the kind of thing to which you could take a saw. The trouble with this sawing-halfway-through lark was that you had no control over where and when the thing was likely to break. Christ, it might even be when he was driving! Even if she was sitting next to him, complaining about his driving, her own imminent decease would not compensate for the depression generated by his own. Ideally, of course, Elinor would be driving her mother somewhere. Somewhere a little more interesting than Wimbledon Hill. Somewhere, well, steeper . . .

Henry sat for quite a long time thinking about the conversation between Elinor and her mother as they hurtled down the Paso della Lagastrella, brakeless. 'Darling, *do* something!' 'I'm *doing* something, darling!' 'Oh darling, we're going to die, oh my *God*!' 'I *know* we're going to die it's not my fault, oh my *God*!' He thought about the soaring, almost optimistic leap the Volkswagen would make as it cleared the edge of the cliff (from Henry's memory of it there was no safety barrier on that particular stretch of the Apennines). He thought about the long, long fall and then the flames, way below. About the immense difficulty that would undoubtedly be experienced by rescue teams.

It was five twenty-nine and fifteen seconds. In just forty-five seconds he would get up from his desk, take his coat and walk past his secretary. He would say 'Goodnight all' (although she would be the only other person in the room), and then he would take the lift down to the chilly autumn street and Blackfriars station, all soot and sickly neon. And from there he would rattle back to Wimbledon and his wife of twenty years.

Henry sat in his chair as the seconds ticked away. But when the large hand of his watch passed the twelve, he did not move. He sat and stared at the desk in front of him, the creamy whorls in the wood, the tanned grain. And he thought about the endless mystery of objects.

2

It was dark by the time Henry reached home. The lights were on in all the houses up Maple Drive. At number 23 the Indian was seated, motionless, in his bay window. On the top floor of 32, Mrs Mackintosh stared nervously out at the dark street. Mrs Mackintosh had Alzheimer's disease. 'Has my husband gone out now?' the expression on her face seemed to say. 'Or is he due back at any moment? Or perhaps he's here somewhere in the house, lurking behind a chest of drawers, waiting to spring out at me.' Only last week she had told Henry (who had lived in Maple Drive for twelve years) that she wished to welcome him to the neighbourhood. On Wednesdays she was driven by her sister to something called the Memory Clinic, where Henry imagined some ghastly psychiatric version of Kim's Game being played. Not that Henry's memory was getting any better. Only the other day . . . Only the other day what? . . .

At 49 all the curtains were drawn and at 51 Mrs Archer had left the front door open, perhaps in the hope that Mr Archer would return. Mr Archer had left her four years ago for a married man with a beard who lived, people said, in Shepherds Bush.

In his own house the curtains were open, the light was on and he could see a young girl with a pigtail, seated at the piano. She was playing 'Für Elise', very, very slowly and cautiously. Next to her was a woman with long black hair, a stubby nose and the kind of jaw found on actors playing responsible sheriffs in cowboy films. As the girl played the woman dilated her nostrils and rose slightly off the piano stool, as if someone was drawing her up by an invisible wire attached to the crown of her head. When the child reached the bottom of the first page the woman darted forward, black hair swinging across her face, for the kind of effortful page turn that would have upstaged Paderewski himself. 'Behold!' the gesture seemed to say. 'I turn the page!' The child struggled gamely on to page two but seemed to suspect that, after a page turn of this quality, anything else was liable to be an anti-climax.

Henry watched the woman for some time. Her broad shoulders. The determined set of her upper torso. Her grim concentration on her child's performance. Mrs Elinor Farr. The mother of his child.

Should he, perhaps, push her off a cliff? They could go down to Beachy Head. Wander along the edge of the cliff. Some remark, along the lines of 'Oooh look! Over there, dear!' And then a smart shove in the small of the back.

But how to persuade her to go to Beachy Head? Let alone to stand near the edge of a cliff. And suppose, as she fell, she clutched on to him? Or, suspecting what was up, dodged smartly to one side when Henry made his move? Henry saw himself in the air, high above the sea and the shingle, spread out like a starfish, Elinor above him, cackling wildly.

She was going to be difficult to kill, no question about it, thought Henry. She had that dogged look about her. Sighing, he let his key into the lock. His daughter was see-sawing, inelegantly, between E natural and D sharp. Maisie had managed, somehow, to make Beethoven's tune sound like a tired police siren; when it dropped a fourth to B natural she paused, fractionally, before playing the note; it sounded, as a result, like a burp or a fart. At the cadenza, she stumbled down the keyboard with something that had elements of a flourish but ended up sounding more like a digital coronary, an awful, shaming collapse of the fingers that, at the last minute, recovered itself and looked as if it might turn into something like the chord of A minor. Such was not its destiny. As Henry removed his coat and set his briefcase down, Maisie's fingers, like demented spiders in a bath, ran this way and that, in any direction, it seemed, that might lead them away from the wistful logic of the melody. All Mrs Craxton's pencilled annotations on the manuscript (*Sudden drop!! Fingering here, Maisie!!!*), all of O. Thurmer's revisions, phrases and fingering, all four hundred and sixteen poundsworth of tutorials suddenly slipped away and Maisie Farr hammered the keys of the piano like a gorilla on amphetamines.

Henry paused on his way upstairs. He loved music. Why was Elinor in charge of Maisie's piano lessons?

He had never really been allowed near his daughter. She had been presented to him, rather in the way she had been presented to her mother, ten years ago, by a Jamaican midwife, in Queen Mary's Hospital, Roehampton. Served up, thought Henry, and not always graciously. Sometimes she was served up garnished with prizes, a certificate of excellence in swimming or a merit card from a teacher, but more often than not she was slapped down in front of him like a British Rail sandwich, garnished with a series of medical complaints. 'She needs grommets!' Elinor would squawk, pointing at her daughter in the gloom of the kitchen. Or else, 'Her chest! Listen to her chest, Henry! It's awful! Listen to it!' And Maisie would stand like some artist's model, exhibiting her diseases as if they were her only claim on him.

Perhaps a few blows to the side of the head with an axe? Or an electric fire tipped into the bath one afternoon? Henry liked the idea of his wife dying in bath gear. The thought of her twitching her last in a plastic hat, face covered with green mud, carried him through to their bedroom (a room Elinor had taken to calling 'my' bedroom) and shored him up against Maisie's rendition of the second subject in 'Für Elise'. F major did not help her any, he reflected, as he struggled out of his ridiculous businessman's shoes.

The trouble was, all these methods were now the staple diet of Radio 4 plays. Just as cliché haunted Henry's daily journey to the train, his socks from Marks and Spencer's, his regular nightly bedtime, his fondness for a cup of tea at ten thirty in the evening, just as he seemed to be destined to be as remorselessly English as the plane trees in the street outside or the homecoming commuters clacking through the twilight towards the village, so his one existential act (hadn't someone called it that?) seemed destined for suburban predictability. Why couldn't he roast her in oil? Hurl her into a pit of snakes? Inject her with a rare South American pois –

The word 'poison' had scarcely formed itself in his mind before

Henry knew, with the sweet certainty that accompanies most forms of conquest, that he had found his *métier*. He wasn't, clearly, the Mad Axeman of SW23. He was not, could not be the Southfields Strangler or the Rapist of Raynes Park. But the Wimbledon Poisoner! He stood up, walked across to the mirror and there studied his reflection. Then he said, aloud – 'The Wimbledon Poisoner'. First ideas were always the best. He removed his jacket, trousers, shirt, tie and underclothes and studied himself in the mirror. A fat man of forty with an improbably long penis and a dense mass of wiry pubic hair. A face, as Elinor was often telling him, like a deviant grocer's. A few thin strands of black to grey hair and a nose that looked like badly applied putty. An out-of-date Englishman.

At the thought of the word 'Englishman' Henry stiffened to attention. He straightened his shoulders (straightened one of them anyway. It seemed to be impossible to straighten both at the same time) and thrust out his chest. Don't be down! There was some go in him yet! By stealth and devotion to his craft he might yet give something back to the class and the country that produced Crippen. What did England produce now, by way of criminals? Louts who could go no further than ill-thought-out violence on street corners. Where were the classic murders that had once held the attention of the world? The patient, domestic acts performed in this country of fogs and mists that had made English murderers the doyens of the civilized globe. These days, the average Brit's idea of a crime was a drunken assault on a Pakistani grocer. He would do it, and he would do it slowly, exquisitely. He grasped his penis firmly in his right hand and agitated it. It stiffened with blood and, like a dog sighting its lead, throbbed with anticipation. Henry removed his hand and wagged his index finger at his member.

'Not yet!' he said. 'We need all our energies for the task ahead!'

He had remembered (how could he have forgotten?) that the suburb had once boasted a poisoner almost as celebrated as Henry intended to be. A really first-grade monster. A beast. A ravening wolf in sheep's clothing. Everett Maltby. Chapter 24 (Appendix), Volume 8 of this book.

Where was the section on Everett Maltby? It was always going missing. Sometimes you would find it wedged next to 'Witchcraft in Stuart Wimbledon' and, later, it would appear in the middle of 'The Impact of the Black Death on South West London'. He padded through to the room that Elinor described as his 'study'. Henry thought of it more as a shrine. It was here that he completed income tax forms, read carefully through the property pages of most of the local newspapers and, most sacred of all, worked on his *Complete History of Wimbledon*. The title alone had cost him two weeks' work. It couldn't be simply *The History of Wimbledon* (there was a book with that title – it didn't matter that it had been published nearly two hundred years ago). It had to be something that would give the prospective punter some idea of the staggering depth and scope and thoroughness of Henry's work. Suggest to them the fact that when they had finished this one they would know absolutely bloody everything that could be possibly known, now and for always, about Wimbledon. That there would be no escape from the great wall of knowledge Henry was propelling in their direction.

He opened the desk drawer and took out a page at random. It was from a rather combative chapter somewhere around the middle of 'Wimbledon in the Ninth Century after Christ'. 'We read', he read, 'in Jasper McCrum's unreliable, tendentious and often plainly wrong book *The Early and Mediaeval Wimbledon* that "in 878 a Danish army took up winter quarters just across the river at Fulham. Nothing is known of its activities, but Vikings normally maintained themselves by raiding the country within a wide range of their base. *So Wimbledon would have been very fortunate to have escaped without some damage*." (My italics.)'

He had hit McCrum pretty hard, thought Henry, but he had been right to do so. Standards were standards. The thought of McCrum cheered him up, and he got up and went over to the bookcase where the offending pamphlet was stored. He opened it and chose a sentence at random. He was not disappointed. 'During the Bronze Age – 2,500 to 750 BC the first metal objects appeared in Wimbledon.' What did the man think he was doing? Had he no notion at all of historical method? The sentence conjured up, for Henry, bizarre images, ancient and modern. He seemed to see men in winged helmets lounging around Frost's, the late-night delicatessen, or peering oafishly into the windows of Sturgis, the estate agent. From there, he allowed the Vikings more licence. They swarmed up Parkside and boarded buses bound for Putney, shouting unpleasant things at the driver-conductor. And then they surrounded McCrum's house and pillaged and put to the sword McCrum and other members of the Wimbledon Society who simply did not understand that –

'You look as if you're going to have a thrombie!' said a voice behind him.

Henry wheeled round, the pamphlet in his hand.

'You're naked!' she said accusingly.

Henry lowered the pamphlet and stood in what he hoped was a coquettish manner. She looked at him stonily. He gave her his best smile, a greeting he normally reserved for waiters. It was going to be important not to arouse her suspicions during the planning stages.

'I'm sorry!' he said, adding in a tone that was intended to be gentle, but came out wheedling, 'Do you find me repulsive?'

Elinor's answer to this was to slam the study door. Henry scratched his crotch reflectively and stared down at his *History of Wimbledon*. Down below the piano started up again. She was playing slightly better this time, but the effect was still markedly sinister. She sounded just perfect for the Wimbledon Poisoner's Daughter.

3

The next morning was Saturday.

Once, a long time ago, Henry could recall being alarmed at the emptiness, the ease, the sheer possibility offered by Saturday. This was no longer the case. On Saturdays Maisie now followed a routine as carefully planned as a day in the life of a nun in a particularly strict order. She went to piano. She went to ballet. She went to drama classes. She went to lessons in drawing, ice-skating, junior aerobics and many other skills which she had absolutely no hope of acquiring. She did not, thought Henry bitterly, as he dragged himself out of bed and weaved his way to the bathroom over Elinor's discarded knickers, go to classes in being thin, or classes designed to allow the participants' to hold one idea in their heads for more than five minutes.

My daughter, he told himself as he brushed his teeth and stared down at number 47's red Mitsubishi, is like me, fat and untalented. Opposite him, the net curtains of number 47 parted and number 47 peered out. Henry did not have to see his thin anxious face, his nervous nibble at his lower lip or the furtive glance to left and right to know that number 47 was performing the ritual known as Is the Mitsubishi Scratched Yet? Ever since the pharmaceutical company for which he worked had given him the vehicle (*given*, thought Henry grimly) number 47 had been watching over it in a manner that suggested an emotion deeper than motherhood, more desperate than romantic love. It was as if he feared the car would suffer from some mechanical equivalent of cot death, would suddenly buckle and blister and bend, hideously out of shape, there before his eyes, at berth, peacefully parked at its usual angle. Sometimes, Henry thought, it would be kindness itself to rise one night between three and four when the suburb slept and drag a sharp stone across the

Mitsubishi's flanks. At least it would end the awful suspense. At least number 47 would know, instead of suspecting, that even expensive objects get old and dirty and die.

Die.

Elinor, now asleep in the bedroom, her square jaw up like a tombstone, her mouth as wide as a new grave, her light snore ticking fitfully, like some tired machine. Elinor was going to die. Henry brushed and spat into the basin, noticing the blood darken the snow-white saliva.

He would get the poison today.

Humming to himself, he went back into the bedroom and put on a pair of grey corduroy trousers, a red shirt and a bright turquoise jumper, stained with food. He looked, he thought as he examined himself in the mirror, more than usually hideous. He rather hoped his wife would wake and catch him like this, unshaven, hair greasy and uncombed, and as he stood beside the bed he farted quite loudly, as if to remind her that she deserved someone as awful as him.

But she did not wake and for a moment Henry was flooded by helpless rage, a feeling that made him want to run to the bedside table, snatch up Elinor's nail scissors and twist them into her neck, this way and that, gouging out blood and veins. 'Excuse me!' he would scream as he slashed at her throat, 'I am here! I exist! Excuse me! Excuse me!'

Giving himself dialogue seemed to calm him and he stood for a moment, arms idle at his side, breathing slowly and heavily. He felt as if he had just run fifty yards, rather quickly. Calm, Henry. Calm. The great thing about poisoners is their control. You don't dash into breakfast and slop paraquat over the wife's Frosties, while hurling abuse at her. You are quiet and slow and methodical. And when she clutches at her side and complains of a slight ache you lean forward solicitously and ask, 'Are you all right, my darling?' You are gentle and considerate. And inside you are the Wimbledon Poisoner.

He was OK now. He bent over, kissed the least precipitous bit of her chin that he could find and went downstairs to find his daughter.

Maisie was sitting in front of the television, glaring sullenly at a man in a pink tracksuit. Getting her out was clearly going to be a problem.

After 'No' her favourite word was 'Why'.

Henry's ploy was simply to lie. 'I thought of going out for some choc bars,' he would say, adding *sotto voce* as his daughter ran for her anorak, 'and I thought we might drop off at the gym/piano teacher's/library on the way . . .'

He promised her a sight of Arfur this morning. He had remembered that Donald, Arfur's father, was liable to be waiting, with other fathers, in his parked car outside the Wimbledon Young Players' rehearsal. Unbelievably, he had actually christened his only son Arfur. Even more unbelievably Maisie thought Arfur was, to use a word too much on her lips these days, 'cute'. Even more unbelievable than either of these details was the fact that Donald was a doctor.

All the men in the suburb had jobs. Henry didn't know any unemployed people. He read about the unemployed in newspapers and saw films about them on television, pacing across photogenic sections of contemporary Britain and muttering darkly about waste and emptiness. The curious thing was that the lawyers, dentists, opticians, salesmen and accountants he knew didn't seem to do much work. Perhaps, he thought as he followed Maisie down the front path, it was that he knew them only as fathers, as people whose primary function was to stand at the edge of swimming pools, dank gymnasia or football fields, their collective manhoods bruised by nurture, blurring with age and helpless love.

Or perhaps they didn't actually do any work at all. Perhaps they only pretended. Perhaps the unemployed were the only people who did any work these days.

Once you knew Donald was a doctor, of course, it was impossible to forget it. His manner, over the years, had come to seem eerily medical. If Henry offered him a drink, Donald would compress his lips, lower his eyes, as if in the middle of a difficult diagnosis, and nod, slowly, responsibly, like a man burdened with some ghastly secret about the state of Henry's insides.

'Thanks, Henry,' he would say, in a tone that indicated this might well be the last drink he would be accepting from his friend, 'thanks!'

The phrase Henry wanted to use whenever alone with Donald's permanent bedside manner was *How long have I got, Doctor?* There was something about the care with which he looked into your eyes that was truly frightening.

The only time that Donald didn't look like a doctor was when people at parties asked him anything about health or physiology. Then he looked like a frightened animal. His composure would vanish, his grey eyes would shift around the room and, muttering something about antibiotics, he would disappear to the other end of the room, where some hours later he would be discovered at some local worthy's side, discussing parking problems at Waitrose with the quiet authority of a great physician.

Maisie had gone round to the passenger door of the Volkswagen and was standing, one hand poised to open it as soon as Henry should unlock it. Henry lowered himself into the driver's seat and stood looking out at her for a moment. It was amazing how little time children wasted. How they went on to the next thing with such satisfaction and certainty. How they went on from being carried and put in things to sitting in the front seat of cars, opening things for themselves, unlocking the tame mysteries of life. She'll be bloody driving soon, he thought, as he clicked open the lock and his daughter settled in beside him. She had her mother's knack of occupying space around her. She snapped the seat belt into position and stared out through the window as if in search of something else to organize.

'Elsie Mitchell says I stink!' she said, as if opening this topic for theoretical debate.

'Who's Elsie Mitchell?'

'A girl in Class Two of course,' said Maisie, 'with a nose like a pig!'

Henry drove.

He turned right into Caldecott Road, left into Howard's Avenue, right on to Mainwaring Road and up the wide thoroughfare that led to Wimbledon Hill. In all these streets, thick with lime trees, estate agents' boards and large, clean cars, there were no people to be seen at all. Henry knew all the houses – the double-fronted mansion with the Mercedes in the driveway, the row of early Victorian workmen's cottages, fastidiously restored, the occasional bungalow or mock Gothic affair with turrets – he knew what each one was worth, and he followed their fortunes, decay, repair, sale, in the way a countryman might watch the seasons. At 29 Howard's Avenue the builder's skip was still outside and the rusty scaffolding blinded its shabby windows. At 45 Mainwaring Road the upper maisonette was still advertising itself for sale – no less than six boards competing for the passerby's attention. Henry noticed all these things with something like affection while Maisie pressed her nose (very like a pig's, Henry thought) to the window of the Passat.

How was he going to turn the conversation round to the subject of poison? Henry could not imagine, when it came to it, the beginning, middle or end of a conversation in which Donald would tell him how to get hold of an untraceable poison.

He could steal some leaves from Donald's prescription pad. But were doctors allowed to order poisons? Why should they be? What were the medical applications of, say, arsenic? Henry realized he had absolutely no idea. He was as pathetically unqualified in the art of murder as he was at golf or philosophy. The problem with this poisoning business was that the preliminary research was horribly incriminating. One minute there you were asking casual questions about arsenic and the next there was your wife throwing up and having her hair fall out. People would put two and two together.

Christ, what were the major poisons?

There was arsenic, cyanide, prussic acid and – the list stopped there. Nobody much used poison any more; that was the trouble. Or if they did it was so modern that nobody got to hear about it. Henry couldn't think of any celebrated poisoners apart from Maltby and Crippen. And after Crippen, what? The line died out, didn't it? And while we were talking about Crippen, it would probably be unwise to choose as a role model someone who had been topped for the offence. He wanted someone who had got away with it.

He was drawing up outside the hall when he thought of Graham Young.

For the moment he could think of nothing apart from the name.

Young had, as far as Henry could remember, been sent to Broad-moor. But hadn't he been a state-of-the-art poisoner? A man who approached the subject with some finesse. Even if it wasn't quite enough finesse to keep him out of the loony bin. From Henry's recollection of the trial, which was, admittedly, not all that clear, Young had been some kind of chemist. There was probably no better way, if one was going to do this thing properly, than to study a celebrated practitioner. It wouldn't be enough to find a poison that would finish her off. He needed to know how to play it when the abdominal pains got started. Was there, for example, a poison that created symptoms that looked like a fairly recognizable disease? And if so, why wasn't every red-blooded English male using it?

Graham Young, yes. Graham Young. Henry had an image of a quiet man in a suit. A man not unlike himself. Something wet and heavy hit the side of his head. He realized Maisie was kissing him. He turned and watched her run up the path and into the hall. Where, though, was Donald? His white Sierra was parked just ahead of Henry, the door open, but there was no sign either of him or Arfur.

Henry got out of the car and sauntered over to the Sierra. No one around. The passenger door was open. And there, on the top of his open bag, staring straight at him, was the white notepad he used for issuing prescriptions. Henry pulled open the door, yanked off the three top sheets and scuttled back to his car. Only when he was safely inside the Passat did he look round to see if he had been observed. He was safe he was safe he was safe.

As he groped his way under his seat, seeking somewhere to stow the paper, his fingers met something cold and hard and sharp. The jack. He'd been looking for that for ages. And if all else failed it would probably be an effective, if unsubtle way of letting his wife know that something rather more serious than Marriage Guidance was required to get them out of their marital difficulties. He wrapped the prescription paper round it and started the engine. He had an hour to get to the library, do his research and return for Maisie. A whole hour. What better way to spend one of those rare breaks in the suburban day than by studying methods of getting rid of one's wife.

4

There were no fewer than four books in the Wimbledon Public Library that dealt with the Graham Young case. One of them – by a man called Harkness – was 400 pages long, contained twenty-four black and white photographs, three appendices and several maps and diagrams. It was eighty pages longer than the standard biography of Antonín Dvořák, the composer, and only seventy pages shorter than the definitive historical account of Rommel's North African campaign.

There were pages and pages of psychoanalytic rubbish, Henry noted, and endless, dreary character sketches of the people Young had poisoned. But there was also a fairly concisely written chapter entitled 'Thallium Poisoning: Odourless, Tasteless and almost Impossible to Detect'. This was just the sort of thing Henry wanted to read.

Most poisons, it seemed, tasted unpleasant. (Elinor did not drink either tea or coffee and only the occasional glass of mint tea. She drank no alcohol and thought most forms of seasoning depraved. Her diet was, in a sense, poison proof.) But thallium, it appeared, was quite tasteless.

Its effects, however, were sensational. Your hair fell out. You had hallucinations. You lost the use of your limbs. You went on to do sterling work in the diarrhoea, headaches and vomiting department and you ended up coughing out your last in a way that Henry thought would be entirely suitable for Elinor. It wasn't just that. Thallium poisoning created a set of symptoms exactly matching a series found in a type of polyneuritis known as the Guillain-Barré syndrome. The first post-mortem on one of Young's victims – Fred Biggs – had found no traces of thallium in the body, although later microscopic analysis revealed there were several hundred milligrams, more than enough to kill him.

It was the polyneuritis that Henry liked. Two years after they had been married, Elinor had suddenly, mysteriously, developed a weakness in her legs, and Henry, who, equally mysteriously, in those days wasn't trying to kill her, had hurried her to the local hospital where the doctors had diagnosed – wait for it – polyneuritis. Polyneuritis was clearly a word like morality that meant so many different things as to be absolutely meaningless. If it meant anything at all, thought Henry, it was something along the lines of *We haven't got a clue*. Henry could imagine the conversation with Donald now. Elinor on the bed, hair falling out, vomiting, losing the use of her limbs and he and Donald, over by the window, voices low, faces discreetly grave. Donald would issue a death certificate for any cause you suggested to him; this case, Henry felt, might be so staggeringly self-explanatory as to allow him to come to a diagnosis off his own bat.

'It's the . . . polyneuritis . . .' he heard himself say, as Donald sneaked towards the medical dictionary, his big handsome head bowed with concern, his grey eyes looking into the distance, in the direction of the local tennis court.

He might even sob. That would be good. If only to observe the embarrassment on Donald's face.

Where should he have her cremated? Somewhere rather low-rent, Henry thought. There was a particularly nasty crematorium in Mitcham, he recalled, with a chapel that looked more than usually like a public lavatory. And, from what he remembered of the funeral (his grandmother's), the ushers looked like men who were trying hard not to snigger. Or should he go completely the other way? Hire a small cruiser and slip her coffin over the side in some ocean that might have some special meaning for her? (The Bering Straits, possibly.) He could . . . but Henry was almost too full of good ideas for her funeral. She wasn't even dead yet.

Half an hour left.

The chief problem with thallium was that it didn't seem to be used for anything much apart from the manufacture of optical lenses of a high refractive index – camera lenses, for example. Henry stared for some moments at the word 'optical'. Why should he need stuff for making lenses? He didn't make cameras, he wasn't an optician –

No, but Gordon Beamish was. Gordon Beamish was a real live optician. He was all optician. He was probably always nipping down to Underwoods for a few grams of thallium. Susie Beamish probably drank it for breakfast. There would be an especial pleasure in using Gordon Beamish's name. If anyone deserved a few years in an open prison it was Beamish.

Like many people who wear glasses, Henry hated opticians, especially opticians with 20/20 vision. Gordon Beamish was a man who made a fetish out of being lynx-eyed. He could be seen most mornings at the door of his shop in Wimbledon Village, arms crossed, mouth twisted in a superior sneer, just waiting for the chance to decode the small print on the front of buses.

'I saw you in the High Street the other day,' he would say, in a tone that suggested that it was quite impossible for Henry to have seen him. Henry had lost count of the number of times Beamish began a sentence with the words 'I notice . . .' or 'I observe . . .' Things were always crystal clear to Beamish; he was always taking a view or spying out the land or finding some way of pointing out the difference between his world – a universe of sharp corners and exact distances – and the booming, foggy place in which Henry found himself every time he took off his glasses. When suffering eye tests in the darkened cubicle at the back of his shop, almost the only thing Henry ever managed to see was the pitying smile on Beamish's face as he flashed up smaller and smaller letter sequences, all of them probably spelling 'You are a fat shortsighted twerp'!

Beamish, thought Henry, could be the fall guy. He liked to think of Beamish in the dock at the Central Court, his counsel blustering on about his client's perfectly normal, acceptable need for heavy metal poisons ('But how do you explain, Mr Beamish, your ordering a quantity of thallium from a perfectly reputable chemist's . . .?') He closed the book, replaced it in the cookery section of the open shelves, and walked briskly to the car. There was no time to lose. It was entirely possible, Elinor being the way she was, that somebody else would try to kill her before Henry got in with his bid.

Indeed, he reflected, as he joined the queue at the traffic lights opposite the library, it was such a blindingly simple, brilliantly obvious idea, it was very difficult to think why everyone wasn't doing it. Why, while they were about it, wasn't she trying to kill him?

Henry drove cautiously up the hill. He tested the brakes when he reached the top. They seemed OK.

Maisie looked, as always, subtly different after her piano lesson. She looked more aware of the world, brighter, more optimistic. This was some compensation for the fact that she was almost certainly no better at the piano.

Donald's son, Arfur, was there, a small, fat six-year-old, who stared at Henry and said: 'I played the piano!'

'Good!' said Henry, through compressed lips. He seized Maisie by the hand and walked back to the car. If he could get hold of something from Beamish, he might be able to lay his hands on some thallium by lunchtime. She could be dead by the time children's television started or, if not dead, at least well on the way to it. He chose a route back down the hill that did not involve too many serious gradients, moving from Roseberry Road to Warburton Drive to Chesterton Terrace and, from there, doubling back along a series of streets with an offensively tangible air of *esprit de corps* – Lowther Park Drive, where people called to each other over their Volvos and, even worse, Stapleton Road, a place that seemed almost permanently on the verge of a street party.

The brakes still seemed OK.

Gordon Beamish was not in his shop – instead, under a gigantic spectacle frames stood a small, rat-faced girl called Ruthie. Ruthie, as if to compensate for her boss's powers of vision, seemed to have every known complaint of the eyes short of blindness. Astigmatism, squints, premature presbyopia, short sight, long sight, tunnel vision, barrel vision, migraine, Ruthie had the lot, and her glasses resembled some early form of periscope; they were a circular, heavy-duty affair, with catches and locks and screws. Somewhere underneath the pebble lenses, tinged both grey and pink, the steel traps and the wires were, presumably, a pair of eyes but they were only, really, a flicker, in the depths of the optician's *pièce de résistance* that towered above Ruthie's nose.

Henry liked Ruthie and Ruthie liked him.

'Is Gordon about?'

'No,' said Ruthie, 'he took Luke to Beavers.'

Beavers. That was a new one on Henry. What the hell was Beavers? Some neo-Fascist organization perhaps? From what he could remember of Luke, the boy would have fitted well into the Waffen SS. Leaving Maisie on the street he went into the shop.

'I'll leave a note for him!' he said.

Ruthie folded her arms, as if to emphasize her lack of responsibility for the shop she was minding. Her eyes, or something very like her eyes, moved in the thick depths of the glass. 'Fine!' she said.

Henry went through to the back of the shop.

On Gordon's desk was a pile of headed notepaper. Henry picked up two sheets. Then he saw something better. In a square, steel tray at the back of the desk was a notepad, the kind of thing given away by small businesses in an attempt to register their names with the public. A. M. Duncan, it read, Lenses, Photographic and Ophthalmic. And underneath the heading, an address. After a quick glance back through the shop (Maisie and Ruthie were staring out at the street in silence) Henry slid one sheet of the printed paper into Gordon's typewriter. What he really wanted to write was:

Henry Farr wishes some thallium to administer to his wife. Please give this to him. He is desperate.

But instead he told whomsoever it might concern that he was Alan Bleath, a researcher employed by the above company and he needed to buy 10 grams of thallium for research purposes. Was that going to be enough? She was quite a big woman. Shouldn't he order a kilo? Two kilos? A lorryload, for Christ's sake! The trouble was, he thought, as he signed the paper, indecipherably, with his left hand, folded it and put it into his jacket pocket, he didn't know much about thallium poisoning, and even less about the making of lenses with a high refractive index. A really thorough murderer would have boned up on both subjects more intently.

Ten grams would have to do. He took a sheet of Gordon's note-paper and typed a short note to Alan Bleath, thanking him for his recent contribution to the stimulating seminar on lenses of a high refractive index, signed this with a fair approximation of Gordon's hand and put it in one of the 'Gordon Beamish: See?' envelopes, addressed to Alan Bleath, 329 Carradine Road, Mitcham. ('Do you seriously expect me to believe, Mr Beamish, that someone came into your office and, without your knowledge, used your typewriter to address a letter?' 'Well, I – ' 'I put it to you that you had always loved Elinor Farr. Your lust for her knew no bounds and when this loyal woman spurned you for her husband of twenty years you wreaked a terrible revenge!' 'No no no! You've got it wrong!')

Actually, thought Henry, as he checked himself in the mirror, no one, not even the police, would be stupid enough to imagine that Elinor could be the victim of a *crime passionnel*. The only passion involved in this operation was an overmastering desire to see her nailed down in a brown box.

He looked, he thought, fairly Bleath-like. Apart from the glasses. He slipped these off and saw a blurred, red disk of a face which resembled a Francis Bacon portrait. Alan Bleath.

'Hurry up!' said Maisie. 'What are you doing?'

'Leaving a note for Gordon,' said Henry.

Let's have a jar! he wrote on Gordon's pad. 'Jar' was the sort of stupid, hail-fellow-well-met word that Gordon would appreciate.

He decided not to go to a chain chemist's. Those sort of places made so much they could afford the luxury of high standards. He wanted an old-fashioned, grubby place with old-fashioned glass bottles in the window. Somewhere run by an elderly couple with no commercial sense. The sort of people who cried with relief when you went in to buy a piece of Elastoplast.

He needed the sort of chemist's he had gone to as a child. If he could remember that far back. These days he had trouble recalling the troublesome fragments of his education he had bothered to mem-orize in the first place; the names of new acquaintances were jumbled together with old verb forms and things he thought were childhood haunts turned out to be places he had only just discovered. But there was somewhere, wasn't there, where once, years ago, he had gone with his mother, or someone fairly like his mother, anyway? Weald-lake Road. That was it! Wealdlake Road!

At the corner of Wealdlake Road, four streets north of Wimbledon station, was the ideal place. A heavy wooden window frame, dusty glass and three big-bellied bottles, coloured with the bright, mysterious fluids Henry remembered from his childhood. He couldn't remember quite when he had first visited the shop but, like Wimbledon itself, it had always been there. Henry had lived in Wimbledon all his life. They would, Henry thought, be glad to see anyone, even a prospective poisoner. They were probably desperate enough to offer a comprehensive after-sales service ('Thallium not right, sir? Try antimony perhaps? Or potassium chlorate . . .').

He parked the Passat and told Maisie he was going to buy some aspirin.

'Can I come?'

'No!' said Henry.

Before she had time to protest he had locked the doors and, removing his glasses as he went, walked briskly over the road. He narrowly missed what he thought was a lamp post but turned out to be a tree, and reached for where the handle was usually to be found on a front door. To his surprise it was there.

He felt perfectly calm as he entered the shop. Not only calm. He felt Bleath-like to a surprising degree. Perhaps this was because he could hardly see more than a yard in front of his face.

'Hullo, sir!' said a blurred, white shape. It sounded old and incompetent.

'Hullo!' he replied, moving cautiously towards it. Then, with the air of a man asking for twenty cigarettes, he said, 'I need 10 or 15 grams of thallium. Do you keep it or should I go to a larger store?'

The blurred white shape came closer. It seemed to be smiling. Why was it smiling? *You are Henry Farr the Wimbledon Poisoner and I arrest you in the name of* – Hang on, hang on. He wasn't the Wimbledon Poisoner. Yet.

In the face of the shape's silence, he continued, breezily. 'I don't know whether a place as small as this keeps registered poisons but I've just moved labs . . .'

Moved labs! Brilliant!

'And I don't know this neck of the woods . . .'

The shape was close enough for Henry to see that it was male.

'Thallium,' it said, in a frankly sinister tone, 'thallium . . .'

Henry wished it would not say the word quite so loudly. And was it necessary to repeat it like that? Or, in so doing, sound like that man in *Journey Into Space* who was born in 1945 and died in 1939? Yes, thallium you old berk, thallium, the heavy metal poison that makes your hair fall out and gives you diarrhoea and you die screaming. That one. Thallium.

'Not Valium,' said Henry briskly, 'but thallium!'

'Yes,' said the shape. 'I remember . . .'

It sounded, Henry thought, as if all this had happened before. As if, on this very spot a hundred years ago . . . what? Some thought, some fragment of memory was tugging at him but he could not quite catch it, as so often these days. Something he had said or somebody had said, something . . . There was, anyway, an atmosphere in this shop, an unpleasant feeling, as if he had just walked through a gateway into a world parallel to our own, where huge and unpleasant moral choices are offered, fought over and discussed.

The shape seemed to be looking through a book, although what the book was Henry could not tell. *How to Spot a Poisoner* perhaps, or *Some Common Excuses Used by Murderers*. Or perhaps he was just trying to find out what thallium was.

'The heavy metal . . .' said Henry, in what he hoped was an offensively knowledgeable tone.

'What do you require this for?' said the shape.

'Work on optical lenses,' said Henry, adding, smartly, 'with a high refractive index!'

'Oh yes . . .' said the shape.

Maybe he was looking at a book that told you things like that. Or maybe people were always popping in here for 10 grams of thallium. Or maybe he was bluffing. He was going to look it up, whip down to Boots and, having bought a few quidsworth, sell it to Henry at ten per cent over the retail value. He was probably willing to sell anything, the glass jars in the window included.

It was spooky, though, thought Henry, it was a spooky shop. Or was it just that what he was doing was spooky?

He moved up to the counter with the air of a man who doesn't like having to go through a routine *once* again but is *prepared* to do so, *all right then here's my card if you insist*! He took out the letter and tossed it on the counter.

'There's my authority,' he said, 'if you need that.'

Bleath was clearly a man impatient of bureaucracy, anxious to get back to his lenses. The shape seemed impressed.

'Do you have any identification, Mr Bleath?'

Bleath put a hand into his breast pocket. Then he transferred the same hand to the back pocket of his trousers and did some not very good patting of both flanks.

'I seem to have mislaid my driving licence!' he said tetchily and then, 'Here's a letter addressed to me!'

It was the way he handed the old fool the letter, Henry decided afterwards, that had done it. He had long ago noticed that if you stared at a customs officer when going out through the green channel, the customs officer stopped you. You had to be careful with officials. And he handed over the letter (which had creased beautifully in his pocket) with just the right note of impatient politeness.

'You'll have to sign the register!' said the shape.

He had done it.

5

The Poisons Register was, like the rest of the shop, a piece of England's past. It was in a thick blue binding and its antique look – the paper was ruled in the way Henry remembered books of his childhood being ruled – gave it the air of a family bible. 'There you are, Mr Bleath.'

He went on to name a sum that Henry thought very acceptable. It was a cheap and easy way of murdering your wife, thought Henry. Very reasonable. Very reasonable indeed. Mind you, in any area of domestic life it was more sensible, in budgetary terms anyway, to Do It Yourself. Some of these types who went in for murder as a professional thing would probably take you to the cleaners as soon as look at you.

He went out, slowly, calmly, ready for the catch question at the door . . . 'Best of luck with the poisoning!' 'Thanks!' *Shit!* Henry replaced his glasses. But the shape, who was now revealed to be an amiable-looking man of about thirty, remained silent.

The air outside smelt good. Up the hill from the south-west a gentle breeze was blowing, and opposite him a huge chestnut tree, already infected with the beautiful rust of autumn, stirred in sympathy with the wind. It was good to know that Elinor would not be breathing this sweet, suburban air for very much longer.

In the car Maisie was studying her music. She looked old and serious. She had scraped her hair back from her forehead and tied it in a ponytail with a pink ribbon. Maisie was always doing things with her hair. Sometimes she piled it up, sometimes she pulled it forward in a fringe, and sometimes she let it hang straight, like her mother's. But whereas Elinor's hair fell, as she herself put it, 'like a great, calm waterfall', Maisie's hair just hung, like old socks on a washing line. And whatever she did with her hair, it still, thought

Henry, didn't do anything for her face – Maisie's face was still there, round as a dinner plate. The kind of face one saw on children by roadsides in Connemara.

He leaned over and kissed his daughter on the forehead. She continued to study her music. After Elinor was dead, he and Maisie could really get to know each other, thought Henry. As he intended to behave extraordinarily well, she would grow to like and respect him (he wasn't entirely sure she did at the moment). One of the advantages of scheduling one's own bereavement was that it was far easier to respond in a mature, caring way to one's partner's decease. Henry had read an article in *The Times*, which said that partners who lost a loved one often blamed the departed for the death. Henry did not intend to do this. He was going to be a tower of strength to all concerned.

'You've been ages,' said Elinor, as he and Maisie trudged up the steps.

'Sorry!' said Henry.

His wife came towards him menacingly. When she walked she moved each hip separately, like a gunslinger moving towards an opponent down Main Street. She drew her right hand out from the folds of her apron and thrust a piece of paper at him, averting her eyes as she did so. It was as if, thought Henry, she wished to have nothing to do with the dispute she knew this word would provoke.

'Waitrose!' she said.

'I thought you went yesterday . . .' said Henry. His voice, he noticed, made him sound frightened. Why was this?

Elinor narrowed her eyes and swung her straight black hair out behind her like a scarf. She moved, as she often did, from pure, concentrated malice, to a vaguely girlish mode, as if she was looking for someone (not Henry) to put his arms round her and tell her everything was all right. A fatherly sort of chap. Henry grabbed the paper and backed away down the path.

'You go to Waitrose now!' she barked.

Was this a command or a statement? It felt like a command, as did so many of Elinor's remarks – but it had the menacing power of a scientific law.

'It isn't my turn!' said Henry.

'It is!' said Elinor.

'It isn't!' said Henry.

'Oh yes it is!' said Elinor.

Henry kicked the side of the kerb viciously. She was being more than usually assertive. Things weren't helped by the fact that he had remembered, in the course of this not very elevated argument, that it was actually his turn. He kicked the kerb again hard and set his lips in a scowl. Why did he always choose to lose his temper over issues in which he was in the wrong?

She's been seeing her therapist again, thought Henry, as he stumbled towards the Passat.

'Can I go?' said Maisie.

Elinor drew herself upwards and outwards. Then, with the fluidity usually only displayed by cartoon characters, she swooped down and around her daughter; her arms cradled each shoulder and her face slid down next to Maisie's. Her voice changed too. It acquired an impossible sweetness, a tenderness that was almost sinister.

'Darling,' said Elinor, 'shall Maisie stay with Mummy and do her cello practice while Mummy helps her?'

Maisie looked trapped. She liked Waitrose. In Waitrose there were Twix bars and Breakaways; there were chocolate digestives and huge jumbo packets of crisps and giant, plastic bottles of Coca-Cola. Sometimes she and Henry sat together in the car, a few streets away from their home, munching chocolate bars, while in the back of the Passat huge cardboard boxes of grains, wholewheat cereal, low-fat spreads and calorie-free, taste-free things to stop you dying of cancer awaited Elinor's approval. She would not have sweets in the house. Simply to smell Coca-Cola made her, she said, violently sick.

'See you later, Maisie!' said Henry.

'We were going to Elspeth's !' said Maisie.

Christ yes! He started to mouth the words 'I'll bring you a choc bar,' but before he was halfway through this soundless sentence his wife's face levelled up towards him. She had the clear gaze of an experienced poker player.

'No sweets!' she said.

'No dear,' said Henry.

Clutching the phial of thallium in his pocket he got back into the car. It was curious. The last place he wanted to be was in the car. Why, every time he got out of it, was he forced back into it?

Today, of course, it suited him to be doing the shopping. What went well with thallium? Curried things? Chicken Dopiaza Thallium Style! But she wouldn't eat curry, would she? Anyway the stuff had no taste. Just give her thallium! Thallium *à la mode de* Wimbledon, served in a little china pot with a spray of basil and a clean table napkin. Elinor might almost accept that. *Nouvelle cuisine* methods of preparing thallium . . . a drop of thallium on a piece of seaweed, chilled thallium, served garnished with a single *radicchio* leaf . . . down home thallium . . . thallium and beans . . . big, tasty, hearty, man-sized thallium burgers served with french fries, pickle and thallium on the side . . . 'It's so *versatile*,' said Henry, aloud, as he drove back down the hill, '*There are so many things you can do with thallium!*'

Shopping with death in mind made shopping almost bearable.

Henry was by far the most cheerful-looking person in Waitrose, as he scanned the loaded shelves for his wife's last meal. Elinor's favourite food was yoghurt. Yoghurt and thallium? Not really. Ahead of him a morose-looking man in a cardigan was sorting through slabs of meat in plastic containers. Once again Henry was struck by the enormity of supermarkets . . . those millions of dead animals, butchered, arranged in parcels, labelled with a SELL BY or a BEST BEFORE date, grouped, not by species or sub-species, but by parts of the body. Whole rows of chicken thighs, galleries of boneless chicken breasts, chicken escalopes coated with breadcrumbs, ready seasoned, free-range, corn-fed chicken that –

Hang on. Ready-seasoned, free-range, corn-fed chicken. Henry pulled one towards him. In a way, he thought, it was a cleaner life being a battery chicken than a free-range, corn-fed chicken. At least the battery chicken knew what it was up against. Stuck in a cell, the light on twenty-four hours a day, at least the battery chicken wasn't going to be fooled into thinking well of people. But the free-range, corn-fed chicken was the victim of a cruel joke. Given a little hope, a little patch of ground . . . so that it would taste better. Soon, thought Henry, feeling, as he often did, a sense of solidarity with chickens, they would label one with THIS FOWL HAS BEEN HAND-REARED AND TALKED TO NICELY. IT DIED PEACEFULLY.

Elinor liked ready-seasoned, free-range, corn-fed chicken. And the fine dusting of the seasoning – the green of the parsley, the black of the pepper, would be a perfect cover for thallium. Even more importantly, Maisie didn't like chicken, especially free-range, corn-fed, humanely killed chicken that had been through Jungian analysis. She liked great slabs of chicken in crispy batter. It would also be comparatively easy – he was getting excited – to sprinkle the thallium on the breast, because Elinor liked breast and he liked leg.

'A little white meat, darling?'

'Of course, my darling!' Elinor would squawk, brushing her mane of black hair away from her forehead. And then the plate, piled high with sprouts and potatoes and gravy and topped with succulent slices of perfectly roasted breast of chicken, coated with a crispy surface of parsley, pepper and thallium, would land before Mrs Farr. And she would spear a piece of chicken and carry it high in the air towards that great black hole of a mouth and, still talking about her therapy, her plans for the future, his inability to understand her as a woman, his crude, male-orientated sexuality, she would munch, munch, munch . . .

'Are you going to make love to that chicken?'

Henry jumped.

It was Donald.

'Oh. Hi!'

'You look miles away.'

'I was.'

Donald peered into Henry's trolley in a companiable fashion. All it contained was a small jar of capers.

'You're a bit behind, Henry.'

'Indeed.'

Donald had got four sponge rolls, three jumbo packets of cornflakes, five loaves of bread, some digestive biscuits, a square packet of something called Uncle Sam's Chocolate Chip Cookies, a

Battenburg cake and two mixed, assorted crisps, in bags that were the size of a small dustbin. Donald approached Waitrose with military precision, working his way steadily through Farinaceous, Vegetables (Salad), Vegetables (Root, Loose and Packed), Poultry, Game, Continental Cuts and Mince, and from there by way of Fish (Frozen) and Fish (Fresh) to Spices, Pickles and Non-refrigerated Ready-packed Sauces, through to Pet Food, Pet Accessories and Household Cleaners.

He nodded his big, handsome head still thick with greying curls.

'Keeping well, though?'

'Fine,' said Henry, 'fine.'

Donald narrowed his eyes very slightly and nodded once again. His perfect profile looked off down the rows of brightly coloured packets. 'Should I tell him now?' his expression seemed to say, 'Or would it be better to let the disease take its course? It won't be long now anyway . . .'

'Elinor's a bit off colour, though.'

'Yes?'

'Well . . . it's a funny thing. I don't know whether I told you . . . but some years ago she was diagnosed as having . . . polyneuritis . . .'

Donald's perfectly formed lips began to tremble.

'I was wondering whether . . . maybe . . .'

Donald looked away, longingly, towards Refrigerated Delicatessen, his clear doctor's eyes, moving expertly from Ready-packed Gravadlax, through Hand-sliced, Oak-smoked, Ready-interleaved Salmon Slices, along the twelve varieties of German and Polish sausage, the pre-packed slices of Waitrose Pastrami and Salt Beef until they reached the orderly rows of Fresh Tortellini, Cappelletti, Paglia e Fieno and Tagliatelle (Green and White).

'Well,' he said finally, 'must get on!'

And with one more nod of that perfect head he was off, working his trolley through the morning crowd with the air of a great surgeon.

Henry put the chicken back in the pile. He paused, then from the back took one that seemed to have got separated from the rest. Its polythene wrapping looked vaguely torn and grubby, as if members of the Waitrose staff had already been playing catch with it. It was past the SELL BY date too. It would do perfectly. It seemed wrong, somehow, to poison a piece of meat in pristine condition.

He threw it in the trolley and went off to look for things Elinor didn't like.

6

Once he had decided on Free-range chicken *à la* Thallium, it was fairly important not to buy anything Elinor might choose as a substitute. If she were to insist on veal goulash, for example, all would be lost. Maisie liked veal goulash. She had heard it was bad for you.

If only she drank something other than herb tea.

Trying not to think about her possible reaction, Henry loaded cured fish, offal, red meat and a bold assortment of vegetables he had never even heard of, let alone eaten. All they had in common was a potential for repelling Mrs Farr. Bags of kohlrabi and okra, sweet potatoes, chillies, Chinese-leaf lettuce and three pounds of a very peculiar thing called an edenwort, which looked like a beetroot going through a severe identity crisis. There was a little plastic notice next to it which read EDENWORT: SLICE IT OR BAKE IT OR USE IT IN CASSEROLES. Or just throw it at the neighbours, thought Henry grimly, as he tipped the edenwort in next to the water-chestnuts and the giant yam.

Checking his purchases against her list as he approached the checkout, he was pleased to find that at no point did the two coincide.

Then he saw Donald, trolley piled high with middle-of-the-road food.

'Hullo there!' called Henry.

Donald nodded, briefly.

'How about a pint?'

Donald considered this offer; his features rippled with thought. If he were a picture his handsome, regular cheekbones and serious eyes would probably be titled 'A Doctor Decides'.

'OK,' he said, in the end. Imaginary nurses sighed with relief. The hours of waiting over! At last they had a diagnosis! 'A jar would be very nice.'

If Henry arrived back after three, Elinor would be at therapy. Maisie would be at ballet. He would have time to stow away the kohlrabi, the offal and the edenwort. And by the time she returned it would be six or six thirty. Teatime!

Time, now Henry was forty, did not proceed in the way it had previously done. Once upon a time, there was waking, which was slow and painful, and then quite a long period, replete with chances and triumphs and defeats and risks, which sometimes, though not always, ended in lunch. Afternoon, Henry remembered, used to be as prolonged and arid as Arizona, and they were followed by things called evenings, which were entirely different and separate from nights. Now – you woke up with a sense of relief and surprise that you were still there, you got up, brushed your teeth, and before you knew it you were watching television. It was dark outside and well past your bedtime. You were also, probably, drunk, but how you got drunk, or where you had been between that first moment of reacquaintance with yourself and now, was a mystery. Apart, of course, from the shops. You had almost certainly been to the shops.

'We could go to the Rose and Thorn!' said Donald.

'Great!' said Henry.

Donald began to place his groceries on the moving counter.

Henry tipped out the edenwort and looked at Donald's back. He looked like a man who would sign a mean death certificate.

What to do with the chicken after the meal? Assuming he phoned Donald as soon as she began to vomit and have headaches, wouldn't Donald ask what they had eaten for dinner? Maybe not, since Henry, unless he got the thallium anywhere near the chicken leg, would be feeling fine.

It was vital, though, to include Donald in the diagnosis of Elinor's condition. He was not only a close personal friend, he was also, to Henry's knowledge, one of the worst doctors in the south-east of England.

'Some bloke came into the surgery,' he would say, sourly, 'complaining of headaches. "What do you expect me to do about it?" I said. "I get headaches. We all get headaches. Piss off out of it!" I said, "You're giving me a headache!" '

'Good for you!' Henry would reply. 'Send him away with a flea in his ear. Psychosomatic, I suppose?'

Donald would pull on his pint (he had to be fairly drunk in order to even start discussing medicine) – 'In fact,' he would say, 'turned out to be a bloody brain tumour, didn't it?'

'Christ!' – from Henry.

'Can you beat it? Can you beat it?'

'Indeed not,' Henry would reply.

And the two men would shake their heads over the inconsistent, bloody-minded civilians who swarmed through a general practitioner's surgery, deliberately misleading qualified men about the nature of their fatal diseases.

Over the pint Henry would make a few more casual references to Elinor's polyneuritis. When Donald examined his wife in the last stages of the illness it might be necessary to lead him to a medical textbook and steer those calm, grey eyes in the direction of the chapter headed 'The Guillain-Barré Syndrome'.

The Rose and Thorn, on the edge of Wimbledon Common was, in the eighteenth century, a favourite spot for highwaymen. The infamous Tibbet, executed at the roundabout at the top of Putney Hill, is reported to have stabbed a man to death there; it has literary associations also. In the nineteenth century, Swinburne, having been thrown out of his local, the Green Man, on the west side of Putney Hill, walked over the common to the Rose and Thorn, where, according to a letter of Watts Dunton, he drank eight pints of strong ale and was violently sick over the landlord's daughter, a woman called Henrietta Luce who later married a distant relative of Trollope's.

Henry told Donald some of this, as he did every time he and Donald used the pub, and Donald nodded and smiled and said: 'Really! How extraordinary!' As he did every time Henry told him these things.

He had got to the point, now, of sometimes saying, 'Yes. I read somewhere I think there was a landlord's daughter called Loo or Loup or . . .'

47

Thus giving Henry the chance to reply, 'In fact her name was Luce . . . perhaps I told you . . .'

To which Donald would reply, a little too swiftly, 'No, no . . . I don't think so . . .'

And then . . . 'Fascinating, really!'

And the two of them would discuss, with some enthusiasm, where Donald could have acquired this information. Their conversations were, Henry felt, the sweeter for having a core of known fact which they could then decorate and refine, like old men in some village discussing last year's harvest.

'Of course,' he said on their third pint, 'the Wimbledon Poisoner used to use the back bar.'

'Is that right?' said Donald.

'Everett Maltby,' said Henry, 'who lived off Wimbledon Hill. He poisoned his wife and his mother-in-law and any number of other people, including some of the regulars at his local.'

'Christ!' said Donald. 'Why?'

'Liven things up a bit, I suppose,' said Henry.

Donald took a deep swig of his beer. He ran his tongue round his lips, as if assessing the taste.

'Can get pretty dull, I suppose . . .' he said.

Pretty dull, thought Henry, I should say so.

'I think I've heard of Everett Maltby,' said Donald.

'It's possible you have,' said Henry. 'He's a well-known local story!'

That must have been where he got the idea from, of course. That was why Everett, suddenly, seemed more real, more frightening than usual. Not that Henry believed in any of that rubbish about possession or reliving history or the power of the myth. That was all so much fashionable garbage, wasn't it? History was what happened to dead people. It didn't act on the living, like yeast. Although . . .

'Wasn't he hanged?' Donald was prompting him.

'Yes, yes,' said Henry, 'in 1888. The mystery really, is why he did it. He was a quiet, apparently happily married man with no enemies. He stood to gain nothing. A complete mystery man. He was a model citizen.'

'Like you Henry!' said Donald.

They both laughed. Then they drank a little. Then Donald said: 'How did they catch him?'

Well, he had confessed, hadn't he? 'Burdened' as he put it at his trial, 'with the intolerable knowledge of my own beastliness!' That wasn't going to happen to Henry though, was it? If a chap hadn't the guts to stand up for his own beastliness where was he? There was, Henry felt, something rather unsavoury about Maltby. Perhaps that was why he had never worked up the notes he had made on the case. At one time he had intended a whole chapter of *The Complete History of Wimbledon* to be devoted to the issue of Maltby, but somehow the chapter had never materialized. For a start, he kept losing the notes, and then, when he had managed to find them and set them out on his desk, he seemed to lack the will to start work on them. There was something decidedly spooky about Maltby. And as they talked the image of the man became clearer and clearer, until Henry wanted to say to Donald, 'No. Don't let's talk about this, shall we? It's too . . . dangerous.' He could see the stuffy front room and the hideous green plant. The heavy oak furniture, the unused piano, the not very attractive daughter . . . He could see Everett's trips up to London, in the days before the electrification of the Wimbledon Railway. He could see Everett sitting at a tall stool, in an office not unlike Henry's, helping to build the wealth of the empire. But there was some detail he knew he didn't want to remember. Why didn't he want to remember it? And why did thinking about it, yes, it did, frighten him?

'How did they, though?'

He had been silent too long. Henry took the route often taken by historians faced with a tricky historical problem. He made something up.

'He confessed,' said Henry. 'It all got too much for him. Guilt. You know? And he broke down. In this very pub, one night, and told everyone that he was the Wimbledon Poisoner. It took him some time to convince them, apparently.'

'I don't think you've ever told me that!' said Donald, sounding peeved to have elicited an original statement from Henry while on licensed premises. Henry, too, felt somewhat alarmed to find himself using his imagination. He tried to steer the conversation back to theory.

'Your typical poisoner,' he said, 'is a drab, quiet creature seeking to call attention to himself by his crimes. But often, so drab is he that even when he barges into the pub waving a bottle of paraquat and shouting *I dunnit*, people just don't want to know. No one could believe that Everett Maltby had done the appalling things he had done. He had to convince them.'

He drank some more.

'Murder,' he said, in the tones of someone who knew a bit about the subject, 'is something we try and classify. Try and put beyond the pale. But we all have a murderer in us. It's just that most of us are not honest enough to admit to the fact. And there are more ways of killing people than by killing them. If you know what I mean.'

'Not sure I do . . .' said Donald.

Henry looked at the clock. It was two thirty. Donald had had enough local history. Like many people, he thought that local history was dull. You could see him wanting to talk about the controversy over the redevelopment of Wimbledon town centre (Greycoat versus Speyhawk, or Caring Architects versus Greedy Planners). Henry did not want to talk about the redevelopment of Wimbledon town centre. As far as Henry was concerned they could fill the whole thing in with concrete.

If he wasn't careful they would get on to the subject of the motorway. Someone, it appeared, was planning to run a motorway through Wimbledon. There were even rumours that it was going to go straight through the middle of Henry's house, a thought that, somewhat to his surprise, filled him with savage pleasure. It was the past that inspired Henry, not the present.

Up at the bar he saw Everett Maltby and, beyond him, Tibbet the Highwayman and beyond him Cicely de Vaulles, who held the fief of the manor house, 250 yards from where he and Donald were drinking. And he touched the thick-ribbed beer mug, brought it to his lips and drank again, sour, brown English beer. History. He had read somewhere, possibly in one of the books Elinor was always reading, that people under totalitarian regimes had no access to their past. This happened in Wimbledon, too. People were simply too lazy to try and remember.

Henry's memory, of course, seemed only defective in matters that immediately concerned him. Who he had had dinner with the night before, and what, if anything, he thought about them. But he was starting to lose track of the things that had made him what he was as well. Where he had been to school, what kind of degree he had got at university. Once upon a time he had read a quite terrifying number of books and accumulated an equally terrifying number of opinions about them. But now his intellectual horizons had shrunk to debates about motorways or endless conversations about the right school for one's child, it was as if he didn't want to remember the Henry who had once promised a little more than that.

To his surprise, Donald was talking about disease. Perhaps he was drunk. Henry felt rather drunk.

'Tell me . . .' Donald was saying, 'this . . . polyneuritis of Elinor's . . .'

'Yes . . .' said Henry.

'Was that when I was treating her?'

'I should think,' said Henry, 'you would have noticed if a patient of yours was diagnosed as having polyneuritis. I mean, I should think you would have something to do with it, wouldn't you?'

'Not necessarily,' said Donald gloomily. 'I might not have noticed it. I might have said . . . "pains in the legs sort yourself out sort of thing." I sometimes do. And she might have gone to a specialist to have it diagnosed. Or perhaps I did diagnose it but I've forgotten. These days I forget what I prescribe and what people have got when they walk out of the surgery. It just goes. I forget everything. I forget where I'm supposed to be and what I've done the day before and whose round it is . . .'

'It's yours!' said Henry quickly.

'You see?' said Donald, with an air of triumph, 'you see? The old brain is cardboard. Complete and utter cardboard these days.'

He got to his feet and walked stiffly to the bar.

Perhaps you only forgot things you didn't want to be there in the first place. That was certainly how Donald felt about his patients.

And maybe that was how Henry felt about himself. And Maltby. Why should he not want to remember Maltby, though? Back to the matter in hand. Come on. Come on. Elinor.

Elinor. All this stuff about polyneuritis was handy, thought Henry, but perhaps a little too neat. One minute, there they were talking about polyneuritis, next minute, there she was dying of it. But Donald's first remark, when he returned with the drinks, was even more eerily appropriate to what Henry had in mind.

'Tell you what,' he said, 'I'll pop up and have a look at her, shall I?'

Henry gulped. Donald drank.

'Most likely,' he said, 'it's stress. She's feeling stressed. She has what we doctors call . . . stress. She's probably in a . . . stressful situation. And so she imagines she has . . . this . . .'

'Polyneuritis,' said Henry.

'That's the one. Well . . .' Donald went on, 'who knows what polyneuritis is? Really? Really? Medicine makes a lot of claims, you know, but basically all of us doctors are pretty well in the dark on most things medical . . .'

Donald was about the nearest he was likely to find to a Murderer's Doctor. But he wasn't too keen on the idea of Donald arriving just as Elinor was wiping the last traces of chicken thallium off her lips. One of the chief requirements of a poisoner was a quiet domestic life. One needed few visitors, an oppressive routine, long silences, broken only by the tick of the clock and the groans of one's victim. It was not a public crime. Everett Maltby had . . . But no. Henry didn't want to think about Maltby any more.

'Are you with me?' Donald was saying.

'Sure,' Henry was saying.

'So I'll pop up about half nine,' went on Donald. 'I'm very fond of old Elinor. I think she's a sweet, no nonsense, old-fashioned girl. She's such a gentle person!'

Henry goggled at him. This remark, it seemed to him, was on a par with 'Stalin was quite a nice guy, basically'. And what had he agreed to anyway?

There was no chance that Donald would diagnose thallium poisoning. Donald couldn't diagnose a common cold. Having him there at the beginning was simply a stroke of luck so colossal that Henry's natural pessimism was trying to turn it into a disaster.

'Make it half ten!' he said.

They ate supper at eight. By half past ten the thallium would be creeping round Elinor's bloodstream. She would be suffering from pins and needles. Stomach cramps perhaps.

She would be pleased to see a doctor.

7

When he got back the house looked empty. The autumn afternoon was paling and the ivy that covered the façade of number 63 dripped with yellows and browns. Opposite, number 47 in huge green wellingtons and baseball cap was talking to number 60. Number 60's wife was shouting something at number 60's children. Or were they number 58's children? Henry pulled the plastic bags out of the boot of the Passat, and lowered his eyes. Number 47 looked as if he were in a conversational mood.

As Henry got through the front gate, number 60 went back up the street towards his wife and number 47 dropped, suddenly and dramatically, on to his knees in front of the red Mitsubishi. For a moment Henry thought that this might be a genuine act of worship, a public act of love towards the vehicle (*I am not ashamed of what I feel about this car! It's the most beautiful thing that ever happened to me!*). But, somewhat to Henry's disappointment, number 47 did not start necking with the bodywork. He started to spray the hubcaps with what looked like toothpaste. Henry was safe anyway. Number 47 was either talking to you or the car; he was incapable of socializing what he felt about the Mitsubishi.

Henry was rather drunk.

How had he got back? Had he gone via Windlesham Avenue and the comprehensive? Or up Abacus Road, where the only black man in their part of Wimbledon lived? Had he gone down to the bottom of the hill and worked his way up to Belvedere Road from the southeast? The suburb was beginning to play tricks on him, to lie about itself. He should never have started making up stuff about Everett Maltby. Few things were sacred to Henry, but local history was one of them.

As he stowed the edenwort and the kohlrabi at the back of the cupboard, he saw his mother's strained, pale face as she boasted, unconvincingly, of her son's prowess to a neighbour. 'Henry's got a real gift for history!' she would say. After he got his lower second at the University of Loughborough, she told Mrs Freeman at 82 that Henry was 'on course for a Nobel Prize'. Could it be, thought Henry, as a shower of yams, bottled gherkins and packets of pastrami disgorged themselves on to the red-tiled floor of the kitchen, that his present bouts of cultural amnesia were a response to his mother's extravagant hopes for him?

'Why have you gone into the law?' she used to say to him. 'You're better than that, aren't you?' In fact, Henry's real problem with the law was that he wasn't quite up to it. Even after eighteen years at Harris, Harris and Overdene he was, he reflected, about as much in the dark on legal questions as Donald was on medical issues. Which was saying something. Henry's mother had, he recalled bitterly, thought that he could 'do better' than Elinor as well. 'It all depends,' Henry had said, 'what you are looking for in a relationship!' In those days Henry had talked like that. Well, if you were looking for the qualities Elinor had displayed in their years together, you could probably only have done better by marrying a man-eating tiger.

But of course, once Mrs Farr Senior had expressed doubts about a woman, it meant Henry was almost duty bound to marry her, just as, as soon as she expressed a political or aesthetic opinion, he immediately experienced a passionate surge of enthusiasm for the view most directly opposed to it. He was almost as hostile to his own mother as he was to Elinor's, even though the politesse observed by his family meant he had not yet worked out a way of expressing it. In the thirty-six years of which he had conscious memory of Mrs Farr Senior, their relationship had never developed beyond the 'isn't it a nice day?' stage. They had never had an argument, apart from one occasion in 1956, when Henry refused to wear a pair of short trousers. Henry's mother still referred to this argument.

'You remember . . .' she would say coquettishly, 'when you made that awful fuss about the trousers . . .'

Thinking about his mother brought Henry back to the matter in hand and, grim faced, he went out to the car to retrieve the chicken.

He had left it on the passenger seat, where it lay, legs in the air, headless rump deep in the upholstery. It was only when he was reaching across for it that he remembered. Those three stolen sheets from Donald's prescription pad. All it needed was someone to go looking for the jack, find their hands curling round them and start asking *why* . . .

You couldn't be too careful. Everything had to be very, very carefully done indeed.

Henry yanked out the jack, groped for the papers and stuffed them into his pocket. Just as he did so, a voice behind him said, 'I've got an awful headache!'

Elinor. Headache. How to respond. Henry tried out a little gasp of sympathy. 'Oh no!' he said. He sounded, he thought, almost openly satirical. 'One of your headaches again!'

This was supposed to be said in the tone of one dealing with news of some immense natural disaster. It came out as positively offensive disbelief. Henry turned to her and held up the jack. Appealing for clemency.

'Look,' he said, 'I found the jack!'

She sniffed.

'Put it in the shed!' she said.

Henry leered at her.

'And I got a chicken,' he said, 'the kind you like!'

And kohlrabi and okra and chili and pastrami and *thallium*!

She frowned at the pavement.

'When you've put the jack away,' she said, 'could you get in the car and go and get Maisie from ballet?'

'Yes!' said Henry.

She thrust her white face towards him. She looked as if she was in pain. Her eyebrows, Henry noted, were curiously thick. Black and bushy. Like a gorilla's, he thought.

'You block me,' she said. 'You block my creativity!'

'Sorry!' said Henry.

She swung her bottom south-south-west and steered herself off up the path. As Henry watched her retreating buttocks, grinding out yet another dismissal, he tried to remember if there had ever been a time, years ago, when he had desired her. Or had she just seen him one day, walking around the suburb where he had been born, and said to him, in that sharp voice she used for all commands: 'Marry Me!'

There was probably a man, somewhere, who could cope with Elinor. Ten feet tall and eight feet wide. With no nerves.

Henry went to the front hall, put the chicken and the jack on the table by the front door and trudged back out to the Passat. It looked smug, Henry thought, about the fact that he was going to have to drive it again. As he drove off down the street he saw the curtains of the front bedroom close. Elinor was going to have her sleep. She always needed a sleep after therapy. An hour or so spent talking with other women about how weak, cruel, uncaring, lazy and insensitive their husbands were always made her tired.

'Oh Maisie,' thought Henry, 'you who are, even now, longing to get your fat little feet out of the ballet pumps that you will never wear gracefully, soon we will be free of her. Soon we will not have to go to ballet or piano or junior aerobics. We can go wherever we like.'

Actually, if he were offered the choice of going wherever he liked in the world, he would probably choose Wimbledon. The tribal customs of Wimbledon were, in Henry's view, as worthy of study as the totems and taboos of the Aborigines of the Northern Territory. The stories of the suburb, the tales that gave number 24, 59, 30 or 47 their right to their homes, these were, in their way, as substantial as the creation myths of the Eskimos. Passats, BMWs, dormer windows, back extensions, wooden garden sheds, all meant something more than at first appeared – white wooden railings, gold name-plates on doors, stained-glass windows in bathrooms, net curtains, numbered dustbins, unnumbered dustbins, sash windows, plate-glass windows, windows with double glazing, windows without double glazing, walls painted white, all of this was part of a body of myth as strange and mysterious as the *Epic of Gilgamesh*. What was the relationship between new roofs and marital discord? Why did people who put adverts for local fêtes in their windows so often neglect the paint on their woodwork? The codes of Wimbledon were too strange and complex to be understood by its inhabitants. It needed some stranger to unlock it, to explain it to itself, to see behind that apparent silence and quietness.

Wimbledon. Its architecture compared favourably with that of northern France (bar one or two cathedrals). Its cuisine was as varied as Hong Kong or Bangkok (you could eat as well at the Mai Thai restaurant, Wimbledon Broadway, as in anywhere around the Gulf of Thailand). Its history, if you skipped a thousand years, was as violent as Phnom Penh's or Smolensk's. The things the Vikings had done in Raynes Park were, let's face it, unspeakable.

Why, Henry wondered, was he getting defensive about Wimbledon? Who was attacking it? Perhaps it was that letter from that bastard up in town. That –

Dear Mr Farr,

Thank you for your letter and thank you for letting us see your nine-volume Complete History of Wimbledon. *It's a massive work and has obviously taken a great deal of your time and trouble.*

I fear, however, that a detailed analysis of a suburb, especially a not particularly well-known one like Wimbledon, would not 'travel' well in our terms. I'm sure you'll understand what I mean when I say that a reader in, for example, Moscow would find your book very difficult to relate to. For a book to have truly international appeal, it must have, well, truly international appeal!

We all loved the chapter about Victorian Wimbledon though. Might not this make a pamphlet of some kind? Perhaps for your local historical society?

Best wishes,

Karim Jackson.

Henry's hands tightened on the wheel as he thought about Karim Jackson's letter. There were people in Moscow, New York, Rome, Paris, Oslo and Naples who were absolutely dying to find out about Wimbledon. Wimbledon was as much a mystery to them as was the Orinoco to Henry. All he had to do, he knew, was get the thing in print.

Why had this Pakistani – if he was a Pakistani – got it in for him?

Why did he take this extraordinarily negative attitude to the most important suburb in the Western world? Was it something to do with tennis? They played cricket in Pakistan, didn't they? Was that the problem? And more importantly than that, what was a Pakistani doing in a position of power and influence in a publishing house? The man (if it was a man) was probably a fairly junior member of the firm; if only Henry could find a way of getting past him to the people really in the driving seat.

He mustn't think about his book. Thinking about his book was almost worse than thinking about Elinor. He would think about what his mother always used to call 'nice things'. 'Think about nice things!' she would say to Henry as she tucked him into bed at night. And, as he coasted towards Maple Drive through the suburb's still deserted streets, Henry thought about nice things. He thought about thallium and the Guillain-Barré syndrome and whether it was or wasn't too late to have Elinor heavily insured.

8

Everything happened very quickly after he had got Maisie back to the house.

Elinor was still asleep. Before she should have a chance to wake and discover the edenwort, Henry got to work on the supper. Maisie sat in the corner of the kitchen with one chocolate bar in her mouth, another in her right hand, another in her lap and a fourth beside her on the draining board, in case anything should happen to the other three.

Henry paused over a half-dismembered edenwort. He had better catch up on Elinor's latest batch of instructions.

She wrote him notes. Notes saying what to get for supper, notes telling him not to leave his shoes by the bed . . . sometimes she left him notes telling him how she felt. About life, about the world, and above all, about him. Since she had started going to therapy, these notes had got longer and more articulate. They didn't start 'Dear Henry', or 'My Dear Husband', but simply began, picking up (as her therapist had taught her) at 'the moment of rage'. There was one, now, lurking in the vegetable basket and Henry moved towards it as one might move towards an unexploded bomb.

Why do you not understand my needs as a woman? You do not commit to the home, do you, Henry? You are (I have to say) intensely judgemental. You block and deny my aspirations to creativity and permanence.

Elinor attended art classes at Wimbledon School of Art. She was particularly keen on pottery, a skill she had, in Henry's view, even less hope of acquiring than her daughter.

You deal death to the need in me to grow and change and become myself. Like a huge wall that shields tender shoots from the light, you do not allow my passions and sensations their scope. I am afraid of you, Henry!

Not half as much as I am of you! thought Henry, as he ran his eyes down the rest of the manuscript (she must have written it before going to sleep).

I am afraid of the male violence that is in you. In a world run by men, for men . . .

Maybe, thought Henry, but, if so, run by other men for other men. I am not one of these men!

A world of cruel greed, rape, nuclear war, phallocentric control, where women are pushed to the sidelines, how can I not be afraid of you? With the fierce hatred that I know is in you? Like a mugger you leap out at me from the dark, and my rights as a woman are violated by your obscene masculinity!

Henry looked at himself in the kitchen mirror, as he crumpled up the other three pages of this latest missive and threw it in the swingbin. He looked, he had to admit, the very picture of obscene masculinity. Glumly, he began to pull out okra and edenwort. If she didn't eat the vegetables, she was almost sure to eat the meat.

Elinor was a star pupil in her therapy class. Having been taught, first at an expensive public school and then at Oxford University, to express herself to order, she found the poor creatures who shambled along to 23 Dorman Road every Saturday, Thursday, Monday and Wednesday absolutely no competition at all. Most of these women had been in what they called 'the therapy situation' for years. Elinor's difficulties were, at least from her description of the classes, bigger and better than those of her fellow therapees. She was a kind of Stakhanovite worker in the field of female suffering, setting new targets for pain, finding each week some new emotional cross to bear. The main topic on the agenda of the therapy class was, to start with anyway, Henry. They all sat around in a circle agreeing what a swine Henry was.

But as the therapy continued, Henry had observed, others were found to be guilty of the capital crime of blocking Elinor's creativity. There were other saboteurs and wreckers, Trotskyists and double-dealing spies, who, sneakily and shamefully, crept about, blocking Elinor's rightful place as an internationally acclaimed oil painter, star newspaper columnist or opera singer. Her mother for a start.

At first, Henry had not been able to believe that her therapist had got it so right. If anyone had prevented Elinor from being an oil executive, or a leading novelist and short-story writer, it was Elinor's mother, a small, heavily built woman with a squint, who lived very near the Sellafield atomic reactor. Principally because Elinor's mother was completely without talent for anything apart from giving men a hard time and had, presumably, passed on her genes to her daughter.

The therapist, apparently, while finding her mother guilty of the hideous and anti-state offence of blocking Elinor's creativity, took the view that she had managed to do this by getting Elinor to love her too much. How she worked this out was a mystery to Henry, since her mother's role in Elinor's life was confined to twice-yearly visits in which she sat in their front room and listened to Elinor telling her how awful Henry was.

He put the chicken in a roasting bag and felt in his pocket for the vial of thallium.

'Ugh!' said Maisie. 'Chicken.'

'It's OK,' said Henry, 'you can fill up on choc bars and then pretend to eat it and when she isn't looking I'll sling it in the bin.'

'Good!' said Maisie.

'I wouldn't touch a mouthful of it myself,' said Henry, 'it's that healthy free-range chicken that she likes . . .'

'Yuk!' said Maisie.

While she was munching her way through her third chocolate bar, Henry took the chicken through to the scullery and carefully anointed its breast with the thallium. On top of the thallium he sprinkled salt, a very little pepper and a coating of tarragon leaves. It was six thirty.

Back in the kitchen, he cleaned the edenwort and the okra and chopped them up small enough to be unrecognizable. He whistled as he chopped and, as he tipped the vegetables into the frying pan, he sang, to the tune of Candyman Blues, the following song:

> Thallium
> Thallium
> Guillain-Barré
> Thallium
> Thallium Thallium
> Thallium Guillain-Barré.

Underneath the frying pan was another note.

You hate women, don't you? Why do you hate women? Why are you so frightened of them? Why do you seek to destroy them? To caricature them? Is it their creative potential that frightens you? Their menstrual power? Their child-bearing power? Is it their fund of womanliness you hate? Don't you hate women, Henry?

Henry couldn't think of a woman he disliked apart from Elinor. And, of course, Elinor's mother.

How would Elinor's mother react to her daughter's death? Henry had a feeling that she would take it well. She had taken her husband's brain tumour like a . . . well, like a man. 'OK,' her square jaw seemed to say, 'Derek has a brain tumour. That happens. We can deal with it!' And she and her daughter had dealt with it. They had coped. They had certainly coped a lot better than Elinor's father, a man Henry had always liked. The news of his impending death had badly ruffled his composure. He had talked wildly about the meaning of life, the emptiness of it all, the lack of scope offered by the Guardian Building Society. Elinor and her mother had clearly found all this in bad taste.

'Daddy is depressed,' they would say, narrowing their eyes and tilting their square chins downward, 'very, very depressed. About the fact that he is dying.'

They clearly felt he should have taken a more manly approach to the brain tumour. A man who had such a positive attitude towards Do It Yourself could surely have used some of that energy to combat the decay of his central nervous system. Henry thought about his father-in-law's funeral, as he placed the Chicken Thallium in the oven, and then checked his watch again. He thought about the dignified posture of Elinor and Elinor's mother, about how good they looked in black, about how they retained their composure even as the oblong box containing Derek slid off through a gap in the crematorium wall. About how, as Elinor and Elinor's mother stood by the flowers in the rain at Putney Vale Crematorium, someone had said to him, 'They're taking it very well!' Of course they were, thought Henry, they couldn't give a toss about the poor bastard.

He would wear his black leather jacket at Elinor's funeral. And the green socks. And the red shoes. He would deck himself out in the kind of clothes that would give most offence to her were she alive. And if Elinor's mother should break down he would sob operatically and people would say to each other, as he stood by the flowers afterwards, 'My, my. He is taking it badly.'

It was six forty-five. He turned the oven on to 250 and put the okra and the edenwort on to a low heat. In approximately one hour she would be getting her chops round the first succulent mouthful of Chicken Thallium. By midnight she would be experiencing severe abdominal discomfort.

Whistling to himself, Henry laid the table, while, in the corner of the kitchen, Maisie finished her last chocolate bar and got to work on a packet of crisps, a tube of Rollos, half a pound of jellybabies and a jumbo bar of Turkish delight. As she ate she cast worried glances up towards the cupboard by the stove, where lay a small sack of potato crisps, some Liquorice Allsorts and two packets of biscuits. Sometimes Henry wondered whether the junk food industry was going to be able to take the kind of demands Maisie was going to make on it in the years ahead.

Occasionally, for some obscure reason of her own, Elinor was pleasant. Henry could not quite work out why, since her pleasantness was not always followed by a request for money or some other favour; perhaps she was remembering something he had quite forgotten, an incident during their courtship perhaps (they must have had a courtship) or a Henry, now lost to Henry himself, who could have inspired feelings such as pleasure. Or perhaps this was part of some internal clock of hers and, at some moments, often weeks or months apart, Elinor was programmed to be briefly but definitely pleasant.

It always threw him.

'Hullo, darling!' she said, as she came round the kitchen door in her black trouser-suit, her black hair swept back under an Alice band. 'I've had a lovely sleep!'

Henry looked at her suspiciously. Why is she saying this? he thought. What has she got in mind?

She crossed the kitchen floor and pecked him on the cheek.

'Sorry I was cross!' she said. Her voice was light, tremulous. Perhaps she was planning to murder him!

'You're making supper!' she said.

'That's right!'

With just a hint of normal, workaday Elinor, she pointed a stubby finger at the vegetables.

'What's that?'

'It's edenwort, darling,' said Henry. 'It's a new vegetable!'

Elinor did not pick up the pan and hurl it across the room. She scooped up a little on her forefinger and nibbled at it.

'It's rather nice!'

'And I've done chicken!' said Henry. 'Free-range chicken. How you like it. All crispy in the oven. Topped with . . .'

'What's it topped with?' said Elinor suspiciously.

'Lovely herbs!' said Henry. 'Lovely fresh herbs from the garden picked all fresh and with no chemicals on!'

'Mmmm!' she said.

And skipped off towards Maisie who, at the first sound of her mother's footsteps, had concealed her cache of sweets under her jersey.

Perhaps, thought Henry, she was appealing to his better feelings. She was making herself difficult to kill on humanitarian grounds. He watched her as she danced a few larky steps with her daughter, singing in an effortfully pure soprano while Maisie shuffled along trying to keep the sweets safe under her jumper.

'Love-lee chicken!' she was singing. 'Love-lee chicken!'

Still in a larky mood, she began to lift her daughter up off the floor. Maisie, like Henry, did not like being lifted. She held herself quite still, staring seriously at her mother, thinking, quite obviously, Henry thought, about Turkish delight. Elinor put her down.

'You two,' she said, 'are so stiff!'

Henry looked across at Maisie. Was Elinor perhaps going to try and top her as well? Never mind. In a very short space of time she would have her feet under the table and those huge jaws would be munching their way into the breast.

And then the doorbell rang.

9

It was Donald.

Elinor was pleased to see him. She it was who opened the door and Henry heard a high-pitched giggle followed by a lengthy squawk of pleasure.

'Donald,' she said, 'it's Donald.'

Henry wondered whether she was having an affair with Donald. WIMBLEDON DOCTOR IN POISON LOVE TRIANGLE, he thought to himself. Or possibly, DOCTOR IN LOVE PACT POISON DEATH WISH PATIENT HORROR.

No. Donald would never do it with a patient. His offence against those who came to him for medical help was less easy to punish. But he was certainly guilty, thought Henry, of liking Elinor and, as he came into the hall, nodding his big head as Elinor fussed round him, Henry wondered whether his wife might not be, *au fond*, quite a pleasant woman. Numbers of people seemed to like her. Neighbours, friends, colleagues. People bought her lunch and rang her up and sent her birthday cards; it seemed a particularly cruel joke that one of the few people who really did dislike her should be married to her.

'You must stay to supper!' Elinor was saying.

'Oh, Elinor,' Donald was saying, 'I couldn't . . .' But he was saying it in a way that implied possible assent. Elinor went to the stove, singing in a high soprano voice 'Donald's coming to supper . . . Donald's coming to supper . . .' When this song failed to make the impact she clearly expected it to make, she turned to Henry as if she was addressing some Yugoslav peasant and did a lot of the kind of lip and tongue work she had used on Elke, their one and only au pair.

'Donald's staying to break bread with us!' she said.

Henry managed a smile. Once again, Lustgarten was on the line to him. 'It was when the friend of the family, Donald Templeton, the trusted and valued doctor who attended both Farr and his wife, came to call that the plans of the man who came to be known as the Wimbledon Poisoner came badly unstuck. Suddenly, to Farr's consternation and disappointment, it wasn't a cosy, deadly meal for two by the fireside, but Chicken Thallium for three!'

Lustgarten stopped by the fire, his hand on the wall, and glared, menacingly, at the camera.

Lustgarten had a point. Did Donald like breast meat? If he did, was Henry going to be able to avoid serving him with any? He tried to readjust his face to make him look less like Macbeth.

'Oh,' he said again, 'great!'

Donald looked at Maisie. 'Only ten!' his big, grey eyes seemed to say. 'Ten years old, and less than a month to live!' Maisie grinned.

'Hullo, Donald!' she said.

Henry attempted to gain some control over the situation. 'Well,' he said, 'we've got a nice, juicy chicken leg for you!'

Donald did not seem unresponsive to this notion. He did not say, 'Actually – I'm a breast man myself!' But then, it was early in the game for such delicate negotiations. Soon, carving etiquette might well be as developed and intricate a ritual as chess and, when it did get that advanced it would probably be in Wimbledon but, for the moment, Henry was faced with the unattractive prospect of involuntary double murder. Was polyneuritis infectious?

'I don't understand it, Doctor! They both started throwing up and seeing flashing lights! Might it be some form of . . . I don't know . . .' (rapidly) '. . . infectious polyneuritis?'

The trouble with this, of course, was that it might lead to another doctor, one more competent than Donald, examining their evening meal. No – he would have to make sure that no breast meat came Donald's way. It shouldn't be too difficult.

'Henry tells me,' Donald was saying in a carefully conversational manner, 'that you've had a touch of the old . . . polyneuritis!'

He said this as if amused by the thought. There was nothing terrifying or frightening about polyneuritis, his half-smile and gentle nod seemed to say, it was just an illness . . . like . . . cancer . . . or coronary thrombosis . . . or Alzheimer's . . . or leprosy! Pretty soon they would all be laughing about it.

'He what?' squawked Elinor.

She shot him one of her more mainline, Elinor-style glances. The standard who-is-this-jerk-and-why-am-I-married-to-him expression. Which, for some reason, then turned into a laugh.

'Silly old thing!' she said, and cuffed him affectionately.

Henry looked at Donald. 'She's a brave little liar!' he tried to make his eyes say. 'She doesn't want to bother you with it.' Donald, who was still nodding his head, did not seem to notice any of this. Perhaps he was just in the kind of trance he went into as a matter of course every time illness was discussed. He had a faraway, Buddhist look in the eyes – a kind of stillness and peace that denoted the complete absence of any mental process.

'I've been a bit depressed,' she said, 'that's all.'

Bit depressed? Bit depressed? You've been behaving like a commodity broker on Black Thursday, haven't you?

'Let's have a drink!' said Henry as he thought this.

'Sherry,' said Elinor swiftly.

A pint mug, my dear? Or shall we decant it into a bucket?

'Surely, my love,' said Henry lightly.

Donald chose Scotch. Maisie had a lemonade. Henry poured himself a Perrier water. He was going to have to keep calm and steady for the task ahead.

'For Farr,' said Lustgarten, 'as he laughed and joked with his old friend in the front room of their Wimbledon home, was already planning exactly where his carving knife would skirt the edge of the poisoned breast meat, digging deeper and deeper away from the tainted flesh, so that neither he nor Templeton would suffer. Farr's doctor was no part of his murderous plan. His venom, both actual and metaphysical, was held in reserve for his wife!'

Henry went to the oven and looked through the grease-stained glass window. He could just make out the chicken. It was still oatmeal-white around the fleshy part of the thighs. But the breast was turning a golden brown – the herbs, the black pepper and the thallium were crisping up nicely. He turned back to Elinor and Donald.

Donald looked, thought Henry, like a perfect blend of Doctor Kildare and Gillespie, the older, wiser doctor of the partnership. Donald was perfectly poised on the edge of middle age – greying curls, the big, sculptural ears, the solidly Roman nose all suggested power, maturity, certainty. Henry concentrated on Donald's face and, as so often these days, found it easier to look as if he was listening by doing the reverse. He timed his nods and yesses and 'Indeeds!' on an entirely mathematical basis, interspersing them with a sort of pucker-cum-squint that could be mild disagreement or the preface to some statement of his own. Sometimes he helped along this impression of participation by opening his mouth and shovelling his chin forward until someone interrupted him.

'Actually,' Elinor was saying, 'we were going to Portugal, but I think we'll be staying in Wimbledon this year. I can't see myself getting out of Wimbledon at all.'

Unless you count the ride up to Putney Vale Crematorium, thought Henry, that'll be a nice little outing for you, won't it? He got up again and went back to the oven. Donald and Elinor had been talking for thirty minutes. Henry marvelled once again at time. Its passage seemed, nowadays, to be the only event in his life. Nothing happened in it any more. It just went. It wasn't the flying thing described by poets. It was the only thing on the horizon, shouldering aside achievement and sensation with attention-seeking roughness, and nothing, not conversation, wine, sexual encounters or the search for knowledge or fame could prevent it. What had they actually done while this chicken was cooking? Bugger all.

Maybe murder was the only way to make all this meaningful. Maybe that was why he was trying to poison Elinor? For a moment he could not quite think why he was trying to poison Elinor. It was just another thing he did – like dealing with wills and conveyancing at Harris, Harris and Overdene, or shouting at Maisie to go to bed. Then he pulled down the oven door, smelt the sweet, fatty smell of the meat and knew that it was probably this very fact that accounted for his decision to go through with the business.

He was poisoning Elinor because she was there.

'Lovely chicken,' said Henry, 'coming up!'

She was smiling at him. My God, thought Henry, perhaps the therapy is beginning to work. Perhaps she is going to turn into a quietly spoken, normal human being. Perhaps that is the point of therapy. For the first year or so it turns you into a kind of psychopathic animal and then suddenly, like a butterfly emerging from the pupa, you sprout wings, your heart opens, you become . . . charming. He looked at Elinor as he brought the chicken to the table.

No. Not yet, anyway. Killing Elinor was, Henry felt, still an ecologically sound thing to do. It would take at least another seven or eight years to turn her into a recognizable human being. Maybe even longer. In fact (Henry went back to the fridge and took out two bottles of wine), if she kept on with this present therapist there was absolutely no hope for her at all. If there was any hope for her, it was indisputable that the outlook was grim for anyone with whom she might come in contact. The woman kept telling her she needed assertiveness training. Elinor needed about as much assertiveness training as Napoleon.

'Lovely chicken!' said Henry. 'Tasty free-range chicken.'

They were looking at him oddly. Elinor took another swig of sherry and Henry arranged wine glasses at each place. Then he went back to the cutlery drawer and, with a skill born of long practice, lobbed knives and forks over to Maisie, who set them down in her customary eccentric manner. Sometimes forks would appear on the right and knives on the left, sometimes (Henry always felt this was Maisie's way of telling people they were not welcome) two knives or only a spoon. Elinor, who usually took it upon herself to criticize all aspects of her daughter's behaviour, was into her third sherry. She and Donald were discussing cars with great enthusiasm. They talked of the Nissan Cherry, the Volvo 740, the Granada Ghia, the Renault 5, the XJ6 Jaguar.

People in Wimbledon, these days, always talked about things as if they were people, and people as if they were things. They lacked confidence in their own values.

Henry was going to add a chapter towards the end of *The Complete History of Wimbledon* in which he planned to deal with the failure of nerve he sensed in the place. Some creature he had met at a dinner party recently (he was, it had to be said, from East Finchley) had had the nerve to tell him that New York was 'more vibrant' than Wimbledon. He had gone on about lofts. People in New York, apparently, lived in lofts, presumably because they couldn't afford houses. 'You have to go there,' he had said to Henry, pressing his face forward, 'it's so alive!' And another man, who should have known better even though he was from Southfields, had announced that Wimbledon was 'on the dull side. It's all accountants and solicitors, isn't it?' What was wrong, thought Henry, with being a solicitor? He thought about Harris, Harris and Overdene. He thought about how Harris smiled at Harris, whenever Henry passed his office door. He thought about the way that Overdene looked at him from his glass cubbyhole whenever Henry was twenty minutes late from lunch. And found to his annoyance that he was grinding his teeth.

Henry breathed deeply. Sooner or later something was going to snap.

'Are you all right?' said Elinor.

'Fine, darling!' said Henry.

The plates were on the table. The group was seated. Henry was carving. Ladies first. Two, three, four huge chunks of Chicken Thallium. Smothered with gravy, garnished with unspeakable, uneatable edenwort and okra. Ladies first. If you don't like the vegetables – have the meat! Ladies first! The plate was on its way to Elinor.

'Leg OK for you, Donald?' said Henry.

'Actually,' said Donald, 'I fancy a bit of breast!'

'Have this!' said Elinor, thrusting her poisoned meat towards him. 'I'm not hungry all of a sudden. Have this!'

10

Of course, in all the books, poisoning was a comparatively simple affair. You made them Horlicks or Ovaltine or tea or coffee. You added the arsenic, the antimony or the heavy metal. And they took it down dutifully. Henry might have known that in his case the operation would prove a little more complicated. He watched, open-mouthed, as Donald beamed down at his Chicken Thallium.

'Well,' said Donald, 'I'd better get abreast!'

Elinor seemed to find this very funny. It was the kind of joke that went down well in Wimbledon. Normally, Henry would have joined in the laughter. Now he watched in horrified silence as Donald cut himself a giant slice of poisoned meat.

'Won't you have any?' he said, desperately, to Elinor.

'No,' she said, 'I might eat later.'

'It's lovely!' said Henry feebly.

'Mmmmm,' said Donald, swallowing a mouthful, 'it is!' He chewed it very thoroughly and, as Henry watched, began to swallow. 'You could die for this!' he said.

Too right you could, thought Henry.

Things were now going very, very slowly. As Henry watched (no one else round the table was eating) Donald lifted another laden fork towards his mouth. Halfway through the trip he decided to make the mouthful even more exciting. He smeared the chicken with eden-wort, okra and gravy, rubbed it round the plate and set if off once more in the direction of his wide, beautifully moulded mouth.

The edenwort and the okra would do it. Surely. Unlike thallium, Henry felt, they were probably odourful and tasteful in the extreme. Enough to make you gag on first crunch, surely. Donald would choke and spit and deposit the whole mouthful back on to the plate. But, as Henry watched, Donald broke into a smile. And not just any smile. It wasn't simply that he was managing to smile with his mouth full – a difficult enough task at the best of times – it was that his smile expressed so many real, positive qualities that it must be designed to sell something. It seemed a shame to waste it on friends.

'Mmmm,' said Donald, 'mmmm!' And then, after a bit of Christ-this-is-so-delicious-it-seems-a-shame-to-go-on-about-it-but-I-feel-it-is-my-duty acting, he went on, 'So chewy. So chewy and fresh!'

He was even beginning to talk like an advertisement. He really liked Chicken Thallium and he wanted people to know that he did. Feeling like an accomplice in this business ('Tell me – how did you get it so chewy?') Henry said, 'Yes. It is. It is chewy. It's a bit tough, the meat. I – '

'What is it?'

'Edenwort and okra.'

Even this did not make Donald crane his neck forward and start retching all over the table. He just nodded and smiled and went on chewing Chicken Thallium, slowly and methodically

Henry tried to think of a remark that would go with an expansive gesture. The sort of gesture that might, reasonably, allow a chap to knock over a bottle of wine and make sure at least half of it got all over Donald's plate. 'But what does it all mean?' perhaps, or, 'For God's sake, we're all going to die!'

He was unable to think of a suitable gesture. With a violence born of desperation, he swung at the bottle nearest to him and the mouth of a bottle of Tavel Rosé landed neatly in the pile of Donald's chicken, allowing pink liquid to pulse on to the plate.

'Henry!' said Elinor. 'What on earth did you do that for?'

'Sorry,' said Henry, 'I slipped!'

Donald was looking foolishly down at his plate. 'Oh . . .' he was saying, 'oh. . .'

He wanted more Chicken Thallium, you could tell. Henry was so infuriated by the childlike look of loss on his face he had half a mind to give him some. Then, getting to his feet, he scooped up the plate. Before he could head off for the dustbin, Elinor gripped his wrist firmly. She had strong hands, and the pressure she put into her grasp felt as if she was about to throw him over her shoulder or come out with some menacingly appropriate comment.

'Hang on! Shall we just run a lab test on this chicken!'

In fact she said: 'Give it to Tibbles.'

Tibbles was Henry's cat. Or, more accurately, she was Maisie's cat. Or, even more accurately, she was no one's cat. Responsibility for Tibbles was a free-floating affair, mainly consisting of whoever didn't want to feed her saying to whoever they thought should be feeding her, 'She's your cat!' She was, of course, in the way of cats, no one's but her own. A small, thin tabby, she spent her life trying to work out the central dilemmas of her life – how to get in and out of the house, and why the fat man called Henry tried to kick her every time the two other people in the house were out of the way. Henry hated Tibbles. He had fantasized about her death almost as much as he had fantasized about Elinor's. Why, now her end was so immi-nent, did he feel a desire to avert it?

'Why not?' he said, and taking both plate and chicken he hurried out to the scullery. 'I'll cut you some leg!' he called.

How much had Donald eaten? Enough to kill him? And, if he had, what was the antidote?

He very much did not want Donald to die. Donald was boring, sensationally incompetent at his job, complacent, vain, narcissistic, almost aggressively narrow-minded. But he was a forty-year-old Englishman. He was someone to drink with, for Christ's sake! He did not deserve death by heavy metal poisoning.

There was a poisons unit at Charing Cross Hospital, wasn't there? Some years ago Maisie had swallowed a whole bottle of vitamin pills and, although Henry had suggested that in his view Maisie's stomach could probably have stood a diet of broken glass, aspirin and raw steak, Elinor had insisted on ringing Charing Cross Hospi-tal. As far as Henry could remember they gave advice over the phone. But he couldn't possibly phone from the house. He could go to a phone box. '...Er... I seem to have swallowed a bit of thallium...' How could he put it? 'I'm doing some work on optical lenses with a high refractive index and I seem to have got some... er... thallium on my sandwiches...' They would want to know where and how, wouldn't they? They were probably in close touch with the police. Oh, Jesus Christ, how long had he got? How long had Donald got? Not long, from the look of the chicken. One thing was for certain. Tibbles had got hardly any time left at all. She was bum up in the air, small head to one side, gnawing her way through Donald's portion and then on to the rest of the poisoned carcass of the chicken, which Henry added to her plate.

If she was well enough to formulate a view on the question – and at the present rate of progress it looked as if she might be – Elinor would take a dim view of the poisoning of Tibbles. Cats did not rate quite as high on her scale of things worth fighting for as, say, dolphins, but their stock certainly stood higher than that of the middle-aged, white, heterosexual male. She seemed unable to appreciate the fact that Henry himself was one of a threatened species, even though that threat was treated with contempt by most ecologists and nearly all women. Perhaps this was why, increasingly, Henry saw life as a struggle between him and the things his wife cared for so passionately – whales, seals, Aborigines, dolphins . . . If it came to a straight choice between a dolphin and Henry (and in Henry's view things had already got that serious) he would go for Henry every time. Would Elinor though?

He stood looking down at Tibbles, breathing heavily. Blood pressure, Henry. Blood pressure. Don't think about animals. Don't think about anything that disturbs you. Think about what your mother used to call 'nice things'. Think about Wimbledon. Think about the rows of quiet houses. Think about the rattle of the electric trains on their way to Southfields and Putney. Think about the neatly kept front gardens and the commuters clacking their way back in the twilight towards the carefully assembled innocence of home.

He was all right now. He cut Donald a generous slice of untainted leg, and went back to the dining table. Now. How was he going to make this phone call? He could not think of a single convincing excuse that would get him out of the house. He would have to use the phone in the hall. Now, while they were eating. He got to his feet.

'Just got to . . . er . . .' Elinor and the doomed man looked at him oddly.

'Make a call,' said Henry with a crispness that surprised him. 'It's a work problem. Tricky conveyancing thing. I think a tort may be involved.'

Elinor was looking at him with what might have been respect. He almost never discussed his work with her, while she, like many other progressive people, regarded the law as a sinister conspiracy to defraud the laity.

'It all hinges on Prosser v. Prosser,' went on Henry, in a world-weary voice, 'as usual . . .'

And, with the purposeful stride of a great barrister on his way to a confrontation in the Old Bailey, he went out into the hall.

It was curious. His attempt to murder her seemed to have given him a new strength in the relationship. He was, suddenly, almost decisive. And that was what was needed. Even as he closed the door behind him, the thallium was on its way down through Donald's oesophagus, slithering towards his stomach and digestive tract, where his body chemicals would turn it into a disease Donald would have difficulty in recognizing. There was no time to lose.

11

Henry dialled the number of Charing Cross Hospital and asked in low tones for the Poisons Unit.

'The what?' said the girl on the switchboard.

'The Poisons Unit!' hissed Henry, in what he realized was a distinctly suspicious manner.

'Can't hear you, caller . . .'

'The Poisons Unit!' said Henry, as loudly as he dared. He tried to say this in a way that suggested that he was always ringing up for a natter about arsenic and thallium, that there was nothing odd about his request.

At that moment Elinor came into the hall. She stood in the darkness, looking at him curiously.

'Hullo,' said a voice at the other end, 'the Poisons Unit.'

'Hullo,' said Henry breezily, 'Henry Farr here from Harris, Harris and Overdene . . .'

'Yes,' said the voice cautiously. Elinor was still looking at him.

'I've got a problem,' said Henry, 'with the conveyancing papers on 56 Northwood Road. I have a real difficulty in locating who has responsibility for the dustbins.'

'This is the Poisons Unit,' said the voice, cautiously.

'I know,' said Henry, 'and I am sorry to bother you at this time of night but my client has given me to understand that this is when you would be available. Tell me, in the lease as originally drawn up would you be able to let my client know whether there was specific reference to the controversy over the dustbins or did this develop after the Maltese took over?'

Elinor folded her arms.

'Tell your client,' said the voice at the other end of the phone, 'that he or she would have a better chance of establishing who is or is not responsible for his or her dustbins if he or she employed a lawyer who didn't address his inquiries to people whose principal concern is pharmacology.' The line went dead.

'Thank you very much indeed!' said Henry with what sounded like genuine enthusiasm. 'That really is most helpful in our terms. I will of course let my client know that Mr Makaroupides takes full responsibility for this and that will take a weight off his mind. Have a nice day!'

He put the phone down and stared coolly at Elinor. 'It's four o'clock in New York!' he said.

'So what?' said Elinor.

'That's where I was phoning. Glyn, Harwood and Schmeiss operate almost entirely out of New York.'

Elinor goggled at him. She had never heard Henry talk like this before. Neither had Henry. But desperation could do strange things to a man. Donald was dying in there, for God's sake. Hadn't there been something in that book about Graham Young? Graham had got him into this. He could get him out of it. Young had, as far as Henry could remember, suggested the antidote for one of his victims himself. Dyner— something . . . dyner—

'Are you all right?' said Elinor.

'I'm fine,' said Henry, 'but this means I'd better just pop out for a second.'

Elinor's eyes were wide with concern. Henry never popped out anywhere. Especially after nine o'clock at night.

'I'll have to go and see Martin Rubashon. He's only just down the road, but this is a face-to-face matter, I'm afraid.'

Who, Elinor's expression seemed to be saying, is Martin Rubashon? And why have I never heard his name before?

'What's a face-to-face matter?' she said.

'The dustbins, of course,' said Henry testily, 'this is a nine-million-dollar contract. I'm not letting it slip over a few measly dustbins!' And with a calm purpose that he did not feel he went out into the street.

As the autumn air met his face, he remembered. Dynercaprol and potassium chloride. That was it. Young had actually suggested its use to the police at one stage of their investigations. All he had to do was stroll down to Underwoods and pick up a bit of dynercaprol and potassium chloride. He didn't fancy another trip to the chemist's he had visited that morning. There was something scary about the place, something, well, Maltbyish . . .

He had, of course, still got a few sheets of Donald's prescription pad. With a quick glance back at the house he ran to the car. Once inside he groped for the sheets in his pocket. He must be careful to disguise his handwriting. Wasn't doctors' handwriting supposed to be hard to read? Henry normally wrote a neat, italic script; it was, according to the more malicious of his colleagues, his only real legal qualification. How much though? How much would Donald need to get him back on the road? And how, come to think of it, was Henry going to get him to absorb the stuff, short of creeping up on him while he was asleep and forcing it down his throat or up his arse? He stopped for a moment, the crumpled sheet of prescription pad on his knee, and wondered whether Donald was really worth all this effort. Might it not be simpler just to let him go? He had had a pretty good life. A pleasant wife (in his terms anyway), a nice house in the suburbs. He had had six glorious years with Arfur.

No. He couldn't do it to Donald. Henry filled in the form and drove down to Underwoods.

Although the pharmacist seemed to have some trouble deciphering the prescription, and Henry had to go through a nerve-wracking pantomime of ignorance about the nature of the chemicals he required, it wasn't long before he was standing once again on the doorstep of 54 Maple Drive.

It might be possible to slip the antidote in some pudding or dessert wine or *digestif*. He had a few hours anyway. And Elinor was just going to have to wait for her merciful release. Henry wondered whether dynercaprol and potassium chloride taken without thallium might be poisonous. He could slip some to Elinor as well. But no, even as he thought this, he realized the hopelessness of the task ahead of him. Killing Elinor was the kind of thing you would need years of study to accomplish. You couldn't just walk into it casually, as he had done, drop home from the office and decide to eradicate her on the spur of the moment. As her mother was fond of saying – it had taken a lot of trouble to get her this far, and this last little step was going to take a deal of organizing as well.

On the doorstep of number 54, Henry stood for a moment in the gloom, flexing his fingers. The Wimbledon Strangler. Inside he could see Elinor talking, with some animation, to Donald, her long hair falling across her face. Donald was nodding eagerly as she talked. She was gesturing about something now, some issue that had excited her, dolphins probably, and as she waved her arms Donald gave her an admiring smile. She was, undoubtedly, in good physical shape. She had a fairly thick neck and her forearms, well, the only way to describe them was meaty.

You could use tights of course. Or piano wire. Like the SAS.

With this comforting thought Henry rang the doorbell, hard, and watched his wife heave herself out of the chair and stump through to the hall. Go for it, Henry! he said, once again to himself, Go for it! The evening has a new agenda. Detoxification followed by strangulation. Go for it, Henry! he said, for the last time, Go for it!

12

Both of them refused all offers of food and drink.

The conversation had turned to law and order. Elinor had begun, Donald told him, by discussing her problems. It appeared she had something called the Madonna Complex. Either she was a Madonna and people didn't give her credit for being one, or else she was trying to be one and people were trying to stop her or possibly she was being forced to be one against her better judgement. Henry couldn't work out, from Donald's description, which of these alternatives was best described by the Madonna Complex, indeed he didn't really listen to a word either of them said. All of his energies were devoted to bringing the conversation round to the topic of food and drink, but Donald, once he had explained, or failed to explain, the Madonna Complex, moved swiftly on to what he described as his problem, which turned out to be law and order.

'Say what you like!' he said. 'Say what you like. If a yobbo attacks my home and family. If some coloured youth breaks into my house and tries to rape my wife . . .' Henry goggled at him. 'I'd strangle the bastard with my bare hands. I don't see why coloured youths should have *carte blanche* to steal my stereo and shit all over my compact-disc player and rape my wife. I don't see it.'

Elinor was looking at Donald, her mouth open. There was, Henry knew, an unspoken contract between them. She was allowed to talk about herself if he was allowed to rave on about black men. The fact that he was soon going to die, thought Henry, gave his words a special poignancy.

'England,' he was saying, 'used to be the most civilized country in the world. Say what you like, you were safe in Wimbledon. Right?'

'Right!' said Henry.

'But now,' said Donald, 'England is a country run by yobbos for yobbos. A country in which respect for law and order takes second place to the problems of some illiterate chocco.'

Henry wasn't sure how to answer this. Hadn't Mrs Thatcher solved this kind of problem? Wasn't it OK to be racist these days? Donald seemed to be describing the bad old days before Mrs Thatcher, as far as Henry could see. Perhaps his memory, like Henry's, was buckling under the strain of being forty. Or else, possibly, the thallium was starting to affect his brain. It would be difficult to assess things like that with Donald. Whatever was the case he, Henry, had better get something down him.

'Whisky, Donald?'

'I won't, thanks.'

'Beer? Brandy?'

'I won't.'

'Cup of tea? Coffee?'

'Not for me.'

Wine? Ouzo? Vodka? Mead? Mineral water? Hot chocolate? Dynercaprol? Potassium chloride?

'Bugger off, friend chocco, I say. Bugger off, friendly neighbouring Paki. And bugger off, Greek and Arab while you're at it. We don't need you. England used to be a country with red pillar boxes and policemen with red noses and decent law-abiding citizens you could eat your dinner off. Now it's a refugee camp!'

Elinor looked pained. Her anguish, Henry noted, went down rather well with Donald.

'Shouldn't we,' said Elinor, 'welcome the refugee? Shouldn't people of all races and nationalities be welcomed by a caring country?'

Donald chose not to confront this vague, if morally positive statement. He was grinning, in a fatherly sort of way, and wagging his hands at Elinor.

'My point, Elly, is this – ' (*Elly? Elly?*) 'Where is the space in all this for the little man? The ordinary, average Englishman. What I would call the little man. Me and Henry, say, who just want a mortgage and a little house and get on with it!'

Elinor started to make more anguished noises.

'How about a cool glass of orange juice?' said Henry. 'Or a sandwich?'

They both looked at him oddly. Elinor narrowed her eyes.

'Washing up, Henry!' she said.

'Yes, m'love!' said Henry lightly.

Oh well. Donald had had a good innings. His time had quite obviously come.

'How about some mineral water?'

'No thanks, old man,' said Donald, 'we're setting the world to rights here.'

Henry started to pack the plates into the washing-up machine. Smeared with grease, fragments of chicken and edenwort, they reminded him, as so often, of his life. Quite decent things, hopelessly botched, needing to be made clean again. That awful doubt came at him again. Maybe Wimbledon wasn't such a great place. Maybe *The Complete History* was what that publisher said it was – a boring load of old rubbish. Maybe – but these were the kind of thoughts that kept Henry awake sometimes at four in the morning, longing for the dawn. They were not to be contemplated. That way lay madness.

Even as a poisoner, not, you would have thought, the most demanding of professions, he seemed to be a complete failure. Seeing him engaged in domestic activity, Tibbles came up to him and began to rub her harsh fur against his legs. In a curious way he would miss Tibbles. Who was going to go first? Her or Donald?

'What the English have given the world,' said Donald, 'is a respect for law and order and decency. I'm talking about justice, you get me? A people who care passionately about fair play, whose legal system is – Christ!'

Henry jerked round.

'You OK?'

'Just got a blast in the gut.'

'Oh,' said Henry, 'have a drink of something!' But Donald was doubled up on the sofa.

Henry rushed through to the kitchen, poured the dynercaprol and potassium chloride into a small glass of water and hurried back to Donald.

'Here,' he said, trying to keep his voice jolly, 'some new tummy thing for you. It'll set you right in no time.'

Donald looked at him suspiciously.

'The best thing for a gyp tum,' he said, 'is – '

'Quickly – ' said Henry, raising the glass to his lips.

Donald spat back the liquid. 'Christ, old man – ' he muttered, 'what are you trying to do? Poison me?'

It was clear that Donald extended his brutal, no-nonsense attitude to medical care to himself.

'No,' he said, 'I'll be all right. Sort myself out in no time at all. I'll be – Oh my God!'

Henry made one more attempt. Putting his left arm round Donald's shoulder, he took advantage of his first relaxation from the spasm of pain, to raise the glass to his lips, push his head back and, as if he were administering medicine to Maisie, roll the fluid past the perfectly kept teeth. There was a gulp and a yell and the rest of the glass (he had drunk at least some) flew up and out and on to the sanded floor of the dining area.

'Henry – ' said Donald, 'what the fuck is that?'

'It's called . . .' Henry paused. 'Globramine.'

The sound of the name seemed to reassure Donald. 'I think I know it,' he gasped, 'though I'm not very good on drugs. I'm rather against a lot of these medicaments . . .'

He was wheezing now, as if in the grip of an asthma attack.

'Let the bastards sort themselves out.'

It was difficult to know, though, whether he had had enough to save him. But at least, thought Henry, the man had a fighting chance. If only Elinor hadn't refused her portion. She must have some radar, he thought, that at the last saved her from the worst effects of his anger and frustration. Which is why it all came back on him. It's a war, thought Henry, between men and women. It's a war, a long, bitter and pointless war, in which towns are burnt, cities taken, allies betrayed . . . and at the end of the war, as after all wars, there is no victory, only the shabby compromise of peace.

He could have murdered her then, in front of Donald and Maisie and the cat. He could have run at her, forced her to the ground and banged her stupid, glossy head until her brains spilled out on to the stupid, glossy floor.

But he didn't. He stood there, clenching and unclenching his hands, trying not to twitch. Am I going crazy? he thought. And when I do, will all this get easier?

'I'll run Donald home!' Elinor was saying, 'you get Maisie to bed!'

'Yes, dear!' said Henry.

As Elinor and Donald shuffled towards the door, Tibbles shouldered her way into the room. She looked left and right and approached the pool of dynercaprol and potassium chloride in a carefully stylish manner. She looked round the room, as if to check that no one else wanted it and then, watched by a sullen Henry, began to lick it up greedily.

Women and cats, thought Henry, women and cats . . .

While Elinor and Donald were gone, Henry practised strangling.

The whole problem was going to be catching her off her guard. And Elinor was never off her guard. Now Henry thought about it, she seemed to enter rooms which he was in carefully, keeping her back to the wall; if he got close to her, she nearly always moved away quickly, usually making sure their bodies did not touch. Henry had always assumed that this was due, on her part, to an entirely natural physical repugnance for him; she moved away from him as one might move away from a bad smell or a dangerous horse. And up until now, the effortless ballet of their lack of encounter had come, in a way, as a relief. He, after all, found her quite as repulsive as she found him and, as the two of them waltzed from oven to sink, from window to cutlery drawer, staring up, down, sideways, anywhere but at each other, Henry had always assumed that this was no more than the usual politesse of a failed English, suburban marriage.

But now he thought about it, weighing up different locations in the house as possible strangling areas, there was a definite pattern to her movements. She was – in the bedroom and the kitchen anyway – quite definitely trying to get behind him, and in clearer ground, the hall, stairs, lounge or garden, she moved fast, certainly too fast to be strangled. This had to be deliberate. Didn't it?

About the only safe areas were the lavatory or the bathroom.

Henry went up to the landing and sized up the lavatory. The chief advantage here was that the door was never locked. Elinor's only defence system was to say, in a tone fractionally the right side of panic – 'I'm in here!' – if ever she saw the door move. It might also be the case, too, that if he timed the attack carefully he might be able to give the verb 'caught short' a transitive sense. They would, however, be facing each other. There was, presumably, a sound evolutionary reason for the fact that no one had yet designed a lavatory in which the occupant faced away from the door, some relic of the time when primitive man was most at risk when at stool, but it did mean that the lavatory user was finely tuned to the approach of strangers.

Henry gave a short run and shouldered his way past the door.

It wasn't entirely satisfactory. She might get her head down and then butt it upwards into his stomach. She had, to hand, the lavatory brush, three toilet rolls and the hardback edition of a very long novel by a Peruvian author with an unpronounceable name. She had her teeth and her two strong arms.

Her teeth. Brushing her teeth. That would be the ideal activity to interrupt by strangulation. It would be late at night, she would have her back to the door and, when brushing her teeth, Elinor went into a kind of trance. He stood at the door of the bathroom, visualizing this most familiar of her rituals. Her left arm by her side, her right elbow out at an angle and her forearm shaking like a pneumatic drill. Her head motionless as her hand moved up, down, side to side, up, down, side to side, the only sound the scritch scratch of the bristles against her perfect ivories. He would do it tonight. He would have to do it tonight. You fell off the horse, you got straight back on and did it again. Go for it, Henry! he told himself. Go for it!

'The deadline,' (this time he spoke aloud) 'is midnight!'

13

Maisie came into the bathroom as he was standing slightly to the right of the basin, arms outstretched, thumbs interlocked, squeezing an imaginary neck.

'Are you practising strangling?' she said.

Henry jumped. 'You should be in bed!' he said.

'Pozzo is depressed!' said Maisie.

Pozzo was a small black furry creature that, years ago, had belonged to Henry. Before Henry it had been Henry's father's. Whether it was a zebra, or a panda or a bear or a seal, cat, ocelot or kangaroo was unclear, but whatever it was, on the grounds of its appearance, it had every good reason to be depressed.

Henry decided to out-twee her. 'Was it sad because its mummy was nasty to it?' he said. 'And shall we make it a pwethent to make it happy?'

Maisie looked at him in disgust. 'Don't be stupid!' she said. He grabbed her, propelled her towards the basin and began to brush her teeth.

'Well, don't you be so disgustingly arch!' he said, brushing her teeth vigorously.

Maisie put out her tongue at him (no easy task for someone who is having their teeth brushed) and made a farting noise. 'You hate Mummy, don't you?' she said.

'Of course I don't!' said Henry. 'I love Mummy. I love Mummy very much and she loves me and we both love you and we all go diddledy diddledy dumpling through the heather on a hot sunny day, like a bunny rabbit with the clap.'

Maisie laughed coarsely. Then, a shade of nervousness entering her voice, she said: 'You do love Mummy, don't you?'

'Oh yes,' said Henry (he sounded, he thought, incredibly sincere as he said this), 'deep down. Incredibly deep down. Millions of miles down in the black, twisted heart of me I do. It's just that I am so evil and perverted and encrusted with slime that it's rather difficult for me to remember the fact.'

Maisie laughed. She was one of the few people in the world who genuinely found Henry funny. Other people, he thought, probably found him funny, but funny for the wrong reasons. Funny because he was forty and not very clever and lived in an English suburb called Wimbledon. Funny laugh-behind-your-hands, thought Henry, funny the way Karim Jackson –

'You're hurting me!' said Maisie.

To his horror Henry saw that as he had been brushing her teeth he had started to grip her neck, hard. There was a brutal, red thumb mark just at the point where her shoulders met her neck. He bent down and kissed it, overcome suddenly with remorse. It was thinking about that publisher that had done it. Why did that bastard have the right to say 'no' to him? Just like that. To ignore something that could (Henry was prepared to admit that *The Complete History* might need work) be one of the most exciting developments in social history this century. It seemed, somehow, monstrously unfair that a decision of such importance to England's cultural future should be left to a person from Pakistan.

Henry wasn't a racist. He just didn't want the bastards to get the upper hand. Didn't they have enough? Couldn't they just ease up a little? Why did Karim –

'Ow!' said Maisie.

He was squeezing her neck again.

'Sorry!' said Henry.

'I won't have any teeth left.'

England was owned by other people these days. After years of greatness it was just a place like any other place. That, somehow, was the worst insult of all.

'Ow!' said Maisie again.

'Sorry!' said Henry.

She turned her plate-like face up to him. 'Can I have my story?' she said.

'Of course, my love,' he said.

Maisie was the only person to whom Henry ever talked these days. She was certainly the only person to whom he started to describe his feelings. In the stories he told her were roads and trees and houses and mountains and monsters and rivers and magicians; but at the centre of the story there was always Henry. Henry, in the story, lived in Wimbledon, but not the same Wimbledon. It wasn't even the Wimbledon of *The Complete History*. It was Wimbledon with some things left in and some things left out. Wimbledon at once grotesque and matter of fact. The suburb became, under Henry's hands, like a vacant lot in Hollywood – full of cardboard houses under an artificial sky. And yet, almost against Henry's will, the real suburb kept breaking in until among the paper houses you could smell the decaying leaves, the acrid exhaust of cars and hear the children shouting to each other under the huge sky on the common.

'What's this one about?' she said, as, holding his hand, she climbed the short flight of stairs that led to her attic room.

'It's about the time I turned into a pig!' he said.

Maisie bounced into her room. 'What kind of pig?' she said.

'A male chauvinist pig!' said Henry.

'Is that a good sort of pig?' she said.

'No,' said Henry, 'it's an awful, rude, wicked, cruel sort of pig.'

'Why did you turn into it?'

'Because,' said Henry, 'I was depressed.'

He lay next to his daughter on the bed and put his arm round her. She looked up at him.

'Why were you depressed?' she said.

'Because,' said Henry, 'my pig wife was going to be made into bacon.'

'Why was she going to be made into bacon?'

'Because,' said Henry, 'she had caught a very serious disease.'

'What disease?'

'It's called feminism,' said Henry, 'and I hope you never get it, because it is absolutely awful and it makes you swell up to an enormous size and when you have it really badly you go round bonking men on the head and blaming them for everything. And your arms grow all hairy and muscly like a man's and you get very keen on boxing and tossing the caber.'

Maisie showed worrying signs of interest in feminism.

'It sounds fun!' she said. Then she looked at Henry suspiciously. 'Anyway,' she said, 'I know what feminism is. It's thinking girls and women are good. What's so wrong with that?'

Henry's stories quite often developed into debates of this kind. In fact, on many occasions, Maisie talked more than Henry.

'There's nothing wrong with that,' said Henry, 'and some feminists are quite nice. But some of them are bad-tempered ratbags who should be locked away in a cellar with a lot of other feminists. I'm not saying that women and girls are bad. I think they're nice. I just don't like being told that boys and men are bad. I think it's stupid and unfair.'

Maisie thought about this. Then she said, 'Well. Boys and men are all right, I suppose. Anyway. Go on with the story.'

'So,' said Henry, 'my pig wife . . .'

It was curious. Here he was, as usual, telling Maisie her story. And a few streets away, Donald was probably in his death agony. Or if not actually in it, well on the way to it. What was so attractive about poison (and Henry had, with some regret, more or less reconciled himself to Donald's death) was that it acted so independently. It was like a good secretary. The sort of secretary you couldn't get hold of at Harris, Harris and Overdene. 'Thallium,' you said, 'job for you!' and thallium picked up the papers, simpered, and went out into the world to do your bidding.

Strangling was not like that.

'You're squeezing again!' said Maisie. 'Why are you squeezing?'

'Because I love you,' said Henry.

'Go on about the pig now!' said Maisie.

'Well,' said Henry, 'my pig wife – '

'What was her name?'

'Her name,' said Henry, 'was Elinor.'

'Oh,' said Maisie, 'like Mummy.'

'Yes,' said Henry, 'but my pig wife wasn't like Mummy. Mummy is sweet and good and kind. But this pig was odious and conceited and impossible to live with.'

'Because it was a feminist!' said Maisie, with a touch of satire.

'That's right!' said Henry. 'Which is not to say that it was odious and conceited because it was a feminist. I repeat. Not all feminists are odious and conceited. But they are not automatically right about everything. And the ones who see life purely as a battle between men and women – which, of course, it is, I suppose, are . . .'

He stopped. Maisie was looking at him doubtfully. He wasn't getting the story right. It was infected with doubt. Somehow the outside world had intruded and broken up the fabric of the tale. What were usually asides, about life, religion, art, politics, had come to dominate the story. He saw himself suddenly, a fat man on a bed, haranguing his daughter about feminism. Was that what he was? Did he, perhaps, really hate women? Maybe Elinor was right. And if she was, perhaps he ought not be trying to murder her?

No. It was just a difficult, demanding task to perform. That was all. It interfered with your peace of mind. From the outside, murder looked like a quiet, sensible alternative to divorce. When you were actually involved in it, when you were down there at the murder coal-face, it could be as complicated and unsatisfactory as marriage.

He had better get Maisie to sleep, though. He didn't really want her to hear her mother being strangled.

'Actually,' he said, 'this story is really about this pig's father.'

'Oh,' said Maisie.

'In fact,' said Henry, 'it's about my father. Who was, of course, in the story, a pig. And although I didn't like my pig wife or my pig mother come to that – I was very fond of my pig father. Because he, like me, was a male chauvinist pig. We all lived in this sty, just off Wimbledon Hill. It was a very expensive sty and like all the other pigs in the street we were very heavily mortgaged – '

He saw Maisie start to open her mouth and, before she had time to ask the inevitable question, said, 'We had borrowed money from the pig bank. Anyway, one day the farmer who owned the street knocked on the door and told us that my pig father was due to be made into *bacon*. There was no way to avoid it. The next day we had to report to the huge, ugly, frightening, hideous abattoir man who, in case you didn't know, lives, actually *lives* three streets away from us! He is tall and cold and sometimes he doesn't only come for pigs he comes for greedy little girls who make pigs of themselves, with too many sweets!'

Maisie was now bug-eyed with fright. Henry leaned across and tapped her on the chest.

'But,' he said, 'my pig wife, Elinor, decided to save my pig father. She decided he was one fat pig in Wimbledon who was not, could not, should not be brought under the knife of the evil abattoir man who lives, in case you need to know, in Clifton Road just off the common, and the story of how she fought off his terrible friend Farmer Dune, and rallied all the pigs of Wimbledon is the greatest story ever told. You will hear how Farmer Dune was himself eaten by a group of pigs. You will hear how pigs decided to own their own houses, and how pigs like me who worked for Harris, Harris and Overdene openly ate legal documents in the street. And you will hear most of all about the abattoir man, the evil, cold-hearted villain who knows no pity!'

Maisie was still bug-eyed. Her chin trembled with anxiety and her big, blue eyes looked far beyond Henry and the bright patterned curtains, at something only children see. He hugged her tightly, unburdened of some inner horror, suddenly carefree.

'I'll tell you the rest,' he said, 'tomorrow night!'

When we will be a single-parent family.

Henry liked the idea of being a single-parent family. There would be programmes about him on the television. Support groups would flash their telephone number at him late at night on Channel 4. He would, he realized, for the first time in his life have a socially accept-able problem. Being fat and forty and hating one's wife and job were none of them socially acceptable. Murder was to make him something he had always suspected he might be, but had never dreamed of becoming – interesting.

For a moment, he wished he could tell Elinor these things. To talk to her, reason with her, confide in her, as people are wont to do when confronting their victims with loaded guns. 'You see, Inspector, you have to die because – ' 'Elinor,' he could see her white anxious face now, 'you have to let me strangle you. I need to grow and change and develop as a person in my own terms. My therapist, Elinor, a man called Graham Young, suspects that the only way forward for me emotionally is to fasten my fingers round your windpipe and squeeze and squeeze and squeeze until your face turns black . . .'

He was squeezing. But not Maisie. This time he was squeezing the bedhead. And his daughter, her big head lolling across his chest, was fast asleep.

Down below, the front door opened and then closed quietly. Henry loosened his fingers from his daughter's shoulder, tucked her under her duvet and, walking lightly on the balls of his feet, moved with a new precision on to the darkened landing. He smiled to himself at the head of the stairs. Not long now. Not long.

14

'Donald is desperately ill!' was the first thing she said, as he met her in the hall. As soon as she had announced this fact, she pushed past him roughly, on her way to the kitchen. This wasn't as bad, Henry thought, as post-therapy hostility. It was more like plain, straight-forward dislike. He felt able to deal with this. One just had to be manly about it.

It was a shame. Strangling really needed a more co-operative part-ner than Elinor. One of those kittenish creatures he remembered from the films of his childhood in the fifties, clad in waist-high, baby-doll nightdresses, women who seemed to enjoy nothing more than lying back among the yellow nylon sheets and allowing themselves to be strangled.

It was feminism that was to blame. Nowadays women carried everything short of CS gas; all of them – at least, all of the women Elinor knew – were fairly well up on the martial arts. He followed her through to the kitchen where, as far as he could see, she was still in operatic mode.

'Desperately, desperately ill!' she said, over her shoulder, then swooped down to the dishwasher, picked up a handful of plates, and marched off towards a cupboard. As she marched she threw remarks over her shoulder, as if in some climactic race with a large orchestra. 'He is in a very critical state, Henry. He is in the throes of this awful thing, can't you see?' Then – 'Chest pains! Dry skin! Pulse slow! Headache!' and finally, 'Poor, poor Donald!'

Well, it was his own fault, thought Henry. If he would go around pinching other people's food! If only he had managed to force down a little more dynercaprol and potassium chloride! Elinor turned to him.

'We've called in Roger From the Practice!'

Roger From the Practice, eh? thought Henry. Well, that should finish him off in no time.

'Poor old Donald!' he said, limply.

'I don't think you care about Donald!' she said, pushing off from the cupboard, like someone striking out in a swimming bath.

Henry felt this was unfair. He liked Donald a great deal; and the prospect of the man's imminent death did nothing to dispel this feeling, since he was the person directly responsible for this state of affairs. Well, perhaps not directly responsible. This business of being responsible for people had to stop somewhere, didn't it? All Henry had done was poison a chicken which the berk had then insisted on eating. There was no way this made Henry 'directly responsible' was there? We had, thought Henry, gone beyond such primitive notions of morality.

'You don't care about anyone! You don't care about anyone but yourself and your narrow little world.'

'Well, what do you care for?' said Henry.

Elinor thrust her square jaw at him. 'Art!' she said, 'Feelings! People! The world around me!'

She didn't, of course, thought Henry, mean the world around her. The world around her was largely made up of Wimbledon. She meant quite a different world. A world of giving women and strong but equally giving men, a world of Bengali dancing, passionately held ideas and seventeen different kinds of psychoanalysis. A world that existed only in her head.

Henry thrust his hands deep into his pockets, glumly. He wondered which row to select from the library of disputes available to him. It was going to be an important row. He could see it now, tucked up in a cassette case. *Last Row Before Strangulation*. Was it going to be the You Are Cold and Unfeeling Row, the Why Are You So Feeble Row, the Fat Row, the Racist Row, the Right-Wing Row, the Left-Wing Row, the Merits of Jane Austen Row, the Driving Row, the Looking After Maisie Row or the Why Are You so Bitter and Twisted Row. After some moments' thought, Henry selected the Sex Row. The Sex Row was always the best. It was so beautifully, predictably ugly. It followed the track it had followed for so many years, awakened the parties to rage, apathy and contempt in precisely the usual places and ended, as it always did, in a drawn game. Henry stuck his lower lip out and in an uncouth voice, said: 'How about a bit of sex?'

Elinor looked at him, blankly.

'A bit of sex,' said Henry, 'you know. We take our clothes off and I stick my penis into you and pull it in and out for a few minutes and white stuff comes out and you say "Is that it?" And I say "There isn't any more where that came from." And you say "Why can't you be more tender?" And I say "Search me, squire." You know. A fuck. You must remember. We had a fuck, didn't we once? A few years back.'

Elinor's mouth had dropped open. She looked now like some domestic cleaning device, mouth open for household filth. Henry gave her some more.

'Or buggery,' he said, yawning, 'that buggery sounds good. I read about it in *Knave* magazine. And that magazine *Hot Bitch*. You have to go to Holland to get it but it's well worth the trip. It's very informative. Or oral. You could suck my cock if you liked. We could turn on the artificial gas fire!'

Here he leered in a conspiratorial fashion. By way of answer Elinor's mouth dropped another few notches.

'Or spanking!' went on Henry brightly. 'I fancy spanking.'

Elinor gave a choking sound. For a moment he thought she was going to hit him, and then her face turned crimson, her mouth started to bang to and fro like a door in a gale force wind and a sound came down her nose that suggested she had just swallowed a quart of White's Cream Soda. Elinor was laughing. It was primarily a Display Laugh, something to indicate that she could rise above Henry, but (this disturbed him somewhat) at the back of her he caught a glimpse of something that could only be genuine amusement.

'Oh, Henry,' said Elinor, now blocking her mouth with the palm of her hand and moaning elaborately, 'you're trying to be funny! Aren't you? Is that the idea?'

Her laughter dropped away suddenly. It was obviously a ploy. She said then, very quickly, like a trick question to someone in the Yes/

No interlude on the Michael Miles Quiz Show: 'Marriage Guidance didn't do much for your need to dump, did it?'

Henry was beginning to enjoy this. 'Marriage Guidance,' he said, 'didn't understand my need for brutally climaxing into tight white bottoms.'

Marriage Guidance had been a bloke called Kevin who, in Henry's view, had had designs on Elinor. She, skilled in the ways of therapy, had after the first few sessions begun dissecting his own motives for him and Kevin, like an obedient dog, ended up nodding slowly as she told him clearly, fully, frankly what he meant when he said what he thought about what she or Henry felt, and how what he thought he thought about what they felt, or said they felt, probably wasn't what he really felt any more than what they said they felt was really deep down what they really felt. Except of course, in her case. Because what she thought she felt was what she actually did feel and she said it, loud and clear and everyone else could go and fuck themselves. This was called 'being in touch with your feelings'.

'At Marriage Guidance,' went on Henry, 'I didn't feel able to discuss my need to tie you to the bed and whip you with my pyjama cord. But that wasn't on the agenda, was it? On the agenda was something called Tenderness with a capital T. Well – ' Henry thrust his face towards her, allowing a small fragment of saliva to trickle down his chin. 'Tenderness is just another aspect of female control. Tenderness is just something that women like because it gives them the upper hand. Tenderness is that hideous, cooing voice you hear mothers using to their children as they get them to do this, go there, stay here. I am so pissed off with being told how men own and control the world. I tell you they don't. They all start out doing what some woman wants them to do. And you know the weapon she uses? She uses Tenderness with a capital T!'

Elinor folded her arms and, shaking her head in the way Henry sometimes did at the motorists who cut him up, she began to pace up and down the red-tiled kitchen. She did quite a lot of snorting, quite a lot of brittle laughter and a very great deal of what Henry took to be assumed inarticulacy.

'Basically . . .' she said, 'basically . . . I think . . . I don't know, but I think . . . I suspect . . . I feel . . .'

Here she raised her square white face up to his and sought his eyes. Then she said, according a miraculously even level of stress to each word in the sentence: 'We're-at-the-end-of-the-road.'

At this point the telephone rang. Henry answered it. It was Donald's wife. Henry could never, would never be able to remember her name.

'It's Donald . . .' she said.

'Yes!' said Henry. He sounded curt, businesslike. Perhaps a little too businesslike, he thought. He sounded like a man whose next line would be 'I'm in a meeting'.

'He's . . .'

'Yes?'

Her voice suddenly swooped into hysterics. For a moment, Henry thought she was going to laugh, and then came a sudden explosion of sobbing.

'He's . . . dead!'

At this moment Tibbles came into the room.

'Roger From the Practice is here!'

Well, I'm not surprised he's dead. I'm surprised you're not all dead!

'He's dead, he's dead, he's dead, he's dead!'

Henry wished Mrs Donald (what was her name?) would stop behaving like an extra in *Oedipus Rex*. So he was dead. Plenty of other people were going to be dead before the night was out. Tibbles for one. She was looking a bit like she had the morning of her hysterectomy. She prowled and paused and placed her feet carefully, all as if she were a normal feline, but there was something woefully uncatlike about her performance. She looked as if she was not entirely sure she was a cat, as if, thought Henry, one, two, three, four, five, six, seven, eight of her nine lives were oozing out of her like blood from a wound.

Henry looked up at Elinor smartly. He said: 'Donald's dead!'

'Oh my God!' said Elinor. 'Oh no! Oh no! Oh no! Oh my God!'

Christ, thought Henry, he's only your doctor!

At the other end of the phone Mrs Donald (what was her name?) was grieving with similar bravura.

'Respiratory failure at 11.30 p.m.,' she said (why did women have to be so scrupulously exact as to detail?) 'and before that he couldn't swallow. He said that he had a violent head pain. And then he had hallucinations. He thought there was a pig in the room.'

'What kind of pig?'

'I don't know. Just a pig. Oh my God! Oh my God! He was so sweet. I loved him so much.'

'I . . . Christ . . . I liked him. He was a nice bloke. A damned nice bloke actually.'

'And oh my God my God just like that! Like that. He's dead he's dead he's dead he's dead he's dead. He'll never come back. He's dead.'

A pause.

'Roger From the Practice is here!'

'Good.'

'He was so good and loyal and honest and brave and sweet and kind. And . . . he was such a good doctor.'

Henry thought this was depressingly typical of the way in which people talked about the recently deceased. Inaccurate would be a charitable way of describing Mrs Donald's description of her husband. He held the receiver a yard away from his ear. Tiny strangled sobs floated out of it and across the room. Elinor swung towards him. For a moment Henry thought she was going to hit him, and then, instead, she seized the receiver from him and, sweeping it down to the floor with her she poured love, support, tenderness and quietness down the line.

'Billykins,' she said (surely this could not be the woman's name?), 'Billykins, this is so awful.'

Henry wandered to the other end of the room. Elinor sat on the floor, allowing her long black hair to fall around her and started saying 'Yes . . . yes . . . yes, I know . . .' and 'Of course . . .' a lot. She listened, thought Henry, the way some people figure skated. Presumably Billykins was telling her about Donald the Gourmet Cook,

Donald the Great Fighter for Social Change, Donald the Novelist. He can't only have been Donald the Great Doctor.

If Roger From the Practice was doing the post-mortem, thought Henry, he should be OK. Roger From the Practice couldn't tell emphysema from the common cold.

'. . . Yes yes, my darling . . .' (Uh?) '. . . my darling, yes . . . we're with you . . . we're with you . . .'

Elinor put down the phone. She stared bleakly across at Henry.

'My God,' she said, sounding a bit like a vicar who has just discovered the Third World, 'this makes one's own problems seem pretty small, doesn't it?'

'Does it?' said Henry.

He sucked on his lips. She put her head on one side.

'I think,' she said, 'that you have instincts and feelings that are not really human at all. I don't think you are human, actually. I think you're like some disgusting little animal, some creature from another planet. I'm sorry for you, Henry. One day you'll wake up and realize how utterly ghastly you are, and I don't think you'll find that very easy to live with. I'm going to bed.'

Flexing his fingers, Henry followed her up the stairs. Behind him, pathetically, Tibbles mewed in the hall. Henry hoped she wasn't gong to make a fuss about dying. Ahead of him Elinor was pulling her dress over her head. She was wearing, as usual, a sack-like dress, one that hinted coyly at pregnancy. Underneath it was, as usual, Elinor's body. It wasn't, actually, if you could forget who it belonged to, a bad body. The thought occurred once again to Henry that someone who wasn't him might have a sexual interest in his wife. If not Donald, then perhaps one of the women from the therapy group. Was he, could he, be married to a lesbian? Such things had happened to more eminent lawyers than he. He heard the sound of the tap running, and then the sound of bristles against gum, ivory and lip. Arms out in front of him, Henry ran up the stairs, thinking, as he ran
– She has three minutes to live.

15

She turned out to have rather longer than that.

For a start, when Henry rounded the bathroom door it seemed, to use a phrase of Elinor's, 'inappropriate behaviour' to run at her. He found himself walking at a steady pace towards those meaty shoulders. Her head, which was rotating at a different speed and a contrary motion to her brushing arm, reminded him of a duck in a shooting gallery. It had a difficult-to-hit quality about it, an almost larky imperviousness to attempts to interfere with it.

Still flexing his fingers, he started to dig them into the base of her neck, or rather, in the area where her neck might be assumed to begin. He found his hands full of dry, papery skin which, as he worked his way closer to her windpipe, came up and away like a curtain of strudel dough. Tossing this first layer of skin aside, he attempted to burrow deeper, only to discover yet more skin, though whether this was the outer skin that had slithered back through his advancing fingers, or a whole new layer was not apparent, but it was pretty clear that finding her windpipe, let alone getting hands round it and squeezing it, was a two-person job.

'What are you doing, Henry?' she squawked. 'Do you want sex again?'

'What do you mean, "again"?' said Henry.

'You only ever touch me when you want sex,' said Elinor. And started to brush her teeth again.

'I don't,' said Henry. 'I sometimes put my arms around you because I need to feel your closeness. I need to touch you tenderly and feel the warmth of your body.'

As he said this, Henry pulled at his nose and raised his upper lip to expose his gums. He looked, he thought, like a nasty species of rodent.

'Shut up, Henry!' said Elinor. 'You just grope my fanny and expect me to respond. Sex isn't just about an animal urge. It isn't like going to the lavatory.'

Henry started to slide down the wall. It looked as if strangling her was not going to be possible. Tonight anyway. Maybe he should go for a contract killing.

'It's a bit like going to the lavatory!' said Henry. 'Anyway, what's so wrong with going to the lavatory? I like going to the lavatory.'

'We had noticed!' said Elinor archly and, shaking out her black hair behind her, she placed the toothbrush, emphatically, in the plastic cup and marched out of the bathroom. On the landing a new thought occurred to her and she re-entered, her long arms swinging, her face screwed up with anger.

'How can you, though?' she said. 'How can you? Your best friend lies dead. Dead. And all you think about is . . . that!'

Here she pointed dramatically at Henry's flies. Henry found he was grinning foolishly. Any sort of attention to his genitals, even if it was the sort of gesture usually used by particularly aggressive barristers, was welcome.

'And stop smirking!' she barked. 'Christ! Anyone'd think from the way men carry on that their . . . things . . . are somehow clever and funny.'

She was down to its level now, her finger jabbing at the zip of his trousers.

Sex between Henry and Elinor had come to a halt some four or five years ago and, from what Henry could remember about it, it was something that was better discontinued. Elinor had spent most of their congress complaining. There were pains in her back, her right arm had gone to sleep, she was stiff, he wasn't stiff. It was lasting too long. It was over too quickly. He was too tentative, too assertive, too submissive, too dominant.

Following her into the bedroom, he decided to continue on the plainly offensive tack.

'Maybe,' he said, sitting on her side of the bed as she reached for a woman's magazine, 'maybe I'm gay!'

She looked at him oddly. 'Don't be silly, Henry!' she said, in a slightly querulous tone. Then she started reading a recipe.

'I often think,' he went on, 'about having sex with men.'

Elinor looked at him over the rim of her magazine.

'Well,' said Henry, 'it would make a pleasant change from having sex with you. Or rather, from not having sex with you.'

Elinor snorted.

'You are just being silly,' she said, 'and offensive!'

'Getting down on all fours,' went on Henry, 'and being rogered by a complete stranger in the open air. On the common. Melting back into the undergrowth, your trousers by your ankles – '

'Henry,' said Elinor, 'I think you are sick. I think you are ill. I think you need treatment.'

'What kind of treatment?' said Henry, licking his lips, 'corrective treatment? A good lashing?'

'Donald,' she said, 'is dead. He's gone. We've lost him. Doesn't that mean anything to you? Don't you have any human feelings?'

If he had hoped that a row might spur him on to a direct, hands on approach to murdering Elinor, Henry was disappointed. Talking to her, as so often, left him demoralized and confused. She seemed to have such endless resources of anger, so many obviously right, sincerely held opinions.

The more he thought about it, the more it became clear to him that this was a job for a real professional. A man with a hatchet face in a blue suit. Elinor would step out of her therapy class one morning, wave goodbye to Anna and Linda and Susie and Tatiana and Ruth and *wham* – several hundred rounds from an M16, the screech of tyres and the howl of brakes as the saloon car roared off down Makepeace Avenue.

'Did you know anyone who had a grudge against her?'

'I . . . can't, officer . . .' Henry would sob, 'she was just a quiet, ordinary housewife . . .'

The trouble was, he thought as he pulled off his trousers, where did one find contract killers? They didn't stick their cards through your letter box or advertise in the Yellow Pages. And very often they were unreliable people, demanding payment in advance or trying to blackmail you. A bit like builders. He had had a lot of trouble with builders last year. As had Donald. They had talked it over in the Rose. If something went wrong with his contract killer perhaps he would talk it over the way he talked over his builder.

'OK, mate?'

'Not so bad. But we've got one of these . . . contract killers on and . . .'

'I had one of those for Billykins. She – '

Donald.

Donald was dead. He had killed Donald. He was a murderer. Henry lay back against the pillow and closed his eyes.

'Sorry, Donald,' he said, in his mind, 'really sorry.'

Donald was very nice about it.

'Look, mate,' he said, 'it happens. Come to the funeral.'

'I will,' said Henry. 'I wouldn't miss it for the world.'

Elinor was looking at him curiously. 'Are you thinking about Donald?' she said.

'Yes,' said Henry, 'I was. I was thinking about what a nice bloke he was.'

'Oh my God!' said Elinor. 'He leaves a great gaping hole in the community.'

'He does,' said Henry.

And indeed he would, very shortly, be going in to a great, gaping hole in the community. In the Putney Vale Crematorium to be precise.

'One minute,' said Elinor, who seemed to have cheered up considerably, 'there he was laughing and joking and having a good time. And the next minute there he was, writhing around on the floor in agony!'

'I know!' said Henry.

'It was like he'd been . . . I don't know . . . poisoned or something!' said Elinor.

Henry coughed. 'I don't think,' he said, 'that that remark was in very good taste.'

It was long after she had gone to sleep and he had prodded her in the ribs to stop her snoring and was, himself, lying awake, staring into the darkness, thinking about Donald that it occurred to Henry that this was the longest conversation he had had with Elinor for about a year and that, after a bad start, she had, once or twice, come dangerously near to amiability.

16

Donald's funeral was, in the planning stages anyway, a magnificent thing.

Billykins, everyone agreed, was magnificent. She was dignified, pale, but, in the playground at least, composed. Arfur seemed positively cheerful. She wore a fetching, knee-length black dress and a kind of Spanish headdress that made her look a little like a sherry advertisement.

'I just want to carry on,' she said, 'as if all this had never happened.'

There were moments when Henry thought she would not turn up for the funeral, so magnificent was she about the whole thing, but as the date approached he noticed she was wearing more and more black jewellery, black scarves, capes, cloaks and jerseys, stockings, blouses and hats. She would deliver Arfur at eight fifty a.m., magnificent in a black coat, black ankle-length dress and black leather boots, and reappear at three fifteen, leaning against the climbing frame in the same ensemble, garnished with a scarf or a single piece of jewellery.

The neighbours, all the neighbours agreed, were magnificent. They called round. They went in and out of Billykins's house, and did something everyone described as 'sitting with her'. Mr and Mrs Is-the-Mitsubishi-Scratched-Yet went up to her in the street and pressed her hands between theirs. They baked cakes and meat pies and wholemeal loaves and they ordered flowers and hoovered the carpets and stairs; in fact, thought Henry, Donald was getting more (and higher quality) attention dead than he ever had alive.

His death, people said 'pulled the street together'. Even Nazi Who Escaped Justice At Nuremberg, at number 42, was seen talking to people in a high, jovial voice, that only increased his resemblance to a Gestapo officer. Mr and Mrs Is-the-Mitsubishi-Scratched-Yet smiled and nodded at people who passed them and tried not to flinch every time anyone went within ten yards of the Mitsubishi. There was, too, at first anyway, wild talk of the honours to be done to Donald. Dave Sprott, the northern dentist at 102, whose carefully preserved northern accent had always seemed to Henry a way of criticizing the London suburb in which he found himself, suggested that they 'hire' St Paul's Cathedral.

'I think 'e's owed that,' said Sprott, 'I think 'e's owed a generous tribute.'

From St Paul's Cathedral to Putney Vale Crematorium did not seem such a short distance to the neighbours, such was their generous enthusiasm for Donald's internment, and when they heard there were plans for a memorial service at Wimbledon Parish Church, some people said it was even better to do it this way. 'Donald', they said, 'wouldn't have wanted St Paul's. What did St Paul's mean to Donald?' This was a fair question, although the same could have been asked about his relationship with Wimbledon Parish Church. But the fact that no one seemed to know where Wimbledon Parish Church was, that no one in Maple Drive had seen the vicar, even at Christmas or Easter, seemed to make little difference. It was, as Nazi Who Escaped Justice at Nuremberg pointed out, the thought that counted. And everyone in Maple Drive, as they cooked, consoled, took out their best suits and thought of even nicer things to say about Donald than the last nice thing that had been said about him, were privately so astonished, so relieved, so savagely glad to be alive that if someone had proposed to bury him upside down in a bucket of horse manure they would probably have agreed it was all for the best.

Two days before the funeral Henry was asked to give a short speech, and although he began by saying he would not be able to talk, didn't think he could get the words out, was no orator, ended, of course by accepting. At the Harris, Harris and Overdene Christmas party three years ago he had made what some considered to be the funniest impromptu speech anyone had ever heard inside the office. At the University of Loughborough there were several people who went on record as saying that you could always get a laugh out of Henry. He didn't see why he shouldn't have a stab at the more serious mode of public address. After all – the man was one of his best friends, wasn't he? It was the least he could do. In one of his private talks with his late general practitioner he said: 'Look old son. It won't bring you back. It won't, you know, make up for the fact that, let's face it, I poisoned you!'

'No no no,' said Donald, 'for Christ's sake, mate. It happens.'

'No, I mean . . .' said Henry, 'I did. I poisoned you. And I'm very, very sorry I did. It was an accident but that doesn't excuse it. And the least I can do is tell them all what a great bloke you are!'

'Were,' said Donald, 'were . . .'

'Christ, mate!' said Henry. 'You see what I mean?'

He wrote his speech several times.

When it actually came to writing rather than vaguely thinking about his address, Henry found it more difficult than he had expected. He had not written much since *The Complete History of Wimbledon* and that book's rejection by ten publishers (he had still not heard from The Applecote Press, Chewton Mendip) had made him a little nervous of putting pen to paper, but he found that if he emptied his mind of everything and forced his hand to fist a biro and then forced that biro across a sheet of paper, some pretty profound and interesting thoughts resulted. He ended by writing twenty-five pages, some of which he read to Elinor late one night. There were also two longish poems in free verse, which he didn't yet feel quite ready to expose to the world. When he had finished the third page she put her head to one side and said in her cross-but-trying-to-be-helpful voice, 'I like the bit about Donald.'

'How do you mean?' said Henry. 'It's all about Donald, isn't it?'

She became assertive-in-spite-of-herself, and marching rapidly from one end of the kitchen to the other, which she always did when entrusting him with a home truth, said, 'It's not, Henry. It's mainly about you.'

'Is it?'

Henry looked at the pages of script he had written in praise of the man he had helped on the way to eternal bliss, and found this to be true. There was a very long story about him and Donald in the Rose and Thorn, a short, rather vulgar anecdote about something that had happened to Donald's wife while crossing Wimbledon Common and a boastful piece about how he, Henry, had amused some French sailors in the bar at the Mini Golf, Boulogne sur Mer. The whole thing was, he had to admit, in very dubious taste.

He started again. He decided to write out a list of Donald's good qualities. *Charity. Skill in Medicine. Standing his Round. Qualities as a Father and Wit.* But the headlines seemed to paralyse him completely. When he got down to *Punctuality* and *Considerateness as a Driver*, he decided to give up and improvise.

'Well, for God's sake,' said Elinor, 'try and make sense. You only make a fool of yourself when you try and speak in public. You were embarrassing at our wedding.'

'Was I?'

'Oh my God, yes,' said Elinor, 'you just sort of dribbled!'

Henry folded his arms over his chest. 'I might, of course,' he said, 'be overcome by emotion.'

Elinor wheeled round, a look of horror on her face. 'How do you mean?' she said.

'I may be in tears,' said Henry, 'I may just . . . you know . . . blub!'

She made the kind of face she made when tasting sour milk. 'For God's sake, Henry,' she said. 'If you do that I shall leave you.'

Henry found such moments of unpleasantness between them almost reassuring. She had been so pleasant since Donald's death that there were times when he could not believe that he was planning to murder her. The trouble was that it seemed almost unfair to Donald not to have another go. Had the man died in vain?

He had probably been trying something far too fancy. Thallium was an Alfa Romeo among poisons, its charm being the fact that it was almost impossible to detect. But was detection such a problem? No one seemed at all interested in how poor old Donald died; he had just keeled over one night. Arfur spoke for everybody when he said, a wondering expression on his face: 'My Daddy just felled over and died!'

What was needed was something down home and businesslike.

Something you could buy over the counter at a supermarket. It didn't have to be colourless, tasteless or odourless, it just had to be got, somehow or other, past Elinor's front teeth, down her oesophagus and into her digestive system, even if to do so it should be necessary to hold her down and clamp a funnel between her jaws. If there was a single reason, thought Henry, why he was once again determined to poison her, it was probably her stubborn refusal to go along with his earlier attempt. There must be something she ate that would act as a cover for paraquat or whatever he was going to use. Some particularly disgusting form of health food, some heavily unbleached flour that could be rebleached.

Bleach. He would start by looking at bleach, and then think of something to go with it. When he went to Waitrose to buy the food for their contribution to what everyone in the street was calling 'Donald's funeral breakfast' Henry spent hours browsing through the domestic cleaners, all of which sounded pretty lethal. *Domestos kills all known germs – Dead!* Their names were harsh, aggressive, Vorticist in tone – *Scour! Blast! Zap!* – and the one Henry most favoured, which seemed from looking at the label to be a sexier version of raw bleach – *Finish 'Em*. It came in a huge blue bottle on the side of which was a picture of something that looked like a bluebottle with twelve legs keeling over, while a housewife in rubber gloves looked grimly on.

There would be especial pleasure, thought Henry, in using a household cleanser against a feminist. Women like Elinor refused to channel their aggression in the direction of household germs. Keeping your house clean was now seen, probably rightly, as a plot by men to stop you doing anything more interesting. No, it was Henry who, on Saturday mornings, scrubbed the kitchen floor, wiped down the surfaces, hoovered the carpets, poured bleach down the lavatories and sinks. But now, a few litres of Finish 'Em would be put to the service of a more crucial domestic task, the elimination of Mrs Farr.

The trouble was – how to conceal the taste? Even hot sweet tea, a favourite refuge for poisoners, would not sweeten the flavour of Finish 'Em and in order to kill Elinor he would need at least half a bottle. And – even assuming he could persuade her to drink it – wasn't it, well, out of the ordinary to find half a litre of bleach in someone's stomach? It was not possible. She would have to eat a bucket of chicken vindaloo to get the stuff down her and, although there had been publicly expressed doubts about the kitchens of the 'Tandoori' Tandoori, Wimbledon, they hadn't, as far as Henry knew, got around to using bleach to liven up their menu.

He had decided to give up, had, indeed, spent several hours trying to think of one thing he actually liked about Elinor when, two days before the funeral, she looked up from a quiche Lorraine ('Billykins says it's about all she could face') and barked: 'What are we going to drink?'

'Uh?'

'At Donald's thrash,' said Elinor, 'we're going to have to drink something. I know it's awful but what? People do like alcohol at a funeral.'

Henry goggled at her.

There had been much discussion in the street on this very topic. Dave Sprott the dentist had suggested a barrel of draught Guinness. Sam Baker QC (almost) from number 113a had suggested that he 'bring along a few bottles of my Australian Chardonnay' but no one could face the prospect of being talked through another glass of uniquely flinty, resonantly expressive Murray River Chardonnay by Sam Baker QC (almost). Vera Loomis, the ninety-two-year-old who lived at number 92 and was known for some reason as Got All the Things There Then? had offered plum wine or home-brewed lager and Susan Doyle, who was reported to watch *News at Ten* while her husband pleasured her, had suggested lemonade shandy. Detective Inspector Rush from 38, known to Henry as Neighbourhood Watch, was of the opinion that alcohol at funerals was disrespectful. He stopped Henry, as he so often did, in the street one afternoon and said, as he so often did,

'Drinking and driving, Henry, wreck lives.'

Someone said that they had heard him suggest that all guests should be breathalysed at the door, for Rush had the reputation locally for being a more than usually dedicated policeman. Henry had been involved in many of these discussions, had indeed had a pint with Dave Sprott to debate the issue, but when Elinor put the question to him he saw, suddenly, how he could not only perform a helpful, neighbourly act, and another last tribute, but also serve something that would, in all senses of the word, Finish 'Em.

'Punch,' he said, throatily, 'I'll make a punch.'

17

Henry started making the punch the evening before the funeral. He got grape concentrate, sugar, cooking brandy and a large bottle of bleach and put the mixture into a large saucepan Elinor used for making marmalade. He didn't boil it, for fear the bleach might evaporate; after the mixture was warm he added twenty bottles of Yugoslav Riesling, two bottles of Guinness and a pound and a half of oranges cut into segments.

Then, reasoning that a little bit of bleach wouldn't harm him, he sipped, nervously, at a teaspoonful of the mixture. It tasted unequivocally of bleach. In fact though, Henry argued to himself, punch usually tasted of bleach. He was simply responding to the fact that he knew there was bleach in the mixture. He was thinking bleach. His toast in the morning tasted of bleach, his pint at the Rose tasted bleached. He would simply add more sugar.

He added three more packets of brown sugar. It still tasted of bleach.

The beauty of it being a funeral was that no one ever complained about the quality of the food and drink at a funeral. You ate what you were given and tried to look as if you couldn't really bear to think about food. Even when things warmed up, it wasn't really done to comment on what was provided. There was, Henry had noticed, a specially reverent way of saying 'thank you' when accepting a cheese and tomato sandwich at a funeral reception and he did not see why people should develop critical faculties just because they were swigging back a wine glass containing a fair quantity of the domestic bleach known as Finish 'Em.

The apparent disadvantage of the scheme – the fact that he was going to end up poisoning not only Elinor and Donald but also most of the inhabitants of Maple Drive, including what remained of

Donald's family (Arfur was notoriously fond of 'Daddy's 'Ine') was outweighed by its brilliantly direct character.

One of the main problems about person-to-person poisoning, Henry had found, was its very intimacy. You had to go to such trouble to persuade the subject to accept the poison and when (or rather, in his case *if*) you managed it, your very intimacy made it all too clear to everyone that you were the one who was slipping them the doctored crumble, the dodgy spaghetti bolognese or the potato salad unusually rich in mineral salts. This way, it was going to be fairly obvious that someone had emptied a bottle of bleach into the punch but, since Henry could not possibly have a motive for murdering the whole of Maple Drive (as far as the police were concerned, anyway), it would be relatively easy for him to gasp in horror and dismay and to take the Wimbledon CID around the places where he had left the bowl of punch unattended. He intended leaving the bowl in as many places easily accessible to a psychopath as possible.

As he mixed away happily (Elinor had retired to bed early) Henry began to see the headlines. WIMBLEDON POISONER – PSYCHOPATH MAY STRIKE AGAIN SAY POLICE! He, of course, would have to take a glass or two, enough to make him moderately sick, but that would be a small price to pay for finishing off Elinor, not to mention Mr and Mrs Is-the-Mitsubishi-Scratched-Yet and Nazi Who Escaped Justice at Nuremberg.

THE BLEACH PRANKSTER: NEW FACTS! They would never trace it to him. Even if he was noticed forcing glasses on to his wife, no one would suspect. Because one of the beauties of this crime was his apparent (or indeed real) lack of motive. Not many people murdered their wives out of dislike. They usually did it for more obvious, sordid reasons; they wanted money, they had fallen in love with someone else or lost their temper. Henry's dislike was a more rational, delicate emotion than that. It was much more, he thought as he moved the boiling pan off the stove and on to the floor, trying to ignore the unholy smell of bleach that came off it as it sloshed against the sides of the vessel, that he had simply woken up one morning and realized, to use a phrase a friend had used about someone else's wife, 'what he had got hold of'. And once he had realized that . . .

To the left of the gas ring was a note. For a moment, Henry thought it would be another few thousand words on the subject of his obscene masculinity, but to his surprise he saw it began 'Dear Elinor . . .' A lover. She had got a lover! Well, this made his activity all the more comprehensible, didn't it? He was picking the letter up when he noticed that it was in Elinor's own handwriting.

> *Dear Elinor,*
> *Mean that! Because you are dear! Listen! Listen!*

Henry detected the influence of therapy here.

> *Do not despair! You are Elinor! Talented cook, linguist, dancer, mother, opera singer and interior designer! Love yourself! Doesn't Irma Cauther have something to say about this?*

(Probably.)

> *Oh, cast off the glooms! Be! Be womanly! Escape from the heavy hands of Patriarchy! But there is one, not far from here, who feels for you as a woman! There is one who would know you, is there not? One who would speak your name and seeks to know the woman in you! Cast off the glooms!*

Really she was getting off lightly with a few glasses of bleach. If there was any justice in the world he should really decapitate her with a spade on Wimbledon Common in full view of her therapy class. *Pour encourager les autres.* And what was all this about one not far from here who knew the woman in her? This sounded, to Henry, dangerously like illicit bonking. And the not far from here made it pretty certain it was a neighbour. He screwed up the note into small pieces and looked around for others. There were, as far as he could see, none. When the punch had cooled he took it out to the garden shed, within easy reach of Tibbles who, since her dose of chicken thallium, seemed to have improved in every conceivable way, and went upstairs to the bedroom. Elinor had woken up and was trying on a black dress that looked more like a kind of solo tent than anything else. With it, she had chosen a pair of black sneakers and a huge black bracelet. She was looking at herself in the full-length mirror by the side of the bed, pulling great lumps out of her stomach and grimacing at her own image.

'I'm fat!' she said, as Henry came in.

'I know,' said Henry, loosening his trousers, 'so am I.'

'God!' said Elinor, and again, 'God!'

Henry did not wash his face or brush his teeth. Instead he pulled off his green boxer shorts, given to him by Maisie last Christmas, and farted in what he hoped was a reasonably light-hearted way. Elinor did not bother to respond. Instead, she said, 'Donald's death has made me think!'

'Has it?' said Henry.

'Yes, darling,' said Elinor.

Why is she calling me darling? thought Henry. What does she want? Did she see me pour the Finish 'Em into the punch?

'I know we're going through a bad patch at the moment.'

Not at all. I think we're developing along the right lines, Elinor. I think there are many positive aspects to our relationship at the present time, not the least positive of which is now out in the shed in a large copper bowl!

'I know sometimes you're almost brutally male, Henry. And unresponsive. But in a way I think this may be a defence mechanism. Because underneath . . .'

A long, long way underneath.

'. . . you are probably quite sensitive. But you are out of touch with that human part of yourself. You've grown a protective skin, a sort of . . . carapace of crudeness to help you deal with the world. And at the moment you've become that outer self. You have no room for good and gentle feelings. Whereas I – '

I am opera singer, talented linguist, cook, mother, feminist!

'I have feelings of tenderness towards people. People I meet as part of my role as mother. People from nearby. There is someone – I'm not going to say his name, but there is someone who I think . . . admires me.'

Henry goggled at her. This was, presumably, a pathetic, almost touching illusion on her part. He decided not to pander to it by asking for the admirer's name.

'It's helped me through this depression, actually. And yes, I have been depressed. I don't deny that. I don't deny that I have some problems of my own,' she went on, although from the tone of her voice it was clear she had no idea what those problems might be. None the less the brisk, no-nonsense manner implied that once she had found what, if any, they might be, like the good feminist she was, she would be out there dealing with them. In fact she might even just dream up a few to even up the score a little. It must be difficult, thought Henry, when you were living with an obscenely masculine, fat, not particularly talented patriarch like Henry. Especially if you were a quote talented linguist gourmet cook and opera singer unquote.

'What problems could you possibly have?' said Henry. 'You're a feminist. Feminists by definition do not have problems. They are simply corrupted by patriarchy, aren't they? All we have to do is to do away with fathers and we're fine, aren't we? Isn't that the idea?'

'Don't be silly, Henry!' said Elinor, in the style of a primary teacher, which once, years ago, she had been. 'We're thinking about our problems. Aren't we?'

She sat up very straight on the side of the bed and continued to address him as if he were sitting on a mat in the Top Infants, wrestling with difficult, dangerous new concepts like add-ups and take-aways and the precise whereabouts of Australia.

'We're thinking about how we can be better as a couple and live in harmony as man and woman. Male and female principle. I believe, you see, that Womb and Phallus must be reconciled in some way!'

'We could do a project on it,' said Henry. 'We could cut out pictures of penises and wombs and – '

'Henry!' said Elinor, in a voice that suggested that if he didn't shut up he might get a clip round the ear. Then she continued in the sort of I'll-be-reasonable-if-you'll-be-reasonable tones adopted by the Russian government to, say, the Lithuanians.

'You seek to control,' she went on, 'it's perfectly natural. It's a very masculine thing. It goes with a whole package of your attitudes.

You're very reactionary, politically. You are racist, as poor darling Donald was. And you are frightened of the world. Frightened of the liberation movements. The movements that seek to free black people, American Indians, Nicaragua and so on. Whereas I seek to go with the flow. To change and grow. To progress, Henry!'

Why was it, thought Henry, that Elinor felt so in tune with the poor and the oppressed of the world? And why was it that this deep empathy with the hard done by inspired her to give him such a hard time? Henry had absolutely no consistent views about anything that did not directly concern him; in his opinion, such views were a rather revolting luxury. Why . . . but Elinor was talking again.

'I was reading this book the other day. About this urge to control experienced by males. Men seek control over women apparently. Whereas women – '

'Seek total world domination!' said Henry, under his breath.

'What?'

'Nothing, dear!'

Elinor looked at him suspiciously. 'The world arms race, for example. Is a product of this urge to dominate, isn't it? And if you look around at the world and try and find the women in positions of power, you have to say, where are they? Where are they?'

Henry started to mutter, into the duvet, the names of women in positions of power. 'Mrs Thatcher,' he hissed, 'Mrs Gandhi. Golda Meir!' OK two of those were dead but they had certainly caused a lot of trouble when alive, hadn't they? When he couldn't think of any more women in government, he added a few authors, actresses, athletes – 'Jane Fonda,' he muttered, 'Chrissie Evert, Dusty Springfield, Adriana Rich!' They were all women, weren't they? They were all doing all right. They were doing a lot better than him. 'Ella Fitzgerald,' he mouthed, 'Kate Millett, Nancy Reagan, Benazir Bhutto . . .'

'What?'

'Nothing, darling.'

Elinor turned to him and laid a hand on his head. 'I just felt,' she said, 'since Donald had that terrible thing happen to him, we have been a bit closer. The horror has brought us together. We haven't dumped so much. We've accepted each other for what we are.'

Talented cook, linguist and opera singer and fat, patriarchal slob.

Henry climbed under the duvet. 'I think,' he said 'I feel – '

These two words brought Elinor out in a kind of rash of solicitude. She swung her whole body round and fixed her eyes on Henry's face as if he were a dying spy with some vital secret to impart.

'I feel,' said Henry, 'that – '

Elinor nodded vigorously. This was clearly the way to get her to shut up and listen.

'I feel,' he went on, 'as a man – '

What did he feel as a man? Nothing much really, apart from pretty fucking confused. He felt he probably didn't know what feelings were any more. What feelings were OK and what were obscenely patriarchal and what merely irrelevant. He had more or less given up feeling, thought Henry, when his mother got started on him.

'Yes,' Elinor was saying, 'yes?'

'Well . . . if we could . . . share more . . .'

'Yes?' said Elinor.

'If once or twice,' he looked up at her soulfully, 'we could share a . . . drink, say. You know? Get really drunk together. Have a few glasses of beer or Scotch or . . . you know . . . punch! The way we used to!'

Elinor smiled, a tight, maternal smile. And patted his hand. 'I know,' she said, 'I know . . .'

She wouldn't have to get very drunk, thought Henry. Four or five glasses of Henry's Stomach Cleanser should do it. Finish 'Em. Finish 'Em all. Her, Dave Sprott the dentist and Sam Baker QC (almost), Inspector Rush, 'Neighbourhood Watch', and Mr and Mrs Is-the-Mitsubishi-Scratched-Yet and Nazi Who Escaped Justice at Nuremberg. By tomorrow night Wimbledon was going to be an easier, cleaner, emptier place in which to live.

18

It was, to start off with anyway, a moving and impressive funeral. It was, as Vera 'Got All the Things There Then?' Loomis, the ninety-two-year-old from 92 pointed out, the best funeral that she had ever attended. It was, she said, adding that she had been to over fifty funerals in the UK alone, the funeral of a lifetime.

She was, she told everyone, particularly impressed with Henry's speech.

At one stage Dave Sprott the northern dentist had suggested they hire a black charabanc and people in Maple Drive, used now to his carefully preserved northern humour, had managed deliberately weak smiles of the kind they managed when Sprott backed them into a corner at someone's Christmas party.

But as Henry remarked to Elinor as the cortège moved away from Darby's, the undertaker in the village, a charabanc might have been a more decent way of moving the extraordinarily large number of people who turned out for what Sprott referred to as 'the big good-bye' for Donald Templeton MD. There were so many limousines and lesser limousines and cars in attendance on the lesser limousines that the queue of cars stretched from Volley's Pizza and Pasta House down to the Polka Children's Theatre on the frontiers of Wimbledon. Some of the delayed motorists were distinctly lacking in respect, one going as far as to say that if he were going to get buried he'd have a bit more consideration for other road users.

In spite of this, to start off with anyway, everyone felt the event was going well. Mr Darby himself, a professionally miserable man in his late sixties, handed Billykins down from the car and into the chapel and, as the mourners crowded in after her, as politely unaggressive as only mourners can be, there was a real, though muted feeling of loss in the air. Inside the chapel there were white flowers, piled almost to the ceiling and, in a brown box a little to the right of a bargain-basement cross, was Donald.

The first sight of the coffin made Henry feel distinctly uneasy.

'Look, Donald,' he said, 'I really am incredibly sorry about all of this.'

'Mate,' said Donald, 'we've all got to go sometime. I'm going today. Very soon you'll be on your way as well.'

'Sure,' said Henry.

'And so,' said Donald, 'will all these people.'

'Very, very, very soon,' said Henry.

Billykins had decided to 'dispense with the burial service as such'. Which, everyone in the street had agreed, was a bold and generous gesture on Donald's behalf.

'What does it mean?' she had asked Henry, a day or so after Donald's death, 'what does it mean?'

'Indeed,' said Henry feelingly, 'what does it mean?'

She had chosen three hymns: 'Say Not the Struggle Nought Availeth', 'Ye Holy Angels Bright' and 'Now Thank We All Our God'. And at the cemetery the vicar, a man who looked as if he needed far more consolation than he would ever be capable of dispensing, had agreed to say a few words before Henry's address. Henry's address, Billykins had said, would be the centrepiece of the occasion. Much, much better to have the sincere words of a family friend than some vicar who didn't really know Donald.

In Henry's hands was a crumpled piece of paper on which was written: 'Skill at medicine 2 mins. Wit and tolerance 3 mins. Father and husband 8 mins. Golfing ability? Tennis serve? Value of house? Poss. tell Biarritz anecdote here (too crude???). Remember: don't be tasteless, Henry!' Lower down the page he had scribbled a quotation from Shelley: 'Life stains the white radiance of Eternity'. This, as Henry looked at it, the piped organ music swelling through the chapel, seemed to sum up the complete irrelevance of English literature. 'Stains the white radiance of Eternity', eh? What did that mean when it came down to it? How many pints would that buy you? In case of trouble, underneath that, Henry had written – 'Death is

Nature's way of telling us to slow down'. And, below that – 'Death comes as the end. The everlasting friend. Sophocles.'

In his researches at Wimbledon Public Library he had not been able to find any really cheering quotations on the subject of death. There were a few of the I-am-not-really-dead-but-just-popped-out-for-a-packet-of-fags sort of lines, which all went on a little long for Henry's taste, and quite a number of death-as-a-viable-alternative-to-life stuff, much of it from the fathers of the early church. Henry had thought of taking this line, but the trouble was, he found, one became almost too jolly at Donald's expense, the implication being that he, the jammy bastard, was well off out of it, while they, the real sufferers, were condemned to a few more years of the horrors of living in Wimbledon.

> The worms crawl in
> The worms crawl out
> The worms play poker on your snout
> Be merry my friends be merry! (Trad.)

was also to be found on Henry's scrappy sheets of paper. Next to it he had written: 'Use this if golf joke goes well!' And on the next page a long, uplifting sentence from a French sociologist, the gist of which was that dying was something we needed a lot of help with. The French sociologist, whose sentence was more like a paragraph, went on to argue that death was something that we needed to share – it needed to be seen publicly. The dying man should be surrounded by his friends and family, should make, as it were, a day of it. To Henry, the idea of being cheered on as you croaked, by Elinor, Mr and Mrs Is-the-Mitsubishi-Scratched-Yet, his mother, her mother, Maisie and anyone else with a few hours to spare was almost completely repulsive. But Donald, to judge from the size of the congregation – they were three deep in the aisles and old Mr Donovan from 21b ('I fought two wars for you lot') had to wait outside the double doors – Donald was not experiencing what the French sociologist called the Lonely Death. He was having, rather, the Oversubscribed Death.

At the end of the second hymn – Ye – Holy – Angels – Bright – Who-o-o-o wait at God's right hand! – Henry found himself being tugged forward by Elinor. He looked up and saw the vicar carrying a book that looked more like an illustrated part work from W. H. Smith's than Holy Writ.

'Not yet . . .' he hissed.

'Donald Templeton,' the vicar began, 'was a man loved, and I mean loved, by all who knew him.'

Which did not, thought Henry, include you, chum.

'Those who followed his career in television, from the role of humble assistant film editor, up through the features department of Granada Television, through to his incredibly successful period as editor of the BBC magazine programme, *Holiday '76*, knew him to be resourceful, keen, and deeply aware, not only of the problems of travel – his chosen speciality – but also of such things as cuisine and interior design.'

Henry looked along the row. Billykins's jaw sagged under her veil. Most of the other mourners were listening to this with the same rapt attention they might have accorded a vaguely accurate account of Donald's life. It didn't really matter, their expressions seemed to say, he might as well have been a short-order cook or a deep-sea diver or a male prostitute. He was just another wally like anyone else. In some ways, thought Henry, the man with whom Donald had been confused seemed to have had a better time of it.

'Later,' went on the vicar, 'Donald Templeton showed himself a skilful cross-country skier, on and off piste, a witty raconteur and an enthusiastic do-it-yourselfer. But, when we think of him today, which I can assure you we do, we think of those left behind. Of Norman, of Jean-Paul and of little Beatrice who feels this as deeply as anyone, including the Sussex branch of the family who, because of the railway accident you all know about, cannot be with us here today. Donald Templeton – '

Whoever he may be.

'Smiles down at us today. His conversion to Islam, his rejection of that faith and the subsequent, troubled period, when the disease had made him all but unrecognizable to any but a few close friends, are things we may wish to pass over today, but – '

Here the vicar raised his eyes to the congregation and a look of panic passed across his face. Perhaps, thought Henry, there was another Donald Templeton. Perhaps . . . But whatever the reason, whether it was that everyone had been so busy reassuring everyone that no one had bothered to talk to the crematorium, whether they had got the time wrong, or whether the vicar had simply had a brainstorm, he now, you could tell, was dimly aware that he had not given an exemplary performance. Whatever the reason may have been, the vicar had no direction in which to go but forward.

'But,' he said, his voice challenging his audience to rise and refute him, 'death, as someone said, is the great leveller. And in my father's house are many mansions. And if ever a man sleeps well after a day's work done well that man is, and I pray God give him rest, Donald Templeton!'

Here, overcome by a mixture of shame, embarrassment and some genuine fellow feeling for whoever it was inside the box some yards to his left, the vicar turned to the coffin and said, in a Shakespearian voice, 'Goodbye, Donald!'

At which point Billykins, perhaps mindful of the more glamorous, civilized life she could have had as the wife of the editor of *Holiday '76*, burst into tears and was comforted by Elinor.

Somehow or other, the vicar got off stage, and disappeared behind the altar, perhaps off to hurl himself into the flames that would shortly be consuming Donald. It seemed, thought Henry, the least he could do. As he left, Henry, pushed from behind by Elinor, crept up in the direction of the coffin.

19

Afterwards he blamed the vicar. Everyone blamed the vicar who, fortunately for him, was nowhere to be found. But Henry knew, however much he might blame the vicar, it was really his fault.

In picking up his notes, he glanced over in Donald's direction. And it was only then that he understood that Donald was actually dead. Up to that moment, Henry had not been quite able to understand the connection between the chicken *à la* thallium he had accidentally served to his old friend and the thing everyone was calling a 'tragic loss' or a 'shocking bereavement'.

At any moment, he had felt, Donald would crop up somewhere in the suburb. He had simply gone missing, somewhere between the Rose and Thorn, the library, the swimming pool or any of the other places where suburban fathers waited for their children. But now he realized with a sense of horror that Donald was actually in the box. That, over there, was Donald. And that woman in the front row, looking up at him severely, was Elinor. It seemed unfair.

The silence in the chapel, broken only by Billykins sobbing, lengthened. Should he, thought Henry, make some mention of the ghastly mistake that had been made? Should he just throw away his speech and talk, as one should, from the heart? Yes, thought Henry, I will. He crumpled the paper in his hands into a ball and fixed the congregation with a stern, preacher's eye.

'I didn't recognize,' said Henry, 'the man that has been described here today.'

This, he thought, went down pretty well.

'I don't know which Donald Templeton he was talking about,' went on Henry, 'but it wasn't my Donald Templeton. I'm not saying that that Donald Templeton wasn't a nice bloke. Fair play to him. I'm sorry he's obviously in the same situation that Donald finds himself.

But no way. No way was my Donald Templeton the producer of *Holiday '76*. I can't think how this . . . cock-up has occurred and I'm deeply distressed by it. Distressed but also, in a way, glad. Because it shows us, I think, that death is a universal thing. It happens to us all, even if we are a producer on *Holiday '76*, whatever we are, however famous and glorious and so on, death comes for us. We are all going to die. Fairly soon. Today, tomorrow, this afternoon. Pretty soon anyway. Pretty fucking soon!'

He had said 'fuck'. At a funeral. He had sworn. At a funeral. Oh my Christ! Oh my sweet Jesus! Oh God! And it had been going so well. He had had them. There, in the palm of his hand. He had been direct, forceful, tough, compassionate, blunt, and then he had said the F word. Why had he done this? He seemed to be still talking and Billykins, doubled up with grief, was sobbing even harder. She looked, thought Henry, like someone who has just run the 800 metres rather faster than they had intended.

'Donald,' Henry was saying, 'was a doctor. He was a doctor. Of Medicine. Not of Law, not of English, not, thank God, of Sociology. But of that art of healing which we all know that his widow, Mrs Donald, needs so much as do we all after the scene that we have here witnessed today. Yes – ' He was back on course now. 'Yes, Donald was a doctor. Not a brilliant doctor. Not a high flyer. Not always, well, right! Often, as we know, to our cost, completely, hopelessly wrong in diagnostic terms. Way off the mark. Quite frequently.'

Billykins gave a juddering sob and started to bang her head against her knees. Elinor was signalling something to him. To stop, perhaps? But Henry couldn't stop. Thinking about Donald in that box, he knew he had to go on, to try and find, in the middle of all this gibberish that was coming out of his mouth, one coherent sentence that would stand as a tribute to someone he had, yes he had thought, was a bloody nice bloke. A wee bit of a racist –

'A wee bit of a racist,' he was saying, *out loud*, 'a wee bit of a racist. But who, I may say, when it comes down to it, and it does come down to it, isn't? Who isn't, in England, these days, fed up to the back teeth with hearing about Mad Mullahs chopping off people's hands for blasphemy and – '

Why was he talking about Mullahs? He must get back to the matter in hand. He found he was looking straight at Sam Baker QC (almost) whose arms were folded and whose face bore a look of intense, sceptical concentration, as if he was listening to his opposing advocate.

'Lawyers,' said Henry, 'like doctors, are the kind of people who live in Wimbledon and this is the kind of person Donald Templeton was. Not, as I say, a lawyer – '

Sam Baker QC (almost) shifted elaborately in his seat. 'But a doctor. And people like Donald, as I say, are used to slurs that are cast at them. They're not ashamed of being English, of being the people they are, of being the quiet, hard-working middle-class people who make up the backbone of England and indeed of America and – '

He caught sight of Sylvie le Perroquet from 109 (Non Merci ce Soir Sylvie). She looked almost frenzied with concentration.

'Of France. But France, America, England, these aren't the issue here. What is the issue is something that unites all those three countries, something that they all have in common, something that is as true of New York as it is of Wimbledon. I am talking, of course, about the situation which Donald finds himself in, the . . . er . . . dead situation.'

They had gone quiet again. He could pull it back. He knew he could. He found he was looking straight into the eyes of 'Neighbourhood Watch'. Inspector Rush normally struck Henry as a dull little man but today his eyes seemed as bright as a squirrel's.

'But death, even in suspicious circumstances, is something that creates a bond between us. Because all of us, of course, are united by death. Death, as someone said, is no laughing matter. It's not a subject for comedy. Except, of course, in the sense that we, all of us here today, English people here today to mourn a loved friend and colleague . . .'

Loved friend and colleague. That was the sort of thing, wasn't it?

'Here to mourn his passing but also, of course, yes, also to have, well, to have a laugh. To laugh because as Sophocles said – laughter is our only response, sometimes, to things. We laugh because the grief is too great, too deep, and that laughter can be as profound and meaningful an emotion as the tears that sometimes come with it, although they come, of course, out of amusement and not out of sorrow. I think comedy is as vital and meaningful as tragedy and I think Donald, if he were alive, which he isn't, would agree, because Donald, like all of us, like all of the English, whether from the north – '

Henry caught sight of Dave Sprott's grey hair and glasses bobbing up and down like some toy hung in the back window of a saloon car.

'Or the south, was an Englishman. Yes. He was an English doctor and I think there are people in the world who think such people are not, intrinsically, interesting. They would rather hear about Aborigines or people who have it away with gorillas because they don't care about the ordinary, decent people. They don't give a fucking stuff about Donald Templeton.'

He had said fuck again. He had said fuck, twice, at a funeral. He glanced down at his notes and caught sight of the words 'Death is Nature's way.'

'Death,' said Henry, 'is Nature's way!'

Nature's way of what? The rest of the quotation was obscured by a fold in the paper. He looked along the row of faces in front of him. They were now devoid of any clue that might guide him. If he could think of a way to stop this he would. But like a man at a party who simply cannot leave, he could not think of a reason why he should step back into the congregation. Was this his punishment? thought Henry.

'I used to drink with Donald,' he said, 'in a pub called the Rose and Thorn. Not a bad pub. A place where you could go to get away from the wife, the "old rat" as it were, although of course Billykins . . .'

Billykins! That was her name! Of course!

'Billykins and he were as devoted a couple as you will find anywhere and Donald loved her with an almost childlike devotion, could not bear to be parted from her, followed her almost everywhere, almost to the extent of hampering her freedom of movement – '

Elinor was looking at him. She seemed to be trying to say something. Stop, presumably. This was all very well. But how did you stop? Once you'd started how did you stop?

'Look,' said Henry, making one last, desperate effort to get this speech airborne, 'look. Donald was my mate. And if Donald was here today, which in a sense he is, although he's . . . er . . . in that box . . .'

Billykins gave the kind of wail familiar to connoisseurs of Greek tragedy. 'Ay ay ay ay!' she said, and then, 'Aieee-ou!!' It was, thought Henry, a primal grief that seemed to have no place in Wimbledon. His speech, ragged and confused though it obviously was, was having some effect. Christ, he was in the box and Henry was talking about him, a man talking about a man. It was simple.

'Look, he's in the box and here I am talking about him as a man, which I am and Donald was, if you hadn't noticed. A man. Yes, one of those phallic monsters, one of those patriarchal blokes that feminism – and Donald of course was no feminist – yes, an ordinary English, forty-year-old male. And what did he want? Really. With his outdated attitudes and his, well, frankly, penis, what did he want? With his mortgage and his little horizons and his contempt for all the fucking rubbish that gets talked these days?'

He had said fuck three times. But they were listening to him. They were actually listening to him. They were leaning forward in their seats, mouths open, hanging on his every word. Henry didn't care any more.

'He wanted,' he said, 'what any man wants anywhere on the globe. A loyal wife, a bit of land to call his, a job that put food on the table, a child that would grow up to love him and that he would raise properly. He didn't want to go to prison or be involved in a war, although I'm sure if it had come to that he would have been on the right side, although, as I should make clear, you never fucking know what the right side is until a long time after. Right? It isn't Tehran though, is it? It might be, it might just be that life in Wimbledon has developed to a higher pitch than anywhere else in the globe. What I am trying to say – '

What was he trying to say? Whatever it was he felt they wanted him to say it. To say it and then leave the platform.

'What I am trying to say is that no human life form, not even Donald Templeton, is completely beneath contempt!'

He realized, as he said this, that it sounded incredibly rude. He did not mean it to be.

'Look mate,' said Donald, 'go on through. Tell it like it is. Go on.'

'I mean by that,' said Henry, 'that I sometimes feel beneath contempt. I'm the sort of ordinary husband and father with not very many views about the world who's led a very simple quiet life and wanted to do good and brave and dangerous things but just never got the chance. And Donald was like that, I think. He was a romantic, you know? He was a wild fucking romantic. He was a man who dared, who wanted more. And I think that's why I liked him, because like him I look up at the sky above Wimbledon and I say "Oh my God. Oh my God, you bastard, I love you!" '

Henry found he was pointing, dramatically at the coffin. They're with me, he thought, they're getting my drift at last.

'That's me and you in there,' he said, in a kind of shriek, 'that's us. That's the next day of our lives. Let's try, shall we, and let that bit that lurked in Donald Templeton out of us. Let's be wild and ridiculous and free, shall we, in memory of him? Let's do it for Donald. Let's go for it. Because he's dead and we'll be dead soon and I think we owe him something, ladies and gentlemen. I am speaking the truth of my heart here because underneath this rather boring exterior I care. I'm not quite sure what I care about but I care. And one of the things I care about that isn't Nicaragua or Poland or anywhere else but right here and part of the country I love and that I am afraid I don't want to see change too much is people like Donald Templeton. Because Donald Templeton is me! I'm in that box with him, feeling what he's feeling, going through what he's fucking going through, man. Thanks Donald! Thanks for everything.'

Here Henry raised his arm in a kind of quasi-Fascist salute in the direction of the coffin and said, voice husky with emotion, 'It's your round, old son!'

Suddenly his eyes were blinded with tears. Convulsed with sobs, he made his way back to his seat where, to his surprise, Elinor, instead of hitting him in the face, put her arms round him. Other people in the chapel were sobbing too. Dave Sprott was leaning forward, his hands over his face, wailing like a child who had walked into his surgery for the first time. Even Sam Baker QC (almost) was white and nervous-looking and his professionally immobile upper lip was dangerously near to quivering.

It was not what Henry had meant to say. Or rather, it was not what he had meant to say at Donald's funeral. But it was, he felt, as he rose to his feet and the strains of 'Now Thank We All Our God' began to filter through to the chapel, something that needed saying.

20

'Come and get it!' murmured Henry under his breath as he carried the bowl of punch into Donald's house. 'Finish 'Em! This should help you forget your troubles!'

To give it some more go, he had added some milk and a carton of orange juice as well as a small plastic container of something called Kleeneezee. It was now the colour of strong tea.

No one actually mentioned his speech, but Dave Sprott grasped his hand and said: 'I know how you feel.'

Billykins just stared at him as if he was a creature from another planet. Only Elinor, when he had put the punch next to the glasses in the hall, barked, *sotto voce*: 'How could you do that, Henry?'

'I'm sorry,' said Henry, 'I was just very upset.'

'It was embarrassing,' went on Elinor.

'Have a drink!' said Henry.

'No,' said Elinor, 'I couldn't.'

'I'm having one!' said Henry.

She set her jaw at him. Over in the corner, Billykins, her head still between her knees, was moaning something. Henry caught the words '. . . awful . . .' and '. . . end the nightmare . . .' but whether she was talking about him or the vicar or Donald was unclear.

'You said you would have a drink!' said Henry.

'I won't!' hissed Elinor. 'I couldn't!'

Then she scuffed her foot on the carpet. An expression appeared on her face that at first Henry could not identify. As she spoke he realized with some surprise, that it was doubt.

'Oh, I don't know,' she said, 'at least you spoke out.'

'Yes!' said Henry.

Why is she saying this? What does she want?

'Grief,' said Elinor, 'is so buried with us, isn't it?'

'Yes!' said Henry.

She gave him a searching glance. 'We repress our feelings, we bundle up into a ball and don't talk about how we really feel. Deep down you probably do care, as you were saying today. Deep down you do care about the environment. About what we're doing to whales and dolphins and the North Sea and the inner cities, and the whole unleaded petrol thing.'

Why bring unleaded petrol into this? thought Henry. I have not formulated a view on unleaded petrol.

'What matters,' said Elinor, 'in anyone, is a spark of caring. Just something that tells you they're still alive. That they're still there. That other people can, well . . . touch them. Don't you think?'

Henry narrowed his eyes. He felt more than usually trapped.

'You feel threatened by my feminism, for example. You feel frightened by my growth as a woman. You feel . . .'

'I feel . . .'

Elinor stiffened with attention.

'I feel . . . frightened by you!'

'What about me frightens you, Henry?' said Elinor, laying a hand on his arm. 'Is it me, my physical presence as a woman, my needs and powers as a mother? Or are you frightened of me as an intellectual?'

'I'm frightened of you as a . . . thing,' said Henry, 'by the way you look at me, by the space you take up. By you. When I hear your step on the path I . . . I just cower!'

Elinor threw back her head and gave a braying, mannish laugh.

'Oh, Henry,' she said, 'you are funny!'

And she cuffed him, amiably, about the shoulder. Henry found this curiously erotic.

He looked around for Maisie. She had been very quiet during the service, although a few days before she had been heard asking what people usually ate at funerals and if there was usually a lot of it. Eventually he saw her in the garden with a whole bowl of rice salad and what looked like a new garden trowel. Black did not seem to have its customary slimming effect on Maisie's figure. She looked, if anything, bigger.

Over in the corner Dave Sprott was, to use his own words, 'settling in' to the punch. Next to him, Inspector Rush stood, glass in hand, peering at it suspiciously. But then Inspector Rush peered at everything suspiciously. Even small children on tricycles. Sprott took a sip, shook his head violently and started to bang himself on the back of the head.

'Wow!' he said. 'Wowza! Got a kick to it, eh?' Mrs Is-the-Mitsubishi-Scratched-Yet, a thin, girlish, fluffy woman, in an even fluffier mood than usual, grinned up at Henry girlishly. 'What have you put in this, Henry?' she said. 'Paint-stripper?'

Henry was beginning to have second thoughts about the punch. What had possessed him? He didn't want to poison the entire population of Maple Drive, did he? Well, at least not in a way that would lead so directly to him. He wasn't even sure any more that he wanted to poison anyone. But as so often in the murdering game, it was a bit late for doubts.

'Let me try it,' said Henry. 'I left it out in the front garden this morning. I hope no one's interfered with it!'

He sounded, he thought, like a character in a Victorian melodrama. Several people, including, he was concerned to note, Inspector Rush, were looking at him oddly. He sipped a glass.

It tasted of almost nothing but bleach.

'I think,' Sprott was saying, 'it has quite a resonant, flinty finish!'

Sam Baker QC (almost) was rolling the punch around his glass and wincing at it. He introduced a minute amount into his mouth and rinsed it around his gums.

'Extraordinary!' he said. 'A very positive nose and plenty of body. It reminds me of a New World wine, aged in the barrel. With a hint of . . .'

'Bleach!' said Dave Sprott.

Everybody laughed.

'Actually,' said Henry, 'if there is anything wrong with it I don't think we should drink it. I left it out in the garden.'

'And put a rat in it!' said Sam Baker QC (almost), accenting as he always did the concrete noun in the sentence. Did he do this, thought Henry, because he favoured anything that might possibly be regarded as evidence? Was it a tic, acquired through long afternoons in the Court of Chancery, where the only way of enlivening sentences might be to stress the wrong word? Or was it simply that Sam Baker QC (almost) was (as usual) trying to make you feel awkward?

'Elinor, love,' said Henry, 'you try it!'

'No no no,' said Elinor, 'it tastes like bleach!'

Sprott drained his glass and smacked his lips. 'It goes down a treat after a while,' he said, in his carefully preserved northern accent. 'It has a nicely balanced quality of well-orchestrated fruit. What have you put in it, Henry?'

'Bleach!' said Sam Baker QC (almost). Everyone (apart from Henry) laughed again. Detective Inspector Rush, who had been rocking to and fro on his heels, started to peer into the bowl.

'I'm a bit worried about this!' said Henry. 'I think we should take a look at – '

'No no no!' said Sprott, dipping his glass in the mixture and taking a deep draught of Yugoslav Riesling, brown sugar and assorted domestic cleaners. 'It's good. It's a bit on the aggressive side. But basically it's good. Has it got Slivovitz in it? Or is it some form of regional tequila?'

'I think,' said Henry, who was starting to sweat with the enormity of his offence, 'that someone may have . . . I don't think we should drink . . .'

But, as so often, people were ignoring him.

'What do you think?' Sprott was asking Mr Is-the-Mitsubishi-Scratched-Yet. Mr Is-the-Mitsubishi-Scratched-Yet made nervous little movements with his hands. He sipped a little, smiled prettily and, casting a nervous glance out to the street towards the Mitsubishi, said: 'It's not unpleasant!'

'Can't we – ' Henry began.

But now everyone wanted to get at the punch. Even Elinor consented to have half a glassful. Henry tried to scrape the ladle along the bottom of the bowl when he served her, reasoning that Impact and Start and Finish 'Em would probably sink through the wine, milk and orange juice, but he was not sure that half a glass would be enough. He was not, to be honest, sure that the solution was going to have any effect whatsoever. The only person who did not accept any of the punch was Detective Inspector Rush who, whenever Henry caught sight of him, was looking down into his glass, suspiciously.

'I'm a little cautious about taking drinks I'm not sure about,' he said to Henry.

'Is that right,' said Henry.

'One never knows,' said Rush, smiling thinly, 'you can't be too careful.'

As the friends, relatives and neighbours of Donald Templeton MD crowded round the punch-bowl licking their lips and holding out their glasses like children in a lunch queue, Henry, who took a couple of glasses himself, peered anxiously round the gathering looking for signs of collapse. There seemed, as far as he could tell, to be a fair amount of that. But then, people in Maple Drive were usually in that kind of state at parties. Part of the trouble was that the subtle blend of Yugoslav Riesling and assorted domestic cleaners was proving astonishingly popular. People said they had never had such a punch. It took a couple of glasses to get you going, they said, but when you got going, they said, you went. Vera 'Got All The Things There Then?' Loomis, the ninety-two-year-old from 92, had to be rescued from tipping the bowl up to her lips with her third glass, and Henry and several others remarked that they had never seen such animation among mourners.

'It's always that way at a funeral,' said Vera 'Got All the Things There Then?' Loomis. 'Once it gets going it really goes!'

Dave Sprott seemed totally desperate for the mixture. He stood by the bowl and making a pretence of serving the other guests managed to drink more than anyone else in the room. After a while it became impossible for Henry to discover how many people had actually had more than three or four glasses. He went out through the french windows into the garden. Would the local crematoria be able to cope with the influx of customers, a day or so from now?

When he returned there were only two or three hardened drinkers standing by the bowl, although Henry was disturbed to note that Inspector Rush was still there, standing just clear of the wall, his glass still full, looking across at Sprott as if he was just about to ask him to come along quietly. Sprott had stopped smacking his lips and muttering that it had a refreshing directness and an unambiguous honesty – but had decanted the punch into a small vase and was tipping it back into his throat, pausing only after each mouthful to slap himself on the back of the neck and shout 'Wowee!' and 'Wowza!'

He showed no signs of frothing. He was distinctly unclammy. And from where he was standing, Henry could observe no signs of cyanosis. It was Rush he didn't like. The detective kept peering over the lip of the bowl and pursing his lips, and then looking back at Henry, and though he kept close to the side of the punch, Henry never saw him drink any.

'I remember – ' he was saying as Henry came into the room, 'dealing with a poisoning case once, which made a great impression on me.'

No one, however, was listening to him. They were listening to Dave Sprott.

What Dave Sprott did do – as he always did, when drunk – was to start to talk, loudly and aggressively, about teeth. 'People's teeth,' he said, his carefully preserved northern accent astonishing the artificial gas fire, the Heal's sofa and the watercolours above the mantelpiece collected by the late Donald Templeton MD over a period of twenty years, 'people's teeth are the expression of their personality. For example, a fact not very well known to those outside the profession is that the Romans considered the teeth were the seat of all the most basic human emotions. Was it the Romans, Edwina?'

Edwina Sprott, six foot two, built like a prop forward, hair on the back of the hands, huge nose, voice like Vincent Price, no breasts to speak of, said, 'No, David! I don't think anyone considers the teeth the seat of all the most basic human emotions. Apart from you.'

Sprott, who always saw in his wife's remarks a wit not at first appreciated by others (until Sprott pointed it out to them) laughed hysterically. 'It is, though,' he said, 'it is. Take anyone's teeth and look at them, and you will find the key to their personality. Take that politician I do. The Labour one. His teeth, in my view, say a great deal about his policies!'

Edwina Sprott towered above him. For a moment Henry thought she might be about to scoop him up in her arms, as a mother gorilla might draw her baby to her, but although she looked as if she might like to do this, she did not. 'It's David Steel!' she said instead.

'It's David Steel you do, David!'

'Christ, so it is!' said Sprott. 'So it is!'

A sure test of their marriage's durability was their capacity to be surprised by each other's anecdotes.

'Christ, he come in for a clean t'other week,' said Sprott, 'and I said to 'im, "Clean?, Clean? This isn't cleaning. This is a restoration job, this is," I said. I told him my theory about teeth and personality and I think what I said may have an impact on the future development of the Liberal Party!'

'David,' said Edwina Sprott, her huge hands dangling in front of her, looking down on her man as if he were a particularly tasty snack in some pastrycook's window, 'you say the weirdest, weirdest things!'

Teeth and celebrities were Sprott's two main obsessions in life. Once started on the subject of celebrities' teeth he was unstoppable. He talked of the role of teeth in history, their importance in the shaping of the modern world, their influence on great events. As he spoke more about teeth he claimed more and more for them. He spoke of his South African cousin whose entire life had been changed by the clumsy insertion of a bridge. He spoke of the relationship between capped teeth and business success, of the obvious link between loose fillings and feelings of sexual inadequacy.

'Aren't you having any?' said Inspector Rush to Henry with a thin smile.

'I won't, thanks!' said Henry. 'I'm driving!'

Rush's enigmatic expression seemed to hint at the absurdity of this excuse. Sprott, meanwhile, tipped the last of the bowl down his throat.

'Teeth,' he said, just before he hit the last of it, 'teeth, the whole of oral hygiene really, is the expression of a society. Britain today is a society in which we have ceased to care about teeth, in which we have ignored the real nature of what we are because – '

And on the edge of what might have been a truly global *aperçu* about teeth and British society, without any trace of cyanosis, frothing, soiling of the air passages, pneumonia, or wrinkled, greyish, leathery hardening of the oesophagal mucous membranes, he whirled round in mid-gesture, clawed at his throat and fell, headlong, on Billykins's carpet.

21

No one was very sympathetic.

Most of the guests were shouting for more punch and Henry, who was dispatched by Elinor to Thresher's for twenty more bottles of Yugoslav Riesling, added it to the more corrosive elements of his recipe, only to be told that the new blend 'lacked fizz'.

Sprott lay face down on the carpet, while Mrs Sprott (who was more drunk than anyone had ever seen her) shouted obscenities at him in a voice that sounded as if it were coming from an even deeper grave than usual. By this stage Henry was back in the room and the group round the punch-bowl had split up; it was Henry who found himself prodding the body with his foot and giving his opinion as to Sprott's state of health. As far as he could tell, Sprott was still breathing. Henry went out into the hall and looked through the open door at the chestnut trees on the green.

Behind him the noise of the party went on. He could hear Billykins shouting something. 'Who wants a widow?' was what it sounded like. Someone, probably Derek Bloomstein, the Other Optician, had started playing the piano.

At least Sprott wasn't exhibiting any of the symptoms of acid poisoning. There was nothing clammy about him. Had Sprott, Henry asked himself, swallowed the stuff in such quantities that it was acting independently of his digestive system? Sloshing around his immaculately cared-for mouth, cannoning into the walls of his gullet and smashing straight through them into the bloodstream?

If it had, he was probably well beyond cyanosis, frothing, or soiling of the lips. He was probably in deep shock. He might, thought Henry, have only minutes to live. If things went on like this there would not only be no one to take his blood pressure or check on his wisdom teeth, there would be no one to sort out his eyes, check out his conveyancing problems or tell him which roofing company to avoid. He had better go back in and get Roger From the Practice to look over Sprott. Except, of course, he couldn't possibly tell the man what was wrong with the dentist. Could he? That would incriminate him, wouldn't it? Could he?

Henry was not particularly fond of Sprott. He had never, for example, liked the mechanical, almost threatening way the man said 'Rinse!' There had also been a nasty incident some years ago, known as The Capping of Elinor's Teeth, in which, in Henry's view, the dentist had steered dangerously close to extortion.

But when it came to it, could he do it? Could he let the man die? Was it fair?

He had already murdered Donald of course. Henry had expected, in the days after hearing the news, to feel some of the things murderers were traditionally supposed to feel. Guilt, for a start. At any moment, as he went between Blackfriars, the Rose and Thorn, St Michael and All Angels Primary School, Wimbledon, and Waitrose PLC he half expected Donald to leap out at him from behind a tree, gibbering, covered in blood and chains. Sometimes, very late at night when he could not sleep, he saw him coming up the garden towards him, blood on his face, soil round his lips and in his right hand a cracked vase in which was, of course, a few drops of fatal thallium ... But on the whole, having become a murderer did not seem to have altered his life. If anything, he felt slightly better than usual.

He had no particular urge, either, to murder anyone else, a thing he had noticed happening to quite a few murderers. Once they had tasted blood, some characters seemed to get a nose for chopping up people into easily manageable portions and leaving them in left-luggage compartments. A slight lowering of their moral standards seemed to bring on an uncontrollable urge to be beastly, an urge Henry did not feel. Even his urge to be rid of Elinor was not, he noticed, as keen as it once was. If he was still wedded to it, it was in the spirit of 'I've started so I'll finish', rather than the almost romantic fervour with which he had first embraced the notion.

He sighed and went back to the denuded front room. Elinor and

Inspector Rush were in the middle of what looked like a rather intense conversation, which seemed, like so many intense conversations, to fail upon Henry's approach.

'You see,' Rush was saying, 'I'm a naturally suspicious man. It's my job. I'm paid to be suspicious.'

He stopped and looked at Henry narrowly. Sprott was still lying face down on the carpet. There was no sign of Roger From the Practice. Mrs Sprott was leaning against the mantelpiece, her mouth open, exhausted enough for silence. Mr Is-the-Mitsubishi-Scratched-Yet was kneeling on the tiled surround to the gas fire. He appeared to be being sick. Glumly, Henry went out into the hall. Some mourners, but not all, were looking clammy. Some were singing. Quite a few were being sick out of windows. On the landing on the first floor, Billykins, veil askew, was sobbing into the arms of Peter 'Where is the Upfront Money?' Furgess from 65.

'Death,' Furgess was saying, 'is certain. You just have to face it, there's no point in moaning about it. It's part of life. It's something that happens. It's . . .' Furgess's face furrowed with the effort of self-expression. '. . . it's . . . par for the course!'

Billykins seemed to find this thought comforting.

Well, death was par for the course, wasn't it? It wasn't such a great event. Perhaps that was why he felt no urge to confess. Henry had never understood why it was that Raskolny-whatever-his-name-was had bothered to turn himself in to the police when no one had anything whatsoever against him.

'Oh!' came a voice from the floor. 'Oh my God! Oh!'

It was Elinor, and something in the basso contralto of her tone, the thrusting, stagy grief of it all reminded Henry of why it was he was trying to end her life some thirty or so years ahead of schedule.

'Oh!' she said again, sounding as surprised as she did when approaching sexual climax (in the days when she approached sexual climax). 'Oh! Oh!'

Henry looked down.

Elinor was sitting astride Sprott's chest, jerking her hips up and out and then allowing them to crash down on his lower ribs; she had both hands outstretched in front of her, made into two fists. She had converted herself entirely to piston action, so that as behind rose, arms descended, thumped on chest and then rose again as behind descended for the next assault. No one else in the room was paying much attention to her. Mr Is-the-Mitsubishi-Scratched-Yet was staring at the contents of his evacuated stomach like an archaeologist contemplating some mystery in the soil. As Henry stared down at Elinor, number 61a (Unpublished Magical Realist) zig-zagged towards him. He looked like a man about to make an awkwardly close relationship with the numinous. Behind him came Vera 'Got All the Things There Then?' Loomis, who looked if anything worse, and the two disappeared out into the hall, presumably to be sick all over 32 and 48 (Ecology-Conscious Pensioner in Green Anorak and Publisher Going Through Identity Crisis).

Sprott did not appear to be paying much attention to Elinor's ministrations. Christ, thought Henry, if Elinor was dropping her arse on to my stomach and then bashing me in the chest with her fists I'd want to make a statement on the subject. Sprott was just lying back, neck up, chin ridiculously forward. Was he, Henry wondered, showing off his teeth? Wasn't there some law against dentists opening their mouths as wide as David Sprott was doing? Wasn't it tantamount to advertising?

It was only when he got close enough to see his eyes that Henry realized that David Sprott was not going to be mending any more teeth for a while.

Dave Sprott was dead.

'He's dead!' shrieked Elinor, as she continued to hit him in the ribs. 'He's dead! He's dead! He's dead!'

This was all getting depressingly familiar, thought Henry. But, to his surprise, this time the news did strike him as genuinely shocking. Perhaps it was the sheer scale of the carnage he seemed to have provoked in his attempt to get through to Elinor. Outside in the hall he could hear people being sick, wailing and calling on God, and found himself saying, 'My God! How awful!'

Roger From the Practice crawled out from behind the sofa. 'Who's dead?' he called. 'Is someone dead?'

He belched and crawled on towards the hall door. Henry put his foot on the patch of carpet directly in front of the newly promoted GP. Roger From the Practice stopped and looked up at him pathetically.

'Yes,' said Henry sternly, 'someone is dead.'

'Who is it?' said Roger From the Practice.

Henry did not answer. Roger From the Practice rolled over on his back like a Labrador waiting to be tickled in the stomach.

'Who is it?' he said. 'Who's dead? Is it me? Say it's me. Oh God, say it's me. Oh God, please, please let it be me!'

22

It very nearly was. But, after a bout of vomiting that would have done credit to a party of schoolchildren going round the Bay of Biscay in February, Roger From the Practice recovered his composure enough to start handing out death certificates the way Napoleon handed out medals.

There were two (Roger From the Practice said) dead on the first landing. One had got as far as the shed before keeling over, and in the downstairs back lavatory, number 61a (Unpublished Magical Realist) had breathed his last in a manner worthy of one of his characters. He had died with his head deep in the Armitage Shanks bowl and his feet at a bold angle. He may not, as someone said later, have turned into a giant ostrich or begun to improvise verses from the Koran, but it was a step in the right direction.

Henry disliked most species of fiction writer but of them all considered magical realists to be the most suspect – perhaps because Elinor was always going on about them at such length. And this particular magical realist was a particularly difficult customer. But however prone the man was to double-park his own neighbours, Henry would not have wished this end on Rufus Coveney, as he was called. Neither would he have wanted Denimed Lout Who Voted Labour and Boasted About It from 129 to have leapt crazily from an upper bedroom and broken both legs in Donald's flower bed.

Henry could honestly have said, as he and Roger From the Practice made a body count, that he had not wanted any of this to happen. And Elinor, who accompanied them, was magnificently human. She consoled, she comforted, she leaned over number 43 (Widower in Blue Suit Who is Rarely in the Country) as he frothed and cyanosed, and with skills presumably acquired in her therapy class persuaded him to think positively about his situation, to enumerate his own personal strengths and maximize 'the plus side of being him' until the ambulance arrived. She gave cardiac massage. She put her fingers down people's throats. She treated the inhabitants of Maple Drive with almost as much care and concern as if they had been Nicaraguan peasants. Henry, looking at her, could not imagine why it was he had wanted to poison such a strong, useful, friendly woman.

This was the whole trouble with murder. On Monday it seemed a clear-cut, straightforward affair. But, by Wednesday, your victim had lost all traces of the things that had made them so eminently killable and, although you felt sure that tomorrow or the next day you would be up to steering them towards a vat of liquid metal or leaving them alone with a naked flame and a mains gas leak, today you just couldn't feel it the way you should. Your resolve weakened.

The real trouble, Henry decided, as he and Roger From the Practice carried another borderline case out into the garden, was people. You just never knew what they would do next. They were so difficult to classify. Sometimes it seemed as if there was no such thing as people, just an endless series of tricks of the light, a history of false impressions.

'Oh my God!' said Elinor, as the first ambulances arrived. 'This is absolutely terrible!'

'Yes,' said Henry, 'yes!'

In the end, only three people actually died at Donald's funeral, and one of these, Vera 'Got All the Things There Then?' Loomis, from 92, was ninety-two and therefore, everyone agreed, didn't really count.

People didn't seem very interested in asking why. There had been, everyone said, 'something not right' about the punch. People had, of course, drunk too much of it. There was talk of analysing what was left of it. But the trouble was – there wasn't any left, which only served to emphasize quite how much the mourners had managed to put away. The person who might have been expected to haul Dave Sprott's remains in to Wimbledon police station and begin the task of cutting him into little pieces was, of course, Detective Inspector Rush. One neighbour had the temerity to ask him whether he intended to do so, to which Rush responded with an enigmatic smile. Mind you, he responded to most questions with an enigmatic smile.

This ought to have reassured Henry. But it didn't. Something about the man's manner made him suspect that he was biding his time. There was something about the way he tipped his hat to Elinor, too, that . . . No. That thought was impossible. Rush was, in the words of Jaspar Cecil, the wine merchant from 83, 'married to the Wimbledon police force'.

That was why his silence was so frightening.

It was two or three days after the funeral that Henry started to study books on toxicology, as a sort of retrospective research effort. He had, he decided, made such a hash of his career as a poisoner that he had no real way of even telling quite how badly he had done. And, in the inquiry that he expected daily, he would have to have some line of defence. All the books he read made him feel a lot worse. But of all of them, from *Lives of the Great Poisoners* to *Some Toxicological Aspects of Pathology*, none made him feel worse than Keith Simpson's *Forensic Medicine*, which he obtained from Wimbledon Public Library.

1. *In a previously healthy subject, the onset, sudden or slow, of symptoms which do not correspond to ordinary illness, should raise suspicion.*
2. *If the source is suspected to be food, endeavour to obtain some of it: trace other persons who partook of it.*
3. *Keep any vomit, stomach wash-out, faeces, units of CSF which come to hand. Seal them and affix labels.*

As far as Henry could see, there were no faeces or stomach wash-outs lying around in Billykins's house, but there was enough vomit on her carpets to keep a team of pathologists in business for a year, and it only needed one person enterprising enough to start picking up bits of it for them to be on to Henry. For several days he went in and out of Billykins's house, offering to take things to the cleaners and watching anxiously for strangers equipped with clear plastic bags and sticky labels. In particular he looked out for Detective Inspector Rush: but he saw no sign of him.

But after a week or so, he grew calmer. People in Wimbledon, thank Christ, didn't think like Keith Simpson. They didn't go round rifling through people's faeces and affixing labels to them. Poison (this is its beauty) is part of everyone's diet. People were always pouring poison down their throats. Looked at in this light, Simpson's work became a comfort rather than a threat. On page 322, he read:

Ethyl Alcohol (C_2H_5OH)

Three forms of poisoning occur:
1. *Acute (fatal) alcohol poisoning.*
2. *'Drunkenness' (insobriety).*
3. *Chronic alcoholic poisoning (chronic alcoholism).*

Further on he read:

Stupor – this is the 'dead drunk' stage at which the patient is roused into response only by the strongest stimuli. To be 'anaesthetic' or unfeeling to injury, to lie in a snoring stupor with flushed face and dribbling lips, is the last stage of helpless inebriety. This is the stage which is likely to be simulated by cerebral disease or head injury.

Even the words used to describe drunkenness, thought Henry (who was by now becoming rather censorious of people who abused their bodies, who subjected them to poison when there was so much healthy, life-giving sustenance around), were a giveaway. *Headbash. Braindeath. Wipe out.* And, if he felt guilt, which somewhat to his surprise he did, it was about the fact that he had not tried hard enough to stop the bastards drinking the stuff. He had even, on the evening after the funeral, suggested to Roger From the Practice that someone had 'got to' the punch but Roger From the Practice, true to his late master's instincts, was unkeen to investigate any theory other than that his neighbours and friends had keeled over as a result of alcohol and stress in fatal doses.

Donald, thought Henry, would have been proud of him. His medical knowledge seemed to be largely derived from reading the colour supplements of newspapers, and his analysis of the party was born out by the local journal, whose banner headline read: 'THREE DIE AFTER DRINKING SPREE FUNERAL HORROR. "MY SHAME!" SAYS WIDOW.'

People did not meet each other's eyes in the street. Nazi Who Escaped Justice at Nuremberg met Detective Inspector Rush at the golf club, and suggested to him that someone should inform the coroner. Rush, apparently, had smiled with enigmatic bitterness, and replied, 'My dear Gunther, I would like to inform the coroner. I am a policeman, am I not? But my hands are tied in this matter. You understand? I am not a free agent in this affair!'

And he had looked, people said, so steely and enigmatic that Nazi Who Escaped Justice at Nuremberg had had to go out and play another round of golf, to get over it. Anyway, nobody had any idea where the coroner was. Even if they had been able to find him he was probably out moonlighting, or had been cut or privatized like everything else in Britain. The fact was that nobody much cared that three more people had croaked. They were all too busy trying to sell their houses at a profit or worrying whether higher interest rates would lead to a slump.

Henry, to his surprise, was getting rather left wing.

Murder, of course, changed you. It sharpened you up, made you less provincial. It gave you an interest. And Elinor, who in the days after Donald's funeral might have been expected to go on even more about his grossness, his obscene masculinity and his record-breakingly loutish behaviour at the funeral of a close friend, seemed positively amiable. There was, of course, nothing like surprising people.

'Really, Henry,' she said one evening, 'you're a mystery, aren't you? You're . . . peculiar!'

She screwed up her eyes as she said this. But from her expression Henry gathered that being peculiar was a better thing to be than obscenely masculine. It might, in the end, be almost attractive. Henry had become a question mark, some difficult, unclassifiable quantity, and his behaviour only intensified her interest. After all, it was not habitual for Henry to jump every time the doorbell rang or give a low cry whenever he heard a police siren heading down the hill ('Good evening, Mr Farr. We'd like to ask you a few questions about a quantity of *bleach* we have found in the stomach of the late David Sprott . . .').

Goaded on by her curiosity about the man she had married, Elinor began, in the evenings, to go over the early history of their relationship, much of which, as she described it, bore no relation whatsoever to anything Henry remembered.

'Do you remember,' she would say, 'that little hotel in Switzerland?'

Henry would look at her glumly across the supper table. What was she talking about? They had never been to Switzerland. Had they?

'That funny little man with the alpenstock,' went on Elinor, 'and the beard. And we went up to that waterfall!'

Here she leered suggestively. Did she mean to imply that they had had intercourse? Henry could not even remember going to Switzerland, let alone having intercourse by a waterfall in that country. Not with her anyway. Perhaps she had done all this with someone else. Some teacher from her primary school days. Or possibly – Henry didn't like this thought – with whoever her secret admirer might be.

Maisie was also, for some reason, a great deal more quiet and submissive. Donald's funeral seemed to have impressed her. She even asked Henry on one occasion whether Mars Bars gave you cancer, to which Henry replied: 'If they do – I recommend we begin chemotherapy on you right away.'

Dave Sprott's funeral, a double date with 61a (Unpublished Magical Realist) was a low-key affair, only enlivened by the sight of Unpublished Magical Realist's family, all of whom remained dry-eyed throughout the proceedings. The person who spoke on his behalf, a cadaverous man with a strong Welsh accent, actually waved a copy of his manuscript (*Decay of the Flying Wolves*) and attempted to give some résumé of the plot to the now somewhat blasé mourners of Maple Drive, SW19. 'After this extraordinary mythical character,' he said, 'half tortoise, half publisher, returns to the mythical country of Rumalia, Rufus is, I think, trying to tell us that the victor, ultimately, is not death and, similarly, in this great, this very plangent image of a toothless wolf alone in the deserted Stock

Exchange, Rufus is saying that the struggle goes on, to be ourselves, whatever we may be. And I think when this manuscript is published it will be a testament to the positive thing in all of us.'

But people get bored with death, even in Wimbledon. Vera 'Got All the Things There Then?' Loomis was scattered in the scattering area, Coveney was taken in a small urn down to Hastings and cast into the sea by one of his relatives (in death he remained unpublished), and the suburb forgot them. Henry became involved in a rather messy divorce in Aldershot and, in spite of what he regarded as one of the most closely argued letters in British legal history, failed to resolve the issue of the dustbin shelters. It seemed for a while as if no more was to be heard from the man who called himself the Wimbledon Poisoner.

'But at number 54 Maple Drive,' said Lustgarten, pacing the length of the quiet street in a long, dark coat, 'Henry Farr, quadruple murderer, planned his next crime. His poisonings may have been the result of bad planning. He tried to tell himself, in the long, lonely nights that followed the tragic deaths of Templeton, Loomis, Coveney and Sprott, that he was not as guilty as he felt. But the fact was that he was now stained not only with the blood of his doctor but also with the blood of his dentist, a respectable widow and a young man whose only crime, apart from the writing of magical realist novels, was to have drunk the lethal cocktail that Farr had prepared for his wife. Although he felt the Furies close in round him, although he was almost sure that vengeance, that justice was about to descend, Henry Farr saw no way back.'

23

Often, as October, sunny and cold, starved the leaves along Maple Drive, Henry Farr thought about not poisoning his wife. He thought about not poisoning her as much as he thought about poisoning her.

As Maisie and Elinor and he walked one afternoon across the common to the windmill, he found himself reflecting that, if he stopped now, there was no question of his ever being discovered. Whereas if he continued, who knew who would be the next to get it in the neck? There seemed to be no easy relation between the people he wanted to die and the ones who copped it. He thought about this as the three of them stood in the wet grass to the south of the windmill, and he read from the local guide, sadly lacking as it was in detail.

'It is difficult to understand why Charles March should have built the windmill in this way. But Wimbledon Windmill bears a striking resemblance to one or two other post mills. It is possible – '

Here he tapped Maisie on the chest, 'Listen, Maisie – it is possible that he simply copied this building out of ignorance of normal wind-mill practice. Do you see? Isn't that amazing?'

'No,' said Maisie.

'I mean,' said Henry, trying to breathe some life into this subject, 'what an amazing dumbo. Just . . . copying a windmill like that. Not knowing anything about normal windmill practice!'

'A windmill,' said Maisie, 'is just a windmill. Isn't it?'

Henry sighed. It was true that since Donald's death he had been making more effort with his daughter; there were times, as a result, when he wondered whether she, not Elinor, was the problem. There were even moments when it occurred to him that he was the prob-lem. He looked across at Elinor.

OK, she was a feminist. That was a harmless eccentricity, wasn't it?

She was a feminist, but when it came down to it she put the things in the dishwasher like anyone else. She mowed the lawn. These days she sometimes even listened to him.

'I'm bored of this windmill,' said Maisie. 'I want to go to the café.'

'Yes, my darling,' said Elinor. 'Yes, of course. Salt and vinegar crisps? Or a sticky bun?'

At the worst point in her therapy (she didn't seem to go quite as often these days) she would never have allowed such words to pollute her lips. The women in the therapy group were of the opinion that poisons in foodstuffs were a direct cause of many emotional and psychological difficulties, one of them having gone as far as writing Henry a note to tell him to lay off the salami, and once the mere mention of the word 'salt' would have brought her out in the kind of rash experienced by someone suffering from a dose of atropine methonitrate or a crafty snort of alkaloids of calabar.

It was Henry who saw the world as under the sway of poisons these days. Poisons, like ugly shapes emerging from a Rorschach blot, were there, behind things, and as he read more and more on the subject, he found himself chanting their names like a litany as he rode the train to Blackfriars, or walked up the hill alone to the Rose and Thorn.

> Ecgonine . . .
> Ergot . . .
> Pomegranate . . .
> Stavesacre . . .
> Papaverine . . .
> Thebaine . . .
> Apomorphine . . .

From acetyldihydrocodin, its salts, to zinc phosphide, from tartar emetic to bismuth, Henry rolled the syllables round his tongue until he felt he was eating the names. He planned delicious meals, which would have as their centre some ragout of veal à *la* alkaloids of sabadilla, followed perhaps by a little side salad of homatropine; he thought about poison as something sweet, something that would be easy to swallow, that would lull you to sleep, get you out of all this.

And, if he was honest, the poisons he dreamed about were no longer anything as vulgar as a weapon, they were not aimed at anybody, not even Elinor.

'I'll have some crisps too!' said Henry.

'Fatty!' said Elinor, almost amiably.

As the three of them waddled across the car park, pitted with puddles, from the woods facing the windmill, where once Henry had dreamed of burying Elinor in a shallow grave, couples walked in the October sunshine.

The couples wear each other on their faces, thought Henry. The Spanish say that the wife wears the husband on her face, the husband wears the wife on his linen. But in England it isn't like that. People simply grow into each other, the way ivy grows into English walls or roses grow into housefronts in any suburb in this quiet island. Perhaps he and Elinor were growing into each other in that way, as they walked, now, towards the steamed-up glass front of the café where couples sat in a silence he might, a week or so ago, have construed as hostile, staring out at their limited, peaceful horizon. Perhaps he and Elinor had just been going through a crisis. They had 'displaced their aggression'. They had, rather spectacularly, 'dumped'. And if four people had had to die, well . . . according to a woman in Elinor's therapy class, you had to 'die to grow'. They had obviously simply persuaded others to go through this part of their therapy for them.

'I want salt and vinegar, chilli beef and cheese and onion!' said Maisie.

'Yes, darling!' said Elinor, with just the faintest trace of strain in her voice.

If there was one thing that made Henry feel he should do away with her, it was Donald.

He really missed Donald. He was surprised quite how much he missed him. He often found himself wanting to say the kind of thing he always said to Donald, things like, 'I don't know, squire . . .' or 'Whichever way you slice it, mate . . .' or even 'Mine's a light and special!' and halfway through enunciating them, turned to find the doctor absent. And, in a way, it was Elinor's fault. If only she hadn't forced her chicken thallium on him, if she had only eaten it up, like a good girl, at the very moment when his hatred of her was as pure as the best poison. And now it was sometimes hard to remember why he was poisoning her; poisoning her wouldn't bring Donald back. Although, thought Henry, as they joined the queue for food, if his death had brought them together perhaps her death would bring him back to life.

'Mmm,' said Maisie, biting into her bun before it was paid for, 'this is yum!'

'Mmm!' said Elinor.

They moved to a table. The Farr family ate in a briskly competitive, albeit communal style. No one spoke while eating; all that was to be heard was grunting and wheezing until the last crisp, the last drop of tea and orange juice and the last fragments of white icing had disappeared down one or other of the Farr family throats.

Someone was prodding Henry in the ribs. Looking down he noticed that it was Elinor. Her mouth full of crumbs, she said, 'What are all those books on poison doing in your study?'

Henry belched and looked at his boots. 'What books on poison?' he said.

'Oh,' said Elinor, '*Great Poisoners of the World, Death Was Their Business, Encyclopedia of Murder, Forensic Medicine, Exit a Poisoner, The Life of "Apple Pip" Kelly the Strychnine Killer, Six Hundred Toxic Deaths –* '

'Oh, those,' said Henry, 'I – '

'*Strong Poison, A Life of William Palmer, the Notorious Staffordshire Poisoner, Hyoscine; Its Uses in Toxicology* by Adolf Gee Smith, *Some Applications of Arsenic in Industry* by – '

She broke off and peered at him. 'Are you trying to poison me, Henry?' she said, and then, looking round the café, in a humorous voice – 'I say, everybody – Henry wants to poison me!'

Then, because it was such a ridiculous idea, she threw back her head and gave a booming, confident laugh.

'I couldn't do that, darling,' said Henry, 'I love you!'

Elinor's eyes narrowed. 'Do you?' she said.

'You're the sun and the moon and the stars to me,' said Henry, 'you're the reason why I get up in the morning and go to bed at night. You give meaning to my every breath. You are my rationale!'

Elinor folded her arms. She looked, Henry thought, like an off-duty policeman listening to some suspect political opinions in his local pub.

'Am I?' she said.

'Yes, yes,' said Henry, 'deep down. You know. Really deep down. Of course you are.'

She didn't look very convinced by this. Did she, he wondered, really suspect him? And if she did, was it the kind of thing she might mention to Detective Inspector Rush, assuming that she and Rush were . . .

'Actually,' Henry found himself saying, 'I just got really interested in poisons. It became a bit of a . . . well . . . a . . . hobby. You know?'

'Well, I always said,' said Elinor, 'that you should have more interests.'

Henry gulped. 'That's right!' he said. 'And I was trying to look at our relationship in the light of that. To make it, you know, grow . . .'

She still did not look entirely convinced. Henry talked more rapidly. 'Did you know,' he said, 'that alkaloids of pomegranate are a deadly poison? Or that the poisoner Neil Cream handed out strychnine to young girls for no apparent motive!'

Elinor's brow furrowed. 'Actually,' she said, 'I am very interested in food additives of any kind.'

'Precisely!' said Henry wildly. 'This is all part of it, you see. I've been trying to . . .' He groped for the word. 'Re-think my attitudes!'

She shook her hair out and for a moment looked like someone he remembered liking, years ago. Why was it that they no longer had a common language?

Henry blundered on, trying to use the words she used. 'I've been thinking about poison as . . . as a mode of communication!'

She looked a little doubtful about this. Picking at the crumbs on the table, she said, 'It is odd though, isn't it?'

'What is?'

'Those deaths. All those people at Donald's funeral. And the punch . . .'

157

'What about the punch?' said Henry.

She didn't answer this question but continued to trace little circles on the damp plastic of the table.

'I was talking about it all to John Rush,' she said, 'I think he knows something. But isn't saying. You know?'

'I know!' said Henry.

'Mind you – ' said Elinor, 'the police never do, do they?'

'No, no . . .' said Henry.

What was all this about *John* Rush?

'They could,' said Elinor, 'be biding their time.'

'I know!' said Henry.

There was a long silence. Henry filled it with a boyishly enthusiastic speech about Mrs Greve, who had poisoned her husband with ground glass in Dublin in the early 1920s. Elinor watched him as he spoke with a kind of sadness he did not understand.

'Actually,' she said, 'it's nice to see you excited about something. There were times when I thought you'd . . . you know . . . given up. There were times when I thought . . .'

She laughed, a little nervously. 'You know . . . you'd . . . poisoned the chicken or something . . .'

Then she clasped his hand, firmly. 'But you wouldn't do a thing like that. You're a confused man. You're a sad man in many ways. But you're not a bad man, are you?'

Henry tried, not very successfully, to look deep into her eyes. 'No,' he said, 'not really!'

'Why would you ever want to poison me anyway?' went on Elinor wistfully. 'What have I ever done to you? You'd be lost without me. Wouldn't you?'

And, with those words, she took Maisie's hand and walked out to the rain-soaked car park.

24

Indeed.

What, when you thought about it, had she actually done to him? Why was he trying to poison her? Didn't this approach to their marriage need a complete re-think?

As they trudged across the common towards the village, Henry realized that few, if any advantages, financial or social, would accrue to him on her death. He would have to get an au pair – some Swedish or German floozy who went out till four in the morning and brought men back to her room. He would have to do even more domestic work than he did at the moment. There would be another funeral to organize. He might even have to speak at it (Henry shuddered slightly at this thought).

Then there was her mother. She would want to help. She would take the train down from Cumbria and sit in the front room and want to talk about her daughter. She would hold Henry's hand and look deep into Henry's eyes and say 'Let's talk about Elinor!' She would go on about how wonderful her daughter was, she would probably describe her talent for opera singing and gourmet cuisine. She might even – Henry started to shake uncontrollably – ask to stay.

There was quite a lot to be said for leaving Elinor alive. From the administrative point of view alone. Where, now he thought about it, was the salt kept for the dishwater? How often did you have to put salt in it? When you put salt in it – where did it go? Did you just chuck it over the dishes like seasoning, or what?

How would he tell Maisie about periods?

They stopped outside a bookshop in the village High Street. Maisie pressed her nose to the glass. Elinor did the same. Then they squashed their lips against its cold, clean surface. They started to laugh.

'Can I buy a book?' said Maisie.

'Of course, darling!' said Elinor.

She wasn't all bad, thought Henry. When the three of them were like this, it almost felt good to be part of a family, knowing you were going back to a warm house, a well-tuned piano, a decent, ordered existence. Didn't married men stand less chance of getting heart attacks than bachelors?

Let's be reasonable, he told himself, as he followed Elinor and Maisie into the bookshop, you're not going to find another woman anyway. You're one of those people who looked interesting but turned out not to be. You didn't show much early promise, but what promise you showed you didn't fulfil. You're just another little Englishman who gets a laugh at parties. That's what you are. The one interesting thing you've ever done is try and murder your wife. Even if you did end up murdering your doctor and your dentist and –

Oh my God, thought Henry, I'm a murderer. I am actually a murderer. He felt suddenly very cold. Why? Why did he feel something that was almost guilt but not quite? As he stood watching Elinor and Maisie he realized it was something very simple. It was the urge to tell someone what had happened, coupled with the realization that he would never be able to do so. That what he had done was a totally private act, that it condemned him to an awful isolation, a world in which every remark or approach, however natural-seeming, was false. 'You are a poisoner!' an unpleasant, small voice in his head began to say.

And this was worse than anything he had felt before. It was worse, precisely because he now knew that he didn't want to poison his wife. With that realization came an inexpressible relief. He felt like a man who has just been told his brain scan is clear. He wanted to rush up to her and tell her the good news (although in that negative way women had she would probably brood over the implications of his original intention). But at the same time as this relief came this stinging, nagging ache. This feeling of isolation that threatened to overwhelm him, and lead him to shout out the truth here, in the shop, on a cold October afternoon.

Hang on, hang on, Henry. This is England, not Russia. For Christ's sake! You've tried to poison your wife. It was something people did. In the heat of the moment. No jury would convict. You had a tiff – you went out and got a shotgun or some strychnine and let off steam. You couldn't have love without hate as that man on *Stars on Sunday* had pointed out. Think positive, Henry.

I have become tougher, he said to himself, I have become more independent. I am better read. I know a lot more about chemistry. Yes, I have lost a valued friend and several neighbours, but for God's sake, if people can't learn from their mistakes and become useful citizens once more, what is the hope for any of us? Crime does not necessarily imply punishment these days – if it ever did. We are more, not less Christian than we were in Dostoevsky's day.

As they approached number 54, he linked his arm into hers. She started at first. Elinor was not used to him touching her. Her therapy group had apparently decided that Henry had something called 'touch taboo'. And, indeed, the pressure of her arm on his felt, at first, a little alarming. But as they turned in through the gateway Henry realized, to his surprise, that he was not actually gritting his teeth. She felt warm and, yes, comforting.

It was amazing how, when you had decided not to poison a person who probably deserved it, the world suddenly seemed a better, more decent, cleaner place. Maybe that was it. Maybe he had been suffering from whatever it was Raskolnikov had had, and hadn't realized it. He had had bad thoughts. He had acted on them. He had been mean and small-minded and thought only about himself and his problems. And look what had happened to him as a result! Years of negative thinking had turned him into a quadruple murderer. But, thought Henry as he let them in to the hall, he wasn't going to lie down under that stereotype. No sirree!

He had been full of spite and bitterness towards the world that lay outside Wimbledon. But now he was going to learn to be generous. Some people flew all over the world and had themselves profiled in colour magazines and had hundreds of women and as much Jack Daniels as they could drink while other people were fat and lived in Wimbledon. That was life! Some people sat up till four in the morning talking about the imagination and the sunset on the north face of the Eiger, while other people watched *News at Ten* and went to bed. That was life. The people with yachts and penthouses and as much sex as they wanted and shares and private beaches and planes constantly at their disposal and suntans and fantastic digestions were not, most of them, happy. Were they! Oh no. Happiness was a more complex emotion than that.

Would he, for example, when it came down to it, swap Maisie and Elinor and 54 Maple Drive for some villa with a swimming pool in Marbella complete with leggy blonde with a first in physics and an insatiable appetite for sex in strange positions with Henry? Would he?

Henry felt a momentary twinge of doubt and pushed it aside. He wouldn't.

Would he exchange his life of struggle, of patient, unrewarded research on a subject that was, possibly, of no interest to anyone anyway? Would he swap his *Complete History of Wimbledon* for some quick, easy, Nobel Prize-winning piece of crap about the state of play in Third World jails? Would he exchange all that lived experience, the forty years of actually being Henry Farr for the cushy way out – I mean, said Henry to himself, who do you want to be? Henry Farr or Graham Greene?

For the briefest of brief moments he thought he was going to scream 'GRAHAM FUCKING GREENE!' and, running from the room, sink the coal shovel into Elinor's neck, but such was the power of positive thinking that the moment passed. He looked round at the sitting room and, his heart growing bigger and bigger, more and more human with each glance, he reached for a pencil and paper. He found himself writing:

Pluses

1. *I have not been found out.*
2. *I have not killed anyone on purpose.*
3. *I have come to terms with my marriage.*

Minuses

But, when it came to it, he could not think of any minuses. From where Henry was sitting, poisoning had been a challenging, bracing way of getting to grips with a mid-life crisis. The *Reader's Digest* would have been proud of him. He was already thinking of Henry the Murderer in the past tense. Something along the lines of 'When I Tried my Hand at Poisoning . . .' or 'My Wife-murdering Phase'. He was entering a new world in which he might learn all those basic skills that had for so long been denied him. For Christ's sake, thought Henry, women are just people. People have problems, don't they?

The awesome thought came to him that, on his own, without any artificial aids or any money changing hands, he, Henry Farr, was experiencing Therapy.

'Open up, Henry,' said a voice within him, 'you are not all bad! You are businessman, father, cook, raconteur! You are murderer, socialite, good neighbour. A murderer is, in many ways, a very positive thing to be. Quite a lot of people would like to be in your shoes. Go with the flow, Henry. Accept the changes in your life! Be well, husband, commuter, solicitor, unapprehended poisoner!'

He was actually grinning to himself when Elinor came into the room. She looked, he thought, almost triumphant.

'John Rush!' she said, in the tones of a butler announcing a celebrity at a party. Then she flung the door wide open. 'He says he wants to see you about something!'

Henry goggled at her as Rush came into the room, bowing slightly as if to acknowledge the importance of his appearance. Before she retired, Elinor, still in larky mood, waved her hand towards him, as if she was proud to have a representative of Law and Order on the premises.

'Detective Inspector Rush,' she said, 'all the way from Wimbledon CID!'

PART TWO

Crime and Punishment

'Don't you see that blessed conscience of yours is nothing but other people inside you!'

Luigi Pirandello, *Each in His Own Way*

25

Henry could tell straight away that, when actually on the job, Detective Inspector Rush was one of the most astute and ruthless detectives of the twentieth century.

There was something about the way he fiddled with his pipe, tamping down the tobacco with the back of a matchbox, biting the stem and, from time to time, squinting along it in a knowing sort of way, that suggested a policeman of almost superhuman intelligence.

But Henry could tell, from the man's drabness, his thin, nasal voice, and his resolute disinclination to discuss anything to do with criminology, that he was a very serious customer indeed. Why else was he parking himself in Henry's front room talking about the weather, about Elinor, whom he seemed to know worryingly well, and, indeed, almost anything but the subject that had quite obviously brought him here. He was clever, thought Henry, very, very clever indeed.

'Your wife,' said DI Rush, 'is a remarkable woman!'

'She is!' said Henry.

'You picked a good 'un there!' went on Rush.

'Indeed!' said Henry.

What was it about Elinor that made her so attractive to such widely different social groups? Policemen, doctors . . . where would it end? thought Henry. Was it simply that, without really being aware of it he had, for all these years, been married to a very attractive woman? The thought was, somehow, frightening. If this was the case – how was he going to hang on to her? Rush was talking again, and something about the look in his eyes told Henry he was getting on to the purpose of his visit.

'I'm sorry to trouble you,' he said, eventually, with what seemed like reluctance, 'but I've been talking to quite a few people in Maple Drive about . . .'

Here he waved his pipe at the window. Once again Henry noted the subtlety with which the subject was being introduced. It was almost as if Rush was broaching it against his will.

'. . . poison . . .'

'What kind of poison?'

The detective inspector seemed to forget, for a moment, which kind. But he also managed to suggest that this very absentmindedness might be some subtle interrogator's ploy. Henry felt an absurd desire to throw himself on the carpet and shout 'I confess! I'm an animal! Take me away!'

'Poison . . .' he said, and paused. Then he gave a short, stagy, little laugh. Henry wished he would stop making gnomic remarks and get on with the real business of the afternoon – alibis, heavy innuendo and possible threats of violence.

'I'm particularly interested in poison,' Rush was saying. 'I look through the local paper and I see someone's been taken ill or found dead somewhere or other and I think . . . I wonder . . . I wonder . . .'

'Yes,' said Henry, 'I expect you do.'

Rush was at the window. He wheeled round, suddenly theatrical, and jabbed his pipe at Henry. 'Three people dead,' he said, 'after a . . .' He paused.

'Drunken spree?' said Henry.

'Precisely,' said DI Rush.

He paced back to the sofa and sat on the arm, looking even more like a man who had been instructed to do all this – walk, sit, tamp down pipe, suck, pause, blow – by a not very good theatre director.

'And of course,' Rush seemed close to laughter, 'there was no inquest. It was simply another party that got out of hand. Three more stiffs.'

'Can I offer you a drink,' said Henry, 'or are you on duty?'

'I'm never off duty!' said Rush. 'I'm always on duty. At four in the morning I wake and I stare into the darkness, thinking about crime and the evil things we do to each other. And about, well, how beastly we can be! I'll have a gin and tonic if you're having one.'

'Surely!' said Henry, trying to keep his voice steady.

He went to the door. Maisie was crouched at the keyhole, eyes round with excitement. She followed him through to the kitchen.

'What have you done?' she said.

'What have *you* done?' said Henry.

'Nothing,' said Maisie, 'I'm a child.'

'Being a child,' said Henry, as he poured the biggest gin and tonic he had ever poured in his life, 'is no excuse.'

He poured one half the size for the detective inspector and, followed by Maisie, went back towards the front room. She installed herself by the crack in the door as he went in. Rush was still standing, staring out at the street, his hands by his side, the pipe now dead to the world. When he heard Henry he wheeled round sharply.

'A nice quiet street,' said Rush in a manner that suggested that it was nothing of the kind, 'in a nice, quiet suburb. Full of nice, quiet houses, and nice, quiet families inside them. And somewhere, in one of them . . .'

His eyes flared dangerously into life. 'A madman. A psychopath. A killer.'

Henry jumped. 'Do you think so?'

'Oh, I know so,' said Rush, 'I know so. I know that somewhere out there, somewhere out there is a man so twisted by hatred and spite, so bent out of shape by life that he couldn't really be called human any more.'

'Golly!' said Henry.

'A man,' said Rush, waving his right arm and pacing up and down on the carpet, 'a man who thinks the world owes him something. A drab little man, obscure, meek and mild, hen-pecked perhaps. Like Crippen, say, with a pathetic pipe dream of his own that will never come to fruition – '

Henry thought of *The Complete History* and gulped. He had the uncomfortable sensation that this man could see right into him, that unlike almost everyone else with whom he had dealings (including Elinor) he knew what Henry was thinking.

'A man who is probably impotent. Unable to connect. Perhaps homosexual, I don't know. But, above all, a man with a warped, vile, grotesque view of the world. A narrow, twisted little man, a moral cripple, a – '

'A beast?' said Henry, in a high, squeaky voice.

'That's it!' said Rush, amazed at Henry's powers of intuitive understanding. 'A beast!'

Rush's face was pale with righteous fury. Henry could see his knuckles whiten round the pipe.

'Most of us,' he went on, 'rue the day the death penalty was abolished.'

'Indeed,' said Henry, 'indeed!'

Rush was clearly not one of your namby-pamby community policemen. He was a copper out to get his man. The sort of person who would work on a case twenty-four hours a day, seven days a week, until he had brought the guilty one to justice. The sort of policeman of whom, in normal circumstances, Henry thoroughly approved. He was not entirely sure, however, that in this case such zeal was appropriate. There was something, he decided, odd and fanatical about the man.

It was the same with the death penalty. Henry had always been in favour of the death penalty. For other people. In his case he felt it would quite simply be unfair. He deserved something for what he had done of course. Light whipping maybe. But death? For God's sake! Would his death bring Donald back? Wasn't it simply an archaic desire for revenge? He drank deeply of his gin and tonic.

'But,' said Rush, 'you've got me on my hobby horse!'

'What is your hobby horse?' said Henry.

'The Wimbledon Poisoner,' said Rush. He laughed, briefly, and from his top left-hand pocket drew a sheaf of clippings. Henry wasn't quite sure whether he was supposed to look at them, and in order not to offend the man – he had in fact an almost insane desire to stay on the right side of him – he stretched out his hand for them. Rush moved his hand away with a larky little smile. He wagged a reproving finger at Henry.

'Oh, no you don't!' he said. 'You're the same as me!'

'How do you mean?'

'A local historian.'

'Ah . . .'

Certain things about the man's behaviour were becoming clearer.

'You remember at the Wimbledon Society,' went on Rush, 'last year. They were telling us about Everett Maltby!'

'Were they?'

Why was he unable to remember meeting Rush at the Wimbledon Society? Surely something as important as a talk about Everett Maltby (he was beginning, now, to recall it) would have marked the occasion as something special. It struck him that there might be something sinister in this lapse. His notes on Maltby were constantly going astray, weren't they? Perhaps, Henry didn't like this idea at all, there was something paranormal going on.

'All areas of the world,' Rush was saying, 'have their particular crimes, and the same is true of districts of Britain. There are, for example, an awful lot of cases of death due to sudden, unscheduled abdominal pain in Wimbledon.'

Henry coughed. 'How do you mean?'

'I mean,' said Rush, 'that crime isn't always a matter of bashing an old lady over the head and running away. Real crime can be very much more subtle. Real crime is often hidden, beneath the surface of an apparently respectable community. The doctor who raises his hat to you in the High Street may be one of the Bus Station Buggers. The bank manager may have a rather over-liberal attitude to accounting proceedings. You take my meaning?'

'Not really,' said Henry.

'I'm coming to you,' said Rush, in a tone that suggested the opposite was the case, 'because of course we're both local history fiends. It's difficult. Quite a few people think I'm way off beam on this one. But I had a hunch you might understand.'

'Understand what?'

Rush flung his arms wide. 'We live on the street,' he said, 'we're neighbours. Let's get together. Let's discuss it. You know what I'm talking about, don't you? You know what I think's going on under the oh-so-respectable surface of this oh-so-respectable manor. I'm talking, of course, about poisoning.'

So this was a social, rather than a business call. Or was it? Was Rush here to frighten him? Or had he some even darker purpose?

'It's just a barmy theory of mine,' he was saying. 'I'm a voice in the wilderness, but I'm convinced, absolutely convinced that there is a poisoner at work in the borough. Here and now!' He gave an enigmatic smile. 'My colleagues think I'm crazy,' said Rush, 'they don't want to know. With them, it's clamp this, clamp that, traffic flow . . . football hooligans . . .' He snorted. 'Football hooligans.'

Then, 'When I first got on to the poisoner, I told a few people, and they were, I have to say, unsympathetic to a degree. But that, if you don't mind me saying so, is the mark of a modern police officer. The door-to-door slog, the house-to-house search, the repetitive, mechanical labour of collecting evidence. Look at the Yorkshire Ripper.'

'Well, indeed,' said Henry, 'indeed, he – '

But Rush ignored him. 'There was no one there who trusted his judgement. Who went out on a limb. Who stood up and said "Look, I have a theory. A crazy theory." Because the psychopath is only to be tracked down by an intuitive guess. He's somebody who otherwise doesn't read as a criminal. He's you!'

He pointed directly at Henry. Henry gave a low squeak.

'He's me! This is the story we're looking at. The Wimbledon Poisoner is out there OK. He's there. He's anyone. He is you and me. He is the dark part of ourselves. You know?'

'Fascinating,' said Henry, 'and . . . er . . . when did you first notice this . . . er . . . pattern of abdominal disorders?'

Rush screwed up his face, paced across to the patch of carpet nearest to the fire, which seemed to be his favourite spot for significant remarks and, wheeling round, did his best bit of pipe work so far, a double lunge, with parry in quarte and passage of waltz-time conducting, followed by a bit of invisible cross-hatching above his ear.

'It clicked,' he said, 'it all fell into place a week or so ago. When I saw you at Donald Templeton's funeral.'

'Let me,' said Henry, 'get you another gin and tonic.'

26

It was horrible. The man was playing some elaborate game with him, waiting for him to crack. He might even be lying about the Maltby talk. Oh Jesus, thought Henry, I am very sorry about the poisoning. I really do apologize. If you get me out of this one I will never ever do anything like it again. I will not think unpleasant things about people. I will not . . .

He poured a gin and tonic about twice the size of his first one, drank it and then poured one twice the size of that for Rush. Important to have the man on your side.

Maisie was still crouched by the door.

'You could bring me a drink!' she said.

'Shut up!' hissed Henry.

'It's very interesting,' she said, 'about the poisoner. Who is it, do you think?'

'You shouldn't be listening to this,' said Henry.

When he had been served with his drink, Rush started pacing the carpet once more. 'But I really started,' he said, 'a long, long time ago. You see evidence, in a case like this, has a habit of disappearing. What looks like a normal death . . .'

He took a fairly pristine-looking cutting from the file and thrust it at Henry.

TEMPLETON, Donald [it read]. *At his home in Maple Drive after a brief illness. Much loved father of Arfur, and devoted husband to Billykins. 'FOR GOD'S SAKE WHY?'*

'She was very upset,' said Henry. 'It's not the best-worded announcement of a death I've ever read.'

Rush snickered. 'It seems pretty carefully worded to me,' he said, ' "brief illness". Not, you notice, "sudden and inexplicable gastric attack", not "after severe abdominal pains". No no no. People aren't interested in that sort of thing. They like to draw a veil over it, don't they?'

He stopped at his favourite patch of carpet and then, as if conscious that he had used this as a base before, moved off towards the window. 'And then,' he went on, 'actually at the funeral, three more deaths! Extraordinary coincidence, don't you think? Extraordinary! But of course no one remarks on it, do they? No one puts two and two together, do they? In the paper we read – '

He handed Henry another cutting. Henry read:

COVENEY, *Rufus. Beloved son of George and Myfanwy. Novelist and critic of note, at Maple Drive after a seizure. 'Go not behind for all is dark before!'*

Henry was studying this quotation and finding it vaguely suggestive when, below it, he saw:

SPROTT, *David. David died peacefully at a social gathering of friends last Tuesday. His funeral will be held at Putney Vale Crematorium, where anyone who wishes a last chance to see him will be most welcome, and afterwards at the family home. Good man, good dentist, good, good, good. 'Farewell.'*

He was beginning to sweat.

'All just slips by, doesn't it?' said Rush. 'Another corpse. Why bother? It is only someone who looks carefully, who studies the evidence, who can put facts together and say "Hang on a tick! There's more here than meets the eye." That's police work, Mr Farr. Constant vigilance. Constant suspicion. It's like having a little man inside who asks nasty questions. I've got a nasty little man inside me and he won't go away. Look at this – '

Rush pushed a much older-looking clipping towards Henry. It read:

PURVIS, *Alan. At Parkside Hospital after a collapse in the Cat o'Nine Tails Bar and Brasserie. O Death where is thy sting? Mourned by Mum, Dad and all at the folkclub.*

'There are others,' said Rush. 'Manning, last September. Severe intestinal pains after an outdoor buffet lunch with a group of salesmen from White's garage, Wimbledon. Pedersen, collapse and subsequent death after ingesting a hamburger at Putney Show. Annabel Lee Evans, only twenty-two, vomiting, diarrhoea and death in May of this year four hours after attending a disco and Bar-B-Q at Southlands College where she ate a meal of curried chicken and coleslaw . . .' He spread his arms wide. 'We're dealing with a maniac. A clever, unscrupulous maniac.'

Henry was inclined to agree with him. He had never met such a maniac in all his life. The man should not be allowed out. But, as Rush continued to pace the carpet, stab the air with his pipe and talk rubbish, Henry wondered whether he might not be misjudging him. He recalled a phrase of Keith Simpson's: 'Almost every event in life is consequent upon a meal.' Just as poisoning was, therefore, hard to detect, it was, by the same token, all the more possible. And once you had fallen under its sway, as Rush had, it offered a hideous but plausible explanation for so many things! In a way, of course, he and Rush were not unalike. Other people would have found them dull. They were dull. They both knew that they were dull. But that didn't stop them.

'A maniac,' said Rush, 'someone who roams the streets, waits his moment, and then, bingo, injects the hamburger, the chocolates, the ham and tomato sandwich, the chicken vindaloo. Lays his little trap and passes on. The poisoner's reward is reading about himself – reading about deaths that *he* made happen. He has a power that no one knows about. *He* made all this happen. He's playing God, don't you agree, Mr Farr?'

Here Rush snaked his head forward at Henry, seeking his interlocutor's eyes, and then, heading back to his favourite bit of carpet, looked around the room for applause. For a moment Henry thought, How does he know? and then, as quickly, realized that he had better not start feeling guilty about poisonings in which he had no involvement. This was taking social responsibility a little too far. He was off the hook, wasn't he? He didn't fit into this guy's theory. Or did he? If he didn't, why was Rush looking at him like that, in that knowing way? Maisie's head appeared round the door.

'Mummy says do you want sandwiches?' she said.

'That would be most kind!' said Rush.

'Chicken mayonnaise or liver sausage?' she said.

'Anything,' said Rush, 'so long as it doesn't contain a registered poison!'

He laughed. A jolly, companionable laugh.

'I'll tell her!' said Maisie.

'It was the deaths in Maple Drive that confirmed my theory,' went on Rush. 'Before then I thought I saw a pattern. And the pattern would evade me. You know? I'd think to myself sometimes, "Rush, you're barmy." No way is there any connection between Julia Neve, who died of quote polyneuritis unquote last February, and Martin Crump the railway worker who died in agony in Roehampton only five hours after eating a meal of peaches, risotto and Continental cheese.'

Elinor appeared at the door, wiping her hands on her apron. Rush looked up at her, sharply, and for a brief moment her eyes met his. *There is one not very far from here who admires me!* thought Henry. He looked across at Elinor as she shook the black hair away from her forehead, and he had to acknowledge that his wife was a very attractive woman. How was he going to keep her? How was he going to put Neighbourhood Watch off the track?

'Are you all right, Henry?' said Elinor.

'Fine, love,' said Henry, 'fine.'

Inspector Rush was looking at him oddly. 'All this talk of poisoning,' he said, 'has put you off your food!'

'Not at all,' said Henry.

'Actually,' said Elinor, 'Henry is very interested in poisoning. He's got a whole lot of books about it upstairs.'

Henry decided it was time to intervene. 'Actually,' he said, 'I am very interested in poisoning. I'm thinking of writing a book about it. The ... er ... Everett Maltby case got me started. I thought ... you know ... I'd look into poisoners as a breed. They're a fascinating bunch. Fascinating!'

Rush's eyes watched him. 'Indeed!' said Rush.
Did he suspect the truth or not?

27

It was worst of all when he talked about Donald.

'What I don't get,' he would say, his eyes on Henry's face, 'is how the poisoner got to that chicken!'

For there was no doubt in Rush's mind that the chicken that had been Donald Templeton's last meal was in the same category as the tubful of beef satay at the Wimbledon Council's Bring and Buy Sale in Aid of Bangladesh; it had been got at.

'Perhaps,' Henry would say, sweating, 'he got at it in Waitrose.'

'How do you mean?' said Rush, a little smile curling at the edge of his lips. *Pull the other one, squire, it's got bells on it! Come on, Farr! Own up, why don't you, eh? Eh?*

'He could have . . . er . . . injected it through the polythene cover. Or else made up a simulated free-range chicken in his own home and smuggled it into Waitrose.'

Rush would look at Henry. A man who could think up something as perverted as this was quite clearly in the running as a suspect.

'Yes,' he would say, 'ye-es. Or possibly he could have introduced some substance into a batch of saucepans. Easy to do. Smear a little carbon tetrachloride round the edge and next time you cook sprouts it's headache and vomiting and bysey-bye to your renal functions.'

'Except,' Henry replied, 'we were all right.'

'Yes,' Rush said, 'you were all fine and dandy. Weren't you?'

And his little detective's eyes travelled up and down Henry's face, and he smiled that smile again, that bleak little policeman's gesture to levity that said *You better watch your step, sunshine.*

'Ah me,' he continued, 'maybe there is another explanation!'

And he laughed, lightly.

He seemed to be constantly round at the house. One night he was in the front room when Henry returned late from a meeting with his divorce in Aldershot (the woman, it transpired, could only make love to her husband with the dog in the room, 'which,' Henry pointed out, 'might or might not be favourable to her case, depending on the kind of involvement required of the creature'). He invited the two of them out for meals at a fashionable bistro in Wimbledon Village, during which he made several off-colour jokes about poisons. Elinor seemed to find them funny, but Rush's eyes, Henry noted, never left Henry's face.

'It would have been so simple,' said Henry at one point, 'if you could have pushed for an autopsy on . . . er . . . the Maple Drive contingent!'

'Wouldn't it?' he said in a quiet voice.

If Henry had had a soul, Rush would probably have been looking straight into it.

'I pushed for an autopsy on Ellen Wilcox of South Wales Road, New Malden,' he said, 'and my, there was a fuss. I'd showed my hand too early. We found nothing. Since when my . . . superiors have been running scared of me. Never mind if a psychopath gets away. Just don't rock the boat. Eh?'

'Indeed!' said Henry.

'We'll get our autopsy,' said Rush quietly; 'one day he'll overplay his hand. He's crazy. He's bound to. And in the meanwhile, maybe we'll get lucky – '

Here he gave a professionally ghoulish laugh. 'Maybe someone'll forget to bury a body!'

Elinor was staring across the table at him, her eyes bright with the wine. 'Your job,' she said, 'must be fascinating!'

'It is!' said Rush, and he looked levelly at Henry. 'There's nothing more interesting than stalking a criminal. Waiting, watching, listening, and then, suddenly, when he's made his mistake – '

Here he leaned forward and rapped the table sharply with a bread roll.

'Pouncing!'

Henry jumped.

'All we need,' said Rush, 'is a body!'

It was almost November, the week before Hallowe'en, when someone told someone in the street who told someone else in the street who almost immediately told someone who told Elinor who told Henry that Mrs David Sprott, widow of the highly insured dentist, David Sprott, forty-two, kept his mortal remains in a small glass jar on a shelf in their bedroom. She also kept, in a drawer in a dresser in the same bedroom, Sprott's false teeth (one of the most closely guarded secrets in world dentistry), his wire glasses and a small fragment of his beard. It was, as Henry said when he heard, almost as bad as having Sprott himself around.

'His trousers,' said Edwina Sprott in her deep, bass voice, 'are still in the cupboard. His boots are still in the hall.'

Bits of Sprott himself! Powdered dentist! Powdered dentist that might contain traces of Finish 'Em, of bleach, of Shine and Zappiton and whatever else he had put into the punch. The trouble was, Henry didn't know whether such things remained in the ashes of a cremated victim. The police had certainly identified traces of thallium in one of Graham Young's victims. Was the same true for bleach? And how much bleach had they drunk anyway?

'Suppose,' he said to Rush one afternoon, 'one had drunk a fair amount of corrosive fluid . . .'

'Yes . . .'

'And suppose . . .'

'Oh, for God's sake!' said Elinor. 'Can't you two talk about anything but poisoning? There are other things in life, you know. There are healthy, normal things! Things that nourish and sustain!'

Although Elinor had given up her therapy class she still retained traces of their style in her speech. The woman in charge had told her, apparently, that she was cured. She was, Elinor told Henry, a fully rounded human being. She was in no further need of therapy.

At first Henry assumed that this meant the therapy class had finally had enough of her. But on close examination he found his wife to be a perfectly pleasant woman in early middle age, with whom he could not, however hard he tried, find any fault. She had had her hair cut, and started to sing as she went about the house. She began to eat normally. She developed an obsession with television programmes involving American policemen shooting at each other.

And she dressed in gayer colours, like a woman who wanted to please a man.

Which man, though? That was the problem.

By the night of Maisie's Hallowe'en party the little bits of Sprott on Mrs Sprott's mantelpiece had become a major talking point in Wimbledon. Almost the only person in the street who had not discussed the issue with Henry and Elinor was Detective Inspector Rush. Rush, Henry decided, was waiting for Henry to make his mistake.

'She's got Sprott in a vase!' he said, as he arrived for Maisie's party, carrying, as he often did when visiting the house, a large bunch of flowers for Elinor. 'The remains of Sprott,' he went on, 'are less than a hundred yards from where we are standing.' And he looked hungrily over in the direction of the dentist's house.

Henry coughed. 'I . . . er . . . know!' he said.

Why was the man mentioning this fairly well-known piece of local gossip now? Because, presumably, he felt sure that Henry was about to make that 'fatal mistake' to which the policeman was always referring. If Rush thought he was about to make a fatal mistake, thought Henry, he had better go right ahead and make one. In the end it would probably be simpler.

Maisie was wearing fangs and a black cloak. Henry had a rubber hammer sticking out of his head and a highly realistic bloodstain across his temple. Elinor was looking, Henry thought, rather ravishing, in a kind of black silk bodystocking. He was looking at her back when Rush approached, and trying to decide whether he had made the right move by resolving not to poison her. She had been showing signs, lately, of a reawakened interest in sex, which Henry was not entirely sure was a good thing. Only last night she had made a number of arch references which Henry thought seemed to imply that they had had anal intercourse in the lavatory of a train between Margate and Ramsgate. He could not remember ever going to Ramsgate let alone buggering his wife on public transport in that area of the country.

'Sprott,' said Rush, his eyes on Henry's face, 'in a vase! Makes you think, doesn't it?'

'Come on!' said Elinor gaily. 'We're going to frighten people!'

The other thing about post-thallium Elinor was that she seemed to have become almost relentlessly cheerful. Especially when in the company of Detective Inspector Rush. This, thought Henry, is probably Her Moment. He would have liked to have had a Moment. Unemployed Journalist with Punk Hairstyle, from 194, was always talking about His Moment which, apparently, occurred in something called The Seventies. Younger people talked about The Seventies as if they were something that actually happened, and not, as they were for Henry, a sort of ghastly blur punctuated by requests for money from the National Westminster Bank's Home Loans Service.

Maybe this was her moment. She was flowering, just as he, Henry, was about to fall into whatever trap it was the detective inspector had set for him. He looked across at Rush, who was wearing a brown trilby and had on a battered, rather dated suit, very different from his usual neat blue outfit. He was also, Henry noted, sporting a small false moustache.

'Who are you supposed to be?' said Henry with just a trace of irritation.

Rush smiled enigmatically. 'I should have thought you would have recognized the allusion,' he said, allowing his smile to curl upwards like paper in a furnace, 'being a keen student of poisoners!'

Henry started to shake.

'Would you?' he said, more than ever convinced that the man was trying to frighten him into doing something foolish.

'I'm Hawley Harvey Crippen,' said Rush, 'of Hilldrop Crescent. The meek little man who wanted to murder his wife. And so bought five grams of hyoscine which he gave her.'

Elinor and Maisie were now some yards ahead of them. Henry found he was talking in a whisper. 'People,' he said, 'do murder their wives, don't they?'

'They do,' said Rush, 'and if they do . . . we often find they're capable of anything. Now – shall we talk about how to get hold of Sprott? For the purposes of analysis.'

28

'Who shall we frighten first?' said Maisie. 'Let's frighten someone who doesn't like me.' She laughed ghoulishly. 'Gives us a lot of scope!' she added.

'I know,' said Elinor, 'let's frighten Accountant Who Talks a Lot!'

She had recently taken to attempting to follow Henry's re-christening of the neighbourhood, without noticeable success. She lacked malice, thought Henry, looking at her and remembering vaguely why it was he had wanted to kill her.

'Let's!' he said.

'The trouble is,' said Rush, 'because that bloody doctor did what he did I'll have a devil of a job to get a look at him officially.' He chewed his lip. 'Evidence, evidence, evidence,' he muttered. 'All I want's a body!'

'Come on, Maisie!' said Elinor.

Maisie made a farting noise with her lips and followed her mother.

'We could ask to borrow his ashes,' said Rush, 'for sentimental reasons.'

'You're a policeman,' said Henry. 'For God's sake! Can't you impound him? Or subpoena him or something?'

Why had he said this?

'I'm afraid,' said Rush darkly, 'there are not many who think as we do. To some the poisoner is a fanciful notion!'

Henry thought he could understand the reasons for this.

'I'm regarded,' said Rush, 'as a bit of a joke!' And he gave Henry that intimate glance, as if to imply that only the two of them knew the real secret. Yes, thought Henry, he knows, but is never going to tell. He's going to amuse himself with me, torment me with this shared secret until one day I can't stand it any more and I find myself screaming to anyone who'll listen – 'I DID IT! I DID IT! TAKE ME

AWAY!' This, of course, had happened to Raskolny-whatever-his-name-was, hadn't it?

Maisie was now running ahead of the group. In her right hand she was carrying a bright red apple. Henry tried to break away from Rush who, without apparent effort, seemed to be able to stay about a yard from his left elbow. Police training presumably.

They were at the corner of Maple Drive. The garden of the house in front of them, piled high with builder's rubbish, looked dark and threatening to Henry. Hallowe'en was quite frightening enough without dressing up as a monster with an axe in your head. Saying the word, hearing the shrieks of the children in the neighbouring streets . . . Over to the right a group of rowdy little girls was approaching, decked out in black hats and coats and rather fetching little broomsticks. 'Trick or treat, trick or treat?' they were singing. 'We have slime that you must eat!'

'What's the apple for, Maisie?' asked Henry.

'I thought somebody might bob for it,' she said. Maisie looked at the apple as if surprised at the fact that she was holding it. It was improbably large and shiny, a fairy-tale apple. Had she had it with her when she came out?

'Where did you get it?'

Maisie looked at it, puzzled. 'I'm not sure,' she said, 'I just got it.'

That was the other thing about children. Just as they had started to stun you into silence with their maturity, their knowledge of sex relations or the IRA they hit you with cluelessness and infantile jokes or a bewildering ignorance about something on which you had assumed they would be well informed. If only, thought Henry, people would be one thing and stick to it. If wives would be nice or nasty, if . . . oh, his trouble was easy to spot. He wanted the world to stay the way it was.

Rush was giving him one of those looks again. Henry tried to move away from him, and went in pursuit of Maisie.

'Who,' she said to him as he drew level with her, 'are we going to frighten?'

'We are going to frighten Jungian Analyst with Winebox,' said Henry, 'and we are going to terrify his wife, Lingalonga Boccherini, not to mention Birdwatching Child Viola Player and Sensationally Articulate Twelve-Year-Old!'

Jungian Analyst with Winebox was a man called Gordon, who for some reason always insisted on being called Gord. He was married to an immensely tall, thin woman with huge eyes and a mournful manner, who for no very good reason was known to Henry as Lingalonga Boccherini. The other two were their children, Caedmon and Wulfstan. Elinor, who was an old friend of Lingalonga Boccherini, had never heard this name before, although she seemed to know to whom Henry was referring.

'Do you mean,' she said edgily, 'Gord and Julia?'

'I do!'

'I don't think,' she said, 'that is a funny or clever way of describing them.'

'They can take it,' said Henry, 'they're psychiatrists.'

'I don't think we should frighten them,' said Elinor.

'Why not?' said Henry. 'Why should psychiatrists be exempt from being frightened! They dish it out all the time, don't they? They tell you you're regressive and introverted and immature and God knows what. They're always going on about the importance of ceremonies, aren't they? Why shouldn't we scare the arse off them?'

'Because,' said Elinor, 'they'll be out frightening someone else.'

Henry began to find this conversation bracing. Gord and Julia were, of course, Elinor's friends. All Elinor's friends belonged to Elinor, although it was understood that if Henry ever acquired anyone interesting (the nearest he had ever got to it was Donald, which was not, Henry felt, very near) then Elinor had rights of trespass on them.

'It's very important,' Elinor was saying, 'for them to express anger. That's why you're such a mess, Henry. Because you don't express your anger.'

Henry felt his neck thicken in his collar and wondered whether not poisoning Elinor might be bad for his health. Gord and Julia didn't need to express anger as far as he was concerned. What they all too clearly felt was that it was a public disgrace that someone as disgusting as Henry should be allowed to stalk about the place unanalysed.

But Henry had seen them *get* angry at him. He had seen their lips tighten when he referred to all psychiatrists as 'shrinks' and to all psychiatric theories as 'bollocks'.

Henry did not like analysts. He was frightened of them. The idea of lying on a couch and telling someone everything that was in your mind! Everything in Henry's mind! That 'open sewer' as Elinor, in one of her less charitable moments, had called it. Where would he start? With the poisoning? The incessant masturbation? The feelings of hatred towards absolutely everyone? The total lack of moral scruple? The compulsive eating? The lack of talent? And what would he be left with if all this were taken away?

'Jungian Analyst with Winebox,' said Henry, 'deserves frightening. Him and his mane of white hair. Walking around, conducting imaginary orchestras. He deserves frightening right out of his sensible, caring, cord trousers.'

'He won't be *in!*' wailed Elinor.

'He'll be in,' said Henry; 'he broke his leg!'

Maisie finally decided the matter. She wanted to frighten Caedmon and Wulfstan. They would not, thought Henry, be difficult to frighten.

Jungian Analyst with Winebox and his family lived in a small cottage on the edge of the common. Here, surrounded by clavichords, violas and books about dreams, they looked out at the south side of the common as the dusk came in through the beech trees.

The party went up through Belvedere Avenue and into Church Road, then left towards the village High Street. Here expensive cars, parked nose to tail, waited for their owners. The village itself wore, as usual, the air of some carefully designed exhibition at Olympia, and Henry, looking at the wooden shopfronts and the come-hither graphics in the windows, the resolutely phoney atmosphere of the antique, saw, the way some people saw skulls under skin and hair, the plaster, the rotten beams, the real, ugly history that held the suburb together.

Everett Maltby had started to frighten him. Perhaps it was the night, perhaps it was Rush, trotting behind him like some apparently biddable dog, perhaps it was the disturbing power his career as a murderer seemed to have given him, but as they crossed on to the damp grass Henry felt haunted by something. This was how Maltby felt, wasn't it? When he watched his wife die? And wasn't that another set of footsteps he could hear behind him on the cold pavement? The footsteps of a man with a pale face and a high wing collar and a handshake as clammy as the evening.

Henry walked ahead of Elinor, and seizing Maisie by the hand ran forward towards the cottage that stood, alone, at the edge of the grass. In a sudden hurry to get this over, he raised his hand to beat out a rhythm on the door, but before he could do so, just as Maisie was preparing to screech a witch's curse, it was flung open from the other side and from the darkness came a howl like a hungry wolf's.

29

'GO AWAY!' shouted Gordon Macrae. 'AWAY! AWAYAWAY!' He had clearly been at the winebox. He did not turn on the light but stood in the shadows, his mane of white hair shaking this way and that. Maisie stepped back, whimpering. Macrae's voice seemed to have been amplified in some curious way.

'It's Hallowe'en!' he shouted, in the same ghostly voice. 'It's Hallowe'en. There are spirits abroad. Away! Away! The damned are out tonight! There is Evil in the air! I feel it!'

All this was fairly standard with Macrae. As the author of a bestselling book about the significance of gesture and a brief but telling study of death and exorcism, he waved a mean arm, and, when he chose, frightened pretty good. Tonight, however, perhaps prompted by the season, he was almost worryingly effective. Behind him, in the pale hall, the even paler figure of Lingalonga Boccherini emerged. She looked, thought Henry, like a crofter's wife, caught at a nasty moment in the Clearances. She was wearing a brown shawl, a brown headdress and stout brown shoes and, as if to emphasize her resemblance to something out of a diorama in the Folk Museum, Aberdeen, she stretched out her hand towards Gordon and began to keen.

'Oh no . . .' said Lingalonga Boccherini. 'Oh no-oo-oo . . .'

Maisie cowered behind Henry. She had clearly not expected resistance. At Hallowe'en you went round and scared people and they gave you sweets. They didn't rush out at you with plasters on their legs, howling and keening.

Jungian Analyst with Winebox produced from behind his back a knobbed walking stick and began to wave it. 'There is a curse out tonight!' he went on. 'A curse! Away! Away foul fiends! Away!'

Then he laughed. Maisie clearly found the laugh the most frightening thing about him. She ran into Henry's coat, as in the remote distances of the hall two figures in pyjamas, of the kind Henry could remember from his childhood, striped flannel jobs with white string cords, crept towards Lingalonga Boccherini. Caedmon and Wulfstan.

Caedmon (or was it Wulfstan?) was saying something. 'Please mother,' he was saying, 'just one more two-part canzonetta before bedtime!'

Lingalonga Boccherini did not hit him hard in the pit of the stomach for this remark. She continued to keen in the direction of her husband.

'Yaaargh!' said Elinor, rather lamely.

Nobody seemed very frightened.

'Hullo, Julia!' she said.

Maisie stepped out from behind Henry's coat. 'Oooowaaieeeiou!' she howled, and then, 'Eaaaargh!'

Lingalonga Boccherini smiled sweetly at her. 'Oh, Maisie . . .' she said, 'lovely!'

And then, from the shadows, came Inspector Rush. He had been standing in the long grass, a little out of sight of the Macrae family, but in two steps he was caught in the yellow light of a street lamp, his neat mackintosh pulled up round his face, his trilby well down over his eyes. He had sucked in his cheeks and stroked his moustache. His attempt to seem sinister was undermined, however, by his voice. Rush was quite simply unable to stop sounding like a man asking you whether you were aware that you were travelling in a bus lane with out-of-date tax disc on display.

'Name's Crippen! Hawley Harvey Crippen. Hilldrop Crescent. Would the kiddies care for a cup of hot, sweet tea?'

Birdwatching Child Viola Player burst into tears. 'Who's that horrid man, Mummy?' he wailed.

'It's Crippen!' said Henry, ghoulishly. 'We found him on the common. He's a poisoner!'

Macrae cackled. He seemed pleased by the sight of his own children's mental collapse. 'Jolly good!' he cackled. 'Jolly good! Crippen! Hawley Harvey Crippen, of course! The man who loved his wife!' He winked broadly at Elinor.

'Poisoners,' said Macrae, not asking them to come in, or to come any nearer his winebox than was absolutely necessary, 'poisoners love their subjects. It's their way of saying "I want you and I don't want anyone else to have you." Julia is writing a paper on it, aren't you Julia?'

Lingalonga Boccherini looked up from Caedmon. Her face had moved, as so often, from melancholy gladness, to sudden, irrational terror. 'Yes,' she said, 'poison is nourishment!'

Rush gazed at her with some respect.

'Poison is all the bad things we think about anyone expressed in chemical form, isn't it? And it's nearly always served with love and attention, to turn the loved one into a victim, the way in which the possessive mother – '

Here Jungian Analyst with Winebox pointed at his wife's head.

'Which of course, as Gordon says, I am – the possessive mother seeks to control her child, of course, very much in the way the doctor controls the patient. Because motherhood, like murder, is controlling. And we say, don't we, that motherhood is "murder". Or that the children have been "murder" today. And that is because, of course, we want to kill them because we love them and because our love is, literally, murder, which is why we want to put arsenic on their fish fingers or whatever!'

Wulfstan started to howl. Jungian Analyst with Winebox laughed and went back into the darkened hall after his son. Lingalonga Boccherini shrank back with the boy in her arms.

'And chop them up!' her husband added. 'And fry them and serve them to the neighbours the way they do in Polynesia! Best thing to do with your wife and your children, in my opinion! Eat them before they eat you! Ha ha ha!'

Caedmon was also looking on the verge of tears. As indeed, thought Henry, will I be if he doesn't let us in and at the Côtes de Nuit fairly soon. But Jungian Analyst with Winebox showed no signs of letting them past his front porch. He paced around in the darkened hallway, waving his arms frantically, free associating, free of charge, into the dank November night.

'The Manichees,' he went on, 'believed that virtue and evil are locked up in certain foods. Rather like saying, if you grasp this, that bananas are immoral!'

'Or toast and marmalade is good!' said Henry, brightly. Macrae looked at him suspiciously.

'Evil dwelleth in the frankfurter!' went on Henry. But this remark only made matters worse.

Macrae gripped him by the collar and, with undisguised dislike, said, 'Food. Don't you see? Food *is* morality. Why do you think we lay such emphasis on "table manners"? Why do we need to control our eating?'

'Because,' said Henry, hoping that Macrae would put him down soon, 'we don't want to get fat!'

'Listen to the words we use about food,' replied Macrae, slackening his grip, 'we offer someone a drink and say "what's your poison"?'

'I'll have a Côtes de Nuit!' said Henry.

'We want, of course, to kill our friend, to punish him for his greed because, of course, the irony of food is that it is a hunger for spirit, as in the communion wafer for example, the sacrament of married life, say, in which we eat each other and no one gets the leftovers. And the irony of poison is that it is a hunger not for death, but for life, for the spirit that quickens! It is a way of bringing the loved one in direct contact with the Almighty.'

Rush goggled at him from out of the darkness. He had clearly never met anyone like Jungian Analyst with Winebox before. The Wimbledon CID, thought Henry, probably used a much tamer species of psychiatrist. But Maisie, who was now clearly out of her depth and anxious to restore some kind of festive quality to this encounter, stepped forward with the apple in her hand. Perhaps, Henry thought later, she was going to offer it to him as a reward for shutting up; in fact it provoked a new torrent of speculation on Macrae's part.

'The apple!' he said. 'Of course! The apple! The apple that we bob for at Hallowe'en is of course the same apple offered to Snow White in the fairytale! What is it? The apple of death in life. The apple of desire that Eve forced Adam to eat in the Garden of Eden. The apple of the female principle. The feminists understand this, don't they? The male poisons the apple to kill his mother, of course!'

'Oh, yes,' chimed in Lingalonga Boccherini, 'because this aspect of nourishment is perceived of as threatening by the male, isn't it?'

Macrae was nodding vigorously. When on this course the Macraes could keep up a kind of antiphonal exchange that, in Henry's experience, could last hours. He began to peer past them in the direction of the kitchen where lay the winebox of Côtes de Nuit.

'But in the folktale, of course,' went on Lingalonga Boccherini, in the dreamy, hypnotic voice that had been largely responsible for her nickname, 'after she has eaten the poisoned apple, poisoned by the wicked possessive mother, who is someone like me really, I suppose, she falls into a faint and she can only be wakened by a kiss from a male, that is to say, a prince, which isn't really a kiss of course but the male urge to rape and violate and explain away the contradictions of the female, very much as you, Gordon, of course try and destroy me sexually!'

'Absolutely!' said Macrae, nodding.

He took the apple from Maisie and held it up high, shaking his white hair out behind him. 'The apple of good and evil, of the carnal and uncarnal knowledge of others! Why else do we bob for it at Hallowe'en? Because of course it represents the evil spirits that are around tonight. Here, even as we speak! And yet of course, we must not, as Adam in the garden did or Snow White at the gate of the cottage, bite into this round, red juicy thing, for it is, of course, tainted. It is the apple of death!'

Here he suited his actions to the words and gnawed a chunk of the fruit away. It had crisp, white flesh and that treasured, sour smell of apples that Henry remembered from his childhood, when his mother . . . Why was he thinking about his mother?

'If we bite into it and chew it we go blue! And choke! And whirl around like this!'

Here he performed what was, even for Macrae, a fantastically good impression of someone dying of prussic acid poisoning. He leapt up in the air, tugged at his collar, gave a ghastly choking sound and, his face blue, fell forward on to the path in front of the house.

It was only when he failed to rise that Henry stooped down beside him and discovered that the psychiatrist was stone dead.

30

The worst thing about being a serial killer, Henry reflected in the weeks after the demise of Gordon Macrae, was that you might not know you were a serial killer. You might think you were jogging along with the occasional regrettable lapse, such as the poisoning of a few people in the road, but by and large, you might suppose, you were a decent enough citizen. And then, one day, you might wake up and discover that when you thought you had been watching the television or mowing the lawn you had, in fact, been out garrotting people on towpaths.

Christ, Henry could not even remember the names of people with whom he had had dinner the night before. He had for years of their marriage offered Elinor both tea and coffee, forgetting she did not like either, and these days was unable to remember talks he had given on (oh, my Christ!) the Wimbledon Poisoner. Suppose he was *the* Wimbledon Poisoner? Not the half-hearted creature he knew himself to be but a real, top-level psychopath.

Because on the inquest on Gordon Macrae it was revealed by a very senior police forensic scientist that the apple contained enough prussic acid to wipe out half the Jungians in Wimbledon. 'And thereby,' said Henry to Elinor, 'saving the neurotics of the district a large amount of valuable time and money.'

Everyone wanted to know where Maisie had got the apple. She couldn't remember. The more they asked her the more she couldn't remember. She didn't seem distressed by their questions, remarking to one particularly insistent WPC, 'I didn't kill him! I didn't like him but I didn't kill him!'

For a time Henry thought she might be following in his footsteps. But even Maisie was not up to the purchase of prussic acid, let alone injecting it into an apple. The more he thought about it, the more

Henry became certain – along with all the national and local press –
that there was such a person as the Wimbledon Poisoner. And that he
was it.

'MADMAN ON LOOSE IN WIMBLEDON!' they said in the London *Standard*. And 'IS THERE A POISONER IN YOUR ROAD?' They published
artists' impressions of a man people had seen behaving suspiciously
near the scene of the crime (which looked, as Elinor remarked,
exactly like Henry). They published analyses of him by eminent
psychiatrists, who were more than usually censorious about the
unknown assassin. All the sketches of the poisoner's character
sounded, to Henry, like Henry.

When, he wondered, as he rattled in to Harris, Harris and Overdene, would he strike again? A client of his in Epsom threatened
suicide if contracts were not exchanged on his house by Christmas.
But Henry could not concentrate on work. He sat staring out at
Ludgate Circus, waiting for the red mist that would send him off
down the road, in a deep trance, for another kilo of antimony.

At times he wondered whether he might not only be the Wimbledon Poisoner but a few other psychopaths into the bargain. His guilt
knew no bounds and, if there was any consolation, it was that
Donald, Sprott, Coveney and Loomis no longer caused him any pain.
They were simply a step along the road for the poisoner, an episode
when, for some inexplicable reason, he had remained fully conscious
while perpetrating his despicable acts.

'WHO IS HE?' asked the local paper. 'CHECK YOUR SUPERMARKET
TROLLEY. HE MIGHT HAVE GOT THERE FIRST!'

In Waitrose plain-clothes policemen loitered ostentatiously near
the shelves full of chicken legs, pre-packed meatballs and pork
chops. They folded their arms and whistled near the cereal packets
and the spaghetti and were seen browsing through Smoked Meats
with the thoroughness of a bibliophile in an antiquarian bookstore.
But no lunatic, syringe in one hand, packet of poison in the other,
was spotted. At dinner parties – although as the poisoner scare went
on there were less and less dinner parties – people made hearty jokes
about bringing their tasters along with them, but it was noticeable
that even people like Surveyor With Huge Gut and Fondness for

Potatoes (24b) toyed with their food in a way that they would not have once done. Tins were popular, although one paper published an account of how someone with a little technical knowledge had been able to inject noxious substances into three cans of Heinz Beans and Burger Bites.

Rush was interviewed everywhere. He even appeared on television news, smiling enigmatically. 'What,' said the interviewer, 'is the poisoner like?' There was a pause and Rush leaned slightly towards camera. Then he said, in a low, serious voice, 'He is, in my professional opinion – a monster.' Several papers profiled him; one, which referred to him as 'superhumanly dedicated to his job', titled its piece 'NO RUSH TO JUDGEMENT'.

He was suddenly a star, and his colleagues and superiors, some of whom trudged with him on his house-to-house searches, clearly resented the fact. They responded by looking at each other significantly every time Rush played with his pipe, narrowed his eyes or in room after room (Henry was actually allowed to accompany him because of what was termed his 'special local knowledge') he made for exactly the same spot of carpet and made exactly the same speech.

There could be only one reason why Rush wanted Henry to accompany him, of course. He wanted Henry to see how close he was getting, to join in at every stage of the game, to watch each clue unroll, to stand helplessly by as the trail that led to Henry and only to Henry was uncovered. But he had no choice in the matter.

The first thing Rush did was to track down those suspected poisoner victims who had been buried and start digging them up as fast as he could. There was, everyone agreed, not much time. The editorial in the *New Statesman* announced that poison was 'well and truly ensconced in the bloodstream of our national life', blamed the low wages paid to employees of supermarkets and demanded swift action. The *Sun* ('GIVE HIM A DOSE OF HIS OWN MEDICINE') led the call for a new, possibly chemically based method of execution for dealing with this kind of pervert. An enterprising youth set up a stall in the High Street, selling Poisoner Products (T-shirts, plastic syringes and Poisoner Peppermints – 'Suck them and you do feel queer!') before he was moved on by a policeman who had somehow got left out of the house-to-house search.

At first, Rush did not have great success with his autopsies. Patricia Leigh Smith who collapsed and died five hours after eating a tuna fish salad at a whist drive in Merton in 1986 had her bones ground up and sifted, but nothing was revealed. But then Hugh Padworth, who collapsed and died six hours after consuming a Bakewell tart at a fête in Putney, was found to contain traces of arsenic ('HE'S A POISONER VICTIM – IT'S OFFICIAL!' *Wimbledon News*). But Rush, like many dedicated detectives, had nothing but an ever-increasing list of suspects to offer an increasingly disturbed public, and his investigations, apart from worrying everyone a good deal more than they were already, did not seem to be leading anywhere.

Maisie was very excited by the poisoner. She had proposed a project at school on Poisons and Poisoning. She had composed a short song, which she sang constantly, the chorus of which went, 'It's good for you! Take it down! Take it down!' Elinor, too, developed a passionate interest in the case. It eclipsed feminism, Nicaragua; even whales, it appeared, were a poor second to the poisoner. She announced that she was starting work on a monograph, provisionally entitled 'The Politics of Poisoning', which, she told Henry, would deal with everything, from prussic acid to salmonella in eggs. 'It is,' she told him, embracing an issue that seemed to give a new dimension to his hobby, 'an additive issue. It's a statement about us because we are defined by what we eat.' But, while all around him were united by their fear of the person who, according to which newspaper you read, stalked or lurked or smouldered through the quiet borough of Wimbledon, Henry grew more and more isolated, more and more frightened by each knock at the door, each ring at the bell. It wouldn't be long now, he told himself, before Rush tired of his game. With each new piece of hard evidence Rush's smile grew wider, until, thought Henry, he was almost nudging and winking at him.

When he finally came to call, one afternoon in late November, when all the leaves had gone from the trees and cyclists and pedestrians walked hunched against the cold east wind that people said would blow till Christmas, it came as a relief. Henry knew, he thought, as he saw him walk up to the house, that he was in the last phase of the game he was playing. He was steady-eyed as he pressed the bell and when Henry answered it he didn't speak or move to come in, just stood on the threshold, the street behind him, his eyes full of enigmatic mockery. Henry took him into the kitchen and offered him a drink.

'Why do you think he does it?' he said, when the silence was becoming unbearable.

'Who knows?' said Rush. 'Resentment against society?'

'It's funny,' said Henry, 'I've got a lot of . . . resentments. Against society.'

'Really,' said Rush, 'and you such a quiet chap.'

It was curiously easy to talk about all this to Rush. Perhaps this, thought Henry, was what it was like talking to a psychiatrist. His words seemed to fall like coins down a well, into a silence that went on and on, waiting for a distant impact.

'Oh yes,' said Henry, 'I mean Gordon Macrae . . . for example . . .'

Jungian Analyst with Winebox! That's what you called him, you callous bastard, didn't you? Eh? Eh?

'And who are these . . . resentments . . . directed against?' said Rush.

He seemed to be speaking very, very gently, his voice no more than breath on a pane of glass. It disturbed Henry's train of thought no more than a small animal might disturb the undergrowth on one of its tracks.

'Oh . . . everyone . . .' said Henry. 'I think . . . people have got it in for me. I think they're out to get me. I think they're all doing better than me.'

Rush's face was not the pinched mask it usually seemed. His skin seemed paper thin, the way Henry's father's had before his heart attack; he had that dried-out vulnerability you sometimes see in old men.

'I mean,' said Henry, 'I might be . . . I might . . .'

Rush leaned forward. 'Might be what?'

'I might be the bloody poisoner! You know!'

Rush nodded slowly. 'Yes,' he said, 'yes.'

Was this it? Was this the beginning of the long journey to the Old Bailey, the endless dashing in and out of police stations with a blanket over one's head? Could he go the whole way now? And confess? He wanted, suddenly, to confess. He wanted to own up to those ghastly thoughts that floated into his head, that, in some awful way, sustained him, the things he didn't speak about even to himself. Because if he confessed he might be like other people once again. He might end this awful, nightmarish isolation.

Henry looked back into Rush's eyes and thought, He understands. He knows about people like me. But could not, for some reason, say the words he wanted to say. He let his head droop and found himself staring at the carpet, at an irregular brown stain to the left of the sofa. Rush was saying something, in that quiet, gentle voice of his.

'I think . . .' he said softly, 'we should get hold of Sprott's ashes. Don't you?'

31

What Henry didn't understand was why Rush didn't pull him in. He was by now under considerable pressure. Any large-scale murder investigation, as Sam Baker QC (almost) reminded Henry at dinner, made a star out of a detective. It also brought him into what could be uncomfortable public prominence.

'WHAT ARE THEY DOING ABOUT THE POISONER?' a story in the local paper asked. Keen-eyed young men in glasses paced the pavement outside the All England Lawn Tennis Club and asked the camera keen-eyed questions to which it did not respond. Rush was interviewed outside Wimbledon police station, where his acting style came in handy. But he was still unable to provide the Great British Public with hard evidence.

'WHEN WILL HE STRIKE AGAIN?' the newspapers asked. And Henry, quivering in front of the television, wondered when he would.

Come on Rush! Make it safe to go into the supermarket!

'Of course,' said Lustgarten, 'Detective Inspector Rush, that keen-eyed and conscientious policeman, had not yet proof in the one case where he thought he might be able to lay an offence directly at the door of the morally maimed creature who lived at 54 Maple Drive. He bound himself closer and closer to Farr, waiting for the sociopath to let slip a remark that might bring him to the modern equivalent of the gallows. And Farr himself, whose conscious apprehension of his inner, murderous self had only arisen in relation to his wife, the feminist, Elinor, could not but accede to the detective's wily request to be "in" on the murder investigation! A cruel irony! As his love burgeoned again for Mrs Farr, it burgeoned, as it so often does, too late! He was doomed! But Fate does not deal kindly with those who step into that no man's land where dwell the lost and hapless souls who bear the Mark of Cain!'

Lustgarten, like Rush, like everyone, was getting rather hysterical.

And it was, as Lustgarten said, ironically true that, as the affair of the Wimbledon Poisoner became first local, then national, then international news, Elinor seemed to grow sweeter and more reasonable with each day that passed. Over supper they would discuss the case and feel genuine retrospective sorrow for (say) Loris Kemp, now alleged to have been poisoned after ingesting a lamb korma at a tandoori restaurant in Wimbledon in March 1987. They often had sex after these discussions. Their congress seemed to grow out of the case. In the middle of a sentence ('But how did he get the stuff into the pickle? If it was the pickle? Did he –?') they would break off and find themselves eating each other over the ruins of the supper table. They did it in ways that were only hinted at in sex manuals. They whipped each other with towels and leather belts. They did it on the floor, surrounded by Maisie's crisps and the remains of their evening meal. They pulled off their clothes as they climbed the stairs and copulated on the landing. They enjoyed long sessions in which physical release was preceded by pleasurable verbal abuse ('You're fat!' 'I know!' 'You're a fat bitch!' 'Yes yes yes, I'm a fat bitch.' 'I'm going to fuck you because you're fat!' 'Yes, oh yes, yes oh, I'm fat!' 'It's *because* you're fat that I'm fucking you!' 'Yes yes yes, oh yes, fuck me, I'm fat!' '*I'm* fat too!' 'Yes yes yes, you're fat!' 'I'm fat and I'm fucking you!' 'Oh God yes. Oh God yes, you are so fat and you're fucking me, oh God!' 'Oh my darling, we're both fat and we're fucking each other and it's so good!' 'Oh yes, we're both fat and we're fucking and it's so good, it's so fucking good and fat!' etc., etc.). In the week in which Rush announced that the deaths of an Irish family of eight in Southfields ('HE KILLS OFF HIS BEAT') were traceable to a kebab served to them by the proprietor of a Greek restaurant in Raynes Park, Elinor and Henry climaxed, simultaneously, a staggering twelve times.

Partly, of course, Henry told himself, this was due to the fact that, at long last, people were beginning to take an interest in Wimbledon. 'Interest' was putting it mildly. Journalists moved into hotels near the village. They wrote long colour pieces about the fear that stalked the borough, and even, in some cases, went into the history of the place at some length. They got drunk in the Dog and Fox and tried to persuade the barmaid to pose for a saucy snap, holding a cheese roll to her lips. And on 10 December, after a particularly gruelling interview with a man from the *Sunday Times*, Rush showed Henry the following letter:

> *Dear Detective Inspector Rush,*
>
> *I am writing to you, at a time when I realize you must be under great pressure, to ask if I could possibly take some minutes of your time. I am engaged in commissioning a book about the Wimbledon Poisoner, to be written by Jonathan Freemantle, who has written several highly praised books about mass murderers. As Jonathan is away in India at the moment, interviewing researchers, I have promised him that I would approach you to see if you would be able to co-operate with us in the planned work.*
>
> *I shall be staying in Wimbledon for a few days in the week after next and wondered if I could buy you lunch and discuss the case with you? I would stress that we do not contemplate a sensational piece but a serious study of some of the sociological issues involved in the Wimbledon poisonings.*
>
> *Yours sincerely,*
> *Karim Jackson*
> *Editorial Director*
> *Brawl Books, London N1.*

'A Pakistani gentleman, I imagine,' said Rush darkly, 'with, I have no doubt, negative views of the force!'

'Seems a fairly inoffensive letter to me!' said Henry.

'I'll put the word out he's coming down!' said Rush. 'He sounds like a troublemaker to me.'

Henry smiled weakly. He could no longer feel as angry as he once had about Jackson. The trouble was, once you had started being charitable, it was very hard to stop. Some of Rush's expressions struck him as grotesquely out of place, until he realized that, once, he had thought and spoken exactly like that. He recognized his old self in Rush and did not much care for it. Involved in all of this was also plain, straightforward fear. He felt about the detective inspector the way snakes are reported to feel about mongooses. As usual with Rush, he was fairly sure that what the man was actually confiding to him was in a kind of code. Was he trying to let Henry know that yes, he knew about Henry's book, about Henry's racism, about yet another unhealed sore? Since his first suggestion that they get hold of Sprott's ashes, he had not mentioned the subject, except very indirectly, and then only as a response to a question of Henry's. In order to get an autopsy, said Rush, he would have to have an inquest; this would create 'bad feeling in the street'. Mrs Sprott didn't want to be bothered with such things.

Of course, thought Henry, an inquest would only prove that Sprott had an unusually large amount of bleach inside him. And Rush wanted more than that. He wanted the only thing that would get him a conviction – a confession. And Henry knew all about confessions. The police used any and every method of extorting them from suspects. Once the detective inspector had declared his hand, all Henry had to do was deny. He was being cleverer than that. He was making friends with Henry. He was slowly and surely creating an atmosphere in which Henry wanted to tell him things, to confide in him. And what better atmosphere than one in which the two of them became partners in a kind of crime. It was as if Rush was a kind of accessory to Henry's guilt.

The policeman's very panic at the thought of not catching the poisoner (already people were suggesting wild and fantastic suspects, from the star of a current TV soap opera to a member of the royal family) had communicated itself to Henry, so that at times, in the way one finishes a sentence for an old friend, he wanted to see Rush's uncertainty resolved.

The other thing that made the advent of Advent more than usually unpleasant was the thought that, somehow or other, Everett Maltby was responsible for all of this. In the days after Gordon Macrae's death Henry went, two or three times, to *The Complete History* to refresh his memory about the Maltby case. On one occasion he got as far as looking out his notes on the poisoner; but when he had got within five or six pages of what he now thought of as the danger area, the paper seemed to weigh on his fingers. It was rather like recalling a party at which one had misbehaved or, more nearly, staying away from a dark room in which something (what?) could be heard moving. It woke in Henry all sorts of fears and anxieties that made him set down the manuscript and stare out of the study window at the bald suburban garden for hour after hour.

It was at such moments that Henry could see himself doing the ghastly things the poisoner was supposed to do. And he found the only company that seemed able to relieve him, the only person with whom he felt able to share anything was Inspector Rush. He was almost getting to like Rush. They spent long hours walking across the common, whole afternoons sitting in Henry's front room, neither of them speaking. If Henry went to the pub, Rush accompanied him; and sometimes the detective would share information about the latest news on the case.

What no one had been able to discover was a pattern in the case. The poisoner seemed to murder (where murder was verifiable) in an entirely random manner. His victims were not exclusively male or female (although, Henry was relieved to note, there were no children); the only thing that united them, as far as anyone could see, was that all the crimes occurred in Wimbledon. Rush was of the opinion that there was no pattern, although plenty of people had identified what they described as his 'target group'. The most popular theory was that he was a man with a grudge against Wimbledon itself, possibly an unsuccessful trader. But no one – to Henry's relief – had, so far anyway, come any closer than that.

'Of course,' said Elinor one afternoon, 'there might be a pattern. But he' (everyone called the poisoner 'he') 'might be deliberately obscuring it.'

Rush leaned forward in the armchair that he now designated his. He looked across at Henry, as he said, 'How do you mean?'

'Well,' said Elinor, 'he might have a real target in mind. And he might not want us to know who that target is.'

'So you mean,' said Rush, 'he goes about poisoning people as a blind?'

'It's possible.'

Henry coughed. 'Sounds a bit cumbersome,' he said. 'If I wanted to murder someone I'd get right in there and do it. Get my hands dirty.'

'You wouldn't, Henry,' said Elinor, with unusual prescience, 'you'd gibber around with all sorts of schemes and make a complete hash of it. Actually – ' here she gave her booming laugh – 'it's such a far-fetched idea of mine it's the sort of thing you'd go for. You never deal directly with anything.'

Henry managed a jovial laugh. 'Oh,' he said, 'so I'm the suspect, am I? I'm the chappie who goes around tampering with the groceries!'

Rush, he noticed, wasn't laughing.

'I'm not saying that!' said Elinor. 'All I'm saying is – it's possible the poisoner isn't a psychopath who kills at random, but a man who wants to kill someone desperately, so desperately that he deliberately kills an arbitrary selection of people in order to conceal his true target. Maybe even from himself!'

Henry gulped. 'How do you mean . . . from himself?' he said.

'I mean,' said Elinor, 'he can't face up to the fact that he really wants to kill the person he wants to kill, so that he kills, almost unconsciously, not simply to lay a false trail, people that he sees as "in his way". He might not even know he's doing it!'

Henry looked briefly across at Rush to see if the detective was watching him. To his relief, he wasn't. Henry's heart was making an eerily amplified noise inside his ribs. He folded his arms judiciously and tried to look as if he was just another wally discussing the poisoner.

'It still sounds a bit . . . complicated to me,' he said; 'what gave you the idea?'

'Everett Maltby,' said Elinor.

The room had gone very quiet.

'Tell us,' said Rush, 'do!'

32

'It was the apple that gave me the idea,' said Elinor.

'How come?' said Henry.

'Well,' said Elinor, 'I like apples.'

Rush stroked his chin reflectively. Of all his Great Detective mannerisms, this was the one Henry found most irritating. Elinor, however, seemed oblivious of him.

'No one knows how Maisie got hold of the apple, do they?'

'They don't!' said Henry.

'Well,' here Elinor sighed deeply, 'I gave it to her.'

Rush shifted in his chair.

'I know I should have said,' she went on, 'but I just couldn't bear to. And what I had to say wouldn't have helped much. And a bit of me – it's really stupid – felt guilty. I felt I was somehow responsible.'

'And where,' said Rush, 'did you . . . obtain the er . . . apple?'

'That's the point,' said Elinor. 'It was just . . . there. On the bowl. I couldn't work out how it had got there.'

Henry was thinking back to the night on which Jungian Analyst with Winebox gave what was positively his last consultation. Had he had time to go out, buy an apple, inject it with prussic acid and leave it on the fruit bowl for Elinor? Probably, was the answer.

'But I can't resist apples. Especially big, red juicy ones. Henry knows I can't!'

Henry wondered whether to admit this was true. As she talked he tried to work out whether being a solicitor would give him less or more rights when he was arrested. Would he only be allowed, for example, one phone call to himself? He wouldn't be any use, though, would he? He couldn't do conveyancing, let alone murder. But Rush wasn't looking at him. His piggy little eyes were fixed on Elinor's face.

'And then I remembered,' she went on, 'about Everett Maltby. That man Henry was always going on about. It was the apple, you see, that reminded me. So I went and looked him up. There's an awful lot written about him.'

'Actually,' said Henry, 'in *The Complete History* I try to – '

What did he try to do? Why had he so thoroughly and completely blacked out on the subject of Maltby? His entire mental processes, these days, could be described as the physiological equivalent of the dot dot dots in *The Murder of Roger Ackroyd*.

'There's a particularly good book,' said Elinor, 'called *A Woman's Weapon*, which is a sort of feminist study of domestic murder in the nineteenth century.'

'Proving,' said Henry, 'that it was a response to male chauvinism, presumably. *Lizzie Borden: Pioneer Worker in the Field of Sexual Politics*. I think – '

'Shut up, Henry!' said Elinor sharply, 'I'm talking!'

Rush was looking at her with a kind of adoration. Why was it, Henry wondered, that his wife was able to inspire uncritical appreciation in so many people who weren't him? If he had been able to look at her like Rush, all this would never have started.

'Actually,' she continued, 'it studies men who killed women and women who killed men. But it's most interested in men who killed, or tried to kill, their wives. And by far the best bit of the book is about Everett Maltby.'

'Maltby,' said Rush, 'didn't only kill his wife. He killed – '

'Norman Le Bone, the butcher,' Henry heard himself saying, 'Genevieve Strong, a neighbour, and – '

'I'm telling this, Henry!' said Elinor. 'Shut up!'

Henry had grasped a new and potentially sensational fact about his memory. It only seemed to function in close proximity to his wife. Maybe Elinor, who had always seemed to know where his tie, socks, shirt or clean trousers were located, had begun to usurp other functions of his brain. Perhaps his little store of knowledge had leaked across to her circuits. Perhaps there was an instruction in his cerebellum that said: COPY FILE TO WIFE.

'And of course,' she said, 'Maltby was born in this very street!'

That was something Henry knew he didn't know. He had never known that. This was something completely and utterly new. Or was it? The trouble was, once you had forgotten something it was pretty hard to remember whether you had ever known it. The best thing to do was to behave as if you were with one of Elinor's intellectual friends, nodding sagely at the titles of books you had never read, films you were never going to see . . .

'Don't tell me,' he said, 'he had a daughter called Maisie!'

'Actually,' said Elinor, 'he did!'

Rush let out a long slow sigh, like a deflating lilo, and taking out his pipe started to do some rather overdone listening, of the kind that suggested he was waiting for a chance to interrupt.

'And his shop,' said Elinor, 'was just off the bottom of the hill. In one of those roads whose name you never can remember. You know? Like Bolsover Street or Atlantis. It's one of those streets you can never find consciously. The only way back to it is to let your mind go blank and hope your feet get you there. I think the chemist's shop is still – '

'He was a chemist,' Henry was saying, 'of course he was a chemist!'

Elinor ignored this interruption. 'Maltby's wife seems to have had some kind of nervous breakdown, and in the spring of 1888, as far as we can tell from her journal – '

Journal? Journal? This was typical of feminist history. Who could have known Mrs Maltby kept a journal? Of course, in his study of the Maltby case Henry had more or less concentrated on the Wimbledon angle; but he had no recollection of where the man lived. He would have remembered that, surely?

'She went off sex anyway. Became very difficult, and Maltby, who in many ways was a very advanced husband – he did most of the cooking, for example, most unusual in a Victorian marriage – decided to do away with her. It seems to have been that he saw no other way out of his relationship.'

Henry looked at the floor. He found, somewhat to his surprise, that he was clenching and unclenching his hands.

'In truth,' Elinor said, 'I see no other way forward, for all sides oppress me like a wall that faces the humblest prisoner in a jail and strong poison is my only helpmeet!'

Maybe she was possessed by the soul of a Victorian poisoner. This certainly wasn't how she normally carried on. Then Henry saw that Elinor was reading from a paperback book.

'You see,' she said, putting the book down, 'I got this ridiculous, ridiculous idea that Henry was trying to poison me!'

'My God!' said Henry, 'surely you didn't!'

He decided to try this line again. He still sounded unbelievably unconvincing. 'Me?' he said desperately, trying to kick start his credibility. 'Me? Poison you? Darling!' He tried a little laugh here ('No, love, no!' from Rush's invisible director).

'Because, you see, Maltby hit on a most ingenious way of getting rid of Helena. He began to poison people in the locality, rather in the way William Palmer did, but, as was argued at his trial, he murdered the butcher, the clerk in the house opposite and a family of five simply to cloak his real intentions.'

'I still don't see,' said Henry, 'what this has got to do with our poisoner.'

He stopped.

'Unless of course,' he said, 'you think I'm sort of . . .' he laughed again, 'possessed! Or something!'

By way of answer Elinor got to her feet. Henry had never heard her talk for so long on any subject not directly concerned either with Maisie's education, her personal therapy or a domestic appliance. He felt vaguely as if his interest in the subject had been hijacked and, looking across at Rush, hoped to see the man yawning or shaking his head sadly. He wasn't. He was looking at Elinor with what could only be described as rapture.

> 'The cup he hands you and the wine
> Are tainted with the hate he bears
> Yet drink it down and ye yield up
> All of your present woes and cares!
> Pour on! Pour on! Drink deeply now!
> Since Faith and Hope and Love are gone,

Let us drink all with Him they call
The Poisoner of Wimbledon!'

This, Henry realized, from the uncomfortable silence that
accompanied it, was poetry. He didn't like poetry. He didn't know
much about it but he knew he didn't like it. Elinor, perhaps sensing
this, gave him some more.

'Since Memory and Reason are
But dust in th'Historic Wind,
Since Love and Justice are alike,
Both impotent and vain and blind,
Let us take meat and share our board
Yea! Let Him feed us and begone!
We have forgot our need to live
Brave Poisoner of Wimbledon!'

Elinor gave no clue as to where this poem might have come from
or, indeed, why she was reciting it, but that was fairly typical of
poetry lovers. They shoved it down your throat at every opportunity,
declaiming it in buses or quoting it with relish at you when you were
trying to do something else. A bit like people who insisted you had
an alcoholic drink, or the worst type of jazz *aficionado*.

Rush didn't seem interested in the poem. 'And where,' he said,
'did you find the apple?'

'In the bowl,' said Elinor, 'by the window. But then anyone could
have got in. It wasn't that that spooked me about it. You see poison is
a spooky thing, as Gordon was saying. It's to do with . . . I don't
know . . . it sounds stupid . . . with . . . loving someone in a way. And
I thought . . . that poem, it's by Edwina Cousins, a Victorian lady
poet who got quite obsessed with Maltby, what it's saying is . . .
poison is to do with obsession. And you see this person, who's doing
all this, now, I mean, I think they got it all from Maltby.'

'Why?' said Henry. 'Whatever gave you that idea?'

'Well,' said Elinor, 'all the people the poisoner has killed, I mean
our poisoner, live in exactly the same streets lived in by Maltby's
victims.'

Rush gave a little gasp.

'And when Maltby did finally kill his wife, he did it with a poisoned apple. Laced with prussic acid. He was a keen amateur photographer you see!'

She looked across at Henry with a smile. 'That's why I didn't tell the Law,' she said, 'I thought it was Henry! Doing his bit for local history!'

Henry bit back a sob. 'Extraordinary!' he said. 'And then, I suppose you thought . . . how absurd! Henry wouldn't . . . er . . . do anything like that. Did you? Is that what you thought?'

33

If the poisoner's intention, as a woman on the *New Statesman* had opined, was 'to destabilize bourgeois society' – he had not really succeeded. Bourgeois society, even in Wimbledon, went right on being bourgeois. People washed their cars and read quality news-papers and worried about their shares as if there wasn't anyone sneaking around Belvedere Drive and Pine Grove waiting to make their diet even more high risk than it already was.

The poisoner had, however, had considerable impact on lunch. People didn't walk into San Lorenzo di Fuoriporta, at the bottom of Wimbledon Hill, with quite the same *élan*. The waiters didn't greet you with the same style, and somehow there wasn't quite the same thrill as you sat at the white tablecloth, toyed with an aperitif and wondered whether to have *linguine alla vongole* or *carpaccio* for your first course. For a start, you couldn't see the kitchens. And this fact that, previously, had made lunch such an entrancing prospect for the bourgeoisie of the borough, rendered it, now, almost unbearable. Who knew what was happening behind those double doors that flew apart and slammed shut behind the sallow waiters as, humming rather effortfully, they made their way from kitchen to table? *He* could have got to the *radicchio* before you did. *He* could have done a thorough job on the *gnocchi*. *He* could have coated the *vitello* with something a bit more lively than a *salsa tonnata*.

Businessmen still gamely went through with the ritual. Many of them said that the British economy would collapse without lunch. The more honest of them said that they didn't know about the British economy but for sure they would collapse without lunch. But you could see from their nervous glances about them, their anxious inquiries about where Luigi was buying his stuff these days ('Don' worry sah – we go alla way to Keeng's Cross! An' we got double locks on alla da doors!) that the pleasure of dining out, that exquisite combination of helplessness and dominance, that highly formalized return to the nursery had lost, both literally and metaphorically, its savour.

The most popular restaurant in Wimbledon, since the poisoner scare had started, was a small Turkish taverna. For a start you could see what the chef was cooking. And the very simplicity of the cuisine – grilled meat and salads – militated against the poisoner's techniques. The restaurant bought its meat from Smithfield, brought it, under lock and key, to Wimbledon, and invited the diners to compose their own salads. BRING YOUR OWN VINAIGRETTE said a sign in the window, DON'T LET YOU KNOW WHO HAVE A HAND IN YOUR LUNCH! Alone of the eateries in the district, they seemed to make a virtue out of the crisis, perhaps because of the healthy tradition of poisoning that had always existed under the Ottoman Empire. When they brought your doner kebab to the table there was always a little joke ('This should finish you off nicely!') and always, in a gesture that was both charming and did genuinely inspire confidence, the proprietor tasted the offered dish before serving. As Henry observed to Elinor one of the great thrills about eating in Mehemet's Cave of Pleasures, as the place was known, was wondering whether Mehemet would keel over and drop dead immediately after nibbling a bit of your shashlik.

It was to Mehemet's restaurant that Henry went, one day in December, to meet Detective Inspector Rush and Karim Jackson of Brawl Books. It was fairly clear, Henry thought, that the policeman had asked him to the occasion in order to tempt him into making one last, fatal mistake. Jackson was, after all, the man who had turned down *The Complete History of Wimbledon*, and Henry had quite often made abusive remarks about him in the detective's presence. It might be true that, when possessed by the soul of the poisoner, Henry was so fiendishly clever that even this mistake would prove fatal only to those who shared his meal. But this thought was no longer of much comfort. Henry wanted to be discovered. He wanted it all to finish. If he was found slipping something into the publisher's humus, so much the better.

Elinor and Maisie seemed pleased that he was going out to lunch with someone from the media. Maisie asked him if he could get Michael Jackson's autograph, and Elinor hinted that a casual mention of her upcoming monograph on 'The Politics of Poison' might earn Henry unspecified sexual favours. But Henry's heart, as he pushed open the restaurant door, was heavy. He did not want to kill again. 'I must not,' he muttered to himself as he scanned the shabby tables, 'bear hatred. I must not feel angry. This man has a right to reject my work. I do not want to kill Karim Jackson.'

'Hi!' said a voice from a table in the corner, and Henry found himself looking at the first man to send back the most detailed account of a suburb ever put together in the English language. 'Henry Farr?'

To Henry's surprise the only concession that Karim Jackson appeared to have made to the Third World was to be ever so slightly biscuit-coloured. In dress, manner, frame of cultural reference and physical appearance he seemed completely English. He was, also to Henry's surprise, really rather charming. Henry waited in vain for him to sneer or boast. When he was told that Henry was the same Henry Farr who had offered him *The Complete History of Wimbledon* he seemed overjoyed. He spoke warmly of 'the vast scale of the book's ambition' and explained that, although it wasn't something they wanted for 'their list' (at which, in spite of Jackson's extreme diffidence of manner, Henry felt a prickle of hostility) he thought it was a splendid piece of work and one which should, in time, find a proper home.

What made all this much worse was that, at any moment, Henry knew he might try to slip something in Jackson's food. Although he had searched himself thoroughly before leaving Maple Drive, Henry knew enough about the workings of the unconscious to know that he might have secreted Jackson's quietus, without his being aware of the fact, anywhere about his person. He might even, thought Henry, have got up in the middle of last night, broken into Mehemet's Cave of Pleasures and doctored a fragment of doner which he might then, by a process so subtle he himself would not even be aware of it, manage to steer in the direction of the publisher. The whole trouble with therapy, he reflected glumly, acknowledging that he was in the middle of some crude, stone age, do-it-yourself version of the activity, was that it stirred up things you never even knew were there. You got to know quite what a bastard you were, exactly how far you were in the grip of things that made you, to use Elinor's phrase, 'stunningly peculiar'.

He had even started reading books on therapy – although there didn't seem to be many of them aimed at middle-aged men – and wondering whether he was something called an anal regressive. He was – Henry took another mouthful of cabbage – obsessed with farting and bottoms. This was something (according to one of the books he had read) you were supposed to have got out of your system by the age of five. Might his poisoning activity be a way of compensating for the unsatisfactory nature of his mother's attempts to breastfeed him (he assumed from everything about himself that they were unsatisfactory, although he would never have dared to broach the subject with Mrs Farr Senior). Was he, in stalking about the place tipping solanaceous alkaloids into vats of rice salad, trying to provide nourishment for the dark impulses that, as Elinor was always pointing out, he had nourished for so long?

'Is your wife green?' Jackson was saying to Henry.

Ah ha, thought Henry, at last the insult, carefully led up to by a show of politeness to put you off your guard. *No, she's blue with pink spots. What colour is yours?*

'Because,' went on Jackson, chewing his chicken kebab very slowly and thoroughly, 'I rather go along with the ecological aspect to the poisoning case. Poisoning as a way of controlling the environment, say, of purging it of the things that one sees as unhealthy. But purging it, of course, by making it, as we would say, "worse". Do you take my meaning?'

'Not really,' said Rush, who was looking white and strained.

'Well,' said Jackson, 'what's healthy to us, a lively society, say, one that's mixed racially – '

Henry tried not to think about racism. Racism brought back memories of Donald. It brought back, too, the disquieting thought that this man had a point. Wasn't it rather absurd to be obsessed with a few square miles of suburb, when one's society offered someone so puzzling, picturesque and likeable as Karim Jackson.

'One in which things are growing and changing, not staying static, is one that someone else might say was "sick". The human ecology of our society actually depends on change and growth, just as the . . . whale needs the plankton, say . . . we need . . .'

He grinned rather charmingly. 'Paki bastards like me.'

Please, thought Henry, please don't talk about racism. Please don't talk about the loss of the British Empire and multi-culturalism and the need for change. I'm sure those things have their place, but it isn't, I'm afraid, in Wimbledon. Yes, I know I shouldn't think these things. I know it's backward of me. It may be why I seem to do these monstrous things. Elinor is always going on about what she calls the 'monster of racism' that lurks in me. But it's how I am. I am trying to be better. I am trying as hard as I can not to murder people, not to think the awful, shameful thoughts that seem to lead on to murder. But it seems that I can't stop. And if you start going on about the British Empire, for whose excesses I was not personally responsible –

'The Amritsar Massacre, for example,' Karim Jackson was saying, 'is an interesting example. Like all of the other show-piece horrors of British Imperialism, it was carried out by decent quiet, home-loving Englishmen, who weren't aware of how racist, how savagely, murderously hostile they actually were to the world outside the world they knew. And our poisoner is a hangover from the imperial past. He kills to forget the horrors he is heir to.'

Henry could feel the hostility rise in him. Make him stop! he prayed. Don't let him go on about Thatcherism and the danger of Little Englandism! Deep down, he intoned in his head, over and over again, Karim Jackson is a nice bloke. He may have a funny name and be the colour of underdone toffee but *au fond* he is, like me, an Englishman. I am not a racist psychopath, I am – hang on, that's wrong. I *am* a racist psychopath but I am trying not to be one. *And this bastard is not helping me any by going on about Imperialism and Thatcherism!*

Henry noticed he was gripping the table hard with his hands.

Jackson was now, to Henry's horror, talking about the Boxer Rebellion. He folded his hands over his ears, then, to try and stop them shaking, held them on to the table. Out of the corner of his eye he saw Rush. The policeman was looking at him with that mocking, enigmatic smile of his. 'Go on!' he seemed to be saying, 'go on! All I need is the evidence of my eyes. An inquest, and then you'll be neatly sewn up, won't you, sunshine?' Henry looked down at his hands. There was something in them. A piece of paper from his pocket? What was it? His hands did not seem to be able to keep still. They were sliding nearer and nearer to Jackson's food. And Jackson was talking again. Henry must concentrate on his face. Then he wouldn't be able to see what his hands were doing. What the eye doesn't see the heart doesn't grieve about. He'll stop me, won't he? The Law wouldn't let a man die, would they? Or would they? Evidence. They want evidence. These days you've got to have evidence. Henry stared at Jackson, willing the man not to say anything Marxist or anti-Imperialist.

'The poisoner,' he was saying, 'is a perfect metaphor for the way we are now. Our fear, our narrowness, our obstinate refusal to see ourselves as anything other than the centre of the world. It's the perfect Marxist paradox. England's very littleness has made her universally relevant. You've no idea of the interest I've had from American publishers and media people about this story. They see it as absolutely central. And yet, in a sense, begging your pardon, Henry, but if it weren't for this who, really, would give a stuff about Wimbledon? I mean it's a nightmare really, isn't it? Wimbledon? It's dead from the neck up. It takes a psychopath to make it interesting, right?'

Henry could not see clearly. The room in front of him was going in and out of focus and Jackson's voice that had, a minute ago, seemed pleasant, cultivated, was booming, echoing, as if they were in some cellar or underground cavern. Jackson's face too was a brown blur and his teeth had gone as white and sharp as a tiger's. All Henry could hear was '. . . Wimbledon . . . not interesting . . . psychopath . . . not interesting . . . Wimbledon . . . not interesting . . . psychopath.' I must get out, he told himself, before I do something awful. I must get out . . . Wimbledon . . . not interesting . . . psychopath . . . not . . .

'Must have a pee!' he heard himself say. Had he actually said that out loud? Or had he said Mustapha Pee the well-known Turkish lavatory attendant, ha ha ha. Foreigners, as Frank Richards said to George Orwell, are funny ha ha ha. Turks and Pakis and Jews and *Oh my God, Henry, what are you saying? Is this the inside of your mind?* And don't be stupid, Henry, just take it calmly, remember the murder of Roger Ackroyd, this isn't that, is it, *dot dot dot . . .?* Oh dot fucking dot, where am I? Could I have put some poison up my arse like they do with cannabis at airports? I am a bit obsessed with my arse. *Oh my God, Henry, this is the inside of your mind, Henry, this is what you are actually like, is it? . . . dot dot dot* where are we? Where are we, are we all right there, are we? Are we all right? What am I doing? Am I all right?

'Are you,' Rush was saying solicitously, 'all right, Henry?'

They were in the lavatory. As far as Henry could see he was not sexually assaulting the policeman. He seemed to be urinating in an orderly fashion, with Rush next to him, doing likewise. But how had he got here? And what had he done in between the table and the lavatory?

'Don't blame you for getting out,' said Rush. 'You probably didn't like listening to our friend from overseas, did you?'

Rush's voice was sweetly insinuating. Of course he was expert at interrogations. He would know how to conjure up the racist, psychopathic monster that was somewhere inside Henry Farr. Maybe this was all part of a ploy to do more than merely convict him. Thirty years in Broadmoor wasn't enough. Henry looked down at the policeman. He realized, with some surprise, that he disliked Rush intensely. That of the two men he would far rather spend time with Karim Jackson. Karim Jackson was better looking, better read, better dressed and far, far better company than Rush would ever be. And yet, such were the appalling limitations of being white and English and living in Wimbledon, he, Henry, was doomed to spend the rest of his life with people like Rush, had indeed, just attempted, or indeed, succeeded, in poisoning a man whose only crime would appear to be that his parents came from somewhere a bit more interesting than Wimbledon.

His fingers stiff and weary, he buttoned his penis back into his trousers and followed the detective inspector out of the Gentlemen's.

At the door, Rush stopped and looked up at him knowingly. 'What disgusts you,' he said, 'is that people like that, black uppity bastards like that come over here, get good jobs and probably white women and plenty of them into the bargain. Isn't that what you can't stand?'

Henry reflected that Karim Jackson had probably an altogether prior claim on white women than he and Rush, on the grounds of hygiene alone. But he did not say that. He stood, listening to the dripping cistern, the door half open, looking down at the inspector's knowing smile, thinking, now the awful rage had passed, How does he know the worst things I'm thinking? Why doesn't he just arrest me? What does he want to make me do?

'He might even,' said Rush, 'try a poke at Elinor! Imagine that! A black man humping your wife!'

These days Elinor's increased libidinous activity had left him so mentally and physically exhausted that such a prospect would come as something of a relief to Henry. But Rush seemed to think it highly likely that Karim Jackson would want to have sex relations with Mrs Elinor Farr, although in Henry's opinion the publisher would probably have to be offered money before he consented to do such a thing.

'Elinor,' said Rush, 'is a treasure!' He sounded, thought Henry, depressingly like Donald. 'I used to see her in the street, long before we even met,' went on Rush, 'and think, "there's an English Rose! There's a perfect specimen of English Womanhood! There's a woman a man could really love!"'

He looked at Henry, the vaguely critical glance with which Henry was familiar from fans of his wife's. 'How,' the expression seemed to say, 'did this fat, badly groomed bastard get hold of such a pearl!' Had Rush been watching him and Elinor long before their fateful encounter at the Everett Maltby talk? Somehow the prospect was even more depressing than the thought that he, Henry, had just poisoned a major force in world publishing, but it might explain why the detective had not yet moved to arrest him. He was Elinor's lover, and he (maybe she as well) was, were playing with him, enjoying the spectacle of his wriggling on the end of the hook. Weren't all police-men sadists anyway? The pleasure of the job was, for them, not the righting of a wrong but the sight of the punishment of the guilty. And my God, was he guilty! As the two men came back into the restaurant, Henry found his lip was twitching out of control. In the mirror above the bar he caught sight of an ill-looking, pale-faced Henry and, his mind a jumble of half-therapized impulses, poisoned apples and sheer confusion at what might be going on in his soul (if he had one), he sat down opposite Jackson.

Jackson was eating a salad and seemed, for the moment anyway, to be in good health. Maybe I didn't do it, thought Henry, maybe . . . Jackson smiled warmly at him, and Henry, his anger quite evapor-ated, found himself smiling back.

'This salad,' said Jackson, 'is delicious! It tastes really sweet! I wonder what they put in the dressing!'

'I can't think!' said Henry, lightly. And breathed deeply again. Just to check, he tasted his salad, very carefully. But as he had feared, it did not taste sweet at all. If anything, it was sharply flavoured. Henry chewed it and as Jackson began to talk once again about the poisoner, he reflected that it was possible that the media person's research might be about to prove a little more intensive than he had anticipated.

34

Of the three people round the table at Mehemet's restaurant, it was almost certain that Karim Jackson was the only one unfamiliar with the symptoms of strychnine poisoning.

There were those who said, after the incident at Mehemet's Cave of Pleasures (nicknamed, in the few months the business lasted after the December incident, 'Mehemet's Hole of Horrors'), that the fatal kebab was not, as Mehemet maintained, of chicken but of guinea fowl, or game of some kind, that had run up against a farmer who was with callous disregard for his fellow men ignoring the Animals (Cruel Poisons) Act of 1962.

But, as Detective Inspector Rush pointed out, his eyes on Henry's face, Jackson had absorbed the poison in a quantity that suggested that the poisoner had been at work.

'Basically,' Jackson said, as the others sat down, 'I'd like to do a book which looks at the suburb and the poisoner together. There's a sense in which this is Sunday supplement country, you know, three hundred words on Gewürztraminer for God's sake, but I'd like to do a book about a locale, maybe even using some of your ideas, Henry, and about a case, an issue – my God, I feel most peculiar!'

Henry looked at the publisher open-mouthed. He ought, he knew, to get on the phone and order some gastric lavage for the man, as soon as possible, but could not think how to do so without incriminating himself. Who would believe a story about 'blacking out' for God's sake, any more than they had believed poor Everett Maltby? It seemed such a shame this man had to die. He was, as Henry had already observed, a little over-impressed with America, but this was a common fault among British people. He was politically naïve, and unhealthily obsessed with his obviously complex racial origins, but beside that, Henry could really find not much wrong with the man.

Added to which he seemed to be offering to publish Henry's book, albeit in a mutilated and over-sensational form. It was a cruel irony, thought Henry, that the one man he was ever likely to meet who took a genuine interest in his life's work was also one of the people whom his baser, unreconstructed, untherapized, unconscious self should have chosen to murder. Did this mean that, fundamentally, deep down, he didn't want his book published? Or was it yet another illustration of the little known law of nature which decreed that if Henry Farr looked like he was getting a break, God would take it away from him?

'You see,' Jackson was saying, 'the movie, which obviously is what I have in mind, has very universal appeal. Englishness is about our only durable export, and this is a sort of hard study of attitudes in the eighties. What I want to do is stay down here.'

'Down here'? What did he mean, 'down here'? thought Henry, forgetting temporarily that the man had only a few minutes to live. Wimbledon wasn't the end of the world, for God's sake.

'I might stay at the Cannizaro Hotel,' went on Jackson, 'named, as I'm sure you know, Henry, after the Duke of Cannizaro, who was also the basis for one of the characters in the *Ingoldsby Legends*, and really get to know Wimbledon. Soak myself in its atmosphere so that I can get it on the page, make people feel that they are there with me and I might – my chest feels a bit funny – '

Henry gazed in baffled compassion at the only man he had ever met who knew the little-recorded fact that Karim Jackson had just confided across the lunch table. It was at that moment that he knew that somehow or other he must have laid his hands on the cursed alkaloid that comes from nux vomica. Jackson appeared to be grinning broadly at him.

Quite suddenly a rigid stiffening of the body takes place, the back becoming arched (opoisthotonus) and the chest more or less fixed so that cyanosis sets in. It is this fixation of the chest which serves best to distinguish strychnine convulsions from those of tetanus.

Cyanosis or no cyanosis, Karim Jackson continued to make his pitch. In the early stages of strychnine poisoning he yet managed to talk of deals, of percentages of the gross profits, of the paperback rights, the mini-series rights, of the intellectual integrity and honesty of the project he was adumbrating as well as its colossal commercial appeal. He spoke – admittedly with some difficulty – of the *Sunday Times Colour Supplement*, of the sharp political relevance the Wimbledon Poisoner had to British society and thereby to the world. He spoke of agents and development deals and full-colour glossy pictures and of the enormous interest already expressed by television producers in the story he was about to try and tell. British publishing would have been proud of him.

'The story has to be told and it has to be . . .'

He seemed to be grinning.

Tetanus spasm is most pronounced in the jaw. The face is fixed in a grim, sardonic smile, risus sardonicus.

'Christ, the deal would be . . .'

After a minute or two the whole body relaxes and the wretched subject lies exhausted, gasping for breath.

'I'm not feeling . . .'

Some minutes later the seizure grips the body again, often fired off by some trivial stimulus. The mind remains clear until death from exhaustion follows a few hours later.

'Look, this is a really interesting . . . Christ All-bloody-mighty . . .'

Treatment is difficult if convulsions are already established. It is hopeless to try and introduce a stomach tube, assuming one can be easily located, for any such attempt will immediately excite another convulsion.

'Wimbledon . . .'

It was, thought Henry afterwards, eerily appropriate that the last word on Karim Jackson's lips should have been 'Wimbledon'. For Wimbledon, that unregarded quarter of south-west London that he had once sneered at, then discovered, and finally, almost embraced, had, in the end, been the death of him. He passed away spectacularly, with the style and flair for catching the attention of the public that had characterized his brief but successful career in publishing. Juddering like a car trying to accelerate in low gear, he jerked forward into the table like a robot and, *risus sardonicus* in full flower (which only increased his nightmarish resemblance to some elegant creature from the metropolis, in the middle of assessing a colleague's reputation), he breathed his last, with twitchy bravura, into Detective Inspector Rush's doner kebab with salad.

'Oh my God!' said Rush. 'Oh, my bloody Christ!' And he looked across at Henry, eyes mute with misery. Rush, you could tell, had had enough of murder. He had had enough of poison. He wanted to go back to traffic control, which was where, unless Henry gave himself up pretty quickly, he was going to be headed. But as well as the misery, Henry saw something else in his face, and it was no longer the superior, enigmatic expression he had feared ever since Donald's funeral. It was pure, unmixed hatred. He knows, Henry thought, he knows what's wrong with me. He led me up to it, made me do it, and still he won't give me the pleasure, yes, the pleasure of arresting me. Because it would, by now, have been nothing but a relief to be able to say, out loud, to someone, even if it was only a policeman, what he was thinking and feeling. He's in love with Elinor, thought Henry, and that's why he's letting me do these things! He fought for the words that would implicate him, and found, to his horror, that they would not come.

Karim Jackson's funeral, which neither Rush nor Henry attended, was a very fashionable affair. Edwina Lush, the fashionable lesbian novelist, author of *Boy's Games* and *The Fearing* gave a dignified, simple address that, those present agreed, enhanced her already considerable reputation as a fashionable lesbian novelist. 'She looked,' said Meryl Johnson, an unfashionable lesbian novelist, 'very boyish. Karim would have been proud of her.' It emerged during the proceedings that his name wasn't Karim at all, but Dave, and that he had adopted his first name at the age of fifteen, on learning that his mother's first husband (not his father) hailed from Rawalpindi. He was biscuit-coloured because he was biscuit-coloured. There was, his closest relatives revealed, absolutely no racial significance in his colour.

There was another headline, the usual rash of comment, and then people forgot about Karim Jackson. Or at least Henry did. He was no longer aware of what people, or indeed journalists, thought. He was scarcely aware of Elinor or Maisie. Only when Rush came to call, which seemed to be every other day, did he take notice of his wife, watching the way she smiled when Rush told one of his endless anecdotes, nearly all of which seemed to deal with the fatal mistakes made by over-confident criminals.

'Your murderer,' he would say, watching Henry keenly over his gin and tonic, 'is a man living in the hell of guilt. He knows – as we know – that one vital piece of evidence will send him to the Old Bailey, and that somewhere in the trail of misery he leaves behind him the one piece of fabric or trace of chemical that will tie him to the crime lies in wait for the observant member of the force! Let's take Sprott, for example!'

'He died!' said Maisie, watching Rush with huge eyes. When he has finally finished playing with me, thought Henry, and married Elinor, he will make a good father to Maisie. Perhaps the three of them will come and see me in Broadmoor.

'I know,' laughed Rush lightly, 'but you see at the time people didn't take kindly to my theories about the poisoner. They thought your Uncle John was barking mad!'

Elinor flushed. 'If people had listened to you,' she said, 'none of this need have happened.'

Rush shrugged. 'No hard feelings!' he said, and bent down to Maisie. He'll bath her, thought Henry, when I'm in Broadmoor he'll bath her and tell her stories. They'll all have a good laugh about me. My God, why don't I do away with him now? One more won't make any difference, will it?

Elinor was looking at him oddly. 'What's the matter with you, Henry?' she said. 'Is something worrying you?'

'Nothing darling.'

I'm a mass killer, that's all! And that man knows it and is waiting for me to crack! Is enjoying the spectacle of my guilt! Wants to make it last!

'So you see,' Rush was saying to Maisie, 'I couldn't get an inquest at the time. I was a voice in the wilderness. But you see, our murderer – ' here he looked straight at Henry – 'probably knows that there is some chemical in the ashes of David Sprott that ties the murder to him!'

Finish 'Em, thought Henry. They probably had people down at Wimbledon police station who could not only spot traces of Finish 'Em in a corpse, but say something pretty authoritative about when and where it was bought. Why, though, did Rush want to hang the death of the dentist on him? After all there were plenty of other bodies around for which he seemed to be responsible – psychiatrists, publishers, Boy Scouts, too, as far as he could tell, and . . .

Henry stopped, and found he was staring at Rush. A terrifying thought had occurred to him. Suppose there really was a maniac on the loose, and the maniac wasn't him. Suppose Rush *knew* it wasn't him. Suppose the man had simply been waiting, all this time, for the moment when he could tie Henry to one murder, and thereby to all the others. That would explain his insistence that Jackson and Macrae had been the victims of random attack, and the reason for his waiting until now before moving in on the remains of David Sprott.

'It's Sprott we need to look at,' Rush was saying, 'and if it takes too long to get the paperwork sorted we shall just have to nip over the garden wall and take the matter into our own hands. Eh, Henry?'

Henry whimpered slightly. 'Yes,' he croaked, 'yes, of course.'

As Elinor went past the policeman to fetch a tray of cakes from the kitchen, he put his arm round her waist with offensive familiarity. She stopped and looked down at him, beaming maternally.

'You picked a good 'un here, Henry!' said Detective Inspector Rush. 'You better watch your back or I'll have her away from you!'

'Don't do that!' Henry said in a voice whose pitch surprised and displeased him.

Rush looked into his eyes and smiled. 'May the best man win!' he said.

And both Maisie and Elinor laughed.

35

There was only one way out of Henry's dilemma, and that was to get hold of the remains of Sprott before the policeman. Rush had been making several references to the paperwork involved in exhumations, in the week before Christmas, and one night, without really planning the business very carefully, Henry added breaking and entering to his list of crimes.

The night he became a burglar began with another of his attempts to talk to Elinor about what he was now fairly sure was a raging affair with a senior member of the Metropolitan Police. He started as he usually did by pretending to discuss Rush the Policeman, rather than Rush the Great Lover.

'Old Rush,' he said, 'has obviously got a theory of who the poisoner is, hasn't he?'

This thought seemed to excite Elinor unnaturally. As she turned towards him, her eyes bright, it occurred to Henry that she and Rush might be working together, the two of them pushing him closer and closer to the edge, until . . .

'Who is it, do you think?' she said. 'Who do you think?'

'Mmm.'

'No, who though? I mean . . .' She propped herself up on one elbow. 'Do you know, Henry, I really did think . . . at one time . . . it might be you!'

Henry's eyes popped open in the dark.

'Well,' she said, 'you are pretty repressed. You are interested in poisons. And you know a bit about Maltby.'

'The Maltby theory is crazy,' said Henry, 'it doesn't . . .'

'But,' said Elinor, falling back on to the pillow, 'I decided you couldn't possibly be the poisoner.'

Henry closed his eyes again.

'The only person you'd want to poison,' she said, in a smallish voice, 'is me.'

Henry stiffened. 'Why should I want to poison you, darling?' he said.

'I don't know,' said Elinor, 'I'm the only person who's nice to you.'

Henry found this curiously touching. 'Would you be nice to me,' he said, 'even if I was trying to poison you?'

'Don't be stupid,' said Elinor, 'how could I be nice to someone who was trying to poison me?'

'I might,' said Henry, 'be trying to poison you in a nice way. Isn't poison an acceptable brand of oral sadism?'

Elinor sat up again, and flailed her left hand in the direction of the bedside lamp. It collided with something that slithered on to the floor. When the light came on, Henry recognized it as a copy of a magazine called *Lifestyle Design*, that was for some reason pushed through their letterbox every month. It was, as Henry recalled, full of articles about how to make *brik à l'oeuf* and which rosé to drink at parties. It was probably all written by Karim Jackson under false names. Oh my God. Karim Jackson! He burrowed back under the duvet.

'If you tried to kill me,' said Elinor, in a warning tone, 'I'd jolly well try to kill you back.'

'I know,' said Henry, 'but you might not know!' He could hear Elinor thinking about this. If she didn't go to sleep soon the dawn would be printing itself on the sky behind the red roofs of Maple Drive, old Mr Grade from 37 would be taking his dog for a walk . . .

'You don't try to poison someone because you love them,' said Elinor, 'it isn't a branch of sado-masochism. It's a sneaky way of doing someone in, that's all. You aren't really trying to poison me, are you Henry?'

'Switch the light off,' said Henry. 'I'm trying to get to sleep.'

'I won't switch the light off,' said Elinor, leaning over him, 'until you tell me.'

'Switch the light off,' said Henry, 'and then I'll tell you.'

He peered up through a crack in the duvet. Her big white face was just above him. She looked fairly serious. There was a pause and then she moved out of his line of vision; a crash as another two magazines hit the floor to join the puddle of glossy pages already there, and then the room was once more in darkness. To Henry's surprise, she did not speak. And, to his surprise, he heard himself saying, 'Of course I'm not trying to poison you. I . . .'

'You what?'

'I love you.'

This sounded, even in the dark, incredibly insincere. She sounded surprised to hear this news.

'Do you?'

'Yes. Yes, I do!'

He heard the sound of her moving towards him under the duvet, like some large animal lost in the underbrush. When she got to the end of her duvet (the Farrs slept under separate duvets 'in order', Elinor used to tell their friends 'to avoid unnecessary body contact at night') she grunted slightly as she moved through the cold patch into his territory. When she reached him, her right hand groped for his body and landed on his stomach. It felt large. Henry wondered, with some apprehension, where it was going to next.

'I mean,' he said, 'I may have thought about poisoning you . . .'

'You what?'

'Well. I mean . . . this last year . . . you haven't been . . . we haven't been . . .'

'I've been awful,' said Elinor.

Henry tried not to sound as if he took this as an offer of submission. 'Well I've been . . . pretty awful . . .' he said.

'You've been dreadful.'

This struck Henry as unfair.

'I don't believe you really have,' said Elinor, 'not really thought about poisoning me.'

'I suppose,' said Henry slowly, 'thinking about doing it is as bad as doing it. Or . . . trying to do it and failing!'

Elinor guffawed suddenly. 'That's pathetic!' she said. 'That's what you'd do, Henry!'

Well, thought Henry, I think I have had rather an alarming success rate actually. I don't call a body count of five too bad for a first-time poisoner. It's just that none of them happened to be you, darling. In fact I may well have murdered thousands of people . . .

'I love you,' Elinor was saying, sounding, Henry thought, a good deal more sincere than him.

'Even though you are a psychopath.'

'Am I a psychopath?'

'A bit of a psychopath.'

Her large hand slid down and landed on his penis. Henry was not sure what to do about this, so he did nothing. By way of response, Elinor made a farting noise with her lips, a gesture that Henry found curiously comforting. Henry propped himself up on his elbow.

'Do you think I could be the Wimbledon Poisoner? And . . . not know I was sort of thing?'

'God knows, Henry,' said Elinor, as she started to move off with elephantine slowness to her own duvet. She had received the comfort she needed. She was ready for sleep. Henry was now wide awake.

'If I was . . . you would sort of . . . stand by me, wouldn't you?'

'Don't be stupid,' said Elinor drowsily, 'of course I wouldn't. Poisoning people is wrong. Especially poisoning complete strangers.'

Henry thought he saw a glimmer of hope for himself here.

'Do you mean . . . poisoning your wife . . . or husband, of course . . . is OK?'

'I don't mean that. But it's . . . understandable. If there's . . . provocation . . .'

Like . . . feminism, possibly?

'Anyone can murder really, can't they? And it could be someone they then realize they love. Like Othello.'

Henry could not think of anyone more unlike him in any of world literature.

'Love is funny. It's mixed up with really horrible feelings, isn't it? If it's any good or it's going to survive children and people dying and your parents and so on, it must be full of the most awful . . . well, poison. But taste sweet, like that poor man's salad.'

Henry did not want to think about Karim Jackson. But Elinor was now wide awake too.

'Actually,' she said, 'it's an awful thing to say. But all that business with Donald somehow got me through depression. I don't know.'

Thanks, Donald, thought Henry, thanks a lot, mate. Donald didn't answer. Perhaps Donald was beginning to have second thoughts about his earlier, generous attitude to being poisoned by Henry. Perhaps he had been talking to Loomis, Coveney, Sprott, Macrae and Jackson.

'I do love you, Henry. Although you're absolutely horrible.'

'Could you ever . . .' said Henry, 'love anyone else?'

'How do you mean?' said Elinor.

'Well,' said Henry, cautiously, 'you must be attracted to other people. Maybe you have . . . you know . . . secret admirers!'

If he was honest with himself, one of the things he had at first liked then disliked about Elinor was the thought that she would not, could not be drawn to anyone else. But now, the very thing that was pulling him back to her was his suspicion that she and Rush were up to something. Was it wickedness and weakness that people liked to see in other people?

'Yes . . .' he said, 'I think . . . you see old Rush is in my view no ordinary policeman. He is someone who has a mind that must make him very attractive to women. Women like you, who are . . .'

He stopped. Elinor was snoring, loudly. Her full-blooded snores were echoed, from upstairs, by a shriller version of the same from Maisie. It was, thought Henry, as if mother and daughter were calling to each other. As she snored, she moved, or rather flailed her left arm in his direction. Henry kicked her hard in the leg. This usually stopped her. But instead of answering with a grunt and a retreat to the edge of her side of the mattress, this time she carried on both snoring and thrashing the duvet with her left arm. Henry got up, went to her side of the bed and, pulling her by the foot, got her as far away from him as possible, so that she was lying diagonally across the corner that was at the opposite end of their bed's rectangle. Her head lolled over the side awkwardly and her right foot protruded from the grubby linen. She looked, even in sleep, uncomfortable. But at least she wasn't snoring.

Henry stumped miserably back to his side of the bed. It had

started to rain outside. Oh my God, thought Henry, poor old Donald. It would seem that poisoning the bastard was the most positive marital move he had made in fifteen years. It seemed to have cheered Elinor up no end. Of course, when it came down to it, people wanted other people to die. It made sound ecological sense. Death and money, these days, were the only way of telling how well you were doing.

'Donald, old son,' he said, 'you didn't die in vain.'

'Absolutely not,' said Donald. 'I look on it as being a kind of kidney donor, really. I go over the top but show you guys the way.'

'Donald,' said Henry, 'I'm really sorry. I'm really, really sorry.'

'For Christ's sake, mate,' said Donald, 'don't apologize!'

The rain was harder now. He was going to have to get up in a minute and go down to the street and when he was finished with the night's work there would be nothing left to link him with the Wimbledon Poisoner. That was all he had to do. And then he could forget about it. Because he wasn't going to kill again. Somehow he was sure of that. It had just been something he did, an illness really, like influenza or jaundice. With the last of the evidence would go the last of his guilt. Come on, Henry. Up you get. Up you get.

Elinor was muttering something in her sleep. Something in the elaborate chemistry of her brain sent a signal along a nerve that moved her tongue, and her voice, though not her conscious self, started to say . . . 'He's a poisonous little man . . .' Henry looked over to see if she was awake. She wasn't. Without her knowledge, polypeptides and neurons hummed and wriggled inside her and she said, again in a bass, mechanical voice . . . 'Poisoning a poisonous person isn't poisonous . . .' Henry looked more closely at her. She still wasn't asleep. But her voice was fading slightly . . . 'Poison a poison . . .' she said and again, 'It's poison . . . poison . . . poison . . .' Then she spoke no more.

All we are is chemistry, thought Henry, as he struggled into his trousers, socks and shoes, that is all we are. But if only we were something more! If only! Perhaps then mankind wouldn't be such a horrible, self-seeking, blind, greedy, poisonous little bunch of bastards. And with that uncomforting, not totally original thought he crept down the stairs, opened the door and tiptoed towards David Sprott's house.

36

David Sprott's dustbins were legendary. 'You could,' as he once told a man from Teamwaste, who was flinching at the sight of what he thought was a maggot, 'eat your dinner off my dustbins.' They seemed to Henry, as he crossed Maple Drive, to be a touching memorial to the man, arranged as they were, like soldiers, facing the street, inscribed, in white painted letters a foot high, SPROTT: 69 MAPLE DRIVE WIMBLEDON. (Who did Sprott think was after his dustbins?) Sooner or later, thought Henry, the rubbish men will come for me. They will take me out in a van or a skip and, like everything else in the suburb, the bedsprings, the cardboard boxes, the Pentel pens, the old cassette cases, the buckled cans of lager, the potato peelings, the floor tiles nobody wanted, the stacks of wet newspaper and the empty, grease-stained bottles of Soave, I will be carried out towards the great ocean of junk.

He started down the side passage; the door, neatly painted and labelled, was closed and locked, but under a brick on the windowsill to his left was a Yale key. Henry eased it into the lock, pushed open the door and, holding his breath, moved forward along the rough concrete of the passage, above him, to his right, the red-brick cliff of the building. Somewhere away to his left a dog barked, and on the hill he heard the sound of a single car.

The window that was usually unlocked was on the far side of the back of the house. To get to it, he would have to cross the french windows, and to his horror, he saw that from within the dining room behind them there was a dim, single light. Surely she couldn't be up? Not at this time? Henry flattened himself against the wall and wriggled round towards the french windows; he must try and blend into the background; he mustn't even breathe; he must move one step at a time and between each step, stop, look, listen.

He stopped. At the far end of the rear wall of the house, screened from him by one of the thick bushes that fringed the fences of the garden, there was a figure. Oh no, thought Henry, please no! For an instant he thought he could make out the shape of Sprott's head, the beard, the glasses, and, as he froze into the wall, he waited for the sound of the dentist's voice, that mocking northern intonation . . . 'Hullo there, Henry? All right, are yer?' But then the figure moved out from the bush towards the window to which Henry was moving, as slowly and cautiously as Henry himself. The moon made the garden, as neat as the fences, the doors, the dustbins, and the thick, empty lilac bushes into a bold, clear woodcut, and the face of the other stranger, in dramatic relief, was a thing of frightening contrasts. The nose twitched and sniffed, like some animal after its quarry, and the mouth was half open, with excitement or fear or both. But it was the eyes that Henry noticed most. The eyes were fixed ahead in a rapture of concentration, as if something in the house was sucking them in, as if the light from the french windows exerted some horrible, unavoidable pull on Detective Inspector Rush.

There could be only one thing he was after, thought Henry. And he could not be allowed to get his hands on it. He stepped out into the moonlit patio and hissed a greeting.

'Rush – ' he heard himself say, 'Rush – it's me!'

The detective stopped and turned towards him. As soon as he saw Henry his face split into a smile, all teeth and lips, that reminded Henry of the *risus sardonicus* printed on Jackson's face, a week or so ago. He knows, thought Henry again, he knows all about me. He even knew I was coming here tonight. That's why he's here. He knows all of the ghastly things I think and feel and don't tell anyone about. And he knows them without me having to explain. He knows all the things only the detective knows about the criminal.

'Well,' said Rush, 'well, well, well!'

Sometimes Henry wondered whether Rush might not be a bit of his own genetic material that had somehow sloped off on its own to some lab and got a dodgy biochemist to set it up as a freelance individual. If he was a cutting off Henry, though, he was probably grafted from the toenail or somewhere up the rectal passage.

Rush continued to smile. 'Are you looking for what I'm looking for?' he said.

Why don't I tell him ? Why don't I just say: 'Fair's fair. Between you and me and the gatepost and Sprott's lilac bush, I did it. Now go ahead and prove it!' What was unbearable, as always with Rush, was the urge to confess, because only with this man was what Henry had done actually thinkable. When with Elinor, Maisie, people from the office or the street, it seemed to have nothing to do with Henry at all. But here, in the moonlight, looking at the policeman, tugging at his upper lip, Henry knew he had killed five people, none of whom, with the possible exception of Sprott and Coveney, deserved to die. Henry decided to face it out.

'Well,' he heard himself say, 'I thought I'd . . .'

'Get hold of the ashes,' said Rush, as if he were referring to the cricket trophy, as if this were the most normal thing to do in the world, 'of course!'

Without speaking, Henry went towards the window and, in silence, began to slide up the sash. It rattled as it rose. The silence between Henry and the policeman became, as he worked, not silence. A car came up Maple Drive. You could hear it from a long way away, falling in pitch and gaining in volume in a graceful curve until it shouldered its way past them, directly outside, with a muted 'pop', followed by the long, slow slide to absence and somewhere else.

Had Rush seen him? Leapt out of bed, taken an alternative route, some secret tunnel perhaps known only to members of the Wimbledon CID that led to Sprott's back garden? Was he intending to confront Henry with the granulated dentist, waving the urn around in a challenging fashion? 'See! Here he is! This is what you've done, you bastard!'

Henry got one leg over the sill. Inside, the house was silent. Rush, who followed him in, led the way across the carpet. As they came out into the hall it occurred to Henry that all this might be some ghastly mistake, that Edwina Sprott might not, after all, have gone on her weekly visit to her sister. If that were the case, however, Rush had clearly got hold of the same inaccurate information for, as they reached the stairs, he spoke again in clear, almost relaxed tones.

'It's a funny thing about poisoners,' he said. 'Most of them want to get caught. It's a club, do you know what I mean? They have to show their cleverness to the world.'

He looked straight at Henry. 'I've studied poisoners,' he said, 'all my life. They're . . .' Here he gave an awkward little laugh, to show that he was making a joke. '. . . meat and drink to me.'

Perhaps Rush was going to drug him and take him back to some private Black Museum of his own. Perhaps Henry was of too great scientific interest to be just chucked over to the boys from legal aid and then sent off to Parkhurst for twenty years. Perhaps he would be taken into Rush's garden shed and nameless experiments would be performed on him. Henry thought he would probably prefer Parkhurst.

'Is there something you want to say to me, Henry?'

'No!' said Henry, rather sharply.

'Are you sure?'

'Yes,' said Henry, 'I'm sure.'

Rush stroked his upper lip.

'It's the loneliness, I think,' he said, 'I think they must have spent night after night wondering . . . is there anyone like me out there? Someone who shares my . . .' Here he laughed again, dry, perfunctory. '. . . enthusiasms. Cream, Young, Crippen, Palmer. The only time they come together is as waxworks. Know what I mean? And what they wanted was probably to just be with someone who would understand. Who'd say the names with them, you know? Hyoscine, gelsemium, aconite . . . You know?'

Henry was sweating. 'I think,' he said, 'we should go on up the stairs.'

Rush smiled. 'Of course, Henry,' he said, 'of course!'

He became suddenly practical when they reached the bedroom. The door was open and, facing them, above the mantelpiece was a 12" by 10" portrait picture of Sprott in his dentist's uniform. He was standing in his surgery with a drill in his right hand, trying, unsuccessfully, to look relaxed. Below his image, in a blue vase, was what remained of him, corporeally speaking, and on either side of the vase were two blue candles, burned halfway down. Say what you like about Sprott, thought Henry, he was a damned good dentist.

'Wait there!' said Rush.

The detective sank to his knees. Henry backed away nervously, while Rush flopped forward on his belly into the Sprotts' bedroom, indicating to Henry that he should do the same.

'Photo cell alarm!' he said, indicating a point about halfway up the side of the door. Henry wondered whether these precautions had been taken before Mrs Sprott's husband had swallowed a litre or so of bleach; in a sense, of course, people's value only became clear when they were dead. When alive Dave Sprott had been treated with amused condescension, now he was getting the treatment handed out to a more than usually influential local saint in Mrs Sprott's church (Edwina was reputed to be a devout Anglo-Catholic).

It didn't take Rush long to check the mantelpiece. He straightened up and from his left-hand pocket took a polythene bag. He slipped the neck of the vase into the bag, and, making sure not a drop of dentist was spilled, upended Henry's neighbour's remains into it. Then from his other jacket pocket he took an envelope and shook its contents into the vase.

He turned to Henry. 'Two rabbits,' he said, 'she should be quite happy with that.'

Then he held up the polythene bag. 'One dentist!' he said. 'Just add water and stir and he'll be back on the job in no time!'

Henry thought this remark was in rather dubious taste, and said so.

Rush's only response was to flash him a crooked grin. 'When you're dead,' he said, 'you're dead. And that's all there is to it. There's nothing else to say.'

Rush seemed able to alter Henry's opinions more drastically than anyone he had ever known. He very much, for once, wanted this remark not to be true. He wanted a flash of light to break in at the window and for Sprott to rear up, twenty feet tall, tearing at Rush's throat with his hands.

'What,' said Henry, 'are you going . . . to . . . do with . . . him?'

Rush smiled slightly. 'What were you going to do with him?'

'I was . . .'

The policeman was still holding the ashes aloft. He looked up at them, as a Chancellor might look at his briefcase on Budget Day.

'I think,' he said, 'the poisoner wants to get caught. I think being caught is the only thing that would relieve the awful, awful loneliness he must feel. The dreadful sense that everything that happens is happening in his head. That there isn't a real world at all, just his own consciousness. And that his consciousness . . .'

Henry gulped.

'. . . is hell. That he's reduced someone to this. That he's brought a man who could walk, talk, be any number of things, to something you could fit into a jumbo matchbox. And the reason he's done it? Shall I tell you the reason he's done it?'

No, thought Henry, please don't!

'Because he can't feel,' said Rush, in a crooning voice, 'he can't feel anything at all. He's dead inside. And to make himself feel, he has to do the most frightful things. He has to kill and kill and kill again and each time he kills he thinks it will be better but it isn't, and so, in shame and disgust, he goes out to kill again, to heal himself, but after the next killing there is still the same emptiness.'

Henry thought it was about time they left. Interesting as this conversation was, this did not seem the time or place to be having it. Somewhat to his surprise, Rush's technique was not having much effect on him. Perhaps he was so hardened a psychopath that he didn't even realize that he wasn't feeling. He was so much of a loony that he thought he *was* having feelings. Tremendous, strong, violent, real feelings. About therapy groups and being made to go to Waitrose and –

'He has to go back to his victims and dig them up and examine them and go through their ashes and test that what he did to them did actually kill them. Because to him, life is a kind of experiment. He has to go back to it and back to it to try and understand it but he never will understand it and that's what cuts him off from normal human feeling and why he never will be human at all!'

This, thought Henry, was a little unfair. He had always hoped that, one day, be might become, if not completely human, at least partially so. He was only forty, for Christ's sake. There was a way to go, he knew that, but in ten or fifteen years he might have acquired the odd natural response. 'Steady on, Rush!' he wanted to say, 'this isn't Russia. This is Wimbledon.'

But Rush was staring into his face with that same, glittering intensity. 'You know that poem about Maltby,' he said, 'don't you?'

'I think,' said Henry, 'I heard a car outside. I – '

> 'Death has no terrors for me now,
> My heart's heavy; let's begone!
> And dine with He who heals all grief,
> The Poisoner of Wimbledon!'

Henry wasn't, for once, lying or exaggerating. He had heard a car outside. And the sound of its engine was familiar. And – oh my God, no, say it isn't so – the door was slamming and he could hear familiar footsteps and –

> 'Let's feast on all his sides of beef
> Let's slaver over cottage pies,
> For he who dines with Maltby, boys,
> Dines marvellously, ere he dies!

> O hurry Southward, didst thou think
> That Phoebus' brightness ever shone?
> No no! The evening comes and brings
> The Poisoner of Wimbledon!'

It wasn't, thought Henry, only his sense of guilt that made this performance so unnerving. Rush's hands shook as he came to the last verse and his mouth, never a very attractive thing at the best of times, wriggled across his face like a snake in a bag. He looks, thought Henry, about as crazy as I must be.

Down below the front door opened. Henry heard what was almost certainly Edwina Sprott's step in the hall. No one could mistake that slow, tombstone tread of hers, the creak and thud of her Doc Martins hitting the stripped pine floor, reminiscent of the opening sequence of *Feet of Frankenstein*, and then the deep boom of her voice, calling up the stairs – 'I'm back, darling!'

37

Henry's first thought was that Mrs Sprott had a toy boy concealed somewhere about the house. Women in Wimbledon, Elinor included, were always moaning on about toy boys, perhaps because if their husbands had one thing in common it was a lack of ludic quality. Accountant's Wife with Over-developed Breasts and New Sierra had, people said, actually got a toy boy, although when finally sighted he was reported to be quite as fat and old and boring as everybody else. Certainly number 12b had had a black toy boy, who had come to investigate her soakaway drain and stayed, but he had only stayed three days and, people said, had left with her television, compact-disc player and fifty-three pounds in cash.

It was only when the widow was halfway up the stairs that Henry realized. She was talking to the late David Sprott.

'I couldn't stand Nelly any more,' she was saying, as she dropped what sounded like a case, 'so I left and came straight on back. I just felt sort of wild and crazy and desperate to get back home. Do you know what I mean?'

Henry thought he did. He started to tiptoe, at speed, towards the large cupboard in the corner of the room. Rush, polythene bag in hand, followed him.

'She was going on about how marvellous she was was Nelly,' said the relict of the man known to some as 'Cap 'em' Sprott, 'and if I have to hear one more time how marvellously that stupid little cow Monica is doing at St Paul's, I shall spit. She reckons she has an IQ of 184 or something – I said "come off it" – and plays the violin without music. I don't condone that myself.'

This conversation brought a new dimension to all those wise words about death being but a brief interruption in our conversation with our fellow pilgrims. It also served to remind us, in Henry's view, how, very often, those conversations should never even have been started, let alone continued across the Great Divide. Death and taxation might be the only certain things, but Mrs Sprott's version of snobbery was probably immune to both.

'Mozart this and Mozart that, I let her know how well Timmy was doing anyway, and why she won't have Mother for Christmas I don't know, it suited me to have her on Boxing Day but oh no, it had to be Christmas Eve. Anyone would think her husband was something interesting. He's only a monkey who reads the news!'

In amongst his second victim's suits, Henry remembered that Mrs Sprott's brother-in-law read the local news somewhere or other; it was a source of mild satisfaction to him that she should be subjected to the incomprehensible, bottomless vanity of this species of person.

'I said had they seen the results of the Lossiemouth by-election but it was pretty clear that they had no interest. I tried them on Nicaragua but they didn't seem to have formulated a view on it. And one of them didn't seem to have any idea of who the member for Bristol East was!'

Sprott, of course, had been kept abreast of politics by his wife, whose capacity to consume weekly journals, TV programmes and even live conferences concerned with political issues was legendary. It was clear that even his death was not going to stand between him and political enlightenment.

'And I heard Kinnock on the radio. That man has no conception of how to orchestrate his power base. He needs to confront Conference!'

Through a chink in the cupboard door, Henry observed her pull the lid off the vase and peer down at whatever Rush had put in it. If it was rabbits she was presumably looking at a whole colony. Whatever it was it seemed to satisfy her, for she replaced the lid with a little smile.

'It's nice to be home, darling,' she said, 'it's nice to know you're there on the mantelpiece.'

Henry looked down. Rush was squatting on the floor, clutching the polythene bag close to him. He looked back out into the room and, to his horror, saw that Mrs Sprott was starting to undress.

She slipped her dress over her shoulders and allowed it to fall to her knees. She was wearing a black bra and black silk knickers that Henry recognized, with a thrill, as coming from Marks and Spencer's. Elinor had a pair exactly the same. She crossed to the full-length mirror in the corner of the room, and looked at herself. Henry heard Rush give a little wheeze of excitement next to him, as Mrs Sprott lowered her knickers. The two men gazed out from her cupboard at something no man other than the late David Sprott had ever seen, the naked, white buttocks, tapering down to a fuzz of black pubic hair and a pair of no-nonsense, meaty, muscular thighs.

Next to Henry, Rush continued to wheeze. Was the detective, Henry wondered, stimulating himself in some way? He looked down and saw Rush, on his knees, eyes fixed to the crack in the cupboard door. His hands, as far as Henry could see, were nowhere near his trousers. The widow Sprott started to unhook her bra, in an extremely sensual manner. She shook it over her breasts, while making little rowing motions with her upper arms, and as it fell to the floor she gave a little twitch of the hips, causing Rush to leak what sounded like a whimper.

Did this, thought Henry, go on every night in the Sprott bedroom? And what about other bedrooms in Maple Drive? Did Mrs Is-the-Mitsubishi-Scratched-Yet, after she had drawn the bedroom curtains, switched on the light in the hall, come down in her dressing gown and gone up in her dressing gown, carry on like this? Was this the reason Mr Is-the-Mitsubishi-Scratched-Yet leapt up the stairs each night, two at a time, minutes after she had gone upstairs? And if this was the case, if things like this, or things even more spectacular than this even, were happening in front bedrooms the length of the street, wasn't it time Henry got a pair of infra-red binoculars and some kind of hide in the front garden?

She turned to them, naked and humming to herself went towards the cassette deck by the bed. She had one of those deep, architectural, solid navels, Henry noted, and large brown nipples. Elinor's were pink. But before he had time to compare and contrast the two women (another aspect, he presumed, of his cold, calculating, psychopathic nature) Mrs Sprott had turned on the machine and the strains of 'Guantanamera' filled the room. It was a song Henry had always enjoyed and, even under these somewhat awkward circumstances, he found himself nodding his head in time to it, and trying, once again, to work out what the hell those words were that immediately followed the opening.

> Guantanamera
> Akeela (?????)
> Guantana-meeera!

And, one more time –

> Guantanamera
> Ah feel ya (?????)
> Guantana-meeera!

And, surely, this time one would get it? Come on! Here it comes again! This time, surely! Surely!

> Guantanamera
> Tequila (?????)
> Guantana-meeera!

But no. They were on to the bit about his poems being flaming crimson and how he was a truthful man who only wanted to bugger sheep. And Mrs Sprott, who had returned to the mantelpiece, was dancing, naked, in front of the photograph of her late husband. Henry did not dare look to see what Rush was making of this. He almost expected the picture of the dentist to register some emotion (surprise possibly) but, like a holy picture, like Mary or Jesus receiving an act of piety, Sprott continued to grin out at the opposite wall, while his widow rotated her buttocks, bumped and ground and . . . oh my God, she wasn't, was she?

Oh yes she was. Now wildly out of time to the music (the man had finished his translation of the lyric and, having demonstrated to his and everybody else's satisfaction that it was incomprehensible in both Spanish and English, was now singing it all over again, in that same, linguistically secretive style), she rotated her hips faster and faster and her elbow jerked up and down as if she was beating mayonnaise.

> Guantanamera
> Ah steal ya (????)
> Guantana-meeera!

Not feeling that this was something he wanted to watch, Henry concentrated on the picture of Sprott, who continued to look at the camera in what he clearly thought was a confident, solid, reasonable fashion. But his wife (it was impossible to ignore her) was pumping her way towards climax, as the guitars, drums and flutes continued their endless circle. Her left hand snaked round her neck and pulled at her hair, then slid down, past her breasts and buried itself in the flesh of her left buttock. She was moving faster, faster and . . . What happens, thought Henry, if the cassette finishes before she does? But through what was probably long practice, both Mrs Sprott and the Havana All Stars – or whoever they were – came to a conclusion at the same time and, dripping with sweat, she started to cast around for her clothes as the tape hissed on in disapproving silence. My Christ, thought Henry, whoever said Wimbledon was dull?

Eventually she resumed her conversation.

'Well,' she said, as she struggled back into her clothes, 'that was very nice, David. Very nice indeed. Thank you very much. I enjoyed that a lot. I hope you were all right. Were you all right? I was. I was fine. Oh, look, you had a good innings really, didn't you? For God's sake, we none of us live for ever, do we? You could be bloody boring, David, actually. You had no interest in politics. You just – ' Here, she sat on the bed and began to sob violently.

Oh my God, thought Henry. Oh my sweet Jesus Christ. I am sorry. I am very, very, very sorry. This is awful. I didn't mean to. I tried to stop them. I honestly did. I tried to stop him drinking the bloody stuff. I really didn't want him dead. I didn't like him. I admit that. But I didn't want him dead. I mean I may have wanted him dead once or twice. But I didn't mean it. Everyone wants someone or other dead some time or other, don't they? Look, I'm really, really sorry.

'Look, Henry,' said Sprott, 'I was insured. I was very heavily insured as a matter of fact. She's better off now than she was with me alive.'

Mrs Sprott continued to cry on the bed. Fat tears rolled down her face, smudging her make up, blurring the lines on her cheeks, reminding Henry against his will that real actions had real consequences. And it was then, he realized afterwards, watching a lonely woman crying on a rumpled bed, in a deserted house, that he knew, whatever else he was, he wasn't a psychopath. He was pretty fucking close, but not there yet. And the only way he was going to get out of this, the only thing that would stop the dull ache the sight of her caused him, would be if he went out to her now and told her everything. Told Rush too. Told all of them what he had done and why he had done it. Atoned, for Christ's sake. Atoned. Because this feeling wasn't containable. It was like a needle in his side or an unstoppable headache that made him, as he stood there in the cupboard, feel he was about to lose his balance.

He probably would have gone out there too, he thought afterwards (in which case the whole thing would have ended differently). The only thing that stopped him was the near certainty that he would have given her a heart attack. And he didn't, no, he positively did not, you could quote him on that, want to cause any more deaths. Ever. He wanted to be nice to people. He wanted to make children smile. He wanted to gladden the last years of grannies and grandpas. He wanted to be helpful, in an unpatronizing manner, to the disabled. He wanted to be all the things his class, his upbringing and his country seemed to militate against. Generous. He had, in the last few months, got rid of so many hostilities, resentments, spites, perversions and jealousies that he must now, he thought, be the nicest guy in Wimbledon. He was poison free, for Christ's sake! He was as clean as a lanced boil! What he was feeling, here in the cupboard, while Mrs Sprott cried into her sheets for a man who was – let's face it – a pretty nice guy as well, was love. Love for her, and for her husband, yes, don't laugh, for Sprott and for Mr and Mrs Is-the-Mitsubishi-Scratched-Yet and Nazi Who Escaped Justice at Nuremberg and Vera 'Got All the Things There Then?' Loomis and Jungian Analyst with Winebox and Lingalonga Boccherini and Surveyor with Huge Gut and Drink Problem and Surveyor with Huge Gut and Fondness for Potatoes and Published Magical Realist and Unpublished Magical Realist and, oh for God's sake, all of them, the whole hopeless, gargoyle crew of them. Because, this was the fact he had never been able to face, let's face it, he wasn't any better or worse than any of these people. He was one of them. He was Fat Man with Bowler Hat and Unimaginable Feelings of Hostility Towards People. He was –

If only I could roll back time, thought Henry. If only I wasn't a quintuple murderer. How simple, easy and pleasant life would be!

And that thought brought him back to the fact that he couldn't roll back time. That he wasn't just Fat Man with Bowler Hat and Unimaginable Feelings of Hostility Towards People, he was Fat Man with Bowler Hat Who Had Poisoned God Knows How Many Innocent People. And that thought made him feel he was falling, falling, the way he had felt that night he tried to strangle Elinor and, to stop that feeling that he was falling, which of course was unstoppable because once you fall you fall, dead people don't come back to life and time will not, however hard you try, go backwards, he felt for a feeling that would stop the falling feeling and found he was feeling, or rather failing to feel, since he was falling, for something that felt as if it was filling the feeling that perhaps he had been failing to feel, the feeling that –

He was gripping Rush's shoulder, hard, the way he had gripped Maisie's shoulder that night, months, although it felt like years, ago. And Rush was trying to brush him off. And Henry's face was pushed into the dark cloth of one of Dave Sprott's suits. And his brushing against it must have started up dust, because of course the poor bastard hadn't been able to wear them where he was going, and the dust swirled about Henry's nostrils and something in the chemistry between dust and nose set off a reaction that, once started, could not, it seemed, even by a major effort of will, be stopped.

Henry sneezed.

38

To understand what happened next, it is necessary to appreciate quite what an effect the presence of the Wimbledon Poisoner had had on the local population. It wasn't, as Nazi Who Escaped Justice at Nuremberg pointed out, that people were afraid to go out. They were afraid to stay in as well. You never knew just where or when the poisoner would strike. The folk stories about him, and there were plenty, said that he was able to slip into any house he wanted. That he was a trained locksmith as well as a trained chemist. Some said, of course, that he was a policeman who talked his way into people's kitchens while pretending to warn them about the poisoner. Others maintained he was a member of the judiciary and still others that he was, in fact, a she-poisoner, a motherly woman who worked in some local school, who had looked after children all her life and suddenly, sickened by all that care and nourishment, had turned to food that blighted, not sustained.

A sneeze in a cupboard meant only one thing to Edwina Sprott. It said *poisoner*, loud and clear.

She didn't move. She stayed where she was on the bed and said, in a clear, nervous voice, 'Please don't do anything to me!'

Neither Rush nor Henry knew quite how to respond to this. 'If you're the poisoner,' she went on, 'don't make me eat anything!'

Rush looked up at Henry, his jagged mouth turned down comically. He was mouthing something. Henry leaned down and made out the words 'Fantastic tits!'

Really, thought Henry, Rush wasn't the sort of man with whom one would have wanted to share any kind of space, however large. Being in a cupboard with him was almost completely unacceptable.

Mrs Sprott was talking again. Her delivery was that of a not very good performer in a West End play. Her lines were put over with a kind of emphasis thought needful to get across basic information to elderly people who have come miles by charabanc, and who, as well as being of low intelligence, are halfway through a large box of Cadbury's Milk Tray. This theatrical manner did not, however, manage to conceal her evident embarrassment at having had an audience for her recent performance in front of Sprott's photograph.

'I'm going out now,' she said, 'and I shall leave the door open. I shall not ask any questions of you. You are free to leave. I am going to take refuge with a neighbour. I promise not to look or phone the police.'

Rush looked at Henry, grinning. Henry ignored him.

'In my opinion,' she went on, 'you are in need of psychiatric help. I bear no malice to you for what you did to my late husband. Hating you won't bring David back. I think you are a poor, sick, creature whose mind is disturbed. You probably don't even know what you're doing. Give yourself up! I am going now.'

Henry was going to give himself up. Not now. But soon. He would go somewhere quiet with Detective Inspector Rush and turn himself in. He had had enough.

It wouldn't be too bad. At least he would find out what he had and hadn't done. Whether he was, like the conkers he had played with as a child, a one-er or a two-er, or a three-er or maybe a fifty-eighter. There would be the trial, of course – bad pencil sketches of him on *News at Ten*, yet more profiles, and after the verdict an endless string of articles and photographs of the exterior of Maple Drive. They would write about Elinor too. POISONER'S WIFE DENIED HIM SEX! THERAPY DROVE MASS POISONER FARR TO MURDER FIVE! 'I LOVE HIM STILL' SAYS POISONER'S WOMAN. Then there would be the musicals, the drama documentaries, the serious studies of the case written by people who would not, sadly, be Karim Jackson; and then a long, long time in Broadmoor with all the other loonies.

Oh, Broadmoor wouldn't be too bad. He had seen a film about it a few weeks ago. About the only drawback to the place, as far as Henry could see, was compulsory group therapy. Although at group therapy would be eager-eyed psychiatrists just dying to hear about his guilt, his blackouts, his sense of isolation.

'She's gone!' Rush was whispering. 'Let's go!'

It occurred to Henry that Mrs Sprott might well be lying in wait for them. She hadn't sounded like a woman about to lie in wait. She had sounded like someone en route for dressing room number one and the smelling salts. But she might, possibly, be planning to conceal herself somewhere and spy on them. It was to this end that Henry removed two jackets from the hangers in the cupboard, and indicated to Rush that they should place them over their heads. It would probably, he thought grimly, be good training for his first appearance at Wimbledon Magistrate's Court.

With the late dentist's jackets over their heads, the two men crept out on to the landing. By pinching the lapels together, Henry managed to conceal his face and preserve a narrow field of vision; it meant that he had to move his whole body if he wished to look in another direction, rather as if he were the front end of a pantomime horse, but at least, as he scanned the landing, left, right, fore and aft, and then one 360° turn, like a radar beam sweeping over the night sky, he was able to be sure that Mrs Sprott had been as good as her word. The two men started down the stairs. The front door was open as Henry, head lowered, made for the street, the jacket hugged to his head like a friar's cowl. Ahead he could see a plane tree, empty of leaves, pointing angrily in all directions. But there was no sign of Mrs Sprott. Henry walked slowly out and down the front path, towards the white gate.

He peered left. No one. Then right. No one. With a short, urgent gesture to Rush, Henry started out to the left, along the pavement.

He couldn't see or hear her but perhaps she was on the phone already. Perhaps, in minutes, Maple Drive would be swarming with dog-handlers, meat wagons, forensic experts and all the other things the police liked to drag along to places where they had no hope of solving serious crime. The trouble was, his field of vision was so restricted by the jacket that he was unable to ascertain whether or not it was safe to remove it. He ran, bent double, zig-zagging like a man avoiding machine-gun fire. Behind him he could hear Rush, breathing heavily and occasionally calling out for reassurance: 'Are we OK?'

Henry did not even want to answer. He was vaguely aware that they were passing number 84 (Stockbroker Who Could Turn Nasty) but, since it seemed easier to keep his head down, he had no idea of what might be ahead or behind him. He noted the pavement, marked with cracks and discolorations, a low wall, painted white, then a privet hedge to the left, a tree to the right, a lamp post, then more discoloured pavement. He stopped. He had come to a bumpy section of kerb, north of which was the gutter. Raising his head he saw he was in Belvedere Road. All he had to do was to slip the jacket off and stroll up towards the common. No one knew him in Belvedere Road. He would go on the common, with Rush, and there he would end all this. He would turn himself over to the policeman. He was just about to slip the jacket off his head, and planning the opening stages of his confession ('Have you ever heard of something called Finish 'Em by any chance?') when, from behind, he heard cries. Not only cries. Feet. Feet slapping the pavement. Not just one person's feet. Quite a lot of feet. Henry juddered round, as awkward as a robot and there, jerked into vision, like something slipping into the perspective offered by a periscope, he saw the line of houses that was Maple Drive. About a hundred yards away a door was opening, and beyond that, another door. Someone was shouting something. Was it Mrs Sprott?

Henry did not wait to find out. Burrowing his head into the dentist's jacket he pushed Rush in the back and the two men ran for the common. He had almost forgotten, in the excitement, that he was the Wimbledon Poisoner. If any of the inhabitants of Maple Drive got to him before the police (Fat Man with Loved Alsatian, for example) he would be very lucky to get as far as Broadmoor, and it wouldn't be group therapy he'd be needing but plastic surgery on a large scale.

'Faster!' he hissed to the detective, almost oblivious of the fact that this was the man to whom he was due to make his confession, 'Faster! Faster! Faster!'

39

The hue and cry, as Henry had noted in volume seven of *The Complete History of Wimbledon*, was a comparatively rare occurrence in the history of the village. In 1788 a man called Paggett had been pursued from the Dog and Fox towards Putney Hill, because – according to a contemporary diarist – he had shouted revolutionary slogans outside a butcher's shop in the village. Enraged local tradesmen had followed him across the common to the Queen's Mere, where 'they caused him to regret his Enthusiasm for the Queen's enemies by using those appurtenances of honest labour viz their true English Hands, to douse him in one of Her own Ponds!'

If anything, thought Henry, the contemporary inhabitants of Maple Drive were a deal more frightening than a few drunken butchers. There were even, Henry shuddered at the thought, a few bond salesmen at the posher end of the street. If what you read in the newspapers was true, the middle classes in the Britain of the late 1980s made your average pack of ravening wolves look like the *corps de ballet* in *Swan Lake*. He thought he could hear more doors opening, more shouts, more feet on pavement, as he ran, quite blind as to what was ahead of him, up towards the village.

After a hundred yards or so, however, he found his pace had slowed, and was, for the moment, unaware of the pressure of anyone's hand on his back. Perhaps his neighbours were so deeply imbued with the philosophy of self-help that, when actually faced with someone who had taken the law into his own hands, they were unable to stop themselves standing back in admiration. Perhaps murder, like everything else, was now part of Mrs Thatcher's enterprise economy. Or perhaps – this was the most likely explanation – they were all a little too scared. Whatever the reason, when he and Rush reached the village High Street, pulled off their jackets and looked back down the hill, they saw no one, only the quiet suburban streets and the cars, parked with loving neatness under the lamps.

It was then that Henry turned back to the village and, in the window of a shop selling electrical equipment, found himself looking at the face of Everett Maltby. He recognized the big, damp eyes, the side whiskers and the high collar. Next to him, with a little shock of horror, he recognized Maltby's wife, and to one side of the couple a pile of photographic plates. It was one of those cardboard displays, of the kind usually used to advertise something. Surely they couldn't be cashing in on the poisoner? Henry felt a chill of disgust at the thought that his perverted desire to kill was being employed to market electrical goods. Then he saw the slogan: WIMBLEDON TRADERS AGAINST THE POISONER. FIGHT THE BLIGHTER! And underneath this was what looked like a list of signatures. Why did people think that signing your name to a petition affected anything? It might, perhaps, have some minimal impact on politicians, but its effect on murderers was probably to spur them on to greater efforts.

'Hullo there!' A figure who had been staring in at the Maltby display turned to face Henry, who to his horror saw it was smiling at him.

'Mr Bleath, isn't it?'

It was the young man who had sold him the thallium.

'I –'

Henry found he was walking towards him across the empty street. Behind him he could hear Rush's footsteps in a dead patrol – one, two, one, two, we'll get you, Farr, one, two, one, two, I'll marry your wife, we'll get you, Farr, one, two, one, two . . .

'Did you call me Bleath?'

'Isn't it Mr Bleath? Didn't I sell you some – '

'Optical lenses!' said Henry wildly. 'Optical lenses!'

What was this man doing here so late at night? Why was he looking in at that picture of Maltby?

'Your shop . . .' Henry found himself saying, 'is near where Maltby's . . . I mean, your shop is . . .'

'Mr Bleath?'

'Maltby lived here . . .' Henry was saying, 'and now there's a poisoner here and . . .'

'Thallium?' the young man from the chemist's was saying in a wheedling, comforting tone. 'Thallium? Thallium? Thallium?'

Henry looked from the chemist to Maltby and back to the chemist again. Remarkable how similar they looked really. Bland. Innocent. That was why they were using Maltby to sell things of course. Like so many poisons he looked sweet and innocent and attractive. Like so many guilty people he looked respectable. Henry could hear Rush's footsteps behind him. One, two, three, don't try and run, Farr. One, two, three, we're going to get your wife, Farr. One, two, three . . . Why was the man in the window looking at him like that? Could he see into his soul? Why was he looking at him so knowingly?

Later of course, when it was all over, he could see quite clearly that the youth was simply a youth (admittedly a youth with a somewhat over-liberal interpretation of the rules governing the sale of registered poisons) and the picture of Maltby simply a picture. That in the affair of the Wimbledon Poisoner everything was precisely as it seemed and that dreams, hauntings, reincarnations and all the other junk beloved of such people as Unpublished Magical Realist were precisely that – junk. But at the time, with the racket in his head and the racket behind him, as he stared at the man who knew him as Alan Bleath, when all this pretence had started, Henry felt himself letting go of everything he had taken for reality. And that falling feeling started again, so that the youth's face zoomed in to his, as it had that day he had taken off his glasses and a voice that seemed like his but was, of course only in Henry's head, started up and he found he was saying, not thinking, the magic words that would release him from all of this.

'I am the Wimbledon Poisoner!'

The youth did not seem very impressed with this remark. Henry tried again.

'I,' he said, 'am the Wimbledon Poisoner. My name is Henry Farr and I am the Wimbledon Poisoner.'

There was, as there always is at moments of crisis, a great deal of time. I must, he thought, be saying it wrong. He started towards the youth and tried out the sentence again, in a calm, I-have-got-to-live-with-this voice. They probably got a lot of basket cases coming up to them and trying to tell them they were the Wimbledon Poisoner.

'I,' said Henry, stooping down towards the youth and gripping his arm, 'am the man who did the poisonings!'

Perhaps this new construction would get the message across. It didn't. The youth was looking at him as if Henry was a rather puzzling piece of modern sculpture or a German expressionist play.

'Look – ' said Henry.

And then time, as time always does, started again, and Henry heard Rush right behind him, heard the policeman's heavy breath and wondered – Why don't you do it now? Why don't you arrest me and get it over with?

'And so it was,' said Lustgarten, 'that the poisoner, Farr, met his end at the hands of the very man who he had feared for so long! At the sight of the innocent chemist who had sold him the thallium a whole host of memories came flooding back and he saw that some evil spirit was working its way through him as it had through Everett Maltby all those years ago. For Justice has a way of finding out the guilty and, in the end, making them confess, very much as Henry Farr the solicitor did, simply to be rid of the intolerable pain of their conscience!'

'Listen!' Henry shouted. 'I am the Wimbledon Poisoner!'

The young man didn't seem at all interested. He was turning from the Maltby display and, with what looked like some urgency, moving away up towards Putney. It seemed to Henry as if he didn't want to hear him.

'I killed them!' he shouted at the retreating chemist. 'I killed them all!'

The man did not even turn round. Christ, thought Henry, what do I have to do to get attention? Steal a nuclear bomb or what?

'I'm a bastard!' he shrieked. 'I am! I put thallium on Donald Templeton's chicken! I did! For God's sake, I did!'

It did sound, he had to admit, pretty improbable. For a moment he found himself wondering whether it was even true, and then, like a man determined to see through a difficult, dull, unlooked-for task, he went on with his confession. It would have sounded a lot better if there had been music on the soundtrack, or if he could manage something a bit more Grand Guignol in the delivery; as it was it seemed, in spite of the sensational nature of its content, a fairly low-grade affair.

'I put bleach in the punch!' he shouted again. 'I get blackouts! I forget things!'

But by now the chemist was running. Perhaps he thought Henry was trying to implicate him in the affair of the Chicken Thallium. Or perhaps, given his carefree way with scheduled poisons, this was always happening to him.

'I inject apples with prussic acid!' yelled Henry. 'I slip strychnine into salad dressing! I hang round supermarkets, for Christ's sake, and I smear aconite on to wholewheat loaves! I'm poison! Hear me! I'm a dreadful, cruel, greedy, stupid, mad thoughtless person! I'm the fucking Wimbledon Poisoner, for Christ's sake! That has to be worth something, doesn't it, you bastard?'

No one, of course, had ever really sat down and listened to Henry. If they had, they tended to get up and walk away halfway through whatever it was he was trying to say. At school, however high he lifted his hand, he seemed to be one of those boys the masters never saw. The least he could have hoped for, he felt, was for people to listen to his confessing to multiple murder. I mean, Christ, he thought miserably, what do they want from me? Some people go on television and talk about absolutely nothing at all and people listen with their tongues hanging out. OK. I'm the quiet little man in the corner. I read a few books and then forgot them. I'm the man who looked like he might do something and then didn't. I'm a . . . well . . . I'm a solicitor, for Christ's sake, but surely, when in a lull in the pub conversation I lean forward and in a piping voice just happen to mention that I chopped up my wife and left her in a bath of acid, people might say 'Hey! There's something going on here!'

'LISTEN!' he shrieked, as the chemist disappeared into the gloom, 'LISTEN! I HAVE MURDERED FIVE PEOPLE! AND A WHOLE LOT MORE PROBABLY! I'M SICK! CAN'T YOU UNDERSTAND? I

NEED HELP! I'M A CRAZY! PLEASE! LISTEN! I'M THE FUCKING
WIMBLEDON POISONER, YOU STUPID, GREEDY, IGNORANT
BASTARDS!'

He was alone in the street. The man had gone. No one was left to
listen to him. Only the man who he had started to think of as his
conscience, as someone inside him nagging at him, indistinguishable
from his very self. It was, of course, as it always had been, to Rush
that he would have to talk. Rush who wanted all of Henry – his wife,
his confession, his very soul. For the first time in forty years, as
Henry turned to face his tormentor he really felt that there was such
a thing as a soul. What else could be giving him such a non-corporeal
ache? What else could be singing in his head like blood pressure,
blocking out the here and now, forcing him to say things he had
never thought he could say?

But there was a kind of insufferable complacency about Detective
Inspector Rush, and his expression, too, suggested that if he had
heard Henry's confession he did not find it particularly interesting or
believable.

'So,' he said, 'you're the Wimbledon Poisoner, are you?'

'I – '

Henry found his voice faltering.

'I've . . .'

'You've what?'

'I've killed people!' said Henry. And now, for the first time, his
crimes sounded real. Prosaic, flat, but terrifyingly real.

Rush smirked. 'Tell me about it!' he said. 'Tell me! Tell me! Do!'

40

The two men, as if by some pre-arranged signal, began to walk up towards Putney. Henry tried to concentrate on his confession. This was, he knew, a very important moment for him. Ideally he would have liked a ring of admiring listeners, a log fire and a policeman who wasn't trying to steal his wife. But he would have to do the best he could. It was going to be difficult, he could see, to get across the pity and the terror of it all. He felt rather as a relative of Aeschylus must have felt, when trying to tell someone about how the great playwright died: 'Well . . . it's like this . . . he was walking along and . . . a tortoise fell on his head!'

'First of all,' he said, 'I put some thallium on her chicken.'

'Pull the other one,' said Rush, 'it's got bells on it!'

Was he, wondered Henry, trapped in some ghastly reworking of *The Trial* by Franz Kafka, in which he was doomed to wander around London trying, unsuccessfully, to convince people of his guilt?

'And then,' said Henry, 'I put a whole load of Finish 'Em in the punch at Donald's funeral.'

This still failed to capture the detective inspector's interest. Perhaps he wasn't saying it right. Perhaps he wasn't expressing enough remorse. The trouble was, although he had felt remorse, remorse wasn't something you could go around feeling for long. Henry was perfectly capable of feeling randy or envious for phenomenally long periods of time, but remorse was, in his experience anyway, something that sneaked up on you, like indigestion.

'Why did I do it? What made me do it? How could I have done it? It seems incredible, doesn't it?'

'Yes,' said Rush, in a small, mean voice, 'it seems completely incredible.'

Far away to their right a pair of headlights raked the darkness of the common and swung away north up towards town.

'I think,' said Henry, 'that I am losing my mind.'

Rush speeded up his pace. To Henry's horror he realized the man was trying to get away from him. Henry stumbled after him through the long grass.

'I'm a bloody psychopath,' he said again, 'I'm a bloody psychopath, man. I'm a crazy. I should be put away somewhere before I do any more damage. I don't know how I got this way but . . .'

Rush turned to him. 'But what?' he said. 'But what?'

'But I have the blood of five people on my hands!'

The trouble was, the more he went over his confession, the more improbable it sounded. Had he really done all the things he thought he had done in the three months since he sat in his office and thought about disposing of Elinor? Or was the whole thing a mirage, a thought experiment?

'You see,' he said, 'Everett Maltby – '

Rush rounded on him again. This time the detective grabbed Henry, and Henry found, to his surprise, that the man had an extraordinarily strong grip.

'What about Everett Maltby?' he said.

'Do you believe,' said Henry, 'that people can possess you? That you can find yourself doing things and not know you're doing them? Like Jekyll and Hyde?'

Rush declined to answer any of these questions.

'Because,' Henry continued, 'maybe the poisoner is someone who's full of . . . I don't know . . . bitterness, bad emotion . . . and maybe this . . . maybe Maltby sort of . . . acts through him . . . or maybe he, I mean maybe I, without knowing it, am acting out what Maltby did. You see? Do you see? Maybe I'm sort of going through what he did, like a puppet . . . like . . .'

Rush's lower lip was working furiously. 'You don't know anything about Everett Maltby,' he said. 'You don't know anything about anything.'

Then he paused. As if the thought had just occurred to him, he said, 'Were you really trying to poison your wife?'

For the first time since the beginning of this conversation Henry felt an important question was being asked. He felt, too, that when he answered it, his answer would count for something. That it really would describe the long years of bitterness and frustration, go some way to explain what Elinor and he had become, how once, perhaps, they had loved each other, but now, whether through time or lack of imagination or weakness on one or other of their parts, they had, quite literally, forgotten what that love meant. And perhaps, in trying to kill her, he had been trying to make that love come alive again, that forgotten feeling, forgotten like so many other things, that was, if it was like anything, like a kind of certainty or a memory of a place he had once visited, oh probably Switzerland, for Christ's sake, who the hell knew?

'Yes,' he said, clearly, simply, 'I wanted her dead. I really did want her dead.'

With a kind of eldritch screech Rush ran at him, his talon-like hands out in front of him. Henry stepped back, fell against a tussock of grass and the detective landed on him, his hands groping for Henry's neck.

This was a bit more like it. At least, thought Henry, we're getting some reaction here.

'There are times,' he said, as they grappled together in the long grass, 'when I'd like to take a fucking pickaxe to her. When she drives me so fucking crazy I'd like to tie her up in a sack and drop her over Hammersmith Bridge. When I'd like to tie her up and throw darts at her. When I'd like to drop her out of an aeroplane.'

Rush was kneeing upwards into Henry's crotch. By leaning forward Henry managed to absorb the blow in his stomach. He pushed out his right hand and clawed at Rush's face, getting a fair bit of cheek and quite a lot of thick, rubbery nose.

'Cunt,' said Rush, 'fucking horrible bastard cunt!'

This, Henry thought, was manly and straightforward talk. At least we all now knew where we stood.

'Don't tell me,' he said, 'you haven't felt like murdering your wife. Not that you've got a wife. But if you had one you'd feel like murdering her. Everybody does. They just haven't got the nerve to go through with it, that's all. They quarrel about property or the children or they destroy each other slowly, over years, when what they really want to do is get their hands round the old rat's throat and squeeze. Everyone wants to murder their wife. It's fair enough!'

Rush, who had not yet managed to make much headway with Henry's throat, was screaming obscenities at him.

'She's owed a crack at me, probably,' went on Henry. 'Why not? What's all this big deal about killing people? At least it's over and done and you can get on with your lives! Christ, it's better than rowing all the time, isn't it? It's better than niggle niggle niggle. Get right on in there and wrap the whole thing up. For Christ's sake, lots of people murder people they really and truly love, for God's sake. Because they don't want anyone else to have them! And they walk out of the courts free men! You can get more for robbing a train than for killing someone! Why is it supposed to be the worst thing in the world to try and top someone?'

Rush was kicking Henry in the shins. He seemed to be trying to say something but Henry wasn't particularly interested in listening to it. What he really wanted to do, he realized, was not to confess but to explain, to justify. In order to shut Rush up he got his hands over the man's mouth and started to bang his head into the ground.

'I don't see,' he went on, 'what Elinor and I want to do to each other is anybody's business but ours. It certainly isn't anything to do with you, you grubby little bastard!'

The policeman's face was turning crimson. Saliva was oozing out of the corner of his mouth. In a few minutes, thought Henry, I shall be up to victim number six. How appropriate that it should be an officer of the law!

'President Nixon and Henry Kissinger,' he said, 'killed hundreds and thousands of people. I know they were only Vietnamese and Cambodians, but they were all fully paid up members of the human race. They do all right, don't they? They get honorary degrees from American universities, for fuck's sake! All I have tried to do is tried to murder a very difficult woman to whom I have been married for twenty years. We're talking about self-defence!'

Rush managed to get one of Henry's hands off his throat.

'Elinor – ' he started to say.

'You don't know Elinor,' said Henry, 'you don't know what she can be like. And in my view nobody who hasn't been married to her for as long as I have has the right to say anything about her. Or just casually condemn me for putting a bit of thallium on her chicken or a touch of bleach in a festive potion. I know Elinor, OK?'

Rush was staring up at him in something like horror. He was no longer attempting to kick, strangle or scratch Henry.

'Sometimes I love her,' said Henry, 'sometimes I hate her and sometimes I want to kill her.'

He realized he had left something out. 'And sometimes,' he added, slightly lamely, 'I do actually try to kill her!'

He now loosened his hands from Rush's throat. 'But I . . . er . . . don't succeed. I seem to succeed in poisoning everyone in the street apart from her. Which is . . . right . . . depressing. I mean I had nothing against Donald Templeton. I had no legitimate grievance against Sprott or Coveney or Loomis or any of them. I didn't know Donald was going to eat the bloody chicken or that that punch at the funeral would be quite so bloody lethal. You knew then, didn't you? That's when you knew, didn't you? And you've been playing with me ever since, haven't you, you bastard? I mean, I didn't want Karim Jackson to die. Well, I may have wanted him to have a nasty accident but . . .'

He wished Rush would stop looking at him quite like that. One thing, he realized, was that he would never be able to explain quite what he felt about Elinor to anyone. He thought they were probably too close, now, even to use a word like 'love'. He hadn't fallen in love or out of love with Elinor and what was between them was a lot more frightening and complicated and, probably, durable, than the meanings associated with that overused and under-explained word. There was no one else in the world quite real to him. That was it. She was the only person associated in his mind with any sort of feeling, and even though quite a lot of the feelings were of the more unpleasant kind, it was probably true that bad feelings were better than no feelings at all. He probably wanted to be a psychopath and she wouldn't let him, that was why he had tried to kill her. But he was as much a disaster at assassination as he was at being whole-heartedly without scruple.

Henry let his arms hang loose by his sides. He rocked back on his haunches and looked up at the moon.

'Anyway,' he said in a rather sulky voice, 'you'd better clap the handcuffs on or whatever you do. Or caution me or something. Because, hard though this may be to believe, I am the Wimbledon Poisoner!'

Rush looked at him. His lip curled slightly, and he said, 'No, you're not.'

He paused.

'I am.'

41

As the French poisoner Eustachy said at his trial, 'It was all a joke!' And Henry, too, as he looked down at Detective Inspector Rush, realized that he had never been fundamentally serious about poisoning. He was not, would not, could not be in the premier league of those who seek to administer toxic substances to persons without their prior knowledge or consent. And, as he scrambled to his feet, it was obvious that if there was to be competition between himself and the detective for what the late Gordon Macrae would have called 'the role of Wimbledon Poisoner', then Rush had the edge on him. He was, to coin a phrase, quite clearly desperate for the part.

'Look,' said Henry, who was rapidly losing his grip on this conversation, 'you may be a poisoner, I don't know. You may be *a* poisoner who happens to live in Wimbledon. But I am *the* Wimbledon Poisoner. I know when I've put poison in something and – '

'Poisoner!' said Rush. 'You don't know anything about poison. You couldn't poison a fucking fruit cake!'

'I think I could actually . . .' Henry started to say. Then he stopped. Rush was walking away from him again, deeper into the darkness of the common, so far from the road now that you could not even see the distant lights in the houses on Parkside. Ahead of them the bare trees lifted their branches out towards each other, touching at the tips in a dead, pleasureless embrace.

'I am the Wimbledon Poisoner,' said Rush, 'and there are no other poisoners worth their salt operating in the district. I am the Wimbledon Poisoner!'

This, thought Henry, was getting like one of those dreary demarcation disputes of the early 1960s. But before he could start rehearsing his life of crime once more, Rush had started to talk again, in a crooning voice, his head rocking from side to side as he spoke.

'Poison is a passion,' he was saying, 'there are so many poisons! So many things that can change the way your body is! When I was ten, you see, I got a chemistry set and – '

'Look,' said Henry, 'I put thallium, got it? Thallium on a piece of chicken that my wife was supposed to eat but didn't! And I put Finish 'Em, got it? Finish 'Em in a punch that my wife was supposed to drink. I'm a poisoner, OK?'

Rush snorted. 'Templeton died, what, four hours afterwards?'

'Yes . . .'

'You don't know anything about poisons,' said Rush. 'You know fuck-all about poisons. If you knew anything at all about poisons you would know that his symptoms were nothing like the symptoms of thallium poisoning. And that the speed of action of the poison was nothing like that of thallium. Christ Jesus, Jesus, Jesus! Stupid, ignorant little man! Stupid, stupid, little amateur cunt! Where was the depilation? Eh? Where was the stomatitis, eh? Loss of energy and weight? Polyneuritis, eh? AND ALL THESE ARE DELAYED, YOU IGNORANT LITTLE BASTARD!'

Henry watched Rush's face very carefully.

'How much did you give him?'

'I don't know exactly,' said Henry, feeling piqued by this mode of questioning, 'a few grams, I . . .'

'A FEW GRAMS, EH? IS THAT IT? A FEW GRAMS? AND HOW MUCH FINISH 'EM DID YOU GIVE 'EM, EH?'

'Well, er . . .' said Henry, with an increasing sense of irritation, 'a bottle, basically . . .'

'A bottle, eh?' said Rush, who had gone suddenly quiet after his outburst. 'A bottle of Finish 'Em. I know the stuff. In dilute solution. Yes? About thirty bottles of Yugoslav Riesling, right? Do you know what's in Finish 'Em? Have you even looked at the make-up of the stuff? It's only a brand name. Do you know what's in it, Mr Wimbledon Poisoner?'

'Well,' said Henry, now definitely annoyed at this series of slurs on his poisoning record, 'it's got . . .'

'Mild alkali NaKOH, or something along those lines. Milder than that. You'd need 80 to a 100 grams neat to finish you off, work out the odds on a few glasses of a dilute solution, try and remember how they died, you stupid, stupid, stupid little man.'

Henry was trying, admittedly not very hard, to remember how they died. He did remember David Sprott talking, rather over-enthusiastically, about teeth.

'The symptoms of atropine poisoning,' said Rush, 'are primarily excitative: restlessness, mental excitement, incoherence, even mania, flushing and dry skin, pupils dilated . . . think back, think back!'

Henry thought back. And he remembered all these things. Looking across at Rush he remembered seeing the man at the edge of the punch-bowl. Could it be possible that . . .

'You don't know anything about poisons,' said Rush. 'If you've read any books on the subject you certainly haven't absorbed the information in them. You've just let your eyes travel over the page for a few minutes and then closed it under the illusion you've actually acquired some knowledge.'

This, thought Henry, was entirely probable. It seemed indeed a fairly accurate description of his normal method of reading. But if thallium hadn't killed Donald Templeton, then what had?

Rush answered his thoughts. 'I wasn't able to get as much atropine into the chicken,' he said, dreamily. 'You see I injected quite a few things at random, and I didn't get much time. They're always watching you. I had to tear the stupid wrapping off. And it would have taken about four hours, I reckon, with the amount I'd managed to get into it.'

The wrapping, of course. He had forgotten that. Did this mean that Henry hadn't killed anyone? He was about to ask Rush about Karim Jackson and Gordon Macrae but, once again, the little man was there before him.

'The trouble about poisoning,' he said, 'the real trouble with it is not how difficult it is to conceal, but how impossible it is to detect. Every day, in every part of the country, people are being poisoned. But nobody cares. Poison is part of our diet. We encourage it. I couldn't get anyone to understand, you see. I'd put something in the food and no one would notice. They wouldn't believe me. The food's all poisoned anyway. It's all poisoned. England's poisoned now.

There's filth in the water supply, there's salmonella in the eggs, listeria in the cheese, there's caesium fall-out in the milk and lamb and – '

Here Rush pressed his face close to Henry's. His breath, Henry noted, smelt strongly of onions. He had, too, a large and worryingly mobile Adam's apple. Henry tried to look away but the policeman's eyes found his.

'There's the Paki poison, isn't there? There's the Jew poison and the Arab poison and all the other poisons that flood in and change the chemistry of the country. So that Wimbledon isn't Wimbledon any more but somewhere else. And England isn't England. It isn't a green and pleasant land any more. It's a brown and pleasant land, isn't it? It's do you want a chapati, isn't it? It's where's my poppadum? Eh? Eh?'

Henry was beginning to suspect that he might be uninvolved in the placing of strychnine in Karim Jackson's green salad. That he might not be the person who had left around a red apple full of hydrocyanic acid for his wife to find, only to have it consumed by a Jungian analyst. He might – this thought was almost too surprising to contemplate – have not poisoned anyone at all. What did you get for attempted poisoning? Six months? If that. They wouldn't be interested in Henry anyway, not with a twenty-four-carat fruit cake like Rush on the stand. He was clearly going to sell a lot of newspapers, thought Henry, provided he could be got to the Old Bailey in one piece.

'What about Gordon Macrae?'

Rush sniggered. 'Macrae got the apple. Isn't that funny? Macrae got the apple. He wasn't supposed to get the apple, of course. But he did. But by then I almost didn't care who got the apple. It was doing it, you see. It was seeing how they died. It was so . . . interesting.'

There was a long silence. Henry didn't feel like talking at all.

'A psychopath,' said Rush, very quietly. 'is someone who doesn't feel anything. You're not like that. You feel a lot of things. I can see it in your face. You're full of feelings. Bad and good, I don't know. I have no feeling. None. Can you imagine that? Can you imagine what it's like to be me? It's like being locked in an empty room day after day after day. Can you imagine what that's like?'

Henry moved away from him slightly. 'Actually,' he said in a shaky voice, 'I think I can.'

Rush didn't seem to have heard this. 'I got the idea from Everett Maltby,' he said, 'that's what gave me the idea. You could poison a lot of people and then you could poison the one person you wanted to kill and people wouldn't think it was you. They'd think, they'd think it was . . . a . . . maniac!'

He started to laugh. His laugh erupted across his face, shaken out of his body, like nausea, rippling across his shoulders, rising in pitch like an operatic soprano and then, suddenly, cutting out, dead.

'It's funny,' he said, 'you can have a fantasy about something. You can think "What would it be like *if* . . ." You know? And then, one day you can decide to put the fantasy into practice. To see what happens. I used to go to prostitutes.'

I'm not surprised, thought Henry. I can only hope the poor things were adequately rewarded for their trouble.

'They were boys mainly . . .' said Rush.

It's a wonder they weren't fucking alligators, thought Henry, who faced by this creature was coming, to himself anyway, to seem more and more like a pretty regular guy.

'It was like it was with the prostitutes,' said Rush, 'it was like a dream, really. It was so easy and slow and curious. And the more I did it the more I wanted to do it. Because I wanted to see what it was like, you see. Because I hadn't really done it. Not really. Because nothing is real to me, you see. I can't feel anything at all. I'm dead inside. Quite, quite dead.'

And, much to Henry's distaste, the little man put his head into his hands and started to cry. He wondered whether he should say something along the lines of 'there there' or 'pull yourself together' or even 'cheer up – it isn't as bad as all that' but, thinking about it, he decided Rush should probably not cheer up because it was quite as bad as all that. It was probably a great deal worse. More to stop the man's tears than anything, he heard himself say, 'Er . . . did you want to kill anyone specific?'

Rush looked up from between his hands, his face grubby with tears.

'I mean . . . did you have anyone in particular in mind? Or was it just . . . anyone?'

Suddenly the detective became angry. 'Of course I fucking did, you stupid, ignorant little cunt,' he said. 'Of course I fucking did. Didn't I tell you I got the idea from Maltby? Didn't I? Didn't I?'

There was a long silence. Henry did not speak. Over in the bushes to their left a small animal of the night moved cautiously through the dead leaves.

'It was Elinor I wanted to die,' Rush said, dreamily. 'I didn't want her to live, you see. I couldn't bear her to be alive. I couldn't bear it.'

Henry might have been expected to feel some vague stirrings of kinship with the man at this point. But if anything could have convinced him that murdering Elinor was the reverse of a good idea it was the news that someone who was not him should have embarked on the project.

'Why?' he asked, somewhat unreasonably given his circumstances, 'should you want to murder Elinor?'

Rush did not answer this. The two men stood some yards apart in the moonlight, a little way away from the black trees. Then, still without speaking, Rush turned again and walked off north, where, against the black and silver sky, they could see the clear, surprising outline of the windmill, its sails like the blades of some infernal machine, poised to deliver just or unjust punishment.

42

Rush was mumbling to himself as, the polythene bag containing Sprott in his right hand, he trudged on about ten or fifteen yards in front of Henry. They had found one of those paths that run across the common and were walking on black cinders; their shoes crackled, out of time with each other. It was very cold.

Rush appeared to be talking about love.

'If you want someone,' Henry heard him say, 'if you want them, really want them, want them to be all yours, then . . . then . . .'

Henry decided not to join in this one.

'Love,' said Rush, 'love . . .'

And then again, 'Elinor. Elinor . . .'

His voice, still addressed to no one in particular, became suddenly quite perky and chatty. 'I first saw her,' he said, 'in the street. And I thought what I thought. She was so pure. So good and pure and sweet. I didn't understand how she could be with you, do you understand? I didn't understand how anyone so pure and patient and sweet and honest and gentle could even dream of loving someone like you. Because you're evil. You're a rotten little compromiser. There's no soul in you, there's only a little snigger about the beautiful things in the world. Oh Elinor! You're so beautiful! And so gentle and so sweet!'

The one thing Henry had never had about Elinor was romantic illusions. She had always been, since the first day he met her, simply Elinor. She had an unavoidable quality. Partly because, even then, she was a fairly wide girl. Henry had met her on the towpath up near Kew Gardens and, from what he now remembered of the encounter, she had, quite literally, been blocking his way. At first he had been rather irritated by this. But on closer inspection there had been something he rather fancied about her.

'What are you looking at?' she had squawked.

'You!' Henry had replied.

Their early courtship had been nearly all on that level.

'Do you want to come out?'

'Well, I'm not bothered . . .'

'Well I'm not bothered either!'

'That's nice!'

'Is it?'

Why was he recalling all this so clearly now? And why had it been hidden from him for the last few months? Memory was so closely related to will, wasn't it? Henry could not, still, recall how he had met the shambling figure walking ahead of him. Rush was someone who had come over him quietly, like a virus. He tried to block out the man's voice and think, think again, what it was about Elinor . . .

They had both known in those early days that something was going to happen. But neither knew quite what it might be. Sometimes it appeared that it was going to be a fist fight. At other times Henry thought they were both waiting for some other person to come along and get them out of whatever it was that they had started. But, somehow, no one else did come along, did they? And so, presumably, they can't have been looking very hard.

'Like a jewel . . .' he heard Rush say, 'like a jewel and that fat bastard crawling all over her and if you could stop . . . if you could stop it . . . if you could make it so that no one, no one . . . ever . . .'

Then a low moan, 'Elinor . . .'

Henry had always found romantic love a demeaning spectacle, and Rush seemed to exemplify the final stages of the disease. The ideal lover worshipped his or her partner without much reference to his or her behaviour; the only way to get the love object to collaborate unquestioningly in the fantasy was to stop it moving, permanently. True lovers didn't fart like Henry or Elinor (actually very few people farted quite as much as Henry or Elinor); they didn't argue about who was going to do the shopping or clean the floor, they went around feeling big, beautiful emotions and making people like Henry feel like vermin.

But who, these days, could afford big, beautiful emotions? And why was it people were such suckers for things that came on grand? At least he had been honest about what he felt.

The more he thought about it, the only thing he regretted about his attempts to murder Elinor was their underhand nature. He should have come at her with a pickaxe that first Saturday. She would have understood. She would have lowered her head, gone for his midriff, nutted upwards into his neck . . . it would have been OK.

'Call yourself a fucking poisoner . . . you couldn't . . . no, you couldn't . . .'

In fact, thought Henry, the level of his incompetence had reached the stage where it was a definite asset. If he went on like this he was going to end up President of the United States. He wondered, idly, how many other people Rush had poisoned in the course of the winding road that had brought him to 54 Maple Drive and the poisoned apple for Elinor Farr.

'We will never know,' said Lustgarten, right on cue. 'Was Rush the man who introduced four grains of veratrine into a selection of speciality rolls at Marks and Spencer's, Lee Lane, in June 1985? Was it the disordered representative of order who made free with the picutoxin on Albert de la Fissolies's first course of chargrilled polenta with chicken livers at a restaurant in Barnes in August 1987? The answer to these questions will never be known. Rush took them with him to the grave, just as he took the secret of the origin of his perverted passion for the lawful wife of Henry Ian Farr, or the precise pathology of his obsession with the case of the celebrated Victorian poisoner, Everett Maltby. Was Maltby in some way haunting the detective, as he had, in his own way, haunted Farr? Only one thing is certain – it is unwise' – here Lustgarten, aware that he was about to deliver a *bon mot* to the camera, smirked – '. . . to interfere between husband and wife, even when they are trying to kill each other.'

Henry stopped. Lustgarten was, as he seemed to be doing more and more these days, anticipating events. What was even more worrying was that very often he seemed to be absolutely right. He was becoming a kind of Tiresias for the media age. Even if he wasn't right about this one, it was certainly true that Henry was in close proximity to a very deranged customer indeed. Rush certainly looked as if he was about to kill someone and, if it wasn't himself, it was probably fairly sure to be Henry.

Just as Henry thought this, Rush turned to him and, as if noticing him for the first time, said, 'I should have killed you first!'

'Do you think?' said Henry, as politely as he could.

'I should have killed you,' said Rush, 'that day I put the atropine in the punch. It would have been easy.'

'I'm sure,' said Henry, not wishing to antagonize the man, 'that for you it would have been no problem at all. You obviously . . . know your stuff when it comes to poisons!'

Rush looked at him narrowly. 'Don't patronize me!' he said.

'I'm not patronizing you,' said Henry, 'I just think that . . . well . . . when it comes to poisoning people you're . . . first class! Obviously!'

Rush sniffed. No one, thought Henry, not even a deranged psychopathic mass poisoner, is immune to flattery. As Rush walked on closer to the hedge that fringes the Wimbledon Windmill, Henry tried a bit more of it.

'Christ,' he said, 'I thought I was a poisoner! I fancied myself at it. I can see now I was a complete amateur. I didn't have a clue!'

Rush was starting to scowl. Henry decided to change the subject. Get his mind off whatever his mind is on. Talk about something that will absorb him. 'I was thinking the other day,' he said, 'about Charles Bravo, you remember the one? Who died on . . .'

'Friday, 21 April 1876,' snapped Rush, 'after being in constant agony since the previous Tuesday, when he had consumed a dinner of whiting, roast lamb and anchovy eggs on toast.' His lip curled slightly, 'Don't try and change the subject,' he said. 'We were talking about how I should have killed you.'

Holding Sprott's ashes high up above his head he moved towards Henry. Henry smelt once again that sour smell of onions on his breath, noticed the folds of skin on the neck, the ill-fitting collar, the watery blue eyes and that awful, yearning expression that seemed to be looking way, way beyond them, but was in fact looking only inside at the mess within him. He judged it best not to back away, but to stand his ground as one might with a dog that seemed threatening.

'And how I still might,' said Rush, 'how I still might! You've had murderous thoughts in you, haven't you? You deserve to die! Don't you? Don't you? Don't you?'

Henry coughed. 'I think,' he said, sounding rather pompous, 'I could learn to be a useful member of society!'

Rush put one clawlike hand on Henry's shirt. He shook his head. Once again Henry had that uncomfortable feeling that this man, only this man, knew precisely what he was feeling, knew the worst things about him, the things he never told anybody, the things he couldn't start to put into words.

'Oh no,' said Rush, 'oh no, no, no. It's too late for that caper. You're going to die, Henry Farr. You're going to die, die, die!'

43

One of the chief drawbacks of poison as a murder weapon is that it does require the collaboration of the victim. Short of forcing a tomato sandwich down Henry's throat or suddenly breaking off to suggest a visit to a nearby Thai restaurant, Rush did not really have much going for him. He could, Henry supposed, try and jab a syringe in him and, indeed, he was waiting for him to make a sudden movement; but the detective, seemingly exhausted by his monologue, stood quite still in the damp grass, the ashes of his victim in his right hand. And then, slowly, wearily, he groped in his pocket and produced his pipe.

Henry backed away a little. It might, conceivably, be a dual-purpose pipe, a blow as well as a suck job. From his inside pocket Rush was taking something from a square box and he was squeezing it into the bowl and . . .

He was putting tobacco in it. He was lighting the tobacco. He was smoking it. Henry breathed out slowly. He looked up at the windmill – the rear end of it, lit from below, looked like a space capsule, the small, rear sail resembling a propeller rather than anything else. The light only faintly touched the four larger sails, waiting in the black sky for some signal that would never come.

'I,' said Rush, in one of those abrupt changes of mood that seemed to accompany his overtly lunatic side, 'am a member of the Wimbledon and Putney Commons Conservation Society!'

'Really?' said Henry, trying to sound interested.

'Oh yes,' said Rush, 'I'm in and out of the Ranger's office. I'm in and out of the windmill.'

He seemed to have completely forgotten about poisoning for the moment, and if the extermination of Henry was high on his list of priorities he gave no sign of the fact.

'It was in a house next to this windmill,' said Rush, 'that, in 1907, Lord Baden-Powell began writing his book *Scouting for Boys*!'

Henry, of course, knew this. Just as he also knew that in 1840 Lord Cardigan fought a duel just below where they were now standing, watched by miller Thomas Dann, his wife, Sarah, and their fourteen-year-old son, Sebastian. Just as he knew that Lord Spencer, the evil bastard who tried to sell off Wimbledon Common for building land in 1864, converted the mill into six small cottages, or –

It was curious, thought Henry. In a way Karim Jackson had a point. There was nothing, at first sight, more fascinating than local history. 'Oh,' you said to yourself, 'just here, in 1846, so and so was beheaded, or just there, over where they've put the new telephone box, there was a pitched battle between some Jutes in 389! Fascinating!' But it wasn't. It was actually completely and totally boring. Who, really, when you came down to it, gave a stuff about local history? Or Wimbledon for that matter?

He gazed at Rush (who was still droning on about the windmill), almost grateful to the man. This, thought Henry, is how I look to other people. How absolutely appalling!

'In 1893 the miller, John Saunderson,' Rush went on, 'was empowered to carry out repairs. He completely rebuilt the roof of the – '

'SHUT UP!' said Henry.

Rush stopped. His lower lip began to tremble.

'I'm not interested,' said Henry, 'I'm not interested. I've had it. I've had it up to here. What do you expect me to *do* with all this information? I'm not interested. Any more than I'm interested in you telling me about my wife and prancing around as if it's clever and funny to go round poisoning people. Well it isn't. Anyone can stick a bit of prussic acid in an apple. A child of two could do it. It's boring and stupid and useless. And it's also wrong. It's inadvisable. It's something that on the whole we should try and avoid. And it's dull, Rush, it's very dull! No one thinks it's clever or funny! It's dull!'

Rush was beginning to look a little like Billykins on the day of Donald's funeral. But Henry, who was beginning to discover the bracing effects of morality on the system, continued in almost sadistic tones, 'I'm not sure I believe you, anyway. Any of this stuff. Isn't it some sick fantasy? I can't see you or anyone else really doing all the things you claim. I think this is just a pathetic way of trying to make yourself interesting. The Wimbledon Poisoner? Come on! It'll never do. There are real and horrible things in the world and you and I are nothing to do with them. The Wimbledon Poisoner? Come on! Come on! Come on!'

He stopped.

From his trousers Rush had taken a small, glass phial. Henry was not sure what it was but, bearing in mind the man's recent testimony, it was a fair assumption that it was not likely to be particularly good for you. Henry's nervousness must have showed in his face, and the policeman, clearly convinced that he was at an advantage, held it as high as the bag of powdered dentist, and began to wave it in Henry's face.

'See!' he hissed. 'See!'

'Yes,' said Henry, 'I see!' Then he said, 'I think you ought to see someone. A psychiatrist.'

So long as he wasn't a Jungian, Henry felt sure he would be sympathetic. Mind you, from the way Rush was carrying on it would probably not be long before he was crossing over to the Other Side, where he could, were he so minded, have chats about his dreams with Jungian Analyst with Winebox, not to mention Sprott, Loomis, Coveney and all the other people he had helped to speed to eternal bliss.

'See!' said Rush again. 'See! See what I have here!'

Actually, thought Henry, Rush was not reachable by any method of analysis yet known in the Western world. He was in the grip of the kind of dementia that could only really be assuaged by hiring Earl's Court and getting a few hundred thousand people together to clap and cheer at every remark made by the sufferer.

'We have so many English poisons,' he was saying, 'yew, yew, yew. Yew with its toxic alkaloid, taxine. And laburnum bark. Laburnum bark. And do you know what the country people call aconitum napellus, which is the flower that makes your pupils dilate and your chest ache and ache . . . they call it monkshood. And they call hyoscyamine henbane. Henbane, henbane, henbane.'

278

His little eyes were bloodshot. All around them on the darkened common was silent. And his voice, now, seemed to be coming from inside Henry's head. If Rush was part of him he was the authentically evil part. Was he now going to come even closer, to sidle up to Henry's mouth, and press himself close to him, put those wrinkled middle-aged lips on his and climb into him, as an astronaut might clamber into a space suit?

'The anemone is poisonous when fresh,' crooned Rush, 'and water dropwort, they call it oenanthe crocata, that's poisonous too. Nature has made it look like the plant they call sweet flag. Some children ate it and died in 1947. Why did Mother Nature do that? Why do you think? I think because she is very cruel, like all mothers, and she plants in her garden things that heal us and things that hurt us and we don't know any more what will heal and what will hurt us. We are living off poison. We have poison in our bloodstream; it has got into our bloodstream and we must drive it out.'

His voice was rising in pitch and his mouth, working this way and that, was dribbling freely. 'I wanted to save Elinor from the poison. You're poisonous, you are, you are poison. I wanted her to be free, I gave her the antidote, we have no antidotes now, we have sold our antidotes, we have no English poisons, we have Paki poison and Jew poison and Nigger poison and you're not listening to me, are you?'

Henry was trying not to listen. But it was proving difficult.

Rush's voice suddenly changed tone completely. 'The earliest form of windmill in England,' he said, sounding rather bright and cheerful, 'was the post mill, which first appeared in 1180!'

Windmills, Henry decided, were much safer territory than the English Naturalist's Guide to Poisons of the Hedgerows. In the interests of keeping this conversation as alive as conversations of this nature could ever be, he said, 'Really?'

'Don't pretend to be interested,' said Rush, 'when you're not! Don't fake it! I can spot fakes!'

He looked across at Henry in a sullen manner. 'Do you think God is a windmill?' he said. 'I think God is a windmill. Worm drive and rack and pinion. Fantail and sailblade. I am His Miller you know. I am God's Miller. He came to me last night and asked me to grind up the bad people in Wimbledon. All of the bad people. Do you think I should grind them up, Henry?'

Henry found this a completely unanswerable remark. Once, years ago, a boy at his school had, in the middle of a history lesson, informed him that all the clocks and watches in Wimbledon were being shipped out at night in furniture vans. What, he asked Henry, who was only fourteen, was he going to do about this? He goggled then, as he goggled now, at a loss to know what to say.

'Jesus Christ,' said Rush, 'died for us, and he broke bread for us but it isn't wholewheat you see, it's processed. It's full of poisons. They put the list of the poisons on the side and God is angry. So I am going to give everyone an antidote to the poisons. Truth casts out falsehood, right? Sodium thiosulphate casts out hydrocyanic acid, that would have done your shrink friend more good than talk talk talk about his dreams, there are no dreams. There are laudanum dreams, what would you give for laudanum? Potassium permanganate. We must cast out the devils in the bread!'

'I see . . .' said Henry, thinking he had found a way of giving this conversation some direction. If he could bring it round to additives in food he felt he was on safe ground. But Rush was looking at him as if he, Henry, was the one who was barking mad. Insanity of course, is very proud of its rules, it doesn't want just anyone to join its club. What was strange about Rush was the easy commerce between the apparently normal and the transparently crazy, and the fact that the building bricks of the edifice Rush was constructing, the words, the phrases, the sentences, some of the ideas, were the currency of the normal, the everyday. Just as poisons were chains of chemicals, which, linked in another order, might create, and not destroy life, so Henry saw cliché, comedy, real pain and even rational intelligence glimmer fitfully in his speech, promise the great human achievement, coherence, only to see them, seconds later, gutter out in the wind and the rain that blew through his skull.

'I am going up into the mill now,' said Rush, 'because my mother is there. She knows all about Maltby of course. She's good with Maltby. There's a man in CID Wimbledon called Maltby and a man called Miller. That's when I knew I was God's Miller and I had to grind him up the way we used to grind the bread so I ground glass in his beef daube, you can see through glass, I could see right into his stomach and in his stomach I saw all this poison, all this poison we read and see and think and feel and never own up to because we are supposed to be so fucking squeaky clean, I am going in now!'

'OK, then . . .' said Henry.

And walking like a man in a dream, clutching the remains of Sprott in his right hand and the phial of whatever it was in his left, Detective Inspector Rush walked towards the Wimbledon Windmill to talk to God.

44

Henry did not attempt to follow him.

Not that he believed God was in the windmill, although, if He was, Henry did not think he was, yet, in a fit state to see Him. What he did feel was that Rush was quite capable of leaping out at him from behind a wooden pillar or a display case of nineteenth-century artefacts.

The trouble was, after Rush had gone and Henry was alone, he suddenly felt exposed, like a man standing under the walls of a medieval castle waiting for the defenders to tip out boiling oil, or an archer to appear somewhere high up on the battlements, his arrow aimed at Henry's heart. The windmill was so still! So quiet!

Perhaps he should go after him. He cut through the wicket gate in the privet hedge and made for the open door. As far as he remembered there was a steep staircase to the left, leading up to a landing. But it was possible that Rush might be waiting for him on the stairs. It would be best to wait below until the policeman made a move.

The trouble was, once he was inside the door, it seemed quite as frightening to stay where he was as to continue up the dark stairs. The only light came from the illumination outside, which from the interior gave one the illusion of being behind the footlights of a *son et lumière*. Henry felt on display, caught, like an escaping prisoner in a searchlight, but in spite of the alarmingly public nature of the place, everything round it was silent. He stood listening for a moment. There was someone on the floor above him. Creak. Creak. Creak.

'Er . . .' Henry craned his neck upwards. 'Rush?'

There was no answer.

'Look . . . Rush . . . if you're hiding up there . . .'

If you're hiding up there what?

'If you are . . . you can't hide for ever . . .'

There was a scurry of feet on the boards of the museum above and the sound of something being dragged across the floor. Was Rush barricading himself in? Henry imagined the noise growing in volume, the creaks, thumps and rattles coalescing, fusing, until in the dawn Rush would, as he had promised, start to grind. The great spur wheel would turn, the governors start to clatter and the unseen hand of some miller open the shutters of the sails through the striking rod and the great stones would start to grind the corn, only it wouldn't be the corn of course, but the suburb itself, sucked into the machine, like smoke from a pipe, squeezed and bruised through the bed stone and the runner stone, shaken out through the hoppers, mounted on the framework they called the horse, shaken by the spindle they called the damsel because it made so much noise, and then poured like liquid meal through the holes into the floor to be bagged up for market. Reaping the sinners!

'Rush?'

Henry was now round the turn of the stairs. In time to see the policeman's legs disappear from the end of a ladder placed against the trap door that leads to the upper part of the mill. Once, in Maltby's day, there was an external staircase up to the fantail stage – now Rush was climbing up through the interior to . . . to what?

With a new confidence, Henry started to follow him. He was on the third or the fourth rung of the ladder when he heard a voice, booming round in the upper chamber – 'Come along, Mother!'

Henry stopped. Then he called up into the darkness above him. 'Rush? Rush?'

He heard what sounded like an old woman's voice: 'I'm tired, Everett!'

Then Rush's voice: 'Not much further, Mother . . .'

'Everett! . . . I'm tired . . .'

Henry climbed further up the ladder and put one hand on the edge of the trap door.

'Everett!' he called. 'Everett! Are you there?'

There was a silence.

Then, Rush's voice: 'They hanged me at Wandsworth in 1888.

They put a rope round my neck and dropped me through the floor. Can you imagine that?'

Another silence. Then – 'The answer to all this is Maltby. He's the answer to all this. Nobody understands, you see. Nobody cares about what happened. Nobody cares about the past. That's what they've done to this country. They've stopped caring about the past. And so we have to go over it and over it. Over and over and over – '

Rush's voice was coming nearer.

'And over and over and – '

'CHRIST!'

This last ejaculation was caused by Rush's slamming down the trap door on Henry's fingers. He heard the policeman cackle as, pushing aside the trap door, he shouldered his way to the upper chamber, in time to see Rush scrambling up the steps that led out to the fantail stage. Henry followed him.

When he got out on to the wooden platform, the thick white sails of the fantail straight ahead of him, like one of those child's toys designed to turn and rattle in the wind, Rush was nowhere to be seen. Down below Henry could see the top of the two yew trees, from this angle and in the theatrical light as dense and sculptured as a cumulus. He looked around him in the cold December night and then, cautiously, went towards the edge of the platform, shielded from the drop by only one whitened spar, at above chest height. Had the man jumped? Then as he came to the edge he heard a laugh above him and, turning, he looked up to see the detective sitting on the edge of the windmill's cap.

'Look at it!' said Rush. 'Look at it!'

He gestured out towards Parkside and the village. From up here you could see the lights, and beyond them the dark incline of the hill; beyond that the far south of the city, spread out into Surrey, Merton, Mitcham, Wallingford, Epsom . . .

'Look at what?' said Henry.

'Wimbledon!' shrieked Rush. 'Wimbledon! Wimbledon! Wimbledon!'

And, unsteadily, he climbed to his feet. He began to walk across the curved cap of the windmill towards the floodlit sails. Away down to Henry's right he heard voices. Someone had been alerted.

'I don't like Wimbledon,' Rush was saying, 'I don't like it.'

This, thought Henry, was in some ways a promising development. If he could get him to talk about –

'I don't like the people!' Rush went on. 'I don't like them!'

Henry decided not to respond to this.

'I don't like the roads or the trees or the houses or the pets or the gardens or the shops or the cars or the – '

He stopped and looked down at Henry.

'Why do you think you're so perfect?' he said. 'Why do you think you're so squeaky clean? Every single thing you do helps to kill someone. Every time you make a plan or buy a drink or phone a friend, you're helping to kill them. Life is a disease, my friend. And how do you know what you put in that food didn't kill? It helped to kill, didn't it? It all helped to kill.'

He held up the polythene bag containing Sprott. 'What counts,' he said, 'is our intention. What counts is our secret thoughts. People put on smart coats and ties and go out to lunch and look almost human, but inside . . . oh, inside . . . And if we do look at the intention, you see, if we do look at the soul, and we judge the soul, how many times a day do we kill or murder or torture or betray or behave obscenely? Everyone is guilty in their secret thoughts. Don't think you're any better than me because you aren't. You're a hypocrite. And your Justice, your dear old Blind Justice is just a way of reassuring yourself that you can see. Well, you can't. You're stumbling along in the dark, groping your way home and you don't know anything about anything.'

The voices below were getting louder. Someone was telling some-one else that there were vandals. But as yet, it seemed, no one could locate the source of the voices. Henry should have called out to them but he didn't. He stood looking up at Rush.

'Morality,' said the policeman, 'morality! What's your morality? Your morality is poison. And you swig it down and roll it round your tongue and you say "that did me good" because someone smacked your bottom when you were a baby and said "now you're better" and you were better. It's a matter of habit, your morality, and you're going to have to acquire some new habits, little man in the bowler hat, because your world is changing and with it your morality. And you're all going to have to get used to the taste of poison. There's poison in Ireland and poison in Africa and poison in Latin America and there's poison right here in Wimbledon and every day you drink it up like a good little man in a bowler hat and you say "My, that feels better! My, that's good poison!" Don't you? Don't you? Don't you?'

Henry felt this required some response. 'I – '

But Rush, waving the polythene bag around his head, silenced him with a scream. 'In here,' he shouted, 'I've got a dentist!'

He shook the bag violently. Sprott's ashes rattled against the transparent, plastic walls of the container.

'Forty-odd years – ' went on Rush, 'of being a dentist! Of being a good little dentist! Of doing his bit for people's teeth! Good boy! Well done! Forty years of standing up and drilling away and thinking you were being some use! And at the end of forty years? What at the end of forty years, eh?'

Here he shook the bag again. Little bits of Sprott dashed against the polythene. There was the possibility, thought Henry, that he would evacuate the man's remains all over the cap of the windmill. But, instead, Rush opened the neck of the bag and looked down into it. What he saw seemed to please him.

'There, there,' he said, 'there, there, there!' And started to shake the contents of the phial in his left hand into the bag. Henry watched. Was Rush, he wondered, extending the range of his poisoning operations to include those already dead? What else would explain the fierce look of concentration on his face as he kneaded the colourless liquid into the ashes of Henry's neighbour? The policeman stirred and poked the dark grains and, as Henry watched, the remnants of a married man of forty-two soaked up the transparent juice in Rush's left hand. As Rush stroked it into the surface of the ashes, the liquid molecules bumped and rolled into the solid molecules, and the dead oral surgeon changed shape, until he was closer to yeast or dough than chaff or meal. This seemed unnatural. When we die, thought

Henry, we do not rise again. We are not put in the oven to prove. We are dust, aren't we? Dust on the wind . . .

But Sprott was yeast, flour and water. Sprott was living bread again, and as Rush kneaded him he acquired that eerie, plastic life that dough, plasticine or clay have in them; he was God's raw material and Rush, the mad miller, the crazy baker, was pushing and pulling him into human form once again. He was a ball now, a dense, rubbery ball, and Rush was rolling him between his fingers, holding him as high as he could, like the communion host, shown to the loyal congregation.

'Take,' said Rush, 'take! Eat! This is Thy Body!'

He started to giggle.

'This is Thy Blood and Body! This is Thy Spirit and Flesh! This Nourisheth and Sustaineth! This is the staff of life, O Jesus!'

His voice rose to a scream. 'This is the Body of God! This is strong poison! This is the acid of the Lord God of Hosts! Bow down! Bow down! This is the Body of Jesus Christ! Eat him for his Burthen is easy! And his . . .'

He started to giggle again. A hideous, unrestrained canter up the scale, operatic, alien . . .

'His Choke is Light!'

And as Henry watched, Detective Inspector Rush began to masticate the paste. He chewed it with elaborate ceremony and seemed to savour whatever it was that had bound the fragments of Sprott together again. Were they, Henry wondered, afterwards, the alkaloids of aconite, were they brucine or emetine or quebracho or yohimbine or cotarnine or curare or colchicum or cantharidine or laudexium, its salts or dyflos?

Whatever they were they were the staff of death. They were part of Detective Inspector Rush's last meal on earth, and from the ecstatic expression on his face you would have thought he was swallowing life its very self. Poison was always his favourite flavour and to eat it *à la* resident must have been the ultimate experience, the equivalent, for a gourmet, of a meal at the Tour d'Argent. How quick acting it was Henry never knew, for the policeman gagged on his former neighbour, slipped and fell forward on to the huge white sail that sloped away from the cap down to the dark garden. There was a scream, a sound of slithering Rush, and then, somewhere out of sight, the dull crunch of a body hitting the earth below. Then, for as long as Henry waited, no sound.

Rush was dead. But he was a psychopathic poisoner. As well as a psychopathic poisoner he was one of the most boring people Henry had ever met. So that was OK. Wasn't it?

Henry stumped down the stairs towards the body.

45

In Rush's home they found, among other things, a detailed account of his poisoning activities. It was this diary, made available to the coroner's inquest, that closed the affair of the Wimbledon Poisoner. When it was published a few years later (to form the basis of a very successful stage play called, simply, *D. I. Rush*) it caused something of a sensation. People talked about the banality of evil, about the lessons for all of us in Rush's ramblings and Henry read bits of it, out loud, to Elinor, when the more decent parts of it were published in the Sunday papers.

November 3rd 1987
Morning overcast. In the afternoon it rained. I put 0.2 grains of gel-
semium in a bun and tried to feed it to the fish. They didn't seem to
want it. In evening hoovered spare bedroom.

It was hard, from the papers, to work out which crimes of Rush's were fantasy. Even a year after his death no one was quite sure how many people he had killed. The natural tendency, of course, was to give him credit for every abdominal disturbance, polyneuritis, seizure, fit and remotely questionable disease in the Wimbledon area for the past few years. He had drawn pictures of some of his victims, and in the downstairs broom cupboard was an electoral roll with a skull and crossbones by the names of at least half of the inhabitants of Maple Drive – which proved, as Henry pointed out to Elinor, that he wasn't all bad. His mother, it transpired, was a schizophrenic who, by a coincidence that turned out to be just that, lived very near to Henry's mother.

Rush was, of course, a monster, but in the course of time he became another sort of monster. A more graphic creature altogether. People who had known him spoke of the strange look in his eyes, of the aura of evil that surrounded him, and many said he had for some years been practising devil-worship. He was said to have heard voices, to have stalked and raped young women and, in the words of one profile, 'to have always been alone'. Nobody, for some reason, asked Henry about him. Nobody ever mentioned the fact that he was incredibly boring. Being boring didn't, somehow, go with being a mass poisoner and psychopath.

In the course of time people forgot about the Wimbledon Poisoner. He went into history, along with Maltby and Seddon and Maybrick and Lafarge and the rest of them. And they forgot about Henry; it seemed extraordinary, really, that they had ever been able to remember him. He was quoted, briefly, in one paper, on the subject of Rush, but the newspapers, to Henry's surprise, were remarkably ill-informed about the true facts of the case. The journalists who hung around Maple Drive and drank in the Dog and Fox were, almost to a man, highly incurious people.

And in the course of time Henry, too, forgot. He forgot more things than he had already forgotten. He forgot about poisoning, or not poisoning, his doctor, his dentist, his wife's psychiatrist, his ninety-two-year-old neighbour, his publisher (he had come now to think of Karim Jackson as his publisher, and even boasted to neighbours about 'going up to London for a chat with his editor') and he forgot not only whether he had or had not poisoned any of these people but even whether he knew who they were or where they had come from. He lived very, very quietly.

He forgot about Wimbledon too, although he continued to live there. He forgot about Everett Maltby and Everett Maltby's wife and Everett Maltby's trial. He forgot about world affairs and local affairs. He forgot about the seasons and the stars and the winds and the rains and almost everything that he didn't absolutely have to remember in order to pay his mortgage, feed and clothe his wife and daughter and get reasonably drunk three nights out of four.

But he did not forget about the time he tried to murder his wife.

It was, of course, about the most interesting thing he had done. Or, to be more precise, nearly the most interesting thing he had done, since he had never actually done it. It was in his mind when they went to bed and when they rose in the morning and it coloured every individual way he looked at her. Because, of course, now he was not burdened with the intolerable weight of having to go through with it, it was, once again, a delightful possibility. If she showed signs of interest in a holiday with Club Mediterranée, for example, or an ill-thought-out fondness for the work of some young radical playwright, there was the possibility, close to hand, of dropping into the Fulham Armoury, buying a hand gun, and simply blowing her head off, one Saturday morning, just before he departed for Waitrose. The more he entertained this possibility, the better behaved she seemed to be, until about a year or so after he had first decided to kill her he realized, with dumb wonder, that they hardly ever argued, that their friends (they seemed to have acquired quite a lot of friends) were pointing them out as a model couple. And it was then that he thought quite seriously of telling her about the time he tried to give her Chicken Thallium. But he never did. Somehow saying the thing out loud would have had a quite unreasonably large impact on their marriage and, as certain adulterers go quietly to their graves with a secret, so Henry Farr hugged his to himself.

One night, about a year after everyone had been talking about the Wimbledon Poisoner, when he was long forgotten, when Maisie had suddenly grown miraculously taller and thinner, when Henry's office had become an almost restful, neutral place of pilgrimage, when Elinor had acquired a whole new range of obsessions and phrases and Henry hadn't even noticed them, they were lying in bed, under their separate duvets, when she suddenly said to him, 'Did you ever try to kill me?'

Henry did not reply.

'There was a time,' she went on, 'when I really thought you might be . . .'

'Really?' said Henry in what was almost genuine surprise.

'Oh yes!'

'When was that?'

She stirred under the duvet. He hoped she wasn't going to come over to his side of the bed. Henry liked his side of the bed. It felt safe and warm. He heard her click her teeth, a sure sign that she was thinking.

'Oh ages ago . . . I don't remember . . .'

'Was it . . . when the poisoning . . . started?'

'No,' said Elinor, 'it was just before all that. One Saturday. Here. There was such a bad feeling in the house.'

'Yes . . .'

'And then poor old Donald . . .'

Henry coughed. He didn't want to think about Donald. 'How was I going to do it?'

'I don't remember.'

Henry turned over and listened to the wind on Wimbledon Hill.

'Well,' he said, 'suppose . . .'

'Suppose what?'

'Well . . . suppose the balance of my mind was disturbed sort of thing . . . and suppose . . .'

'Suppose what?'

'Suppose I did . . . well . . . only once, of course . . . get this . . . mad urge . . . to . . . do away with you . . .'

Elinor sat up in bed. Henry stayed very still.

'How do you mean?'

'Well . . . I don't know . . . suppose . . . well, say we'd been having a row and then we were walking . . . well, near a cliff, say . . . and I had this urge to . . . push you off . . . say . . .'

'And what then?'

'Well . . . suppose . . . you know . . . I . . . had a go sort of thing . . . you know? What would you . . . er . . . do?'

'I'd divorce you,' said Elinor, 'and I'd phone the police and have you sent to prison.'

'Fine!' said Henry.

There was another pause. Eventually she slid down to a supine position in the bed. But he could tell from the tense quality of her stillness that she was not asleep.

'I just wondered!' he said, brightly.

'Because you don't want to kill me, do you Henry?' she said.

'Oh no!'

Elinor coughed. 'Good,' she said.

He heard her snuggle further down into her duvet.

'You couldn't really say anything else, could you?' she said.

'No,' said Henry.

Then she stirred in a lazy way and yawned. 'I'm very strict about things like that!'

'I know,' said Henry.

The silence was of a different quality now. It was restful, autumnal, like the season, like the leaves on the plane tree outside, that were turning, as they had turned a year ago when they were both different people, as they would be tomorrow.

'You can't go round murdering people!' said Henry. 'It's just not on!'

Elinor chose not to answer this uncontentious remark. The pause between them lengthened, and then, in the last moments that preceded sleep she spoke again: 'You think I'm stupid,' she said, 'but I'm not. I know all about you, Henry. And I'll tell you one thing about us. It's till death us do part. That's the way it is. Right?'

'Right!' said Henry.

She was snoring quite soon after that, but Henry lay awake for a long time, staring into the darkness, waiting for sleep that would not come. He thought about Elinor, and why he was still with her and what it would be like in the weeks and months and years to come. If there was one single thing that she had that was worth something, it was her mysterious quality. She was so hard to explain. He still didn't quite know what she would do next in any given situation. He still wasn't sure what she did or didn't know about him and what she was planning to do with whatever information she had picked up about him. Killing her would have been a very stupid thing to have done. There was, he decided, as he turned over to address himself to sleep, quite a lot of mileage in her yet.

They Came from SW19

For
Ned, Jack and Harry

PART ONE

1

The worst thing about my dad dying was my mum telling me about it.

When I get to forty-two, I hope they shoot me. I know quite a lot of forty-two-year-olds and they are all a real problem. It is a very diffi-cult age. My biology teacher is forty-two, and when I found that out, it explained a lot of things about him.

Forty-two-year-olds – I've noticed this – rarely bother to finish their sentences. You find them hanging round the corners of the house, pouring each other drinks, lighting each other's cigarettes and saying things like, 'Bobbo, of course . . . ' They don't need to say any more than that. Everyone knows what follows. Mere mention of the name 'Bobbo' is enough to activate hundreds of Bobbo stories which everyone has been telling twice a day ever since the 1960s. The Good Old Days! Get with it! The world is changing!

Mum is forty-two.

I know this because she says it, on average, about eight times a day. She always says it differently. Sometimes she sounds really surprised, as if she'd only just been handed her birth certificate. Sometimes she says it as if it is some horrible truth that must be faced. But mostly she says it as if it were my fault.

It isn't my fault! I know if I weren't fourteen she wouldn't be forty-two, but the two things are not, as my biology teacher would say, 'causally related'.

The day my dad died was a hot, dry day in early September. It didn't look like the sort of day on which people died. It was more like the sort of day you expect at the start of a holiday. Even the sky above the tiny roofs of Stranraer Gardens was, from what I could see of it, the deep blue of the sea on travel posters.

I didn't even know he was ill. They had called Mum while I was at school and she had left for the hospital before I got home. She got back from St Edmund's at around eight o'clock. I was sitting in the small room at the head of the stairs – the one he always used to call his office. The front door opened and slammed shut, and the wall next to me shook nervously. My dad was always very proud of the fact that we lived in a six-bedroomed house. It's meant to be a three-bedroomed house, but the Maltese plumber who had it before us put up an amazing number of walls and partitions and screens. From the outside it looks like another dull little terraced house, but when you're inside it you feel like a rat in a maze.

Immediately I heard the front door I switched off his computer. I knew it was her and knew the first thing she would do would be to listen at the bottom of the stairs to see if she could hear the hum of the machine. I've tried muffling it with scarves and old raincoats, but the house is so small that she always hears. She's frightened that it's going to rot my mind and turn me into a hunchback.

She's left it too late. My mind is rotted to compost and I am about as close to a hunchback as you can get.

She waited for a moment at the bottom of the stairs. Then she went through into the kitchen and I heard her moving around in an aimless sort of way. From the kitchen she went into the hall. I heard her making a small, mewing noise.

After a minute or so, I heard her come up the stairs and wait on the landing. Why was she waiting? Had I done something wrong? Of course my mum always moves around the house quietly and fearfully, like a woman listening hard for the nastier kind of burglar. But, as soon as her face came round the door, I knew we were looking at a problem. She worries about everything, but this time I could see it wasn't my inability to practise the saxophone.

She has long, grey hair, and she was brushing it back from her face. She looked like she did the day she told me about – to use her own words – 'the marvellous thing men and women do with their bodies'. For a moment I thought she was going to give me an update on this particular bulletin – the disgusting thing men and women do with their dachshunds, perhaps – but instead she said, 'A terrible thing has happened, Simon!'

She left it there. I was obviously supposed to say, 'What, Mother? Do tell me!' But I didn't. I just carried on looking at the floor. I have very bad eye contact, she tells me. Bad eye contact, bad posture and terrible skin.

'Norman has gone from us!'

Hey, Mum – where's he gone? Barbados or what?

'He's gone, Simon! Gone! Gone! Gone!'

I was getting the message. He was gone. But where, Mum? You know? Be more specific.

She put her hand up to her forehead and started to rub it anxiously. She flinched a little as she did this. Then she lowered her face towards the floor and snaked up sharply so that she was looking into my eyes. 'He has gone,' she said, 'to Higher Ground!'

Something about the way she said this suggested to me that she was not referring to the Lake District.

She sat down heavily on the black sofa in Dad's office. The one he intended to use for clients. I used to fool about and pretend to be a client sometimes, which seemed to amuse my dad a great deal. Mum, looking slightly out of place in the room, brushed the hair back from her eyes. Then she looked off into the middle distance, as if she was trying to find her own personal spotlight.

'O dear Lord Jesus, who died on the cross for us!' she said – she really did – 'Oh God! He was forty-three!'

I did not like the use of the past tense, my friends.

'Oh my God!' she said again, and then, clenching her fists tightly and drumming them against her forehead in double-quick time, she squeaked, 'What does it all mean, Simon?'

This is typical of the way forty-two-year-olds talk. They cannot hold an idea in their heads for very long. A thought occurs to them and out it comes – like bread from a toaster. You have to go through their pronouncements very carefully and decode them. What did all *what* mean?

She got up from the sofa and came towards me. About three yards away, she stopped and shot out both arms. She looked as if she was about to sing. For a moment I thought she *was* going to sing (my mum is capable of such things when we are alone together). But she just stayed there, her arms at an angle of roughly 110 degrees to her body. I didn't give her any encouragement. After a while she put her arms down in the sort of resigned, hopeless way in which people take apart tents or deconstruct folding tables.

'You must,' she said, 'listen to the Lord Jesus!'

She didn't say this with much enthusiasm. Then she stepped back and looked at me sadly. She always looks cold, does my mum.

'I wish you'd tell me your emotions,' she said in a small voice. It was typical really. Something was my fault again. I was supposed to throw myself into her arms, or what? And what emotions? I'm fourteen. I don't have emotions.

Now that her arms were well and truly down, she seemed inclined to test out the old legs. She walked north-north-east, in the direction of the very large colour photograph of me that hangs on the wall next to my dad's desk. I put the points of my fingers together and looked over them at a spot about a foot above her head.

Then she gave it to me straight: 'Norman is dead!'

She paused dramatically. And then added, 'A heart attack.'

Why didn't she say this earlier? Why did it take three minutes of pacing round the room to lead up to it? But, now she was in specific mode, she kept on coming with the facts.

'He died', she went on, 'at five fifty-one. Our time.'

I want to know what time he died in New York, Mum! That'll make it easier. If I'm to get a fix on this event, I'd like to cross-reference it internationally. I want to know what effect this will have on the world money markets.

'His breathing', she went on, 'became "laboured and stertorous" at about three forty-five, and by teatime he was in . . . '

Here she paused, obviously confused about what he was in. Finally she came up with, ' . . . serious difficulties.'

She was making him sound like he was entered for the Fastnet Race. Although – maybe dying is like ocean racing. I wouldn't know. I just wished she'd stop giving me all this blow-by-blow stuff. But she had started and she was going to finish.

'At four-o-three a man called de Lotbinniere came to give him cocoa and take his temperature. But that was a mistake.'

I should think so. From the sound of it, Dad was well past the hot-drinks stage. I looked up. I could see her wondering how far she should go along the de Lotbinniere front.

I hunched my shoulders and sucked in my cheeks. For some reason I found myself wishing I could lay my hand on my glasses. It would have been nice to have something between my eyes and the rest of the world. To take my mind off what she was saying, I started to think about this de Lotbinniere character. What was he doing wandering around hospitals waving thermometers in the faces of dying people? Shouldn't someone put a stop to his activities?

Mum had moved on from de Lotbinniere. She had that glazed expression you often see on her face when she is trying to tell you any story in which she is the main character.

'I went out for a cup of tea from the machine, which was at the end of the corridor by the glass doors and did soup as well. Hot, thick tomato soup, it said. Although I wanted tea . . . '

A haunted look came into her eyes. I could not have said whether this was to do with the soup-versus-tea controversy, or the death of the man to whom she had been married for twenty years.

'It gave me the soup which turned out to be oxtail. And while I was getting my change he had a second coronary thrombosis.'

This would in any normal person's hands have been the end of the story. But not for my mum.

'I was weeping profusely, of course. And hurling myself at Daddy and attempting to take him in my arms.'

This was not something she had done much of when he was alive. Or going through what passes for life at 24 Stranraer Gardens. But, clearly, Norman Britton was a lot more of an attractive proposition now he was no longer with us. Dead people can't answer back can they? Dead people do just what they're told.

'And de Lotbinniere returned at this point and approached me from behind.'

I had known that she would have to return to de Lotbinniere. There is a weird logic to my mother's tales. The small parts always run away with the main narrative, although they themselves are often upstaged by the things that really obsess her – like brands of instant coffee or the design of furniture covers.

'Paul de Lotbinniere is a graduate chemist from Leeds and is only doing nursing as a temporary thing. He hopes to have his own gardening business, although it's proving immensely difficult at the moment. Apparently people have lost interest in gardening.'

Paul de Lotbinniere, eh? Come on, Mum, tell me more, do! Approached you from behind! De Lotbinniere! My man!

I had gone back to looking at the floor. It seemed the safest place to look. Just behind the desk, my dad had stencilled a large thing that looked a bit like a rhubarb leaf with bits chopped out of it. In the middle he had written my name and my date of birth.

SIMON BRITTON

MAY 1ST

1976

He had left spaces for all the brothers and sisters who were supposed to come pattering along after me. Who, mercifully, failed to appear. As I began to look at it, I began to think that this was how my dad's gravestone would look. A name and a date or two and a bit of the old fruit-salad carving.

I didn't cry or anything but decided to move my eyes away. There was a feeling in the room, although I couldn't have said precisely where. I couldn't have said what it was either, but I did know that that was the only good thing about it.

' . . . a cup of tea with de Lotbinniere while he wrote out the certificate and they took Norman away. Oh darling, darling, darling!'

I couldn't work out whether this referred to me or Dad or de Lotbinniere. So I said nothing.

She was on the move again for the next remark. She went over to the black bookshelf in the corner. She put one hand on it and peered in my direction. She seemed to be having trouble getting me in focus. I could see her quite clearly. She has a chapped look, does my mum. She's been cured, like a herring, in the tiny kitchen that my dad could never afford to replace, and round her eyes is a web of small lines etched into her skin. They're marks of worry and of ageing, I know, but sometimes I imagine they're long-healed cuts from a razor and that it's my dad and I who made them.

'He always wanted to be buried at sea.'

This was news to me. I somehow couldn't see Mum and Dad ever having the kind of conversation in which they would get round to talking about such things. But I still said *nothing*. I have to live here. You know?

Mum continued: 'I said, "Why?" He said because he loved the sea. I said, "I like John Lewis's, but that doesn't mean I want to be buried there." He loved John Lewis's. We must remember to be positive about this.'

With this remark she shuffled across the bare, polished floorboards, arms out. At first I thought she was going to try for a clinch, but at the last moment she decided against it. She stood about a yard away, looking suddenly bleak and small and miserable. And then she remembered to be positive. It wasn't that big a deal. Her husband had *died* that was all! I could see her worried little eyes looking for the pluses, and eventually she found one of them.

'He will be in actual, direct contact with Derek and Stella Meenhuis! And he will actually be able to see and touch and experience fully the Lord Jesus Christ!'

Fond as I was of Derek and Stella Meenhuis, I couldn't see that it was worth dying in order to get in touch with them again. Neither am I one of those people who think it will necessarily be a big deal to look God in the face. But my mum had got on course now and she came closer to me, anxious to apologize in case she had mistakenly given the impression of being disconcerted by watching someone die of a heart attack.

'We are going to *talk* to him!' she said, in the sort of eager way she used to recommend one of our cheap holiday breaks in a caravan park on the South Coast. 'We are going to talk as we have never, never talked before, Simon. This isn't bad, darling! It's just . . .'

She struggled for the inappropriate word and, in the end, found it: ' . . . just . . . *different*!'

2

I have a very bad attitude towards death. I'm terrified of it.

I know this is wrong. I know that there'll be bright lights and that Jesus will lift me up in his arms and that I will find myself in a large and harmonious choir – something that is never likely to happen to me while I am alive – but I don't *look forward* to stiffing.

I couldn't even work up much enthusiasm on my dad's behalf. While my mum started on one of her favourite topics – the precise geographical layout of heaven – I found myself looking round the room to remind myself of the few small things that had been his, before the loving hands of the Almighty cradled him in bliss eternal. It's pathetic, I know, but looking at furniture he'd sat on, or pictures he'd looked at, seemed to help.

As she droned on about the wonderful quality of the light Over There (she always makes it sound like one of my dad's brochures for his holiday cottages in Connemara) I looked down at the old man's desk. Below me, just to my right, was a pair of his glasses. He left them there, beside the Anglepoise lamp, because he only used them for reading. Next to the glasses was a letter that he must have been looking at before he got up to walk to wherever he had his first heart attack. At the bottom of the page the guy had written, rather optimistically, 'See you Thursday.'

You should never say things like that. You never know if you're going to see anyone on Thursday. When you kiss goodbye to your wife (or whoever) in the morning, don't say, 'See you tonight.' That's tempting providence. Say, '*Might* see you tonight.' And if she gives you a hard time about it, you just tell her. There is no guarantee.

I saw those glasses horribly clearly. As if they were correcting my sight, from where they lay, on the shabby wooden desk. I could hear everything very precisely too. In the street outside, someone was playing a radio. The song on the radio was the Pet Shop Boys singing 'What Have I Done to Deserve This?' I could hear the Maltese plumber's water pipes singing along with them and, above my mum's head, see the shelf that my dad had put up in the spring of 1986. It took him the whole spring to do it, but it still slopes, dangerously, towards the floor.

My mum shook her lank, grey hair and blinked like something from the small-mammal house. She'd moved on from the nature of Heavenly Light and had got on to how we would all float around like *spacemen* when we reached the Halls of Jesus and how we would not need to eat *as such* but would always be sort of *three-quarters of the way through a most delicious meal*. Something about my expression must have told her that even this was not going to get me to look on the bright side of this issue. She looked at me rather plaintively and said, 'Auntie Diana will be so pleased to see him!'

I didn't agree or disagree with this.

'They always had so much in common,' she went on. Then she folded her hands together, lowered her head and, without asking anyone's permission, went straight into public prayer.

My mum is a leading member of the First Church of Christ the Spiritualist, South Wimbledon. Why didn't I mention that? What do you take me for? It isn't something I advertise. Only a few people at school know. It is, for reasons that will become clear, impossible to keep it from the neighbours, but whenever I am out with First Spiritualists I try to make it clear from my posture and expression that I am absolutely nothing to do with them.

I don't know whether there was ever a Second Spiritualist Church of South Wimbledon, but, if there was, I guess the First Church soon ran it out of town. The First Church has some very heavy characters in it *indeed*. In spite of a Youth Drive and the Suffer Little Children campaign, not many of them are under forty-five. But even the wrinkliest members can still act funky.

Four years ago, for example, my mum and I were on the Used Handbag Stand at the twice-yearly Bring and Buy Sale, when Rita Selfridge offered to buy my mum's trousers. The ones she was wearing. She offered her five pounds for them and asked her if they

309

qualified as Used or Nearly New. My mum didn't do anything – she never does if people are rude to her – but my mum's friend, Mabel, who is seventy-five, threw herself at Rita Selfridge and bit her, quite badly, on the neck.

The First Spiritualist Church of South Wimbledon was founded early this century, by a woman named Ella Walsh. They don't actually use the word 'founded'. What she did was to 'renew' a body known as the Sisters of Harmony and Obedience, a Church which had been in her family for over a hundred years. Ella Walsh was the great-granddaughter of Old Mother Walsh of Ealing, of whom you may have heard. Old Mother Walsh was a prophetess who lived in a hut very close to what is now the North Circular Road. She had a dream in which she saw a huge snake wind itself around the planet. Fire came out of its mouth, and it bore the inscription TWO THOUSAND YEARS GO BY. It talked as well. It said that a woman was coming who would save the world and make it whole. She would be announced by a boy prophet 'of pure heart and mind' and, when she came into her ministry, 'all mannere of thynge would be welle'. If she didn't, it was going to gobble up the world. Some snake!

After Old Mother Walsh died, her memory was kept alive by her daughters and granddaughters. The Walshes bred like rabbits. Eliza Walsh, for example, had no fewer than six phantom pregnancies as well as the twelve that produced babies. Finally, around 1890, just after the Walsh family moved to Wimbledon, Ella Walsh, the Mother and Renewer of the Sisters of Harmony, was born.

Ella took the Sisters in a new and exciting direction. She kept some of the rules and regulations and printed a limited edition of *The Sayings of Old Mother Walsh* and added her own angle. She brought in Spiritualism, and soon there just wasn't room for much of Old Mother Walsh's doctrine, even though scraps of it survived and were still about when I was young. 'Evacuate the noise of the bowel in your own place!' for example. Members of the First Church still rush out of the room if they suspect they are about to fart.

Like all Churches, the first thing it did was to set about getting some money in the bank. Ella Walsh met a guy called Fox, and, more importantly, got in touch with his brother, who had died four years earlier in a boating accident near Chichester.

Fox was *loaded*.

Ella Walsh and Fox spent many a happy hour talking to Fox's brother. He was, it turned out, feeling pretty good about being dead. Apparently being dead was a lot more fun than being alive. They had snooker and whisky and quite good boating facilities over on the Other Side. And, after they'd contacted Fox's brother, they called up all sorts of other people – including Robespierre and William Thackeray. It was all such fun that Ella married Fox and Fox gave her thousands of pounds to build the First Spiritualist Church.

She must have creamed off most of the money, because the First Spiritualist Church makes your average scout hut look like the Taj Mahal. It is a kind of tin and concrete shack, somewhere at the back of South Wimbledon station, and I'm always hoping some enterprising businessman will see that it has restaurant potential and offer us money for it.

It has no restaurant potential.

On the back wall there is a letter from Sir Arthur Conan Doyle, thanking the First Spiritualist Church for all their help and saying how great it was to talk to them. The letter is signed, in his absence, by one Rebecca Furlong, and it's only when you look at the date that you realize it was written fifteen years after Sir Arthur snuffed it. He sounds pretty chirpy, and gives no indication, in the text, that he has croaked. He doesn't really mention much about himself at all. But maybe after you've been on the Other Side for a certain length of time it all gets pretty samey. Certainly, dead people seem pretty keen to get on down to the First Spiritualist Church of South Wimbledon, so there can't be a lot happening over there.

If I ever die they won't see me for dust.

Pike and Hannah Dooley won't have the chance to ask me how am I doing and do they have skateboards in the afterlife. Marjorie can use every single one of her internationally renowned psychic tricks on me and I will guarantee not to respond. And Quigley, oh Mr Quigley – he can rap the table for as long as he likes but I will not be answering!

They did great business, apparently, after the First World War. In the early 1920s you couldn't get in. Just before the war, Ella and Fox had had a daughter called Rose and – guess what! – she turned out to be a Psychical Prodigy. Rose, as far as I can gather, was a real all-rounder. She wasn't as hot on Jesus as her mum had been, but when it came to automatic writing, Ouija board, ectoplasm and something rather dodgy-sounding called cabinet work, there was no one to touch her in South London. About the only thing Rose Fox didn't do was levitate, but, as she was nearly sixteen stone, that is hardly surprising.

I saw her when she was in her mid-seventies. She rolled into Sunday service supported by Mr and Mrs Quigley and gave us this big speech about how the spirits never talked to her any more. The last time anyone from the Great Beyond had given her their valuable time was, apparently, during something called the Suez Crisis, when she had had a short conversation with the late Admiral Nelson. 'They want me to join them,' she said. 'Their silence beckons me!' And then, as people frequently do down at the First Spiritualist Church of South Wimbledon, she burst into tears.

I quite often burst into tears on my way there. On one occasion, when I was about seven, my mum had to untwist my hands from about every gatepost in Stranraer Gardens. 'It's not as if it's the Spanish Inquisition,' she used to snap.

No, it was the First Spiritualist Church of South Wimbledon! That was what was worrying me. If it had been the Spanish Inquisition it would have been fine. I thought I knew where I stood with the Spanish Inquisition.

Some people blamed Rose Fox for the decline of the First Spiritualist Church. She went too far, people said. There were all these poor bastards who had lost relatives in the First World War, trying to get in touch with them. But with Rose it was hard to hear anything through the table-rapping or the squelch of ectoplasm being flung about the room by men in black jerseys. She started to take photographs of the spirits too, and that is how she came to be accused of trickery.

'Did I ever tell you', my dad said to me once, when we were

walking, as we often did, in the direction of the off-licence, 'about how Rose Fox was photographed beneath the spirit reality of Franz Josef of Austria?'

'I don't believe you did,' I replied.

Whereupon, from his pocket he produced a black-and-white photograph of a plump woman in a loose white dress. It was hard to make out what was behind her – a chair, a table and what looked like a wardrobe of some kind. But what was directly above her head was easier to see. Hanging in the gloom, at a height of about five feet, was the gigantic face of an elderly man with mutton-chop whiskers and a helmet with a steel point on it. I happened to know, because we were doing it at school, that the face balancing on Rose's bonce was that of the last ruler of the Austro-Hungarian Empire.

'My God,' I said, 'it looks just like him!'

'It does, doesn't it?' said Dad.

He wrinkled his lips appreciatively, as if he was already tasting the first drink of the day. 'It also', he went on, 'looks amazingly like a photograph of the old boy that appeared in the *Illustrated London News* in June 1924!'

That was typical of my dad. He always took great delight in any reports of trickery. And anything that reflected badly on Rose Fox, who was a great heroine of my mum's, always went down particularly well.

The worst thing Rose Fox did was not to organize spirit photographs of internationally famous dead people – it was to get married. She got hitched to a man called Stuart Quigley, in the year the Second World War broke out. Quigley died in 1950 and was so boring that no one could bear to speak to him much, even after he'd croaked. But, before he opened that last little door into the unknown, he managed to make Rose pregnant. And so it was that in 1948 Rose Fox gave birth to the man born to make my life a misery – Albert Roger Quigley, MA – part scout leader, part amateur opera singer, part Christian, part Spiritualist and 100 per cent complete and utter arsehole.

Quigley is an assistant bank manager. My mum once took me into his branch to show me his name, which is written up on a board. He is billed just below someone called Mervyn Snyde, who looks after International Securities. I think they are making a grave error of judgement in letting anyone know he's there. Quigley, like quite a few other members of the First Church, is downright sinister. It was quite horrible to think that someone like him should be left alive when my dad was dead.

I didn't start crying until after my mum had left the room. But the thing that started me off wasn't the fact that Quigley was still above ground. Or the thought of my dad lying on a slab with all his dental-work showing. It wasn't the thought that I would never see him again, because he still seemed too real for me to imagine that as a possibility. I mean, that guy in the letter, right? He'd planned his Thursday round Norman, you know? And I had so many things that I could have been doing with him, now, tomorrow, the day after tomorrow, that it was literally impossible to believe that he wouldn't be doing *any* of them.

The thing that started me off was the last thing my mum said before she headed off down the stairs. She tried a tentative embrace, patted my head vaguely and went across to the door. She looked, I thought, almost pleased with herself as she turned back to me. I didn't crack. I just kept right on looking at her, with my head slightly to one side. I think I was trying to look intelligent. My dad always used to say that intelligence was the only thing that made humans bearable. Which makes his ever being involved with the First Spiritualist Church even more puzzling.

'Over There,' she said, 'they are probably organizing some form of official welcome for him!'

I goggled at her. All I could think was that my dad hated parties. Especially official ones. In order to avoid replying, I looked out of the window. Over Here, the late afternoon sun was slanting down on to the impassive red brick of Stranraer Gardens. I could see our cat slink into the opposite garden, her shoulders pressed towards the ground.

'We are going to be talking to him in the very near future,' she said. Then she walked back towards me and nodded significantly. 'I am sure that he has a great deal to discuss with you. And I have a very great deal to tell *him* now that he has Passed Across!'

There was something almost menacing in the way she said this. She straightened her narrow shoulders and gave me a blink from those worried little eyes of hers. 'Conversations with Norman,' she said, 'are only just beginning!'

With a kind of smirk, she bounced out of the room. I could hear her steps on the stairs, sounding, as usual, a note of warning, of some kind of trouble on the way.

That would be the last thing the poor old bastard wanted. He finally gets through with the mortgage and the weekly shopping and putting the rubbish in a grey plastic bag and trying to fit it into the dustbin, when what? She's calling him up and telling him the news about the latest jumble sale and my failure to pay attention in French. I would have thought the only plus about being dead was not having to listen to her any more.

She'll have him back before he knows it, I thought. *She'll send his ghost out to Sainsbury's.*

It was Sainsbury's that did it. I suddenly saw my dad wheeling the trolley round the delicatessen section. The way his face lit up at the sight of the salamis and the smoked fish was beautiful to behold. I saw him purse his lips as he sorted through the bottles of *rosé* wine, trying to find that special one that was going to make an evening with my mother bearable. I saw him finger his paunch at the check-out counter and grin when he caught sight of the chocolate biscuits, Swiss rolls, soft drinks and all the other things I had managed to smuggle aboard the wagon. I saw his big, round face and neatly combed, balding hair, and I saw the heavy gold ring on his left hand. I saw him. You know? I saw him.

It was only then that I thought: *He's not coming back any more. I'll never see him again as long as I live. And I may not see him when I die, either.*

I put my face down on his desk then, and cried like a baby.

3

A friend of my mum's once said that my dad looked a little seedy, and at the time I was very offended. But there was some truth in the remark. When I saw his clothes, without him, in the weeks after his death, I could see that that was what they were. The suits were neither flash nor respectable. The jerseys were all torn and ragged, and the pairs of shoes (my dad loved buying shoes) were never quite expensive enough to achieve whatever effect he had intended.

But he was more than his clothes. None of his possessions made sense without him. And what made it even harder to understand that he really had died was the fact that, as is usual in the First Spiritualist Church, he was not buried. Not by us anyway. A day or so after he was transferred from the hospital to the funeral parlour, the undertaker rang my mum and said, in an unctuous tone, 'Will you be wanting to arrange a viewing, Mrs Britton?'

'No,' said my mum.

'What I mean is,' said the undertaker, sounding a touch peevish, 'he is here at the moment. If you want to see him . . . '

He hasn't run off or anything! You know?

I was listening to all of this on the extension – which is the only way you ever find out anything in our house – and this last remark was followed by the longest pause in British telephone history. I seriously thought my mum had gone off to make a cup of tea.

Eventually the undertaker said, in a wheedling tone, 'He looks very nice now.'

Come on down! We've laid on tea and biscuits and a video!

'He really does look at peace. It's amazing what we can do!'

I thought this was a bit much, frankly. I wouldn't have said my dad was a good-looking guy, but I didn't think he needed the services of an embalmer to make him palatable.

'No one,' said my mum, eventually, 'will be coming to see Norman.'

'Oh . . . ' said the undertaker, going back into peevish mode. 'If that's how you feel . . . '

In that case we'll take him out of the window. He's taking up space! We'll screw the old lid down and get on with it.

'Anyway,' the guy said finally, 'he will be here till about a quarter to five . . . '

So boogie on down while you have the chance! I mean, what do you require here? A funeral or what?

'No, thank you very much,' said Mum. 'Thank you for the opportunity of a viewing, but in this instance the family must decline.'

The guy on the other end of the line was obviously dismayed at this unwillingness to test-drive his mortician's skills.

'My Church', said my mum, with a certain amount of prim pride, 'does not believe in burial as such. We give you *carte blanche* as far as Norman's corpse is concerned. Do with it as you will!'

'I see,' said the undertaker.

You could sense him trying to work out what this signified. Did it mean absolutely anything went? Were they to be allowed to stick him in a trolley and wheel him round the local supermarket? Or give every last bit of him away for medical research?

'You do . . . er . . . want him buried?' he said finally.

'Buried? Not buried? What's the difference?' said my mum.

'Well,' said the undertaker, 'to us, quite considerable.'

'Is it?'

'Well, we don't usually find ourselves dealing with non-burying situations. Cremation and burial are, so to speak, our *raisons d'être*.'

'Quite,' said my mum, rather meanly.

It was possible, of course, that the guy was wondering whether to give my dad the full five-star treatment. *Burmese mahogany,* you could hear him thinking, *silver-plated handles, top-quality professional mourners.* Indeed, when the bill came in, it looked as if we had been charged for exactly that.

'Are you a Hindu?' he asked eventually, with some caution.

'Certainly not,' snapped my mum.

He was well and truly stumped now.

'Well, Mrs Britton,' he said in the end, 'we shall try and dispose of your husband's body in a way that we hope will be suitable as far as you are concerned.'

'What you do with his body is irrelevant. I will be talking to Norman in the next few days, and I assure you that one of the things we will not be discussing is his funeral.'

'Indeed,' said the undertaker. Then, clearly desperate to regain some professional self-respect, he said, rather brightly, as if none of this conversation had taken place at all, 'Would you like any photographs of the event?'

My mum started laughing at this point. I was rather with her actually. 'Photographs?' she said. 'Photographs?'

I think the guy was simply wondering whether he would be required to furnish proof that he hadn't sold the cadaver to some fly-by-night surgeon.

'Norman', she said pityingly, 'has gone to a place more beautiful and more peaceful than anything you could imagine. You can't take photographs of it and stick it on the mantelpiece. You can't get package holidays to it. But those of us who have talked to people who have had first-hand experience of it know it is utterly, utterly beautiful!'

'I'm sure,' said the undertaker feelingly.

And, leaving the poor sod trying to work out for himself exactly what place she was talking about, Mum put the phone down.

This must have happened about a week after Dad died. But I don't remember much about the days that followed that first, awful conversation with my mum. Perhaps because the night that followed it was so eventful.

It was hot that autumn. The evening they took him to the hospital went out like a Viking funeral. I didn't cry for long. I was frightened she might hear me. I cleaned up my face and sat looking out of the window. The plane-tree opposite looked how I felt. It hadn't even got the energy to turn brown. But the sun was going gently, winking back at me from the windows of the neighbours' houses in the way it can do, even when someone you care about dies. A few streets away, on the main road, a police car or an ambulance made the noise I most connect with cities – the pushy, important wail of a siren.

Down the street I caught sight of a few stalwarts from the congregation, trying to park a car. You can never keep them away from a death. But they were on the job with unusual speed. Maybe someone Over There had tipped them off.

Like many other things in the First Spiritualist Church, the parking was a team effort. Hannah Dooley, in a tweed skirt and a double-breasted jacket, was waving madly at the bonnet, while Leo Pike was sneering at the boot through his gold-rimmed glasses. I couldn't work out what his expression meant. Maybe it just meant that Pike drove a large, uncontrollable Ford that was at least ten years old. This was a brand-new Audi. The guy in it was important business.

The door opened and Quigley got out. Yo, Quigley! New wheels! You tapped into the bank's computer, or what? Pike held the door for him. No one cringes quite like Pike. Humbling himself in the sight of God is not enough for him. He would crawl to me if I let him. As I watched his wintry little face, his shoulder hunched in his tweed jacket, his constant, half-bowing motions as Quigley emerged, I found myself wondering, once again, how it was that someone so humble could be, on occasions, so fantastically menacing.

Hannah Dooley loves Pike, but the reverse is not the case. Maybe Hannah loves him because she loves all the things people throw away, and Pike has the look of something left out for the binmen. Left out but not taken. If I was a refuse disposal operative, I would have nothing to do with him, but Hannah Dooley gives him the kind of tenderness she bestows on old chairs and smelly bits of carpet. She pulls them out of people's gardens and waves them at the householders who are guilty of casting them aside. With her wrinkled face bright with eagerness, she calls, 'Are you *really* throwing this away?' To which my dad always used to reply, with scarcely controlled fury, 'We are trying to, Miss Dooley. We are trying to!'

Quigley was followed out on to the pavement by his wife and daughter. The wife is called Marjorie, and says things like, 'Is there a plentiful sufficiency of baps?' The daughter is called Emily. She is good at the cello. Need I say more?

Some years ago, Marjorie, Emily, Hannah and Pike (who is a kind of unofficial chairman of these three) all decided that I was going to learn to play the saxophone properly. They bought me the examination syllabus. They bought me a year's supply of reeds. They used to leave my instrument outside my bedroom door after evening prayers at our house. But they had reckoned without me. They couldn't actually wrap my lips around the horn and inflate my lungs until I made a noise. Only my dad was allowed to hear me practise.

Hannah Dooley shambled up to Quigley and started to whisper something in the great man's ear. Quigley likes Hannah Dooley, but you never know which way he is going to go. I could see his big, bushy, black beard waggle up and down as he nodded at something she said, then he shot a quick glance at her when he thought she wasn't looking. Sometimes he stroked the ends of his beard and lifted his nose rather sensually as he did so. Quigley is proud of his beard. I think it's the kind of beard that conceals a great deal more than the owner's face. When he had finished the listening/stroking routine, he turned smartly and walked towards our house. Even from the first-floor window you could see that his hand was in his right trouser pocket and was grasping his balls firmly. Just in case anyone tried to give them ideas.

The *whole* Quigley family was wearing flared trousers, including Emily. Flares and bright colours. When someone croaks in the First Spiritualist Church, you let the relatives know you don't feel negative. Pike was last across the road, waiting, as he usually does, for a car to come into sight before scampering in front of it, like a spider. Pike is really keen to rip through the gauze that separates us from Sir Arthur Conan Doyle. Maybe he thinks he'll get his hair back on the other side.

Quigley rang the bell. You could tell it was Quigley. He hit it hard, as he always does. He kept the volume very steady and – the giveaway this – he left it that extra five seconds, as if to say: *It's no use hiding behind the sofas, guys! I know you're in there!* Downstairs I heard my mum scurry out of the kitchen and scrabble at the door.

There was a pause as she opened it, then Quigley said, 'Great day for Norman!'

'Yes,' said mum, rather feebly.

'He's crossed!' said Hannah Dooley.

'We're so pleased for him,' mumbled Pike.

'Yes,' said mum, again sounding as if she was past feeling pleased for anyone.

I heard Quigley's big feet come into the hall. 'Have you experienced him yet?' I heard him say.

I assumed he was talking about my dad. He certainly sounded very up about the whole dying business. And I knew to my certain knowledge, that, after me, my dad was Quigley's least favourite person in the Wimbledon area.

'I . . . I'm not sure,' said Mum.

Mum is never fantastically sure about her spiritual powers. And the Quigleys do nothing to bolster her confidence in this area.

'I sort of . . . had a whiff of him on the stairs.'

'Yes!' This from Mrs Quigley.

'But then,' said Mum, 'he was always on the stairs.'

He was actually. He was always on the stairs or in the hall. He hung around his own house like he was a lodger did my dad. As I sat listening to the Quigleys, I could almost see the poor old sod. I could see his ragged little moustache, his beaky nose, and I could hear his voice, rolling the words round his mouth like he was a voice-over for a cheese commercial: 'I never wanted to be a travel agent!'

That was a frightening one. There were guys out there who could just *make* you be a travel agent. And presumably the same people were lying in wait for me. They could saunter up and offer me even worse fates than the ones they had forced on my old man. 'Ever fancied being a *greengrocer*, Simon? If you want to keep the use of your legs, I advise you to get your head round the old *fruit and veg*.'

The Quigleys clumped through to the kitchen.

'Ohhh,' I heard Marjorie say. 'You've got a new bin unit!'

She sounded really excited about this. Hearing her reminded me of my dad's reaction the first time he had seen it. He had said it was the most elegant wooden sculpture to surround a plastic bucket he had ever seen. He also said it was something called 'post-modern'.

Which, I think, is a term of approval. He was at Oxford, my dad, but he never did anything with it, apparently.

'It's actually a bin-*housing* unit,' my mum was saying.

I sat on the stairs and pulled at my T-shirt. If you can fluff it out, it makes you look as if you have quite a respectable chest. When I had finished fluffing out my T-shirt, I held out my right arm and tried to coax out my bicep. It did not seem to be its night.

Downstairs they started laughing about something. Emily was joining in, the way she always does. I sat there, thinking about my dad. I couldn't face going downstairs and telling everyone how terrific it was that he had stiffed. The window alongside me, which looks out over what Dad always called 'the most disgusting back passage in London', was coated with fine, grey dust. Why did we always live in places that other people had tried, and failed, to care for? And why was it we could never make them right? Once upon a time, years, years ago, I could have sworn we had lived in a big, clean house where the lights always worked and there was a garden you could go into without stepping in something nasty.

I suppose Dad had made money once, a long time ago. Well, he certainly wouldn't be making any now. If they have cash on the Other Side it's probably a bit like those currencies they have in eastern Europe. Not even worth earning.

After a while I heard a snuffling sound on the landing. When I investigated, I found Pike rifling through the airing cupboard. He was holding up a green jacket.

'Was this your father's?'

'Yes,' I said.

'Nice jacket,' said Pike.

I went up to him and took it from his hands. I'm only fourteen but I'm as big as Pike. I put my face very close to his and said, 'I'd better hang on to it, don't you think? In case he drops back for it.'

Pike snorted. 'Oh,' he said, 'you don't come back in the body. You don't come back as yourself.'

'What are you coming back as, Pike?' I said. 'A natterjack toad? That might be a big improvement come to that . . .'

Pike snickered. 'Toads are nice.'

'Compared to you, Pike, the toad is Man's Best Friend!'

I heard a cough in the hall below. There, looking up at us, was Quigley. I could see more than I wanted of his teeth and nostrils. He spread his arms wide, as if he was about to conduct an imaginary choir – something he quite often does at bus-stops or (alarming this one) when driving the car.

'Simon,' he said. 'We have come a-visiting!'

The last time my Dad had seen Quigley was in the First Spiritualist Church Five-a-Side Football Team. Quigley had somehow got them a game with a nearby public school, and an enormous boy called Hoxton had put no fewer than eight goals past my dad.

'Jump high high high, Norman!' Quigley had called in a light voice as they ran back after goal number nine had slipped past my dad.

'And stuff the ball up your arse!' my dad had called in a loud, fruity voice.

'New car,' I said.

Quigley smirked. 'The Lord rewards His own.'

Pike was slobbering over the banisters. It was time to go.

'Well, Mr Quigley,' I said. 'I have to be going out now.'

'Simon,' said Quigley, 'don't you want to get in touch with Norman? He's very, very, *very* strong at the moment. This is a very crucial time in his spiritual development.'

I heard my mum call: 'Will you have some root beer, Mr Quigley?'

The First Spiritualist Church disapproves of all alcoholic drinks unless they are made 'at home and cleanly in the sight of the Lord'. Which leaves the more adventurous a lot of scope for 300-per-cent-proof spirits of the kind that are best taken in through the scalp. The last time my dad had finished off a bottle of his home-made gin he had tried to put a pair of his underpants on Quigley's head. Quigley had beseeched him in the sight of the Lord to abjure 'strong wine and wickedness'. After that I was sent to bed.

I started down the stairs.

'I'm sorry, Mr Quigley,' I said. 'I have to go out.'

Quigley put his head to one side. 'And where is young Simon going to, I wonder? Is he going to tell us where he's going, do you think? Or what time he's going to be back? What do you think, Mother?'

This was to Mrs Quigley, who, with my mum beside her, had appeared at the kitchen door.

'I'm going,' I said in a quiet, patient voice, 'to see if any Unidentified Flying Objects have landed on the Common. I'll be back for supper. OK?'

4

It is a perfectly reasonable assumption that there are intelligent beings somewhere else in the universe. They may be more than intelligent. They may be very, very intelligent. So there is a *possibility that they are on their way to the earth*. And if they do get to land I don't see why it shouldn't be in sw19. That's my position.

If you look at the literature, you will discover that the aliens have landed in quite a number of suburbs all over the world. A group of squat but distinctly humanoid creatures dropped in on a residential district just outside Munich in the winter of 1979. A bunch of 'leathery-faced people in cloaks' were seen coming out of a large silver object in a commuters' sector of Barcelona as recently as 1989.

I am not saying I have seen them. But a hell of a lot of perfectly sane people *have*. I am not denying that irresponsible individuals invent sightings. Or that the ufological movement has as many crazies associated with it as, say, the Conservative Party. I do not believe, for example, that Hans Kluigtermeier was, and I quote, 'anally raped by a group of nine entities in red cloaks just outside the town of Poissy-le-Vaugin in northern France, *last September*'. But the volume of evidence is so considerable that it is irresponsible to ignore it. Why, I ask you, should we be the only intelligent life anywhere in the galaxy? They are out there. And they may well be on their way here.

My friend Mr Marr is actually an electrical engineer. I mean he really does go out and mend things for the Council. No one has tapped him on the shoulder and tried to take him away in a van just because he chooses to clip on the old infra-red binoculars and get out there on the Common every night, clutching a tape-recorded message saying WELCOME in thirteen languages.

There are those who say he *should* have been taken away in a van years ago. I know this. He knows this. But he is pretty calm about it.

'I know I may never see them, Simon,' he says to me sometimes. 'But if they *do* come, and if they decide to come to Wimbledon, I want to be there to see it!' Which seems reasonable.

He's a bit like those people at the January sales. You know? Who camp out for weeks in advance because they're terrified of missing a bargain. Or the guys who doss down outside the Royal Albert Hall because they want to be first in with a chance to hear some brilliant cellist.

He was waiting for me on the corner with his Thermos.

'Who knows', he said, as we walked up the hill towards the War Memorial, 'what will come out of the sky tonight?'

I didn't answer this.

'It's a nice, clear night for them, anyway,' he went on.

'Indeed, Mr Marr,' I said. 'I hate to think of them getting wet.'

He laughed. He does have a sense of humour does Mr Marr. You can take the piss out of him and he doesn't mind.

'Weather is no problem for the aliens. They laugh at weather.'

I didn't ask how he knew this. Partly because, on the corner of the street, I could see Purkiss and Walbeck waiting for us. Walbeck was jumping up and down on the pavement and grinning. As we got closer, he pointed a finger at the sky and shook his head violently. Purkiss laughed.

Purkiss is small with a shock of black hair and the beginnings of a hump. Walbeck is huge but lost. They both wear anoraks. Walbeck is deaf and dumb. But he is fantastically talkative. I've worn out many an envelope in conversation with Walbeck.

As usual, Mr Marr just nodded to them as we passed and they fell in behind us. He lets them come along, but they're not top-quality ufologists. They're apparently very unscientific in their attitude to the beings who are hurtling through space-time towards Wimbledon Common. I often worry whether the four of us are *enough*. You know? What will it be like when they spin down out of the upper atmosphere and cop a load of me, Mr Marr, Purkiss and Walbeck? Will they be impressed?

'You're a dark horse, Simon,' Mr Marr said as we climbed the hill towards the Common. It was dark now, but still warm. We were moving past bigger houses than ours. Houses that seemed to put out their secrets for all to see, but were, nonetheless, more mysterious than the cramped terraces of Stranraer Gardens. 'You never say what's on your mind.'

'Do you reckon?' I said.

He looked at me sideways.

'But you're on the right side, anyway!'

Mr Marr reckons that we as a society are not doing enough about the extraterrestrials. When you think of all the money that is put into medical research and the English National Opera – why can't we put aside a few quid to welcome the boys in the saucers. You know? I mean, what are they going to think?

He's particularly keen on what he calls 'instrumentation'. I think this comes from being an engineer. He has instruments for listening to them, instruments for picking up their lights, instruments for talking to them and an amazing variety of gadgets for making the long night watches easier. Things to rest your head against, things to put your feet on, little chairs to make sure you are pointing towards the night sky at the right angle and little trays that enable you to have your dinner and keep your eyes on the Crab Nebula at the same time. We all miss a lot of stuff, Mr Marr says. We wander around looking at the ground – and up there there's a party going on!

His wife died ten years ago. She was apparently the most beautiful woman you could ever wish to look at. Her name was Mabel. I've seen her photograph and it obviously doesn't do her justice. She has just the one head, but she definitely has an alien look about her. She was a terrific cook though, Mr Marr says.

'Well . . . ' he said. 'Anything happen today?'

'My dad died!'

He was the first person I had had to tell. For some reason it made me feel tremendously important. It didn't seem a difficult thing to say. It was the sort of thing real men said to each other. I was so concerned with actually saying it, rather than thinking what it meant, that it came out wrong. I wanted to sound serious but unweepy. Instead, I sounded positively chirpy about the whole business.

Mr Marr stopped. 'Oh Simon!' he said. 'Oh *Simon!*'

He's from the North is Mr Marr. He has this funny voice and this great big tuft of ginger hair that sticks up in surprise from his head. He's really nice.

'Should you be out tonight?'

'It's OK, Mr Marr. Honestly.'

Purkiss looked at Walbeck. He pointed at me. Then he raised his hands above his head. Then he pointed at the ground and made what looked like shovelling movements. They could have been something different, of course. It's always hard to tell with Purkiss.

Walbeck was looking at him, as usual, in total puzzlement. I don't think he and Purkiss really communicate. They resent being so much together, I think – which, from both their points of view, is an entirely understandable reaction.

Mr Marr took over. He set himself in front of Walbeck and said in a slow, clear voice, 'Simon's father is dead.'

Walbeck nodded seriously. Then he turned round and started to wander off down the street. Maybe he thought Mr Marr had said, 'Go home to bed.' It's that bad with Walbeck.

Mr Marr turned to Purkiss. 'Bring him back,' he said, 'and don't try to tell him things. Write them down, OK?'

'Yes, Mr Marr,' said Purkiss, in a high, squeaky voice.

Somehow all this was helpful. When I'm around Purkiss and Walbeck, it almost seems a plus that I am me. Mr Marr was making off up the street with big, confident strides, clearly anxious not to miss any aliens.

I must say that it felt like a good night for them. Although it was late summer, it was still warm. That wind seemed to promise something. There was no one now on the quiet, wide streets that surround the Common. The thought that out there, somewhere between the stars and the moon, was my dad's soul (I believe in the soul) gave the night a special feeling. As we came up to Carew Road and headed towards the War Memorial, I kept my eyes on the planets.

Over to the left was something that I thought might be Venus. It turned out to be the masthead of the Sun Life Assurance Building. I looked to see if I could make out the Great Bear or Orion's Belt, but all I came up with was a group of stars that seemed to be laid out in the shape of a condom. Was there, I wondered, a star called Durex Major? When you looked closer, however, you could see that it looked more like an aubergine. Or, indeed, a Renault Espace.

I see condoms everywhere. I am obsessed with them. It's pathetic. The chances that I'll ever get to use one for anything remotely like the purpose for which it was intended are very, very low. The best thing I could do with one, really, would be to pull it over my head and breathe in deeply.

I gave up and looked at the moon. You know where you are with the moon. It was in the usual place – just to the right of Wimbledon Public Library – and it was the usual colour – De Luxe Oatmeal, the colour we've painted our bathroom. It has lost its glamour has the moon. Too many people have been there. These days, they say, the Sea of Tranquillity is littered with probes and undercarriages and the remains of astronaut picnics.

It's the far galaxies that get to me. All I want to hear about is Sirius Four and Betelgeuse and Star BXY5634256 in the Milky Way. Stars that are light years away, and moving away from us at speeds you couldn't begin to imagine.

Khan says it's all to do with something called String Theory. Khan is in my class, and, although he is only about three feet high and his father is an Islamic sex-maniac, he does know about physics. Apparently the world was all string before it was what it is now. Or something like string. It's full of things that are so dense that matter sort of pours into them – white dwarves and black holes. And it makes a noise too. There's a sort of background hum out there, like static on a radio. There's Solar Wind and Solar Dust and Bargons and Protons and, according to Khan, something called Axion Radio, which is not a local broadcasting station but some vibration that happened *minutes* after that key moment 150 billion years ago when everything was in excess of 1 billion Kelvin. Don't ask me who Kelvin is – some friend of Sharon's or Tracy's I suppose.

I don't *know*. That's what makes looking at the sky so absolutely amazing.

'I liked your dad,' Mr Marr was saying, while I thought about the universe. The War Memorial was in sight now. Beyond it was a dark patch of grass and the shallow pond next to which Mr Marr always takes up his observation post. 'He was a nice bloke.'

'Yes,' I said, 'he was a nice bloke.'

My dad always used to say that you should be very suspicious of people who said you were a nice bloke. It means they really despise you, apparently.

My dad said a lot of things that were quite hard to fathom. I didn't think it was true that Mr Marr despised him. Dad despised himself, I suppose. At least he said he did. When he wasn't claiming to be the greatest unpublished novelist in western Europe.

He hadn't always been a travel agent. He had been a lot of other things while he was trying to be a novelist, but he had ended up as a travel agent. Which, apparently, was the worst possible thing that could have happened. Some jobs, he used to say, go quite well with writing. A guy called Trollope worked at the Post Office. Melvyn Bragg is a television personality. But, according to my dad, there has never been a really successful writer who was also a travel agent. The two just do not go together.

'He was a disappointed man in many ways,' said Mr Marr, who had moved into the past tense a touch too easily for my liking, 'but he was a man of real calibre.'

I nodded. I just do not *get* remarks like that. *Calibre!* Get serious why don't you? Mr Marr would never have said that about Dad when he was alive. He used to drink with him sometimes, but I don't think he knew him well enough to decide whether or not he was of *real calibre*. Whatever that may mean. And, what, while we were at it, did he mean by 'disappointed'? It wasn't his fault they made Dad become a travel agent and forced him to marry my mum.

Mr Marr was practically running now. He always gets like that when he's close to the action. It's as if he expects the aliens to sneak in a landing before he's in place. And that somehow, if he *wasn't* on his canvas chair on the edge of the Common, it wouldn't really count. You know? Like when you tell yourself that if you don't get to the red light before it changes you'll die at school today.

He put up the canvas chair. Walbeck and Purkiss, as usual, hung back in the darkness. Walbeck, his head tilted so far that the point on the end of it practically brushed the back of his jacket, was staring at the stars like they were the faces of old friends. What's so great about Walbeck is that he *really* expects them. Any moment now. He just can't wait to start nodding and waving at the little green guys, and trying to get them to write him messages on the back of that envelope he carries with him.

'Walbeck's frisky,' I said.

Sometimes he seems to pick up what you say. As I made this remark, he started to frolic on the patch of grass, waggling his head to and fro, and grinning as he did so. Mr Marr looked at me. He had a deadly serious expression on his face. 'Tonight', he said, '*is* the night!'

It was funny. He says that every night. The fact that, so far, in ten years of watching there has not been a sign of them only makes him more convinced that he is getting closer to the moment when, from a saucer hovering over the birch trees, a steel ladder is let down on to the Common and entities start shinning down it and asking the way to the nearest fast-food restaurant.

My dad was like that about his book. Every time he got a letter back from a publisher, he was convinced that, this time, it wasn't going to start:

Dear Norman Britton,

I am afraid we are having to return the MS of *Jubal's Lyre* to you. Much of it has a Dickensian breadth but ultimately it fails to convince. The drawings, however, impressed us all!
Yours,
A. Bastard

Things were always just about to get better for my dad. Which is perhaps why he got on so well with Mr Marr. 'The thing about old Marr,' Dad would say, 'is that he's committed. You know?' Sometimes he would add, with a little wink, 'There are those, of course, Simon, who maintain he should *be* committed. If you take my meaning . . . '

I sat next to Mr Marr on the grass and I could see that he was sort of quivering, like a retriever. As I looked up at the sky, I could have sworn I heard a distant humming sound.

Watching for the aliens is always a nerve-racking business. You never know when they are going to come. Every time a car backfires or a plane flies in low over Raynes Park, Purkiss and Marr are up and gibbering like loonies. Quite often Mr Marr has started the tape and we're halfway through 'We hope you had a pleasant journey and that our atmosphere is proving satisfactory' before we all realize that we have been straightening our ties for a 150 c.c. Kawasaki.

Tonight was different. Tonight was the night. There is some mysterious force at work in the world, because I swear I had foreknowledge. Even before all this happened, I *knew* that something was on its way and that, by the end of the night, my life would be utterly changed.

5

We were about twenty minutes into the session. Purkiss had already frothed at the mouth at a Boeing 747. Walbeck suddenly started rubbing the top of his head with the palm of his hand.

'What does that mean?' I asked Purkiss.

'It means', said Purkiss, 'that he's hungry.'

I didn't get this.

Purkiss looked rather superior. 'It's his impression of a cheese-burger,' he said.

From the High Street I saw an elderly man in a dark grey suit walking towards us. Jacob Toombs. Toombs is an elder of the First Spiritualist Church, which means he can do anything he likes apart from shag the choir in full view of the rest of the congregation. He was walking in a very peculiar way. Each time he lifted his foot he waggled it around in the air before placing it, very carefully, on the ground in front of him. He looked as if he was trying to avoid dog turds.

Toombs was elected an elder a few years back, after a pretty dirty campaign in which a lot of famous dead people endorsed his candi-dature heavily. He's pretty extreme, even by First Spiritualist stan-dards, but I couldn't work out why he was carrying on like a man trying to walk along two separate tightropes at the same time. Then I remembered.

'Place the foot carefully upon the ground,' Old Mother Walsh is reported to have said, 'and hurt not any living thing with the soles of thy feet.' Toombs was trying to make sure he was doing right by the local insects. Every so often he stopped and peered closely at the pavement to check they were all all right. Then he looked over his shoulder.

About twenty yards behind him I could see my mum, Pike,

Hannah Dooley and the Quigleys, all waggling their feet like astronauts. They were on their best behaviour because Toombs was there. Why had they brought him to see me? If they'd brought Toombs with them, it must be serious.

Toombs looks great, which is more than can be said for most members of the First Spiritualist Church. He has a hawklike nose, fierce blue eyes and a great mane of white hair. It's when he opens his mouth that the problems start. You think he's going to make with some deep remark about the meaning of the universe. In fact, what you usually get is, 'There's nothing worse than a bad-mannered dog!' Or, 'The English abroad often wear shorts.' That, for Toombs, would be a *pretty bold* statement. He is usually a lot less controversial than that.

He was staring at me now as he got closer. Was he staring deep into my soul? Or was he trying to remember whether he or his wife was taking the kids to school in the morning?

When they got close enough they sort of formed up in a line – something the members of the First Spiritualist Church are incredibly good at doing. Then Quigley coughed and stepped forward a pace. 'Well, Simon,' he said. 'Mr Toombs has got something to say to you.'

A look of panic ruffled the calm of Mr Toombs's handsome face. *What was it?* his expression seemed to say. Quigley looked sideways at him and muttered something. I couldn't hear what it was. Then Toombs took two paces forward from the line and cleared his throat. 'Simon,' he said, eventually, 'your father is dead!'

A lot of people seemed keen to emphasize this fact. As if I hadn't heard them right the first time. As if I might have thought they'd said, 'He's in bed,' or, 'He has a bad head.' *I am getting the message: he is dead!*

'But', Mr Toombs went on, 'there have already been very strong messages coming through from him.'

'What kind of messages?' I asked.

I didn't care for this. They seemed almost pleased about whatever it was my dad had had to say. All I could think was that this sort of behaviour was not typical of Norman. He was not a talkative man.

'Messages about his deepest feelings.'

This was even weirder. The one thing my dad never liked to talk about was his deepest feelings. And he hated other people, especially my mother, talking about *their* deepest feelings.

Mr Toombs was nodding solemnly. Quigley stepped up to the elder, whispered in his ear and then retreated to the line, combing his beard for nits as he did so.

'There have never been quite so many messages coming through so soon after a coronary thrombosis,' said Toombs.

'Really?' I said.

Purkiss and Walbeck were busy clocking all this. Mr Marr had the bins trained on the front gates of Cranborne School. He was absolutely motionless. From the look of him you would have thought a green man with horns and a ray gun was drifting out past the Porter's Lodge at that very moment. But maybe he was just trying to ignore Quigley and company.

'And we are of the opinion', went on Toombs, 'that Norman has something very important to tell *you*.'

He prodded me in the chest with his forefinger. I looked straight at him.

'That is why we have come,' he went on rather menacingly. 'We want you to join with us now in trying to make contact with him. We must find out exactly what his problem is.'

'His problem', I said, 'is that he's dead.'

Quigley gave a superior laugh. 'We have a very simple view of the world don't we, Simon?' Then he turned to Mr Marr, who, like Nelson, was keeping his eye to the lens. 'How are the "little green men"?' he asked.

Mr Marr did not respond to this. He twitched slightly though. He hates aliens being called 'little green men'. As he says, we don't know what shape or size or colour they'll be. And why be so sexist? They may be hermaphrodites.

Mrs Quigley weighed in next. The First Spiritualists often talk like this. As if they all had one sentence in mind and had agreed to share it out between them. As if they were all controlled by some central brain.

'The feelings are very, very bad,' she said, in a low voice – 'very, very negative. We feel he has something very, very important to tell us. And he can't quite get through.'

'Maybe we need a bigger aerial,' I suggested.

Mrs Quigley looked intently at me. She gave me the impression I had just uttered a great and important truth. 'Yes – maybe we do!'

I just stood there looking at them. Then my mum said, 'Please, Simon. For me. Will you? For me.'

This is it with mums. There you are, trying to have a rational conversation, and then, suddenly, they're looking deep into your eyes and reminding you that, just over fourteen years ago, you were in their womb. So – you were in their womb! So, just because you were inside them they think they have some kind of hold over you! Actually, Mum usually says something even more embarrassing than that. So embarrassing that I can hardly bring myself to write it down: 'I carried your maleness inside me for nine months and a day.'

I was frightened she was going to say something along those lines now. Right here, in front of Emily and everything. So I did the quite tactful thing I do at such moments. I sucked at my teeth and looked at the ground. But I could still feel her looking at me. Eventually, I looked back at her. She had come out as she was, in her flour-covered apron. She seemed smaller and more frightened. The way she always does when the Quigleys are around.

I smiled and said, 'OK.'

Walbeck pointed at the sky and shook his head vigorously.

'I'm sorry, Walbeck,' I said, making sure he had a good, clear view of my mouth, 'but they probably won't come if I stay. You know?'

I'm sure it's true, actually. I'm sure none of this would have happened if I'd been there. Nothing ever happens when I'm around. I have to be surgically removed to create an event. If you see what I mean.

They were still looking up into the night sky as I was led away by the delegation from the First Spiritualist Church. Mr Marr was drinking deep, straight from his Thermos. Purkiss was sitting cross-legged on the grass, trying to read *Flying Saucer Review*. And Walbeck, his big, round face anxious and pale, was looking after me. Every so often he would point up at the stars and give me a rather woebegone thumbs-up sign. He puts a lot into his gestures, and when I gave him one back I tried to make it worthy of his very high standards. I got my thumb to sit up straight and then I made it quiver like a dog that has sighted a rabbit. Walbeck is a connoisseur of sign language, and even he looked impressed.

'I got this terrible feeling,' said my mum as we turned down towards Stranraer Gardens, 'that something was wrong. Just after you went out.'

Mrs Quigley came in here, before Mum said anything embarrassing. 'Emily', she said, 'had a very strong feeling in the toilet.'

'Well,' I said, 'Dad spent a lot of time in there.'

Everyone nodded seriously at this remark.

Mum clutched my arm. 'I went into the spare bedroom,' she said in a low voice, 'and he was *there*! He was ever so tangible, Simon. And he isn't happy about something.'

Quigley nodded seriously. 'He has a lot to tell us – a great deal to say. We all feel it.'

Dad had absolutely nothing to say to Quigley when he was alive. I couldn't see why being dead should have made him any more communicative. But, in the First Spiritualist Church, people tend to get a lot livelier after they've croaked. Guys who, when they were alive, would not give you the time of day can't wait to tell you how terrific it is on the Other Side and where they went wrong in the brief period of time allotted to them to hang around South Wimbledon.

Dying is a big event for the First Spiritualist. I sometimes think that what would really suit them would be a gas explosion right outside the church – and then the whole lot of them could get blasted over to where the action is.

I noticed that they had formed up into a kind of protective shell around me. Pike was a little way ahead, over to my right. Hannah Dooley, Mr Toombs and Mrs Quigley were behind to my left. The north-west exits were covered by my mum and Quigley. Emily hung in close to my offside rear in case I should try to bolt west-south-west as we came in to Durham Gardens.

'Well,' said Quigley, in a conversational tone, over his left shoulder, 'has Jesus Christ entered your heart yet, Simon?'

'Not yet, Mr Quigley,' I said. 'But you never know!'

'You never know,' he repeated, with somewhat forced cheerfulness.

The big thing in the First Church of Christ the Spiritualist is honesty. Everyone is very honest with everyone else. If you have body odour, people will tell you about it. You know? And they are razor-sharp about Faith. It's not like the golf club. You don't just join. It's not really enough to be born into it, which is perhaps why so many people leave – especially around my age. They are always asking you whether you *really* believe, and whether Jesus has *really* entered your heart.

I think the only reason I haven't left is that I have nowhere else to go. While my dad was alive, none of it seemed to matter too much.

'Norman,' Quigley had once said to him, 'are you happy with the Lord Jesus? Are you comfortable with Him?'

My dad had given him a cautious look. 'I think we get along pretty well. You know?' And he turned to me and gave me one of his broad winks. Then he raised his right buttock and mimed a farting movement.

He never really liked conversations about JC. And he never talked to me about those things. Maybe now he was dead he would have a bit more to say about it all. I found myself quite looking forward to his views. What he said, of course, depended on which of us got to him first.

We were marching, in good order, down Stranraer Gardens. We were coming up to the shabby front door of number 24. We were waiting patiently while my mum groped in her apron for the key. We were stepping over the threshold.

Mrs Quigley stepped in first, her long red nose twitching with excitement. As she moved down the hall she was practically pawing the carpet in her excitement. When she got to the bottom of the stairs she turned round and flung her arms wide. 'Yes,' she said, 'oh *yes*! He is very strong. Very, very strong. Still!'

If anyone was going to get on the line to the late Norman Britton,

her face seemed to say, it was going to be Marjorie Gwendolen
Quigley.

6

Mrs Quigley is a sensitive. I don't mean she *is* sensitive. She's about as sensitive as tungsten steel. She is *a* sensitive, the way some people are bus conductors or interior designers. She is in touch with things that dumbos like you and I did not even know existed until people like Mrs Quigley clued us in on them.

She knew, for example, that Emily was going to fail Grade Four Cello. Not because Emily Quigley is tone-deaf and has fingers about as supple as frozen sausages, but because she *knew*. The way she *knew* that ferry at Zeebrugge was going to roll over and kill all those poor people. Why, you may ask, did she not get on to the ferry company and tell them not to bother with this particular service? Or, indeed, get at the Associated Board of Examiners? She *knew*, that was all. It was fate – right?

She usually keeps quiet about her prophecies until they have been proved correct, but occasionally she will go public a little earlier than that. Remember the nuclear war in Spain at the end of 1987? That was hers. Or the tidal waves off Boulogne in the August of the following year? Seven thousand people were going to die, according to Marjorie Quigley. A lot of us thought that house prices would be seriously affected.

She was extra-sensitive tonight. After she had pawed the carpet, she lifted that long, spongy nose of hers and sniffed the air keenly. Her nose is the most prominent thing about her face. The rest of it is mainly wrinkles, that dwindle away into her neck. On either side of the nose are two very bright eyes. They are never still. They come on like cheap jewellery.

'Norman!' she said, as if she expected my dad to leap out at her from behind the wardrobe in the hall. 'Norman! Norman! Norman!'

'He wath in the toilet,' said Emily. 'I had a thtwong feeling of him in the toilet!'

You could tell that nobody much fancied the idea of trying to make contact with Norman in the lavatory. Marjorie's nose and mouse-bright eyes were leading us to the back parlour, scene of some of her greatest triumphs.

They always have the seances in the back parlour – a small, drab room looking out over the back garden. It was here, a couple of years ago, that Mrs Quigley talked to my gran. Never has there been such an amazingly low-level conversation across the Great Divide.

'Are you all right, Maureen?'

'Oh yes. I'm fine.'

'Keeping well?'

'Oh yes. On the whole. Mustn't grumble. You?'

'We're fine. How are Stephen and Sarah?'

'Oh they're fine. They're all here and they're fine.'

It really was difficult to work out who was dead and who was alive. My favourite moment came when la Quigley, running out of more serious topics, asked my dear departed gran, 'What are you all doing Over There?'

'Oh,' said Gran – 'the usual things.'

The *usual things*, my friends! They are dead and they are still running their kids to piano lessons and worrying about whether to have the spare room decorated. What was the point in dying if that was all you got at the end of it?

I had the feeling, however, as Mrs Quigley settled herself at the table, that tonight's rap was going to be a little more heavy-duty. The team got into their chairs and pulled themselves up to the table like they were the board of some company discussing a million-pound tax-avoidance scheme. Only I remained outside the circle.

'Come,' said Mrs Quigley. 'Come, Simon!'

I came.

Have you ever been to a seance? Do you imagine something vaguely exciting? With the curtains drawn and the doors closed and the night wind banging at the window? A weird, black-magic affair, where people push glasses around on heavy tables, or levitate, to the sound of heavy breathing? With the First Spiritualist Church of South Wimbledon, it isn't like that at all.

For a start there is no build-up. You draw the curtains, yes. But after you have taken the hand of the person next to you, off you go. There are no preliminaries apart from a short prayer, which Quigley was giving out as I sat down.

'O Jesus,' he was saying, 'all of us here at 24 Stranraer Gardens are very keen to get in touch with Mr Norman Britton, of this address, who died earlier today at a hospital in the Wimbledon area.'

That's Quigley. He gives it to Jesus straight. Like he was talking to Directory Enquiries or something.

'You' – I could tell from the way he tackled the first letter of the word that he meant Jesus – 'see everything. You see wars, famines, victories, defeats and also, of course, You see . . . us!'

I breathed out. Once Quigley gets on to the Lord it's time to go out and get the popcorn. Those two can talk for hours. Or, rather, JC can *listen* for as long as Quiggers can dish it out.

'Tell us, Lord,' he went on, 'about Thy new arrival. How is he? And can He . . . '

Here he stopped, aware that he had vocalized the first letter as a capital and that he wasn't supposed to be talking about Jesus but about my dad. He gulped and struggled on, careful to demote the late Mr Britton to the status of mere mortal.

' . . . can *he* – Norman Britton, that is – talk to Thy children here at 24 Stranraer Gardens on today Wednesday the Fifth of September?'

That's Quigley. The date. The time. The map reference.

Jesus said nothing. He never does. People do not expect him to.

'And,' went on Quigley, 'Lord, if Norman has a message for any one of us here – any word of advice from Thy Kingdom on the Other Side – please may he come forward and speak as we trust in Thy mercy to reveal him!'

There was absolutely no response to this.

Quigley, rather like a guy on the radio, filling in time between records, prayed a bit more. 'Thy crop has been a good one, Lord, and the economy, as far as we can tell, is moving out of recession and into Steady Growth.'

Here he stopped, clearly aware that he was losing all grip on his capital letters. To mask any confusion he might be feeling, he squeezed his eyes tightly shut and drove forward into the next sentence. 'But Britain still lacks a spiritual dimension, Jesus, and many people live their lives in complete ignorance of Thee.'

He lifted his head at this point, opened the Quigley peepers and looked round at the assembled company. His gaze ended on yours truly. I could have sworn he was trying to pick me up! It was only one step away from 'Hi, let's go back for a cup of coffee!' You know? There was that much sincerity in the old Quigley glance.

There was still absolutely no sign of Norman.

Quigley ploughed on bravely. 'Television is about to be deregulated and, as a result, there is a danger that pornography will be pumped into our homes. Old values are under threat. Motorways . . . '

He stopped. He now had his head bowed over the table. His fingers masked his forehead. He peered over them at the assembled company. He obviously hadn't quite got the heart for motorways. Once again he looked in my direction. I had adopted the sort of half-and-half attitude to prayer I had perfected for the rather less intense religious services on offer at Cranborne School, Wimbledon. I sat at a slight angle to the vertical, with my eyes hooded like a hawk's. This was the only concession I made to the spiritual. You could see this freaked Quigley. Was I on the team or wasn't I? Was I working for the opposition?

'Motorwayth', said Emily Quigley, picking up the ball and moving well with it, 'are an evil, Lord! They blight the beautiful countwythide. Thupport and thuccour uth in our thtwuggle to thtop thith ditheathe that thweatenth the thtandardth of the Thouth-Eatht!'

She has no shame, Emily. She looks for the nineteenth letter of the alphabet and she works it in whenever she can. Content-wise, however, she had clearly scored a hit. People were nodding as if they all felt this was something that needed saying.

My mum's eyes were blinking very fast. She pulled at her straggly grey hair and, in the reedy, worried tones she always used to talk to him, she said, 'Norman . . . '

This was clearly something that had to be stopped. The guy had not yet had clearance from air-traffic control and here she was weighing in with a direct address, using his first name. You could tell from the way both Quigleys looked at her that the death of her husband had not improved her standing in the very competitive field of psychic phenomena.

Mrs Quigley made her move. I felt her hand flutter in mine slightly. And then, one or two firm tugs at my wrist. On the other side of her, Emily started to brace her right shoulder. She knew her mum. When Mrs Quigley goes for it, you get out the protective clothing and nail the furniture to the floor. She is serious business.

'Oh!' said Mrs Quigley. 'OH! Oh! Ohhhh!' We all knew the main show had started. There is a fantastic amount of upstaging in the First Church of Christ the Spiritualist, but nobody was going to give Marjorie Quigley anything to worry about. They knew a class act when they saw it.

'Oh!' she said, as if someone was pushing a large cucumber up her bum. 'Oh! Oh! Oh! Ohhhhhhhh!'

Then she started to tug hard at my hand. I held on as hard as I could, but she was moving into top gear. On her other side, Emily had whipped away her hand as if someone had just passed a few thousand volts through it. Her mum was sort of snaking forward and then bouncing back in her chair, then giving us a few good pelvic thrusts, before starting the whole movement over again. She looked as if she was in the middle of some complex, experimental swimming stroke.

'Oh!' said Mrs Quigley, as if she was getting used to the cucumber – even, perhaps, to like it a little. 'Oh! Oh! Oh! Oh! *Ohhhhhhhh!*'

She was bucking like a rodeo rider now. At any seance the rule was always to give Mrs Quigley a good strong chair, because there was no chance it was going to keep its four legs on the floor for any longer than was absolutely necessary.

On the other side of the table, Quigley was waving his hands. 'O *Jesus*!' he was saying. 'Oh *Jesus Christ*!'

It was hard to tell whether Quiggers was talking to the Son of God or was merely in a panic at the unexpected violence of his old lady's seizure. She always gives good value, but this one was a real corker. Everyone else was, quite literally, keeping a low profile. Pike's profile was so low his nose was hitting the table. Toombs, one hand in my mum's, the other grasping Hannah Dooley, was getting his head well down between his knees. He looked as if he was about to chunder all over the carpet. Only Marjorie's old man, who had broken away from his two tablemates and who had bared his lips above his yellow teeth, like a nervous horse, was giving it anything at all. But he never fails her.

'O Jesus,' he said, 'are you come amongst us?'

As if in answer to this, Mrs Quigley gave a loud howl and headed for the floor like a rugby forward crossing the line. My hand snapped out of hers. She must have gone about five yards. Then she started to writhe.

Mrs Quigley writhes brilliantly. She does an aerobics class with my mum, who says she can hardly get her knees in the air. But get her in a darkened room and mention Jesus a couple of times and she is doing things a world-class athlete could not manage. She goes in about eight different directions at the same time.

Quigley got to his feet, his eyes shining. *This*, his expression seemed to say, *beats anything at the National Westminster Bank*. 'What is it, my sweet one?' he said. 'What is it, my sweet precious?'

Mrs Quigley started to grunt. The grunt was new. I thought it was pretty good. I don't think Quigley was too sure about it. He kept looking at her as if she was about to drop her drawers and flash her gash at us.

'Darling,' he said, reaching for her hand. 'Darling . . . Darling . . . What is it, sweet darling?'

It's a normal day, Quigley. I always do this. Remember?

Quigley looked up at the light fittings. 'Jesus,' he said, fixing his eyes on them, 'what is the spirit that is in her? Jesus? O Jesus? Jesus? Jesus?'

Jesus was still saying *nothing*. Mrs Quigley started to bang her head on the floor. Over on the other side of the table I saw Pike sneak a look at his watch.

She made us wait for it. She always makes us wait for it. But when

345

the voice comes out it is always good. This time it had a weird, distorted effect on it. It was hard to see how she could have possibly produced this timbre on her own, but what la Quigley doesn't know about voice production could be written on a very small postcard. A guy from the Society for Psychical Research once frisked Marjorie just before she got in touch with the late Elvis Presley. Although she was clean, she made, I am told, a noise like a container ship's fog-horn and broke three windows.

But this voice was really creepy. It had a sharp little edge to it. It sounded lonely. There was an ugly ring to it, too, as if it belonged to someone who had mean, nasty things to say about the world.

Whoever it belonged to, it was calling my name.

'Simon!' it said. 'Simon Britton! Simon! Simon! Simon Britton!'

Everyone looked at me.

'Yes?' I said, in as calm a voice as I could manage. 'That's me. What exactly can I do for you?'

7

You don't talk directly to the dead.

Over There, just like over here, you always have to go through someone if you want to do things properly. It's a bit like when I used to phone my dad's office and his secretary would say, 'I'll see if he's in.' I knew this meant that he was in but that she wasn't sure if he wanted to talk to me.

The dead are like that. They are guarded by a whole load of spirits, with names like Peony and Goldenrod, and by the time these have kept you hanging round for hours, telling you their life stories, you sometimes wish the dead would hire competent secretaries.

Sometimes you get crossed lines. You're looking for Aunt Elsie or little Camilla, but Lloyd George or Philip Larkin or somebody like that barges in and tells you what a great time they had on earth.

This voice of Mrs Quigley's was a *spirit*, right? The next thing on the agenda was for us all to start asking it who it was and where it came from. Spirits don't volunteer any information. They don't walk around with ID cards pinned to their robes. And they have to be wooed. Sometimes there are things they don't want to tell you. Sometimes they are too busy to talk to you.

I was buggered if I was going to woo this spirit. I didn't, to tell the truth, like the sound of it. It rather freaked me out in fact. And so, as so often happened at our seances, it was a member of the Quigley family who led us further down the passage to that Other World that lies in wait for us all.

'What ith your name?' Emily said.

There was a pause while Mrs Quigley thought of a name. 'Gossamer,' she said eventually, in a thick voice. Was this another celebrated spirit? A founder member of the Durex empire?

My mum is always good with the lower spirits. She'll spend hours asking them how they float and what they eat and are their clothes comfortable. She often asks them really personal questions about their habits. I've heard them get quite offended.

'Are you at peace, Gossamer?'

The voice took on a slightly babyish quality. 'I . . . at peace . . . '

'Oh good,' said Mum. 'Oh *good*!'

'I at peace, but . . . '

Quigley moved in, fast. 'But what?'

He tends to threaten the more junior spirits as if they are hostile witnesses in a cross-examination.

'Gossamer?'

Mrs Quigley was writhing again.

It sometimes occurs to me that it was only during seances that the Quigleys could say what they really felt about each other. Normally Mrs Quigley was subject to the usual restrictions that apply to married people. She had to sit there and grit her teeth while her husband went on about the mortgage rate, the need for competitive small business and the very real power of Jesus' love. In the middle of a seance she was at liberty to grunt and throw herself around the room and ignore everything the assistant bank manager said to her.

'Gossamer?'

'Go away!'

'Gossamer?'

'Fuck off!'

The spirits often use bad language. Especially when Quigley is asking them personal questions. I have often thought of going into a trance myself simply to have the pleasure of telling Quigley to go and fuck himself with an iron bar. As yet, I fear, I have not had the nerve to do so.

'*Gossamer?*'

Mrs Quigley's voice became plaintive and girlish.

'What-a matter?'

Quigley looked as if he was trying to resist the temptation to honk into his inside jacket pocket.

'Gossamer . . . have you a message for Simon?'

'Methage for Thimon?'

Gossamer had gone babyish in a big way. Quigley responded by trying to out-yuck him/her/it.

'Yes. What message for li'l' Simey? What message 'oo got?'

Mrs Quigley came back with the sort of scream Dracula comes out with when faced by garlic or wooden stakes. She drew her knees up to her chin and started to bang her right arm on the floor in pretty strict rhythm. At the same time she pushed her crotch up at Quigley as hard as she could. He looked impressed. When her voice came through, it was a tiny croak, distant and far-away. 'Simon?' it said. 'Are you there, Simon?'

'Is this Gossamer I'm talking to?' said Quigley in a no-nonsense voice.

It didn't sound like Gossamer. It sounded like someone on a car-phone going into a tunnel.

'Gossamer gone . . . ' said the voice. 'I am not Gossamer.'

'Who are you?' said Pike, clearly feeling the need to be included in all this.

'An old spirit,' said the voice – 'one from the dawn of time. A tired spirit. A tired spirit that wants to sleep.'

'What was your name?' said my mum – 'when you were on the earth?'

Mrs Quigley thrashed a little. There was dead silence in the room.

'On earth,' said the spirit, 'I bore the name of Norman Britton.'

'And what', asked Quigley keenly, 'was your address?'

'Address?' said the spirit, feebly. 'How do you mean – "address"?'

It obviously didn't know about addresses. They don't have addresses over there, guys. There is a marked absence of the Filofax.

'Which house . . . ' said Quigley, sounding a bit like my mum talking to a Swedish lodger we had once, 'which *house* did you *live* in?'

'I . . . '

There was a tense silence. Then Mrs Quigley frothed lightly, twitched a little and said, 'I Gossamer. I come back!'

Everyone looked pretty cheesed-off at this. I think we all felt we had had Gossamer. He was fine as far as he went, but it was time to make contact with new and more exciting shades.

'We want to talk to Norman,' said Quigley, keenly, 'not to Gossamer. Can you put us in touch with Norman? Norman Britton.'

'He was a travel agent,' said Mum. 'He had a shop in Balham High Street.'

Quigley glared at her.

'Norman,' he said, in an insistent tone. 'Norman Britton.'

'I Gossamer,' said Mrs Quigley, brightly.

This whole thing was beginning to resemble a bad transatlantic phone-call. Should we, you could see Quigley wondering, just leave a message and ask the guy to ring back? If we did get through, were we going to get any sense out of him?

'Why can Norman not sleep?' Pike asked.

Maybe because of all you guys getting on the line and asking the old spirit pointless questions! You know?

'Is there something that troubles you?'

Mrs Quigley groaned. Long and low and quiet. 'Ohhh! Ohhh!'

'Thay if you have thinned!' said Emily Quigley. Typical Emily. She'd never have dared talk to my dad like that when he was alive, even during the period when he was into the High Anglican Church, Putney. I was quite prepared for my dad to get on the line and start talking about his period of Error – which is how the First Spiritualists referred to his going over to another Church. But he didn't.

'What is your message for Simon?' asked my mum. 'What do you want to say to him?'

He didn't answer. This was, I have to say, absolutely typical of my dad. You could ask him a question and he would take literally days to reply.

'Want to say . . . '

'Want to say what?' Quigley sounded like a man trying to encourage his pet snake to dance.

There was no reply.

My mother, in a rare moment of independence, said, 'You frightened him off!'

'Don't be *stupid*!' said Quigley. 'Don't be *utterly stupid*!'

He was crouched over his wife, massaging her hands. Eventually that voice came out of her again. It was the one I didn't want to hear.

The voice of a child alone in a large house at night. It had fear in it, but it also had the things that make you afraid – darkness, and the things that come out of darkness and make you afraid to go to sleep. It was like a sinister baby – something very young that has already had another life and is only pretending to look at the world for the first time.

'I lived my life . . . I drank my wine . . . I broke my bread . . . '

'Yes?' said Quigley. 'Yes?'

Suddenly the voice changed again. It dropped an octave. It really was a bass voice, a voice thick with cigarettes and whisky, rich with the things that had helped to end its owner's life. It was my dad, I swear it. Although it was Mrs Quigley's lips moving, it was his voice I heard.

'Simon, old son . . . ' he said.

It was so *like* him, you know? Right down to the way he couldn't finish sentences. I couldn't help myself. I just couldn't help myself. I wanted to talk to him so much. I wanted him to say the things he always used to say to me. Not big, important things but just those ordinary remarks that let you know you're still here and ticking over. I was so desperate to hear his voice I didn't care if it came from the mouth of Marjorie Gwendolen Quigley.

'What, Dad?' I said. 'What's the matter? What do you want? What's the matter?'

Very slowly, Mrs Quigley started to lift her head off the floor. It wobbled loosely during the ascent, very much as Mum's does when she is doing her aerobics on the bathroom floor. Madame Quiggers did not look well. She always says that intense mediumship can damage you permanently and that very intense spirit possession can take thirty years off your life. If these calculations are correct, she could well be joining Norman for a face-to-face confrontation rather sooner than she had anticipated.

What was weird was that she was looking straight at me, but she obviously couldn't see me.

'Oh Simon,' said my dad's voice, seeming to come from the pit of her stomach. 'I am . . . I am . . . condemned!'

'Condemned to what, Dad?'

'To walk the earth.'

I could see Pike give a nervous glance out of the window. He takes these things very seriously does Pike.

Suddenly Mrs Q started to writhe again.

'Walk the earth where?' said my mum, in a rather worried voice. 'In any particular place? Or sort of roaming about across the sea and so on?'

Although this was clearly exactly the next question on Quigley's mind, he gave her a pitying look.

Mrs Quigley was working up her writhing and thrashing nicely. When she was at domestic-blender speed, the cucumber-up-the-bum effect was reintroduced. It now sounded as if a team of construction workers were hammering it into place. 'Oh!' she said. 'Oh! Oh! Ohhhhhhh!'

'Where, Norman?' said Mum, who really did sound genuinely concerned about the quality of the old man's afterlife. 'Where are you?'

The voice came again, and it was still my dad's. He could have been in the room. You know?

'Repent, Simon!' he said, in a deep, hollow voice. 'Repent! You hear me? You must repent!'

Repent of what? Was it my fault he had kicked off? What had I done that was so wrong?

'Free me, Simon! I beg you, free me! Free me!'

By now Mum was practically screaming. 'Where, Norman? Where are you?'

Rio de Janeiro? The Algarve? Have you come back as a lighthouse keeper in South Uist or what?

With a snap, Mrs Quigley rose to a sitting position. It was not what any of us expected her to do, but, like a great actor, Mrs Quigley often throws in something very low-key, bang in the middle of a high-dramatic passage. It surely does keep you watching. Quigley, her ever-faithful support act, ran to her side. He raised his hand to her face and kept it there for a full thirty seconds. Pike's eyes were starting out of his head on stalks. Hannah Dooley was openly weeping.

This time Mrs Q gave us a new voice. It was my dad still, but he sounded as if he had been put through a mixer, and someone had added echo, reverb and a few hundred dBs of extra bass on the way. It had a threatening ring to it, too – some traces of that earlier spirit voice. The voice that reminded me of a frightening and frightened child.

Mrs Quigley's tongue lolled out of her mouth. She started to laugh. Or, rather, something inside her started to laugh. It wasn't a very pleasant sound.

'In what part of the world,' said my mum, in pleading tones, 'are you condemned to walk?'

'Wim – bel – don!' said my dad.

8

Great!

Not only does he die, he is condemned to walk the earth and find no rest. Worse than that, he is condemned to roam around Wimbledon for the next few thousand years. Have a heart, O Spirit of the Universe! Wimbledon is bad enough for an afternoon. With house prices the way they are, quite a few people are stuck there for rather longer than that. But at least they can look forward to stiffing.

My dad was one of the undead. He was not being allowed to pass to the Other Side. He was going to miss the tea parties and the organized games. Although he wasn't an enthusiastic Spiritualist, he often said he looked forward to seeing Auntie Norah again after she fell under the train at Norwood Junction. But even that was to be denied him. *What had he done to deserve this?*

He used to get ratty about the neighbours. He could be quite vicious when asked to Hoover the front room. But he was not what you would call a bad man.

He said what he thought did my dad. Maybe that was his crime. I remember the two of us came across a large poodle having a crap on the pavement outside our house. Dad picked it up by the collar and hurled it and its half-ejected turd into the middle of the road. Whereupon a woman in a fur coat threw herself upon him and demanded to know what he was doing with her dog. 'Give me your address,' said my dad, 'and I'll come round and shit on your doorstep!'

He was basic. He was noisy and loud, and he was earthy to the point of being gross. Whether he was singing an Irish song called the 'The Galway Shawl' or clapping me on the back or trying, unsuccessfully, to kiss my mum, he was very much of this world rather than the next one.

But he wasn't a bad man.

I could think of no good reason why he should have been doomed to roam up and down the local streets or float in and out of the Wimbledon bookshops, trying to pick up the latest paperbacks with his see-through fingers. I did not understand why it was that Mr Lustig, the deputy headmaster, was going to be allowed to walk through him on his way to church, or why the Thompson family, from three doors down, whom he had always hated, should be allowed to shoulder their way through his thick chest and big, balding head on their way to the pizza parlour.

It was to do with something I had done. It sounded to me as if he was being punished for something I had done. What *had* I done? For a moment I thought he might have been trapped on the earth he had enjoyed so much because I hadn't appreciated him properly. And then it occurred to me that I had probably done quite enough bad things on my own account to allow something like this to happen.

I have done plenty. I am an averagely bad person. Fourteen earth years give you plenty of time to plumb the depths of human depravity. We cannot all be Emily Quigley. I have done things that would make your glasses steam up just to *mention*. You know? I am a sinner.

I do, for example, from time to time, indulge in a spot of self-abuse. I say 'from time to time'. That isn't quite accurate. I wank like a man demented whenever I get the opportunity. And I do seem to get an awful lot of opportunities. Nobody gets me to go on mountaineering trips or enter for swimming galas or any of the other things that are supposed to be good for masturbation. They let me get on with it. As a result, although there are times when my hand does come off my chopper, I have to admit that they are fairly well spaced. I don't think it's going to make me go blind, but it must be having some effect. Maybe I'm going deaf. People are always saying I don't seem to hear what they're trying to tell me.

Could my wanging off until the sheets crackle be the reason why my dad had been condemned to waft through Wimbledon for the foreseeable future? I seriously thought about this possibility as I went to bed that night. But, then, you are not rational when someone you love kicks the bucket.

I lay awake, I remember, staring out at the moon above the street and trying, unsuccessfully, to keep my hand off my dick. There's a poster on my wall. It's of Bruce Lee, the Master of the Martial Arts. Looking at Bruce no longer gives me the thrill it once did. I keep it there because it reminds me of how simple and decent things used to be when it was enough to watch Chinamen kicking each other. As I gazed up at Bruce's iron-hard stomach and the three red sword wounds on his chest, it reminded me of the good old days before pubic hair. I missed them.

The Quigley family had stayed over, something they did quite a lot of if they thought one of us was in spiritual danger. They were always trying to insinuate themselves into our house when my dad was alive. But he used to do things like open the front door and call 'Homes to go to!' if they stayed past ten. Any later than eleven and he would appear in his pyjamas and begin winding the alarm clock.

'We need to be with Sarah,' Quigley had announced after the seance was over. We had asked Jesus, and Jesus had thought it was a fantastically good idea that they stayed. Toombs and Dooley had gone for their bus, and Pike had shambled off to his second-hand Ford, dubbed by me Lethal Weapon III.

I could hear Quigley snoring. He didn't just snore, he made a sort of satisfied grunting sound in between snores. At one point I could have sworn his old lady was giving him a blow job. I kid you not – the noise he made was remarkable. But, when I got up to check, it turned out Mrs Q was sleeping with Emily in a room at the back of the house. Quigley was capable of sucking himself off, mind you. There are no limits where Quigley is concerned.

At about four I got up and went for a walk. I walked along the landing and looked in on my mum. She was lying with her nose in the air, giving out a light snuffling sound. Mrs Quigley and Emily were locked together in a rather awkward-looking clinch. Between them was Emily's teddy bear, whose name, in case any of you are interested, is Mr Porkerchee.

I went back to my room and looked down at Stranraer Gardens.

Surely, I thought to myself, they wouldn't make him roam Stranraer Gardens? Death brought you some privileges, surely? He might not deserve the Elysian Fields, but he hardly deserved *that*.

And then I saw him. He was standing outside number 20. Everything about him said *ghost* in very large letters indeed. And, if he wasn't actually roaming, he looked like a man on the verge of roaming. He looked pretty condemned to wander to me.

He was wearing white, as ghosts tend to do. A kind of long smock, almost down to his ankles. He was barefoot, of course, and there was, you had to admit, a kind of ghostly yellowish glow about him – although that could have had something to do with the fact that he was standing under a sodium lamp.

The only other serious effect death seemed to have had on him was to deprive him of his glasses. But, I guess, Over There, you have no need of glasses. It certainly hadn't made him any more decisive. He was just hanging round looking vague – the way he used to when he was alive. Maybe, I thought to myself, he hadn't been assertive enough to get through to the Other Side. He looked a bit like one of those guys you see at airports, waiting for their luggage to come round on the carousel.

I just assumed it was an optical illusion – in a couple of minutes, I'd look back and it would be gone. Either that or we'd get a few special effects – a shooting star or a voice booming out round Stranraer Gardens telling us our days were numbered. But my dad proved to be as low-key posthumously as he had been when above the sod.

I lay down on my bed, closed my eyes and counted to a hundred. Then, very slowly, I pulled myself up to the window and looked out. He was still there.

That was when I got really frightened. At first I lay, not moving, listening for some other effect that would tell me that what I was seeing was supernatural. They do that in films. They play the music and you *know*. When it really happens, you do not know. It's like death itself. One minute you are worrying about where the next cheeseburger is coming from, the next you have stepped into another world.

I didn't dare look again. I lay there, sweating, in the darkness. Then I decided to wake up Quigley.

I mean – this was his field, right? And, appalling as his old lady was in most departments, she had been proved 100 per cent right about this one. She had said he would roam Wimbledon, and there he was – roaming. I also felt, and I'm almost ashamed to say this, that it would be useful to have an adult male around. Quigley the Squash Player is quite famous in the Mitcham area. When he starts to call you Sonny Jim you run for the door if you are wise. When he carried the cross in the pageant organized by the First Church (yes he *was* playing his hero) he almost threw it across the room when he got to Golgotha.

Without daring to look out of my bedroom window, I tiptoed along the landing. Quigley was in the spare room, lying under the grubby duvet, his right foot protruding from one end. It looked more like a vulture's claw than a foot. His beard was bolt upright. It looked, as usual, as if it had nothing to do with Quigley. As if it had just perched on his chin for a couple of hours and was soon going to flap off to join its pals. His mouth was wide open and his arms were folded across his chest. I looked at them for some time, wondering how he managed to keep them there while remaining asleep. Maybe there was some religious significance to it.

I shook him hard by the shoulder.

'Mr Quigley!'

'Uh?'

'Mr Quigley!'

His eyes clicked open. His head jolted back into the pillow. Then he sat up, ready for action.

'Simon? Yes?'

He is a leader of men is Quigley.

'Mr Quigley . . . I . . . '

I stopped. I just didn't know how to describe what I had seen. Then I said, 'I've seen my dad!'

Quigley's chin went into pleats. His nostrils flared. He described a very small 180-degree turn with his head, while keeping his eyes fixed on mine. 'Simon, where have you seen him?'

'In the road outside.'

Quigley nodded. *I was wondering when this might happen*, his expression seemed to say. But he didn't seem in a hurry to get over to my bedroom to check out the phenomenon. I was surprised by this. I would have thought a guy with Quigley's background would have been reaching for the specimen jar and getting on the line to the Society of Psychical Research before you could say astral plane.

'Yes!' he said. 'Yes!'

I suppose he might have been frightened he might not see the apparition. As it was, his old lady's talents had been confirmed by an unprejudiced observer. It was also possible that the prospect of actually seeing my dad roam Wimbledon, rather than talking about it, made Quigley a touch nervous. My dad could have come back for any number of reasons. One of them might even be Quigley.

'Let us pray, Simon,' he said. 'Let us kneel in prayer.'

'All right.'

He grabbed my hand and sprang out from under the duvet, keen as ever to get on the line to Jesus Christ, God the Father or whoever else was on the switchboard at four in the morning. He was stark naked.

I kid you not, he had the biggest chopper I have ever seen in my life. It was gigantic. It bounced around furiously for a moment or two, and then Quigley, as if he had only just remembered it was there, jammed both hands over it. I thought at first he was going to start twanging it backwards and forwards, like a piece of elastic, but instead he said, 'O Lord, Thou seest my nakedness!' I didn't say anything. I left this between him and Jesus Christ of Nazareth.

Quigley did not quite have the neck for the full-frontal nude approach to the Almighty. Or maybe he was just cold. He wrapped his balls in the duvet and knelt by the bed. For a moment I thought he might still, in fact, be sound asleep. Maybe I was asleep. Maybe we were all of us dead to the world and it was only my dad, out there in the lonely street, who was really alive.

I knelt. I don't mind saying that. I knelt.

Look, I was impressed. It isn't every day you see a ghost, is it?

'O Lord Jesus Christ,' said Quigley, 'help this boy! Help him through the difficult phase he is experiencing and return him as soon as possible to Thy bosom where so many others of us ... er ... nestle.'

There was a pause. Then I said, in my own time, in a low voice, 'Yes, help me!'

I needed help. It was either Jesus or an optician. I mean, either I was cracking up or else I had got the world badly wrong. Maybe it was a mistake to go around being proud of being so cynical. I was cynical.

'I am cynical, Lord,' I heard myself saying *out loud*.

Quigley was nodding furiously. 'Yes, Lord, he is! Alarmingly so for one of his age.'

I wasn't sure I went all the way with this. But then, to my surprise, I found myself saying, 'I do awful things!'

Quigley shot a glance in my direction. He seemed keen to know more about this aspect of my life.

'Fleshly thoughts?' he said, in a rather wheedling tone.

'I ...'

I stopped. I realized I didn't want to discuss my need to pull the wire with Quigley. Not, at any rate, as we were both placed at the moment. There was only a duvet between me and his enormous whangdoodle. Once I had got on to the subject of my dick, maybe Quigley would bring up the subject of his own equipment, and from there we would go on to discuss our private parts generally, after which it would probably be time for a bit of the old *gay sex*.

'I'm mean ...'

Quigley's eyes were shut tight and he was chewing his moustache furiously. This was what he really enjoyed. Impromptu prayers at 04.00. Brilliant.

' ... I'm selfish ...'

Prayer is a very insidious thing. My advice is: don't start! Once you start, it is really hard to stop. Because it was true. You know? I really am mean and selfish. I give my mum a fantastically hard time. All she is trying to do is keep the house clean and give me a good education, and I sit at the table, pick my nose and think about nothing except the next television programme, the next video and the next chocolate biscuit. I sit like a mule and I undermine her. I know I do this because this is what she tells me about fifteen times a day. Which is why it is getting worse. I am getting really *good* at sitting like a mule. No one undermines like me, apparently!

So, as I started to list my faults – well, the clean ones anyway – it came as a fantastic relief. I felt I was talking to a real person, and that there was nobody else in the world I could talk to like that. I mean, not even Greenslade! You can say things to Greenslade, but not *those* things. I was praying. I was talking to Jesus!

'I am conceited as well. I think I know all the answers.'

'You don't know all the answers, boy!' my dad used to say to me. Especially if we were talking about current affairs. Along with 'You're a long time dead,' and 'The mind is its own place,' it was one of his favourite sayings. As I said it I started to blub. *Again!*

Look – it had been a hard day. And as I said it I saw him as he had been in life, sitting at the wheel of our car while my mum went into the shops, reading a travel book and biting his lower lip. I saw him laughing like a hyena down the phone or coming out with one of those brief, completely inexplicable things he used to come out with at the dinner table: 'There are passages in Tennyson that force one to conclude he had experienced air travel. How can this be?' I saw him in life and I saw him in death. I saw him out there under the street lamp, *roaming*. And I sobbed my heart out.

Quigley put a manly hand on my shoulder. He kept the other one (thank *Christ*!) on the duvet. 'Cry, little one,' he said. 'Cry out your pain and your sorrow and your sin!'

That is normally the kind of line that would send me reaching for the sick bag. Not then.

That's what I mean about praying. I was enjoying it. I could see the man on the other end of the line. He looked a bit like Peter Falk in *Colombo*, except he was in pyjamas and he smiled more than Peter Falk. He was as real, as solid and as lifelike as that hologram I had seen out in Stranraer Gardens.

'I'm sorry . . . ' I was saying. 'I want to believe in you. I am sorry. I am sorry . . . '

I was talking Quigley's language. He let go of the duvet and put both his lean, muscular, Christian arms round me. There was nothing between me and the Quigley organ but my brushed-nylon pyjamas.

'Go to the window,' he said. 'He will be gone. He is at peace.'

9

Quigley was spot on.

There was absolutely no sign of my old man anywhere in the street. I checked out the upper atmosphere, but he wasn't whizzing around the chimney-pots either. Quigley stood beside me. He had given up the duvet. He seemed to enjoy the opportunity of flaunting his tackle at old Mr Walker opposite.

'He has gone, Simon,' he said, 'and Jesus is a bit like that.'

'He doesn't hang around either, you mean?'

Quigley laughed amiably. Now we had prayed together I was obviously going to be given a lot more latitude.

'Jesus can do anything for you. He can bring your daddy back and he can take him away. He can bring joy or sorrow, pain or pleasure.'

They had said he would be roaming and he had roamed. I had prayed and he had disappeared. The First Church of Christ the Spiritualist was scoring very high marks indeed.

'I'm sorry,' I said. 'I'm sorry I was cynical.'

'That's all right, Simo,' said Quigley, putting his left arm round my shoulder. I saw his willy bounce up and down and his balls go jingle jangle in the direction of old Mr Walker. 'All I want to do, young shaver, is to love you and cherish you!'

'How do you mean?' I said, a touch nervously.

Quigley squeezed me, rather hard. 'Your daddy is with Jesus, and he's got a lot of personal things to go through before he is really at peace. But we're going to be talking to him about that and getting him to come to terms with what his problems are. And you're going to help!'

I wiped a tear from my cheek. I must have looked a right dickhead. 'Yes, Mr Quigley.' I sniffed.

'Because' – here he stabbed me with his forefinger in quite an aggressive manner – 'what *you* do and think and feel affects *him*. How you behave affects *his* spirit.'

I was past debating this remark. You know the bloke who fell off his camel on the road to Damascus and started to hallucinate? St Paul – that's the guy. I think that what I had experienced was probably very like what happened to him. And, just as St Paul resolved to keep off the hand-jobs and stop frenching the local Syrian girls, so I started to think how I could change my life so as to make things easier for the late Norman Britton.

'You have come to Christ!' said Quigley, raising his eyes to heaven. 'O Jesus!'

I looked sideways at him. Now I was almost a Christian, you would have thought I might find him a little less repulsive. Weren't Christians supposed to love their neighbours – all of them – even Quigley? I looked into my heart but found there was still no space for Albert Roger Quigley. If anything, I realized, I found him even more repulsive than usual.

'I am going to wake the others,' he said, his chopper waggling excitedly.

I must say I would not have relished being hauled out of bed at four in the morning to be told that some idiot had just come to Christ, but this is the kind of thing Christians *adore*. They like anything a bit showbiz. You know?

'Marjorie!' he boomed, as he headed out on to the landing. 'Sarah! Emily! O Jesus!'

Was he going to put any clothes on? Was all this proving too much for him? Was he *ever* going to get any clothes on?

'Oh, Simon!' I heard him shout. 'Little Simon has come to Jesus!'

I heard Mrs Quigley squawk from the landing below – 'He's what?'

She didn't sound at all wild at the news.

'Simon has come to Jesus! Oh Marjorie! Oh Sarah! Oh Emily! We are getting such messages! We have seen visions, my children!' I went to the window and looked down at the street, at the very spot where I had seen my dad. I could see the actual section of pavement where he had been standing. I wanted to go down and mark the place. You know? Like pilgrims do. A placard: NORMAN BRITTON APPEARED HERE. And I felt fantastically sad too, as if I had just learned something, but didn't yet know what it might be.

It's funny. Everyone has been young but none of them really remembers. None of them remembers how complicated it is. How sometimes time goes too fast and sometimes it goes so slowly you want to get up and push the hands of the clock round. How you never get the things you want when you want them because all you know how to do is to want. You want so much, so many things. And none of them seem to be for you.

When I turned round, my mum, Emily, Marjorie and Albert Quigley were filling up the door to my bedroom, beaming at me like I was the school photographer.

'Oh Thimon,' said Emily, 'thomething thtupendouth hath happened! You have theen Jethuth'th light!'

I was beginning to have doubts about the wisdom of having prayed with her dad. If I went back now there was going to be a major incident. It occurred to me that there was something pre-planned about all of this. As if they knew, or had somehow contrived all this to happen, not *just* because it was good to get a guy to come to Jesus but because . . .

Because what? I didn't know. And it certainly wasn't an issue I could raise out loud. My mum was peering at me. She looked, I thought, vaguely disappointed.

'Let's get on our knees,' said Quigley, who seemed to feel uncomfortable when he was off them for more than ten minutes at a time, 'and thank Jesus!' To my relief, he was wearing pyjama trousers.

The others had no difficulty in coping with this. They swarmed into the room, found themselves a nice quiet space and got the old knees in contact with the carpet. I was the last to get down, after one more nervous glance in the direction of the street. Quigley was in touch with Jesus before I even hit the deck.

'Thank you, Jesus,' he said, 'for showing little Simo his daddy.'

Here he flashed a quick look at Marjorie. Once again I had the uneasy feeling that there were things on the agenda that little Simo was not going to be told. There was a desperation about the guy. As if he wanted me to go further. To get a full confession down in writing so as he could use it for . . .

For what?

'And now,' Quigley went on, 'Simo is going to talk to you about his new-found faith!'

He is? I looked up at the rest of the family, who were all waiting for me to begin. More praying. In those days I was naïve enough to think that prayer is conversation without the hypocrisy. And when I started to pray I made the fatal mistake of saying exactly what was on my mind.

'Jesus,' I said, trying to keep my tone matey without being offensive, 'you know how much I . . . er . . . liked my dad and how much I . . . er . . . want to see him.'

You could tell this wasn't enough for Quigley. He shot me one short, fierce glance. I tried again.

'If he really is walking the earth, then tell me . . . tell me why . . . '

A strong right arm gripped mine. A fierce, bearded face was thrust into my line of vision. 'Simon,' hissed Quigley, 'you don't make deals with Jesus!'

Why not? He's supposed to be a nice guy. He's a Jew, for Christ's sake – why not make deals with him?

'Faith,' said Quigley urgently, 'is a leap. Faith is a jump. You must believe, Simo. You must have faith. And then blessings will flow!'

Mrs Quigley nodded furiously at this. My mum was looking at me, red-eyed. She looked as if she was beginning to have doubts about the session.

'There is no time left,' said Quigley. 'You must believe *now*! *Now! Now! Now!*'

You can't take Jesus back to the shop, guys. He doesn't come on approval. He is even harder to dispose of than a subscription to the *Reader's Digest*.

'I . . . '

'Do you want your father to be at peace? Do you want his soul to find rest? Do you want to be able to talk to him? To hear his voice sweetly like the . . . ' Quigley groped for a simile ' . . . lark,' he said eventually.

I looked around at the circle of faces. 'Well,' I said cautiously, 'I . . . '

Quigley started to tremble violently. 'Don't play games with Jesus Christ!' he said, in the tones of a man addressing a baby crawling towards a live electricity cable. 'Don't mess around with the Living God, Simo! This is an *urgent* matter!'

But why? Why was it suddenly so urgent? He was upping the stakes the whole time. I knew for my own sake that I had to say I believed in something. I didn't particularly want it to be Jesus. But there didn't seem to be any alternative.

'I . . . '

'Say it, Simo, please say it! I beg you!'

Did he get commission or what? I felt I was on top of a cliff. I was going to step off and fall through the air. I was going to fall the way a seed falls, blown by the wind. And there, on the shore below me, was my dad. He would be waiting for me when I got there. And, if I said the words, he would be alive again.

'I believe . . . '

There was a hiss like air escaping from a cushion. Quigley was breathing out slowly. Why should just saying these words seem so important? I could change my mind about them later, couldn't I? I quite often said things I didn't believe. Would repeating the magic formula make it true? And what would it lead to?

From the expression on Quigley's face I suspected it might lead to plenty. Did he see me as some kind of potential Messiah? The First Spiritualists are always looking for the 'boy prophet of pure heart and mind'. Fox reckoned she had found him in a thirteen-year-old Bengali youth from Manchester, and Mr Toombs had made some pretty big claims for a Scottish farmer's son.

'I believe in . . . '

'In what, Simon?'

'In Jesus Christ.'

There was a nasty moment when I thought I was going to be expected to go on and say exactly what it was I believed about Him.

And maybe to tell everyone why I believed whatever it was I did. But, before I was forced to get down to specifics, Quigley picked me up. His strong hands held me under the armpits and he sort of shook me at the window, as if I was a new baby of which he was especially proud.

'Alleluia!' he said.

They actually say that sometimes down at the First Spiritualist Church.

My mum, Emily and Marjorie came in right behind him: 'Alleluia!'

And then Marjorie stepped forward. The two of them folded me in their arms. I looked across at my mum, still on her knees in the far corner of the room. There was no way I could move. It was as if I suddenly belonged to this rather unappetizing couple. I looked up at Quigley's face, flushed with triumph. Once again I had the impression that this had not been done entirely for my, their or even Jesus Christ's benefit.

'Mrs Danby,' said Quigley, 'will be very pleased.'

His old lady smirked at him. 'Mrs Danby will be *delighted*!'

I had heard that name before. I couldn't have said where. It brought with it all sorts of memories – a smell of something sweet and heavy, like perfume. A noise like distant music, with light falling in long lines from a high window. And a feeling of longing for something that I knew I could never have.

But it also brought with it a voice that said, 'Don't ask too many questions about that name, Simon. Watch, wait and listen.'

I looked out of the window once more before I finally went back to bed. There was no sign of him. It was like he had never been there.

10

When I woke next morning I could have sworn I heard my dad's voice on the stairs. The sky at the window was the same pale blue as the day before. A breeze ruffled my face gently.

'What do you fancy for breakfast?' That was always his first remark of the day, as he stood outside my bedroom in his grey towelling dressing-gown.

'What is there?' I would reply.

There would be a panic-stricken pause, and then he'd say, 'Beans . . . I think.' Or maybe, '*Pain au chocolat* . . . possibly.' He never knew what there was.

So I'd get up and the two of us would stagger down to the fridge. We'd stand there, side by side, staring in at the pork pies and the tomatoes and the milk bottles, and then he'd groan. 'Me and drink are *through*!'

It was only when I opened my eyes fully that I realized I hadn't heard him at all. No one had said anything to me. Perhaps they were hoping that Jesus would wake me. I did, however, seem to have acquired a truly staggering hard on. Maybe this had frightened Quigley off.

As I swung my feet out on to the carpet, I looked down at my erection resentfully. What use was it? What was it supposed to be *for*? As things stood, there seemed to be no chance of anyone taking it seriously for about another ten years. By which time my balls would probably have started to drop off.

My chest did not seem to have got any bigger during the night. My left arm was still slightly shorter than my right. I went to the middle of the room, closed my eyes, flexed my knees and allowed my head to loll to one side, thereby bringing myself into the first Tai-Ping position. 'You are focused, Simon,' I said to myself. 'You are in harmony with the Law!'

I allowed my trunk to roll forward and lowered my head between my knees. It is quite easy to fall flat on your face while perfecting the second position of Tai-Ping. Maybe Europeans are the wrong size, or maybe it's just me. I stopped short of full *bei-shin* and began the duck-jumps backwards and forwards across the room. But I hadn't the heart for *ten-shang-lai*. I groped for my school trousers under the bed, while listening hard for the Quigleys.

At the back of the house, from the kitchen, I heard what sounded like voices raised in song. As far as I could tell, whoever was doing it – and one of them was certainly Quigley – was also adding a sort of primitive drum beat by banging a wooden surface, hard. I looked at the clock. It was seven forty-five.

'I'm H-A-P-P-Y. I'm H-A-P-P-Y. I know I am, I'm sure I am because . . . ' Drum roll. ' . . . Jesus loves me!'

Bully for him. I was beginning to have second thoughts about Jesus Christ. I know he can heal the sick and raise the dead, but does he also have to make people carry on like the Treorchy Male Voice Choir at a quarter to eight in the morning?

When I had safely covered every bit of naked flesh, I made my way down the stairs towards the noise of the singing.

The kitchen door was closed. I put my ear to it. Things seemed to have gone quiet. For a moment I had this fantasy that the Quigleys were lying in wait inside – hanging from the curtain rail upside down, perhaps, or concealed under brooms and buckets in the scullery cupboard – and, as soon as I opened the door, they would spring out at me like a shower of surprised bats. I bit my lower lip and pushed open the kitchen door.

The first thing I saw was Mum. She was standing over by the stove waving a spatula. She wasn't wearing the faded floral apron, the one that Dad always said made her look like an Irish chambermaid, but a bright new plastic affair. She looked as if she had spent the night rearranging her hair.

I was about to say something, but before I could there was a drum roll from the table and Mum started singing *on her own*.

MUM: I put my fingers in his garments.

His flesh seemed cold and pale.

On his hands and feet there were some marks so neat . . .

At which point the Quigleys came in, in four-part harmony:

QUIGLEYS: I think they had been made by a nail!
MUM and QUIGLEYS: *Oh Jesus!*
MUM: I rolled away the stone into the garden!

I felt more than just a little queer!

In his chest and side there were some wounds you could not hide . . .

Here the Quigleys leaped to their feet and, with a sort of loosely choreographed thrust forward with the right arm, sang:

QUIGLEYS: I think they had been made by a spear!
MUM and QUIGLEYS: *Oh Jesus!*

While they went through the next bit – which was about how Jesus then pitched up waving a spear and a bunch of nails and saying how they were no problem for Him – I made my way to a vacant place at the table. I could see that on every plate was something I had only ever seen before in a hotel – a full English breakfast. There were sausages and tomatoes and eggs and bacon and fried bread and mushrooms, and, in the centre of the spread, a gigantic pot of steaming coffee.

All of the Quigleys looked amazingly clean. Their flares looked as if they had all just come back from the dry-cleaners. I wouldn't put it past Quigley to take a trouser press with him wherever he goes.

When they'd finished, they all started chuckling, and Quigley, switching all his attention to me, said, 'People call us the Mad Quigleys!'

I'm not surprised, I almost said, as I grabbed what looked like my plate and, after checking whether I had got as much as Quigley, started chomping into the fried bread.

I somehow could not connect myself with the person who had prayed to Jesus. How had I managed to do such a thing? As I pounded bits of sausage into the egg-yolk, I wondered whether praying could be related to wanking. It was often hard to believe, in the morning, that you were the person who had been pulling his wire so energetically the night before.

Quigley was buttering his toast as if in time to invisible music. 'Well, young shaver,' he said, 'Jesus lives!'

There seemed no tactful answer to this. I just hoped no one was going to mention last night.

On the other side of the table, Emily was trying out what could have been a wink. 'Hallo, fwend,' she said.

'Hi,' I said, reaching for the toast.

Quigley's right arm shot out and grabbed my wrist. 'Haven't we forgotten something?'

I paused. 'Sorry,' I said, and put my hands back under the table.

After a decent interval, I said, 'Could you pass the toast, please, Mr Quigley?'

This, I thought, was about as good as you could get at 07.58 in the morning. But it wasn't good enough for Quigley. He grinned like a loony and waggled his head from side to side. 'Nope,' he said.

Christ, what did he want? 'I beseech toast, O great Quigley!' 'I fall on my knees, O Quigley, and crave the boon of toast!'

'Er . . .'

Quigley waggled his forefinger saucily. 'Jesus!' he said.

Could you pass the toast, please, Jesus? Was that it? And would it then rev up on the plate and fly in low over the salt and pepper?

Quigley pushed his face close to mine. I could see egg, sausage and tomato being ground to pulp by the Quigley teeth. 'Thank Jesus.'

He seemed quite chirpy about this. We were, after all, on the same side. For a moment I felt genuine remorse about not having thanked Him.

'Thanks, Jesus,' I said in a firm, manly voice. And then, in case there should be any doubt about this, I added, 'For the toast.'

Quigley beamed at me. 'Yes,' he said, 'thanks for the toast.'

'And,' I said, 'for the hot chocolate.'

'We haven't got any hot chocolate,' said my mum, swiftly.

I like hot chocolate. My displeasure must have showed on my face, because Quigley came in with, 'It's a boy child, Sarah.'

I knew this. I gave him a friendly smile and reached out, once again, for the toast. Once more Quigley's arm reached out and grabbed mine. Was I ever going to get any toast?

'Could I,' I said patiently, 'have some toast? . . . in the name of Jesus,' I added, thinking that the mention of His name might prod Quiggers into action.

He just sat there beaming. 'Not till you say the password,' he said.

A guy could starve to death here, surrounded by all this bacon and sausage and egg and fried bread. In many ways, Quigley was like a computer game. You know? You paid a lot of money to be frustrated. I just could not figure my way through his latest move.

'Pleath, Mithter Quigley, could I have thome toatht?' said Emily.

For a moment I thought this was merely a rather formal way of her addressing her old man. Then I caught on. 'Please, Mr Quigley,' I said, 'could I have some toast?'

'Good,' said Quigley, beaming. 'Good!' And he passed me the toast.

It was that simple. I was able to eat bread in my own home. I was in with the in-crowd.

The rest of the meal was uneventful. They didn't have grace after the meal. Nobody asked the Lord to make sure I had a good day at school. I was not handed a boxful of bibles to give out in break. I tell you, I was grateful when I pulled my blazer off the banisters and headed for the front door. Whatever it was they had in mind for me, it was clear that I was a high-priority project for the people at the top of the First Spiritualist Church. If they kept this up for long enough, I was going to start telling the folks up at school that they should welcome the Lord Jesus into their hearts. I tried to imagine myself saying this to Greenslade. It was neither easy nor pleasant.

For some reason, that morning, I decided to walk up the hill, instead of taking the bus up the main road. I started thinking about those extraterrestrials. There *had* been something odd in the atmosphere last night. I had never seen Mr Marr so certain that he was going to get a result. I went up through Elam Gardens and Holtfield

Park, trying to figure out this Christian thing and whether it might have anything to do with the visitors from outer space. Could you be a Christian ufologist? I didn't see why not. There were people, according to Mr Marr, who reckoned Jesus came from outer space.

The first thing I saw when I came off Parkside and across the Common was Mr Marr's little canvas chair, his telescope, his night binoculars and the ten or twelve back numbers of *Flying Saucer Review* that are always to hand when he is waiting for the subjects of the periodical to show up. Everything was arranged just as it had been last night. It was like the lunch table on the *Marie Céleste*.

I was standing there trying to understand what all this might mean when a hand clapped me on the shoulder and a noise like an old goods train being shunted started up in my ear. Walbeck only makes one greeting noise and it is very distinctive.

He held up a small, grubby piece of paper, on which were written the words THEY TOOK HIM AWAY IN A SPACESHIP.

I looked at Walbeck. He pointed to the chair and the bins and the magazines. Then he nodded. He looked, I have to say, very serious indeed. I tried some direct speech.

'Where to?'

Walbeck gave me an odd look. *Where do they take people in space-ships? Margate?* He was writing. When things get bad, Walbeck writes.

ANOTHER GALAXY, OF COURSE!

Of course! He started to cover the paper again. I could see that it was covered with fragments of Walbeck's previous conversations. Discussions about joints and timber sizes (Walbeck is a carpenter by trade) lay next to words of comfort addressed to his elderly mum, and sometimes ran into them, so you got sentences that looked like ARE YOU ALL RIGHT THERE MUM FOR TEN INCH NAILS? Or I GOT YOU SOME OF THAT FISH YOU LIKE FROM THE BUILDER'S MERCHANTS YOU IDIOT!

The message intended for me read: PURKISS AND ME WENT FOR A HANBERGER THEN WE WENT FOR A KIP AT PURKISS'S PLACE AND WHEN WE COME BACK AROUND SIX IN THE MORNING WE FOUND . . .

I turned the page. On the other side was written SIX SQUARE FEET OF CHIPBOARD.

Walbeck always runs out of paper at the crucial moment. We went back to lip-reading.

'What did you find?'

Walbeck pointed at the chair, the magazines and the binoculars. Then he shrugged.

'Maybe he went home.'

Walbeck shook his head furiously. Then he made the conventional sign for Purkiss, which is a kind of crouch plus leer, and did a fluttering movement with the fingers of both hands. They had been to Mr Marr's and he was not there. I just *knew*, the way I had known about my dad. I knew when we left him peering up at the sky that something awful was going to happen. It was all laid out so neatly on the grass. Mr Marr would never leave his binoculars, and the canvas chair cost £15.99!

I wanted to stay and find out more. But we had run out of paper. There is a limit to the amount you can glean from pointing at things and grinning like an idiot. As I turned to go, Walbeck pointed at the arrangement on the grass. He looked really sad suddenly. Then he pointed at the sky and raised his shoulders in a questioning sort of way.

'I know, Walbeck,' I said. 'Why should they take a nice guy like Mr Marr? He was on their side, man. Why should they take him?'

I walked on towards school trying to work this out.

The same reason they had come for my old man, of course. Because life isn't any fairer on the other side of the solar system than it is here. They come for the nice guys and leave the bastards behind. It's always people like Mr Marr and my old man who get tapped on the shoulder by the small men with green leathery skin and fifteen fingers on each hand.

There *had* to be a connection. I didn't yet know what it was, but there had quite clearly been an unusually high level of psychic activity in the Wimbledon area last night. The energy that was capable of lifting an electrical engineer off the Common might well have something to do with the fact that a forty-three-year-old travel agent had been dragged back from the grave to haunt 24 Stranraer Gardens.

11

Just before I got to the school gates, I got out *Tricolore 4* and started to read it. It lets people know you're a serious person, doing something like that. And, besides, I am in correspondence with a girl called Natalie, who lives in Clermont-Ferrand. As far as I can make out, Clermont-Ferrand is even worse than Wimbledon. I was deep into the bit where Olivier and Marie-Claude are trying to buy some cheese in La Rochelle. *Tricolore* never gives you the stuff you really need to say to French people, like, 'Can I hold your hot body to me?' It is all about how to ask for a full tank of *'super'* from the friendly *'garagiste'* and what to say when they have run out of cardigans in Nogent-le-Rotrou.

I was late. We were almost into First Period.

As I came up to the gates, I looked cautiously over the book and saw Khan and Greenslade. Khan was sitting on his games bag. Greenslade was going through his pink nylon rucksack with an expression of desperation on his face.

'Est-ce que tu as oublié tes condoms?' I said.

He gave me a superior smile. 'This is no time for you to be a dickhead, Britton. I have *lost* my geography project!'

I never mind people saying I'm a dickhead. It's the key to my popularity. I'm pretty controlled, if you know what I mean. I wait before I speak, and if I'm not sure what to say – which is quite a lot of the time – I just give this mysterious smile. Greenslade says it makes me look like the village idiot.

This morning, for some reason, I really felt like blurting out what was on my mind. Not about my dad. About the aliens spacenapping Mr Marr. It was only when I thought about saying it out loud that I realized how crazy it would sound. Thinking how crazy it would sound made me wonder whether it was true.

'Tell Baines you'll bring it tomorrow,' said Khan in a deep voice. Khan is always calm about things. I think it's because he is so good at physics.

The three of us moved through the gates towards 4C, or Cell Block H as it is known. Behind us, Limebeare was getting out of his dad's BMW in that special way people get out of expensive cars.

What possible *reason* would they have for spacenapping Mr Marr? He was an engineer. Maybe that was why they needed him. Maybe something had broken down out there on Alpha Centauri and he was the only guy able to fix it. Maybe the know-how of the London Electricity Board was the only thing that could save the atmosphere of some lump of rock light-years from SW19. They would set Mr Marr down, hand him a nine-headed spanner and, after he had done the job, he would be on his way back to Wimbledon.

Maybe they needed my dad *and* Mr Marr. You know? Maybe that was why he had appeared to me last night? Maybe they had ways of breathing life back into people so as they could do their evil will – although I could not, for the life of me, think why entities from a distant planet should want a travel agent.

'Why are we always late?' asked Khan, as we trudged along the corridor towards the classroom. He sounded as if he was going to get philosophical about this.

Maybe they had heard about him. Dad always said he was the best man in South London if you wanted two weeks in Provence with swimming-pool and maid provided. Maybe the fame of Sunnyspeed Tours had spread. And if there are galaxies where life-forms exist, on the other side of the long dark spaces that lie outside our solar system, why shouldn't the life-forms need travel agents?

'Flasher will kill us,' said Greenslade, looking morosely down at his feet. Greenslade is tall and thin. There is always a gap between his shoes and the bottom of his trousers.

What, while we were at it, did Jesus Christ have to do with all this? Was JC somehow mixed up in the mysterious events of last night? What did I mean by 'Jesus Christ' anyway? I had certainly been pretty glad to talk to him, or indeed Him, last night, hadn't I? Suppose He really did exist – not in the way Quigley thought, but as a kind of mysterious energy source. We didn't necessarily mean the same thing when we said 'Jesus Christ'. Any more than Sarrassett Major and I mean the same thing when we say 'football'. Sarrassett Major means huge guys throwing each other at a ball, neck-deep in mud. I mean hanging round the goal and talking to Greenslade.

We got into class just before 'Flasher' Slingsby. I moved into my desk, carefully chosen because it is in the darkest corner of the room. If you sit very still, people think you are part of the furniture. Flasher came in, threw his briefcase on the desk and started to pace around, draw pretty shapes in white chalk and talk the incomprehensible rubbish for which teachers get paid.

I just sat there, my head in my hands, thinking about all this stuff and trying to make sense of it.

'Britton! What have I just been saying?'

I looked Mr Slingsby straight in the eye. 'You were talking about triangles, sir.'

This was safe ground. There was one on the board, for Christ's sake!

'What about triangles, Britton?'

'Well . . . about how they are . . . amazing, sir.'

There was muffled laughter. Britton was at it again.

'In what way are they "amazing", Britton?'

'Well, sir, they are equilateral. Sometimes.'

Mr Slingsby was enjoying this. He positively twinkled as he said, 'And is that what I was saying? That they are "equilateral . . . " '

Here he gave the class a conspiratorial wink. They responded well. ' " . . . Sometimes." '

I looked round at the faces of the class.

'I'm afraid,' I said, 'I wasn't paying much attention.'

'Oh!'

Mr Slingsby sounded almost delighted at this news. He tapped his desk with his finger and gave me about twenty seconds to sweat.

'Indeed. And why were you "not paying much attention", Britton?'

I paused. I let him hang there for a good half-minute. Then I said, 'Because my father died of a heart attack yesterday afternoon, sir.'

I have seen guys dropped across, but none like 'Flasher' Slingsby was dropped across that day. 4C were giving his performance very close attention. He looked, I thought, like a man who has opened his desk and found his wife's head in it. I didn't say anything. I just looked at the floor.

'Britton, you . . . '

'I what, sir?'

He had dug the hole. He had jumped in. It was now up to him to play himself out. The lads were definitely with me. Greenslade had folded his arms and, his head on one side, was studying Flasher's body language as if he was going to write an article about it for the school magazine.

'You . . . you shouldn't be here!'

I wasn't going to let him get away with that. I raised my head and looked straight at him. 'I thought it might take my mind off it, sir.'

I have never really let anyone at Cranborne School know too much about the First Church of Christ the Spiritualist. People can use information like that. People think I'm kinky enough as it is. Sometimes people ask why I have to leave early on Friday afternoons, but I do not – repeat *not* – tell them I am off to Gather in the Lord's Fruit in a High and Seemly Way (which is why Mother Walsh deemed the hours between three and six thirty on Fridays to be sacred). I say I am going to the dentist. They must be really worried about my teeth.

Flasher had turned a light pink. 'You . . .' He was opening and closing his mouth like a fish.

'It was very quick, sir.'

Flasher did not wish to know this. But I kept right on telling him.

'He was having a pint in the pub at lunch-time, sir, and by early evening he was . . . You know?'

My God, you could see Flasher thinking, *this could be me!*

'Simon, I'm . . . '

First-name terms! I kept my eyes on his face, waiting for his next move.

'How old was he?' he said eventually.

'He was forty-three, sir.'

You could tell he was dying to get the conversation back to sines and cosines and all the other wonderful things left to the world by Leibniz and Descartes. But there was no way he could do it.

I looked over in Greenslade's direction. Greenslade was carving a primitive figurine out of his rubber. Next to him, Khan was hunched forward across his desk. He looked as if he was about to put Flasher right on some tricky point of mathematical theory. The windows in our classroom are really high. I could only just make out the pale blue of the sky outside.

Flasher coughed. 'Don't you want to . . . be with your family at this time, Britton?'

'Not really, sir.' *It's actually quite a relief to be here! Have you seen my family?* 'I just feel . . . '

I started to play with my pencil.

Feelings are weird. Here, where I was surrounded by people who were actually *sympathetic* to a person when they heard that a close relative of his had failed to make it, I didn't really feel sad at all.

'I thought it would be better if I just carried on, sir.'

Flasher squared his shoulders. He is a captain in the Territorial Army. A year ago I was with him on Army Cadet Force manoeuvres in the Welsh Mountains. Limebeare, who was, for some unknown reason, a corporal, stole a bazooka from the armoury and shelled the village of Aberfach for three hours before being arrested by the local police. They handed him over to Flasher, and Limebeare said afterwards that he would rather have served three years in Carnarvon jail than pass the afternoon he did with Slingsby.

'Yes, Britton. Yes. I quite understand.' He looked at me in a somewhat worried way. 'I never know what goes on in your mind, old son,' he said. 'You're a secretive chap, Simon . . . '

You could see that he now thought he was in the clear. We had had this out man to man. Although how he could say I was a secretive chap was, to me, a complete mystery. I'm an open book.

He came towards me between the grim wooden desks, and for a moment I thought he was going to put his arm round me. I wasn't finished yet.

'I *thought* it would . . . but . . . I don't think I can quite . . . manage it, sir.'

Flasher looked at me narrowly. For a second you could see him wondering whether this might not be a wind-up. You could tell he still thought this was a strong possibility, but it wasn't a chance he could afford to take.

'Would you like to go home, Britton?' he said.

'I think I'd just like to walk on the Common and think about things.'

No pupil of 4c had ever requested such a thing before. If this went on, it wouldn't be long before we started ordering hot chocolate and croissants to be brought to the desk.

'Is that all right, sir?'

'Absolutely, Britton. Absolutely!' said Flasher. 'But . . . '

'Yes, sir?'

'Don't do anything foolish, will you?'

'No, sir,' I said, in a voice that was meant to suggest that I was about to pen a short note describing Flasher's insensitive attitude to the bereaved and then swallow a few dozen Nembutal.

I got to my feet. Everyone was looking at me. I wondered whether to tell them the whole story. But I wasn't sure that Flasher was ready for my dad's coming back to life. He had not really had time to adjust to Norman's death.

I stopped at the door and gave him my best and bravest smile. 'Thank you, sir, for being so understanding about my problem. There are times when geometry just doesn't seem at all relevant.'

'I realize that, Britton,' said Flasher with some humility.

Very slowly and quietly I closed the door behind me. I could feel the lads' appreciation as I headed off down the corridor. A round of applause would not, I felt, have been out of place. All I needed now was to bump in to Mr Grimond, the games master, and for him to ask me what the *bloody hell* I thought I was doing.

Mr Grimond would fit quite well into the First Spiritualist Church. He is stark, staring bonkers. He has been known to hold boys upside down on the rugby pitch and swat the ball with their heads. He regards brain damage as character-forming, which, for someone of his level of intelligence, is an entirely consistent position.

I walked out through the main entrance, past the picture of Sir

Roger de Fulton, a rather dodgy-looking customer in a blue dressing-gown, and the huge pokerwork version of the Cranborne School motto QUID AGIS? Or 'Wha' Happenin'?' as we translate it. There was more sunshine outside than Wimbledon could really accommodate. The streets seemed rich with possibilities – the way they do when you know you're supposed to be at school.

I thought I had better go down the hill and take a look at Mr Marr's house. In my right-hand jacket pocket I could feel the weight of his front-door key, the one he gave me three years ago.

As I passed south of the War Memorial, I could see Mr Marr's chair, standing out on the Common. Next to it, all his stuff was still laid out. It looked lost, like someone's drawing-room suite abandoned in a junk yard.

Mr Marr had given his key to no one else. I was the only person he trusted. He had told me to use it only in emergencies. But this, to me, looked like an emergency.

'There may come a time, Simon,' he had said to me, as he handed it over, 'when people from another galaxy who are not kindly disposed to us – and such people are probably out there – may . . . you know . . .'

' "You know" what, Mr Marr?'

'Well . . . MIBs for example. You know?'

I knew. 'MIBs' stands for 'Men In Black'. In Deepdene, Ohio, in 1958 Mr and Mrs John Wearing saw a large flying saucer three miles out on the highway to Sawmills Bridge. It was hovering over a petrol station. There was, according to Mr Wearing, 'a sort of perspex shield where the driver's cab might have been situated', and he claimed to have seen a large 'blob-like creature' with its nose pressed to the windscreen. It let him know, without using earth language, that the whole of the midwest of America was in grave danger.

Fine. These sorts of thing are always happening.

Two days later, after the Wearings had contacted the local newspaper and given an extensive interview, two men in black suits turned up. They wore dark glasses and black trilbies but were by no means the Blues Brothers. In 'cracked, automatic voices' they warned Mr and Mrs Wearing that they had better not speak of these experiences to *anyone*. I'm not, actually, quite sure why or how the Wearings allowed the story to get out. I mean, I hope they're all right. You know?

'If I should disappear without trace, you know what to do,' Mr Marr had said to me.

'I know what to do!'

'Here's the number. Memorize it and destroy it.'

He gave me the top-secret telephone digits of a very senior guy in the Wimbledon Interplanetary Society. I was to ring him only in an emergency because, apparently, British Rail took a very dim view of his receiving calls about non-terrestrial business during office hours.

There was still no breeze at all. It was dead still that September. On the house-fronts in Columba Road, the roses nodding on the brickwork, as big as soup plates, looked as if they were waiting for something. And, as I turned into the cul-de-sac where Mr Marr lived, it seemed to me that the whole suburb was holding its breath.

I had forgotten the number of the chairman-for-life of the Wimbledon Interplanetary Society. I could not even remember the name of this rather crucial person. It would have been good to talk to someone about all of this, I thought to myself, although, from the little Mr Marr had told me about him, he sounded pretty flaked. Anyway, by making the call I would be admitting what had really happened. There was still a chance that Mr Marr had been taken ill or something, or had decided to go and see a relative.

Except he didn't have any relatives. And, if he had been taken ill, there was a card in his jacket pocket saying who he was. We take no chances in the Wimbledon Interplanetary Society. 'Be always on your guard,' Robert du Carnet, the secretary, had said at the last Annual General Meeting. 'Don't let *them* choose the time!'

We know that the things from hyperspace may want to blast us to bits. And that people who don't even believe they exist will be at even more risk than we are. We have a duty to survive, Mr Marr says.

He chose this particular cul-de-sac, for example, for very good reasons. He liked to feel his back was secure. Although, as I often pointed out to him, the aliens could easily come at him over the tennis-courts. His house is a funny little semi-detached affair, with bulging windows and wooden beams stuck to the bricks that are supposed to give it an Olde Worlde appearance. There are three uncared-for rose bushes in the front garden. There's a white one for him, a red one in memory of her and a yellow one he planted just for me. He always said I was the son he never had. The white and red ones were supposed to grow into each other, but they never managed to do it. They just sort of droop grimly at each other across the ragged lawn. I don't know what this says about the old Marr marriage. My bush has gone crazy. It grows out in all directions and showers petals all round it.

The front curtains were drawn, which was odd. I was a touch scared. I peered through the frosted glass in the front door. All I could see was the shape of Mr Marr's bicycle. Through the letterbox, I could see the usual pile of letters, plastered with stamps from all over the world. They write to Mr Marr from everywhere about sightings, landings, close encounters of the fourth kind and all the other things that those boring radio telescopes down at the Mount Palomar observatory fail to pick up.

I fitted the key in the lock. I pushed open the door and looked down the hall. The first thing I thought was: the blobs or the androids or the giant green lizards from Venus or whatever they were had paid Mr Marr a call.

12

Every drawer in the house had been pulled out. But it wasn't like burglars. Things had been piled neatly on the floor, as if someone was packing for a long journey. Underpants were in one pile, socks another, and by the door there was a neat line of shoes. Over by the window the aliens had made a start on the reading matter, which, as it was mainly about them, was unsurprising. They were halfway through a book called *The UFO Report 1991*. It was open at a chapter entitled 'Disturbing Encounters in Northeast Brazil' by Bob Pratt.

A sentence on the first page caught my eye. *'If a UFO were to land in my backyard I would certainly not run out to embrace it. I would be very wary – and with good reason.'* Somebody had underlined this remark. It wasn't Mr Marr, because he never writes in books. He's fussier about how they look than he is about what's in them. I say some*body*. Some*thing*. Something which had used a Biro. I looked round carefully. There was a kind of chill about the place. I got up and went through to the kitchen.

Whoever had paid Mr Marr a visit had tried to make a piece of toast. Not very successfully. It was possible, of course, that these guys could handle speeds faster than light but a British toaster had them baffled. Mr Marr's toaster is, as it happens, a particularly dodgy piece of equipment. But why should they take the things out of the drawers? I sat on the bed and tried to think.

Could it be a burglar? But if it was a burglar, where was the broken window or the forced lock? I checked all over the house and there was no sign of any such thing. The next thing I did was to ring Mr Marr's office and ask if he had shown up for work. A woman at the other end said he hadn't. She sounded very surprised. 'He never misses,' she said. And then, 'Are you his son?'

That made me feel peculiar. I said I was his nephew. I don't know why. She didn't have any idea of where he might be if he wasn't at work. Which figured. There just wasn't anything else in his life. I was really getting worried. First my dad and now Mr Marr. What was happening?

Why were all his things out on the floor, as if someone had been packing? Was it possible that he had run away? Had he done something awful and decided to leave without telling anyone? Surely he would tell me if he was in trouble. Wouldn't he?

Or was he playing them along? I thought about this as I loosened my school tie and paced about the empty front room, feeling like a detective. I quite liked this line of approach. Maybe he had expressed keenness to visit their galaxy, but asked if he could pack a few things first. The blobs or the lizards, or whatever they were, follow him back from the Common and stand over him while he makes preparations.

'Come on, Marr,' they say, 'Threng, our King, is waiting.'

'I'll be right with you,' says Mr Marr, 'I'm just packing a pair of *boxer shorts* . . . '

All the time his eye is on the phone. If he can call me or Purkiss or, preferably, someone better qualified than either of us, he is in with a chance.

I sat back on the bed. This great detective I once read about used to go to the scene of the crime, close his eyes and visualize. Very often it turned out that he tuned in to what had actually happened. I closed my eyes and tried to *see* the aliens with Mr Marr . . .

He brings them back to the house and plays for time. But they don't give him that chance. The clothes pile up. More and more drawers are opened. Finally the blobs tap him on the shoulder and say, 'It's time to go, Marr!' That's when he makes the toast. Will there be anything to eat in the Crab Nebula – you know? But he's nervous. He burns the toast. The blobs are getting restive. Their ship is parked up by the War Memorial and at any moment some local is going to start asking questions.

Come on, Simon. You need more than this. This is just guesswork. You need some sign. If he really had been spacenapped (I wasn't yet sure that he had) he wouldn't go down without a fight. He'd leave some sign, wouldn't he? He'd leave a clue. For me or Purkiss or Walbeck.

He'd ask to go to the lavatory. Of course.

'Lavatory?' say the aliens. 'What is this?'

The aliens have progressed light years ahead of us. They have no need of toilet facilities on their planet. Marr gives them a GCSE lesson in biology and they laugh behind their flippers at how primitive we are. He explains the cultural need of humans to lock the door when they go to the bathroom. And then . . .

I was already walking towards the bathroom. The door was closed. I tugged at it hard. When it opened, the first thing I saw was the mirror. It was flecked with tiny white spots. Mr Marr had been spitting at it for years. On the washstand in front of the mirror were four or five tiny, deformed pieces of soap. But, in the middle of the glass, dead in the centre, someone had scrawled a single word: HELP!

They had used lipstick. My first thought was: *Where did Mr Marr get lipstick?* But then I realized. It was probably his wife's. He keeps all his wife's things, just as they were. There are even pairs of her stout, sensible shoes in the back kitchen.

You see, I do think we *know* things before they actually happen. There has to be a sense beyond seeing or hearing or taste or touch or smell. Not everything they tell you down at the First Church is idiotic. Great scientists, like Einstein for example, sort of *suspected* things like relativity before they had had a chance to prove them. He had an idea and found that the facts fitted it. I had had an idea and it was looking as if the facts fitted it only too well.

Other stuff in the bathroom had been disturbed. The cupboard on the wall had been ransacked. Toothpaste and toothbrushes were on the floor. Someone had opened a bottle of shampoo and sprayed it around the place like it was champagne at a Grand Prix.

I pinched the bridge of my nose with my thumb and index finger and began to visualize.

Mr Marr is surprised at the mirror. The aliens follow him and catch him writing. 'This is going to the lavatory, Marr?' they say, their metallic voices sounding a bit like Flasher Slingsby at his most evil.

There is a struggle. They cover him with poisonous slime or zap him with a laser gun. Then they have fun! They play with earthling cosmetics! Because, deep down, these aliens are just a bunch of kids. And then, suddenly bored, they tuck him under their flippers and saunter back through Wimbledon.

No one sees them. No one would blink twice if a 400-foot reptile wandered through Wimbledon Village after eleven at night. It is *dead*!

I was not jumping to any conclusions, but I thought we could well be talking spacenapping here. At least, it seemed as possible as any other explanation. Quite *how* this linked up with what I had seen outside 24 Stranraer Gardens the previous night I didn't know. But one thing seemed pretty certain. I had been wasting my time talking to Jesus about it. It was not His department. This was a very practical issue, with very serious implications for me and everyone else in the Wimbledon area.

I was just about to go into the living-room when I heard a sound outside. A kind of scratching at the front door. I had closed it. Hadn't I? I sat on the edge of the bath. Maybe I had. But Yale locks were not likely to present much problem to the heavies from the other side of the Red Shift. I stayed where I was, listening to my heart knock against my ribs.

Finally I went out into the corridor.

There was no sound coming from the front door. But someone or *something* was moving along the gravel at the side of the house. I inched my way towards the front room. If I could get down the path and out into the street, maybe I could at least warn someone before they dragged me up the old ladder and added a fourteen-year-old boy to their collection of souvenirs from the planet earth.

I breathed deeply and got ready to sprint.

Pathetic, isn't it? When they really do come in large numbers, we'll be out there putting up everything we've got and they'll wade through us. We'll be like those Aborigines faced with Captain Cook, the first white man they had ever seen. They thought he was the spirit of their ancestors and ran away.

I reached for the door handle. As I did so I heard someone try the back door. Two short turns and then a knock. It *was* burglars. They had done over Mr Marr and now they had come back for me! I thought I heard steps moving away. They would try the front again. I almost ran to the back door and opened it in one swift movement. I found I was looking at Purkiss.

I gave a little squeal. I was inches from Purkiss's big, thick glasses, long, greasy hair and big, bloodshot eyes. I've never been able to find out what he does for the Parks Department. I think they just leave him around in open spaces to deter flashers. His mouth was twitching, the way it does when he has something to say.

'Where is he?' he said eventually.

'I don't know, Purkiss,' I said. 'I really don't know.'

At this point Walbeck emerged from behind a bush. He scurried across the gravel, waving as he did so, and scanning the sky for signs of alien craft. He looked, I have to say, very worried indeed. He had his piece of paper with him, but I think we all felt this wasn't a time for writing.

'They'll come for me next!' said Purkiss.

I looked at Purkiss. I didn't, somehow, think this was likely. I don't really think an alien would bother with Purkiss even if he landed on him on his way to somewhere else. And it seemed downright impossible that the said alien, having nobbled Mr Marr and got him halfway to Saturn, should suddenly stop, snap his fingers and *go back* for Purkiss.

Walbeck was hugging the line of the wall. Every so often he would point at the sky and shiver violently.

'He didn't show up for work,' said Purkiss.

'I know,' I said.

Purkiss opened his bloodshot eyes wide. 'There's no sign of him!'

'We don't know whether they have actually taken him,' I said. 'That's one possibility. They could be keeping him somewhere. They could be still here. You know?'

Then I stopped. What was I saying?

'We don't actually *know* that it's aliens.' Walbeck crouched down and put his hands on his head. He turned down the corners of his mouth, pointed up at the sky again and then gave us the thumbs-down signal. It was as well he hadn't been around when they did actually show up or he would have let the earth down pretty badly. The sight of these two had calmed me, however, and, when I spoke, I was surprised to find I was talking quite slowly and clearly.

'We just have to be careful. From what I've seen so far, guys, if these *are* extraterrestrials, they're not the "Hi, let's party!" kind.'

Walbeck was now curled up in a ball, whimpering. Purkiss knelt down beside him and started to stroke him as if Walbeck was a frightened dog.

'But, as yet,' I went on, 'we don't know. We don't know what they look like or what their methods are. They could look like . . . Purkiss for all we know!'

We looked at Purkiss. It lightened the mood somewhat. Even Walbeck grinned and indicated, as only Walbeck can, that he hoped they didn't look anything like Purkiss.

'Should we tell the police?' said Purkiss.

We all know the police are useless at dealing with non-earth-based crime. All they are good for is holding the crowd back around the saucer while the boffins get to it. Some of them try feeling the old alien collar, and they are usually reduced to a small heap of cinders for their pains. Visitors from other planets just do not fit into police procedure. And I had the feeling that if we told the police it would all turn out to be our fault.

'Tell no one,' I said urgently. 'I am going to keep a careful watch for any other manifestations, and as soon as they happen we will move. In the meantime, who knows? They may bring him back!'

Purkiss nodded. 'In the case of the Poznan Twelve,' he said, 'Mr and Mrs Vrchlika said they had been enhanced by the experience. It was only the dumplings that experienced material alterations to their state.'

'Sure,' I said.

We didn't mention the twelve-year-old nun in Santa Monica, though. Or the experiences undergone by the director of the Lycée Municipale in the West Cameroun in the spring of 1981. All of us knew enough about spacenapping to be aware that it could go either way. Some days it was all wet kisses and talk of mutual cooperation.

The next minute it was out with the old steel scalpels and heigh-ho for penetrating the earthling body in a variety of disgusting ways.

We were all pretty tight-lipped as I locked the back door and went out the front to join them. Say what you like, my friends, all the evidence seemed to suggest that a respectable engineer of amazingly regular habits had, suddenly and for no obvious reason, disappeared without trace.

As I headed, unwillingly, back towards Stranraer Gardens, I felt that I was the owner of a heavy and awesome secret. Something that I could tell no one. Not even the character I had found it so welcome to have words with last night. No, not Albert Roger Quigley – Jesus Christ. You remember? His writ runs from Galilee to Tuscaloosa, but in none of the texts do we find any mention of His having control over things far out in deep space or of His Voice having the power to command among the spirals of twisting stars.

13

'Why', said Greenslade as we sat at the lunch table, a few days after my dad had died, 'do you eat meat with a spoon?'

I didn't answer. I chewed a lot and gave him some of my village-idiot face. All around us, boys in black blazers were cramming food down their faces. Out on the rugby pitch, Mr Grimond was shouting at Extra Quintus. The sky wore the same blue it had chosen for the day I saw my dad for the last time.

'You could cut it,' said Khan, leaning over and studying me over his glasses, 'and *then* eat it with a spoon.' He gave me a shrewd look. 'Is it true that your parents are very religious?'

I gulped and said nothing.

Members of the First Spiritualist Church always eat meat with a spoon. They were commanded to do so by a geezer called Lewis, who was big in the Church in the 1930s and who, for a time, posed a bit of a threat to Rose Fox. 'Forks,' he used to say, 'do the Devil's Work. And knives grieve the spirit.' He had pretty definite views on cutlery did Lewis. He gave out some heavy notes about the correct method of holding your spoon as well. And towards the end of his life he got into condiments. 'Do not pass the mustard' was the general drift. I still flinch if someone at school offers me the stuff.

'Didn't you say your mum was a nutter?' said Greenslade, looking at me keenly. I shrugged. Then Khan nudged him with his foot.

'I'm sorry, Britton,' he said. 'Your dad . . . '

'That's OK,' I said, getting to my feet. 'Actually, my mum and dad belong to this Church and you . . . '

I looked down at their faces. I realized that I wasn't going to be able to talk to them about the First Church of Christ the Spiritualist. And I felt sad, because I wanted to explain it, but I didn't even know where to begin.

I never have friends back to the house. You can just never tell whether anything embarrassing is going to happen. But Khan and Greenslade had met my dad a few times. Once when he came to pick me up after a school trip that is still known as *Die Screaming in Koblenz*. That was in the days when he drove a motor bike. And once when he made a spectacle of himself during Mr Hammond's production of *The Caucasian Chalk Circle*. Nobody could hear what he was shouting – I think it was about the death of Communism – but my mum said it was as well they couldn't.

'What's with the games bag?' said Khan. 'I thought it was a free afternoon.'

'I'm playing squash with a friend of my dad's.'

I don't know why I said Quigley was a friend of his. I tell lies, sometimes, for absolutely no reason at all – except to see the expressions on people's faces. Both Khan and Greenslade looked rather serious as I picked up my bag and headed for the sunlight.

I think I had agreed to play squash with Quigley because he was the only person I could think of to talk to about Mr Marr. Mr Marr hadn't showed up at any of the places where he should have been. It was time I told someone.

Once, of course, I would have told my dad. I talked to him about the extraterrestrials quite a lot.

'What you've got to watch,' he used to say, 'is Krull of Varna. He's the boy to watch.'

He was not convinced by the evidence, I'm afraid. I had shown him the black-and-white photographs of a Pleiadean Saucer, taken by Albert de Roquefort of Autruches in the Rhône Valley, and he was not impressed. In fact he laughed a lot.

'I'm not saying,' I used to say to him, 'that that is a genuine photo. But that doesn't prove they aren't there, does it?'

'I'm sure they are,' said Dad. 'But where?'

This was where it got sticky.

'Well, they're there. At the moment. But they're on their way here.'

'Well,' Dad would reply, 'call me when they show. I'd like to be there to see it . . . ' Then he'd put his arm round me. 'What size do you think they run to? And do they have corkscrews on their heads? That's the thing!'

I could almost hear his gravelly bass voice saying this. I saw again his blue jersey with the food stains down the front and smelt his breath, acrid with garlic from the La Paesana Restaurant, Mitcham.

Quigley had been suggesting we play for almost as long as I had known him. 'Come down to The Club, young shaver,' he used to say on Sunday mornings. 'Do you know it?'

'No,' I'd reply. 'What's it called?'

'It's called,' Quigley would answer with ill-concealed pride and excitement, 'The Club. And it's one of the most exclusive squash clubs there is. It is *over the road from the All England Tennis Club!*'

I couldn't see why this was such a big deal. But Quigley always got a thrill from things like that. The whole family dine out at a hamburger place off Piccadilly just so as he can say they are 'off to a little bistro in Mayfair'. I wouldn't put it past him to lug a Thermos down Pall Mall so as he could tell us all he had 'dropped in at the Palace for tea'.

When I got to it, however, I must confess I was impressed. It had smoked-glass windows and a character in a commissionaire's uniform outside. I couldn't think how Quigley got the money to pay the membership. In the car park, every third car must have cost more than our house.

I sauntered up to the desk and put my games bag down in a firm but casual way. The guy, who was in a sort of mauve serge suit with THE CLUB written in the top left-hand corner in discreet lettering, was looking at me rather oddly, so I pushed my glasses back up my nose and gave him one of my businesslike looks. 'Simon Britton,' I said, using a voice I had heard my dad use when on the phone to the bank, 'for Roger Quigley.'

'Roger' to the outside world. 'Albert' to those lucky enough to feel close to the great man.

You could tell from the man's face that Quiggers was pretty well thought of here. There was a ladder, Emily had told me, and Quigley was at the top of it. Occasionally some puny stockbroker who fancied his chances, just because he had played in the Olympics or something, would try and move in on The Boss, as Quigley was known. And the guy would have to be carried out by teams of paramedics.

As I said the word 'Quigley', the man himself appeared. He was wearing a loose cream shirt with a drawing of a hairy geezer and what looked like a signature underneath it. As he saw me, Quigley pointed to it. 'Alberto Loosali!' he said, as if I was supposed to know who this was.

'Right,' I said.

Quigley went to the desk. Stuffed into his bag was a racket that looked as if it had been tested at speeds of several hundred miles an hour. He was wearing a pair of green track-suit trousers. Even his buttocks had a taut, menacing air. I was beginning to feel tired just watching him sign me in.

'Loosali,' said Quigley, 'beat Rumero in Athens!'

I had absolutely no idea who either of these characters were.

Hoisting his bag over his shoulder, Quigley jogged off towards a door marked MEMBERS ONLY. I followed him, marvelling at the change in posture he had achieved simply by wearing trainers that looked as if they were worth about £200. You knew, just from his equipment, that Quigley was the business as far as squash was concerned.

'I'll go easy on you, young shaver,' said Quiggers, 'for dear Norman's sweet sake!'

I'd played squash with my dad. He was banned from his club for smoking while playing. But before they gave him the boot we did play. Just once. It was the funniest thing I can remember.

'Oh *no!*' he would shout, as he ran across the stone floor, waving his racket. 'Oh *no!* This is going to be a *disaster!*' His forecast was usually correct.

Quigley's approach was very different.

He was the only guy I've ever met who took a shower *before* playing. 'I like to be clean for the experience,' he said. He looked like a man who would not need to shower after the game.

I had to get in the shower with him, which was a pretty sobering time for me. Partly because he made very free with the old Quigley chopper, shampooing it and hosing it down as if he was about to enter it for some competition, and partly because he insisted on singing as we stood, man to man, under the steaming water.

'Praise God I am not blessed with pain! Praise God I am in bliss!' he carolled as he towelled himself down and sprayed talcum powder on what had to be the biggest cock in South London. No one laughed.

A thin guy in the corner asked whether I was Quigley's son. And Quigley, as he got into some figure-hugging shorts, said, 'I am all the father he has, Walter.'

Walter looked impressed. As we went out to the court, he said to me, 'Lovely man, lovely, lovely man!'

Maybe Walter had an account at Quigley's bank. I don't know.

Greatly to my relief, there were no spectators.

I was wearing a baggy pair of jeans, which Quigley had been pretty sniffy about. 'We must be properly clad,' he had said. But I knew, from the moment he closed the door to the court, that I was by no means underdressed for the event. About the most suitable garment to have worn would have been a suit of chain mail.

He started by suggesting a 'knock-up' and then, almost immediately, whacked the ball against the rear elevation at about the velocity of light. It came back at me with such force that my one thought was to find some quiet corner, pull a rug over my head and let the ball finish whatever it had to do.

But there is no place to hide on a squash-court. It is just you and the ball. And, when you're playing with Quigley, it doesn't feel like one ball. It feels like an angry swarm.

The ball snaked round like a heat-seeking missile, cutting off my line of retreat. As I stood there, my racket held out in front of me like a serving-spoon, it made contact with the wall to my left and ricocheted back towards me. It seemed annoyed that I had missed it.

'Move into the ball!' yelled Quigley.

I ran, hard, in the opposite direction.

'It's spinning!' he yelled. 'I've put top spin on it!'

It looked like he had done a lot more than that. It looked like he had brainwashed the thing. It was coming after me like a Dobermann pinscher. I swerved to my left and the ball hit the far wall of the court. It showed no sign of slowing up. After the way he'd hit it, it could be whanging around the four walls for the foreseeable future.

Quigley, his buttocks thrust out behind him, was bouncing up and down on the spot. 'Thar she blows!' he yelled. He seemed pleased with the way things were going. 'She comes on hard, me dearios!'

I have a pretty hazy grasp of the rules of squash. When Dad and I played, the idea seemed to be to keep the ball in the air for a few minutes and then award the points to the person who seemed to need them most.

Quigley and I hadn't finished knocking up yet, and already I was wondering if The Club kept an oxygen cylinder handy. The ball headed off in the direction of the service area, travelling waist height at about thirty miles an hour. With a kind of feeble cry, I set off in pursuit.

I was getting angry. You know? I was fighting back.

I caught up with it – or, rather, it caught up with me – as it was setting off from the rear wall on another leg of its journey south (or was it north? Or west? Or east?). I held out my racket, with the right arm fully extended, drew back my left leg and drove forward, hard. The ball hit me in the chest.

'Stretcher case!' yelled Quigley, in the grip of almost unbearable excitement. 'Give that man a jelly bean!'

With these words he danced up the court, his long legs waving elaborately, like a crane-fly's. When he finally got the ball in his sights, he swept it up against the back wall. My one thought was to get as far away as possible from both him and it before he started whacking me into play as well.

'Give it welly!' he shouted as I shambled to the nearest corner, listening to the irritated whine of the ball. 'Give it welly, young shaver!'

I did not, I have to say, give it welly. I did not give it any kind of footwear. I gave it a kind of reedy sob as it slammed into some other surface that I had not known was there. How many walls were there in this court? And which way up were we? I was beginning to feel as if I was in a space-flight simulator. As if Quigley might appear above me at any moment, grinning, as he slurped across the ceiling upside down.

This time I stayed where I was. I tried to look like a man waiting for his opportunity. I stood on my points. I held the racket with both hands. I ducked. I weaved. I gave the ball some pretty nasty looks. But I did not make the mistake of actually moving in its direction until it had finished whizzing round the court and was trickling towards the door.

It was time for a bit of conversation.

'Mr Quigley,' I said, 'did I *really* see my dad out in the street the other night?'

This did, at least, prevent Quiggers from scooping up the ball and sending it back into orbit. I was doubled up. My face felt like a large, red balloon and my shirt was dripping with sweat.

'How d'ye mean, m'deario?' said Quigley.

'I mean, was it *real*? Or was it like a dream or something?'

Quigley picked up the ball and folded his long fingers round it. Up in the gallery a couple of members had come in to watch The Boss humiliate me.

'Life,' said Quigley, 'is a dream and a passing show. Hallo, Bertie!'

'Hallo there, Big Man,' said Bertie. He was a guy of about seventy, wearing a blue blazer and a yachting-cap. Had he, I wondered, come into the wrong club? Or was this a sort of special drinking outfit?

Quigley put a hand on my shoulder. 'You saw what you saw, Simey,' he said. 'You saw what God wanted you to see. You were led by God's will. Because he wants you, Simey. He wants you for Our Church and for Jesus. Make no mistake about that, young shaver!'

Quigley made these remarks in a loud, audible voice. A couple more spectators had come in behind the person in the blazer. One of them seemed to be wearing what looked like a sombrero. The other, a man of about eighty, nothing but a fluffy, white towel. They seemed to be nodding keenly. Maybe they were Christians, planted there by some committee of the First Church of Christ the Spiritualist.

'What I mean,' I said in a low voice, 'is that there are things in the world, in the *universe*, that we can't explain. Aren't there? About why we're here and what we're doing here and what it's all about.'

'Yes,' said Quigley. 'Yes, me laddio – there are things in the universe that are pretty hard to make out. There are!'

He thrust his face into mine. He did not appear to have sweated at all.

'Sin is one of them,' he said, 'and wickedness is another!'

This wasn't a lot of help. I wanted some basic questions answered here, not the usual stuff about being good or bad.

'I mean . . . ' I said, 'suppose someone . . . well . . . disappeared?'

'Who's disappeared?' said Quigley, sharply.

'Well,' I said, wondering if it was safe to say this out loud, as I did so, 'Mr Marr.'

Quigley laughed. 'Oh, Mr Marr! Well, if *he's* disappeared we know where to look, don't we? It's simple. Eh?' He prodded me in the chest. 'Spacemen got him!'

He found this very amusing. So too did the guys in the gallery. There were all chuckling to themselves as Quigley handed me the ball and suggested I try to serve. He laid some emphasis on the word 'try'. I was about to suggest that I went to lie down for an hour or so. Instead I held the ball gingerly between the first and second fingers of my left hand and braced myself for more pain.

'Beef!' said Quigley. 'Beef in the service!' I wafted the racket backwards and forwards a few times. The air resistance was pretty rough. Before I hit it, I had one more go.

'But if you saw something weird, and you had an *explanation* for that. And it was aliens. I mean, that was the one that made sense, then . . . '

Quigley came over to me. He looked troubled. He thought I was still on about my dad.

'Norman has a lot of unfinished business here. He was a man very much *in medias res* . . . '

'Was he?'

'Look,' said Quigley, 'we've had messages through about Veronica. He's talked about the Veronica business a lot. And about Mrs Danby too.'

From the way he said this, it sounded like he and Marjorie had been giving the old man some retrospective marriage guidance.

'Who's Veronica?' I said.

He stopped. He looked a trifle cagey.

'There are some messages from the Other Side that are not suitable for young people's ears.'

He cuffed me. I think it was meant affectionately, but I staggered a few yards from the effect of the blow.

'I don't think the little green chaps have anything to do with your daddy's continuing presence on the earth,' said Quigley, 'and I have to say to you that if I saw one of your aliens I'd go up to it and I'd give it a good hug! I'd say "Cor lumme, Alien – haven't yer heard about the love of Jesus?" And I'd take its little green heart to my bosom. Because the love of Jesus isn't just for you and me, Simo – it's for Venusians and Droids and the old ninety-foot green monsters from the planet Zog too!'

I was getting nowhere with this. It would be hopeless to tell him about Mr Marr. I had been stupid to even try. Why had I ever imagined that Quigley would understand? I braced myself for the service.

'Your dad did some very, very wrong things. He didn't always do right by you, I'm afraid. But God will forgive him for that. What we mustn't do is shut Jesus out from our hearts, because for as long as we do we hang around the places we loved and the ones we cared for *like ghosts*!'

I hit the ball as hard as I could. It helped to imagine that it was Quigley's head. It sort of trickled down from the racket and dragged itself up to the rear wall of the court. It was already looking tired as it made contact. It came down, rather meekly, towards the Quigley feet.

Quigley looked at it sternly and did a sort of on-the-spot gallop. His long arms swirled his racket round in the air. The last movement was the sort of thing I had seen conductors do when they were in front of large orchestras that were playing loudly. There was a rush of air through the court and the squash ball was back in business.

It really had it in for me this time. It clearly thought I had no business to be on the court. It went straight for my head. I held up my racket, purely in self-defence. The ball hit it dead centre and whizzed back against the rear wall. With a stab of fear I realized we were into a rally.

'Good!' yelled Quigley. 'Whammo, whammo, whammo, good!'

He plunged after it like a man possessed.

'Beef in the service!' he yelled. 'Beefo, beefo, beefo, beefo, good!'

There was an ache in the whole of my upper body. Water was running off my hairline like snow in a heatwave. When Quigley made contact with the ball it howled back into play, and, to my surprise, I managed to spoon it back to him.

He was well away now. He was past caring how the ball had got to him. 'Just keep it going, young shaver! Last man to the ball's a cissy, eh?'

Quiggers didn't really need a partner. Once the ball was in motion, he just went. All I had to do was to look keen and occasionally wave my racket at the ball. He would grunt as he ran past me to bash it back into play – 'Nice try, Simo! Keep it coming, eh?'

After a minute or so there was just him, the ball and the walls of the squash-court. He ran from side to side, grunting and thwacking and yelling, and I moved, very gradually, towards the more suitable role of spectator.

I can't remember at what point I stole towards the door. All I do remember is that Quigley was volleying and forehanding and backhanding and the spectators were cheering and waving. And suddenly I was tiptoeing back towards the changing-room. I could still hear him grunting and thumping as I made my way out of the front door of The Club, *en route* for anywhere that wasn't 24 Stranraer Gardens.

What had I seen that night my dad had died? And where had Mr Marr gone? None of the adults who made it their business to tell me things could tell me anything about this affair. The only person I could have talked to wasn't around. I thought about him as I slouched off down the road. I thought about sitting with him after our squash game, him with his head in his hands, me sipping a Coke. But, no matter how hard I thought about him, it wasn't going to bring him back or explain why the world had got so hard to understand since he died.

14

The afternoon had clouded over when I got out of The Club. There was a line of grey clouds, lying like boats at anchor, above the hill. I slung my bag across my back and walked back down Wimbledon Park Road. I headed away from home, towards the big main road, noisy with lorries and bright with the signs of tobacconists and fast-food places that never seem to close.

I felt low. I stopped just before I got to the main road and tried to see if I could see my right bicep. It was still acting cagey, even though I took off my blazer and rolled up my shirt sleeve. There was still a vague depression where my chest ought to be. Maybe that was why I was so hopeless at all forms of sport.

But I didn't really feel bad about being thrashed by Quigley. I think it's important to rise above such things. I'd rather people thought I was intelligent than superbly muscled and well co-ordinated.

I felt my bicep again. It seemed to have disappeared completely.

What I felt bad about was that I had actually wanted to confide in Quigley. That's how desperate I was. And it reminded me how much I wanted to have a normal family. You know? The kind that they have in that soap-powder ad where they've made a home movie and dad laughs when she gets the stains out. I mean, I know it's schmuck. I know they're only a bunch of dead-beat actors, but sometimes I wish I could step inside the screen and become part of them. Khan gets kept in to do homework most evenings. Greenslade's dad hit his brother with a cricket bat. And Richthofer's mum – who isn't really his mum – had an affair with a chiropodist. But, compared to my family, they are all *normal*.

I can't understand how my mum and dad ever got together. You know? I can remember dad coming in one day, when we were on holiday in Dorset, grasping me by the arm and saying, in the serious voice he used to talk about religion, 'Always remember, Simon, I love your mother very much.'

Why was he telling me? Why did I have to remember? It wasn't helped by his adding, as he went back out to start having another row with her, 'She hems me in boy! She hems me in! But *by God* I love her!'

He should have been on the stage really. But he joined the First Church of Christ the Spiritualist as a substitute.

I mooched down the main road, games bag on my shoulder. Why couldn't we do the things normal people do, like go to bowling-alleys? Why did the First Spiritualist Church believe that the Charrington Bowl, Kingston, was 'unclean and filthy with the work of the whore'? Why did we have to eat fish on Wednesdays? Was it absolutely necessary to follow Ella Walsh's instruction to 'avoid Ireland like the plague'? I'd quite like to go to Dublin. You know?

For some reason I turned off left down Furnival Gardens. Thinking about it afterwards, I decided that it must have been exerting a strong psychic pull. It doesn't look like a road with any spiritual significance. It isn't on a ley line or anything. At first sight it's just another long, pointless South London street with too many cars parked in it. But, as I trudged up it, I started to feel weirder and weirder. It wasn't simply that I felt depressed, although, if I had had a guitar and if I had been able to play, I'd have sung the blues. As my eyes wandered from the dirt-stained pavement to the greyer sky, I could feel a presence in the air. And it was *him*.

You always knew Dad was around. You knew it from his cough or his habit of breaking into song or his preference for bawling at people he wanted to go and see rather than walking around and trying to find them. Some people, like my mum, aren't really present and correct even when they're there, but there was never any doubt about Dad. The broken veins on his cheeks, the half-smoked tipped cigarettes, the low growl before he delivered an opinion about something – they were all so *vivid*.

I couldn't believe he'd died, you see. All I wanted was a middle-aged man with a big nose. That wasn't so much to ask, was it? Surely whatever spirits arrange the world could lay that on for me? I looked hard across the street, in between the cars, up towards the road ahead that was rising to another main street running across it, watching for that familiar face and listening for that unforgettable voice.

In one of the houses on the other side of the street an upper window was open. Loud classical music was coming out of it. I imagined someone lying on the bed, staring at the ceiling and watching the breeze stir the grey lace curtains this way and that. Up to my right I could see the black railings at the beginning of the patch of waste ground, and, ahead, nothing but roads and houses and, beyond them, houses and roads, cluttered with people as lonely and scared as me. The suburbs are hell. They go on and on and on, like Sunday afternoons.

He came out of a house about 150 yards away. He looked up and down the street, as if he was frightened of being followed. Then he looked up at the front bedroom window. He wasn't wearing white. He didn't *look* in the least ghostly. But he was wearing the sort of clothes he would not have been seen dead in, when alive. For a start he was wearing a hat, which is something my dad never ever did. 'Headgear,' he once said to me, 'is an unnecessary indulgence, except when the temperature is below zero.' But, although I was a fair way away from him, I could have sworn it was my dad. If it wasn't him, it was an incredibly good simulation. He didn't see me. He turned and walked up the hill, past the waste ground.

I thought hard about what Quigley had said. Was it all my fault that my dad was forced to walk the streets of Wimbledon? I remembered him once saying to me, the year we went to Cornwall, 'I stay for you, boy. You know that, don't you? I'm here because of you.' And when they argued, which was a lot, it was often about me. I could hear them at the other end of the house, as I lay awake in bed. 'You don't appreciate him,' one of them would say, and the other would answer, 'No, no. It's *you*! It's you who doesn't appreciate Simon!'

Had I made them both unhappy and was this why he couldn't be at peace? Or was I dreaming all this, making some poor, innocent, middle-aged person look like my old man, simply because I so much wanted to see him again?

The figure I was following – I still wasn't certain it was my dad – didn't look at all depressed to be hanging around South London. In fact, once it had got going, it looked pretty pleased to be here.

If it wasn't my dad, then what was it?

Supposing we weren't dealing with something as local as space-napping. Supposing we were talking invasion. Suppose the extra-terrestrials had moved beyond the initial, exploratory stages and on to one of their favourite ploys: full-scale invasion of planet earth. Method? Bodysnatching. Aliens, as I am sure you know, are no slou-ches when it comes to taking people to bits and reassembling them, programmed to do the will of the War Lord of Ro or the Headless Things of Jupiter.

Sure. Crazy, I know. I didn't, as yet, actually *think* this. But it was as good as any other explanation on offer.

The normal procedure is to pull a guy behind the hedge on his way to the office, strap him to a bit of Venusian technology and drain off the old cranium before you can say 'Bob's your uncle.' After this, the individual heads on into town – the only clue to the fact that he has been taken over by aliens being a slightly glassy look about the eyes and a tendency to give all words in any sentence a roughly equal amount of stress.

Why not dead people? You know? Dead people are perfect. We leave them lying around the undertakers' for days, just waiting to be reanimated by the guys from Orion or a highly developed corner of the Magellan Cluster. Stiffs from all over South London could be swarming towards some prearranged meeting-point, their expressions devoid of all traces of emotion. Maybe what I had seen outside my window in Stranraer Gardens had come to me courtesy of the same firm that had lifted Mr Marr!

If it was a simulation, the extraterrestrials had done a fantastically good job. It even walked slightly to one side, the way my dad always did. It stopped, just as it got to Garratt Lane, and hitched up its trousers in exactly the way he used to do.

I still hadn't got a close look at its face.

It turned right into the next main road and headed off south. The funny thing was – they hadn't got the clothes to fit. The suit jacket hung limp and awkward from the creature's shoulders, and it was wearing huge brown boots. They were not the sort of thing Dad would ever wear. It's a standard mistake the aliens make. They run up a pair of trousers out there on some moon of Jupiter and they never get it *quite* right.

They had also reckoned without human psychology. They probably didn't know about families and how humans sort of, you know, *like* each other. Their planet was probably not unlike the First Church of Christ the Spiritualist, and when people died they hung out the bunting. If my dad was alive, he would have let me know.

As I watched the entity tiptoe down the highway, I remembered Dad on the night I passed Grade Two Saxophone with merit. He was practically going up to people in the street on the way to the restaurant, grabbing them by the lapels and shouting *'Merit! You hear me? Merit!'* in their faces. I remembered him at the table in La Paesana too, his face flushed with wine, his fists clenched aloft – 'Nail the bastards! That's what you've got to do, Simon! Nail the bastards!'

It's funny, when I think about any of these gatherings, although my mum must have been there, when I try to picture them I can't see her. It's as if she's been painted out, the way Trotsky was painted out of all those photographs after the revolution in Russia. It was my dad and me. It was always my dad and me.

Whatever was slouching down Garratt Lane, its hands deep in the unfamiliar earthling pockets, was something else again.

I started to feel angry.

Why had I believed that garbage from Quigley? Why had I ever assumed that any of this was my fault? How had I got into the absurd position of believing that, just because I occasionally pulled my wire, my dad had been forced to roam some of the least attractive parts of South London after his death? People will believe anything, that's the fact of the matter. It's all too easy to dismiss a new idea – like, things from the Crab Nebula are trying to take over the planet – simply because it sounds strange. Why is believing *that* any stranger than believing that God punishes sinners? Or that Britain is a democracy? Or any of the other crazy things adults ask young people to believe?

Steady on, Simon, I told myself. *Let's sort out what's possible here. What do we actually think, Britton?*

Why shouldn't a take-over of the world begin in Wimbledon? It's as good a place as any other to start restructuring the DNA of earthlings. It's got the edge on northern Brazil, where, according to Bob Pratt, there is a phenomenal amount of this sort of thing going on.

I kept a respectable distance from the creature as it moseyed down through South Wandsworth. Was it headed for Tooting Bec and a quiet pint with some finned, semi-amphibious pile of green blubber with four heads? It wasn't an obvious monster. It looked, superficially, quite normal. But the more closely I looked at it, the shakier it looked as a human being. Everything looked a bit ... *put on*. Very cleverly done and very neatly thought out. But missing the thing that divides us from the rest of creation: humanity.

I don't think I would have said anything if it hadn't started running for the bus. Sometimes you only *see* a person when that person does a particular thing. As it thrust itself down on its right foot, it jerked its elbows down at the ground as if it was going to use them to lever itself forward – exactly the way my dad used to do. 'In my youth,' he used to tell me, in a way I have to say I didn't entirely trust, 'I was something of an athlete.' It was the exact movement, I swear. I couldn't help it. I called, just once – 'Dad!'

Immediately I had called his name I regretted it. I felt that I had been ridiculously naïve. If this thing was from the other side of the galaxy, it would be ready for such eventualities. It probably had a tape packed with all the things my dad ever said. In my dad's case it wouldn't need to be a particularly long tape, because he only ever said about thirty or forty things, in fairly strict rotation. It had probably got them all in there, stacked away neatly in its nasty little alien head. 'Mine is a pint,' and 'I am easy, old son!' and 'Have you seen the *Writers' and Artists' Yearbook* anywhere?'

But they never, as I said, get humans *quite* right.

It turned and looked towards me. Just for a moment I saw something behind its eyes I thought I recognized. But then it wasn't there any more. Its face changed and what I saw on its features was extra-terrestrial panic, as if someone was getting on the line to it and calling 'Re-turn to ship! A-bort mi-ssion! The hu-man-oid earth-ling has re-cog-nized you!'

It lowered its hat so that it covered its eyes and ran for the bus. The trousers really were *laughable*, my son. I mean, this was supposed to be my dad, right? The man for whom time stopped at some moment in the 1970s. This thing's trousers were trailing on the pavement, and made of some coarse tweed, quite unlike anything Norman Britton had ever worn. It was bent over double as it reached the bus. Whether this was because it was still under orders to keep its face away from the light or whether it was because it was finding our atmosphere difficult I didn't care to guess. The atmosphere in Garratt Lane is not great, even for humans.

'Dad!'

I couldn't help it. I called again. Not being a highly disciplined blob from a star system billions of years older than our own earth but a flesh-and-blood boy of fourteen, I was a little at the mercy of the old *emotions*. But it didn't turn. It had to get to grips with the amazingly primitive transport devices still in use in the Wimbledon area, to look with some degree of confidence into the eyes of driver-conductors and tell them it had not got the right change.

It made the bus. The bus pulled away. I was left there on the pavement.

The real road-to-Damascus moments are the ones you work out for yourself. No one helped Archimedes, right? There was just him and the bath. What I went through on the pavement that evening was a revelation. I knew I wasn't crazy. I had never felt so utterly and completely sane. But I knew, the way you know the answers to a difficult exam when you've prepared the paper really well. These guys weren't buddy-buddy-give-us-a-football-pitch-to-land-on-and-let's-get-pally. They were devious. They were unscrupulous. They were unbelievably good at genetic engineering. And they were *here*.

I would have to be very careful who I started trusting with all this information, though. In some ways, the violent ward of the local

mental hospital was an attractive alternative to number 24 Stranraer
Gardens, and this was probably just where the extraterrestrials
hoped I would be placed. But I didn't think I was ready for it yet. I
needed a sympathetic audience. Not necessarily ufologists – they do
not need convincing about *anything*. But people who would spread
the word. People who would let me get through the details of this
story without trying to take my temperature and asking me where I
stood on mind-expanding drugs. I needed a fairly large body of
people who were good at believing things. Who else, my friends, but
the First Church of Christ the Spiritualist, South Wimbledon?

As I crossed back towards Wimbledon Park Road, a hymn from
my childhood came into my mind:

> Tell them the word!
> Tell them the word!
> Why don't you ever just try?
> If you have some news
> That you really mustn't lose,
> Come along and Testify!

I found myself singing this out loud as I walked towards Stranraer
Gardens thinking about the extraordinary things I had seen and
heard since my father's death. And when I got to the chorus, I
practically shouted it into the faces of the astonished passers-by:

> Testify! Testify!
> Take your troubles to the Lord!
> Testify! Testify!
> Dare to face the Fire and the Sword!
> Are you down and glum?
> Oh has the Saviour come?
> Have you news you really want to cry?
> Step among us brother!
> We're the ones! No other
> Will let you really Testify!

I thought about Old Mother Walsh's prophecies. I thought about
Lewis. I thought about that snake with TWO THOUSAND YEARS GO BY

on it. And I thought about all the crazy things people believe. Just to keep themselves sane.

> Step among us brother!
> We're the ones! No other
> Will let you really Testify!

PART TWO

15

One Sunday morning, about a week after I had seen my dad for the second time, I was lying in bed when I heard voices in the street below. They were singing. Not loudly, but loudly enough for half past six on a Sunday morning. Among the voices, I thought I recognized Roger Beeding's and Hannah Dooley's.

> Mother-life God she is calling Thee!
> Mother-life God she is calling Thee!
> Holla! Holla! Holla!
> Awa-a-a-y!

We have very patient neighbours.

I got up, staggered to the window and, while keeping my head below the level of the sill, attempted to close it.

My first thought was that I was 320 duck-jumps behind and if I was ever going to make the state of *shai-hai* I would probably have to spend a whole weekend duck-jumping. My second thought, which did not occur to me until I was crawling back along the floor towards my bed, was that today was the day when I was due to Testify. That was what the choir outside was for. I had been called upon to show my newly strengthened Christian faith before the whole congregation of the First Spiritualist Church. Praying with Quigley wasn't enough. I had to tell the people. He was very emphatic about that.

I got back under the duvet and felt my balls, for reassurance. These were probably one of the few things of mine not due to be on show at the First Church of Christ the Spiritualist later this morning. As Quigley had said to me, last night, 'Speak the whole truth of your heart when you testify, Simo!'

There is a sign outside the First Church that reads

ARE YOU A CUSTARD CHRISTIAN?
DO YOU GET UPSET OVER TRIFLES?
JESUS ISN'T. COME ON IN AND JOIN HIM.

If I was a Christian at all – and I wasn't sure that I was – I thought I was probably a custard Christian. Or maybe not even that. Maybe I was a jelly Muslim or a sponge-cake Buddhist. *The whole truth of my heart.* The thought of morning service is always a pain, and the prospect of this one made me stick my head back under the duvet to block out the already brilliant day.

I had also remembered that the Quigleys were still living with us. 'We're having building work done,' Quigley had said, 'so we can camp out with you!' He had said this as if he was doing us all a big favour.

My mum came in at about 07.15, holding out my black suit and a white shirt that she had just ironed. She stood looking at me from the end of the bed.

'Oh, Simon!' she said. 'Oh Simon!'

'Yes, Mum?'

She put the shirt and the suit on a chair by the window.

'I wonder if Daddy will come through today. I must say, I hope he manifests himself. He'd be so proud!'

I thought there was a very good chance of his showing up. Quite often there are more deceased members of the congregation present on Sunday mornings than there are living punters.

'Would he?'

She looked at me narrowly. She was rather less convinced about my conversion than the Quigleys. I had been doing my best to mime the odd prayer since my dad died, but I had a feeling she saw through me.

'You're not going to be silly, are you?'

'No, Mum. I just wasn't sure whether he *would* be proud. I mean, Mum, was he religious or what?'

'He was . . .'

She stopped. I found myself wondering what exactly my dad *had* been. He had been religious. I knew that. Even if he wasn't always

sure quite what religion he belonged to. She had told me how they
met at a First Spiritualist Church 'Convert the Heathen' session outside the Anglican church in Putney. Pike, Quigley and Mum used to
wait behind the hedge, rattling tambourines and waving placards
saying ARE YOU REALLY GOING TO MEET THE LIVING GOD? as the congregation filed out and chatted to the vicar about the problems of
British Rail.

Dad had had some kind of religious crisis later, but I didn't know
too much about that. He had mentioned it to me, in a roundabout
sort of way, but I could never work out when it had happened or
how old I was when it occurred. It was funny I couldn't remember.
But your own past can be a closed book, even at fourteen.

My mum, as mums tend to do, had divined my state of mind
rather shrewdly and moved over to the bed in a thoughtful kind of
way.

'Norman . . . '

At first I thought she might be addressing him directly. Then I
realized we were into genuine past-tense mode. She sighed slowly.

'I very nearly married a man called Flugtermans,' she said ' – a
dentist.'

Why was she telling me this?

'I met him at a tennis club, and he was a very, very attractive man
indeed. And very fond of me. But I didn't continue the relationship
are these your socks?'

'Yes.'

'They're stiff with dirt! And your father was not, I have to say, a
handsome man although he was . . . '

'Available,' I said.

She gave me a sharp look.

'Anyway,' she went on, 'then he went to Portugal and everything
changed of course you should really have some new blinds but
they're so expensive and they warp.'

I knew better than to interrupt. Sooner or later, out of monologues
like this, some really vital piece of information was liable to emerge.

'Of course,' she said, 'I know you still blame me for what happened at Angmering.'

I kid you not, I had not a clue as to what she might be talking about. People assume that parents and children will understand each other. It doesn't work out like that. They share experiences, but they don't seem to share the same memories of them. Family business is strange.

I can remember my dad opening the newspaper once and saying, 'There is going to be a war in China.' And I can also remember him standing in the hall with my mum and her saying, 'I am going out!' and him, for some reason I will never understand, bursting into tears. Why did he cry? And was he even the same guy as the one with markedly dodgy views about the international situation in the Far East?

'Gorbachev is a genius!' was another one of his. Only to be followed, a few weeks later, by 'Gorbachev is an idiot!'

How could you explain this human stuff to Globo, Arch Lord of the System of the Blabbenoids? You couldn't. You know why? Because it doesn't make sense.

I looked at Mum as she moved towards the door. She seemed pleased to have got this off her chest. Whatever it was.

'In Angmering . . . ' I said, cautiously.

She suddenly got angry.

'With Veronica, for Christ's sake!'

I still didn't get it.

She went to the window and looked down at our drab patch of suburban garden. She sighed. 'I'll never forget that night in Lisbon!' Then she turned to me: 'Always be faithful and true, Simon. Always be honest and faithful and sincere in your dealings with others where are your trainers?'

'On the floor.'

'Keep them out of sight!'

Then she puckered her lips and allowed her breast to heave one or two times. This is usually a sure sign that she is about to quote from the collected works of Old Mother Walsh, and this, indeed, is what she did: ' "Shoes are remarkable, warm, bright and neat. The best place to keep them is on your feet." '

And with these words she thumped off down the stairs, leaving me to collect my thoughts for the hard task of Testifying.

I rolled out of bed and, feeling I was doomed to the state of *hei-hei*, or eternal sloth and uselessness, I wondered whether I could find a pair of unstiff socks.

The choir outside seemed to have stopped, but downstairs I could hear the Quigleys. Marjorie, who has a carrying voice, was saying, 'Isn't Testifying the best thing? Mrs Danby says it's the *best thing!*' She sounded rather girlish as she said this. Then I heard Quigley's low bass, but couldn't make out what he was saying.

I took one last, depressed look at myself in the mirror above the electric fire and clattered down the stairs. As I reached the landing I heard Mrs Quigley say, 'We're having the patio done. Then we're getting a *completely* new roof.'

They were getting a good deal out of staying at our house. Some people have to rent places. And, while we were at it, how the hell were they managing to afford these improvements? My dad always used to say that *we* could not afford lunch, although, I have to say, this did not stop him eating it.

They were all in the clothes traditionally worn when people are going to Testify. My mum was wearing a sort of large red sack and a conical hat that made her look like a gnome in a pantomime. Mrs Quigley was wearing a loose white robe with a hat and a veil rather like a bee-keeper's. She looked like a worker at a nuclear power station. Women at Testifying must be 'loose and bright', as Old Mother Walsh once said. The men are their usual uninspiring selves.

Mrs Quigley held out her arms as I came into the hall. 'Oh my darling, darling boy!' she said.

I had been getting a lot of this. I had so far managed to avoid being kissed by the old bat, but I had the strong feeling that, by the end of the day, she and I were going to be getting physical.

I stayed where I was. She decided against physical contact. Instead, she looked up to the ceiling from where she got quite a lot of her inspiration. Quigley was smirking next to her. *The whole truth of my heart!* How was he going to take the news of the hijacking of

419

earthling bodies by extraterrestrial beings? I was going to have to be extremely subtle about this.

'Jesus,' said Mrs Quigley in sharp tones, 'can you see this boy?'

'Thee him,' said Emily. 'He'th blethed!'

My face didn't crack.

'Today,' said Quigley, 'is a very great day in your life. You're going to stand up in front of a hundred or so of your closest friends and tell them your deepest, most private thoughts.'

This seemed to me to be a pretty fair definition of hell, but I tried to look like a man who enjoyed such occasions.

'You're going to tell them,' said Quigley, 'what *you* think about . . . about . . . *everything*!' And then, with a kind of war whoop, he picked me up under the armpits and carried me out to the choir waiting outside. He was incredibly strong.

As we thundered along the road, he whispered in my ear, 'And after you've Testified, Simon, you'll be Confirmed in Faith. In ten days. Think of it! Cor blimey, mate, you're not just Simon, old lad. You're Simon pure!'

Bergman had a barmitzvah and I went. Everyone there was Jewish apart from me. There was a lot of chanting, and afterwards we went to a posh hotel and I got a free hat. Bergman, at the end of it, was officially a man. As far as I am concerned, Bergman has been officially a man since the end of the Upper Removes. He is one hairy guy. But it was nice to see all these old geezers with huge noses treating him as if he *was* a man. In the First Church of Christ the Spiritualist you are Confirmed in Faith, which means you are officially a berk. There are no free hats.

Quigley held me up with one free hand and opened the door of his car with the other. He threw me across the front seat, and the choir applauded – whether this was for my benefit or to register approval for Quigley's strong right arm was not clear.

He wanted me Confirmed in Faith did he?

Being Confirmed in Faith is the full masonic job. I've never been able to find out what goes on at the ceremony, but, from what I've heard, there is more to it than rolling up your trouser-leg. I know that the male members of the congregation 'play loudly on the organ and show their bodies'. I know a fair amount of water gets chucked around, and at some point I think you are expected to wear your underpants on your head. But in between all these things something happens which is only spoken of in hushed whispers. Maybe they paint your balls green.

All this stuff dates back years, to Old Mother Walsh and her Sisters. When they baptized people they stayed baptized. You know? There was none of this dip-the-finger-in-the-water-and-let's-talk-about-the-Test-Match bollocks. They used to run down into the Nerd, or whatever river it is that runs through Ealing, and throw themselves in, yelling about the love of Jesus. Water was cheap and unpolluted in those days.

He was really moving fast was Quiggers. He couldn't wait to get me sewn up, could he? *Why the big hurry?* I wondered, as Mum, Emily and Mrs Quigley got into the back of his brand new car and he thrust it out into the traffic.

One of the areas where Quigley really needs a lot of help from the Lord Jesus is in the driving department. But I have never heard him confess his unworthiness in this field of human endeavour. He snarls at motorcyclists, accelerates hard at the back of buses, and views the red traffic light as a challenge rather than a warning.

As we careered down towards South Wimbledon, I remembered other trips I'd taken to church. Mostly I thought about going with my dad. I thought about running along beside him as we came up to the main road opposite the church, about his taking my hand and singing, 'Hold my *hand* – I'm a *stranger* in *Paradise*!'

And, as I thought about that, another image came into my mind. A heavy, silver casket was swinging backwards and forwards and there was that smell in the air – a smell of old leaves and perfume and musty, clinging sweetness. There was music, too, and those long shafts of light that fell from a high window, somewhere over to my right. For the first time, I could feel my father very close to me, his face very dark and serious. He was talking to someone. Someone I couldn't see. I wanted to see who it was, but I couldn't. He was mumbling. The words he was using weren't English. They were some old, runic language I couldn't understand. But there was something even stranger than that about him. He was on his knees. Why? Why was he kneeling? And to whom?

'We are come to the Temple,' said Mrs Quigley, as Quigley reversed into a parked car.

The street was packed with members of the First Spiritualist Church. It was Day Release at the loony bin. Over by the door of the church I could see Meriel Viney, wearing a kind of white sack and a pair of what looked like tennis shoes. On her head was a hat that looked as if someone had dropped a large meringue on her head. She was chatting away to Roger Beeding and to Roger de Mornay. There were, I found myself thinking, a hell of a lot of people called Roger in the First Spiritualist Church. What was it about the name that made them want to funk on down and start praising the Lord? We had no Peters, no Colins, only one David and, though there had been a Kevin a few years back, we were now understaffed in that area too. But you just could not keep the Rogers away!

It's for old people, our Church. Old people called Roger.

Right outside the church, directly in front of Roger Beeding, was a large Rolls-Royce. Sitting in the back seat was a woman in a long, cream dress and a hat the size of a toddler's swimming-pool. She was smoking a small cigar and sported a face that was a lot less elegant than the hat.

Quigley is down on smokers. Cigarettes are the work of the Devil. But smoking was obviously kosher as far as this old bat went. He rushed up to her as she got out of the Roller, took her right hand and thrust it into his beard. 'Oh!' I heard him say. 'Oh!'

Mrs Quigley looked pretty pleased as well. She had the air of one who might head for the pavement and start writhing at any minute. 'Mrs Danby,' she croaked, 'I'm so pleased! Mrs Danby!'

So this was Mrs Danby. It was strange. I couldn't remember ever having clapped eyes on her before. But she was looking at me as if we were long-lost friends. She was smiling so hard the gauze on her hat wobbled. And, as I met her eyes, I did have a memory of something, although I couldn't have said what. It was to do with a smell and some music and a steel thing swinging out and back, out and back, like the pendulum in the story by Edgar Allan Poe.

'This', Mrs Danby was saying, 'is one of the greatest days of my life!'

She simpered at me. I was beginning to feel like a ritual sacrifice. I mean, had the First Spiritualists moved on? Was I going to have it off with this woman and a couple of goats? Give me the goats any time, I thought, as I was shuffled towards her.

'Has Norman come through?' I heard her say.

'We have been in *constant* touch with him,' said Quigley, as if he was reassuring the chairman about the Exports Division.

The old bat beamed. 'How is he?'

'He is doing fine, Mrs Danby,' said Marjorie.

Who was this woman? And why would she not take her eyes off me?

'What's he doing over there?'

Everyone looked at Mrs Quigley.

'Oh, he's been . . . jetting around,' she said at last.

'Yes,' said Mrs Danby, shaking her head winsomely, 'he was always a busy soul was Norman. Has he made new contacts?'

'He feels very, very fully occupied,' said Mrs Quigley, 'but we are getting some very serious indications that he has been . . . having a personal rethink.'

Mrs Danby nodded gravely. 'Yes,' she said. 'Oh yes. When we fall, how we do fall!'

I couldn't work out what she meant by this. In fact, I couldn't work her out at all. She was wearing high-heeled shoes – which is very unusual for a First Spiritualist – and she was smirking at people as if she was at a cocktail party rather than morning service.

Behind her I could see into what is rather optimistically known as the vestry – which is nothing more than a curtained-off area of the floor, rather like what you might see in a hospital casualty ward. Pike was standing by a wooden rack of pamphlets, including *What Has Old Mother Walsh to Say to Us?* and a large, colourful one for the kiddies entitled *Daddy isn't Dead, He's Just Gone Out for a Bit*.

Mrs Danby started up the steps, and we followed her. When she got to the large graph that shows the state of the church-roof appeal, she stopped and looked down at the waiting crowds as if she was a

423

victorious politician looking down on her compliant voters. To avoid catching her eye, I looked at the graph. As far as I could tell, the roof seemed to be consuming money faster than we could give it.

She grabbed my hand and turned her wrinkled face to mine. 'You don't remember me, do you?' she said.

I didn't reply. I wanted to ask her if she was, by any chance, called Veronica, but I didn't dare.

She tossed her head and looked around at the congregation. 'I have not been to Service these few years,' she said. 'I have been in the Outer Darkness!'

Perhaps she had been abroad, to Africa or something. That would explain why I didn't recognize her. She was hard to miss, even among such a handpicked collection of fruitcakes as the First Spiritualist Church.

'I was close to your father during his great crisis,' she said, 'and it was I who led him astray. Into other fields, other woods, other pastures that seemed sweet but were full, as it turned out, of stinking weeds!'

They had been on country rambles together, was that it?

'And now', she went on, 'I am hearing Norman again. I am hearing him loud and clear. You are helping me, Simon. And when you are one with us, when you have plunged your head in the cold, clear waters of baptism, then my great sin will be forgiven. I stole the father and gave Him back the son!'

I didn't like the sound of any of this – especially the bit about plunging the old head in the cold, clear waters of baptism. But there was nothing I could say. I still had this uncomfortable feeling that I did know her. That she belonged to some time, when I was a little kid, that had somehow been barred from my memory.

Down below, Roger Beeding was beginning the traditional question-and-answer routine that always comes before you go into the morning service.

BEEDING: Shall we go in and worship?

CONGREGATION: Let us.

BEEDING: How shall we go in and worship?

CONGREGATION: On our feet.

BEEDING: How shall we worship when we are within?

CONGREGATION: On our knees.

BEEDING: How shall we go before the Living God if He
    appears before us?

CONGREGATION: On our bellies . . .

I used to have a friend, the only other boy of my age in the
congregation, before he went to Nottingham. He and I had a version
of the Introit that went:

BEEDING: How shall we stand in the church?

CONGREGATION: On our heads.

BEEDING: What may we hold when we are within?

CONGREGATION: Our penises.

BEEDING: How may we hold them?

CONGREGATION: Well and tightly . . .

I thought of him now – he was called Mike Jarvis and he was a
great skateboarder – as the congregation swept up the steps, past me
and Mrs Danby, and Pike triumphantly pushed back the curtain to
reveal the inner sanctum of the First Church of Christ the Spiritualist.

It was a sight as familiar to me as my own front room. A large,
empty room with high, narrow windows through which the bright
day filtered slowly on to various shades of brown. Brown linoleum
on the floor, brown chairs, arranged in neat rows, and, on the walls,
pictures and photographs and testimonials from dead Spiritualists,
all of them, it seemed to me, written in faded brown ink and confined
to faded brown frames.

At the back of the raised platform at one end of the hall was a
wooden cross, about six feet high. That, too, was brown. As we
trooped in for the service, the sun caught it and, for a moment, I had
a vision of what it must have really looked like, all those years ago,
when they nailed poor old JC up before the people, one bright day in
Palestine.

At the far end of the hall, Quigley was showing Mrs Danby to
what looked like a comfortable chair. There aren't many of those in

the First Church. And, up on the platform, Roger Beeding was calling the faithful.

'How are we now?' he called.

'We are in the church!' called back the congregation.

'How are our voices?' he called.

And they replied, 'They are rich and fruitful!'

Mr Toombs raised both his arms. He looked like Dracula about to make a maiden flight. 'Let us,' he said, 'praise the Lord!'

We had started. There was no going back. And all I could think, as the service began, was *the whole truth of my heart! I am supposed to tell the whole truth of my heart!*

16

In the autumn of 1924, the young Rose Fox was visited by the spirit of Wolfgang Amadeus Mozart. He told her that, in a previous life, *she* had actually been the composer of *Eine Kleine Nachtmusik*, and, while she was in a trance, he dictated his new work to her – a Concerto in G for harp, oboe and string orchestra. The piece was performed in Wimbledon Town Hall in 1926, and the consensus was that, in 130-odd years, Wolfgang had not really developed musically. Some people were so bold as to suggest that he had now lost his grip and was writing pretty fair garbage.

It didn't stop at Mozart. It turned out that Rose Fox had been an awful lot of people in previous lives – mostly male, and all of them, apart from a rather dull-sounding galley slave in 34 BC, rather famous or important. These people have always Done Things in previous lives, perhaps to make up for their rather undistinguished efforts while being alive and in their own bodies.

Anyway, one of the people Rose Fox had been was John Wesley. And, from what I hear, her Wesley was a lot nearer the mark than her Mozart. He dictated to her many of the hymns that are still in use by the First Church of Christ the Spiritualist – many of whose tunes are exactly the same – bar one or two notes – as the ones the *real* John Wesley cobbled together in the eighteenth century. Rose's Uncle Eustace, who lived upstairs in her parents' home when she was a girl, was, incidentally, a staunch Methodist.

The better Wesley went down, the more she did him. Mozart didn't write much after the concerto for harp, oboe and string orchestra, apart from an unfinished Requiem Mass, which no one could be persuaded to perform. But Wesley went on to write hymns, give advice and generally add shape, colour and texture to the ritual life of the First Spiritualist Church.

He was pretty gnomic by all accounts. He didn't say, 'Right, men – come in by twos, line up facing east and bang your foreheads on the floor!' He would come out with lines like, 'Let your words to God be as the noise of Esau!' Which meant that, for a couple of weeks, an amazing amount of shouting went on. So much so that Wesley came back with, 'And yet softness be a virtue.' He did sound a bit Mummerset from time to time.

One of the first bits of advice he gave the First Church was, 'Bend the knee, but not unwisely.' With the result that, to this day, the guys spend a lot of the service in a kind of crouching position.

He also said, 'Wave thine extremities and be joyful.' Which led to all sorts of strange behaviour. People finally settled on a kind of threshing movement of both arms, which, when combined with the crouch, made the congregation look like a group of canoeists on a particularly tough stretch of water.

But the most important thing Wesley told Rose Fox was, 'Let there be constant movement in thy church.' He stuck to that. In fact he kept on repeating it. And he made it clear that he wasn't talking about regular reallocation of senior positions in the Church. So, by the late 1980s, the services resembled the kitchen of a fast-food restaurant during a busy lunch hour. People would get up, go to the opposite end of the room, jig about, go back to their seat (or, better still, someone else's), get up again and jog round the perimeter of the hall.

As Rose got older, Wesley's orders got stranger and stranger. Most people agreed that things had gone a bit far when he told the Church, in 1982, to 'Face north-west whenever possible.' Did this mean when in the middle of the service? Or did it mean just what it said? Were we going to be looking at guys backing into the path of oncoming lorries in order to preserve the decencies? How about the old *sexual intercourse*? Were Spiritualists going to be forced to do it in strange, and possibly overexciting, positions?

I'd love to be forced to do it in strange positions. It's my dream.

Most people ignored this commandment, although I have heard it said that Pike was to be seen with a compass on a number of occasions, trying to align himself correctly. It turned out the reason we all had to face north-west was because it was the direction 'from which Rose had come forth'! She was born in Liverpool. A year or so later she told everyone that they must make an annual pilgrimage to that city, where she had a cousin in the catering trade who was prepared to give them all cheap rates, but by that time Rose was losing her grip on the faithful.

We started with Healing. People are always being Healed down at the church. It is certainly easier to get the medical treatment dished out by Roger Beeding's wife than it is to get to see your local GP. She does patients in job lots, which is a system I could recommend to the Mayberry Clinic, Wimbledon.

'Stand before if you wish Healing,' said Beeding, and his wife – a short, dumpy woman called Clara – walked out in front of the congregation, her eyes tightly shut.

In a high, squeaky voice, she said, 'Come to me in Jesus' name!'

The usual bunch of hypochondriacs shuffled forward. Clara Beeding opened her eyes and looked quite relieved to see Jasper Lewens, Tracy Johnson and the guy with the wart. She had dealt with a case of peritonitis in 1985, and apparently it didn't work out too well.

'It's my neck,' Jasper Lewens was saying in a rather whingeing tone. 'It won't leave me alone!'

Before Lewens could moan on any longer, Clara Beeding put out her hand and touched the side of his head. 'Your pain,' she said, with fantastic confidence, 'is going!'

Jasper started to rub his neck furiously.

'O Jesus mine,' went on Clara, 'see the pain! See how the pain is going from this man! See how it leaves his body and becomes at one with Thy Word!'

Before he had a chance to respond, Clara had moved on to Tracy Johnson. Tracy has a thing I can only describe as Non-specific Pain. Some weeks it's in her head, some weeks it's in her chest and some weeks it's in her legs. This week it was in her womb. 'O Lord Jesus,' she kept saying, 'it is in my womb!'

Tracy isn't as easy to deal with as Jasper. She likes to make sure everyone knows exactly where the pain is, how long it goes on for and whether it's burning, stabbing, singeing or a combination of all three.

But, before she could really get under way, from one side of the church, the one that leads out to the dustbins, came a group of three or four people one of whom I recognized as Sheldon Parry, the born-again television director. Sheldon, who is a really nice bloke and very fond of children, was pushing an elderly lady in a wheelchair. She looked quite happy to be in the wheelchair. Or maybe she was happy at the fact that, in a few minutes, after a couple of minutes' contact with Clara Beeding's right mitt, she would be skipping around with the best of them.

Clara did not look best pleased to see her. The peritonitis wasn't her only disaster. She had gone badly wrong – so my dad said – with a case of genital herpes. You could tell that she was looking forward to doing her number on the wart. She knows where she is with a wart. But she didn't flinch. She turned away from Tracy Johnson and went straight to the woman in the chair.

'O Lord!' she said, speaking extra loud to drown out Tracy mumbling on about her womb. 'O Jesus, who made the blind see and the lame to walk, look down on this woman!'

The old lady looked up at her. Clara stretched out her hands and held them above her client's head. She was not going to back down on this one, you could tell. 'You can walk!' she said, in a throaty voice.

'No I can't!' said the old lady, sounding rather perky. 'I can't walk at all. That's why I'm here.'

Clara gave a little, silvery laugh and stretched out her hand again until it was about an inch from the old lady's permanent wave. 'Rise up!' she said. 'Rise up and walk!'

The old lady struggled for a bit and then subsided back into her chair. 'I can't!' she said, sounding rather apologetic. 'I really can't. I'm sorry, but I can't walk!'

For a moment I thought Clara was going to give the old woman a piece of her mind. Didn't she understand? You don't get *better* down at the First Spiritualist Church. You get Healed. The two are not necessarily the same thing at all. And she hadn't said *when* the disagreeable old trout was going to walk. It might be next week or a year next Tuesday. She might, at least, look a bit grateful at Mrs Beeding's taking all this trouble over her.

Before things could get really awkward, there was a movement from the other end of the hall. It was Quigley. He always knows when to provide a distraction. 'I have News!' he said. 'I have Great News!'

There is always News at morning service, and it is usually Great News. It can be news of a member of the congregation's promotion or someone's marriage or – even better – someone being run over by a lorry, but there is always news. On a slow day, Quigley just goes through the newspapers and rambles on about whatever comes into his brain. One year, I remember, he gave us half an hour on John McEnroe being slung out of the Men's Singles.

This morning, I had a horrible feeling that the news might be something to do with me.

Quigley pushed his way forward towards the platform as the woman in the wheelchair was hustled away and the man with the wart returned, rather miserably, to his place in the congregation. Quigley had with him, I noticed, a brown box.

'I have News,' he said, 'about one of Us!'

I coughed nervously. Quigley leaned down, picked up the box and, from it, pulled out something that looked like a waffle iron.

'This,' he said, 'is a paper-stripper!'

People nodded seriously.

'It strips off,' said Quigley, archly. Quite a number of heads turned in my direction.

'It strips off old wallpaper so that new paper can be hung. New starts be made on old walls!'

Suddenly his face grew dark with anger. His voice climbed a couple of octaves. 'But stripping paper isn't the answer,' he yelled – 'it isn't the answer if the wall is basically *no good*!'

People nodded some more.

'This paper-stripper,' he went on, 'isn't doing God's work! Because God, like us, cannot work with substandard materials. We are going to throw it aside!'

The man next to me looked a touch apprehensive. The paper-stripper was about a foot long and nine inches wide. It looked as if it was quite solidly constructed.

'Away you go, old paper-stripper!' screamed Quigley, as he raised the device high over the heads of the congregation. 'You are only so much *rubbish*! Go forth!' And, suiting the action to the words, he hurled the metal object towards the opposite wall, narrowly missing Hannah Dooley as he did so. It crashed into the flowerpots on the whitewashed ledge under the window, raining pottery, bits of geranium and John Innes Number 3 Compost all over the congregation.

They loved it. You could hear them gasp as Quiggers reached out his arm to them.

'But in this Church,' he said, 'is a virgin piece of wall. A piece of wall that is clean and firm and decent even when the paper has been stripped away from it!'

I had a nasty feeling that I was part of this do-it-yourself metaphor. I stood there looking up at him, wishing that someone would demolish me.

Mrs Quigley, as always, was on cue. 'Have you got News, Albert?'

He looked at her blankly. *Yes*, you could see him thinking, *I have damaged a vitally important piece of domestic equipment!*

'News for us, Albert?'

Quigley was still reeling from the impact of his great gesture. He was, of course, the man who had once brought in a cup, painted black on the inside and white on the outside, and, after pointing out its close resemblance to the soul of the average sinner, had jumped up and down on it, foaming at the mouth. But the paper-stripper! This was something that would be hard to beat.

'News?'

'News!' said Quigley, and then looked across at me. For a moment I thought he was going to get back to the DIY metaphor and start to try to get them to see me as undercoat or Jesus Christ as primer, but, instead, he recovered himself enough to say, 'Great News!'

There was a sort of rhubarb effect from the pit. 'What news?' 'Great news?' 'What be this news?' 'News, they say!' etc. etc.

Quigley looked in the direction in which he had hurled the paper-stripper as his old lady repeated, 'O Jesus, Great News!' She raised her hands above her head, trying to get this going. 'O Jesus Christ!' she said.

You could see that the temperature needed raising. A few people came back with 'O Jesus!' or 'Yes, Jesus!' but nobody was ready for talking in tongues or, indeed, listening to people talking in tongues, which I have often thought is much the more taxing of the two options.

'Is it News about a boy?' she asked, reminding me of an actor working with someone who has completely forgotten his lines.

Quigley was looking at her blankly. 'A boy . . . ' he said, his heart still with the wallpaper-stripper.

'What's the boy's name?' asked Pike.

Short of giving the guy cue-sheets, there was not much else we could do. Quigley's eyes shifted, weasel-like, from me, to Pike, to his old lady. At the far side of the church, old Mr Pugh, who had swallowed about half a kilo of compost, was coughing furiously.

'Yes,' said Hannah Dooley, who gave the appearance of one prepared to be genuinely surprised by the answer, 'What *is his name*?'

Quigley very slowly raised his right hand. I had the impression that if he didn't come through on this one soon his position was going to be in very grave danger. Life at the top end of the First Spiritualist Church has a sharp, corporate edge to it. But, before our eyes, he seemed to find strength. The first two fingers closed together as if he was a little kid pretending he had a gun. He extended his arm fully and began to waggle it in an arc across the faces of the congregation.

'It's a very special name,' he said.

It was still hard to tell whether he had actually cottoned on to what the name was. But quite often Quigley will keep his audience in such a state of suspense that he forgets what it was he intended to say.

'O Lord!' said Mrs Q. She looked a bit happier now. Hannah Dooley was looking as if she might do something usefully hysterical at any moment. The woman next to Mr Pugh seemed to be in tears, but that might have been due to the compost.

'It's a beautiful name,' said Quigley. 'A beautiful and holy name!'

'Yes,' said Pike, his eyes glinting madly behind his wire glasses, 'but what *is* the name?'

He sounded, I thought, a touch peevish about this – although years of supporting Quigley might make any man edgy. I wasn't sure. A strange change had come over Leo in the last week or so. Of all of the First Spiritualists, he was the only one who seemed, in some way, to have been affected by this business with my dad. Why should that be?

'There's an S in it!' said Quigley, who was still keeping his cards pretty close to his chest.

'Ohhh!' said the congregation.

This was all getting a bit like the Paul Daniels show.

'There's an I in it!' said Quigley.

'Ohhhh!'

'And an M and an N and E!'

I wondered who he was talking about. A new recruit called Smein possibly.

'And an O!' said Quigley, sounding a bit perturbed.

Maybe he was talking about someone called Simone. Or a new Japanese Christian called Monsei. Not that it mattered. No one is liable to comment on a renegade E in the First Church. Quigley was now back on course, and you could feel the relief in the audience.

'It's a SIMON!' he said.

'Ohhhh!' moaned the punters.

The paper-stripper was forgotten. He could have flung fifty paper-strippers at them now and they wouldn't have minded. 'It's a SIMON!'

Or a Smonie or a Nemois.

I felt myself propelled towards the stage. Terry Melchett, the supermarket manager, whose wife left him for another woman, gave me a hard shove in the small of the back. Kate Melville and Sue d'Argy Smith, whose daughters left the Church, as so many do, just before they became nubile, each took a hand and gave it a sharp pull, and over their heads came the long arms of Gordon the Bachelor, whose fingers stroked my hair, as countless other key personnel in the body of Christendom, South Wimbledon, stroked, shoved, pulled and all but *carried* me towards the stage on which I was supposed to pour out the secrets of my heart.

'We're going to sing!' shouted Quigley.

There is no order of hymns in the First Spiritualist Church. You sing as the spirit moves. Sometimes two different sections of the congregation will be belting out two completely different numbers.

'What are we going to sing?' called someone at the back.

There was a lot more rhubarb, along the lines of 'Yes, what?' and 'What *are* we going to sing, brothers?' and then Mrs Quigley cut in over the top of this with a cadenza that would not have disgraced Dame Kiri Te Kanawa.

'Te-e-e-sti-fyyy!'

We all looked around. There was a hunting-horn quality to this which suggested that someone else was supposed to get up and answer. They did.

'What shall we Te-e-e-stify?' sang young Mr Pugh.

'We shall tes-ti-i-i-fyy,' sang Mrs Quigley, to a tune that seemed to be completely of her own devising, 'to-o-o the-e-e Lor-or-ord!'

'Give me a one!' said Quigley.

Over by the piano, Mary Bunn squirmed on her piano stool and gave him a one.

'Give me a two!' said Quigley.

Next to Mary Bunn, Big Louie the Jamaican, on drums, gave him a two.

'Give me a *three*!' said Quigley.

Next to Big Louie the Jamaican, Sylvia Margaret Williams, our seventy-nine-year-old bass guitarist, gave him a three.

Quigley leaped into the air like a monkey that has sat on a bunsen burner and gave a sort of primal grunt. The First Spiritualists needed no encouragement. They had done this before and they would do it again. As one voice they went into one of Rose Fox's greatest hits:

> Testify! Testify!
> Take your troubles to the Lord!
> Testify! Testify!
> Take your troubles to the Lord!

> Take your troubles –
> Oh take your troubles –
> Take your trou-ou-ou-oubles –
> Take your troubles to the Lord!

There is more, I fear. I don't think it was dictated to her by John Wesley. But, when in doubt, it is the one we always reach for. Great truths are always simple, right? And, whatever else you might want to say about this number, you would have to admit it was simple. The tune sounds as if it was dictated to Rose Fox by a three-year-old child.

The band hit their instruments harder and harder and the congregation started to stamp in time.

> Testify! Testify!
> Take your troubles to the Lord!

The walls were shaking. On the roof above me, the shabby light-shades shook on their long flexes. The glass of the windows shook in its wooden frames. Mary Bunn, hitting the keys harder and harder for Jesus, lifted herself off the stool and brought her bum down with a crash as she laid down chord after chord. The congregation were like different parts of a huge engine, each one passing a movement on and the recipient taking it up and changing it. It was as if there was a wave of water and the wave turned a wheel and the wheel turned a cog and the cog turned a piston and the piston punched out a wave, bigger and more overwhelming than the first wave, turning a bigger wheel, a bigger cog, a bigger piston and then finally a wave that seemed enough to swallow everything in its path. The whole crowd was shouting, like some awful, natural machine.

> Testify! Testify!
> Take your troubles to the Lord!
> Testify! Testify!
> Take your troubles to the Lord!

As I got closer to the raised platform at the far end of the church, it was as if the sound was pushing me forward. The sound was shaking the roof and rocking the floor. It was rapping in my back as I was pushed past Roger Beeding and Roger de Mornay and closer and closer to the eight steps that led up to the low wooden platform on which was the gigantic cross and the large black-and-white photograph of Rose Fox.

It was only when I was actually up there and the music had stopped, and I found myself looking down at a hundred or so expectant faces, that I remembered the magnitude of the task in front of me. I had not only to Testify as to how, where and when the Lord Jesus had entered my heart but also give the punters a detailed account of the innermost secrets of my heart. What I felt about life, my immediate family, the Church and the wider issues facing society. Such as the full-scale invasion of sw19 by extraterrestrial beings.

I did not feel confident of my ability to do any of these things. But I was dead sure that the last item would take some getting round to.

'Hi, guys!' I said, eventually, 'I'm Simon Britton. Remember me?'

17

This got a laugh.

People do laugh in meetings of the First Church of Christ the Spiritualist. In fact they do just about everything short of brushing their teeth, but this was what I would call a really *good* laugh, if you know what I mean. I felt they were really pleased to see me. They were genuinely amused.

Suddenly, Testifying didn't seem such a big deal. You know? I was just going to tell them about all the things that were on my mind, about my dad and about Jesus and about aliens taking over the . . .

I looked round at the faces. They didn't look ready for aliens. Not yet. Not in sw19, anyway. I must work round to the subject gradually.

'Basically,' I went on, 'I'm fourteen. You know?'

There was another laugh. A sort of happy, let's-all-be-friends-there's-no-problem kind of laugh.

'And', I went on, doing something a bit casual with my hands, 'being fourteen can be a hass! Right?'

'Right,' said a small, fat man in the front row whom I could not remember ever having seen before.

Sooner or later I was going to have to turn this conversation round to Jesus Christ. I figured it was better to start with Jesus. They knew where they were with Him.

'I'm at Cranborne School,' I said, 'and I'm doing GCSE in two years' time.'

This didn't go down quite as well. I could feel them getting restive.

'In biology, chemistry and physics,' I continued, 'geography, IT, English, French, Latin, Spanish and maths. Which is not my best subject!'

They did not want to know this.

'But', I said, 'I haven't come here to talk about my exam prospects!'

'No,' said a voice from the back of the hall, 'you have not!'

I flung my arms wide.

'Right, too right!'

What had I come here to talk about? Jesus Christ.

'Jesus Christ!' I said.

'Amen,' said Quigley, rapidly.

'Amen,' said everybody else.

This seemed safe ground. It wasn't too committing. It was giving everyone a lot of pleasure. And it was certainly an improvement on my thoughts about the core curriculum. I tried it again.

'Jesus Christ!'

'Amen,' said Quigley.

'Amen,' said everyone else.

Maybe I should just go on doing this all night. You know?

'Jesus Christ!' I said.

There was a pause.

'Amen,' said Quigley, rather grudgingly.

'Amen,' said everyone else.

I was going to have to get to the point.

'The other day, my father died.'

They liked this. A sort of appreciative hush fell upon them.

'He went out to the . . . er . . . pub, and he had a heart attack and he died!'

'Alleluia!' said the strange fat man in the front row, who was clearly new to this sort of thing.

'But,' I went on quickly, 'very soon after this, he turned up outside our house at 24 Stranraer Gardens!'

There was a lot of nodding. This was par for the course, they seemed to be saying. You kicked off, you had the death experience and back you came to tell people about it.

'When did you make contact?' asked old Mr Pugh, who seemed to have recovered completely from the compost. I really was going to have to get round to discussing the extraterrestrial problem. We could be here all night rapping about the finer points of mediumship.

'It all depends what you mean by *making contact*. And who you're making contact with. We all talk about making contact, don't we? It's one of our big things as . . . er . . . Christians, which of course we all are. But this contact I am talking about is a terrifying, although of course in a way wonderful, but also terrifying, form of . . . er . . . contact.'

This was very well received. I've noticed that in sermons of any kind it is important not to state your hand too early, or too clearly. You have to dress it up a bit. You know? You may have come there to say something really basic like 'Sin is Bad!' or 'God is Good!' but it is crucial to start by talking about your Auntie Renee's operation or why your dog was sick in the back of the car on the M4. Were they ready for me to get closer in?

'What I have to say,' I went on, 'is *so* important and *so* . . . vital that at first it may be difficult to believe. You may say, "Oh no! That Simon's a loony!" You know?'

'We won't!' called Quigley, with what I feared was misplaced optimism.

'You may say, "Cart Simon off to the nuthouse!" You know?'

'Amen,' said Hannah Dooley.

'Alleluia!' said the fat man in the front row.

It was now or never. I had to go in, and go in fast.

'If I were to tell you,' I said, trying to look each one of them in the eye, which is not an easy thing to do with ninety-odd people, 'that Wimbledon was being invaded by alien beings from another planet, you would probably laugh and call me a lunatic. Right?'

They did not look as if that was the case, actually. If anything, they seemed rather receptive to the idea of talking about invasion of the locality by monsters from deep space. The fat man in the front row was shaking his head vigorously. He obviously wanted aliens on the agenda of the First Spiritualist Church.

'But,' I said slowly, looking round the hall, 'I think I have evidence – *clear* evidence – that something of this sort is going on, right here, under our very noses in our . . . ' I groped for the right word and found it ' . . . Christian community.'

We were on course here. We had said goodbye to GCSE options

and we were on course. The awful thing was that, as I said it, I began to have serious doubts about it. As if what I thought and what I said were two completely different things. But I found myself looking straight at Pike. And he was leaning forward on his chair, his hands clasped together. He was nodding! He seemed so attentive, so clued in to my every word, that I suddenly found the confidence to go on. In a kind of rush I went back to the main menu.

'Well, I can't be very specific about them. About who they are or why they are doing it or what they want. But all I can say is that I am *certain* that there is, as I speak, an extraterrestrial presence in the area. They are *here*, guys. As is, of course, Jesus Christ!'

I thought I had better bring things back to Jesus. And it certainly did help. People were nodding seriously, as they tended to do when you mentioned JC.

'I know that a lot of people find this sort of thing ridiculous. A lot of people dismiss it out of hand. But I don't think they should. Impossible things can be true. I *saw* my father, I am telling you – out in the street. And he's dead!'

At the back I could see Quigley purse his lips. He did not, I have to say, look at all pleased. *Jesus*, I thought to myself. *Work in Jesus. Now!*

'Jesus,' I said, 'healed the sick and raised the dead.'

'Alleluia!' said the fat man in the front row.

'And a lot of people found that ridiculous!' I realized as I said it that this could sound a little tactless. Especially in view of the fact that, in the far corner, the old lady in the wheelchair was making determined but unsuccessful efforts to get up and walk.

'Not,' I went on, 'the sick and the dead, of course. They were very glad to be helped in that way. But the cynics, who refused to believe the *evidence* of their eyes. People who scoffed. People who sneered at what others truly believed.'

This was good. Quigley was looking foxed. Everything I was saying was, so far anyway, completely acceptable Christian dogma. As far as I knew. Although what is and is not acceptable in the First Church of Christ the Spiritualist changes from minute to minute.

'Aliens,' I went on, 'are somewhere out there in the universe. It stands to reason that in such vast space there must be some other beings. Are we saying that God has absolutely no imagination at all? That all he can come up with is a few rotten old . . . humans?'

This was even better. The old direct questions seemed to be quite a good technique. You could see them struggling for answers and coming up with nothing at all. I tried a few more, in quick succession.

'Has something happened in your life that you can't explain? Have you seen something that just doesn't fit into the normal pattern of things? Do you have a feeling, for example, that you are being watched?'

'Alleluia!' said the fat man in the front row. He was on my side, guys. He could stay. I raised my voice slightly. At the back Quigley was looking very worried indeed. If he was going to interrupt, he had left it a little late.

'Are you,' I continued, 'unable to lay your hands on familiar domestic objects, and have you come to the conclusion that someone must be moving them?'

Hannah Dooley, who is notoriously absent-minded, was nodding furiously. I paused dramatically and raked the audience with my eyes the way I had seen Quigley do.

'Who do you think might be responsible for all these things you can't explain? Who do you think might be here, even as we stand here in Christian worship? Who might be walking among us even as we pray to the Lord Jesus?'

'Aliens!' shouted Pike with sudden tremendous enthusiasm.

'Aliens!' yelled Hannah Dooley.

'Alleluia!' said the fat man in the front row.

Quigley was white with fury. I saw him whisper something to Mrs Danby, but she didn't seem to hear him. But it was too late for Quigley. 'If you really want something, boy,' my dad used to say, 'then go for it!' I went for it.

'Aliens,' I continued, 'are right here at this moment! They have landed! And I have *conclusive proof*!'

There was more rhubarb. 'He has proof!' 'Conclusive proof!' 'He says he has proof, Mabel!' etc. I stopped for a second and tried to think what my conclusive proof was. The thought of describing it out loud to over a hundred people made it feel less convincing than I thought it had been.

'A close friend of mine called Mr Andrew Marr has *disappeared*!'

I saw Pike's weatherworn little face watching me with intense concentration. 'Aliens!' he yelled. He was getting the idea quickly, guys. Years of intensive training in the paranormal had taught him how to draw these kinds of conclusions with consummate speed.

'Aliens!' I said. 'And these same aliens have also . . . '

Here I paused again. I gave the next three words a great deal of lip and tongue work.

' . . . taken my father!'

Here I raised my hand to heaven and shook my fist at the sky. My voice rose an octave or two as I screamed, 'Give him back, you bastards!'

'Give him back, you bastards!' yelled Pike.

'Aliens!' yelled Hannah Dooley.

'Alleluia!' said the fat man in the front row.

Quigley made his move. But both he and I knew it was too late. He sounded positively mealy-mouthed as, with a great show of wonder and puzzlement, he started to say, 'These aliens . . . '

'Yes,' I said, sticking with the simple idea, 'Aliens! These aliens!'

'Aliens,' said Pike, dead on cue, 'are come amongst us, my friends! Hear! Hear the word of the Lord!'

If there had been any danger from Quigley, it was headed off, once again, by Pikey, who dashed into a space by himself and, springing up and down like a goblin, started to shout, 'Hear the word of the Lord!' at regular intervals.

I could see Quigley was about to make another move, but before he could do so I held out my hands, palms downwards, in a gesture much favoured by Mr Toombs in his last ecclesiastical campaign. 'Let us pray,' I said.

'Oh let us pray!' said Hannah Dooley.

'Pray!' squeaked Pike. 'Oh let us pray!' He looked up at the ceiling. 'Old Mother Walsh,' he said, 'prithee the snake not be come!'

This went down very big with the lads. When she was feeling down, Old Mother Walsh was always going on about how the snake was slithering in our direction. It was entirely feasible, of course, that it should be at the controls of an interplanetary vehicle of some sort.

'Old Mother Walsh,' Pike said again, 'let not the snake come out of the sky!'

There was much murmuring of assent at this. You would have thought, from the way they were all carrying on, that they were all closet members of the British Interplanetary Society. Quigley was looking at me in open horror now. You could see that my attack had taken him completely by surprise. Even if he had wanted to try unmasking me, he wouldn't have dared. This was the most exciting News the First Church of Christ the Spiritualist had heard in years. They were bored with all this let's-hear-it-for-Galilee-purify-your-heart rubbish. Even talking to the dead can pall. They wanted Simon Britton.

'Let us pray,' I said, 'that this . . . alien menace be . . . dealt with! By the . . . proper authorities and by . . . '

'Jesus Christ,' said Quigley, smartly.

'Alleluia!' said the fat man in the front row.

'Amen,' said Hannah Dooley.

'Because,' I said, looking straight at Quigley, 'don't let's kid ourselves. There are other planets and there *are* people on them, and from time to time those people may well want to get on board ship and head down here. And if we *refuse* to believe that, we're being like the mockers and the sneerers who refuse to believe in the Lord Jesus Christ. Because belief . . . '

Here I raised my right hand and pointed my index finger straight at the bearded one. He didn't flinch. He looked straight back into my eyes.

' . . . is the important thing in the world. And arguing for what you believe, however stupid or illogical or plain mad it may seem. And standing up for what *you* choose to believe against those wicked people who just want you to believe what they tell you. Who just want to take over your mind and not let you think for yourself. Who . . . '

'Who welcome the snake!' said Pike.

I had a sudden vision of a reception committee for the snake. It wasn't difficult to imagine it wriggling out of a cigar-shaped object on Wimbledon Common.

Pike did a sort of wild leap and whirled round to face the congregation. 'Aliens!' he said, sounding like the compère at a Hallowe'en party.

What I had said had clearly got to Pikey in a major way. Maybe I was more eloquent than I thought. It was only much later that I remembered my speech had been more or less word for word something my dad had said to me once. It was funny – when my dad had said it to me it seemed like the rather tired, friendly sort of thing that parents often say to you. Spoken, or rather screamed, by yours truly in the First Church of Christ the Spiritualist, it was *dynamite*.

It certainly put the wind up Quigley. He didn't say anything at all as, led by his former lieutenant, the congregation swarmed up to the dais and lifted me high on their shoulders. Yelling 'Aliens! Jesus!' and 'Aliens are come!' and 'Prithee the snake not be here!' in about equal proportions, they carried me round the body of the hall. I shook my hair back and waved my arms above my head as Pike mopped and mowed in front of me and the band struck up an impromptu tune.

I could have been old JC himself, I tell you, riding into Jerusalem on his donkey, ready to spread the Good News. I could have been one of those prophets who foretold him. I could have been almost anyone I chose that day. I had testified all right. I had put Unidentified Flying Objects right back on the agenda where they belonged, and, from this day forth, the First Church of Christ the Spiritualist was never going to be the same again.

18

That, more or less, is how the First Spiritualist Church experienced its last and greatest schism. I mean, it was ripe for it. I sometimes like to think it was my eloquence, but the fact of the matter is that if I had got up on my hind legs and suggested a bit of Karaoke instead of the morning service, they would have leaped at it. They were ripe for change, and, as it happened, I couldn't have chosen a better subject with which to widen the scope of the Church's activities. Or, indeed, to discomfort Quigley.

There was, as I subsequently discovered, quite a high crossover between ufology and fundamentalist Christianity. Hannah Dooley knew a bloke in Birmingham who had been set on by a group of small 'pod-like' creatures while out walking his dog. They did a number of very unpleasant things to him and left him, dazed and confused, at New Street station at two in the morning. Mr Toombs had been a founder member of the British Premonitions Bureau in 1967 (it registered 500 premonitions, most of which were concerned with major transport disasters). The place was a powder keg.

It wasn't only ufology. There were six clairvoyants, four water diviners and nine people who had had direct contact with poltergeists. They all wanted space. Sheldon Parry, it turned out, was a life member of the Society for Psychical Research and had been deeply involved until he had lost his library books. They all needed to express what they felt.

All I did was get things started. There had always been schisms in the First Church of Christ the Spiritualist. There had been Lewis, the guy who was down on cutlery and condiments, and much earlier a bloke called Evans, who maintained that Old Mother Walsh was really a man in drag and that it behoved members of the Church 'to wear the clothes of the other kind'. Evans was arrested in Piccadilly in 1908, wearing 'lace petticoats and stays and drinking from an opened spirit bottle'.

And there were a lot of memories. You know? Since the days of Ella Walsh, the real main event had been table-rapping, but people in the Church still talked about Old Mother Walsh and her prophecies. It wasn't only the snake with TWO THOUSAND YEARS GO BY on it. There was a whole lot of other stuff scheduled for the beginning of the second millennium: green rain, black snow, animals learning to talk and a heck of a lot of red-hot hail. One guy had already arranged to sell his house and go and live in the Caribbean in 1998 because, as he said, 'You might as well have a decent last couple of years.'

I don't think I would have made quite so much impact, however, if it hadn't been for the fact that, while they were carrying me round the church yelling, 'Aliens!' 'Jesus Christ!' and 'The snake cometh!' the roof fell in. I say 'fell in'. In religion these terms are relative. You know? One minute Jesus is a sort of cross between Batman and Captain America, next thing he is 'just a bloke with a few special powers', and before you know it he is a deranged Jew with a no more than ordinary claim on our imaginations. A couple of sheets of corrugated iron broke loose and fell on Mr Pugh's head. That was all. But it was enough. In a week or so you would have thought a crowd of angels had wafted in from Putney singing my name and crying 'Hosanna!'

The burning bush, right? I mean, did it? You know? Or did it just look kind of . . . reddish?

Nobody said much to me after the service. As we trooped out of the hall, the old lady in the wheelchair was still trying to get up, and Clara Beeding was kneeling in front of her. I thought I heard her say, 'Go on, you can do it!'

A couple of people came up to shake my hand as we got into Quigley's car. He stood back, a tight smile on his face, as Roger de Mornay said, 'A beautiful, beautiful, beautiful speech!'

Once we were inside the car, Quiggers allowed himself a full-blooded sneer. 'Well, well,' he said, 'little green men!'

I didn't speak. In fact nobody said much on the way back. Just as we came into Stranraer Gardens, Mrs Quigley said, 'We have worked so hard to bring you to the Lord, Simon! You cannot know how important to the Church this is. Mrs Danby . . . '

Here Quigley cut her off sharply. 'Don't let's talk about Mrs Danby. I'm sure we can manage Mrs Danby, Marjorie!'

There was something really horrible about the way he said this. A pure flash of creepiness. I missed my dad more than ever as I went into the house, ahead of the others, and climbed the drab stairs to lie on my bed, looking out at the bright blue sky above the street.

After a while, the door to my bedroom opened and my mum's head peered round it. Her mouth was turned down and her little eyes were beady with worry. She blinked at me for a minute or two and then said, 'Aliens!'

I didn't respond. She clicked her tongue in the way she does when I eat peanut butter straight from the jar.

'Spacemen!' she went on.

I sighed.

Mum went over to my window and looked down at the street. In a small, far-away voice, she said, 'Mr Quigley's awfully cross with you and Pike. He's very worried. He's very worried indeed. And he cares about you, Simon. He thinks about you and prays for you all the time. He does!'

She went out then and left me alone.

The next week saw a constant procession of Spiritualists in and out of our kitchen. Some of them came to talk seriously with Quigley and to shake their heads at me. Rather more, including Pike, came to shake me by the hand and ask me detailed and unanswerable questions about the nature of the extraterrestrials who had landed in the Wimbledon area. Once or twice, at mealtimes, I thought Quigley was going to speak to me about the matter. But he didn't. Usually he likes to get you alone, as, I have noticed, a lot of Christians do. So, when he suggested that we all go 'to furnish the larder' on Saturday morning, I thought I was reasonably safe.

Normal people go shopping. First Spiritualists go to furnish the larder.

Shopping is a tricky one for them. You have to be very careful when prowling along the shelves. A First Spiritualist doesn't drink coffee, or eat white bread or cheese (apart from Gorgonzola – the Good Cheese as it's called), and faced by a frankfurter is liable to scoot off into a corner, whimpering. Nobody quite knows who decided all these things were dangerous and evil, or why they did so. But they take the rules pretty seriously. Branston Pickle is 'harmonious and honest', but all forms of sausage are, basically, in league with Beelzebub.

One of the reasons they go shopping in groups is because not everyone agrees about which foods are OK and which ones are going to plunge you into hell-fire. Someone will reach for a jar of fish-paste only to be brought up short by another member of the party reminding them that fish-paste is unclean, while someone else may get as far as the checkout with a year's supply of baked beans, when, across the crowded shelves of the supermarket, comes a voice reminding them of the danger they are facing.

There are a lot of scores paid off when shopping. My dad used to love chocolate cake, and, whenever they were having a row, my mum would remember that chocolate was 'a poisonous thorn in the side of Creation'. At other times the two of them would wolf down a whole packet of After Eight mints with no apparent difficulty.

This Saturday we went with the Quigleys, Hannah Dooley, Pike, the Clara Beedings (as Roger and Clara are known) and, to my surprise and dismay, Mrs Danby. She showed up in her Rolls in the car park of the supermarket, and, although there was a lot of nodding and smiling and remarks about coincidences, it was pretty clear that her presence had been arranged for someone's benefit. I suspected it might be mine.

I hate going around in groups. Especially groups of people from the Church. I'm terrified we might see Khan or Greenslade on a day when everyone has decided to follow Mother Walsh's directions about placing the feet on the ground without damaging the old insect life. But on this particular day we looked almost normal. Everyone was very friendly, and there was much jolly laughter as we passed the frankfurters and Quigley made as if to ward off the evil eye.

He waited until we were browsing through the chilled fish before raising the issue: 'Do you really think that Old Mother Walsh's snake is *actually* going to wriggle down Wimbledon High Street when the time comes?'

I didn't ask what time he meant. The time of Snakes Wriggling Down Wimbledon High Street presumably.

'Er . . .'

My mum was piling tinned ravioli into the trolley. She looked like a small animal that expected to be surprised at any moment.

'I don't think you do, do you?' said Quiggers, 'I think you think, as I do, that Old Mother Walsh wasn't talking about a *real* snake. She was talking about the snake that is in all of us all the time!'

What snake was this? A tapeworm perhaps?

'A lot of the simpler souls,' said Quigley, 'probably think a great big snake is going to slither out at them and start gobbling them up in a few years.'

You could see from Pike's face that this was exactly what he thought. If this snake did show, I thought, please God it liked the taste of men with beards.

'Cor lumme, young shaver!' said Quigley. 'Your little green chaps are no more than that snake really, are they? They are a way of saying, "The world's in pretty bad shape, Jesus, and pretty soon someone will come along and give us pain and suffering and woe." '

I looked him straight in the eye.

'No they're not. They're just *there*, that's all. And I never said they were green. What I said was, it looks as if they're here. You know?'

Quigley laughed. He was still being Mr Nice Guy. My mum had finished shovelling the ravioli into the trolley. She and Emily and Mrs Quigley were headed for toilet tissues at a brisk pace.

'Little talk with Jesus?' he said, and, halfway through reaching for a tube of tomato purée, he closed his eyes and froze solid as if overtaken by a large quantity of molten lava. I waited for him to finish.

When somebody pressed his PLAY button, I said, 'People think I'm stupid because I think there's something in this alien business. But I'm not!'

Quigley grabbed my arm. 'No, li'l' Simo,' he said. 'You are not. You are special! You are favoured.'

He rocked to and fro, his eyes half-shut. On the line to Jesus once again. ' "A boy will come 'fore the snake's unfurled, and preach the woman to save the world!" ' he said. A bloke who was trying to get at the tomato purée gave him rather an odd look, but Quigley was not bothered. I recognized another of Old Mother Walsh's rhymes.

' "Go to the river in ones and twos, but be sure you put on your overshoes!" ' I quoted back at Quiggers.

He became enormously excited and, as the rest of the party started back towards us with a huge mound of lavatory paper balanced on the ravioli, he hopped from foot to foot, clutching my arm. Only Pike, I noticed, had stayed with us. He was watching Quigley, a sour look on his chapped little face.

'That,' said Quigley, 'is the point. Old Mother Walsh didn't always mean what she said to be taken *literally*. But, by God, the end of the world is coming and, by God, a pure and holy boy will preach the woman who will *speed his coming*!'

With these words, he pointed dramatically at Emily Quigley.

If anyone was going to be chosen to usher in the end of the world, she could well be the girl to do it. She had the face for it. Was this the deal? Did Quigley see me as some kind of John the Baptist figure? If he did, it wasn't surprising he was trying to get me Confirmed in Faith. Anything to make Emily Quigley look good. I may not be pure in heart, but, since Mike Jarvis the skateboarder went to live in Nottingham, I am about the only fourteen-year-old boy in the First Church of Christ the Spiritualist.

It gave me a spooky feeling, actually. Maybe he had a point. Maybe what I was saying wasn't so very different from what Old Mother Walsh had given the troops all those years ago.

He could see I was wavering and he held my arm tightly as the others came up. 'Extraterrestrials', he said, 'may well be on their way. I don't dispute that. Who knows what the Lord will send us on Judgement Day? But, cor lumme, snakes and aliens don't have to be taken literally. All we know is that, as Mother Walsh said, *when the pure boy preaches the woman ...* ' – here he gave Emily a meaningful look – ' . . . something pretty nasty is going to be heading in our direction. Don't call it aliens, Simo, call it Sin. Call it Wickedness. Call it Pain and Suffering!'

Pike gave him a curiously malevolent look. 'Call it aliens!' he said, in a rather spooky, hollow voice. 'I know it's aliens!'

Quigley looked rattled. But, before he could say anything, Mrs Danby emerged from round a large pile of tins of tuna-fish. She was carrying an armful of cat-food cans and smirking to herself. Quigley, with a short, convulsive movement that was halfway between a bow and a twitch, took my hand and led me towards her. 'Here's your boy,' he said. 'Shall we away the noo?'

This whole thing had a prearranged feel. What were they going to do to me now? Take me out to a patch of waste ground and kick my head in for spreading dissent?

'Where are we going?'

'We have a sufficiency of ravioli,' said Mrs Quigley, 'and . . . er . . . Norman has something to say to us!'

'What?' I said.

They all started to look at each other rather furtively. Mrs Danby dumped the cat-food in the trolley and came close to me. She smelt of dried flowers and pepper. There were bags of skin under her neck, and she had a deep, posh, drawling voice, like an actress in an old film.

'Norman has specifically asked to talk to us at Mr Quigley's house,' she said. 'Even though the kitchen is only half-completed!'

'Maybe', I said, with a completely straight face, 'he wants to see how the units are getting on.'

Mum gave an eager little nod. 'Yes . . . yes . . . maybe he does!'

I marvelled, once again, at the rapid change in my father's attitudes after his death. The last words he had spoken to me on the subject of kitchen units had been really quite abusive.

I wasn't at all sure about this. Look what had happened at the last seance. And, since then, there had been Mr Marr's disappearance and my Dad's own, frightening version of the Second Coming. I couldn't bear the thought of hearing that voice again – the low, small voice like that of a child alone in a house at night.

'Do we have to?' I asked.

There was suddenly a very, very tense atmosphere. All of them were looking at me. Mum started to sing, in a light, quiet voice – something she only does when she is nervous. They had clearly been leading up to this all week.

'Oh, Simon,' Mrs Danby was saying. 'I led your father down dark and narrow ways. Ways strewn with thorns and brambles and alive with venomous snakes! And now the whole Church is in danger!'

Quigley nodded vigorously. 'I think,' he said, with a rather savage look in Pike's direction, 'that we are in need of Guidance. Splits in the Church, Master Pike! Splits in the Church! Remember the Lewis Doctrine! Remember the Schismatics of New Malden!'

I had not heard anything about these guys. But as, presumably, they had been wiped off the face of the earth by someone pretty close to Ella Walsh or Rose Fox, there seemed little point in asking about them.

There was nothing I could say. I am fourteen. I have no rights. I followed them out into the car park and sat, miserably, in the back of Quigley's car as, in a mood of forced cheerfulness, we drove towards the Quigleys' house behind Mrs Danby's Rolls. I was squashed between Pike and Hannah Dooley in the back seat. The summer still hadn't gone away, although we were almost out of September. Above us, great masses of cumulus clouds stood out in the sky like old-fashioned sculptures.

The Quigleys live further out than us. To get to their house you drive down arterial roads lined with buildings that are neither warehouses nor shops. They squat on ragged patches of grass like abandoned containers, painted bright colours, stuffed with more than anyone could want of Do-It-Yourself Equipment, Garden Furniture or, in one case, Pure Leather.

The Quigleys live next to a park. Their house is semi-detached. It is worth £300,000. So Mr Quigley keeps saying. I wouldn't live in it if you paid me twice that amount. It is a big, square box, painted dirty white, and, although he is always knocking through, extending, repapering and spring-cleaning, there is something dead about the place. The furniture stands around listlessly, as if it is waiting to be sold. In the garden, the flowers and vegetables are as neat as Mr Quigley's accounts. There is an apple-tree up against the fence that separates them from their neighbours, but it has been given a kind of Buddhist monk's haircut. It does not look capable of bearing fruit.

The sun was still bright as we approached the Quigleys' house but it didn't seem to have reached their road, which was the same as it ever was: dank and green and desperately quiet.

The first thing I noticed was that the whole of the top half of the house was swathed in what looked like green plastic bandages. There was scaffolding rearing up the face of the house from the front garden and, next to the front door, a large notice saying:

GORDON BRUNT

GENERAL BUILDER

SINCE 1964 SERVING SOUTH LONDON

Next to the notice was a fat man in blue dungarees and a white hard hat. He looked as if he might well be Gordon Brunt. He also looked as if his mission might be to make South London completely and utterly miserable. As the crowd of us came out of the car, he leaned backwards over Mr Quigley's fence and spat, slowly and deliberately, into the geraniums.

'What do they do, Marjorie?' said Quigley, with sudden and violent passion.

Mrs Quigley was curiously calm as she replied, 'They take our money. They abuse us. They leave their *filthy newspapers in the loo*!'

When she actually spoke to the guy she was quite amiable. 'Hallo, Kevin. Are there problems?'

Kevin looked at her blearily. 'It's a bastard this one, Mrs Q,' he said. 'It's a real bastard!'

Quigley coughed. 'We need,' he said, rather stiffly, 'to use the house for prayer.'

Kevin looked at him suspiciously. 'You what?'

'We need,' said Quigley, with deliberate, offensive clarity, 'to use our dwelling to talk to the Lord Jesus Christ.'

Kevin looked at him doubtfully. 'I'm not sure about that,' he said. 'The plumbers are in.'

454

At this moment a loud banging noise came from one of the upstairs windows. Quigley, who seemed not quite in control of himself, grabbed the man by the ears. 'This is my house, wherein I dwell. And I would be grateful if you could get up there and tell that *oaf* Duncan to stop whatever it is he is doing!'

I hadn't understood, until now, why it was so important for the Quigleys to make contact with my dad at their house. Now it was clear. When he's at home, Mr Quigley is even more masterful than he is in other people's houses. The man shambled off into the house, and the rest of us picked our way across the front garden.

As we came into the front hall I heard Kevin yelling up the stairs, 'Stop the hammering! They want to pray!'

'You what?' said an invisible plumber.

'They want to pray!' said Kevin.

A large, hairy youth came out of the bathroom at the head of the stairs. He was carrying what looked like a huge steel club. 'Why can't the idiots pray somewhere else?' he said. Then he saw Mr Quigley and his hand went to his mouth. Quigley clearly had a master–slave relationship with these people.

'We will be in the back room,' said Quigley in tones of quiet authority, and, watched by several more astonished employees of Gordon Brunt Ltd, we all filed through into Quigley's dining-room.

The ceiling had been removed and we were looking up at where the roof of the house once had been. That, as I had seen from the outside, was shrouded in green plastic, and, as all the windows seemed to have been boarded up, there was scarcely any light at all. It felt as if you were in the middle of some enormous forest where the trees had grown together, blocking out the day.

Quigley pushed the seance table into the middle of the room, grinning at me over his shoulder as he did so. 'We're rough and ready, young shaver,' he said. 'But we're homey, aren't we?'

His confidence, which had slipped a little since my Testifying, was coming back. Here, surrounded by his family, his vast collection of Gilbert and Sullivan records, his several hundred bound copies of *What Car* magazine, his three watercolours of Wimbledon under snow and his collection of rare antiques, he was a man again. Even though all these objects were shrouded in heavy-duty plastic, he was a man again.

'Shall we pray?' he said, in an insidious voice.

'Yes!' said Hannah Dooley.

Mum sat at the table and pushed the grey hair back from her eyes. She pressed her hands together. They were red and raw from cooking and washing, and the lines on her face seemed to have multiplied since I last looked at it. 'Norman,' she said quietly, 'is very, very near.' Mrs Danby, who was dressed in sporty tweeds, as if for a shooting party, gave a superior kind of nod. I wondered whether there was anything in the teaching of Tai-Ping that could get me through the next half an hour. I though about *sei-sei-ying*, or the condition of being a birch leaf in early autumn, but did not find it helpful. What was needed here, rather than meditative technique, was a pump-action shotgun.

I had no choice. They were all sitting waiting for me. With a mounting feeling of dread, I went to a chair at the far end of the table from Quigley and lowered my head in the gloom. Quigley stretched out both his arms across the table and looked up at what was left of his roof.

'O Jesus, we seek Thy help. As our Church is itself in a confusion Thee Thyself often experienced when on this earth in places such as, for example, Gethsemane, which was, by anyone's standards, a pretty tough time for You. Hear us now as we attempt to contact Simon's father and help him in the great spiritual work that awaits him in this prime time of his boyhood!'

He shot me a quick look from under those bushy brows. I kept my eyes down. Emily was looking at me in a way I found frankly flirtatious.

Suddenly Quigley stopped praying. His old lady was bearing down in her chair and generally showing signs of getting off the psychic runway in double-quick time. She hadn't even frothed yet.

I was two down from her, but I could see Hannah Dooley wince as Marjorie started. Quigley stopped, clearly expecting her to give it a bit of movement, but, instead, she went into a sort of mammoth clench. She bound her brows and bit her lower lip and generally carried on like someone with serious constipation. After a quite incredibly long time she said, shaking her head wildly, 'No!'

Everyone looked a touch put out. In twenty years of psychic work, Marjorie Quigley had never yet refused her fence. I looked up and saw Emily looking at her mum in consternation.

Her mum shook her head again. 'No no no no no!' she said. She gave a huge sigh. 'There's no one there!'

Look. This was ridiculous. We're going out to lunch or what? We *knew* there were loads of people there. We'd only just put down the phone to them. The woman was just not doing her job and getting through.

She started to tap herself on the forehead. 'Total blank,' she said. 'Nothing there at all!'

We did her the favour of pretending that she was not talking about her own lack of brains.

She bit her lip furiously. 'Damn!' she said, like a tennis player who has just lost a point. 'Damn! Damn! Damn! Damn!'

Mrs Danby leaned across and took her hand. 'Gently,' she said. Then she looked at me and sighed. 'Norman always liked to go gently.'

This struck me as amazingly suggestive. Why was she looking at me like that? I looked across at Mum and found she was looking at Mrs Danby with an expression I did not recognize. It could have been fear or sympathy or irritation or a combination of all three. I thought about her and about Dad and the Danby woman. I had no idea, really, what any of them thought or felt.

Mrs Danby was simpering at Mum. When she'd finished simpering, she said, 'I blame myself!'

My mum looked vaguely hurt. She scratched herself behind the ear and said, 'Oh don't do that, Mrs Danby!'

'If it hadn't been for me,' Mrs Danby said darkly, 'Veronica would never have gone to that wine and cheese party. Or to Angmering for that matter.'

Everyone started to sigh and shake their heads. Mrs D held up her claw-like hand. Quigley started to ooze humility. He bowed forward over the table. He got his head so low you could practically see the cleft in his buttocks. 'Oh Mrs Danby,' he said, in the tone of voice he usually reserves for Jesus Christ. 'Oh Mrs Danby!'

Mrs Danby smirked. She didn't have to do a lot to get results. But I've noticed that a certain amount of loot helps to invest even your most casual remarks with a certain significance.

Mrs Danby shook her lizard-like head and pointed at me dramatically. 'When all's well with the boy,' she said, 'we will come into our own!'

I felt they had money on me. You know? Like I was a horse or something.

Mrs Danby was well away. She broke her hands free of the grip of those on either side of her and pressed her palms to the table. 'Thou seest me, Lord,' she said. 'Thou seest this boy also. Help him! Grant that he be not in Error! Help him back to the circle! And may he be the healing of the things I wrought with his father!'

'*Wrought*', eh! What had she and my dad wrought, I wondered? Suddenly I was in Error! Error is pretty bad. If you're in Error you are one step away from the thumbscrews. If there had been less enthusiasm among the congregation for ufology, maybe they would have devised a public punishment for me.

People who fail the Church are sometimes made to appear at morning service 'as they were first made before God', which these days usually means in their underclothes. If they have been just very bad, and if they have someone to stand up for them, they are given three strokes of the whip, usually by Sheldon Parry, the born-again television director, and then made to put on a short green smock for the duration of the service. If they have been very, very bad and are not well connected inside the Church, the man with the wart gobs all over them, people chuck potato peelings at them and then they are turned out into Strathclyde Road in their underpants.

I was moving dangerously close to the potato peelings. This much was obvious. I checked under the jeans to make sure I wasn't wearing the Donald Duck boxer shorts.

'Yes,' said Quigley, looking at me. 'Grant that what he has seen may not be a thing sent to tempt him!'

Pike made a kind of snuffling noise, and Mrs Quigley tried once again. She took the hands of those on either side of her, lowered her head and gave a constipated grunt. She grunted until sweat stood out on her brow. She grunted so hard there seemed a very strong chance she might drop a turd right there and then. But, after a minute or so, she shook her hands free, waggled her head furiously and said, 'Nothing. Nothing. Nothing.'

They were in a meeting, guys! Mozart was talking to Rose Fox. Rose Fox was talking to Vivaldi. My dad was tied up with Dickens or waiting for General Franco to turn up.

'Damn!' said Mrs Quigley, 'Damn! Damn! Damn!'

'Precious . . . ' said Quigley.

'Fuck!' said Mrs Quigley. 'Fuck! Fucking arseholes!'

Everyone looked at her oddly. It was OK for her to do this kind of thing when in a mediumistic trance, but this wasn't quite that, was it? She was, allegedly anyway, *compos mentis*. If this kind of thing was allowed to continue, she might well start swaggering into Sunday service and shouting things like 'Bugger!' or 'Piss off!' if she found someone in her seat.

'My darling . . . '

It was then that it happened.

Leo Pike, in forty years of attending Spiritualist seances, had never made much impact on the spirit world. He had an aunt in Leicester who had died of double pneumonia in 1964, but she had never wanted to speak to him. In fact, none of the dead, famous or unfamous, had ever shown any interest in Pike. And, as far as I had been able to judge, the feeling was pretty mutual. In all the years I had been watching him, he had, as far as I could tell, absolutely fuck-all interest in them. You could wheel in Julius Caesar and Pike would just sit there, peering at him through his gold-rimmed glasses.

You can imagine my surprise, then, when Pikey, without prior warning, started to hum like a top. At first I think most of us thought it was some electrical appliance. Then we noticed that the Pike head was sort of pulsing backwards and forwards like a mechanical toy.

Nothing unusual in that. Pike's head quite often pulses backwards and forwards like a mechanical toy. In fact, he has an extraordinary repertoire of mannerisms, all of which could be reasonably mistaken for possession of one kind or another. There isn't a moment when the lad isn't twitching or jerking or going into spasm. So, at first, we saw nothing unusual in his bonce doing the rhumba on top of his neck.

Then his toupee started to slip.

Pike's rug was a topic of endless fascination in the First Spiritualist Church. I can still remember the day when it walked into all our lives. I must have been about nine, but I still remember my dad putting his back to the door, after Pikey had gone home from a seance.

'Did you *see* it?' he said in hushed tones. 'Did you *see* it?'

'Sssh, Norman,' said my mum. 'Don't let's talk about it.'

But it was impossible not to talk about it. One minute there he was with a few scraps of grey hair plastered across his scalp – the next he looks like a prizewinner at Cruft's Dog Show. This wasn't just any old wig, you know? It looked like it had been grown in a tropical rain forest.

For weeks we had talked of little else. How was it held on? Was it stitched? Was it pure will power? Was it, perhaps, Blu-Tack? One woman was prepared to swear she had seen Sellotape on the back of Pike's neck.

And now it was moving. The more his head jolted backwards and forwards, the further down his scalp it crept. By the time he had finished rocking, his fringe hung over his eyes. When he finally spoke, it was as if his voice was coming out of a large, brunette bush.

'O Lord,' he said, in a high pitched voice. 'O Lord!'

We all just goggled at him. I mean, no one had ever seen Pike do this before. Right? Then he slewed round hard in his chair. His wig was now at a slight angle. He looked as if someone had just hung a mop on his nose.

From behind the toupee came a deep, deep voice. 'How y'all doin'? it said, in a strong American accent. 'An' how's little Nelly?'

19

No one had an answer to this.

For a moment I thought Quigley was going to tell him to snap out of it. But then my mum said, in a timorous voice, 'Do you mean Nelly Woodhouse that was with the Guardian Building Society?'

There was a silence. Then Pike said, in the same Texan drawl, 'Don't rightly know, ma'am. Don't rightly know.'

Mrs Danby was looking at Pike with a new respect. This all went to show just how far Quigley had slipped since I Testified. Time was when no one would dare open their traps in front of Mrs Quigley.

'The spirits wander,' said Mrs Danby, 'and find their homes in new bodies.'

Everyone nodded with fantastic respect. *'The spirits wander,' right? You heard Mrs Danby. She said the spirits wander, and she has a Rolls Royce, guys!* I thought to myself that, however far they had wandered, if they ended up in the body of Leonard Arthur Pike they must be really desperate.

Pike started to sing 'Home on the Range' in quite a loud voice. I had never heard Pike sing in real life, so I couldn't tell how this spirit voice matched up to the real one. Whoever was talking to us from Over Yonder, however, knew *all* the words.

> Oh give me a home where the buffalo roam
> And the deer and the antelope play . . .

I thought there was a strong chance that some of the lads might join in, but this proved not to be the case. Pike gave us all four verses, including the one about the wagon train being painted green, which I had never heard before. When he had stopped, there was silence. Nobody could follow that. We all looked at Pike. What was he going to do next? Would it be with or without music?

'I'll mosey on down now,' he said, now sounding as if he came from Alabama rather than Texas. 'I'll mosey, ah guess.'

'Stay, spirit!' said Mrs Danby. 'Who are you?'

Pike gave a deep chuckle. 'Tex,' he said. 'Tex is my name.' Then he started to sing 'Home on the Range' again.

I don't think we would have worn all four verses again (especially the one about the wagon being painted green) but, when he got to the line about the deer and the antelope playing, he burst into tears.

'What's the matter, Tex?' asked my mum.

'Little Nelly!' said Pike, now sounding vaguely Australian. 'Little Nelly Woodhouse died on the prairie!'

That was all we could get out of Tex. Mrs Danby tried. My mum tried. Even Quigley abandoned his dignity and had a go. But Tex had nothing more to say to us. I still wake up at night and think about Nelly Woodhouse. It was haunting, somehow.

There followed the longest silence I can ever recall at a seance. Pike just sat there with a toupee and tears all over his face, and we sat there staring at him.

After three or four minutes Quigley said, 'He's in deep, deep trance.'

'Yes,' said Mrs Quigley, 'he is very, very far away.'

Mrs Danby nodded.

'I have been where he is,' la Quigley continued, 'and it is a bleak and lonely place.'

'Yes,' said Mrs Danby.

Mrs Q was finding her way back into the action.

'It is a place,' she went on, 'where the soul is buffeted by winds, and violent storms and feelings from the old, old time.'

'Yes,' said Mrs Danby.

Before Mrs Quigley could start drawing us maps of the terrain on the far side of the Veil, Pike gave an absolutely agonized scream. It really was scary – I kid you not. What was even weirder was, it sounded like his own voice.

'Mr Marr!' he yelled. 'Mr Marr!'

I leaned forward. 'What about Mr Marr?'

But Pike went on screaming. It was a horrible sound. As if someone was being hurt, badly. The sort of noise you imagine coming from a torture chamber. *'Mr Marr! Mr Marr! Mr Marr!'*

'What about him?'

Then a new voice came out of him. It was a mechanical, grating sound from deep in his throat. I'm not easily spooked, but I didn't like this voice. It reminded me of the voice that had started all this, the night my dad died. 'I serve a different master,' said the voice. 'I serve other gods!'

It was well weird. No one was holding hands any more. We were all staring at Pike. As we watched, his wig fell forward over his nose and landed on the table in front of him. No one tried to pick it up. Pike continued to stare ahead of him, but his eyes weren't focused on anything.

'Where are you from?'

Pike gave a glassy smile. His head turned to me, just the way Mrs Quigley's had done when she passed on that first message from my dad. And, when he spoke, I'll swear it was my father's voice coming out of him. It sounded just like him.

'I'm a long way away, Simon,' said my dad. 'I really am a long, long way away.'

'Dad . . . '

Then the mechanical voice cut in on him, like a radio changing channels. 'Our planet is dying,' said the mechanical voice. 'We have no food or water. Help us, please! We have no food or water.'

Quigley's eyebrows drew in tight. He wasn't sure about this at *all*.

'Our sun is weak,' said the mechanical voice. 'Our canals are dying. The moon is in its last quarter. Help us, please!'

'How can we help?'

That's my mum. If she met an alien in Wandsworth High Street, she'd be telling it the way to the supermarket and offering it free babysitting before you could say 'flying saucer'.

I wasn't sure what Mrs Danby thought of all this. She was gazing at Pike in bewilderment.

Before Quigley could interrupt, I leaned forward and said, 'From which planet are you?'

I practically spelt this out. I wanted this thing to hear me loud and clear. It didn't, however, answer me directly. Which, if you think about it, isn't surprising. Anyone – even an advanced being from the other side of the universe – who is forced to use Leo Pike as a channel of communication is bound to experience transmission difficulties.

'From which *planet*?'

Pike's head was still facing me. At my last question there was movement behind the eyes. You could see a thought stirring, but you couldn't say if it was Pike's or not.

Then the voice started again, cracked and dry. 'Our planet is old and tired. The craters are dying. There is no night now. We need food and water.'

Whinge, whinge, whinge, eh? When we finally meet beings from another galaxy, all they do is moan! As I was thinking this, Pike started to laugh and the voice took on more colour. It didn't sound mechanical now. It sounded sneaky and mean, like a kid that thinks it's got away with something.

'We got Marr,' it said. 'We fixed Marr good!'

'Which *planet*?' I said again.

I was getting annoyed, as well as frightened. But before I could say any more, my dad's voice came back.

'Don't look any further, Simon, please,' he said. 'It's too dangerous. Please don't look for me any further. We all have to die, my darling. I didn't want to go! I didn't want to leave you! But I'm dead. You must stop looking for me . . . '

'Dad . . . ' I almost shouted.

But, as I did, the mechanical voice came back, loud and clear. 'I am Argol, from the planet Tellenor in the constellation of the Bear. And I bring death with me. I am the bringer of death to your world!'

Pike clambered to his feet and tried to walk forward. The table was in the way, but he was still trying to move. Emily Quigley started to scream. Pike's legs went up and down like someone walking the wrong way along a travelator. He still stared straight ahead as he ploughed into the heavy dining-table.

Then, suddenly, he picked it up and flung it across the room. Pike isn't a big guy, but he did this like he had been in secret weight-training. As the table fell against Mrs Quigley and my mum (who started to cry), Pike just kept on walking, like a robot responding to an invisible signal. When he got to the wall, he didn't stop. He just kept trying to walk through it.

'Leonard . . . ' whimpered Hannah Dooley. 'Oh Leonard . . . '

'I am not Leonard,' said a sneering, robotic voice. 'I am not *Pike*. I am Argol from the planet Tellenor in the constellation of the Bear. And I bring death with me. I am the bringer of death to your world!'

We knew this. But we were still interested. No one had ever seen Pike express an opinion about anything. His job was to open car doors for Quigley. Now here he was walking into walls! Mrs Quigley could roll. She could froth. Although she seemed not to be doing a lot of that these days. But did she walk into walls? We were looking at a very serious contender indeed.

Mrs Q was looking rather critically at Pike's performance. And he was certainly not getting the kind of back-up she got from her old man. He was just quietly walking into the wall, while the rest of us stood around in an awkward half-circle.

From a room somewhere else in the house came a loud gurgling sound, followed by a scream. It was hard to hear what was being said, but someone had put a nail through a pipe. None of us paid this any attention. I looked at Pike, my mouth open. How had he got hold of that name? Why 'Argol'?

I'll be frank. In a way, I thought he was putting it on. I mean, I thought there *were* aliens, or something like aliens, out there. But I wasn't sure they were the kind of entities that come from other planets. They could have been the kind you find here. It is easy to make up someone to look like someone, isn't it? And to play on someone's fears and hopes. Could they have got an actor to pretend to be my dad? It was possible. Somebody was trying to freak me out, and, from what I could gather, it might well have something to do with the Quigleys, with Veronica and this Mrs Danby.

But what I thought and what I believed had been moving further and further apart in the weeks since my father had died. What I was prepared to believe now, although it changed from day to day, was something frightening and surprising and new. Belief is spooky.

It's something you use to get you from A to B, I guess, and right now that seemed a long way to me. Besides, for reasons I will come to shortly, the name Argol was familiar to me.

'Look, Argol,' I said, trying to get the boy-to-alien tone just right, 'if that *is* your name. How did you get here?'

Pike's face was now pressed firmly into what was left of the Quigleys' wallpaper. He had stopped using his legs. He was just concerned with getting his nose as far into the brickwork as humanly possible.

'I think,' said Mrs Quigley, sniffing the stale parlour with her long, dog's nose, 'that there's a bit of *play-acting* going on here!'

Pike leaped into the air. He sort of bounced off the wall as if he was on a piece of elastic and someone had just yanked it from the other end. He whirled round, stood in a kind of ape-like crouch and started to swing his arms in front of him. Mrs Quigley backed away nervously. It was, I thought, the last time that she would make sarky remarks about a fellow medium's performance. When Pike spoke again it was in that mechanical voice. But there was nothing human about it at all now. It was 100 per cent artificial. It sounded like a menacing version of my Amiga 500.

'Why do you not believe?' it said. 'Why do you pretend you are the only beings in the universe? Why should that be, my friends? Why do you not recognize us? We are here. We are among you.'

Quigley folded his arms. He was starting to get annoyed with Pike, you could tell. 'Just in Wimbledon?' he said. 'Or are you all over the place?'

Pike started to walk towards him. His mouth was open and he was dribbling down his front.

'Leonard!' said Quigley, his voice shaking slightly. 'Don't be . . . '

Pike's face started to distort. One hand came out in a kind of claw and swiped at Quigley. My mum jumped and screamed. Hannah Dooley, her nostrils flared, was muttering something to herself. When the voice came back it was the full robot job – an awful, grating sound. 'We landed in Wimbledon,' it said, 'and soon the rest of the planet will be ours!'

With these words the forty-eight-year-old accounts clerk leaped at

Quigley's throat and, pinning him to the floor, started to bang his head on the dust-sheets that shrouded the household's £700 Persian carpet.

20

This was, I thought, just what Quigley needed.

He was not of this opinion. He got his hands round Pike's neck and started to squeeze. But Pike kept on banging his head against the floor.

'Look,' said Quigley, 'let's be reasonable about this, shall we?' Not an easy thing to say when someone in the grip of an alien being is trying to make scrambled eggs out of your brains. 'Let's . . . er . . . discuss . . . '

You had to hand it to Quigley. But Pike would not stop. His face was dark purple and there was that look in his eyes again. I didn't say anything, guys. I had remembered where I had heard that name before.

'Leonard . . . '

'I do not know of *Leonard*,' said Pike. 'I am Argol from the planet Tellenor in the constellation of the Bear. And I bring death with me. I am the bringer of death to your world!'

And death number one looked set to be that of Albert Roger Quigley. Mrs Q was pulling at Pike's cardy, and even Mrs Danby was weighing in on Quigley's behalf, but Pike kept right on banging.

'Argol,' said Quigley finally, 'I beseech you in the name of Jesus Christ – Argol!'

Pike stopped banging and a slow smile spread across his face. When he spoke he sounded more like Pike than anyone else. 'Argol,' he said, with childlike delight. 'Do we have to bang our heads on the floor before we understand? *Argol*. It isn't difficult to say, is it? You can say *Persil* can't you? You can say *Daz* and *Flash* and *Bold*. You can say *Argol* can't you? Argol is my *name*, lunkhead!'

Quigley remained cool. If he wasn't such a complete bastard he'd be a great guy. But, say what you like about him, he was probably the perfect bridge between us and a being from another world, especially when that being proved to be as mean and nasty as Argol looked to be.

'Argol,' he said, 'please let go of my head! OK?'

'All right,' said Pike.

Then the breath seemed to go out of him, like air out of a lilo. He fell forward on Quigley's chest. But, just as he did so, he gave us one more burst of the mechanical voice: 'Andrew Logan Manningtree Marr, born Glasgow 1946, died Wimbledon 1990. Marr knew too much. Andrew Logan . . . Manningtree. Manningtree Marr. Operation Majestic. Operation Majestic UK8.'

There was a clicking at the back of his throat. I stepped away from him towards the wall. What he had just said, if that was what he *had* said, was as frightening as anything else that had happened since my dad died.

He went on: 'Operation Majestic UK8. Marr knew too much!'

Then Pike, or Pike's body anyway, flopped all over Quigley as if the two of them had just been exchanging bodily fluids.

Pike did not move. After some time, Quigley said, curtly, 'Get him off me!'

Mrs Danby, Mrs Quigley, Hannah Dooley, Roger Beeding and my mum rolled Pike off him. Pike curled up on the floor. He seemed, as far as I could tell, to be fast asleep.

'Let us pray,' said Quigley.

'Yes,' said Mrs Danby.

What a man! He has just been pulverized by a being from the other side of the galaxy and what does he do? He is right on the line to Jesus. He didn't even get up. He just rolled neatly over on his side and commenced talking to the Big Man.

'Jesus Christ,' he said, as if he was an experienced soldier talking to a rather dumb general, 'there are many impostors in Thy world and many of Us have failed to Grasp the . . . er . . . Meaning of these Things.'

He stopped. When he has those upper-case problems, you know he is running out of steam. Then he said, in a thick voice, 'Is he all right?'

'I think so,' said my mum.

I looked at her. It was weird. Since my dad died she had got smaller and smaller. If she went on this way, you'd be able to pick her up soon.

Everyone has their moment, right? And hers was the day he croaked. It was like he hadn't done anything really interesting until he kicked off. He couldn't surprise her. Maybe dying is the only honest thing we do. As I looked at her, I thought of her shrinking, like someone in a fairytale, and how one day I might hold her in the palm of my hand with her little voice squeaking commands at me as if she was a mouse I'd picked up in the garden. I didn't like that idea. I figured I ought to be the person to make her grow, but I just didn't know how.

'He was in the grip of some Force,' said Mum. 'I was reminded of that poltergeist in West Germany!'

Quigley shot her a glance. 'Let us pray,' he said again. 'Let us pray that Our Church, which We have built up through Thy Faith and trust, will . . . hold together . . . and that . . . although there are Beings that . . . '

There was a pause. Then a thin, hopeless little noise came out of him, like a half-hearted fart. To my horror, I realized Quigley was crying.

We were getting to him. We were getting to him. Me and the aliens were finally getting to him.

No one moved. We had seen a lot of people cry in our time, but this was the first time that Quigley had done us the honour. We let him finish. He did make a pretty thorough job of it. He started with a series of gulping sobs, went through to a noise like a drain emptying out and finished up with a sort of throaty sob.

Mrs Danby went to him and put her arms on him. 'Albert,' she said, 'I want to help you. I want to help. I promised the money to the Church and I want to give it. But I must see the boy's faith, do you see?'

'My dear . . . ' began Quigley. But she was having none of it.

'We all know how I led Norman astray. How I led him out of the garden and into a rough and stony place where naught but thistles and brambles grow! How I made him betray what he *believed*!'

This whole thing was about what you believed. My dad and I had talked about these things so rarely. We just never seemed to get round to them. It was always the joke or the next argument or the next meal at La Paesana with my dad. And yet he must have believed in something.

He said to me once, when he was driving me to school, that there was nothing left to believe in these days. I said to him, 'But you believe in . . . well, in . . . in what Mum believes, don't you?'

He gave me a kind of bleak look. 'I'm not sure, old son. I'm not sure what I believe in any more. I thought I knew, but it's . . . it's so hard . . .'

I looked out at the school. The school he'd wanted me to go to so that I could be as clever as he had once been and go to Oxford the way he'd done and not waste it as he had been foolish enough to do. I leaned across to kiss him goodbye and I said, 'Believe in me, dad!' As a joke, right?

But he put a hand on my shoulder and said, in that philosophical, gravelly voice he had, 'All we have to believe in is our children. And yet we betray them!'

He said things like that, my dad. But not usually in the early morning. Usually when he'd had a few. Betray? I mean, be serious! Who said we trusted each other in the first place? It is nearly the year 2000, my friends.

I looked up. Mrs Danby was staring across the darkened room at me. Upstairs the hammering and shouting seemed to have stopped. Her voice sounded shaky.

'You know . . . Simon was to be . . . was to . . . ' She looked at me sort of pleadingly. 'And now he has *changed* us all! Hasn't he? He has made us think!'

You can say that again, was what I read on Quiggers' face.

'You know . . . ' Mrs Danby went on, 'are there beings from other worlds? Here? In Wimbledon? It's perfectly possible, isn't it?'

She laid a hand on Quigley's shoulder. 'I cannot give the money until my doubts are resolved. I am deeply confused.'

471

She spoke for all of us here.

She shook her head wildly. 'Too much, Albert! Too many things that cannot yield their secrets!' And, with these stirring words, she went outside to her Rolls-Royce. Although why anyone with a Silver Cloud needs to worry about things yielding up their secrets is still a mystery to me.

Whatever they were talking about had had a very bad effect on the Quigleys. Mrs Quigley was hyperventilating and giving me some very dirty looks indeed.

My mum dabbed her eyes with her handkerchief and said, 'Arnold Bottomley had a seizure when he was on a canal boat and it took four of us to hold him, although he had been so easy-going on other trips, especially the Greek one that I didn't go on. He did quite well at Sussex University!'

Nobody responded to this. Nobody knew whether the seance was over. Were we still talking to Jesus?

Very slowly Pike got up. He shook his head. Touched his face. Realized he hadn't got his glasses. Then he said, 'Where am I?'

'32 Strathclyde Road,' said my mum.

'At the moment . . .' said Quigley ominously.

'You what?' said Pike.

Quigley too sat up now. The two men looked at each other in silence. Somehow or other Pikey found his glasses and, in the course of getting them hung on his ears, discovered his rug was missing.

'Oh my *God*!' said Pike softly.

'Yes,' said Quigley, 'Oh my *God*!'

Pike, on all fours, started to pad around the floor in search of the missing toupee. I could see it over by the wooden boards that had been nailed across Quigley's windows. It looked like a sleeping dog on the white sheet. I didn't like to point it out to him. I just wanted to get out of there.

'Spacemen . . .' said Quigley, with a sniff. 'Spacemen . . .'

'You what?' said Pike.

'Spacemen!'

Pike's bum was in the air as he groped his way forward. Suddenly Quiggers was on his feet and, before anyone could say anything, he

472

was taking a brisk run-up at the Pike bottom. Moving like a man who has played more squash than he need, he spun round, drew back his right and booted his wigless ex-sidekick right up his grey-flannelled arse.

'Argol from the planet Tellenor,' he said. 'Argol from the *fucking* planet Tellenor!'

'Who?' said Pike, as he fell face forward into his rug.

But Quigley was not to be stopped. He was raining kicks into all the softer bits of the body chosen by the being who was to bring death to our world. If Argol had any bollocks at all, I thought to myself, this could well be the end of Albert Roger Quigley.

Rog did not, however, disappear in a white sheet of flame. He just kept right on kicking Pikey, and Pikey kept right on taking it. Their relationship was right back on course. There was absolutely no sign of Argol. Maybe he had zoomed off into another body. You know? Maybe he *was* in the body but he just liked getting kicked by earthlings. Maybe they were into S & M on the planet Tellenor.

Pike was curled up into a ball, like a hedgehog, clutching his wig to him the way a kid might hold on to its teddy before going to sleep. Rog just kept on putting the boot into him. Each time the toecap went into his stomach, Pike moaned quietly, his knuckles tightening round his toupee.

In the end, Quigley put his hand on his hip and stepped back a pace. 'Now,' he said, 'what was all that about, *please*! Argol from the planet Tellenor! And as for Mr Marr – did you ever see him more than twice in your life? Eh, "Argol"?'

'Who is Argol?' said Pike, evenly. 'And where is the planet Tellenor?'

If this was an act, it was a good one. It certainly threw Quigley, because he turned his attentions to me. Breathing heavily, he reached for my shoulder and pulled me towards him.

'We are going to bring you to heel, boy. You hear? We are going to stop your troublemaking. You hear? We are going to draw the reins in very, very, *very* tight!'

'Albert . . . ' began my mum tentatively.

Quigley turned on her. 'There's something bad got into your son,

473

Sarah, and Mrs Quigley and I are going to have to do something very serious about it. He is going to *have* to be Confirmed in Faith. You hear me? He *must* be. You hear?' Here he grabbed my arm and squeezed it, hard. 'Even if we have to drag him kicking and screaming before the Lord. Our Church needs funds. You understand, boy? Our Church needs you!'

I was scared. But not just by Quigley. I was scared because if what Quigley had said to Pikey was true and he really *didn't* know Mr Marr, how come he had access to his full name and date of birth? The only person in the world who knew those was me. For some reason he hated that middle name of his. It was almost as closely guarded a secret as Operation Majestic UK8.

Oh yes, there is such a thing. That was the real reason I was sweating as I went to bed that night. Operation Majestic UK8 is *dynamite*. Nobody else, apart from those directly involved – and, of course, Mr Marr – knew about that stuff. It's dangerous even to mention it to people, according to Mr Marr.

But Pike knew about it. If it *was* Pike talking. Not someone or some*thing* using his poor little body to give us a dreadful warning.

21

You may find this hard to believe, but Operation Majestic 12 really happened. You can look it up in *The UFO Report*, by Timothy Good, if you like. It's the most convincing evidence we have of an alien invasion of this planet, and a matter of public record.

In 1952, according to the American nuclear physicist Stanton Friedman, a top-secret briefing document for President Eisenhower was leaked to the public. It revealed that the wreckage of a flying saucer was allegedly recovered seventy-five miles north-west of Roswell, New Mexico, in July 1947. Admiral Hillenkoetter's report for the CIA noted, among other things, 'that the characteristics of the human-like bodies were different from homo sapiens; that there were strange symbols on portions of the wreckage which had not yet been interpreted'. And 'that it was strongly recommended that Operation Majestic 12 be kept accountable only to the President of the United States'.

There is objective evidence that something odd did happen near Roswell in 1947. We know for a fact that the area was sealed off and that army and rescue services were called to the scene. And that no one, not even the press, was allowed near. Stanton Friedman, who has years of experience in the design, development and testing of advanced nuclear and space systems, concludes, in his 1990 report, that *the leaked documents are genuine*.

Before you say, 'Then he is barking mad,' think hard about this. There are plenty of things they don't tell us about. And Operation Majestic UK8, like its American counterpart, is one of those things. The reason you haven't read about it, even in the official UFO journals, is that it has been kept so secret that not even the ufologists know about it.

Operation Majestic UK8 refers to a set of documents shown to Mrs

Thatcher *in secret* in 1984. These documents refer to a spaceship that crash-landed on the island of Jura in the Inner Hebrides in the autumn of 1983. (Autumn, as you will have noted from this manuscript, is a busy time for the extraterrestrials.) An alien who was brought from the wreckage in a container to the Mill Hill Medical Research Centre survived in our atmosphere for three days, five hours and twenty-five minutes. According to the UK8 papers, a full-scale invasion of the earth was planned, although, from what the creature told them, the research scientists concluded that it would be *eight or nine years* before the 'fleet' was fully prepared.

The alien, who was, according to the scientists, 'of humanoid form', was from the planet Tellenor in the constellation of the Bear, identified subsequently by scientists as probably belonging to star system BG4543/2221 in the Beta Principis cluster. Mr Marr reckoned that he conveyed 'certain information' to the scientists, including that his planet was controlled by a creature. The creature's name was *Argol*. Hardly anyone knew this apart from me and Mr Marr. How could Pike have possibly known? Wasn't it likely that the thing that had got into him at the seance was really from the planet Tellenor? It hadn't been like any other seance I had ever seen . . .

I thought about this the day after Pike went crazy. It had been a particularly bad day at school. 'Dummy' Maxwell had told me I had a 'hunted look' about me. I ask you! My dad always used to say that he didn't pay teachers to make personal remarks.

I was sitting with my feet up, watching a film about a Puerto Rican mass murderer. First of all Emily Quigley came in.

'All Daddy wantth you to do,' she said, 'ith to thay that alienth ith only an ecthpwethion! He thinkth tho highly of your thtwength!'

I ignored her. The Puerto Rican mass murderer was letting off a pump-action shotgun into a bus queue in downtown Los Angeles.

After a few minutes she went out and Quigley came in, waving a piece of paper. He grinned madly at me and said, 'Well, young shaver! This should sort you out!'

He put his hands on his hips and gave me a kind of larky look. 'Why do you always look so *sullen*, fellow? Gosh! Jesus ain't arf depressed at seeing his children down in the mouth, me deario!'

I kept my eyes on the screen. I never look sullen. Especially when I am watching Puerto Rican mass murderers. This one was now sobbing over his attorney's shoes. Quigley waved the paper over my face.

When its flapping had started to irritate me, I snatched it from him and saw that it was ruled like a timetable. On it were written, in crude capitals, things like:

> 07.45–08.10 – HOOVERING
> 08.10–08.15 – CHRISTIAN WORSHIP
> 08.15–08.25 – BREAKFAST (optional)

I went back to looking at the screen. Events move swiftly in these films and it's very easy to miss things. The Puerto Rican mass murderer was now in bed, surrounded by a crowd of admiring listeners, lawyers, policemen, close relatives and beautiful women. Obviously the only way to get respect is to make with the pump-action shotgun. You know?

Quigley reached forward and turned it off. I turned it on again. I was quite calm. At this moment my mum came in.

'Do you think,' Quigley said to her, 'that the little bloke should be watching this . . . ?'

'Oh . . . ' said my mum. She sounded scared.

Behind her came Mrs Quigley, who was holding a frying-pan. 'It's only some rubbish about a Puerto Rican mass murderer . . . ' she said. 'He's got off by the blonde one in the wig, anyway!'

I knew she had psychic gifts, but I could not work out how she was so clued in to this film. Surely there was no way she could have seen it before.

Quigley started to pace up and down the room as the mass murderer, who had now leaped out of bed and on to the window-sill of his hospital suite, announced his intention of travelling the sixteen floors between him and the pavement without the aid of lift or stairs.

'You, me laddio,' said Quigley, 'are on pindown! You will be picked up from school by Marjorie or me or your mother or all three of us from now on.'

I kept my eyes on the screen. I tried to imagine Greenslade and

Marjorie Quigley together. I just could not do it, somehow. It seemed hard to believe they were in the same universe.

'Golly, Simo, you are making it hard for us,' Quiggers went on. 'We want a pure boy that we can hold to our bosoms and we get a kind of . . . I dunno, ol' matey . . . a kinda *monster*!'

The Puerto Rican mass murderer had decided to jump. His attorney's girlfriend was holding on to his legs as he went through the things that were wrong with his life, in broken English. 'Itta steenk!' he was saying. 'It alla steenk, thees life!' I knew how he felt.

My mum and Mrs Quigley were now sitting on the arm of the sofa, their eyes glued to the screen, as Quigley paced around the room.

'There is to be no hanging around the High Street and staring into shop windows,' he went on. 'There are to be none of those "hamburgers" either.'

You could really hear those inverted commas click into place. What was he trying to do to me? We were talking Colditz here, guys!

'There are no phone-calls in or out. There are no little "subs", and there are no trips to the newsagents either, me deario. Until you stop this upsetting talk and this . . . divisive rambling about . . . '

'Aliens,' I said, rather irritably. I knew he was trying to rile me, but I was determined to keep calm. I thought about *sang-sang-dang*, or the state of being a rose-bush in early May. It helped.

On the screen they had let go of the Puerto Rican mass murderer's trousers and he was on his way to the sidewalk, head first, at about seventy miles an hour. It was better for him really. He didn't look the kind of guy who could have taken a long prison sentence.

' "Sin is a busy old thing when out! See how it travels, Lord, all round about!" ' said Quigley, who often reaches for the wise words of Old Mother Walsh when things are getting tough.

After the mass murderer hit the deck, I got up and, resisting the temptation to fold my left forearm over my right elbow, make a prong of the middle finger of my right hand and then lift it in Quigley's face while telling him he was a motherfucking asshole, I went to the door. 'And don't look so sullen, me laddio!' he called after me.

Sullen? I wouldn't know *how to*, my friend. I had risen above him and was now in the state of *dung-hai*, or complete and utter superiority to Quigley.

What was really getting to him was the fact that alien-fever was proving hard to eradicate in the First Church of Christ the Spiritualist. I thought about his notion that 'alien' was just another way of saying 'devil', or that Old Mother Walsh and her snake weren't, actually, any more real, although just as powerful, as Argol and the things from Tellenor. It didn't stand up. I don't say I knew what was happening, but, whatever it was, it was *real*. You know? I hadn't even dared go near Furnival Gardens since I saw my old man for the second time.

I would have to go down to Mr Marr's house. And, with this new regime in force, tonight would probably be the last chance I had to do it. I decided to wait until they were all asleep. I lay on my bed with a computer magazine and, from time to time, went to the window and looked down at the darkened street. I could make out the spot where my dad had stood that night.

Down below, Quigley shouted goodnight at me and I shouted back, and, at last, my mum tiptoed to the door and, looking fearfully around her in case Quigley saw, blew me a little, damp kiss. 'You can be so sweet, Simon,' she said, 'but you're such a stubborn thing!' I didn't answer. I might have provoked even worse charges. Then she said, 'You're so like him. You're so like poor, poor Norman!'

Quigley was always the last to go to bed. His routine was monumental, guys. When everyone was in bed he would go round to every window, double-check if it was locked and then, before he came upstairs, place a few key obstacles in the path of any potential intruder. I swear he was obsessed with burglars. He spent a lot of time swaggering about the place, flexing his muscles and telling everyone what he was going to do with those 'foolish little feller-me-lads' if they showed up.

I had to wait for what seemed like hours. But, eventually, after several tours of inspection of the windows and much talk of the need for Banham locks, Quigley, exhausted by his own vigilance, staggered to bed. Minutes later he was making a noise like a pneumatic drill. I slipped out of bed, got into a pair of jeans and a T-shirt and headed down the stairs.

It was like a slalom down there. There was an ironing-board, two kitchen chairs and a couple of broken wooden boxes snaked around the front room. In the back kitchen was a dresser, three pails of water a yard or so apart and a small scattering of drawing-pins. In the front hall – in case any burglar should choose to throw himself through the fireproof glass in the window or slice through the mortise lock with a flame gun – was a selection of things to trip over. There was a rubber ball, a few of Emily's textbooks and a sort of forcefield of nails resting heads down and points upwards towards the unseen burglar's face. As I discovered this arrangement, I began to feel almost sorry for any potential thief. After fighting his way through all this, he would have to face an angry and almost certainly stark-naked Quigley.

The street was empty. In one house, on the corner, there was a light on in the front bedroom. A middle-aged woman, wearing what looked like a turban, was looking out at the night. I don't know what she was looking for, but she didn't see me. There was a warm wind on my face and hands as I made my way towards Mr Marr's place.

I didn't look up at the sky. But I really felt they were looking at me. Like you do in the supermarket sometimes, when you can sense something behind you and you turn and there's this camera, mounted at the edge of a shelf, swivelling its one black eye this way and that, like some malevolent goblin at the door to a secret cave.

I didn't look behind me either. They were *here* weren't they? They could be keeping pace with me, along Forrest Avenue, down Gladewood Road, and across up through Park Crescent. Maybe they had got people in every third house. Maybe Mr and Mrs Lewis at 119 Cedar Avenue were not in their usual positions, snoring back to back in the bed they bought twenty years ago. Maybe they were out in the garden, walking around stiffly, expressionless as vacuum cleaners, as they prepared the Giant Pod for Argol of the planet Tellenor.

I had a feeling that, when Argol finally showed, he was going to look a lot more scary than Leo Pike. I had heard his sound-bite, and he sounded like a man who meant business.

Looking in front wasn't really safe either. Suppose Argol, or someone like him, suddenly leaped out of someone's driveway to give me a taste of his galaxy's latest in combat weapons. The Jura alien had had a lot to say about Tellenorean life-forms. Much of it, Mr Marr said, was just too horrible to tell me. He didn't want me to have nightmares, he said. I thought about what they *might* be like. In a way, not knowing made it worse. I used to feel that way about Old Mother Walsh's snake when I was a little kid. Now it's something to laugh at, but then . . . I was feeling more and more like a little kid with each day that passed.

As I turned into Mr Marr's I was shaking. I had to force myself down the street to his house. I had to force myself up the path to his front door. And, when I fitted the key into that lock, my hands were trembling.

Listen – no one could have got into Mr Marr's. I had the only key. No one had forced any doors or windows, because they didn't need to, did they? On Tellenor, according to the Jura alien, they have mastered the technique of passing through solid objects – one of the things Mr Marr said was worst about the Tellenoreans was that you never quite knew when they were there.

If it was them, they had been through the house very, very carefully. Since my last visit they had had another go. Someone or something had been through the fridge and taken away a few samples of earthling diet – a chilli con carne and a cold lasagne that was probably even now being scoffed by a load of blobs up in the ionosphere. They had also started to take away literature. They had been pretty systematic. Most of the stuff missing was from Mr Marr's extensive collection of material dealing with invasions from other galaxies. And the huge file dealing with Operation Majestic UK8, which had taken pride of place in Mr Marr's top-secret collection of UFO papers (in the cupboard under the stairs) was nowhere to be seen.

I thought about the police. But if these beings had left any fingerprints I had the strong feeling they wouldn't be the kind you get down at Scotland Yard.

He had kept the file under a pile of back numbers of the *Wimbledon Guardian*, because, as he said, 'there were a number of people who would be only too happy to see all documents in the case suppressed'. At one point, I seem to remember, he'd kept the papers in the fridge – which is why the top sheet had a large blob of sweetcorn in the top right-hand corner.

Our Tellenorean friends had taken the *Wimbledon Guardian* as well as the UK8 papers. I didn't like to think why they needed the local paper. By now, probably half the small ads in the current issue had been placed by aliens.

I was scared, though. I was really terrified.

And then, as I came out from under the stairs, I heard something moving upstairs. Two creaking boards and that was it. I stopped. I listened hard. I could hear my heart tap against my ribs. My face suddenly felt very hot, and then, as suddenly, very cold. There was silence. I wanted the silence to go on, but, as I listened, it felt as if I was racing it. That the thump of my heart was challenging it to go on and not to be broken by a . . .

Crrreak . . .

There was something up there. And, while I was not in possession of definite proof, my money was on it coming from somewhere a little further away than the Fulham Palace Road. As I changed from listening to walking mode, I tried to work out whether it had feet or flippers or ran on rollers. The noise had an insistent quality – like a small animal gnawing away at something or gathering food and stopping every few minutes to listen, as hard as I was listening in the dark of Mr Marr's house.

I did not want to find out if it was friendly. If it was friendly, how come it was scurrying around stealing magazines and not coming out into the open and asking who was in charge round here. Everything seemed to indicate that it was our friend Argol, or some flunkey of his. I tried to remember if Mr Marr had ever said anything about how Argol looked. Was he a thing or a person? Hadn't someone said something about his teeth? I was almost sure they had. His *teeth*! My Christ! The gnawing was starting again. Not content with stealing Mr Marr's library, the bastard was chewing up his bedroom furniture!

Then I heard the humming. A high-pitched noise that seemed to come from the head of the stairs. It wasn't the kind of sound an engine made – or a dishwasher or a television or any of the things I was used to seeing round the house. I only realized what it was when I got to the front door. It was a human sound, but unlike one I had ever heard before. It was more like the noise dogs make sometimes – a see-sawing musical phrase, as if it was talking to someone you couldn't see. That was it. Human and yet definitely *not* human.

I looked up at the bedroom window as I closed the door behind me. I saw Pike's face pressed to the glass. He looked as if he was lit from below, and his nose and cheeks were spread out in a white, lifeless slab against the window pane. But his eyes were glinting, as if he was looking at something no mere human could see. Or – and this thought only occurred to me when I was out on the street and running for the hill as fast as I could – as if there was something else behind his eyes, looking out at the world, waiting for the awful moment when it would start to take apart our little corner of the planet, piece by shabby piece.

22

They had done something to my dad. And now Pike was under their control.

The only comforting thing about this was that, although they were well placed to take over my brain, they had, so far at any rate, declined to take up the offer. Maybe I secreted some hormone that gave the average Tellenorean a violently unpleasant feeling. Or perhaps Argol had an enlightened policy towards young people. Maybe it was going to be like the Cultural Revolution in China and we were all going to be given the chance to team up with the aliens. Certainly, if offered the choice between Quigley and an eighty-foot beige monster with a corkscrew head, I knew where my allegiance would lie.

I tried to remember what else the documents had said. A lot of them, of course, were so secret that Mr Marr couldn't even show them to me. They were, he said, the kind of documents you eat rather than read. The guys at Mill Hill who had worked on the Jura alien had been very cagey about this, apparently, but I think Mr Marr said there was a lot of stuff about mind control. The Tellenoreans don't talk the way normal people do. They just sit there by the fire projecting their thoughts into each other's brains, like me and Greenslade. In fact, it was rumoured that one of the Mill Hill guys had had his brain messed around with by the visitor who screwed up the landing in the Hebrides.

The trouble with this alien business is that you cannot trust your senses. As Jenny Randles says in *Abduction* (according to Mr Marr, the only really reliable guide to the spacenapping phenomenon), 'Of course I am making no assumptions about what it means to have been abducted [by aliens], but if some researchers are correct *many of*

*you reading this book might have undergone an abduction experience with-
out consciously realizing it.'*

It was possible that all this business with my dad was a deliberate
ploy by Argol and his pals to destabilize yours truly. After all, I was
close to Marr, wasn't I? And he was the only guy on to them. Maybe
my dad was really and truly dead and what I had been looking at, in
the road outside our house and in Furnival Gardens, had been a
hologram put out by the Tellenoreans. Maybe it was me they were
after. Maybe the reason I had Testified the way I did was a kind of
double bluff on Argol's part. Maybe *they had already got to me.*

I was running now. Putting one foot after the other in a style I
have developed during cross-country runs organized by Cranborne
School, I allowed my head to sort of loll forward and my legs to
patter after it, leaving the middle bit of me completely free for
inflation and deflation. At any moment I expected one of the masters,
placed at strategic intervals to stop a guy taking short cuts or lighting
up a Havana cigar, to leap out from a place of concealment, brandishing *The Times* and bellowing, 'Come *on*, Britton! Come *along*
there!'

As I panted into Stranraer Gardens, following the no-hopers' rule
for cross-country – *never run in a straight line* – I was flailing my arms
left and right and zigzagging at an angle of about ten degrees to the
horizontal.

Everything in Stranraer Gardens was as still as I had left it. The
trees in the street were shamming dead. Every last bit of unkempt
hedge in our front garden was taking the same attitude it had always
taken. In whatever street we live, our garden is always the shabby
one. 'Gardening vexeth the spirit,' my dad used to say to me with a
broad wink whenever my mum asked him to get out and cut the
lawn. Whenever she said to him, 'But, Norman – don't you want to
sit in it, like other people?' he would reply, rather grandly, 'A garden,
my dear, is a place for passing through as quickly as possible on the
way to the pub.'

I stopped a few yards from the house. All around the fences, the
parked cars and the neat roofs was that weird stuff you get just
before dawn in the suburbs – it isn't light or darkness but some other

thing entirely – shadowy, ghostly, but so much itself you feel you could reach out and run it through your fingers.

I got my breath back. With that stupid feeling of relief you get when you're home, I pushed open the door, tripped over what felt like a set of billiard balls and fell headlong into a carefully arranged selection of this week's vegetables. As I went face first into about two kilos of potatoes, a large hand seized hold of my T-shirt from behind. The hand pulled me up towards the ceiling.

'Where've you been, my laddio?' said Quigley's voice, quiet but deadly. 'What have you been a-doing of?'

'I've been . . . '

That was as far as I got.

'It's been on the *Common* looking for little green *men* has it? And holding their little green *hands* and having little green *drinks* with them and having little green *chats* about their little green *planet* . . . '

'Listen . . . ' I said.

He was hitting me really hard. It was only when I swung to the left and broke free for a moment that I was able to observe that he was wearing my dad's grey towelling dressing-gown. My dad wasn't a tall man and it only just covered Quigley's enormous willy. It made him look as if he was wearing a mini-skirt.

'What are you trying to do to our Church, Sonny Jim?' he hissed. 'Why are you trying to split us in two? After all I have done for you!'

I could not think of a single thing that Quigley had ever done for me. But now was not the time to tell him. He hit hard.

'Do you know what hangs on Mrs Danby's covenant?' he said. 'Have you any *idea*?'

I had an idea what the covenant was. It sounded as if all this was as much about money as it was about religion.

From upstairs I heard my mum shout, 'What is it? What is it?'

Quigley went mad. He started to clout me around the head, yelling, 'Burglar! Burglar! Burglar!'

'Burglar?' came a cheeping from the back bedroom.

'Burglar!' yelled Quigley. 'Burglar!'

Pronouncing the word seemed to bring him to his senses. He stopped, looked over his shoulder and put both his hands up to my face. 'O Jesus Christ,' he said, looking over my shoulder as if JC had just wandered in from the garden, 'did you die for this boy?'

I kneed him in the balls as hard as I could.

'Jesus Christ!' he said, doubling up in pain.

'Oh, screw Jesus Christ,' I said. 'Screw him. And screw his mother Mary too!'

Quigley gave what I can only describe as an eldritch screech and came at me with both arms, legs and the front bit of his head. 'Blasphemer!'

Mrs Quigley was now at the head of the stairs. 'Burglar!' she screamed.

'What is it?' called my mum again.

What indeed? A burglar who blasphemed? Who broke into your house in the middle of the night and, after paying the usual compliments to your stereo, got on with the job of pouring scorn on your most cherished convictions?

Quigley beat me through into the back kitchen. I heard my mum's voice. 'Simon!' she called, in feeble tones. 'Is that you?'

'It is!' I yelled. 'The one who was in your womb for nine months and a day, remember? And, if I didn't think this bastard who's making so *fucking* free with my dad's house would follow me there, I'd jump right back in this minute!'

'He called Albert a bastard!' yelled Mrs Quigley.

'Well he is,' I said. 'He is a bastard. He's a complete and utter bastard, if you want to know.'

'He thaith Daddy ith a bathtard!' came Emily's voice.

Quigley clouted me smartly across the side of the head. I fell to the floor and crouched, Pike fashion, in a corner of the kitchen, covering my face with my hands. Quigley went to the door to check there was no one around, then, unable to stop himself, ran back to me and twisted my ear hard. 'Stop play-acting,' he said. 'I didn't hit you hard!'

'Let go of my lugs.'

He started to shake my head about. It was not going to be long, I reflected, before I made my contribution to discussions in 24 Stranraer Gardens via a Ouija board.

I sensed, rather than heard, my mum come in. Quigley had made sure he had stopped hitting me as soon as he heard her on the stairs.

'Mum . . .'

'Oh, Simon . . .'

Quigley leaped back, pulling down my dad's dressing-gown with a surprisingly prim gesture. I looked up at my mum. I noticed that she was crying. Those little eyes of hers were red and angry, and her chin quivered helplessly above her neck as she came towards me.

'Why do you let him do this to me, Mum? Why don't you stand up for me? Don't you love me, Mum?'

My mum dabbed at her eyes. She didn't answer.

'If Daddy was alive he wouldn't let him do this to me! Why do you? Why do you let him? You don't love me, do you? You don't even like me, do you? Why don't you like me? What have I ever done to you?'

Unable to answer this to her or my satisfaction, my mum started to cry. But they weren't her usual tears. Usually she cries like the rain we had on a holiday once, up in Scotland – a soft, grey drizzle – but this time her body shook with real sobs.

Quigley joined in. He's a big guy, but he seemed to have got to like crying. It was him, not me, that went to her and got hugged. He needs a lot of help. I don't think he finds himself any easier to live with than the rest of us.

'Help me through it, Sarah!' he was saying. 'Help me through this!'

Help me through the hitting-Simon experience! Why won't you?

I could see my mum's face on the other side of Quigley's shoulder. I could also see something I had absolutely no wish to see at all, which was Quigley's bottom. It was long and sausage-shaped and coated with fine, black hairs. It peeked out from under the rim of my dad's dressing-gown with a horrible sauciness. Mum's eyes were signalling to me – something far-away and desperate. I could not work out what it might be.

Eventually Quiggers rounded on me. 'Now, Simon, apologize to your mother for that disgusting, manipulative little display. Could you?'

488

I was obviously not taking the punishment right. I was not observing the Christian decencies for getting thumped. How tactless could I get?

'I'll never apologize to you, Quigley,' I said. 'I hate you. And I hate your creepy wife and your creepy daughter and I wish you were all dead. I wish you were dead and my dad was alive. I think you stink. I think all religions stink, actually, but Christianity stinks worse than any of them.'

There was silence.

Just in case I hadn't made this absolutely clear, I added, 'I'll never forgive you and I'll never apologize to you and I'll never do anything you say.'

He was still looking pleased with himself.

'Why is it so important to get me back in your rotten little Church, Quiggers?' I said. 'Is there some grubby, horrible reason? I bet there is. Well I tell you, Quigley, by the time I'm through with it there won't *be* a fucking Church. The aliens are here, Quigley.'

He twitched slightly, like a lizard's tongue. I pushed on, sensing a weak spot.

'They've got into your congregation, Quigley, and they're going to wreck the Church. They are. You're finished here, I tell you.'

It was then that my mum came over to me. She knelt next to me and, peering into my face, she said, 'Testify, Simon. Please. Come back to Jesus. Please. I don't want you to be damned. If you'll be Confirmed in Faith I'll never ask you to come to the church again. And Mr Quigley will go. He will.'

She stroked my hair then, very gently, the way she used to do when I was a little kid.

'I want you to be saved, that's all, darling. And then we can get on with our lives. Please, Simon.'

I looked up at her.

She put her hand to my cheek. 'It's like Mr Quigley says – you're a pure boy! You are!'

I remembered some of the nice times we'd had. Me and Mum and the old man. Laughing at things or sitting together round the table and my dad making jokes and . . . Why is life such a bitch? Why does it lay these things on you? Why does it pull your heart two ways? And why do feelings always surprise you?

I wish we were machines. You know? People go too far.

23

'Why,' Greenslade whispered to me, 'isn't semen an element?'

Up behind the desk, 'Pansy' Fanshawe was preparing to see how sodium reacted with something whose name I could neither remember nor pronounce. Pansy had a far-away expression on his face. He looked a bit like a sorcerer as he stirred the mixture in a small clay crucible.

'It's a pretty big element in my life,' I said.

On the other side of me Khan sniffed. He doesn't like us talking like this. If Khan ever whangs off, it is probably for the purposes of spectroscopic analysis.

Pansy looked up wildly. He is about sixty and they should have retired him years ago, but he has nowhere else to go. I sometimes think they may not be paying him. 'Now,' he said, in a quavery voice, 'molybdenum is . . . '

He stopped in mid sentence, as he often did. I stared at him intently. It was about a week after my showdown with Quigley and I should have been at Harvest Festival. I have to avoid the last period on the second Friday in October, which is when the First Church of Christ the Spiritualist celebrates 'the rich goodness of God's vegetables'.

I was supposed to be there. But I wasn't. Outside, on the sun-soaked Common, they were piling up French loaves and bottles of Beaujolais. But I was staying inside, learning about what the world was really like, or, rather, what Pansy Fanshawe thought it was like.

After the night Quigley had kicked my head in, I had finally seen something I should have seen a long time ago. I didn't have to do any of these crazy things they made me do. I didn't have to stand up and tell the whole truth of my heart unless I wanted to. I didn't have to say shit to Jesus Christ if I didn't feel like it. I had stayed in bed on

Sunday morning, even though Quigley had nearly kicked the door down and then burst into tears all over my duvet. 'We need you, Simo,' he said. 'We need your deep love! We need your purity!' I was lying there thinking about fellatio at the time. How did they actually *do* it? Did it hurt?

He didn't need my purity. He needed me to sweeten Mrs Danby. But I didn't need him. You see, it was really my dad that made me go along with the Church, even though he didn't really involve himself. Somehow he managed to make it fun, the way he made so many things fun, and, now he was either dead or else taken over by some force I could not even begin to understand, there was nothing whatsoever to keep me in the Church.

'Now,' said Fanshawe, 'stand well back, because there may be a bang!'

Pansy's chemistry lessons are mainly a question of lobbing stuff out of the cupboard into a crucible and trying to get an explosion going. Most of the time he doesn't even know what elements he is trying to combine. He's closer to a mad chef than a chemist.

Khan was trying to say something. He looked worried. 'Sir,' he said, in his precise, slow voice, 'under certain circumstances, compounds of the substances which you are attempting to combine may have a reaction in which, say, the sodium . . . ' He did not get to the end of the sentence. With a mad gleam in his eye, Pansy lobbed a small chunk of brown rock into the crucible. There was a colossal bang and the sound of the clay crucible hitting the desks, walls, windows and members of the Fourth Form. Thackeray started screaming.

Greenslade and I had hit the floor early. We know Pansy. When we raised our heads above the desk there were clouds of smoke blowing across the chemistry laboratory. Fanshawe was giving a kind of war whoop as, through the grey fumes, I saw the unmistakable figure of Quigley.

He stepped in front of the class like a demon king making his appearance in a pantomime. Behind him I could see my mum, Emily and Mrs Quigley, who appeared to be carrying a large sheaf of corn. It was, I think, the worst moment of my life so far. I was absolutely terrified that Greenslade or Khan might discover that I was anything to do with these people. How had they got in here? I seriously thought of crawling through the smoke to the door.

But it was too late. Quigley was pointing at me, dramatically. 'I think this boy must come with us,' he was saying.

Fanshawe clearly thought that Quigley was the product of the chemical reaction he had just engendered. He was goggling at the First Spiritualists like a medieval alchemist who has just raised the Devil. 'Are you . . . er . . . a . . . parent?' he said feebly.

My mum stepped forward as more smoke billowed across the laboratory, circling around the faces of pupils, master and visiting religious maniacs. 'I am his mother,' she said, in a quiet voice, 'and he is excused today's last-period chemistry to attend a Christian service.'

Pansy looked at her as if he was trying to work out how to combine her with deuterium and to calculate the effects of the resulting explosion.

'It is,' said Quigley, with quiet dignity, 'a festival of the faith to which Simon belongs.'

Greenslade gave me a sideways look. I raised my eyebrows, resolving, as I did so, to let him know my side of the story as soon as possible. There was no point in fighting this one. Not in front of twenty-three members of the Fourth Form. I got up and walked, with some dignity, towards the door. When I got level with them, I rounded on Quigley. 'This is the *last* time, scumbag!' And, with that, I stalked out into the corridor, as Pansy, still dazed from the effects of the explosion, meandered feebly after my mother, muttering about notes and the headmaster's policy on being excused important school activities.

'Where's Pikey?' I asked, as they marched me towards the car. Quigley did not answer this. Since Pike's behaviour at the last seance, he had been banished from the Quigley presence. I noticed that the assistant bank manager was biting his lower lip and grinding his right fist into his left palm.

As we got to the car, I stood back from them and said, 'You can do this to me once, but you can't go on doing it. I don't believe, you see. I don't believe any of that rubbish you talk.'

Emily Quigley looked really distressed. 'Thimon,' she said, 'it'th like in *Narnia* when Athlan thaith to Edmund that he mutht have *faith*!'

'*Narnia*,' I said, 'is bullshit. Give me Wimbledon any day.'

I looked straight at her. 'Why do you believe all this rubbish? It's crazy. You all know it's crazy. It's only habit keeps you doing it. If you once stopped and thought about it rationally, you wouldn't believe any of it.'

I looked back at the school buildings. I was amazed at what I was saying. And yet I knew, as I spoke, that this was what I had always thought but had been too frightened to express. Silently, we all got into the car.

There was a mood of quiet desperation about Mr and Mrs Quigley. As we drove up towards the Common, they looked at each other briefly, then looked away.

'Has Pikey left?' I said, 'Has he joined the true cause? Is he out looking for the bastards who stole my father?' They didn't answer this, but my mum leaned forward and patted my hand absently.

In the boot was a large pile of tins of tuna-fish and a harvest wreath that had clearly been designed by Marjorie Quigley. We were coming to the end of the day, and the light was starting to fade.

The First Spiritualists were camped out at the edge of a grove of birch trees. There weren't many of them. When I was a child I could remember gatherings of two or three hundred people, but there were fewer than a hundred out on the dry grass. Someone had told me that no fewer than twenty people had left the Church after my speech, many of them to join the Raelian Society, a group that exists to set up embassies on earth for alien intelligences wishing to make contact with earthlings.

'What's keeping them away, Quiggers?' I said. 'Is it the weather or what?'

Quigley twitched, then decided to ignore this remark. As we walked towards the circle of Spiritualists, he turned to me and said, in a high, pleasant voice, 'I know you will come back to us, Simo! The Lord Jesus will make a way for you!'

'Listen, Quigley,' I said, speaking in a clear voice, 'Jesus Christ is out of the picture. When beings from another planet get started on you they will *laugh* at your beliefs. You'll be like some savage to them, clutching a wooden idol.'

Although they could all hear me, no one responded to this remark. Quigley looked more than usually Christian.

The First Church of Christ the Spiritualist was arranged in a huge circle around a large pile of groceries. The produce did not seem to be of high quality. The recession seemed to have hit Harvest Festival rather badly, I thought. I saw a lot of tins of spaghetti. Old Mother Walsh had urged her followers to 'bring living things and offer them to the Lord', and there is an account somewhere of the Sisters of Harmony sacrificing a sheep. These days people bring hamsters and terrapins and rabbits and dogs, but nobody quite has the nerve to pin them down on a slab and cut their throats. As we sat down a little way away from the rest of the group, I saw a small girl waving her hamster's cage at the sky. 'There You are, God!' she was shouting. 'There's Hairy! You can have him if You want!'

There are a lot of children at Harvest Festival. It's quite a jolly occasion. Looking at it now, I suddenly started to feel old. Older than anyone else there. A group of little kids were doing what is called the Carrot Dance, over by the groceries. It's a crazy thing where one child pretends to be a carrot and the others top and tail him and put him in boiling water. As I watched them, I thought about all the crazy things the people I've grown up with believe and do. How we bury people, how we marry people – First Spiritualists are always married as close to 3 February as possible, and, when the bride has made her vows, someone pours a bottle of milk over her head ('to feed her young') – how we pray, how we hang sheets out of the upstairs window to celebrate a birth, how we seem so utterly and completely deranged and yet feel so utterly and completely sane.

For a moment I wondered whether the First Spiritualists are any crazier than other people. People who pride themselves on being rational won't walk under ladders. Famous physicists talk about

God without really knowing what the word means. Much of the faith of my mother and father's Church would seem bizarre or laughable to Greenslade and Khan. But to me, standing there in the autumn sunlight, it suddenly seemed natural and comforting. Maybe because, at last, I had finally lost it. I was no longer part of the First Church of Christ the Spiritualist. My dad was dead, and he was never coming back.

Over by the birch trees, Mervyn Finch had started to play his squeezebox to Vera 'Got All the Things There' Loomis, and a few of the adults were dancing the old dances that have been passed down for nearly 200 years. Old Mother Walsh's 'Rabbit, Skip O'er the Lump of Bacon' and, my personal favourite, 'Who's Away to Jesus?' Hannah Dooley was pressed close to Sheldon Parry, the born-again television director, crooning softly to herself. Clara Beeding was chatting amicably to the man with the wart. The sun was over the rim of the Common now, and there was the beginnings of darkness in the tangled trees.

'Danth with me, Thimon,' said Emily's voice at my elbow. I looked down at her, as the music grew louder. She was so full of hope and decency and trust. And that voice! Emily was, according to her mother, an absent-minded girl, but she never forgot to lisp. *Why not?* I thought to myself. *This is the last time I'll be part of these people.* I took her hand and led her into the centre of the dancers, as the light failed over Wimbledon.

24

We went through every dance in the book that night. We even did 'Goodbye to Clonakilty' (a title no one in the Church has ever been able to explain), and, when it was quite dark, the group over by the trees lit a fire and we went into 'Ella Walsh's Foxtrot' or 'Bless the Lord and Shame the Devil'. You grab your partner by the waist and sort of waddle for a bit, then stamp four times, hard with each foot, on the ground. It's a dance designed for fat people who are not light on their feet. After you have stamped, you raise your right hand and, for some reason, shout, 'Shame the Devil!' Except at Christmas, when some people yell, 'Stuff the Turkey!' I usually try and say something different from both of these. Such as, 'Rinse the Saucepans!' or 'Phone Your Auntie!'

In the slow bits, I moved away from Emily and waggled my ears. It's something I have only recently learned to do, and she seemed to appreciate it.

As the music pounded on, I pulled Emily this way and that across the baked earth. It was almost dark. Over to our left, in the field that lay between us and the road, was the shape of a horse. A solitary man walked his dog home, up in the direction of the Windmill. And, all around us, people were swaying and shaking, clapping and singing, as the beat grew wilder and wilder.

Emily cannoned into me, her face red with pleasure. 'Why do you believe in alienth?' she said.

'Because I think they're there,' I replied.

She grinned. 'Thatth why I believe in Jethuth!'

I grinned back.

'Why believe in alienth, though?' she went on. 'Alienth are thuch a complicated thing to believe in!'

I thought this was rather a shrewd point. Maybe away from her mum and dad she was capable of being a human being. I shrugged. 'You've got to believe in something,' I said, 'and I believe in aliens.'

I couldn't stop dancing with her. I moved with her, close, towards the centre of the circle and that crazy pile of groceries. I took her by both hands and I started to swing her in a circle, singing as I went, shouting the words of the song over and over again.

Quigley wasn't dancing. I saw him by the camp-fire, standing next to my mum, watching me hungrily. Maybe he thought he was going to get me back into the Church, but what I was doing was strictly pagan. I was dancing for dancing's sake, not for Jesus'.

I was almost at the centre of the group when I saw the light in the trees. It was a reddish glow, moving unsteadily towards where we were at a height of about fifteen or sixteen feet. It would weave towards us then veer away crazily. Sometimes it would stop and shine downwards, as if it was scanning the earth for something. Then it would move off on course again. I could see a vague shape behind it.

I was the first to notice it. Then Emily, following the direction of my gaze, watched the light, or lights, as they swayed through the trees towards us.

Mr and Mrs Ian Gilliemore, who were taken from their Hillman Avenger on the night of 24 September 1958 and subjected to scanning by a 'big light' from a group of midgets in the traditional green cloaks, reported seeing 'a sort of dancing light' just before the midgets struck. They said the light moved in just the way this one seemed to be doing.

Other people had seen it now. A guy next to me was nudging his friend and pointing at the trees. My arm was tingling, like it's supposed to do when the Neptunians come at you through the undergrowth, foetal implants in hand. I went hot, then cold.

Word was spreading among the crowd. Even Mervyn, whose hands were flying across the keys of his accordion, was seen to gape up towards the thing dancing like a huge firefly in the dusk. The music slowed and then stopped. People stopped dancing and stood in silence looking over at it. They looked just the way they did when they turned to the altar on Sunday mornings. There were whispers, too. 'They're here!' I heard one man say. And another, 'It's true! They've come!'

Quigley, who was now standing next to Mrs Danby, a little away from the rest of the congregation, was watching open-mouthed. Next to him, I saw my mum push her grey hair from her temples. There was an expression on her face I hadn't seen in a long time. She looked hopeful. She was eager to welcome whoever was coming to her out of the darkness. She was going to exchange knitting-patterns with the Visitors, and ask them if they would like a hot drink after their 17 million light-year journey to Wimbledon. That was the most common look on people's faces. Hope. Stronger than you saw it in church. More various, shifting, fading, like the light at the end of a day, as the lights came closer and closer towards us.

Maybe they wanted the groceries. You know?

Were they lights or was it just one light? It seemed to have changed colour. It was white now, and behind it you could see the shape. It didn't stop but came on towards us out of the trees.

Next to me a woman gasped, 'It's here . . . It's . . . ' Emily clutched my hand and stepped back. Now it seemed at least twelve feet in height, roughly humanoid in shape and wearing what looked like a plastic bucket on its head. Its legs – if it had legs – were covered in what looked like a large brown sheet, and the light seemed to come from a kind of lamp attached to the back of what could, or could not, be its head.

As it came on across the grass, quite a few people dropped to their knees and pressed their palms together in prayer. Emily held my hand even more tightly. 'Jethuth . . . ' she was saying, 'Jethuth . . . Jethuth . . . '

I held my ground. Even at this distance, in the gloom, I could see that the thing on its head that looked like a plastic bucket actually *was* a plastic bucket. In fact, I thought I recognized the bucket. The large brown sheet was quite clearly a large brown sheet, and the thing at the back was none other than my bicycle light.

'*Roughly humanoid in shape*', was, too, a fairly accurate description. Because, as the creature swayed around in front of us, it was becoming obvious, even to the more short-sighted of the congregation, that we were looking at Leonard Pike. 'I come', he said from inside the bucket, 'from the planet Tellenor!'

There was quite a good reverb effect on his voice. The woman next to me was quite clearly not at all sure whether this was Pike. From the look on Quigley's face, it was obvious that Pike was soon going to wish that Pike was not his name.

I couldn't figure this. If the Tellenoreans *had* got into Pike's body, wasn't this a slightly odd thing to make him do? Were they not as bright as we had supposed? Were they complete idiots? Or were they, perhaps, a nation of satirists? Perhaps they had come all those billions of miles for the purpose of taking the piss out of us.

As I waited, Pike started to fall, jumping clear of the stilts that had been holding him up. The bucket, miraculously, remained on his head. 'I come,' he said again, 'from the planet Tellenor.'

He was losing his audience. 'And I come from Epsom, mate!' said a voice at the back. There was a gust of laughter.

Pike, aware that the bucket was not helping him, removed it. The effect was startling. In the darkness, Pike's face, illuminated by the bicycle light, looked positively ghoulish. He was breathing rapidly, and his pinched, chapped little face was urgent with venom. He looked crazy with fear.

'He *was* taken,' said Pike. 'He was taken from the grass. Here on the Common. And I can prove it.'

With a shriek, he pointed his finger at Quigley. 'He's lied to you,' he said. 'He's a liar and a fraud. He's a cheat.'

Quigley looked white.

'Ask him what he's done with the money! Ask him what he *plans* to do with Mrs Danby's money! Ask him where it's gone!'

Quigley didn't speak. He started to open and close his fists, but he didn't say anything.

'They are here!' said Pike. 'Follow me! Don't follow the liar and the cheat! Follow me! I'll take you to the spot where they took him! I've looked through the accounts! Follow me!'

If Quigley had ever had a chance of regaining his grip on the First Spiritualist Church of South Wimbledon, he had lost all hope of it now. There was an awful conviction in Pike's voice. You just knew that what he was saying about Quigley was true. You knew.

Quigley just stood there, his immense arms loose at his side, as the mass of the congregation, murmuring among themselves like extras in a bad production of a Shakespeare play, swept after Pike as he turned and, bucket in hand, ran off across the Common towards the spot where Mr Marr had been sitting the night the aliens came.

25

He was yelling something as he ran. Something about somebody dying. I couldn't tell who. Something about how he, Pike, was guilty. Guilty of what, though?

As we got to the narrow road that runs past the spot where Mr Marr used to watch the night sky, he turned and held up his hands towards the stars. '*Help!*' he screamed. Once.

I'd heard (or was it seen?) that cry before. Where was it?

'*Help!*' yelled Pike, again.

Of course. On the mirror in Mr Marr's bedroom. HELP! scrawled in lipstick.

The First Church of Christ the Spiritualist was, as its leading members were fond of saying, on the move. It was, literally, going places. Every single member of the congregation was haring through the bushes of Wimbledon Common in search of flying saucers. If ever there was a flight from the true religion, this was it.

We stopped on one side of the narrow road. Pike was on the other, jumping up and down like a man with a swarm of bees in his underpants. It was as if he was on the other side of a river that no one knew how to cross. And the road had the look of water, silvered under the rising moon.

Pike was pointing to the grass near to where Mr Marr had been sitting that night. 'Look at it!' he yelled. 'Look at it! It's where they landed!'

One or two of the braver spirits moved closer to the road and peered across at the grass. You didn't see it at first, but you saw if you held you head at the right angle. About twenty yards from where Mr Marr had been sitting, the grass had been flattened. It lay as if some giant hand had combed it out and then blow-dried it, in a perfect circle.

It was curious. No one wanted to cross the road. It was as if there was a force field there. As if Pike was behind an imaginary glass wall, cut off from the rest of the Church. As he railed on at us, more and more people came up to the edge of the tarmac, looking across at him, helplessly, in the moonlight.

'I'm guilty,' Pike was saying. 'I'm guilty too. Jesus, forgive me. Oh forgive me, Jesus!'

'Jesus forgives you,' said someone over to my left.

This was standard with the First Church. You went out – you had a good time. You drank gin. You coshed old ladies. You embezzled Church funds. And Jesus forgave you. But Pike looked like a man who would not, could not, be forgiven. As if whatever he had done had cut him off from the mercy he had been seeking for so long.

'It was here,' yelled Pike, 'on the road! Here!'

I looked at Quigley, who was standing well away from the crowd. His face was still that dead white colour. He was looking at Pike as if he expected him to change shape, to flower into some awful creature.

'I'm a murderer!' yelled Pikey.

He moved towards us across the road. Instinctively – as if faced by some poisonous animal – people moved back a little. Pike stopped in the middle of the tarmac. Somewhere, over on the other side of the Common, a truck moved up from below the hill and, headlights hooded, started across towards Parkside.

'I'm a murderer!' yelled Pike again.

'Leo,' came a voice that I recognized as my mum's. 'You're not a murderer!'

Pike's face reddened with fury.

The truck turned right by the big houses at the south edge of the Common and started along the straight stretch, where we were standing. Pike turned and saw it. For a moment I thought he was going to stand there facing it, daring it to stop. Then he moved back towards the circle in the grass on the other side of the road.

'Who did you think you murdered?' called my mum, in a bewildered tone.

The truck was coming closer. You could feel the earth shake as it changed down, ready to turn out into Parkside.

Pike's face was distorted with anger. 'Marr, of course. I murdered Marr, you morons! Right here I murdered him!'

His lips puckered up. 'It was . . . it was like spacemen took him. It was. He was lying here. He was dead in the road. I wasn't driving fast, honestly! When I came back, he was gone. He was lying here.'

He gestured towards the centre of the road. He seemed very intent on showing us the precise spot where Mr Marr's body had lain. That was all that seemed to matter to him. Then, with a blitheness I had never associated with Pike, he stepped two paces back into the path of the oncoming truck.

It hit him in the chest. The guy was quick on to the brakes, but not quick enough for poor old Pikey. By the time the truck had stopped, Leo was under its offside wheel and starting the long, complicated journey to the spirit world.

It's some consolation to reflect that of all the UK citizens undergoing the death experience, Leo was probably the one most prepared for it. He had spent nearly all of his forty-eight years in the First Church of Christ the Spiritualist, and during that time he had witnessed literally thousands of encounters with people from the Other Side. He had never missed a seance or a service, and he died, as Mr Toombs said the next Sunday, a 100 per cent, fully operational Christian.

But his death and the mystery surrounding it spelt the end for the Church in which he had worshipped for so long. It wasn't the Wimbledon Crop Circle, as the shape in the grass came to be called, that destroyed it. Most people agreed that Pike had been out the night before working on it with an industrial fan. It was tiredness that finished the First Church. That and the fact that it lost faith in the nearest thing to a charismatic it had had since Rose Fox. In fact people seemed to be losing interest in aliens. One by one, over the next few weeks, they just drifted away. You could see it in their faces, minute by minute. They were getting that worried look you see on people's faces on the Tube. They were becoming, at long last, ordinary.

The elders started to investigate Quigley and the Church funds the day after Pike's death. The Quigleys were still living with us. Gordon

Brunt and his friends had taken away a wall without putting in the proper structural support, so the whole of the left side of Château Quigley had collapsed. They had also done something terrible to the boiler, and discovered dry rot in the airing-cupboard.

I heard a lot of the commission of inquiry. One night I heard Quigley shout, 'Would you bleed me dry?' All I heard of the answer was the low bass of Mr Toombs and the nasal falsetto of Roger Beeding. But, from Quigley's face when he came out, I gathered that that was precisely what they were intending to do with him.

Sometimes, in hushed voices in the evenings, I heard my mum and the Quigleys talking about money. But nobody said anything to me about that, nor about where Mr Marr's body had gone after Pikey ran into him with Lethal Weapon III.

One evening, after he'd been answering more questions from Toombs and Beeding, Quigley came into my room when I was doing my homework. I didn't look up. There was something scary about him these days. He just came over to my desk, looked down at what I was writing and whispered, almost to himself, 'You're as bad as your bloody father!' Then, with the back of his hand, he hit me, hard, across the side of my face.

One day, towards the end of October, I came home from school late to find my mum, Marjorie and Emily sitting in Quigley's car outside the house. My mum looked as if she was in the middle of being kidnapped. She gave me a weak smile and a fluttery little wave. It gave her, suddenly, the helpless look of royalty.

I tapped on the glass, and she wound down the window. 'What's going on?' I said.

'We're off to write prayers,' said Mrs Quigley, answering for her, as she tended to do these days.

'Do come, Simon,' said Mum.

The back wall of the First Church is littered with scrap pieces of paper on which are written things like PLEASE HELP AUNTIE JOAN THROUGH THIS PHASE OF THE TREATMENT or DEAR GOD, HELP ALL THE PEOPLE I SAW ON WATERLOO STATION THIS WEEKEND AND PRAY FOR ALL, ALIVE AND DECEASED, AT 110 HOLDEN ROAD, FINCHLEY. I wasn't sure for whom they would be praying. Under the present circumstances it could equally well have been me or Quigley.

'Where is he?' I said.

They all looked shifty. 'He's out the back,' said Marjorie. 'With Danzig.'

Danzig! It sounded as if Quigley had passed beyond the reach of prayer. Who the hell was Danzig? A German missionary, perhaps. I turned my back on them and marched towards the front door.

'Danzig,' called my mum, as I disappeared into the house, 'looked as if he might do it. So Roger stayed with him.'

This was getting even more mysterious. As I went through the drab little hall, I wondered whether there was an overseas branch of the First Church of Christ the Spiritualist and, if so, whether it contained a man called Danzig. He sounded like a guy with a problem.

As I came to the door that leads out to the garden I heard Quigley's voice. 'No, Danzig,' he was saying in a coaxing sort of way. 'No, no, no. Not there, Danzig. There! There! See? There!'

Had Quigley finally come out of the closet? Was he trying to get Danzig to do to him what no other man had ever done? I suddenly had a clear mental picture of Danzig – a hairy-chested man with a gold medallion and tight, white trousers.

I walked through on to what my dad used to call 'the wide green spaces of 24 Stranraer Gardens' and heard Quigley's voice again, this time low and thrilling. 'Yes, Danzig,' he gasped. 'Yes, yes, yes! There! Good! Good! Good!'

I turned to my left and saw a large Labrador. It was squatting on the flower-bed. Its back legs were straining furiously and its face wore a fixed and glassy expression. It was almost certainly going through the final stages of the digestive process. Quigley peered down at its bum. He looked pleased. 'My dog,' he said. 'Hundred and ten quid!'

The animal gave a final grunt and expelled whatever it had to expel. There was certainly a lot of it. When it had finished, it hared off across the garden as if it had done something clever.

'So,' I said, 'they're off to pray.'

He was wearing one of my father's ties. My dad always claimed to have gone to public school, but he was never precise about which one. The ties all looked as if they came from a jumble sale. I never liked him wearing them, but I liked them even less round Quigley's neck.

'To pray for you, Simo,' he said.

'They needn't bother, Quigley,' I said.

He came over to me then. He was breathing heavily. I could see everything about him very clearly. The black hairs on his hands. The ridiculous, wiry neatness of his hair. The pallid, clammy surface of his skin. 'You need help, boy,' he said.

'Listen,' I replied, 'pretty soon the whole of south-west London is going to be under the iron heel of Argol of the planet Tellenor. I should move on out if I were you.'

Quigley sneered. 'You never believed any of that rubbish, did you? It was just a stick to beat me with, wasn't it?'

I didn't move back, although he shoved his face close to mine. 'No,' I said. 'The really pathetic thing about all of this is I did. I still almost do believe it. That's how badly you bastards have fucked up my brain!'

Quigley started to twitch. 'I'm not leaving, Simon,' he said. 'I'm going to be here for the rest of your *life*.'

I still didn't move.

With a sort of grunt, he wound his hand back and again clouted me, hard, on the face. It hurt a lot, but I didn't let him see that. I just stood there. After a while he didn't seem to see me. He turned to the dog and said something to it. For a moment I looked away, and when I looked back he was gone. A minute later I heard the car engine start. I was alone in the house.

My dad was dead. There were no aliens. Or, if there were, they were playing it so cool as to be almost unnoticeable. There were no ghosts or gods or any of that stuff. There was only the unlimited prospect of Quigley. It was time to go.

I went back into the house and, when I was sure no adults had sneaked back in to spy on me, I went upstairs to my bedroom and started to pack.

I didn't take much. A few computer magazines, some cash I

pinched from Quigley's drawer and my Abbey National card. I have £300 in there, which is quite a lot of money. My dad always said it was for when I got married. If I hung around here any longer, it would all go on a nose job for Emily Quigley. I took two paperback books, a toothbrush, my Ventolin inhaler and a copy of the repeat prescription, four T-shirts, two pairs of jeans and my other pair of trainers. Everything I really care about fitted into my games bag, which, according to the principles of Tai-Ping, is how it should be.

I looked round at the picture of Bruce Lee, the travel poster of Malaysia my dad gave me, my certificate of merit for Grade Two Saxophone, my 320 computer discs, my colour picture of an iguana and the tattered remains of a portable snooker table we got when I was twelve.

I thought about Mum and wondered whether to leave her a note. I decided not to – simply because I couldn't think of what to write.

Outside, the October day was darkening. I headed down the stairs into the silence of the early evening. When I got out on the street, I would just keep going. The sun was almost gone, but that was OK. I'd find a field or a park bench, and early next morning I'd head on down to the sea. Somewhere or other is a place my dad took me once, where there are tall stone buildings huddled above a blue sea, donkeys, and guys in grey suits with open white shirts and faces that look like their owners have had time to consider every move they make. Somewhere there's somewhere that isn't Wimbledon. Some place that isn't full of narrow grey streets and closed-up lives and people like Albert Roger Quigley.

I had one call to make before I hit the road.

There's a pub about four streets away from us where I used to go with my dad. Sometimes he'd look across at me, when my mum was deep in a copy of *Psychic News* and there was nothing on the television, any time from May to October. He'd say, 'Fancy a pint?'

'Don't mind if I do.'

Not that I ever drank beer. I'd sit with a Coke and some crisps and watch him drink. Watch him sip in that amazingly slow way that adults do. Watch him stretch, yawn, look across at me and come out with those perfect forty-year-old clichés they use to make the time pass easily and without controversy.

'It's a hard road, Simon.'

'It is, Dad. It is.'

It *is*.

I wasn't going to drink or anything. I'm not one of those fourteen-year-olds who go to pubs. I look my age. You know? I'm a straight-down-the-middle ten-plus-four wonder. One of those aimless youths you stumble over on their way from the pinball machine to the nearest shop that sells electrical equipment. A blurred, white, not-quite-grown-up face in the crowd.

The garden there, where we used to sit, has a swing and a slide and is framed by a huge chestnut-tree. This mother was in the terminal stages of yellow. From time to time, a leaf would detach itself and sashay down to join its friends, slicing sideways, plunging head-long and then ripple-dissolving to the damp grass. There was dew on the white steel tables and a feeling that, at any moment, a man would come out of the bar and start stacking the chairs away. It was just dusk, when things start to look not quite themselves. I watched the light drain away and felt the cold clawing at the earth between the tables. The end of the year.

I sat at the table we used to use and tried to think what I really believed. I felt I ought to be thinking something momentous. It isn't every day you run away from home. Surely I had got some things clearer since he died?

I hadn't. I was just as confused as that day she came in and told me the news. Did life go on like this, I wondered? Did it offer absolutely no solutions? Is it all punishment from now on in?

There were a couple of drinkers in the far corner, but no one noticed me. I was just getting up to go and make my way on down to Greece when I felt a hand on my shoulder and heard a deep voice. 'Hi, kid!'

I looked up. It was my dad.

26

I jumped. For a moment I was right back in my bedroom that first time. I blinked. I closed my eyes and opened them again. He was still there. Viewed from close up he showed absolutely no sign of being controlled by an extraterrestrial intelligence. The guys from Tellenor were probably so good that they had overreached themselves and programmed free will into him. You know?

He was holding a pint of beer in his left hand, and, when he smiled, I could see the fillings in his teeth. The dentalwork was a perfect match. They had worked wonders on the timing too. He drank, wiped the froth off his mouth, put the glass on the table, readjusted it, dropped his hand and then put it behind his head.

I sat there, waiting for him to dematerialize. He didn't. Instead he did a couple more fortysomething things. He pursed up his lips, looked at me, then away, and then, after shifting carefully on his seat, he farted.

What more do you want? It drinks beer! It picks its nose! It farts! We will never catch up with this galaxy, no matter how hard we try. They mimic our greatest achievements in a way that puts our own selves to shame.

'I was not as surprised as I thought I was going to be,' he said eventually, 'to hear myself pronounced clinically dead!'

I goggled at him.

'I hadn't been feeling terrific,' he went on, 'since I got into the hospital. A coronary thrombosis doesn't exactly leave a guy feeling perky!' He yawned. 'They don't really check on you very closely. It's very much a wing-it *oh-he-looks-a-bit-stiff* situation. I mean, they don't hold a mirror to your lips or anything.'

'They don't?'

'They do not, old son. They thump your chest a few times and call the old crash unit and then they grope around for your pulse, but it's a very amateurish affair really.'

He wasn't wearing the suit he'd been wearing in Furnival Gardens. He was wearing jeans, a sports shirt and a cardigan. For some reason I found the cardigan really offensive. It wasn't the sort of thing my dad would wear at all. Maybe the aliens had got into shopping.

'I don't think that your average British doctor is very good at diagnosing death,' he went on. 'I don't think it's taught at medical school. I wonder the mortuaries aren't full of people banging on the doors and trying to get out!'

'Do you mean,' I said, 'that you weren't dead?'

He grinned. 'I didn't experience myself as dead. Although that was the medical profession's analysis of my condition. At first I thought I might be having an out-of-body experience. Then I thought it might be an in-body experience – that my soul was to be confined to my body for some sinister theological reason.'

I reached out across the table to touch him. He took my hand and held it in a very un-Tellenorean way. This was him, all right. This was my dad, just as he had always been.

'What did . . . '

'I think the first clue I had that I might still be on the team was when your mum pitched up to inspect the body.'

'You mean . . . '

'They got me out of the ward and put me under a sheet in this side room. I lay there quite quiet. I could hear everything that was going on, but I couldn't move or speak.'

I tried to picture him under the sheet. The light filtered through. Like lying in bed in the morning when they call you to get up and you lie there, listening to the noises in the street below, wondering whether you'll ever get up and join them.

'I heard the nurse ask her if she wanted to take a last look at me. She said she didn't think that would be necessary.'

'Typical!'

'I was a bit pissed off,' said my dad. 'I mean, it isn't every day you get the chance to view your old man's corpse, is it? It's an experience, isn't it?'

There was a pause. Then he sucked at his teeth and went on.

'She was actually surprisingly complimentary about me.'

'I know,' I said glumly.

'They all were. The nurse said I had been a very good patient. Christ, I'd only been in the hospital for about ten minutes before I snuffed it!'

It must have been weird lying there. Presumably trying to move a leg or an arm or get your mouth to move. And hearing these voices from a long, long way away. Voices that had been chattering away at you all your life.

'The nurse said I was very good company, which I thought was praise indeed for a guy who had just had a coronary thrombosis. Then your mother went on about how I had always wanted to be buried at sea.'

'That's what she said to me.'

He scratched his head. 'Did I ever say I wanted to be buried at sea?'

'Not in my hearing.'

'She seemed very convinced of the matter. From the tone of her voice, I thought I was not going to be able to avoid being slung in the box and slipped off the Isle of Wight ferry. I just couldn't *move* or *speak*. You see?'

I could picture my mum and the nurse, who, for some reason, I had decided was Irish. A short, plump woman from Galway.

'She said I was an interesting and sad man in many ways.'

'Who? The nurse or mum?'

He gave me a strange look. 'Your mum, of course. Do you think I'm a sad man?'

'No,' I said, rather shortly.

He took another deep draught of his beer. He looked up at the pale white sky above the half-ruined trees. He looked like a guy glad to be alive. With each minute that passed he was getting less and less extraterrestrial. But, at the same time, more and more *alien*. I didn't recognize some of his gestures. He'd got a new one where he crossed his feet, and a new version of his smile. It seemed to stay on his face for slightly longer than was necessary.

'Anyway,' he said, in a conversational tone, 'then they took me down to the morgue.'

'Christ!'

'Indeed. Ganymede, they call it. I mean, the guys who took me down were *real* incompetents. They treat the dead with absolutely no respect.'

He sounded rather civic about this. As if his experience was going to lead to a campaign for the rights of corpses or something.

He looked at me thoughtfully. 'She didn't cry or anything. It was just sort of "Shall we take him down then?" and Bob's your unc.'

'She was . . .'

'She was pretty calm about the whole business. I could have done with a bit of weeping and gnashing of the old teeth. We got a very low-key response.'

Well, that wasn't how she had behaved at home. Hadn't she said she'd gone wild? I didn't feel like finding out whose version of events was true. I was too busy holding on to the edge of my chair and waiting for him to rise twenty feet in the air.

'We had our problems, but . . . ' He sucked his lower lip. 'It makes you think, being in a mortuary.'

I could see that this might well be true.

'It makes you think, when you hear people call you Charlie as they sling you on the slab.'

'Why did they call you Charlie?'

'I think they call all the stiffs Charlie. I mean, they're dead. They don't count, do they? That's it. Sling them aside. You know? Pickle the bastards in formalin and donate their remains to medical research.'

We were on to Dead Lib again. He looked quite morose at the treatment handed out to cadavers. Then he took another long drink of beer.

'We don't understand life, do we?' he said. 'I mean, it's here and it's so *sweet* and we don't understand it.'

'I don't understand it,' I said. 'I haven't got a clue, I tell you.'

It was amazing, really, that he had managed to recover from the heart attack so easily. He looked, I have to say, absolutely great. Still, I suppose this was what happened in the Middle Ages. You rolled around, went blue and your eyes shot up into your head. And then, if you made it, off you went to till the fields or whatever. I had heard the National Health Service was in a bad way, but I didn't realize that do-it-yourself, take-your-own-chances medicine had reached this level of intensity.

'I started to come round when they put me on the slab. I was lucky not to go straight in the fridge, I tell you.'

'I bet!'

'The word "autopsy" kept running through my mind. You know? But they were at the end of their shift. They closed the old door behind them and there I was, alone with a few dozen stiffs. Assuming they *were* stiffs and not a fresh consignment of medical mistakes.'

He narrowed his mouth into an O shape and pushed his eyebrows up into what was left of his hair. There was still foam from the beer on his moustache. I watched the bubbles wink in the ghostly light, glisten, and then die. You could see the pulse beat in his neck. You could smell him too – a whiff of new soap and old changing-rooms. You could see the broken veins on his nose and see the puffy skin above his eyelids, bunched up like old crêpe curtains. And you could watch those little blue eyes that never quite met yours. It was my dad all right.

'I don't know how long I was in there before I sat up and looked around. I know I banged on the door, but no one heard. And when I looked down at my ankle they'd put this label on me.'

'What did it say?' I asked. 'FRAGILE? Or THIS WAY UP?'

He grinned. 'You are a witty little bastard, aren't you?' Then he yawned. I could see the red trap of his throat.

'Actually, it said NORMAN BRITTON, C OF E.'

'Did it?'

'It did,' said my dad. 'Not NORMAN BRITTON MA OXON. Just NORMAN BRITTON, C OF E. After forty-odd years of being a good boy and paying the mortgage and . . . '

I could see that it had been an upsetting experience. But what did he expect them to write? NORMAN BRITTON, NOVELIST AND TRAVEL AGENT?

'Anyway,' he went on, 'I wandered round and checked out the corpses. They all had labels on. You know? And there was one just next to the door that must have come in while I had been lying there, unable to move. It didn't have a name on it. Just a ticket that said UNIDENTIFIED RTA. It was a real mess, I tell you. Looked as if some-one had been practising three-point turns on its chest.'

He shuddered. I said nothing.

'And I thought to myself: *What's it all for?* You know? Did I want to go on being NORMAN BRITTON, C OF E? What's so great about my life?'

I couldn't, for the moment, think of an answer to that. So I still said nothing.

'There are big pluses about being dead,' said my dad. 'You don't have to take the dishes out of the dishwasher and put them in the dish rack and then take the cutlery out of its little plastic box and then put it in the cutlery drawer making sure that the *spoons* go in one compartment and the *knives* in another compartment and the *forks* in another compartment except there are always *forks* in the *spoons* compartment and *knives* in the *forks* compartment when you get there so it's hopeless it's always too late to get things right it's a total frost honestly is life you are a lot better off dead in my opinion. Do you know what being dead felt like?'

'You tell me, dad!'

'It felt like a good career move.'

Of course. That long white robe I had seen him in that night was a sort of hospital gown. They dress them up like ghosts. But how had he got down to Stranraer Gardens?

'They brought some other poor sod in,' he said, as if in answer to my question, 'but I was over behind the door and they didn't see me. I just slipped out, walked down a corridor, out through a side exit and came down to home. I just stood there looking up at it. You know? Wondering whether to take up my life or walk right out of it.'

He put one hand on mine. 'I changed the labels,' he said. 'I put

515

my name on the road-traffic-accident victim and I walked out with
UNIDENTIFIED clutched in my paw.'

He seemed to find this next bit difficult to say. His eyes were
watering as he started it, and he looked away from me again,
towards the deserted white tables around us.

'It was so *strange*,' he said. 'Sometimes I think there's something at
the back of all this that's so . . . so bloody bizarre. You know? Roots of
coincidence and all that . . . '

'What, Dad?'

He looked straight at me.

'The body they brought in during the night. The one on the slab.
The unidentified traffic accident. I saw the face. It was your mate. Mr
Marr. The guy who sat out on the Common, waiting for the spacemen to come. I walked out free, you see. And the undertakers buried
him.'

27

It was at that moment that Mr Quigley passed the entrance to the pub garden. He stood under the street light, looking back from where he'd come. He shook his head and clucked to himself like the White Rabbit in *Alice*. He was carrying a bag of shopping. He looked annoyed about something. I got the impression he was looking for something to hit. Probably me. He didn't see me.

'What's up?' said my dad.

'It's Quigley, he's after me!'

'Quigley!'

It was now quite dark in the garden. For some reason we were both whispering. Out in the street, Quigley shouted off to his left. He was calling to someone, but I couldn't hear what he was saying. It sounded as if he was calling a dog.

'What's going on with Quigley?'

'Oh,' I said, 'he's had a lot of heavy conversations with you. Apparently you've repented of your wicked life.'

'I have!'

'Sure,' I said. 'I've been talking to you myself, you know?'

Dad looked away.

I said, 'Quigley's a bastard. He's living with us, and he treats me like shit.'

My dad looked back at me. I tried to think of the worst thing that Quigley had done.

'He's gone and bought a dog!'

I wasn't asked for any more information. But I gave it just the same. I told him about how he'd hit me. About how I was some kind of prophet as far as he was concerned and he was desperate to have me Confirmed.

There was a bit of a silence when I'd finished, and then Dad said, with a grin, 'Quiggers is right about one thing, old son. I had a really wicked life, and I repent!'

Somewhere in the distance I heard the growl of thunder. I looked up at the sky and saw that the clouds were one dark, lurid, compact mass. My father looked really ghostly in the light from the street, and for a moment I found myself thinking: *He is a ghost. He really did die. This is all a story.* As I did so, he got to his feet. His face changed suddenly. There was none of the humour you usually saw in it, and there was a fixed look about the eyes that I found almost frightening. He rose, slowly and mechanically, staring ahead of him and beyond me. Then he lifted his right hand with the index finger extended.

Behind me I heard a kind of yelp. It wasn't a sound I ever remembered him having made, but certain things about it made me think it came from Quigley. There was a thump as his shopping hit the floor.

My dad still didn't say anything. He just stood there, staring past me, his arm flung out in front of him and his attention fixed on what had to be the assistant manager of the National Westminster Bank, Mitcham. Dad didn't speak. He didn't need to. I could hear Quigley give a sort of low whimper, but otherwise he said nothing. The silence in the garden was as loud as Marjorie Quigley's trousers. It went on and on and got louder and louder.

And then, finally, my dad spoke. Not in his normal voice but in a low, throaty baritone that reminded me of Vincent Price in *The Haunted Palace* – my dad's favourite picture: 'Albert Roger Quigley, do you remember me?'

It was fairly obvious from the noise coming from behind me that the man in question did remember him fairly clearly. In fact, as far as I could judge from the old hearing system, the effect on Quigley was fairly stupendous.

I mean, look at it from his point of view. My dad had recently been cremated. Quigley had sat there while the good people from the Mutual Life Provident Association had come round and told my mum the news about her death benefit. He had, in fact, been in close personal touch with the guy's spirit via one of the finest psychic talents in south-west London. He just *did not* expect to come across the late Norman Britton in the garden of the Ferret and Firkin at half past six in the evening. And he certainly didn't expect the said Britton to be pointing at him in a manner usually affected by people like Darth Vader or Banquo.

I turned round in my chair.

Look, I have seen people surprised in my time. I have seen people very surprised. I have, on occasions, seen very, very, very surprised people. But I have never seen anything like the expression on the face of Albert Roger Quigley that evening. He looked like a man who has just stepped into an empty lift-shaft. His mouth kept opening and shutting like a mechanical shovel, but no words – not even a direct appeal to the Lord Jesus Christ to be excused this experience on health grounds – passed his lips.

It was, in one sense, a stupid question. I mean, how short did Dad expect Roge's memory to *be*? But the way he delivered it would not have disgraced your average member of the Royal Shakespeare Company. It wasn't just that he was pitching it lower. He gave each word an incredibly fruity emphasis. When he got to the R in Roger, he vibrated the old tongue on the palate with the brio of an international string player. The finger, too, seemed to be going down fantastically well with Quigley. He was staring at it the way a cat looks at a dinner-plate. Would he ever get over this initial shock period? Was he going to have a thrombie right here on the spot?

Come on Quigley, pull yourself out of it! Deal with the situation! This sort of thing should be right up your street. Think of the articles. Think of all the hands-on psychical research that is just coming at you free of charge. Make with the sketch maps of the area. Measure the ambient temperature. Get down the witnesses' names and addresses. This is a one-off, my friend. If you move quickly you could bag this one – jam it into the specimen bottle and whip it off to the Society for Psychical Research prontissimo!

He did not, I fear, seem to be prepared to experience the phenomenon in a truly objective, scientific way. He was kind of staggering, with one hand held to his temple, and from time to time making a noise like water running out of a bath.

Dad, warming to his role, moved a couple of steps forward, his arm still flung out in front of him. He looked, I thought, a touch over the top. 'Quigley,' he said in a spectral voice, 'repent!'

There was another growl of thunder. Behind Quigley, Danzig appeared at the entrance to the garden. He lowered his head and, whimpering, sidled towards his master. Quigley looked ready to repent. He looked ready to tear his clothes apart. He looked rather less rational than his dog. 'Oh!' he said finally. 'Oh! Oh! Ohhhhh!'

He gave me a quick look to check that I was really there, and an even quicker look round the garden to see if there were any other responsible local citizens around to witness this triumphant affirmation of an afterlife. But the drinkers at the far end of the garden were gone. There was only me and this spirit in the gloom of the garden.

'Oh!' said Quigley, again. 'Oh! Oh! Ohhhhhh!'

'Quigley,' said my dad, moving into the shadows away from me, 'I am in hell! And you will join me here!'

Quigley stared at me. It was weird. Once my dad had got started, I had started to believe him. To believe his act. You know? When I think about it now, he *was* an actor. He was a guy who could *be* something for a brief period of time and then he vanished like the spirit he was impersonating. When I looked at him in the darkness, I began to wonder if all of what he had told me earlier could be some trick on me, played by the spirits who had sent him.

'How can you sit there?' said Quigley. 'How can you *sit* there?'

I opened my eyes and gave him a puzzled look. 'What do you mean, Mr Quigley?' I said. 'What are you staring at?'

'*That!*' said Quigley, 'That . . . that *thing*!'

Quigley gestured feebly towards my old man. Then he turned to face him. Dad was flaring his nostrils and giving him a wild stare. I thought he was going well over the top, actually. But Quigley was not in a mood to ask why my dad had returned to earth. He was not in the mood to ask rational questions. I don't think he'd have noticed if someone had dropped a set of kitchen units on his head from 30,000 feet.

Dad took a couple more steps towards him. Quigley started to whimper. 'No,' he moaned, 'no!'

'Yes, Quigley,' said my dad. 'Yes, Quigley! Yes! Yes!' He looked as if he was all set to strangle the forty-four-year-old assistant bank manager.

My dad always was something of a ham. The sensible thing to do, having made the initial impact, was to walk off in a slow and menacing way, leaving Quigley to gibber. But Norman was determined to give full value for money.

'Do you know what hell is like, Quigley?'

'No,' whispered Quigley.

'Hell is being blown across vast empty spaces with the wind at your back and dust in your eyes. Hell is the taste of your own vileness, Quigley. The sour smell of your own wickedness and wrongdoing.'

If this was the kind of stuff he had put in his novel, it wasn't surprising that he hadn't found any takers for it. But it was still kosher as far as Albert Roger Quigley was concerned.

'Who are you talking to, Mr Quigley?' I said, in what I hoped was an awestruck tone. 'Who is it that you can see in the garden?'

'O Jesus!' said Quigley, suddenly remembering who was supposed to be in charge around here. 'O Jesus Christ, help me! O Jesus Jesus Jesus! Jesus Christ!'

'There is no Jesus Christ,' said my dad, in solemn tones. 'There is no God of the Christians. There are no prophets in your world, Albert Quigley.'

I hoped he wasn't going to start rubbishing the Koran. You never know when those Muslims might be listening.

Quigley dropped to his knees, his face white and shaking. 'Oh Lord,' he whimpered to himself. 'Oh dear Jesus Christ!'

'There is no Jesus Christ, Quigley,' said my dad, in a very authoritative way.

Quigley looked up at him, dog-like. 'Who is there?' he asked, pleadingly.

'There is no one!' said my dad. 'There is no one beyond this life. Those who return, return as themselves, condemned to live out the circle of their lives again and again!'

Thunder broke again, and this time there were two or three brief flashes of lightning. The chestnut-trees opposite me were suddenly vivid green and, as suddenly, dark again. The brick wall round the garden broke into focus and faded to black. Once again I had the feeling that what my father had said to me in the garden could all be some horrible trick. That he really had died and that what he was telling Quigley was the truth. Not what he had told me.

Quiggers was gibbering. 'What . . . There must be . . . What is . . . ' It was almost as if he'd stopped seeing Dad at all. That made it all scarier. Because *I* started to believe that I wasn't seeing him. That the familiar switchback nose and scraps of grey hair were going to melt away into the darkness. 'There must be . . . *something*!' Quigley said. 'There must . . . God . . . '

My dad came back well. He raised his hands above his head and then stretched them both out at the unfortunate First Spiritualist. He was now doing quite a lot of acting tormented. His head was wobbling violently, and there was dribble down his chin. Whatever he did would have gone down well with Quigley. The presentation was right. Albert Roger was very involved with the performance. He had suspended disbelief completely.

'There is nothing,' said my dad. 'There is nothing. No faith. No light in the darkness, Albert Roger Quigley! Nothing but the smell of your own loneliness and guilt!'

This was very much the kind of stuff that Quigley was used to dishing out. But it didn't look as if he was capable of taking it. He hunched up his shoulders. He looked as if he was about to cry.

'What's the matter, Mr Quigley?' I said again. 'Who are you talking to?'

There was no stopping my dad. I wanted to say to him: *Get off! Quit while you're ahead!* And a bit of me wanted him to stop the way you want an actor in a film to stop. Because he is so damned real that you think this pain and suffering is *really* him. You know?

'Death,' said my dad, 'is not a journey to some pleasant place. Death is simply the stopping of your heart. The end of sensation. The not being able to smell or taste or screw. Death is death. And there are no spirits. There are things. Fleshly, heavy things that come back to mock and torment you!'

'Argol,' cried Quigley, who was, rather gamely I thought, trying to make some radical alterations to his cosmological system. 'Argol of Tellenor!'

Dad laughed. The laugh was really horrid. It was low and cracked to begin with, then it rose up the scale, eerily, and shook out its top notes across the damp, half-lit glade until I really did think that my father had come not from the hospital but from some horribly, cold, empty region that lies in wait for us instead of all the heavens we have dreamed up to make things bearable.

'I am not he of Tellenor,' said my dad, who was always good at bluffing. 'I am he that was Norman Britton when on the earth, now returned to haunt you, Albert Roger Quigley, and to tell you that you are an evil man and that you will fall as I have fallen! Down and down, until you can fall no further!'

There was another roll of thunder, and once again the lightning lit up the garden and the surrounding trees.

As the sky's noise faded, my father moved into exit mode. He walked, slowly and stiffly, towards the ramp that led from the garden to the street. As he approached Quigley, Quigley started to sob. Then my dad paused.

'What must I do?' asked Quigley – always a man anxious for instructions.

My dad gave him the sort of look that only someone declared clinically dead can manage. 'I will come again, Quigley,' he said, 'when you least expect me! I will haunt your dreams and yea your waking moments!'

'What must I *do*?' said Quigley, understandably keen to get on the right side of this spirit.

'Touch not my son, Quigley,' said the old man. 'Leave him be!'

I found myself wondering who we could haunt next. There were a few members of staff who could do with a visit from beyond the tomb.

Dad did a bit of sneering, then he said, 'Farewell, Albert Roger Quigley!'

'Farewell,' said Quigley, clearly anxious to keep up the tone necessary for spirit dialogue.

My dad started off again towards the street. From the back he looked even better. He kept the shoulders stiff and he rolled a little, like a sailor back from a long voyage.

Quigley ran towards me like a kid let out of primary school. 'Can't you see him? Can't you *see* him?'

'See who, Mr Quigley?' I said, widening my eyes just a touch. 'See who?'

My dad was almost out into the street. I had the strong impression he might be tempted to come back and give us a bit more front-line colour from the other side of the grave. I leaned closer to Quigley, who, in a kind of transport of enthusiasm, grabbed me by both ears and squeezed my head hard. 'Oh my God!' he said. 'Oh Jesus! Oh God!'

You see how hard it is to get people to adapt? If he thought about it rationally, on the basis of the evidence presented to him, he had no basis for trusting Jesus Christ any further than he could throw him. But there he was, reaching for familiar things, as we all tend to do when scared out of our brains.

After a while he let go of my head and started to cross himself furiously. He was doing quite a lot of this, I noted. And it wasn't exactly the kind of thing endorsed by the First Spiritualist Church. Perhaps all this was going to push Quigley towards Catholicism – often, so my dad used to say, a good port of call for those on the way to a nervous breakdown.

'I have been a bad person,' he said.

This was no more or less than the truth. I had been telling him so for the last few weeks. But would he listen to me? Would he hell!

'I have done awful, awful things . . . '

Yes, Quigley. I know.

' . . . To you, li'l' Simey, and to the Church I love.'

He pushed his face close to me. He smelt of garlic.

'I have embezzled Church funds!' he said.

Sure. We gathered. What we really wanted here was a tape recorder. I mean, where did he think I thought he *got* his new car and his loft extension and his fridge-freezer?

'I masturbate,' he said, in thrilling tones.

I did not want to know this. Not at nearly seven o'clock in the garden of the Ferret and Firkin. Not anywhere, actually. I mean, we all do it, Quiggers. We get down in the darkness and from time to time we pull the wire. But we don't boast about it.

'Your father,' he said to me in a kind of sob, 'has just appeared to me in this garden!'

I tried to look impressed.

'He has told me some very important things.'

'Are you feeling OK, Mr Quigley?' I said.

'Oh Simey!' he gasped.

Then he did something really vile. He flung his arms around me and pushed his beard in my face. Something soft and dry touched my face. I realized, with some alarm, that these were the Quigley lips. The bastard was kissing me!

'I think', I said, trying to duck, 'that you should go and lie down.'

Preferably not on top of me! I knew nothing of Quigley's sexual life, but it was entirely possible that Marjorie and Emily were not enough for him. He was a red-blooded assistant bank manager. Up at the pub window I could see Mr McIvory, the owner. He's a tolerant man, but I just wasn't sure how he'd take me being frenched by a middle-aged man in the garden of his public house.

'Look,' I said eventually, 'fuck off and leave me alone. OK?'

'Fuck off and leave you alone!' echoed Quigley, as if I had just taken pi to sixteen decimal places off the top of my head.

'Yes,' I said.

'Yes,' said Quigley.

And then – do you know what he did? He started to back away, just as he had when he saw my dad. He wound his way back over the leaf-strewn grass like a toy duck. His mouth gaped and his hands flapped. I held up my hand very much in the manner of Salvius the tribune greeting Glabriolix the slave and giving him news of the Emperor's dog, Pertinax.

'Quigley,' I said, 'wait!'

He waited. He was in a suggestible mood.

'Oh Simon!' he said, looking at my face as if he was trying to memorize it for some exam. 'Oh Jesus, young shaver! Oh me deario!'

He put his hand to his mouth. 'I must tell the world!' he said.

This might work better for me than his lying in a darkened room, which was what he really needed to do. We had to get him telling his story as soon as possible. Preferably to a tough-minded clinical psychiatrist.

He turned on the balls of his feet and spread his arms wide. He was keen to tell everyone the Great News about my dad coming back to life to expose Christianity. With a man of Quigley's energy and commitment behind him, I decided, it would not be long before Norman had a cult all of his own in south-west London.

'Tell the world!' he almost shouted, and ran, swiftly, out towards the street.

After he had gone, I sat back at the pub table. My dad's glass of beer, half-empty, was still there. But Quigley, if he'd noticed it, would have seen nothing unusual in a spirit getting outside of a pint of Young's Special. If you were a ghost and you could choose who you could appear to, Quigley would be a good bet.

I don't know how long I was sitting there, but eventually my dad came back and sat down in his chair opposite me. He looked the way he looked when he had been telling jokes and there were no more jokes to tell. His face looked old and crumpled and sad, and, as he picked up his glass again, I had the strong sensation he was about to tell me something I didn't want to hear.

28

'I'm in love with somebody else.'

I didn't say anything.

'There's another woman in my life. Has been for six years. I love her, you see? I just can't . . . '

He paused. I didn't help him out.

'I can't live without her.'

It was, I decided, a *ridiculous* cardigan. Had she bought it for him? He just didn't look himself at all. He was sort of smirking as he said all this stuff. In a way I found very irritating. I tried not to listen. I thought that, if I didn't listen, soon he would stop and then we would go home and life would start again, the way it had always been before. But he kept on talking, and I couldn't stop myself from hearing.

'She's called Veronica,' he said, 'and your mother knows about her. Has known about her a long time. And it's why she and you and . . . and why we . . . '

He stopped.

'I don't love Mum any more, you see?' he said. 'I don't love her.'

I looked up at him. Straight in the eyes. 'Is that where you've been? With this Veronica woman?'

'That's where I've been, and that's where I want to stay.'

He drank again. But this time as if he wanted to get the beer over and done. As if he suddenly didn't want to be here at all.

'I met Veronica at the Anglo-Catholic church in Putney – St Mark's. When Mrs Danby took me there. The old bat led me astray in more ways than one. After I started with Veronica, Mrs D went back to the First Spiritualists.'

'But you kept going to these Anglo-Catholic geezers?'

A lot of things were becoming clearer. That smell of oil and candles and that light from a distant window and him on his knees, mumbling. He must have taken me there.

'She seemed pretty keen to get me on the team,' I said.

Dad leaned forward and tapped me on the knee. 'She felt guilty. She offered a covenant to the Church if I came back or you were Confirmed in Faith. A lot of money. But I wasn't going to go back . . .'

He looked away. He had that look he used to get on Saturday mornings after he had come back from the shops. As if he was looking at his life and not enjoying what he saw. As if there was a whole load of things behind him and nothing in front but age. You know? As if the night was coming in and he couldn't stop it.

'In the end, Veronica and I packed in Christianity.' He tapped me on the knee. 'Make up your own mind,' he said. 'Look at the world and make up your *own* mind.'

I kept my eyes on his face. 'Do you believe there is a God?' I said.

'Yes,' he said, slowly.

From the way he said it, he might have been talking about Krull of Varna. The thought didn't seem to bring him any comfort. Or make the prospect of that long night any easier.

'But I don't know what I mean when I say that word. It's just something I say . . . because I have to say it . . . Because it brings me some comfort.'

'Like Veronica,' I said. I had to say it, guys. I could not help myself. I just did not like the sound of this woman. She was young, probably. Younger than my mum. Nearer to my age than his, I felt sure. She sounded fat and self-important, I thought.

'I know you'll be OK, Simon,' my dad was saying. 'You're very tough and very smart and you're your own man. You always have been.'

He put his hand on my hand again. I moved it a little way away.

'Will this Quigley guy be finished now?' he said. 'Now they've rumbled him? He will, won't he? I mean, if he causes trouble you can call on me, you know?'

I just looked at him, blankly.

'If I thought you couldn't look after yourself, you see . . . '

I wasn't sure I cared for this 'look after yourself' stuff. I never like it when people say that to you. It was the same as this 'make up your own mind' line. I wasn't sure I *could* make up my own mind. You know?

'What are you telling me?' I said, in a flat voice. 'I don't get you.'

'I'm going away, Simon. I'm going away and I'm not coming back.'

It's funny. I knew he was going to say that. Just the way I knew my mum had bad news when she came in on me in Dad's study all those weeks ago. The evening he died.

'Where are you going?' I said, evenly.

'Veronica has a place. It's a long way away from here. We can start all over again. You know?'

'How can you start all over again?' I said to him. 'It doesn't make sense. You only get one life, don't you? How can you start it over again? It's started already, hasn't it?'

'Darling . . .'

I didn't like him saying that. He sounded like Quigley. He reached for me again, and this time I moved even further away from him. I'd had enough middle-aged men slobbering all over me for one day.

'I'm sorry, Simon,' he said. 'I'm sorry.'

And they were all apologizing!

'I didn't realize that Quigley . . . I mean, if it's that bad, of course I'll . . .'

'I can handle Quigley,' I said in a steady voice.

'Are you sure?'

'If I can handle you, I can handle Quigley.'

'Simon – sometimes I don't know . . . I don't . . .'

'Look at life,' I said, nastily, 'and *make up your own mind, guy*!'

He changed tack then. He gave up trying to grab me. He started going on about the life insurance. He knew just how much he was worth. He said that his not coming back was much the best option for all of us. He was insured with four different companies, he said, which was probably another reason Quiggers was hanging round. 'Dying on your partner,' he said, 'is much fairer and more financially beneficial to them than divorcing them.'

He put his head in his hands then. He was a bad man, he said – a weak, bad man.

'You're not bad,' I said – 'you're really nice!' It wasn't true that he was bad.

He cried a lot, but I didn't cry. I didn't see why I should. I'd done my crying for him the day they told me he was dead. Funnily enough, that hadn't seemed at all real. It was only now it was like he was really dying.

When he'd stopped feeling sorry for himself, he handed me a piece of paper with a number on it. 'If this Quigley gets too much,' he said, 'write here. Give me a bit of time to get settled. It's a box number.'

'What's wrong with your address?' I said. 'I won't tell anyone. You can trust me, guy!'

He looked at me. He looked all crumpled now. Those new clothes she'd bought him looked even more stupid than they had before. He said something – I forget what, but it was pretty clear he didn't trust me. Or maybe Veronica had got to him on the subject. I thought about how I'd walked around all those weeks and what I'd felt about him and the crazy things I had found myself believing. And I thought: *Where were you when I needed you, Dad? Where were you when you died on me? You know?* He had done nothing.

There was a lot of stuff about his life too. About his novel and his business. That was in all sorts of trouble, apparently. If he did come back to life, he was in real problems with the bank. Although isn't that what life *is*? Being in trouble with the bank. He went on about Mum. How she had always held him back. How he had never really been able to write because of her. I couldn't figure this. What did she do? Start banging on the ceiling every time he took out his Biro? I mean, she goes on – but what the hell? They all go on, don't they?

'When you're my age,' he said, 'you'll understand.'

'I won't,' I said. 'I understand now.'

He pushed the glass along the table. 'Come with us,' he said. 'You'd like Veronica. Come with us!'

'To Box 29? You reckon?'

As I said this, I realized it was too late for me and him. That I wasn't going to leave. Ever. And that he didn't really want me to. He had said that just to be polite. Oh, he was polite. He was polite and good fun and a hell of a laugh at parties. But, at the end of the day, you couldn't trust him.

'Your mum needs you,' he said.

I'd noticed. But I hadn't noticed him clocking the fact until the day he decided to bugger off to Box 29 with Veronica. I was almost ready to tell him I couldn't face Quigley on my own. But I couldn't find the words. And they wouldn't have had any effect.

When it comes down to it, grown-ups think about themselves. After that they think about other grown-ups. And a long way after that they think about children. Children really are on another planet as far as they are concerned.

'I want you to look after her,' he said.

'Well,' I said, '*you* don't seem to be intending to do it, do you?'

Then I looked back at the table. I was giving that table a lot of attention. Suddenly I felt I was talking to my mum. Because it was feelings and stuff. Me and Dad never talked about that much before. She did all that. But, now we were talking about it, I felt this great weight on me. As if we would never have the time to say all the things we needed to say to each other. As if we just didn't have the words for them. You know?

'Well,' I said, in the end, 'you'd better bugger off. You're taking a risk being here really, aren't you? Someone from the Mutual Life Provident might drop in . . . '

'Veronica's got the car . . . ' he said.

She had a car and everything! He was made up!

'Look, Simon . . . ' he muttered, as he got up, 'I'm sorry. I am so sorry!'

'Don't be,' I said.

He came at me again and I could tell he was going to make another stab at a heavy masculine embrace. I just sat very still, waiting for him to go.

'You're very angry with me now,' he said, 'but one day . . . '

'I'm not angry. I'm fine. Just fine! OK?'

There was a pause.

'What's she like?'

'Veronica?'

'Yeah.'

'She's . . . ' Another long silence. 'She's funny.'

He looked at me. His eyes seemed to be coming from a long way away.

'Like you, Simon.'

He was wearing jeans. That was my dad – always trying to keep up with things. But I figured the jeans wouldn't last long. Veronica would be working on something to go with the brown shoes and the cardigan. She would reshape his whole wardrobe. And when she'd finished that she'd start on him. He wouldn't be allowed to fart or pick his nose or put his feet on the table. After a while he wouldn't be my dad at all. He'd be Veronica's husband.

'Write,' he said, 'won't you? Because I can't. Write. OK?'

'Sure,' I said.

Then, at last, I looked him straight in the eyes. 'I won't give you away,' I said. 'I promise you that. I won't tell anyone anything about any of this as long as I live. I swear it.'

'I know, Simon,' he said.

He made a half-hearted move towards me, but I gave him no encouragement. I didn't even look up as he went up the ramp into the street, so I'm still not sure when he passed out of the garden and into the rest of the world. Sometimes I picture him walking out with his head held high and his step straight. Other times I see him sort of shuffling, as if the world had finally got to him. As if he was suddenly old and tired and defeated.

But mostly I try not to think about him at all.

Quigley never recovered from that evening. He told quite a lot of people what he'd seen. He even told the people at work, who were most impressed. He went through a brief period of chatting to the customers down at the bank about how he had seen someone come back from the dead. In a garden at twilight. But, although they were amused at first, I don't think they liked it and, after a while, he was sent for treatment. He told the doctors all about how my dad had come back to life in this grey cardigan and had told him the secrets of the universe.

Nobody's bothered about Pike or how or why he went through Mr

Marr's pockets, cleaned out his ID, took his keys and squatted in the house to acquaint himself with the principles of ufology. It is as if Marr, Pike, my dad and Quigley had never been. As if they were all part of some troubled dream I was having.

Quigley's in a mental hospital near Tooting. He went in just before Christmas last year. Mum and I go to see him sometimes, and we agree that he is a much nicer person than he used to be. He tells us about Old Mother Walsh and how the snake is coming for him. It has five heads, apparently, and is from the planet Tellenor. Lewis set it on him. It has a number on it, but not the number of the second millennium. It is marked with a 24, the number of our house. He's worked Argol in there too. Argol is on his way in a kind of steel tub, apparently, and when he gets here we are *for* it. The only thing you have to be careful not to mention is the First Church of Christ the Spiritualist. I don't understand the details, but apparently Mrs Danby got her lawyer on to him about some financial thing. She herself left the Church and is going to leave all her money to the Battersea Dogs' Home. She wrote my mum a long letter saying that I was a Devil Child and the best thing my mum could do with me was have me exorcized. My mum wrote back and said that she didn't have that kind of money.

'She's an old hag,' said Mum.

'Oh, I don't know,' I said – 'I think I could do with a bit of exorcism!'

Mum and I get on a lot better these days. We'll never be close, if you know what I mean, but we've got something worked out. Mum has been a lot more cheerful since Quigley was declared bankrupt, insane and guilty of fraud. She's got bigger. Her eyes, which used to be dull and filmy, have got some of their sparkle back. She and Hannah Dooley left the First Spiritualists and founded a Household Church. They've called it the Fellowship of Christian Spiritualists of 24 Stranraer Gardens, and they have a lot of fun, singing and dancing and playing the tambourine in the back room downstairs. Once or twice my mum has even gone into a light trance, and, though she hasn't yet contacted anyone interesting, we have great hopes of her.

They reckon it was all Quigley's fault. That Old Mother Walsh had it right and that Ella Walsh should never have led the Church into the ways of men. They are quite down on men, but they seem to like me.

Mrs Quigley and Emily still live with us. They had to sell the house – what remained of it after Brunt had finished with it. Mrs Quigley doesn't say a lot, and what she says she says quietly. Sometimes, if she's good, my mum lets her chop the vegetables. Emily turns out to be really quite decent. She has had a crisis of faith since her old man was put in the bin, and, a month or so ago, she took all her C. S. Lewis books out into the garden and burnt them. For some reason, shortly after the First Church of Christ the Spiritualist took its number out of the phone book, she started to forget to lisp. Who knows, one day I may marry her. On the other hand, I may not.

I used to think sex was all about condoms and fellatio and getting girls to show you their underwear. These days it seems something more mysterious, but also somehow more real. As if it's just over the horizon, waiting to happen to me, as weird and wonderful as all the things that happened last autumn.

I think about the aliens quite a lot. I still think they're out there. I think they're still spacenapping people, if you want to know. Not in the obvious way. I don't think they cruise into our atmosphere in *saucers*, exactly. But, whatever name you choose to give it, *something* gets into humans one way or another and makes them do things that are very hard to understand.

I'm staying as far out of it all as I can. I'm based on the moons of Jupiter from now on, and the only time I'll come back to earth will be strictly on a day-trip basis. I'm behind that glass that separated us from Pike that night on the Common. I never wrote to that box number. I never will. I keep the piece of paper in a tin next to my dad's glasses – the ones he'll never come back for – but I know I'll never use it.

You see, I was a little kid a year ago and I made the mistake kids make. I let things get to me. I let them all get to me – Quigley and Pike and my mum and Mr Marr. Most of all I let my father get to me. I let him get under my guard. But I'll never let anyone do that again.

From now on I'll never let anyone under my guard. No one gets close to me. Not ever.

East of Wimbledon

For Suzan

'I shall have you hanged,' said a cruel and ignorant King to Nasrudin, 'if you do not prove that you have deep faith and wise perceptions such as have been attributed to you.' Nasrudin at once said that he could see a golden bird in the sky and demons within the earth. 'But how can you do this?' the King asked. 'Fear,' said the Mullah, 'is all you need.'

from 'The Subtleties of Mullah Nasrudi',
in *The Sufis*, by Idries Shah
(The Octagon Press, 1964)

PART ONE

1

'We teach here,' said Mr Malik, 'Islamic mathematics, Islamic physics and of course Islamic games – '

'What,' said Robert, feeling it was time for an intelligent question, 'are Islamic games?'

Mr Malik gave a broad wink. 'Islamic games,' he said, 'are when Pakistan wins the Test Match.'

He spread his hands generously. 'You, of course, among your other duties, will be teaching Islamic English literature.'

Robert nodded keenly. His floppy, blond hair fell forward over his eyes, and he raked it back with what he hoped was boyish eagerness. He should really have had a haircut. 'In that context,' he said, 'do you see Islamic English literature as being literature by English, or Welsh or Scottish Muslims?'

They both looked at each other in consternation. Perhaps, like him, Mr Malik was unable to think of a single Muslim writer who fitted that description.

'Or,' went on Robert, struggling somewhat, 'do you see it as work that has a Muslim dimension? Such as . . . *Paradise Lost* for example.'

What was the Muslim dimension in *Paradise Lost*? Robert became aware that the room had suddenly become very hot.

'Or,' he went on swiftly, 'simply English literature viewed from a Muslim perspective?'

'You will view English literature from a Muslim perspective,' said Malik with a broad, affable grin, 'because you are a Muslim!'

'I am,' said Robert – 'I am indeed!'

He kept forgetting he was a Muslim. If he was going to last any time at all at the Islamic Independent Boys' Day School Wimbledon, he was going to have to keep a pretty close grip on that fact.

He had decided to pass himself off as a Muslim shortly before his twenty-fourth birthday. His father had waved a copy of the *Wimbledon Guardian* at him as Robert was being dragged out of the front door by the dog. 'Could be something worthy of you in there,' he had said, prodding at the Situations Vacant column. And, out there on the Common, on a bench facing a murky pond, Robert had read:

ARE YOU A BROADMINDED TEACHER OF THE MUSLIM FAITH? ARE YOU YOUNG, THRUSTING AND KEEN TO GET AHEAD, WITH GOOD INTERPERSONAL SKILLS? ARE YOU UNDER FIFTY-FIVE WITH A CLEAN DRIVING LICENCE? WE WANT YOU FOR A NEW AND EXCITING ALL-MUSLIM VENTURE IN THE WIMBLEDON AREA.

It was the word 'broadminded' that had caught his eye. It suggested, for some reason, that the job might lead to encounters with naked women. There was certainly something breezily sensual about the man now facing him across the desk.

He seemed pleased to see Robert too. There was no hint of prejudice in his eyes. Robert had feared the headmaster might be a sinister character of the type given to chaining people to radiators in downtown Beirut. He had stopped watching the news shortly after the hostage crisis. In fact, these days he found that, by lying on his bed with the curtains closed and deliberately emptying his mind, he was able to forget most of the unpleasant world events that had troubled him for the first twenty-four years of his life. He was no longer quite sure, for instance, who was the current leader of the Labour Party. With serious mental effort he was hoping to achieve the same state with respect to the president of the United States, the names of the countries of central Europe and almost every geopolitical incident not located within a five-mile radius of Wimbledon Park Road.

Mr Malik grinned, got up from his desk and crossed to a large map of the world on the wall next to the window. Ruffik or Raffik, or whatever his name was, had been taping it to the wall when Robert came in for the interview. Already one corner had come adrift. North-West Canada lolled crazily out into the room. Timber forests brushed lazily against the deserts of Saudi Arabia, as the August breeze sidled in from Wimbledon Village.

'All of the world,' said Mr Malik, jabbing his finger in the vague direction of America, 'will soon be Muslim.'

'I hope so,' said Robert, knitting his brows with what he hoped was a typical convert's expression, 'I hope so!'

Mr Malik stepped smartly to his left and looked down at the green lawn that stretched between the Islamic Independent Boys' Day School and the High Street. Beyond the wrought-iron gates, flanked by two dwarf cypresses, girls in summer dresses, their legs and shoulders bare, walked homewards, calling and laughing to each other. Mr Malik gave them a tolerant smile.

'Muslim ideas and Muslim thinking are making great strides everywhere. Even in Wimbledon. Look at yourself, for example!'

'Indeed!' said Robert.

He hoped they weren't going to get into a detailed discussion of how he had seen the light, or whatever it was you saw when you converted to Islam. If the headmaster asked him which mosque he went to, he had already decided to say that he always visited the nearest one to hand. *What does one need*, he heard himself say, *except a prayer mat and a compass?*

'Were your parents Muslim?' said Malik.

Robert blinked rapidly and said, 'Our family has been Muslim for as long as any of us can remember.'

'Since the Crusades!' said Malik.

They both laughed a lot at this. But the headmaster of the Islamic Independent Boys' Day School then leaned back in his chair, folded his arms and gave Robert a slow, shrewd glance.

'My grandfather converted during the Second World War,' said Robert. 'He served in the desert, and I think that had a profound effect on him. He was involved with the Camel Corps, I believe.'

Malik was nodding slowly. He had a big, well-sculptured nose. Tucked under it was an elegant moustache. But his eyes were his most notable feature. They flickered on and off in his face like dark lanterns, expressing now amusement, now scepticism, but mostly a resigned acceptance of human weakness.

'You were brought up as a Muslim?'

'No, no,' said Robert hastily, 'My . . . er, father was a . . .'

Malik was looking at him steadily.

'A Hindu!'

If the headmaster was surprised at the volatile nature of the Wilson family's religious convictions, he showed no sign of it. He got up and started to pace the threadbare carpet around his desk. 'Our boys,' he said, 'are sent to us because their parents wish them to become part of British society and yet to retain their Muslim identity.'

'I must say,' said Robert, with the unusual conviction that he was speaking the truth, 'that I don't really feel part of British society!'

Malik ignored this remark. He gave the impression of a man speaking to a large and potentially hostile crowd.

'Their parents,' he said, 'want them to be lawyers, accountants, businessmen, doctors. But they also want them to be brought up in a Muslim environment. By Muslims.' He gave Robert another shrewd, appraising glance. 'Such as yourself, for example!'

He should not have worn the sports jacket, thought Robert. Or the grey flannel trousers. He should probably not have come at all.

'Are you keen on games?' went on the headmaster in his fruitily accented English.

'Mustard!' said Robert. 'Keen as mustard!'

Mr Malik savoured this out-of-date colloquialism like a world-class wine-taster. He nodded slightly and then, backing towards the window, placed his left hand, knuckles outwards, over his ribs, and his right hand, palm up, to about head height. At first Robert thought he was going to be made to swear some Islamic oath. Then he realized he was supposed to get up from his chair. He did so.

'Let's look over the facilities,' said Mr Malik, rubbing his hands, briskly. 'As the brochure is not yet printed we can't look at the brochure, can we, old boy?'

Robert found he was laughing immoderately at this remark.

Malik opened the door and waved his hand, expansively, over to the right. 'Chemistry labs!' he said.

This sounded like something out of the *Arabian Nights* – a command for the chemistry labs to appear. It certainly bore no relation to the rather shabby stretch of corridor, leading to a narrow, circular staircase, towards which the headmaster was pointing.

'Impressive!' said Robert.

Malik's eyes narrowed. Robert wondered whether this might be taken for a satirical remark. Then he realized that the headmaster was doing something natural to politicians or actors – putting on a face to match some titanic thought that probably did not exist.

'Yes,' said Mr Malik, looking off into the distance. 'Yes, it will be. I can see it. It will be! It will be . . .' He paused and allowed himself a smile ' . . . mustard!' Then he was off.

They walked, at some speed, towards the other end of the corridor. From there, a more impressive staircase – square, wooden, vaguely Jacobean in appearance – led down to a hall decorated with hanging carpets and peculiar bronze objects that looked a bit like cooking-utensils. It reminded Robert of an Afghan restaurant he had once visited.

Mr Malik did have something of the *maître d'* about him. As they clattered down the stairs, he waved his hand at the far wall. 'Praying area!' he said.

Robert had read something about this. Wasn't the general idea to line up against the wall and bang your head against it? Or was that Jews?

Why was he so appallingly ill-informed about the religion to which he was supposed to belong? How long would it be before Mr Malik rumbled him? Why had he even bothered to read the damned advertisement? He should have gone back to the video shop in Raynes Park. Maybe not. He thought of Mrs Jackson's face as she returned one of the staff's bootleg copies of *Let's Get Laid in LA*. He had given it to her in good faith. It had said *Fantasia* on the box. And by all accounts the children at Barney Jackson's eighth birthday party had enjoyed it a lot. He could go back to the Putney Leisure Centre for God's sake! Some people had spoken highly of his skills as a lifeguard. No one had actually *died* in the accident. Or the Wimbledon Odeon!

He shuddered as he thought of the Wimbledon Odeon.

Malik walked along the hall, opening doors and flinging them back against the wall of hanging carpets. He barked back over his shoulder at Robert. 'Large airy classrooms for the senior boys,' he said. 'Slightly smaller rooms for the slightly smaller boys. And here – ' He came to the last door in the hall – 'a very, *very* small area that will be used to accommodate the very, very small boys during their early weeks at the Islamic Boys' Day Independent School, Wimbledon.'

He didn't seem entirely clear about the title. Was it the Islamic Boys' Day Independent School Wimbledon, or was it the Islamic Day Boys' Independent School Wimbledon? They would need to have made their minds up by the time they got the notepaper.

So far, Robert had seen no sign of notepaper.

He peered in at the last room. It was the size of a generously proportioned cupboard, with a narrow skylight in the top left-hand corner of the far wall.

'This,' said Malik in the tones of a man who was about to lock him in and leave him there, 'will be your room.'

'It's lovely,' said Robert.

'That which Allah has in store is far better than any merchandise or muniment. Allah is the most Munificent Giver!'

This was obviously a quotation of some kind. Whatever Allah was dishing out, he clearly wasn't sending a fortune in the direction of the Islamic Day Boys' Independent Wimbledon School.

Even so, the place was clearly not without funds. The school occupied a fairly large eighteenth-century house which, although its walls bulged crazily and its ceilings were pregnant with age, had a grandeur about it that suggested some old-established colonial concern. How many pupils would there be?

Robert bowed his head and tried to look like a Muslim. Mr Malik looked at him with concerned curiosity. 'Do you wish to use the facilities?' he said.

'I'm fine, thank you, Headmaster,' said Robert. Should he, he wondered, have worn a hat? A turban of some kind?

'Over there,' said Malik, gesturing towards a door on the other side of the hall, 'are the kitchens.' All Robert could see was a large porcelain sink, lying upside down in the corner of the room. It did not seem to be connected to anything.

Mr Malik waved airily at the front door. 'Language laboratories,' he said. 'Information technology – or "IT" as it is known. This is the 1990s for God's sake, Wilson!'

He said this in tones that suggested that Robert had just proposed some alternative date. *Am I looking too combative?* thought Robert as he followed the headmaster out into the rear gardens of the Wimbledon Islamic Day Boys' . . . He really must try and remember the correct word order. Did he want this job or not? The Boys' Islamic Day . . .

'Playing-fields!' boomed Mr Malik. He threw both his arms wide and closed his eyes. He was obviously seeing playing-fields. Robert saw a large, shabby lawn, bounded by a high wall. There was an apple-tree in the far left-hand corner, and, next to it, a dilapidated climbing-frame.

'We have put the gymnasium in the orchard,' said Malik, 'and hope our boys will acquire healthy bodies in healthy minds. Tell the truth, Wilson, and shame the Devil!'

Robert tried to stop himself from twitching. He did not succeed.

'As for you sinners who deny the truth,' said the headmaster, peering closely at his prospective employee, 'you shall eat the fruit of the Zaqqum tree and fill your bellies with it. You shall drink boiling water; yet you shall drink it as the thirsty camel drinks!'

'Indeed,' said Robert.

It was time, he felt, to ask a few keen and thrusting questions. *Interview them, old lad*, he heard his father's voice say. *Make the terms yourself. Be tough, Bobbo. You're too soft on people!*

'Where,' he heard himself saying in slightly querulous tones, 'is the staffroom?'

Malik gestured to a battered wooden shed about halfway down the garden. 'The staffroom,' he said smoothly, 'is located in the Additional Science Block Complex. Science and technology are vital, Wilson. Crucial!'

The door to the Additional Science Block Complex opened, and a small, wizened man in dungarees appeared. Robert recognized him as the man who had been taping the map of the world to the wall earlier. He addressed Malik in a language that could have been Arabic, Punjabi or, indeed, Swahili. He sounded annoyed about something. Malik shrugged, grinned, and, as they turned to go back into the house, said, 'Talk English, for God's sake! We are in bloody England. Don't come on like an illiterate wog! Please!'

The man in the dungarees narrowed his eyes. He did not look as if he knew any English. What, Robert wondered, was his role in the Wimbledon Islamic Boys' Day School? Groundsman? Janitor?

'Rafiq will be giving classes in macroeconomics,' said Malik, 'and he will also be dealing with engineering. He can make *anything*. He is one of my oldest friends. Even though he is from the University of Birmingham. You are an Oxford man, of course.'

'Indeed,' said Robert.

Robert had been to Oxford. He had been there for the day in 1987. It had seemed a nice place.

'I read classics,' he said, trying to remember whether that was what he had said in the application, 'and I was lucky enough to get a first-class degree.'

This seemed to go down quite well.

Robert had noticed quite early in life that people tended to believe what you told them. Even people who were professionally suspicious – lawyers, policemen and certain kinds of teacher – were never suspicious about the right things. The only difficulty was remembering what you had said about yourself, and to whom. Only the other day a neighbour had asked him how the viola recitals were going, and there was an elderly man in the village who still insisted in talking to him in Polish.

'Oh God, yes,' said Mr Malik with some enthusiasm, 'the classics! Virgil. Homer. Horace. Harriet Beecher Stowe. Longfellow.'

He was heading back towards the school. Just to the right of the back door Robert noticed four or five battered wooden desks, piled crazily on top of one another. Malik waved at them. He seemed to feel that they spoke for themselves. As they went back into the hall, he said, 'Do you have a blue?'

A blue what? thought Robert.

Malik's eyes narrowed.

Robert considered a moment, then said swiftly, 'Cricket. Rugby football.'

'Well, Wilson,' said Mr Malik, 'we will take up references, of course. But I think we may well find ourselves working together at the beginning of the first term. I like the cut of your jib!'

'Well, Mr Malik,' said Robert, 'I like the cut of *your* jib!'

'Yes indeed,' said the headmaster – 'it is not a bad jib!'

He went, with some solemnity, to a cupboard next to the door leading to the smallest of the classrooms. 'You will work here,' he said – 'with the very small boys.' From one of the shelves he took a small, leatherbound volume. With some ceremony he handed it to Robert. 'You will have a copy of this, of course,' he said, 'but I offer it as a gift. I will be in touch as regards our terms of employment.'

He stared deep into Robert's eyes.

'Payment is on a cash basis,' he said. 'I like you, Wilson. I want to work with you!'

He put his hand on Robert's arm and pushed his face so close that their noses were almost touching. 'I think you have a good attitude!' he said throatily.

Then he went to the door, flung it open and sent Robert out into the glare of the August afternoon.

It was not until he was at the door of the Frog and Ferret that Robert looked at his present. It was an edition of the Koran, translated by N. J. Dawood. Slipping it under his jacket, he walked up to the bar and ordered a large whisky.

2

He had got it out and was looking at it furtively when Mr Malik walked in and glared fiercely around. Robert shrank behind a pillar, and, to his relief, the headmaster did not appear to have seen him. He watched, as the headmaster strode up to the bar, tapped it imperiously with the edge of a fifty-pence piece, and said, in a loud, clear voice, 'A pint of Perrier water, if you please!'

The barman unwound himself from his stool and walked over to his customer. He muttered something, and Malik, addressing his reply to the whole pub, said, 'A pint. A bottle. Whatever. I am parched!'

Robert drained his whisky and shrank down into his chair. As soon as Malik turned back to the bar, he would make a run for it. Did he have a peppermint about his person?

No.

Malik gave no sign of turning back to the bar. He had the same, grand proprietorial attitude to the Frog and Ferret as he did to the Wimbledon Islamic Day Boys' Independent School. 'My mouth,' he said fruitily to the assembled company, 'is as dry as a camel's arse!'

No one seemed very interested in this. Robert recognized Vera 'Got All the Things There' Loomis over in the corner, smacking her lips over a glass of Guinness. Over by the window was Norbert Coveney, the brother of the man who had died in the Rush poisoning case three years ago. He did not seem pleased to see Mr Malik. The barman poured two bottles of Perrier into a pint glass, with almost offensive slowness.

Malik eyed him hungrily and then, with a theatrical flourish, turned back to the almost deserted pub. 'Give a poor wog a drink, for Christ's sake!'

The inmates of the Frog and Ferret did not respond to this.

Although, thought Robert, from the look of them they would not have been much impressed had Malik yanked out his chopper and laid it on the bar as a testament of his good faith. Standing by the door with a pint of porter in his hand was Lewis Wansell, the downwardly mobile dentist, popularly known as 'Die Screaming in Southfields'. 'They work all hours,' he was saying, to no one in particular. 'They come here and they work all hours. What chance do we have?'

The headmaster turned his back on the company, applied his lips to the edge of the glass, and sucked up his mineral water.

Robert rose and started to tiptoe towards the door. 'Hey,' said a voice behind him, 'you forgot your book!'

Mr Malik turned round just as Robert got to his table. Robert, wondering whether it was a punishable offence to bring the Koran on to licensed premises – let alone leave it there – scooped up the volume and walked towards his new headmaster. He ducked his head as he did this, widened his eyes, and flung open his arms. This was intended to convey surprise, delight and a dash of Muslim fellow-feeling. As it was, he felt, he gave the impression of having designs on Mr Malik.

'We meet again,' he said.

Mr Malik did not smile. He nodded briefly. 'Indeed.'

Robert held the Koran up to his face when he got within breathing distance. The sweet, heavy smell of the whisky climbed back up his nostrils.

'I'm always leaving this in pubs,' he said, waving the sacred book, rather feebly.

This was not what he had meant to say at all.

'I mean,' he went on desperately, 'quite often, in the past . . . I . . . er . . . have left it in pubs. In the hope that people will . . . er . . . pick it up and . . . read it. Rather like the Bible.'

'Do people leave the Bible in pubs?' said Mr Malik, in tones of some surprise.

'They leave it in hotels,' said Robert – 'the Gideons leave it in hotel bedrooms. And I shouldn't be surprised if they left it in pubs. Or even carried it round and sold it. Like the Salvation Army magazine.'

The headmaster was looking at him oddly. Why, having made a mistake, was he busy elaborating on it? Then Mr Malik said, 'Have a drink, Wilson, for God's sake. We are friends, for God's sake. Have a pint, my dear man! Have a pint of beer!'

This offer surprised Robert considerably. As far as he was aware, this was not the kind of thing devout Muslims were supposed to say to each other. Perhaps it was a trap.

'Just a Perrier for me,' he said, rather primly.

Malik winked broadly at him. 'Righteousness,' he said, 'does not consist in whether you face towards the East or the West. I myself am having a bottle of Special Brew.'

Robert coughed. If this was a trap, it was a carefully prepared one. Once you had said you were a Muslim, could they do what they liked with you? Was it a case of one sip of Young's Special and there you were – being stoned to death in the High Street?

'Just the water please, Headmaster,' he said. Mr Malik gave a broad and unexpected smile. It gave him the appearance, briefly, of a baby who has just completed a successful belch. '*Headmaster!*' he said. 'That is what I am!'

He snapped his fingers. The barman gave him a contemptuous look and ambled off in the other direction. A small, leathery-faced man was waving a five-pound note at him from the other end of the bar.

'They serve the regulars first . . .' said Robert.

'They serve the white chaps first,' said Mr Malik – 'and who can blame them?'

The barman finished serving the leathery-faced man. He gave Mr Malik a measured stare. He looked at the headmaster as if he was an item he was trying to price for a jumble sale. After a while he walked back towards them.

'A Special Brew, a Perrier water and a large Scotch for my friend,' said Mr Malik.

Robert gulped.

'Isn't that what you were drinking, old boy?' said Malik.

'I was . . .'

How did he know this? Had he made a special study of infidels' drinking habits?

The headmaster was looking up at the mirror above the bar. Robert followed the direction of his gaze. He found himself looking at the reflection of a man in a shabby blue suit, who was peering into the pub from the street. Apart from the fact that he had chosen not to wear a tea towel on his head, he bore a sensationally close resemblance to Yasser Arafat. Behind him, in a slightly less shabby blue suit, was a man who looked like a more or less exact replica of Saddam Hussein. Both men had two or three days' growth of stubble on them, and both were wearing dark glasses. This could explain why they seemed to be having trouble making out what was going on in the interior of the Frog and Ferret.

Both men seemed to be hobbling slightly. Perhaps, thought Robert, as they pressed their noses to the glass, they had been involved in some industrial accident. They looked as if they had been working together, for years, on the same, grim production line.

Their effect on Mr Malik was profound. He looked like a man who has just opened a packet of cornflakes and been greeted by a Gaboon viper. Ignoring the barman, he reached out for Robert and squeezed his forearm. Without turning his head, he said, grimly, 'Well, the Wimbledon Dharjees are upon us.' He carefully knitted a crease into his forehead. 'And not, I fear, the best type of Dharjee!'

Robert wondered whether the two men were brothers and this was their surname. Wasn't a dharjee something you ate, like a bhajji or a samosa?

Mr Malik started to move away along the bar, keeping his face, as far as possible, away from the visitors.

'Hey!' called the barman.

'Gentlemen's lavatory,' hissed Malik. And before anyone had time to question him further he was gone, moving with surprising speed for a man of his size.

Just as he left, the two men opened the door and started to hobble their way towards the centre of the room. It was only now that Robert was able to see what was making them limp: both were wearing odd shoes. Robert's first thought was that this might reflect some kind of financial crisis in the immigrant community in Wimbledon. But then he noticed that each of them, on his right foot, was wearing what looked like a slipper. Not only that. As they moved into the pub they both stopped from time to time and wriggled their right feet anxiously. Did they suffer from some form of verruca, some ghastly mange that affected only the toes of the right feet?

When they reached the bar, the man without the tea towel on his head pushed up his glasses and peered round. He had small watery eyes. With his glasses on his forehead you got to see more of his nose. Yasser Arafat, Robert decided, was better-looking.

'Can I get you anything, gents?'

Yasser Arafat sneered. The barman sneered back. Then both men came over to where Robert was standing.

'A beer? A glass of wine?'

Both men ignored the offer of service. This was more or less the reverse of the usual situation in the pub. The barman screwed up his face into a tight ball. With a shock, Robert realized he was trying to smile.

'A soft drink of some kind?'

Saddam Hussein leaned his elbows on the bar and, looking sideways at Robert, said, 'I see you know the man called Malik. The big man. We know his business. He teaches here in Wimbledon.'

His appearance and delivery gave the impression that he had got this information from some oasis a few hundred miles south of Agadir. It suggested, too, that he was not looking for the headmaster of the Wimbledon Islamic Boys' Day Independent School in order to offer him a low-interest mortgage or a new kind of double glazing.

Robert decided to reply cautiously. 'Is he,' he said, 'a friend of yours?'

This seemed to amuse Yasser Arafat. 'Malik,' he said crisply, 'is a slug and a blasphemer!'

His friend leaned his head over his shoulder and cleared his throat loudly. The barman's mouth dropped a notch and he started to ask, in hostile tones, whether both men breezed into their own living-rooms without buying a drink.

'He is,' said his companion, 'excrement.'

This seemed a little harsh to Robert. There was, he had to admit, something not entirely trustworthy about the headmaster, but to call him 'excrement' was, surely, to overstate the case.

'He is,' said the man without a tea towel on his head, 'the vomit of a dog!'

For a moment Robert thought Saddam Hussein was going to spit on the floor. But his eye had been taken by the book, now lying on the counter of the bar. He looked at it suspiciously. 'What is this?' he said.

Robert coughed. 'It's the . . . er . . . Koran.'

They did not seem impressed. Perhaps he had not pronounced the word correctly.

'I haven't actually . . . er . . . read it yet,' he went on, brightly, 'but I intend to in the very near future.'

He had rather hoped that the book might provide a talking-point. But, if anything, its presence seemed to intensify the men's suspicion of him. He did not feel it prudent to tell them that he had just embraced the Muslim faith, partly because he was not sure that they *were* Muslims and partly because he was afraid they might ask him what he was doing with a large whisky and a bottle of Special Brew. Robert's voice died away.

'This is the Koran?' said the man who looked like Yasser Arafat.

'It is indeed!' These men, Robert decided, could not possibly be Muslims. Muslims would, surely, have felt the need to express some enthusiasm at finding an English punter leafing through it. 'And from everything I hear it's quite a book. It's had enormous . . . er . . . influence . . .'

It was fairly obvious that he was telling them nothing new. In fact they were looking at Robert, as people tended to do, as if he had some satirical intent.

The man without a tea towel on his head reached forward and touched the book with his index finger. He withdrew it very quickly, as if the volume carried some electrical charge. 'I have learned this book by heart,' he said.

'Good Lord,' said Robert, 'why did you do that?'

This was obviously the wrong thing to say.

'He carries it in his heart,' replied the second man, 'and he speaks its truth to all who will listen. To those who will not listen he does not speak.'

'Very sensible,' said Robert.

'He cuts them as he would slit the throat of a chicken.'

'Fair enough,' said Robert, 'fair enough!'

Malik seemed to be spending a long time in the lavatory.

The barman seemed now almost pathetically anxious to please the new arrivals. He was rubbing his hands and smirking. It was clear to Robert that the best way of getting service out of him was to look as if you were about to gob on the floor. He seemed to be trying, not at all successfully, to attract their attention.

'This is what one day will be done to Malik and those he serves!' said Saddam Hussein. 'He will be dragged in the dust and he will be pierced with knives. This will happen to those who serve him also.'

Perhaps, thought Robert, these men were from the Merton Education Authority. There was a clattering sound from out by the gentlemen's lavatory.

'You know him?' said the man without a tea towel on his head.

'I'm afraid I don't. Not *know* exactly . . .' said Robert.

'I think you do,' said Saddam Hussein. 'I think you will be a teacher at the Islamic School. I think you are Wilson. I think you live in Wimbledon Park Road. I think you are a hypocrite Muslim!'

News certainly travelled fast, thought Robert. He had only sent the application in on Monday. How could they possibly know these things?

'We have read your application,' went on Saddam, 'and we know about your sports abilities. But we do not think you write like a true believer!'

'It will be a school for pigs and blasphemers,' went on his friend, 'and all who teach in it will die.'

'We are all going to die,' said Robert, as cheerfully as he could.

'Tell your friend,' said Saddam Hussein, 'that we are watching him. And we will watch you also.'

'OK,' said Robert.

'And tell him,' the man went on, 'that we have something that will make him and his friends ashamed to face the daylight. Something that, when our people read it, will make him and his friends crawl through the dung!'

Robert tried to keep very still. The man's face was now pressed closely into his. He smelt sweet and musky. *I should probably investigate alternative ways of making a living as soon as possible*, thought Robert.

'When the time comes,' the man was saying, 'we shall distribute this among our people. They will read and understand. And then, when the time of his Occultation is over, the Imam will come to us.'

The man who should have had the tea towel on his head was rummaging in his jacket pocket. It occurred to Robert that he might be looking for a gun.

Eventually the man pulled out a small parcel and set it on the bar, a few inches from Robert's copy of the Koran. He looked into Robert's eyes. 'When you see Malik, give him this box. Let him read and understand that he will die. And that all who serve him will die. And that the staff and pupils of the Wimbledon Islamic Independent Boys' Day School will burn in hell-fire when the day comes. And we know the day, my friend! It is coming!'

Robert was about to protest, once again, that he had only just met Mr Malik. But these men seemed worryingly well informed about aspects of his life about which even he was vague.

The first man made a complex, guttural sound and pushed the box towards him. Robert picked it up. It was wrapped in green paper.

'If I see him,' he said, 'I'll do that.'

The man grabbed him hard by the wrist. He was breathing hard. 'You will see the Imam, but the Imam will not see you. Because, as it is written, hypocrite Wilson, the Imam sees not as we do! This, too, tells you you will be consumed in the fires of hell that do not cease!'

'I'm sure,' said Robert. 'I'm sure!'

Everyone will burn in hell-fire when the day comes, he reflected, as he walked out into the glare of the street, but the day, for Jew, Christian and Muslim, has been a hell of a long time coming.

3

When he got home, he found his parents making a cassoulet. This was slightly better than finding them making love, or in the middle of an argument. They did all these things with a great deal of noise and enthusiasm.

'What have you been up to today, Bobkins?' said his father.

Robert stared out of the window at the featureless lawn. Badger, the family's lurcher, was sitting in the middle of it, staring hungrily at passing flies.

'I got a job,' he said.

His father looked at his mother. They smirked at each other. Mr and Mrs Wilson were always convinced, each time their son took a new job, that this one would, in Mrs Wilson's phrase, 'lead to something.' She was, in a sense, right. She had been positive that Renzo's the Delicatessen was going to lead to something, although she could not have predicted that the 'something' was going to be the loss of Mr Renzo's thumb in the slicing-machine. She had been positive that Bearman and Studde, the estate agents, were going to lead to something, and, although Mr Bearman's suicide was not quite what she had had in mind, there was no doubt that Robert's presence in the firm had, in Mr Bearman's own words, 'changed it, changed it utterly!' Disaster had a way of following him. That was why for the last nine months he had stayed indoors as much as possible.

They beamed at him now from across the kitchen.

'What . . . er . . . is the job, exactly?' said his father.

Robert looked back at him cautiously. Both his mother and father encouraged him to use their Christian names, but calling them Norman and Sylvia had never helped him to feel more intimate with them. Nor had it helped to quell the guilt he felt every time he saw their eager little eyes brighten at the sight of their only son. He knew he was nothing to be proud of – why didn't they?

'I'm going to be a teacher,' he said.

'Great stuff!' said Mr Wilson senior, as he chopped a red onion into a frying-pan. 'I'd give my right arm to be able to teach. They do *such* an important job! And they're not really appreciated, are they?'

'You would be a marvellous teacher, Robert,' said his mother, 'and it's marvellous they've seen that without asking for all those stupid qualifications!'

'Qualifications!' said Mr Wilson senior, shaking the frying-pan violently. 'Who needs 'em?'

Norman Wilson, as he was fond of reminding people, had no qualifications. This could have been why the accountants for whom he had worked for twenty years had, early last year, asked him to leave. He did not seem worried about not having a job. 'I've got the redundo, old son,' he used to say, 'and now I can get on with my writing.' No one in the family knew what he was writing, apart from the occasional cheque.

Robert's mother walked swiftly towards the fridge. For a moment he thought she was going to grab it by the handle and throw it over her left shoulder, judo style, but at the last moment she veered off to the left and, grabbing a tin of haricot beans, trotted towards the door that led to the garden. Out on the lawn, Badger reared up, his face wild with excitement.

'No, no, no!' screamed Mr and Mrs Wilson, in perfect synchronization. 'Go away! Go away! Go away! Bad dog!'

Badger sat down again. He looked depressed.

'What will you teach, exactly?' said Robert's mother.

'English,' said Robert, 'Greek. That kind of thing.'

'Do you know any Greek?' said his father.

His mother was coming back, now, towards the sink. On the way she had acquired a corkscrew and a bag of potatoes. She threw the potatoes, viciously, on to the worktop. Out on the patio a small breeze stirred her geraniums.

'I picked up a bit,' said Robert, 'when I worked at the kebab place.'

They both seemed impressed by this.

'What kind of school is it?' said his mother.

Robert wondered how much to tell them. He decided that they were not quite ready for the Wimbledon Boys' Islamic Independent Day School. He would break it to them gently over the next few months.

'Oh,' he said, 'it's for boys. Small boys. Not big ones, as far as I can make out. And it's new. I'm getting in on the ground floor.'

His father pulled hard at the cutlery drawer. The handle came away, easily and smoothly. The drawer stayed where it was.

'Who built this kitchen?' said Mr Wilson senior. Nobody answered this question. With a sigh, Robert's father placed the handle in another drawer, picked up a carving-knife and began to attempt to lever the drawer open. This activity seemed to calm him.

'That girl of yours is waiting for you in your bedroom.' He turned to his only son and gave a suggestive wink. 'I wish I had young girls waiting for me in my bedroom!' he said, squatting on his haunches in front of the drawer and driving the knife in deeper. There was a splintering sound from inside the kitchen unit.

Robert's mother looked at him, a dreamy expression on her face. 'It seems only yesterday,' she said, 'that you and Maisie and Philip Chung and that Schnitzler boy were working for your GCEs. In this very kitchen!'

Philip Chung and the Schnitzler boy had, of course, managed to get some GCEs. Philip Chung and the Schnitzler boy had moved away from Wimbledon. As had the Borrage brothers, Susie Parsons, Linda Haddock and Janet Fitzpierce who did it with anybody. Only he and Maisie were left. Was it really eight years since he had left Cranborne School?

As he clumped up to his room, he thought about Maisie.

Of all the projects he had started, none had been more enthusiastically taken up by his mother and father than Maisie. The daughter of local advertising man, Marco Pierrepoint, she was thought by many people in Wimbledon to be beautiful. There were those who said she was too plump. Gary Brisket, the music scholar, who had gone to Cambridge and never come back, always maintained that 'she had the biggest jacksie in sw19,' but, like many other boys in the neighbourhood, he had walked out with her for a while, and, when she told him she was in love with someone else, had cried, briefly, behind the pavilion at Cranborne School.

She was always falling in love. If not with people, then with things. One week she would be a vegetarian, the next a passionate student of the French troubadours. For months last year she had visited a gym in Putney every day, announcing her intention of 'building up my pectoral muscles'. She had only just stopped in time, thought Robert, as he peered at her through a crack in the bedroom door – her breasts were already the size of Rugby balls.

We're like brother and sister, Bobkins. That was what she always said, however much his mother winked, nodded and leered every time Maisie came to the house. If they were brother and sister, he said to himself, as he stood there on the landing, taking in that smell she had of pepper and vanilla and lily of the valley, he had been horribly close to incest for the last eight years. He stood for a moment outside his room, sniffing hard.

'Is that you, darling?' she said.

'Afraid so,' said Robert.

She had a flowery look about her too, he thought as he studied her through the crack in the door. He never really got the chance of a good look when he was in her presence. Maisie liked you to put in a great deal of work when talking to her; Robert was always too busy pulling funny faces or staring deep into her large, black eyes to appreciate what was on offer.

'Are you peering at me again?'

'Sorry.'

As he came into the room, Maisie rose and offered him her left cheek. Robert swooped in. As his lips made contact, her scent exploded in his nose.

'Mark's left me.'

'Oh *no!*'

'He has.'

She sat back on the bed and began to cry.

Robert wondered whether to put his arm round her shoulder. It seemed a rather forward thing to do. He had, after all, been in the room for over a minute. Physical contact with Maisie was usually limited to arrivals and departures. Perhaps he could embrace her and then rush out of the room muttering something about a previous engagement.

Her shoulders were heaving. Her large breasts shook under her crisp, white blouse. Robert put his hand carefully round the back of her head and landed it, as tactfully as possible, on her right shoulder. When it was clear she wasn't going to nut him or knee him in the groin, he gave the shoulder a little tug, and ten stone of Maisie fell against him, her long, black hair brushing against his face.

'I loved him so much . . .' she said.

'Yes,' said Robert – 'he was a really nice bloke.'

This didn't sound quite right somehow. Which one was Mark anyway?

Maisie started to laugh and groped for a handkerchief in her bag. 'He was a *bastard*, you *idiot*,' she said. 'He was a complete *sod*!'

'Why?'

Her voice had a note of genuine irritation as she said, 'Because he left me, stupid.'

Robert remembered Mark now.

'He was in the Air Force, wasn't he?'

Maisie was giving him a peculiar look.

'Or was it the Territorial Army?'

She started to laugh again. To try to prolong her mood, Robert took from his jacket pocket the parcel intended for Mr Malik.

'What's that?'

Maisie's eager, greedy eyes had begun to sparkle.

'Is it a present? Is it for me?'

'Of course,' said Robert. 'Of course it's for you.'

'Oh, Robert,' said Maisie, 'you are *sweet*!'

Robert wondered whether to take his hand off her shoulder. He did not trust himself to do so. The area between armpit and thigh, smelling as it did of soap, perfume and clean linen, was not one where he felt able to sustain the fiction of a brotherly embrace.

'Can I open it?'

'Of course, darling.'

She gave a little squeak and grabbed the box.

Maisie was experienced at unwrapping presents. She crooked her index finger under the string and yanked hard. As the string broke, the green paper fell away and the two of them found they were looking at a beautifully inlaid box, about the size of a packet of Kleenex. It was decorated with whorls and loops in what looked like ivory, but the material of which it was made, though it felt like polished wood, was probably something more valuable.

'Oooh, it looks valuable!' said Maisie. 'Is it onyx or something? Is it a valuable box, Bobkins?'

'It is a very valuable box.'

He coughed nervously.

'And what's in it, Bobkins? Is it just the box, or is there a bracelet in it? Is there a lovely bracelet in it?'

Robert wiped his forehead. 'There might be,' he said in paternal tones. 'Let's see, shall we?'

There might, of course, given the nature of the man who had given it to him, be animal excrement in there . . . or a poisonous tarantula . . . or . . .

'It's precious stones!' gasped Maisie as she slid her long, polished nails between the lid and the case, trying to force it up. 'It's joolery! Say it's joolery, Bobkins!'

'It might,' said Robert, 'be jewellery.'

There were those in Wimbledon who said that Maisie was spoilt. Her father was always giving her things. When he had been made creative director of Swan & Jenkins, he had bought her a car. She had run it into a wall after two weeks and had never driven again. There were those who said that, now she was in her twenties, her father should stop addressing her as 'the sexiest little princess in Wimbledon Park Road'. It was widely agreed that she should not sit in Pierrepoint's lap quite so much. There were those who said that she had been given too much, too often, too young. But it was impossible not to give her things – her pleasure in them was so fierce and childish.

Suddenly the lid sprang up. They found themselves looking at a silver locket, face down, wreathed in the same designs as the cover of the box. Underneath it was a roll of paper. At first Robert thought this must be wrapping, but, as they leaned their heads into the box, he saw that it looked more like medieval vellum than anything else. It was covered with writing.

'Oooh,' squeaked Maisie, 'is that Arabic?'

'It is,' said Robert in an authoritative voice. 'That is actual Arabic writing.'

It certainly looked like the stuff you saw outside halal meat shops in the Shepherd's Bush Road. And if it wasn't, Maisie would not be likely to know. Her father had managed to find her a job in the rare-prints section of Sotheby's, but, although she had been there nearly a year, she still seemed invincibly ignorant about all forms of calligraphy.

'What does it say?' said Maisie, clearly under the illusion that the early stages of conversion gave one unusual facility with the language of the Koran.

'It says,' said Robert, trying to look as if he was familiar with the incomprehensible squiggles, 'that you are more beautiful than rubies and that the dawn is not equal to your eyes. And your breasts are like . . . er . . . sand-dunes.'

Maisie looked suspiciously from the manuscript to Robert. 'I'm not sure I like the sound of that. Is that all it says?'

'It's a poem by a well-known Arabic poet,' went on Robert.

'What's his name?'

'Hoj!' said Robert, after a long pause.

'I think I've heard of him,' said Maisie, as she reached for the locket and started to scratch her nails into its side. Maybe, thought Robert, there was something nasty in the locket.

'It's a love-poem. Written in the tenth century, and it compares the beloved to the stars in the sky and the . . . er . . . Zaqqum tree and says her thighs are like . . . pistons!'

'Did they have pistons in the tenth century?' said Maisie, who was having no luck in her attempts to open the locket.

Robert, who was now getting quite involved with Hoj's love-poetry, ignored her. He was about to give her the details of Hoj's brief and unsatisfactory life in and around Baghdad a thousand years ago, when she gave a quiet shriek. The locket had flown open to reveal a black-and-white photograph of a boy of about ten years old. He had a thin, sensitive face, with black hair brushed neatly in a parting, such as you saw above the faces of British children of the fifties. On his right cheek was a huge strawberry mark. He was wearing a neat white shirt and, rather oddly, considering the rest of his appearance, a pair of dark glasses.

Maisie did not seem to like him being in her locket.

'Who's he?' she said, accusingly. 'Did you get it in an antique shop?'

The simple thing would have been to answer 'Yes.' But Robert was unable to resist a more complex response.

'It's a traditional Arab gift,' he said. 'When you're fond of some-one, you give them a picture of a little child.'

Maisie looked at him oddly. 'For luck, sort of thing . . .' she said.

'That's it,' said Robert.

'Like Joan the Wad the Cornish Pixie?'

'Exactly like Joan the Wad the Cornish Pixie!'

She was still not happy about this. Her voice was anxious as she said, 'And he's just . . . *any* child. He isn't someone you know, is he, Bobkins?'

'It's just a custom,' said Robert – 'like . . . kissing under the mistletoe.'

'Oh, you are sweet. I don't want to know *what* it is. I just want to know it's from you and it's because we're friends and that in spite of all your problems we love each other. How much was it?'

Robert winced slightly and put his fingers to his lips. Maisie flung both her arms round him and kissed him full on the mouth. She looked up into his eyes. 'Sometimes,' she said, 'I wish you weren't gay.'

Robert wondered whether this was the moment to tell her he wasn't. The only trouble with this would be explaining why he had said he was in the first place. He could not, for the life of him, remember why he had told Maisie he was a practising homosexual. Maybe he hadn't. Maybe it had been her idea.

Thinking about it now, as she sprawled across his pink duvet, her black hair in an artful pool beside her, he decided it was probably Maisie's idea. She had most of the ideas in their relationship. If you could call it a relationship.

'Is it still just casual sex?' she said – 'in parks and so on?'

Robert shook his head vigorously. 'I'm through with all that. I want a serious relationship now.'

Who with? her expression seemed to say. Her eyes narrowed slightly as she moved down the bed.

'This boy in the photograph . . .' she began, rather sharply.

'Absolutely not!' said Robert, primly. He just managed to suppress an urge to tell her that he went in for older men. Especially those involved in the outdoor life. *Lumberjacks*, he almost heard himself say – *anything with broad shoulders and hairy legs!*

A year or so ago, just after she had broken up with Guy Hamilton-Barley, he had planned a spectacular conversion to the opposite sex. They had had dinner in an Italian restaurant in Wimbledon Village, and Robert had told her he had been having erotic thoughts about women. She had replied, rather briskly, that although they looked like women they probably weren't.

There was another of those silences between them. Maisie put her head to one side and watched him carefully. She clearly expected him to say something interesting. 'I love Robert,' she would say to mutual friends – 'he's so *funny*!' Robert had never thought of himself as funny. When people laughed at things he said, which they quite often did, he usually took it as a personal insult.

What could he say to interest her?

'I'm thinking,' he said, eventually, 'of becoming a Muslim.'

She seemed to like this idea. 'I think that's wonderful, Bobkins,' she said. 'I think that's absolutely wonderful. Will it involve travel?'

'I don't think so,' said Robert.

He was beginning to find this conversation oppressive. You would have thought she would have put up a bit more of a fight for Christian values. He got to his feet and went to the window. The German next door was mowing his lawn. Beyond him the Patersons were playing tennis against the Joneses. *Why couldn't they find another way to compete with each other?* thought Robert. *Like – who could jump off the highest building head first.* Over to the left, a huge plane-tree, dulled by the August heat, cast dappled shadows on his father's lawn. Badger was lying on his back doing complicated cycling movements with all four legs. As Robert watched, the dog righted himself, shot out his tongue to the left of his snout and chomped his jaws together smartly.

He had never planned on staying in Wimbledon. He had always thought, somehow, that, like his friends and contemporaries, he would go somewhere glamorous and far-away. York, say, or Brighton. He had applied, years ago, to a polytechnic in North Wales. They had not even replied to his letter. He was still here, eight years after leaving school, in the beautifully kept room with the pink duvet, the twenty or thirty paperbacks and all the loving tributes to his childhood. *'We're the lost generation!'* Martin Finkelstein, the clever boy from South Wimbledon, used to say. *'We're the children of the eighties! We have no hope!'* At least Finkelstein had gone on to get a scholarship to Cambridge. Maisie and Robert were people who had even managed to go missing from the lost generation.

He felt just as much a Muslim as he felt like any of the other things he occasionally owned up to being.

'There's a guy called Malik,' he said. 'He's sort of my spiritual mentor. I'd like you to meet him.'

It was only as he said this that Robert realized that he really did like Mr Malik. Almost more than anyone he had met in the last five years. Not that he had met many people in the last five years.

'I'd love to meet him,' said Maisie. 'Is he young?'

It occurred to Robert that he had absolutely no notion of Mr Malik's age. He could have been anything from twenty-five to fifty. Was this, perhaps, in part due to his religion?

'Is he Pakistani?' said Maisie. 'I adore Pakistanis! Is he like Imran Khan?'

'I'm not sure what he is,' said Robert. 'He's not English, that's for sure.'

Except that there was something quite incredibly English about Malik.

Maisie was peering at the manuscript. 'Read me a bit,' she said in the slightly bossy squawk she acquired whenever she was genuinely excited.

Robert screwed up his eyes and gestured to the first page. 'All that,' he said, 'is about your breasts. Or her breasts, rather – Hoj's woman's breasts.'

Maisie looked at the letters dubiously. She held the manuscript out in front of her at arm's length. 'I suppose,' she said, 'you have to hold it upside down or back to front in order to read it. They do write back to front, don't they?'

'They do,' said Robert crisply, anxious to get off the subject of Arabic, 'but I quite often read the Koran in English.'

Maisie's eyes flickered. She seemed impressed. 'You're really serious about this, aren't you?' she said.

'Very serious,' said Robert, whipping Mr Malik's Koran from his jacket pocket. 'I never go anywhere without a copy of this. Believe you me, it makes quite a read!'

Maisie shook her head in something like wonder. The most interesting thing about Robert, up to this moment, her face seemed to suggest, was his impression of John Major. But now . . .

Robert flicked through the Koran's pages. It looked pretty menacing stuff, even viewed at high speed. It also seemed worryingly long.

'You're not reading it backwards!' cried Maisie, in an accusing voice, 'you're holding it the right way up!'

'It's in *English*!' said Robert.

Not that reading it upside down or back to front would, as far as Robert was concerned, have made much difference, as he riffled through snappy chapter headings like 'The Blood Clots', 'He Frowned', and one entitled simply 'Sad'. There seemed to be four pages devoted to the Greeks, and a useful subsection on 'Kneeling'. Once again he found himself wondering whether he had the necessary stamina to be a Muslim, even an imitation one.

As he put the book down, the doorbell rang. He heard his mother's steps in the hall and then heard her clear, confident voice call up the stairs.

'There's a man here with a package for you, darling!'

With a sense of foreboding he could not quite explain, Robert tiptoed out on to the landing. A small man in a motor-cyclist's helmet was waiting at the door, holding a large brown-paper parcel. The fact that he looked as if he came from the Middle East did not disturb Robert particularly. But he found, as the messenger came into the hall, that he was checking the state of the man's footwear carefully, and was absurdly relieved to discover that he was wearing the same kind of shoe on both feet.

4

'Robert's thinking of becoming a Muslim,' said Maisie, brightly, over the dinner table.

After a brief, horror-struck pause, his father said, 'That's terrific!'

'Yes,' said his mother with alarming speed, 'it is terrific! It's great! It's wonderful!'

'Yes,' said Maisie, 'isn't it?'

Robert's mother helped herself to cassoulet.

'What are you going to call yourself?'

'Ahmed,' said Robert.

'Are you allowed cassoulet?'

'I'm not sure,' said Robert – 'I'll have to check.'

He heaped two pork sausages on to his plate and added some beans, a hunk of bacon and three or four stewed tomatoes. His father was splashing wine into Maisie's glass. '*If I ever had a daughter,*' Mr Wilson used to say, '*I'd like her to be like Maisie!*' Badger approached the head of the Wilson family and gave him a deep and soulful look. Mr Wilson gave him a carrot.

Next to Robert on the table was a package. On the outside he read, in clear, firm capitals:

FROM THE ISLAMIC BOYS'
DAY INDEPENDENT WIMBLEDON SCHOOL.

Underneath this were a few Arabic letters and under them, in quotation marks, the words, LET US WORK TOGETHER. In the top right-hand corner of the parcel was a large, printed message, warning people that it contained valuable documents. Someone had sellotaped the package together and someone else had torn off the Selloptape. Inside were a few sheets of paper.

As his mother and father heaped cassoulet on to their plates, Robert took out the first sheet. This was headed simply:

BROCHURE

Under this he read:

> Muslim values and Muslim tradition are everywhere in ferment. We read in many newspapers of the need for Muslim schools, but we have to ask *What kind of Muslim schools? Are they to be a narrow, sectarian enterprise that only succeeds in alienating an already alienated Muslim population from a country where, like any immigrant community, it wishes only to belong?*

Next to this, in capitals that could only be Mr Malik's, he read:

I.E. NO LOONIES NEED APPLY

Robert read on as Maisie forked food into her face. Robert's father was asking her whether her father was any better. Maisie was telling him, in a cheerful, brightly inflected voice, that Mr Pierrepoint was not expected to live beyond October or November. 'We rather hoped he'd be around for Christmas,' she was saying, 'but it looks as if not, I fear. Although that may be for the best. He *loathes* Christmas.'

Robert spilt a small amount of gravy over Mr Malik's next paragraph.

> The Independent Boys' Day School (Wimbledon Islamic) will provide a fully comprehensive education in the background of a supportive and caring Muslim environment. Although the medium of instruction will be English, and skills for dealing with the UK will be taught (we all are aware, I feel sure, of the 'Old Boy' network) we orientate our classes around a fully comprehensive awareness of the need to achieve in UK terms and yet maintain a wholly authentic, if modern, Islamic identity.

Next to this, Malik had written:

I.E. GET THE LITTLE BASTARDS SIX 'A' LEVELS
AND A PLACE AT OXFORD AND CAMBRIDGE.

Robert's mother was telling Maisie that it was wonderful that she had such a sense of purpose in life. Sotheby's, she was saying, must be a wonderful place to be. 'You are surrounded, my dear,' she went on, 'by beautiful things!' She looked, mournfully, at the men in her family as she said this. 'Some young people,' she continued, looking at Robert, 'just seem to *drift*.' Robert kept his eyes on the brochure. Badger sidled up to him and placed his long head on Robert's left knee. Robert gave him a bean.

English literature and the classics will be taught by Dr Robert Wilson of the University of Oxford, a 'Varsity' man who is also a practising Muslim and has adopted the name of Yusuf Khan.

Next to this Malik had written:

HOW DOES THE NAME GRAB YOU? I THINK
IT HITS THE RIGHT TONE BUT WE CAN
CHANGE IT IF YOU PREFER.

Alongside him will be 'Rafiq' Ali Shah of the University of Birmingham, who will teach macroeconomics, engineering and practical artwork, and a fully qualified, all-male teaching core of experienced Muslims.

Robert's father was peering over his shoulder. Robert adopted a Quasimodo-like stance, hugging his plate to his chest as he turned over the page.

Lightly glued to a thick sheet of cream woven paper were several black-and-white photographs, clearly lifted from the pages of magazines. There were pictures of classrooms and laboratories, and one of a large, well-equipped gymnasium. A tall Indian-looking boy was balancing on his hands, watched by a group of rather suspicious-looking men in white coats. A caption underneath read ST EDWARD'S SCHOOL, BOMBAY. At the bottom of the page was a photograph of an Olympic-size swimming-pool. Malik's text read as follows:

Classrooms and laboratories offer the student the chance to grow and learn, in a pleasant and relaxed environment, while our swimming-pool will enable those who wish to 'swim' to do so whenever they feel the need. But we will also be mindful of the need of boys to fulfil the five obligations placed on Muslims, including, of course, the daily prayers, which will be an integral part of school life. The school's own mosque – built with funds supplied by the National Bank of Kuwait – will supply this!

Robert turned over the page. He found he was looking at what looked like a full-colour reproduction of the Taj Mahal. Next to it, Malik had written:

ACTUAL LIFE-SIZE OF PREMISES. SERIOUSLY
THOUGH, BASIC FUNDING IS IN PLACE BUT
ALL IDEAS WELCOME.

Underneath the photograph he had proposed the following text:

Financial backing for the school has been made available by Mr Shah, a leading figure in the Wimbledon Dharjee community. Mr Shah is a prominent local businessman whose interests include the 'Sunnytime' newsagent's and confectioner's and a tandoori restaurant in Raynes Park.

There were no other photographs on this page. Instead there was a raggedly typed series of paragraphs, headed:

STAFF BIOGRAPHIES
MALIK, J. (BA OXON, FIRST-CLASS HONOURS IN FRENCH, ENGLISH AND MATHEMATICS)

Mr Malik's family are from Pakistan but he was brought up and educated in the UK at Eton and Oxford, where he founded his successful company CORPORATE PRODUCTS LTD, now trading as RECESSION BUSTERS. He is a member of the Diners Club.

There was a space underneath this next to which the headmaster had written DASHING PHOTO OF SELF HERE! Underneath this was the photo of himself that Robert had enclosed with his application. It made him look more than usually like a tapir.

YUSUF KHAN ('ROBERT WILSON', MA OXON, FIRST CLASS IN
CLASSICAL LANGUAGES. RUGBY FOOTBALL AND CRICKET BLUE)

Yusuf went to Cranborne School, Wimbledon, and is a recent
convert to Islam. He is twenty-four years old, a fine games
player and a dedicated teacher of the young! He wrote to us,
asking to be included in our venture as follows –

With a thrill of horror, Robert recognized a (slightly doctored) paragraph from his letter of application:

I am a practising Muslim, based in Wimbledon, who is keen to develop
my interpersonal skills in relation to other Muslims. I have taught at
several non-Muslim schools and am keen to work with others of my
faith in a supportive and fully Islamic environment! Wilson is six feet
two inches, fond of opera and married with six children.

Next to this Malik had written:

I HOPE YOU LIKE THE OPERA IDEA. AND ONE OF US HAS TO BE
MARRIED. IT MIGHT AS WELL BE YOU! I WANT TO DO A MAILSHOT
OF ALL PARENTS WITH ISLAMIC NAMES WHOSE CHILDREN FAILED
TO GET IN TO CRANBORNE SCHOOL. URGENT WE TALK RE THIS.
POSS CHANGE NAME OF SCHOOL? LOSE REFERENCE TO ISLAM? I
AM ANXIOUS FOR A BROAD BASE, WILSON. YOUR VIEWS, PLEASE,
SOONEST!

The final staff biography read:

'RAFIQ' ALI SHAH (MSC BIRM UNIV.)

'Rafiq' is a close personal friend of Mr Malik and has been
closely involved in the Foundation Trust for the Islamic Boys'
Wimbledon Independent School. He is a talented and modern-
thinking scientist, with a great flair for doing and making practical things, from furniture to jewellery! He will be taking the
boys in all aspects of crafts and sciences. 'Rafiq' also hails from
the Wimbledon Dharjees, a group distantly related to the Nizari
Ismailis, whose full history is available in a pamphlet written by

Mr Shah, our patron, entitled FROM BAGHDAD TO WIMBLEDON. A BRIEF HISTORY OF THE WIMBLEDON DHARJEES!

Mr Malik had not been sure about this last sentence. He had crossed it out and, next to it, written:

'BRIEF' IS SOMETHING OF AN UNDERSTATEMENT. THE BOOK IS TWO THOUSAND PAGES LONG AND NOT RECOMMENDED TO ANYONE OUT OF SOLITARY CONFINEMENT. REMIND ME TO 'CLUE YOU IN' ON THE WIMBLEDON DHARJEES!

Next to Rafiq's name he had written:

POSS NOT MENTION RAFIQ'S BACKGROUND HERE. CERTAINLY NO PICTURE OF THE UGLY BASTARD. WE DO NOT WANT LOONIES!

No, thought Robert grimly, they certainly did not want any more loonies. His mother had always told him that he had no grip on reality. He wondered what she would have to say about Mr Malik.

Someone had clearly opened the package after Mr Malik had finished with it. It wasn't just the broken seal that told him that: there were grimy fingermarks across the photographs that could not possibly belong to neat, well-perfumed Mr Malik. Could this be something to do with the two men in the Frog and Ferret? They certainly had an unhealthy interest in and knowledge of Robert's involvement with the school, and they looked like men who would have few qualms about intercepting people's mail.

'Won't you get involved in fatwas and things?' Robert's mother was saying. 'They can get awfully steamed up can Muslims, can't they?'

Robert found he had started to sweat. He rearranged his face, rather primly, and said, 'People in the West are very ignorant about Islam.'

He certainly knew nothing about it whatsoever. Everyone at the table, he realized, was looking at him. People always seemed to want him to speak, and he tried to oblige in his usual manner – by saying the first thing that came into his head.

'It isn't just about going down to the mosque,' he went on, in a stern, authoritarian voice.

'What *is* it about?' said Maisie, her eyes shining.

People certainly sat up and listened when you told them you were a Muslim. It was a talking-point.

'Well,' said Robert weightily, 'as far as I can make out – and it's early days yet – it's about . . .'

What *was* it about? His father was looking at him in that eager, doggy way in which he looked for exam results, sports results, girl results and all the other results Robert had not, so far, been able to deliver.

'It's about . . .' he began again.

Perhaps if he waited long enough he would receive some kind of divine guidance on this essential point. It did not, however, seem to be forthcoming.

'It's about the fact that Allah is . . .' he groped for the right word – 'very important. He is absolutely crucial. He is a . . . well . . . er . . . God!'

His father nodded, keenly, anxious not to interrupt his son's flow. 'I think,' he said, 'that Al-Lah is the Arabic word for "God"!'

'Is that right?' said Robert, trying not to sound too surprised by this fact. 'Well, of course, I am rather new to it. You probably know as much as me. More, probably!'

Mr Wilson shook his head and gave a slightly superior smile. 'Muslim . . . Christian . . .' he said. 'What's the difference basically?'

This seemed to have brought them full circle. As Robert was not able to enlighten anyone on this point, he contented himself with a kind of shrug.

Mr Wilson, who was showing worrying signs of being well-informed about the Islamic world, went on, 'The thing Muslims are very hot on is the Koran. They look at it morning, noon and night. They can't get enough of it. It is to them the *crucial* book!'

Robert's mother clearly felt her son was being upstaged. She cleared her throat delicately, smoothed her greying hair, and looked at Robert, as she often did, as if he was a nervous dinner guest whom she was determined to encourage.

'What's the Koran *like*?' said his mother. 'And how did you get involved with it? Did someone give you a copy on a station or something? A sort of missionary? Or was it someone at the door?'

Robert paused. Then he said, 'I just . . . er . . . picked it up,' he said – 'in a bookshop. And found it . . . you know . . . unputdownable!'

He didn't think they looked ready to be told about the school. His mother was gulping air, rather fast, and patting down the back of her hair – something she did only when seriously concerned. And his father's attempt at bluff, common-man-style interest in his son's conversion could not conceal the rising panic in his eyes.

'You should read it,' said Robert.

He, too, should get around to reading it – preferably in the fairly near future.

'They chant it,' Mr Wilson senior was saying, 'from the top of those high buildings they have. Will you be doing that? Do they have any of them in Wimbledon?'

'Any what?' said Robert's mother, with a little sniff of disapproval as she rose from the table and started to clear away the plates.

'Any of the tall things Muslims shout from in the mornings,' said Mr Wilson. 'I doubt they have any of them in Wimbledon.'

'There are *masses* of Muslims in Wimbledon,' said Robert's mother, 'but I've never seen them shouting from high buildings. At any time of the day. There were hundreds of them at Cranborne, and they were all very well-behaved.'

She looked, darkly, at Robert. 'They did very well in exams,' she said, as she stacked the plates on the sideboard. Then she turned to the group at the table, and, putting a hand, rather theatrically, to her close-cropped hair, said, 'Shall we have coffee on the *terrasse* and look at the garden?'

She was always saying things like this. She was never happier than when moving guests around her house in the interests of gentility. No sooner had you got comfortable than she was urging you to take *digestifs* in the conservatory, or *biscuits* on the lawn, or *gâteaux* on the roof. She pirouetted, briefly, in the middle of the wooden floor and waved a hand towards the upper part of the house. '*En route, mes braves!*' she said.

Mrs Wilson would have been happier in Versailles than in Wimbledon Park Road. But she was making the best of it.

'Ça sera superbe, chérie!' said Mr Wilson, rising bravely to the challenge of her French. 'That was absolutely *delicious*!'

Her food was always delicious. Her judgements always sound. Her dress sense always impeccable.

How did people manage to be happily married? thought Robert, as they trooped up the stairs. What was the trick of it? A dedicated cultivation of a certain kind of insensitivity, presumably. Years and years and years of managing not to notice things that might annoy you.

The Wilsons' *terrasse* was a wrought-iron balcony, jutting out from the back of their corner house. It afforded a view not only of the garden but also of a large group of communal dustbins belonging to the flats that overlooked their house. It also, as Robert's father was fond of saying, offered an unlimited chance to enjoy the advantages of a burnt-out car, a large concrete shed with the words CHELSEA WANKERS written on it and the street that led away from all this, up the hill to a part of Wimbledon the Wilsons had never been able to afford. Not that it had stopped them dreaming – Mr Wilson had expected promotion right up until the moment he had been made redundant.

They had only just sat down when a car screeched round the corner, climbed on to the pavement, and stopped a matter of inches from a neighbour's garden wall. It was a silver Mercedes, about the size of a small swimming-pool, but its bodywork was badly rusted, and the engine sounded as if it was trying to absorb a few kilos of iron filings. It roared ambitiously, then died. The driver's door opened to reveal the headmaster of the Wimbledon Islamic Independent Day School (Boys).

He looked anxious. He almost ran towards the Wilsons' house, then stopped, with a theatrical flourish, just short of it and, shading his eyes with his hand, looked up at the balcony.

'Wilson!' he said, in deep, urgent tones. 'Wilson! You must come! You must come now, Wilson! Urgent school business! Wilson!'

Robert found he was getting to his feet. Maisie, for some reason, was doing the same. She moved to the iron railing at the edge of the balcony and peered down at Mr Malik like a keen student of aquatic life who has just spotted a new species of tropical fish.

'Bring your wife, Wilson,' said Mr Malik, 'and also your children if necessary. But come! I beseech you! I beg and implore you! Come!'

Mr Malik was stretching out his arms. He looked like a man about to fish out a small guitar and continue this conversation to musical accompaniment.

Robert's father and mother were both, in different ways, narrowing the distance between chin and neck, a gesture that, like tortoises, they often used when threatened. His father was making rapid, worried clicking noises at the back of his throat as he too rose and moved – in a racially tolerant manner – towards the edge of the balcony.

'Is he . . . one of . . . *them*?' whispered Mrs Wilson, with the kind of clarity actors affect when playing a deathbed scene to a large theatre.

Robert, as he made his way down to Mr Malik's car, followed by Maisie, did not attempt to answer the question. He would have described Mr Malik, to almost anyone, without being quite sure why he was doing so, as '*one of us*'.

5

Mr Malik beamed at Maisie, and rubbed his hands together briskly. 'You have a beautiful wife, Wilson!' he said.

'Oh, we're not married,' said Maisie, swiftly. 'I'm just a very, very old friend of his. Are you Robert's spiritual mentor? You see Robert needs help, because he's – '

Before she had the chance to say anything more about their sex life, Robert grabbed her arm and steered her towards the car.

'What's the problem, Headmaster?'

'We are going to collect a pupil!' said Malik.

This, Robert felt, was somewhat alarming news. It was, after all, the middle of August. He had assumed, from the deserted look of the school, that, like every other educational establishment in England, they were on holiday. Perhaps, he thought, as he and Maisie got into the back seat, the Islamic school year was different.

'We have to go to them if they won't come to us, Wilson,' said Mr Malik, who was watching Maisie with some interest. 'We have to get out there and pitch!'

Robert felt nervous. For some reason he did not like the idea of Mr Malik being so close to his territory. And he liked even less the fact that his employer seemed prepared to adopt Maisie. He found himself wondering where the headmaster might live. Did he, perhaps, live above the school? He gave the impression of a man who had simply appeared in the middle of Wimbledon, like a djinn in a fairy story.

'Who is he?' hissed Maisie. 'Is he a mullah?'

'I don't think so,' whispered Robert, in reply – 'or if he is he keeps very quiet about it!'

It was also, thought Robert, a bit late in the day to be starting

lessons. Perhaps the Islamic Wimbledon Boys' Day Independent
School was going to be working a night shift.

Maisie turned to Robert. 'I think he's *sweet*!' she shrieked quietly.

Malik ignored the remark, but put one large, well-manicured hand
up to his hair. The back of his tropical suit, Robert noted, was powdered with dandruff.

'Are we going to pick all the children up ourselves,' said Robert,
'or will some of them get to school by public transport?'

'A school,' said the headmaster, giving him a curious glance, 'can
develop in various ways. The majority of the boys will obviously
arrive under their own steam – although, Wilson, I have to say that at
this particular point in time we do not have any boys!'

He gave a rather mad laugh as they drove, at some speed, up
Wimbledon Park Road towards the Village. To their right was the All
England Lawn Tennis and Croquet Club. As they passed its steel
gates Robert felt the usual surprise that such a monument should be
there at all. Although its windows caught the sun, and behind the
barbed-wire-crested wall you could see the military green of its oval
stands, it had the air of some sinister scientific research establishment – a place designed for something darker than tennis.

'Although the school is not fully operational,' said Mr Malik, 'we
will collect this boy now.'

He turned round and looked Maisie full in the face, as he acceler-
ated towards an oncoming lorry.

'His parents wish us to "hang on" to him until we are ready to go.
He has fallen under harmful influences and needs the support of a
typically stable "UK" background. He can stay with you, Wilson!'

This seemed a slightly unusual way of proceeding. Robert had
never heard of a school in which pupils were acquired on a door-to-
door basis. But, of course, education, like so much else these days,
was a business.

'He is a very intelligent boy,' said the headmaster, as if in answer to
Robert's unvoiced doubts, 'which is why I want to get my hands
on him at double-quick speed. I think I am going to give him a
scholarship.'

'Oooh!' said Maisie, who seemed to have no problems adapting to the curious pace of life in the Boys' Wimbledon Independent Day Islamic School. 'What in?'

They had somehow survived the lorry. They were now headed, at about fifty miles an hour, for someone's front garden. Malik bashed the horn two or three times, took his hands off the wheel, and waved his arms expressively. He braked hard, and the car hit the kerb and bucked across the road like an angry horse.

'Oh,' he said, 'physics, Greek, Latin, French. That sort of thing. A general scholarship. He is a first-class boy.'

'How did you find him?' said Robert. 'Did you advertise?'

Malik laughed in an open, friendly manner. He rapped on the horn as if to emphasize his good humour.

'Precisely, Wilson!' he said. 'I advertised. I put an advert in *Exchange and Mart*!'

He seemed to find this thought very amusing. When he had reasserted control over the Mercedes, he said, in a suddenly sober voice, 'Actually, Wilson, that is not at all a bad idea.'

He paused, as if considering something.

'I must tell you something, my dear Wilson,' he went on, 'about the extraordinary history and traditions of our Wimbledon Dharjees. I am sure you have seen them about the place.'

'I'm afraid,' said Robert, 'I haven't.'

'They are a very fine bunch of chaps,' said Mr Malik thoughtfully – 'not unlike the Bombay Khojas. But of course based in Wimbledon as opposed to Bombay. They are distantly connected to the Nizari Ismailis, of whom I am sure you have heard.'

Robert tried to look as if he had heard of at least some of the people Malik had mentioned.

'But,' went on the headmaster, 'there are bad eggs amongst them, as there are everywhere. Strange secrets and stories from the dawn of the Islamic era!'

Robert nodded.

'That,' said Malik, 'is all you really need to know. Some of the Dharjees are first-class chaps and others are really awful ticks. I will tell you which ones are which.'

When they reached Wimbledon Village Malik drove north,

towards the large houses that face the Common. About half a mile further on, he turned right through a pair of huge iron gates. As they came in to the front drive, the gates closed, silently, behind them. Something made Robert look up at the window above the front door.

A young man was wagging his finger at an elderly woman in a white headscarf. He looked as if he was telling her off about something. She cowered away from him as if he was about to strike her.

'That's the bloody woman!' said Mr Malik. 'Been filling the boy's head with a lot of absolute rot!'

These were obviously Dharjees to be avoided. Assuming they were Dharjees and not Khojas or Ismailis. Whatever any of these things might be.

'Do you know the parents?' said Robert.

'Very well,' said Malik. 'They are professional acquaintances. We play golf together when we can get the chance.'

The front door of the house opened and two men in dark-grey suits came out. One of them looked more like a well-tanned version of the Duke of Edinburgh than a man from the Indian subcontinent; in profile, Robert decided, he would look well on a postage stamp. He half expected him to call for polo ponies. His companion was a small, round, jolly-looking character. The taller of the two called, in aristocratic English tones, 'My dear Malik! This is so kind!'

They walked towards him, in almost perfect step.

'This is *frightfully* good of you, Malik,' went on the tall man, 'and I am so sorry to bother you with our troubles!'

'There are lunatics, my dear Shah,' said Malik darkly, 'everywhere.'

'My dear, there are,' said the tall man. 'And the sooner we can get the boy lodged away from our people the sooner it will die down.'

He beamed at Robert. 'We are delighted to have an Oxford man on board,' he said. 'You must have been up at the same time as the Crown Prince of Dhaypur!'

'I think I remember him,' said Robert cautiously. He was aware that this must be Mr Shah, the school's principal backer. It was important to make a good impression.

'We always called him "Lunchtime Porker"!' said Mr Shah.

Mr Malik laughed, and it seemed wise to do the same.

'There were quite a lot of us Muslims up at Oxford,' said Robert, 'and we all used to hang out together. Go to the same clubs and . . . er . . . listen to the same sort of music.'

They were looking at him oddly. Why had he opened his mouth?

The tall man's demeanour would not have been out of place at Greyfriars Public School. There was a peculiarly English reserve about it. But Mr Shah's friend was obviously more in touch with his emotions. In the manner of a man who had been waiting to do this for some time, he suddenly seized the headmaster, lifted him clear of the ground, and rocked him backwards and forwards. Robert could see Malik's neatly shod feet pedalling wildly as his new friend hoisted him up higher and higher. Perhaps he was going to put him over his shoulder and burp him.

'Wilson,' said the headmaster, 'this is Mr Shah, our benefactor, and another member of the Wimbledon Dharjee community, Mr Khan. Mr Khan is here on business.'

The second man put the headmaster down and grinned. 'I am a vastly inferior variety of Dharjee,' he said, 'and I am honoured to meet you, Wilson! Mr Shah, I fear, will have nothing to do with my proposals! You are welcome at my restaurant at any time of the day or night. Except on Wednesdays.' Mr Shah was looking vaguely discomforted. Mr Khan, right arm forward, marched towards Robert.

To Robert's relief, the man did not look as if he was about to give him anything less formal than a handshake.

'Should I cover my head with something?' hissed Maisie.

'Why?' said Robert. 'I think you look very nice.'

Maisie looked impatient. 'I'm a woman,' she said, 'and I've got bare arms and a bare head!'

She said this as if trying to excite him in some way. Before he had the chance to find out any more about this, she had backed away towards the car, opened the back door, and started to grovel around on the seat.

If she was looking for something to cover her head, she was out of luck. As far as Robert could remember, all there was on the back seat was a damp chamois leather. The thought of Maisie appearing with this perched on her head made him twitch uncontrollably.

Neither Malik nor Mr Shah nor Mr Khan seemed very bothered about this. Mr Khan, the restaurant-owner, seemed to have decided that a handshake wasn't enough. He was clearly anxious to get stuck into Robert in a more serious way.

'Oh, Wilson, my dear chap!' he was saying, in a tone of voice that made Robert feel like a jelly at a children's tea party – 'Oh, Wilson, Wilson, Wilson! You will be friends with a poor restaurateur, won't you?'

He leaped into Robert's arms and got to work on his hindquarters, watched with some embarrassment by the Duke of Edinburgh look-alike.

'Are you . . . er . . . Dharjees?' said Robert through a mouthful of Mr Khan's jacket. Both men laughed uproariously at this. Robert made a mental note to find out more about this particular Islamic sect. It was hard to connect the two men in the pub with these two rather jolly creatures.

'Where is my teacher?' came a small voice down to Robert's left.

Robert looked down and saw a boy of about ten years old. He had neatly brushed black hair, a dark-blue jersey and baggy grey shorts of the kind worn by boys at an English public school. He was stand-ing very straight and very still.

There was something strikingly familiar about him. Robert felt sure he had seen him somewhere before. That, surely, wasn't possi-ble. He knew very few adults and hardly any children. Had he, perhaps, seen this boy on television? Perhaps he was a prince of some kind. What had Malik said: 'fallen under harmful influences'?

'Hello there!' said Robert, in a jolly, yet formal, voice. He was trying to sound like a schoolmaster (on his application he had claimed four years' service at a fictional prep school called The Grove) but he had not yet managed to acquire the manner. He sounded, he thought, like a paedophile. To make things worse, he discovered he had put his hand on the boy's shoulder.

'Are we going to have all Dharjees, or will there be any normal Muslims?' he asked, to fill the awkward silence.

Mr Malik and Mr Shah gave him tolerant, slightly weary, smiles.

'Normal Muslims!' said the school's benefactor, in an amused tone. 'I think we are *fairly* normal Muslims, don't you, Malik? I think it is you that is the "weirdo"!'

'Wilson,' said his headmaster, 'is a comparatively recent recruit.'

Mr Shah nodded in a kindly manner. 'What made you convert to Islam?' he said, in the studied, neutral tones of someone asking someone else about their children.

'Er . . .' Robert looked wildly about him. 'I was desperate!' he said eventually.

Mr Shah took his hand. 'These are desperate times, Wilson,' he said – 'desperate, desperate times. A spirit walks the land, and it is an ugly, intolerant spirit, and many of us are frightened – frightened unto death!'

'I am desperate,' said Robert, looking over towards the Common. (Had he seen a glimpse of one of the men in the pub, there, among the birch-trees about a hundred yards away from them?) 'I am absolutely desperate. I am thinking of going to Mecca.'

All three men nodded slowly. They seemed sympathetic to the idea. Robert tried to remember where Mecca was. He was going to have to bone up on this kind of fact if he was going to be able to hold his own in this section of the Wimbledon beau monde.

'We are talking fifty a week for the boy,' said the restaurant-owner. 'He eats anything apart from cheese.'

Robert nodded and tried not to look confused. He had not thought that the school fees would be so reasonable. Perhaps there was a special offer on. Perhaps they were going to wait for the school to become fashionable and then treble the prices. Anything was possible at the Independent Islamic Wimbledon Boys' Day School.

'He is called Hasan,' said Mr Shah, 'after a great ruler of the Ismailis!'

He knelt to the little boy's level and put his hands on the lad's shoulders. He patted his face.

'Hasan I Sabah,' he said, 'and Hasan the Second. On his name be peace!'

Then he embraced the child. 'You are Hasan of our house!' he said, in a low, gentle voice. 'Go with Wilson.'

Robert looked down at the little boy. He was still standing absolutely still. His thin shoulders, his delicate wrists and his finely drawn neck gave him a lost air. Something about him made Robert's heart lurch. The boy turned his head, and Robert caught sight of a huge strawberry mark on his right cheek. Now he remembered where he had seen him before. The hair, the features, even the slightly desperate, pleading stance of the shoulders, were those of the boy in the photograph in the locket that he had given to Maisie only that afternoon.

It wasn't only this, though, that chilled him suddenly, made him feel, for reasons he could not have explained, unaccountably nervous. The little boy was oblivious to the sun, and the blue sky, and the terraces of thick, green leaves on the chestnuts that faced the house. He was not wearing glasses, as he had been doing in the photograph, and now Robert was able to see that his big, pale pupils were jammed uselessly in the porcelain of his eyes, staring endlessly at nothing.

6

Perhaps, thought Robert, as they climbed back into the car with Hasan, he had simply failed to notice an adjective in Malik's prospectus. Perhaps he was going to work in the Wimbledon Independent *Blind* Islamic Boys' Day School. Or – this seemed rather more likely – Malik was having to take what he could get. His manner to Mr Shah had been positively servile.

'Don't you want to wave goodbye to your dad?' Robert asked his new pupil.

'Mr Shah is not my "dad",' said the little boy, in a curiously precise voice. 'I am an orphan. I am brought up among his servants. I think I speak for his servants. For all the poor of the earth!'

The headmaster cut across them. 'My dear Hasan,' he said, with more edge than Robert had seen him use before, 'you have been listening to that nurse of yours!'

'I can't help listening to her, Mr Malik,' said Hasan, 'because she talks to me.'

The little boy sat, quite still, between Maisie and Robert. One frail hand rested on Maisie's knee. She seemed confused by him. She had not found anything to cover her head or her arms, but Mr Malik seemed to find this situation quite satisfactory. In fact, as he studied her in the driving-mirror, Robert could have sworn the headmaster was licking his lips.

Robert patted Hasan on the knee. He felt the need to say something reassuring.

'Well,' he said, with slightly forced cheerfulness, 'we are all in the hands of Allah!'

The little boy wrinkled up his face. Maybe the Dharjees were such a specialized variety of Muslim that they had not yet caught up with Allah. Someone would certainly need to tell him before he started at the Boys' Wimbledon Day Independent Islamic School. Or possibly, once again, Robert had slipped up on pronunciation.

'I presume,' he said cautiously, as they started down the hill, 'that the majority of the pupils will be . . . you know . . . your basic . . . Muslim.'

Mr Malik grinned. He seemed to find this line of approach immensely amusing. 'Who knows?' he said.

'Well,' said Robert, 'there can't be much demand for . . . er . . . Islamic games among non-Muslims!'

Malik grinned again. 'Who knows?' he said.

Here he winked at Maisie.

'They're very fatalistic,' she hissed. 'It may not be the will of Allah that you get any Muslim pupils. You may get coachloads of Unitarians or people who really wanted to get into the Royal College of Music. But you can't do anything about it. It's fate!'

Malik nodded vigorously. 'Your wife is right,' he said. 'What is willed is willed. We simply have to do our best. In fact, some Islamic theorists think it makes bugger all difference anyway.'

The car leaped round a corner, scraped a lamppost and bounced sideways down towards Robert's house. There was, thought Robert, a lot to be said for a religion that relieved you of all responsibility for your destiny. Especially when you were being driven by Mr Malik.

'I could eat a cake,' said Hasan, in a small, thoughtful voice, 'with jam on it.'

No one offered to respond to this remark.

Robert leaned forward across the passenger seat. 'Tell me, Headmaster,' he said. 'Those men in dark glasses in the pub – '

Malik did not seem keen on this line of conversation. 'My dear Wilson,' he said, 'don't even think about them. If they come up to you in the street, cut them dead. They are NOSP, if you take my meaning. Not Our Sort of People!'

He caught Maisie's eye in the driving-mirror and gave her a broad wink. 'My dear girl,' he said, before Robert could finish his sentence, 'are you also of the Muslim faith?'

'It seems,' said Maisie breathlessly, 'a very attractive option.'

Malik grinned. 'It is,' he said. 'It is an attractive option. It is, I would say, very *user-friendly*!'

Maisie nodded. 'Yes,' she said. 'It has a rugged, masculine feel to it!'

Malik's hand went up to his neatly combed hair. He patted it into place with a small smile. 'It is not,' he said, 'a religion for softies!'

'I'm amazed Bobkins sort of embraced it,' said Maisie, 'because you see he is a practising – '

'Catholic!' said Robert. 'I mean I *was* a practising Catholic!'

'Catholics, Buddhists, Muslims – you Wilsons have got the lot, I would say, my dear boy,' said the headmaster as he jammed on the brakes and the Mercedes jerked to a halt outside Robert's house.

Hasan jumped off the back seat like a puppet on a string. He made a small, whooping noise. As far as Robert could tell he had enjoyed the experience.

Malik leaned his arm across the passenger seat and looked into the back with intense frankness. 'I want you to look after Hasan, Wilson,' he said, 'because Hasan is a very, very important little boy. I do not want you to let him out of your sight. Do you understand?'

Robert gulped. 'He will be staying with . . . er . . . me?' he heard himself say.

'That is correct, Wilson,' said the headmaster. 'There are people who are trying to . . . get to him, if you take my meaning.'

Perhaps, thought Robert, other schools were trying to snaffle him. Scholarship boys were obviously a valuable commodity. The boy quietly sat between Robert and Maisie. He was not very large. They could put him in the back kitchen with the dog.

'Right, Headmaster,' said Robert.

'And,' said Malik, 'even when you are in the house, watch him carefully.'

Robert looked apprehensively at Hasan. Was he, perhaps, liable to violent fits of temper? Could he have a serious incontinence problem?

'Look,' said the headmaster, 'I am sure I am worrying about nothing. I've simply seen something I probably did not see. But, for the first few days anyway . . . keep him away from windows.'

'On religious grounds?' said Robert. Perhaps Dharjees were against windows.

'Absolutely,' said Malik. 'Absolutely. On religious grounds. And if anyone comes asking for him at the door, or comes up to you in the street and expresses an interest, you haven't seen him. Right?'

'Right!' said Robert.

'Especially,' went on the headmaster, 'those gentlemen in the pub.'

'With the peculiar shoes,' said Robert.

Mr Malik wrinkled his brows and gave Robert one of those swift, shrewd glances that hinted at a complex, subtle person behind the actor's manner. 'You noticed that, did you?' he said. 'There is probably no significance in it. After all, my friend, we are the other side of August the eighth!' And with this inexplicable remark Mr Malik leaped from the car, opened their door, and, like a chauffeur, bowed them out on to the street.

Robert trudged up the steps to the front door, after Maisie and Hasan. Mr Malik got back into the car. Robert turned back towards him but, before he had a chance to say anything, the headmaster had driven off towards Southfields.

There was quite a lot that Robert wanted to ask. Had they acquired this pupil by entirely legal means? Where were the other pupils going to come from? What was so dodgy about August the eighth? And what was the problem with windows as far as Muslims were concerned? Were they, perhaps, unclean?

Robert added one more biggie to that list as he turned back to Maisie and the little boy. How was he going to explain away the arrival of a ten-year-old blind Muslim boy in his parents' house? Not to mention the fact that Hasan seemed to be looking for house-guest status for an unspecified period of time. Mr and Mrs Wilson were almost irritatingly tolerant people. They had been kind when Robert had failed all of his GCEs apart from woodwork. They had not minded when he failed to pass his driving-test or, indeed, when he failed to show any aptitude for anything apart from walking round Wimbledon Common with Badger. But on this occasion he might well have gone too far.

'Isn't he *sweet*?' said Maisie.

'Will you give me some tea?' said the little boy. 'And a cake with jam on it?'

Robert looked down at his new charge and felt as if he was falling through space.

The boy took his hand and pressed it to his face. 'You are a kind man,' said Hasan. 'I can hear it in your voice. I can tell a great deal from people's voices.'

'What can you tell from mine?' said Maisie.

The little boy paused. 'You are a very wise woman,' he said. 'You are very strong and clever and brave.'

Clearly Hasan's voice test was not an infallible guide to a stranger's personality. Or maybe he just said this to all the girls. But there was something impressive about him. He could have been very clever, or very well born, or very, very lucky. Or, possibly, simply *look* as if he might have been any of these things. But there was something about him . . .

As usual, Robert had forgotten his key, and, as usual in the Wilson house, no one was answering the door. Somewhere deep inside the family home, Robert heard his father shout, 'I'm on the lavatory!'

'*I'm* on the lavatory!' came his mother's voice, making its normal, easy transition from gentility to an almost bestial directness of approach. 'They'll have to wait!'

'It might be someone interesting!' yelled his father.

Whatever he was doing in the lavatory didn't sound very demanding.

'Surely you've finished by now!' yelled his mother. Over the years, the two men in the Wilson family had made so many inroads into her natural delicacy that now, at nearly fifty, she would sometimes seem to parody maleness, to flaunt it at its possessors, in an attempt at that last, desperate act of criticism – sarcasm.

'Get your arse on down there,' she yelled – 'only make sure you wipe it first!'

Robert heard his father guffaw. They still had the capacity to amuse each other, even if they left him stone cold.

Before this conversation could become any more specific, Robert leaned on the bell, hard.

'I'm coming!' yelled his father. 'Hold your horses!'

Hasan, his head and shoulders still eerily still, was smiling in a benign manner at the letter-box. He continued to hold Robert's hand tightly. Robert tried to look natural, and failed.

'He's coming!' said Hasan, 'I hear him!'

There was a clumping sound from within the house. The door opened, and Robert found himself, once again, looking at his father. He took in the long, shaggy hair, the wire glasses, the beaky nose and the slightly anxious expression. Mr Wilson senior always looked as if he had just remembered that he had forgotten something. This was, indeed, quite often the case.

It was possible, he thought to himself, that his father would never work again. In which case he, Robert, would be the only earner in the household. He would have to try to do this new job in a thorough and conscientious manner. He would be a *good* teacher. He would be the inspiration of a whole new generation of British Muslims. He saw himself, sitting cross-legged in a stone courtyard, surrounded by eager little children from the Third World, dressed, like him, in long, white robes. Did Muslims sit cross-legged? Or was that the followers of the Maharishi Yogi or whatever his name was?

'Hello there!' said Mr Wilson to Hasan. 'And how are *you*?'

He was talking as if to an old friend – a manner he quite often affected with complete strangers. Behind him, Mrs Wilson had appeared. She was bobbing up and down beside his left shoulder, jabbing her finger towards Hasan.

'Who is *he*?'

This question was voiced silently, with a great deal of lip and teeth work. She could have been presenting a programme for deaf people. Robert did not answer her.

'Is he one of *them*?'

Robert nodded.

Mrs Wilson looked determinedly saucy. She clearly hoped that social life in Wimbledon Park was going to look up now that her only son had become a Muslim. *Let them all come*, her expression seemed to say. *Baggy trousers, prayer-mats – wheel 'em in!* She pranced out of the front door. 'Welcome to our house,' she said to Hasan, in the low, solemn voice she used in the Wimbledon Players. 'Welcome! And peace be on you and on your house!' She bowed low as she said this, and walked backwards into the hall.

Behind the kitchen door, Badger was making small, high-pitched noises from the back of his throat.

Robert took one last, despairing look back at the street as he followed his mother inside. There was a man standing in the shadow of one of the plane-trees opposite. He was wearing a shabby-looking leather jacket, jeans and a check shirt. Although he was of Middle Eastern appearance, at first Robert took him for a punk, because his jacket was ripped at the back. It looked as if it had been torn in the interests of fashion. And, although it was hard to judge at this distance, there was definitely something suspicious about the man's shoes.

Mrs Wilson did not seem unduly alarmed at the prospect of having acquired a paying guest. As they went into the front room, she announced her intention of giving Hasan her husband's office upstairs. 'You never do anything in it anyway,' she said in a cheerful voice, 'and at least he won't notice the wallpaper. It's amazing the way he gets about, isn't it? For a blind person, he's very quick on his feet!'

She made no attempt to modify her voice. Perhaps she had decided that Hasan was deaf as well as blind.

'Where's he from?' said Robert's father, clearly feeling, like his wife, that the little boy was not up to responding to direct questions.

'Bangladesh,' said Robert, aware that his parents liked definite answers.

Hasan walked into the sofa, fell on to it, and curled up like a cat. He smiled to himself. He seemed pleased to be in the Wilson house. 'The time of my Occultation is not yet come!' he said.

Robert thought this was probably good news. He thought of asking the little boy when he thought his Occultation might be. They might need to get in special clothing, or warn the neighbours.

Hasan, as if sensing Robert's curiosity said, 'I must not speak of these things. It is forbidden to speak of them!'

Maisie, standing over by the bookcase, next to Mr Wilson senior's collection of country-and-western records, wore a solemn, almost religious, expression. 'They're very strict are Muslims,' she said, in the kind of voice that suggested she wouldn't mind them being a bit strict with her. She cast her eyes down to the floor. 'Especially towards women!' she added.

Robert looked at her and at Hasan. It was obvious that the Independent Boys' Day Islamic School Wimbledon was going to change his life in more ways than he could anticipate.

He went over to the window and looked out at the street. The man in the ripped jacket was still there, although he was no longer watching the house. Now he was able to take a good long look at him, Robert could see that there was something strange about his shoes. One of them was a normal black leather boot. The other was a slipper-like creation of vaguely Eastern design. As he stood there, looking up the street, the man lifted it from the pavement and rubbed it against his leg, as if his foot was infected with some curious itch. Then he looked back at the Wilson house and stared, insolently, in at the blank suburban windows.

PART TWO

7

There had been difficulties with local planning officials. There had been opposition from local residents. Herbert Henry, the taxi-driver, had told customers in the Frog and Ferret that its effect on house prices would be catastrophic. 'Would you like to live next door to a Muslim school,' he said, 'considering what they get up to?' When asked *what* they got up to, he had muttered darkly that he knew a thing or two about Muslims and ordered drinks all round. His son Alf, the skinhead, had said that he would personally strangle any Muslim he found messing with his wife, adding that if Tehran was such a great place why didn't the bastards go back there?

Henry Farr, the solicitor from Maple Drive, who could be *so* funny when he chose, had said, in his comic colonel voice, that 'Johnny Muslim can be quite a tricky customer!'

But, somehow or other, Mr Malik's school was in business. He opened, five weeks behind schedule, in mid-October. It had been, as the headmaster pointed out to Robert, a desperate scramble to get any of the punters in at all. A mole working inside Cranborne School had supplied them with a mailing-list of all Muslim parents whose children had been rejected by 'This is a Christian Country' Gyles, the Junior School headmaster, and Robert and Maisie had been through the telephone directory, picking out anyone with a Muslim-sounding name. Apart from a few Sikhs and a very irritable Hindu from East Sheen, most of the targeted persons seemed quite pleased to be asked.

Teachers had been more difficult. 'There are not many people in Wimbledon who have your qualifications,' Mr Malik had said to Robert in the pub. This was not surprising. Since his appointment, Robert had awarded himself a degree from Yale, an honorary doctorate from Edinburgh University, two novels and a successful season with the Chicago Bears football team.

They had interviewed a man from Bombay who claimed to have a degree in physics but turned out to be a defrocked dentist, and they had nearly offered a job to a man from Sri Lanka who seemed to know everything about the school apart from the fact that it was supposed to be for Muslims. He turned out to have escaped from an open prison in Dorking. Finally they had hired an almost completely monosyllabic man from the University of West Cameroun called Dr Ahmed Ali. All he had said at the interview, apart from 'I completely agree with you' and 'You are absolutely right, Headmaster!' was 'Let's get this show on the road!'

'He's a dry stick, Wilson,' said Mr Malik, 'but he is 100 per cent loyal. And I am looking for 100 per cent loyalty. Everything else can go hang!'

Dr Ali was to teach maths, chemistry, philosophy, geography and world events. He was, presumably, at this very moment, teaching one or some or all of these things in the large, airy classroom he occupied next to Robert's. As usual, no sound whatsoever came from his room.

Robert was not teaching. He was in the state – now, after two months of the autumn term, agonizingly familiar to him – of being about to teach. *At any moment*, he told himself, *I will find myself up on my legs, waving my arms around in the air and giving.* His mother was always telling him that it was important for teachers to give, although what they were supposed to give she did not say. What did the little bastards want?

He sat at his desk and looked at his class. They looked back at him. 'Right,' he said, threateningly, 'I am going to call the register.'

Mahmud put up his hand. 'Please, sir,' he said, 'I want to go to the toilet.'

Robert sighed. 'Right,' he said, even more threateningly. 'Does anyone else want to go to the toilet?'

No one moved. Fifteen small faces, in various shades of brown, studied him impassively.

'*A Muslim should enter the lavatory with his left foot first, saying,*

"*Bismillah Allahumma Inni a'udhu Bika min al-Khubthi wa al-Khaba'ith*"
(*In the name of Allah, Allah in You I take refuge from all evils*).'

'I know what'll happen,' said Robert. 'Mahmud will go to the toilet
and then you'll all want to go. You'll all rush out after him, won't
you? I want you all to think very hard about whether you *really* want
to go to the toilet.'

The pupils of the reception class at the Independent Wimbledon
Day Islamic Boys' School did not enter the lavatory with their left
feet first. They ran at it, screaming, in large numbers. Like children
everywhere, they seemed to find lavatories hilarious.

Robert had read the chapter on lavatories in *Morals and Manners in
Islam* by Dr Marwan Ibrahim Al-Kaysi of the University of Yarmouk.
It was tough stuff, and here, as in so many departments, the Inde-
pendent Boys' Islamic Day Wimbledon School was falling short of
Dr Al-Kaysi's, admittedly high, standards.

Morals and Manners in Islam was the only book on the subject he
had been able to find in Wimbledon Public Library. Apart from Mr
Malik, it was Robert's only real guide to his assumed religion. But
was it right? Was Al-Kaysi on the money? He certainly seemed to
strike few chords with Class 1.

'If you really, *really* want to go,' Robert went on, 'then now is the
time. There will be no other chance for the rest of the lesson. From
now on in it's do-it-in-your-pants time.'

His class laughed. They liked him. And Robert, in some moods,
found the company of boys under ten both soothing and stimulating.

Sheikh, a small, pale boy of about seven, leaned forward in his
desk. 'Is this number ones and number twos, sir?' he said – 'or is
there any flexibility on that?'

Sheikh was going to do well. His father described himself as a
lawyer, although, like most of the parents and many of the staff
of the Wimbledon Islamic Independent School (Boys' Day), Robert
suspected he was not being entirely open about his status.

'We must all pull together in the various departments!' Mr Malik
had told Robert, Rafiq and Dr Ali at their first staff meeting. 'We are
going for maximum expansion. You are in on the ground floor of
something very, very exciting!'

It was true they had kitchens now. And once, through the open door of his classroom, Robert had seen Dr Ali using a Bunsen burner. But there was still an alarmingly improvisatory air about Mr Malik's school. Rafiq, for example, who had not changed out of the grubby overalls that he had been wearing on the day of Robert's interview, seemed to spend most of his time painting the walls of his classroom. And the headmaster had a disconcerting habit of offering jobs to people he met at dinner parties. A man called Harris had been offered a shadowy role as Exterior Liaison Officer, and Mr Malik was always talking of 'finding something' for Maisie.

Maisie, in her turn, was always hanging around the school. She had bought her own copy of the Koran and was to be seen reading it on her way to work in the morning. She was on page 124 and pronounced it 'riveting'.

It was two weeks away from Christmas. Outside, in the street, there were Christmas trees and coloured lights in the windows of the shops. People pushed along the pavements of Wimbledon Village, grey faces stung into crimson by the wind, and, on the Common, the last scraps of last year's leaves bowled crazily through the defeated grass. A winter's day in the 1990s.

Or, alternatively, a winter's day in the 1380s. That was the period according to the Islamic calendar. In here it was the 1380s.

Or was it? Robert had not quite mastered the Islamic calendar. But, since no one he had met in Wimbledon Islamic circles seemed to use it, it did not prevent him from holding his head up in the staffroom. It was something to do with the year of the Prophet's birth, or the year in which he had gone to or come from Mecca or Medina, but Robert could never remember which.

He really must get hold of another book. *The Bluffer's Guide to Islam* – that was the kind of thing he needed.

The class were looking at him. They were silent, rapt. They viewed Robert as an exotic form of entertainment. Mafouz, a tiny, pale, Egyptian boy, had said to him a week or so ago, 'Sir – I am not allowed television. But you are better than television!'

He must use this moment to demonstrate his familiarity with Islamic law. 'Now,' he said, pacing in front of the blackboard, 'if you do go to the toilet, and if you do a number two – '

The class laughed. Robert continued: ' – which hand do you use to wipe your behind?'

This, he thought, was pretty basic stuff. It was there, clearly set out in Dr Marwan Ibrahim Al-Kaysi's indispensable guide to how to get ahead in the Islamic world. And here they were, nearly twenty-odd children, gaping back at him as if he had just asked them to run through the periodic table.

'Sir,' said Sheikh, 'you don't use your hand. You use paper.'

This went down very well with Class 1. They rocked on their heels. Robert, mindful of Dr Al-Kaysi's injunction to Muslims on page 139 – *'A Muslim should avoid: 1. Being nervous, highly strung or liable to sudden anger and 2. Bad relations with others'* – smiled benignly back at them.

'You use your *left* hand!' he said, slowly and clearly, in the tones of one who knew a thing or two about Islamic *adab*.

'Ergh!' said Sheikh. 'I won't shake hands with you then!'

What did their parents teach them? Did they even attend the mosque on a regular basis? And, if so, which one? It wasn't a question Robert felt he could ask. Anyway, the mosque was one of the many subjects he felt it safest to avoid until he had plucked up the courage to go into one.

When the school had started, Robert had expected tobacconist's sons, monolingual Turks, or youths with swarthy faces and hooked noses, clad in sheets. But, as Mr Malik kept reminding him, this was not the target audience of the school. They were after upwardly mobile Muslims. Perhaps because they were the only people able to afford the fees.

The children Robert was attempting to teach were, although they didn't know it, the latest recruits to the mysterious section of English society known as the lower upper middle class. They were the sons of dentists, ambitious businessmen and fairly successful academics. The vast majority of them had tried, and failed for one reason or another, to get into one or other of the local preparatory schools. Their parents were sending them to the Wimbledon Islamic Day

Independent Boys' School because they wanted them to grow up English.

The only truly exotic one among them was Hasan. He sat, as usual, at the back of the class, his little shoulders eerily still, his face tilted to one side, as if drawing warmth from some invisible light-source. He never spoke to the other boys, and they never spoke to him. At the end of each day, as he had done since the beginning of the autumn, Robert took him home, where Mr and Mrs Wilson petted him, fed him, and put him to sleep in the spare bedroom as if he were their own son.

'Let me remind you,' said Robert, 'of one of the *hadiths* of the Prophet. Who knows what a *hadith* is?'

No one knew. Not even Mafouz or Sheikh. *No wonder the Islamic world is in such a mess*, thought Robert angrily, *they don't even know what a* hadith *is. Where have they been all this time?* Or (he did not like this thought) were they winding him up? Were they all pretending to be ignorant in order to trap him into making some punishable blunder?

It was possible they didn't know. They spent so much time in Zap Zone at Streatham, scampering about in clouds of dry ice, zapping each other with laser guns, so many hours watching *Neighbours* or running up and down shopping-malls, playing Super Nintendo, they had probably not had time to go anywhere near a mosque or get their heads round the basics of Islamic education. Ayatollah Khomeini, he thought grimly, had a point. He wouldn't let the Iranian people watch *Neighbours*. He knew where such behaviour leads.

'A *hadith*,' said Sheikh eventually, 'is a saying of the Prophet.'

'Good, Sheikh,' said Robert. 'Good!'

Sheikh was an important man to have on your side.

They knew, all right. They were just not telling him. With the uncanny prescience of children, they had divined that he was a fake. They had gone home and told their parents. Mr Mafouz, a big, jolly man who worked for a travel agent, was compiling a dossier on him. He would send it to Baghdad or Cairo, and, within minutes, men even more serious than the two in the Frog and Ferret would be on their way to Wimbledon with automatic rifles.

One of the men from the pub (the Yasser Arafat look-alike) was also working for the school. Mr Malik had given him a job as a janitor. 'Aziz is a shifty fellow,' Mr Malik had said, 'and he is on no account to be allowed near Hasan. But he is first class with the mop and broom. He cleans as he sweeps as he shines!'

Aziz spent most of his time skulking about the corridors, snarling at people or banging his pail loudly immediately before and immediately after daily prayers. 'He is that kind of Dharjee,' the head had said, when Robert asked him about this. 'What more can one say?' And he added, as he laid his finger to the side of his nose, 'It is not advisable to discuss religious questions with him!'

Robert was not about to do so. His principal endeavour was to stay off the subject of Islam except when alone with the children. But Mr Malik was always bringing up the subject. He seemed fascinated by the details of Robert's conversion. Robert had been vague about them on an embarrassing number of occasions.

It might be simpler, in the end, to actually *become* a Muslim. Was it, wondered Robert, something one could do by post?

'A *hadith* is a saying of the Prophet. A man called Bukhari went around after Muhammad died and spent sixteen years compiling his collection. He talked to over a *thousand sheikhs* in Mesopotamia and – '

Where else? All this information, derived as it was from chance remarks of Mr Malik's, threatened to slip away from his memory even as he was talking. Robert put a lot into the delivery of the speech. He tried to make it sound fresh and exciting. He spoke slowly and clearly and smiled a lot. But Class 1 looked back at him listlessly.

'Well,' Robert went on, aware that he had lost his audience, 'someone called Abu Quata . . . Abu . . . Anyway, someone called Abu told Bukha . . .'

Was it Bukhari or Bukharin? Robert groped for a familar name.

'Anyway *Muhammad* said to this chap that when you go to the toilet you shouldn't wipe your bum with your right hand.'

They were bored. He thought he was on safe ground with lavatories, but they were bored. The only thing they wanted to hear was that the Prophet had said that everyone could go to Zap Zone and stay there for the rest of their natural lives. Robert thought of the day he had taken Class 1 to Zap Zone, and shuddered.

He went to the far side of the classroom. He climbed on one side of the desks, stood on tiptoe, and, forcing up the skylight, eased his head through into the icy December wind. The class, used to his eccentricities, waited patiently.

Robert looked across at the High Street. There was the man standing near the gates of the school. It was Aziz the janitor's friend from the pub. The one who looked like Saddam Hussein. He was always hanging around near the entrance of the school. Sometimes the two of them could be seen muttering together in the playground.

Robert peered back at Hasan. All this was something to do with the manuscript. Why else had Hasan's picture been put with it? But what else were they after? And why had Hasan been entrusted to him?

He was getting paranoid. This had to stop. No one was after him. He was pretending to be a Muslim. He was indulging in a little harmless deceit. That was all.

As he stood there, a woman, heavily swathed in black drapes, turned into the driveway of the school and started towards the front door. It wasn't until she got within a few yards of him that he realized it was Maisie. Robert looked back at his class. They were watching his legs with polite interest.

'What are you doing in that?' said Robert. 'You look as if you've climbed into a bin-liner, Maisie.'

'The name,' said Maisie, 'is Ai'sha.'

She held up her right hand, and brandished what looked like a Batman mask on a stick. 'You shouldn't really be looking at my eyes,' she said.

'I don't see how we can avoid that,' said Robert, 'unless you use some kind of periscope.'

'Don't be stupid, Bobkins,' said Maisie. 'You must stop being stupid. We must be friends now. We are Muslims.'

'We' are Muslims! Uh?

'The Muslim,' said Maisie, in a complacent tone of voice, 'is the brother of any other Muslim. He should not oppress or surrender him.'

Robert recognized this quotation – it was one of which Malik was particularly fond. The headmaster had a large store of quotations designed to show what a nice, easygoing bloke Muhammad was. He did not dwell on the hyena spotted in blood that Abraham was going to throw into hell on the Day of Resurrection, or on the necessity of chopping male infidels into small pieces.

'When,' said Robert querulously, snatching a glance back at Class 1 as he spoke, 'did you become a Muslim?'

'This afternoon,' said Maisie. 'It's as easy as falling off a log.'

'Something you'll be doing rather a lot of,' said Robert, 'if you insist on wearing those ridiculous clothes.'

How did one become a Muslim? It wasn't really a question he could ask at this stage. But, however you did it, Maisie was clearly keen on doing the job properly.

'Mr Malik's converted me!' said Maisie.

Robert had still not been able to discover the headmaster's first name, although on occasions Malik had asked to be addressed as Abdul, while making it clear that this was not his name. Apparently – he told Robert – anyone at his school who was not 100 per cent white had been referred to as 'Abdul.' Mr Malik had been brought up in Cheltenham and had attended a public school, although he was never precise about which one.

'How has he done that?'

'He sort of lays his hands on you,' said Maisie – 'it's extraordinary!'

Robert did not like the sound of this. He looked back, briefly, at his class, resolving to have a word with the headmaster as soon as possible. Saddam Hussein, on the other side of the street, lifted his right leg and scratched his toes against his left calf. He was, like Aziz the janitor, definitely wearing one shoe and one slipper. Robert started to withdraw his head.

'I'm going to come and work at the school,' said Maisie. 'I've given up Sotheby's.'

'What are you going to do?'

Maisie smirked. 'I'm not going to *teach*, obviously. I'm a woman. I'm not capable of teaching. I shall probably do something humble, like work in the kitchens making Islamic school meals.'

This was not wholly bad news. The food at the Boys' Day Islamic Independent Wimbledon School was unspeakable. It was cooked by a woman, or something that looked like a woman but could have been a giant panda. She was reputed to be a relative of Mr Malik.

'Anyway,' she went on, more urgently, 'I need to talk to you. I've found out something rather alarming.'

Robert looked across the street. Saddam Hussein was still scratching his right foot. What was with these guys' feet?

'It's about that bit of paper you gave me. With the locket with the photo of Hasan in it.'

'What about it?'

Maisie looked sulky. Robert looked back into the class. He could just see Hasan, sitting, as usual, quite still, his hands resting lightly on the desk in front of him. He realized, suddenly, he didn't want to know who or what the little boy was. He simply wanted him to go on sitting there.

'You told a fib, Bobkins. It isn't about Hoj or Hoj's woman's breasts. It's about something rather disturbing!'

The man was now working his right foot out of its slipper. Why was he doing this? The temperature outside was down to nearly zero.

'What?'

From the class there were the beginnings of whispering. Soon the whispering would become talking, and soon the talking would become shouting. After the shouting would come screaming, biting, dancing in circles, waving the arms and legs and many other things not recommended by Dr Marwan Ibrahim Al-Kaysi as truly Islamic behaviour.

'I'll tell you when I see you. But it's rather worrying. It's all to do with some people called the Assassins!'

With these words, Maisie snapped her mask up to her face and went up to the front door. Over on the other side of the High Street, Saddam Hussein had straightened up. In his right hand he was holding his slipper. He waved it, mockingly, at Robert. Somewhere inside the building the bell went for break.

Robert drew his head back inside the classroom and, taking a deep breath, climbed down from his desk.

8

Robert climbed the stairs to the staffroom. They had moved in from the garden during a cold spell in November. On the landing, looking out over the High Street, Aziz, wearing new brown overalls bought for him by the headmaster, seemed to be waving to his friend. When he heard Robert, he scuttled away down the corridor. His right foot, Robert noted, was half in and half out of his slipper. From below came the sound of small boys damaging furniture. Break, as always at the school, was unsupervised. 'We all need a break,' Mr Malik used to say – 'including the staff!'

Two open wooden crates, piled high with computer keyboards, were stacked against the wall outside the headmaster's study. They were labelled MALIK. BIRMINGHAM. THIS WAY UP. Robert knew their presence would not be explained. They would be taken away one day, like the seven hundred cans of dogfood, or the fifty television sets, and never seen again. There were no signs of monitors or printers. Mr Malik seemed to specialize in bits of things. One week there had been fifty fridge doors outside his office, another week forty or fifty bicycle frames, although Robert had not so far caught sight of a single chain, tyre, wheel or handlebar.

Robert stopped and put his ear to the headmaster's door. When he wasn't teaching, Malik was usually on the phone, and you could hear him through the wall. Often he seemed to be selling things. This week it was cars.

'Listen,' Robert could hear him say, his voice booming in the barely furnished room, 'I can let you have the Cortina for *nothing*. I am serious. It will cost you absolutely nothing at all. And it is a car with a great deal of character!'

Then the headmaster laughed. He was always laughing. It was, in Robert's experience, a sign that things were not going well.

Robert then went up to the staffroom door and listened. There was, as usual, no sound from within. With a familiar feeling of dread, he pushed the door open.

Rafiq was over by the window, reading a technical magazine. He turned to Robert, gave him the thumbs-up sign, and returned to the study of a complicated diagram. The science and engineering master was always amiable. His sign language was, on the whole, positive. But Robert could have wished the man would get some false teeth.

Opposite him, sitting well down in his chair, staring hard at the carpet, was Dr Ali. Dr Ali had not spoken to anyone since he had got the job. There were times when Robert wondered whether he was capable of speech. Robert had once put his ear to the door during one of his colleague's classes and had been able to hear nothing from Class 2 but an eery silence. In Dr Ali's right hand was a book entitled *Basic Mathematics for Schools*. It was not one of the textbooks supplied by Mr Malik from the Lo-Price Bargain Bookstore, Clapham. It looked about thirty or forty years old. Perhaps the man had picked it up in West Cameroun.

'When are the next prayers?' said Robert in a cheerful, optimistic voice.

Both men looked at him closely. Neither attempted an answer to this question.

'I lose count,' went on Robert, 'but I've got the feeling we're due for another bout of banging the forehead on the carpet.'

He knew, as he said this, that it was not a good thing to say. But the more he repeated the simple daily rituals of Muslim belief, the more he felt the urge to adopt a brusque, English attitude to them. It was as if he was frightened they might lay a claim on him. As if he might actually *be* a Muslim, in spite of himself.

'I can't wait,' he went on, aware that – as usual – he was making things much worse. 'You've no idea how much it means to me to be part of all this.'

Still no one spoke.

Sometimes, during the ritual prayer, now he had got over the early stages of wondering when to get on the floor, when to rise, and exactly how to get the fingers up to the earlobes, he found himself begging to be excused any significance in his actions. This happened, for some reason, when he was close to Dr Ali.

'A good Muslim,' said Dr Ali, 'should pray five times a day. I do not think we do this.'

Robert was so surprised to hear the mathematics master speak, he found his mouth was hanging open like a fish's. What Dr Ali said was certainly true. Although they had started, at the beginning of term, to pray five times a day, it was already down to two sessions. And Mr Malik, who generally led the school, adopted such a histrionic attitude that it was often difficult to tell whether he was praising God or auditioning for him.

Next door, the headmaster was on another call. 'I have had sight of the manuscript,' Mr Malik was saying. 'Wilson gave it to the girl. It is a sign that they are serious.'

It sounded as if whoever was on the line did not agree.

'My dear Shah,' said the headmaster, 'this is stuff from the dawn of time. It won't go away ... any more than ... Robin Hood or King Arthur will go away. They will try anything to get to Hasan!'

His voice dropped. Robert leaned back in his chair so that his ear was touching the wall.

'We must hold our nerve,' Malik was saying, 'and have someone look at the damn manuscript. They won't move until nearer the time, anyway. Now Wilson must – '

His voice dropped even lower. Robert gave up the attempt to eavesdrop. When he looked up, he realized that Dr Ali was looking at him.

'Have we met before, Yusuf?'

'Oh,' said Robert, weakly, 'I don't think so.'

Dr Ali did not take his eyes off his face. 'Were you ever,' he went on, 'at the University of West Cameroun?'

'Oh no,' said Robert, 'I've never been out of Wimbledon!'

He was beginning to find Dr Ali's conversation even more disconcerting than his silence. In order to escape the gaze of the doctor's large, black eyes, he studied the rather grubby lapels of his suit. He concentrated upon the doctor's neat, white shirt, his thin, anxious neck and his general air of having just surfaced from some particularly nasty branch of the Inland Revenue. Perhaps he wasn't going to talk any more.

'Things are going on at this school,' went on Dr Ali, in a whisper, 'of which it is difficult for a good Muslim to approve.'

'Really?' said Robert. His voice, he thought, sounded curiously squeaky.

Dr Ali kept his eyes on Robert's face. He drew up his bony index finger, stood it to attention next to his aquiline nose, and wagged it furiously. 'We shall assemble the sinners!' he said. 'Their eyes will become dim with terror and they shall murmur among themselves, "You have stayed away but ten days!" '

'Indeed!' said Robert. He spotted at once the no-nonsense tones of the Koran, and, as always when The Book was being quoted, kept his eyes on his chest and tried to look like a man willing to leap off his chair on to all fours, ready for total prostration at any moment.

'Hell lies before them,' went on Dr Ali, in conversational tones. 'They shall drink stinking water; they will sip, but scarcely swallow. Death will assail them from every side, yet they shall not die. A dreadful torment awaits them.'

He hadn't yet said who 'they' were, but Robert had a fairly good idea that some of them might well be unemployed young men pretending to be Muslims in order to worm their way into jobs that should have been occupied by the Faithful.

Dr Ali looked over his shoulder. Rafiq seemed occupied with his magazine. The next remark was hissed directly into Robert's ear, and Robert felt his neck lightly sprayed with saliva. 'Trust nobody,' Ali said. 'Do not trust Malik. Malik is vile with the knowledge of his vileness. He crawls on the ground like a snake. He is loathsome, and spotted.'

This did not seem a helpful thing to say about one's headmaster. Had Mr Malik known quite what he was taking on when he hired Dr Ali?

'I am trying to get through to the Islamic Foundation,' went on Ali, 'to warn them of what is going on here. Of the laxness. Of the vileness. But since my revelation they do not listen to me.'

'When did you have your revelation?' said Robert.

'I had one this morning,' said Dr Ali. 'But I have them all the time. I have never spoken of them before to anyone here.'

This would explain why the good doctor had got in here. Mr Malik had been at pains to exclude what he continued to call 'the loonies' – that is to say, anyone whose attitude to the practice of his faith was, in the headmaster's opinion, excessively enthusiastic. 'Islam,' he was constantly telling Robert, 'is not a faith that pries into a person's soul. We have never really had an Inquisition, never really persecuted people for their beliefs. We have always recognized the danger of self-appointed visionaries.' Somehow or other Dr Ali would seem to have slipped through the net. Robert decided to try and find out a little more about him.

'When did you have your . . . first . . . er . . . revelation?' he asked in a low voice.

'At the Business Efficiency Exhibition at Olympia,' said Dr Ali. 'A vast pillar of fire rose up through the floor and decimated the display of the Nugahiro Corporation's new range of lap-top computers!'

'Did anyone else see it,' said Robert, 'or was it just you?' He leaned forward and spoke quietly. Rafiq was studying his magazine with the kind of intense concentration often assumed by those who are listening to other people's conversations. 'It could have been industrial espionage!'

Ali ignored this remark. 'I have seen it subsequently,' he went on. 'I have seen it come down from the sky with a noise like thunder, and I have seen within it the bodies of those who were Too Late!'

'At Olympia?' said Robert weakly.

'I have seen it in Wimbledon,' said Dr Ali. 'It has been lowered over my head many times, and then, as I have reached up to smite it, it has passed before me and consumed many people. I have also heard the sound of mocking laughter.'

'Is that right?' said Robert.

He wondered whether Dr Ali had confided this fact to Class 2. It could explain the terrified silence that reigned every time they were locked up alone with him. He had better get to the headmaster and warn him.

But, now that the mathematics master had decided to trust him, he seemed unwilling to let Robert go. He grasped his sleeve urgently. 'I must talk to you during the nature walk,' he went on, 'and tell you what is going on here.'

He indicated Rafiq with a brief nod of the head. 'What is his game?' he whispered.

'He teaches engineering and design,' said Robert.

Next door, Mr Malik was back to talking about cars. 'It has done forty thousand miles,' he was saying. 'It has forty thousand on the clock, and that is how many miles it has done. Take it or leave it. It has a new engine. It has rust protection. It is a beautiful car, I swear to you.'

Robert got up and, muttering something about marking, made as if to leave. To his consternation, Dr Ali started to follow him. When they got to the door Robert looked over his shoulder at Rafiq, but the engineering master was still deep in his magazine.

'Tell me,' said Ali, 'why do they bring their filth before us and spread it on the ground like raiment?'

'I don't know,' said Robert slowly. 'I haven't actually – '

Dr Ali smirked in triumph. 'The Dharjees will be consumed in eternal hell-fire,' he said, 'and out of their loins will come many-headed creatures. They will be torn limb from limb and cast into a lake of serpents!'

There seemed little point in continuing this conversation. Robert was far more interested in finding out where they stood on footwear, but this was clearly not an area that interested Ali.

'I must get on with Sheikh's essay,' said Robert – 'it's twenty pages long!'

Dr Ali gave a sniff of disapproval and, falling once again into his customary silence, slouched back to his chair. He did not, as usual, read or stare out of the window or make tea or do any of the things Robert assumed one usually caught teachers doing in off-duty moments. He sat, slumped back, chin on chest, staring down at the intricate patterns of the carpet, in a seemingly unbreakable silence.

Robert went next door to the headmaster's study and tapped at it nervously. Inside he could hear Malik's voice. The headmaster sounded tense. 'You are welcome to come and inspect us any time you like,' he was saying. 'Come and have a look over the gymnasium. Have lunch in the canteen. Sit in on one of my lessons. I am an Oxford graduate. You may learn something.'

Robert opened the door. Mr Malik waved him in. As Robert closed the door behind him, the headmaster put his hand over the telephone. 'Spies,' he mouthed. 'Government spies!' This meant he was on the line to the local education authority.

Beckoning Robert to a seat, he continued to talk into the mouthpiece about the school, about its playing-fields, its concert hall and several other items that, so far at any rate, existed only in his imagination. He seemed to be making some impression on the person at the other end of the phone.

Robert looked round the headmaster's study. It was decorated with photographs of his relatives. Mr Malik had relatives everywhere. He had aunts in Bombay and brothers in Edinburgh, cousins in North Africa and sisters-in-law in Australia. The only place they did not appear to have penetrated was Wimbledon – which was perhaps as well, since it left Mr Malik as the sole source of information on the Malik family history. This left him an enormous amount of scope for demonstrating the kind of narrative energy that most English fiction-writers would have given a great deal to acquire.

'My mother,' he would sometimes say, 'was an Englishwoman called Perkins. She married my father for sex. Purely for sex. And he was never quite sure why he had married her at all.'

His mother wasn't always called Perkins. She wasn't always an Englishwoman either, although more often than not the headmaster gave one of his parents British nationality. Not that it mattered. Mr Malik, Robert reflected, as he sat watching the headmaster discuss the school's proposal to take boarders, build an indoor tennis-court and a hard playing-area and organize a Community Service scheme, was a creature of his own imagination. He needed far more than the normal ration of two parents, each with only one identity apiece.

'We'll do that,' Malik was saying. 'We'll have a pint! We will! Absolutely, my dear boy! We will!'

He put the phone down. He looked at Robert. He did not smile.

When he spoke, his voice was trembling. 'You have deceived me, Wilson!' he said. 'Why have you deceived me?'

Suddenly, to Robert's consternation, the headmaster burst into tears. This was not what he had expected him to do. The headmaster of Cranborne School had made it his business, during Robert's nine years in the place, to make sure that other people did the crying.

Unsure of what to do, Robert started round the desk. He had a strong urge to put his arms round the man, and indeed was about to do so, when Malik thrust him away, sobbing.

'Don't touch me! Ai'sha has told me about your proclivities!'

Robert backed away towards his chair, trying to work out whether this was the deception to which the headmaster was referring. Even if he had been a screaming queen, he thought, it wasn't something he was bound to mention on the application form for a boy's public school. What did the man expect?

'What proclivities?' said Robert, who was not entirely sure what the word meant.

Malik raised a tear-stained face towards him. 'What you do in your spare time, Wilson,' he said, 'is absolutely your affair. There is, I am glad to say, no direct allusion to the activities in which you engage in the Koran or in the Hadith of the Prophet, although from what I know of the blessed Muhammad – may God rest him and grant him peace – it is not something of which he would approve. He was a man's man, Wilson.'

Robert coughed. 'I want to stress, Headmaster,' he said, 'that . . . er . . . the . . . proclivities referred to were . . . er . . . a phase!'

Why was he so incapable of truth that he wasn't able to deny something that was patently false? Perhaps because denial seemed such a crude affair, and truth so lamentably one-dimensional.

'I am through it, Headmaster,' he said, 'and out the other side.'

This, somehow, did not seem quite enough.

'It is an unspeakable thing,' went on Robert. 'It is the loneliest thing in the world to wake up in the middle of the night and realize you are one of . . . *them*!'

Mr Malik seemed to find the lack of political correctness in this remark reassuring. He held out his hand to his junior master and composed his face into a solemn expression of trust. 'Very well, Wilson,' he said. 'And now, I beg you, I beseech you, to reassure me that you are not also one of those unspeakables of which I think we both know the name only too well.'

Robert could not think what he meant by this. What else was he supposed to have been up to? Cross-dressing, perhaps? Where did Islam stand on that one? He tried to recall some of Marwan Ibrahim Al-Kaysi's dos and donts. *'It is indecent for a Muslim to look at his private parts and his excretion.'* Was that it? He was always looking at his private parts. Or had Maisie invented even more ghastly crimes for him. *'Dogs are not allowed in the dwellings.'* Maybe she had accused him of doing appalling things with Badger.

'What do you ... think I ... er ... might be, Headmaster?' said Robert.

Malik looked puzzled by this remark. 'Why, Wilson,' he said – 'a *Twenty-fourther*, of course. What did you think I meant?'

This, thought Robert, had a definitely sexual ring to it. Was it some ghastly anal version of *soixante-neuf*?

'A Twenty-fourther,' went on Mr Malik, 'like that damned Aziz and his friend! A group that threatens to split the Wimbledon Dharjees *right down the middle*! That endangers the security of this school, Wilson!'

'Do you mean,' said Robert, 'those people who wear peculiar shoes on their right feet?'

The head seemed amused by Robert's obvious ignorance of the subject. 'They do indeed wear "peculiar shoes", my dear Wilson! They do indeed! And you know why?'

'I'm afraid I haven't a clue,' said Robert.

Mr Malik leaned forward. The muscles in his neck were quivering. Robert could not remember seeing him as disturbed as this. *'So as they can whip them off at a moment's notice!'* he hissed. *'So as they can get their damned toes out and waggle them at people!'*

Robert's expression had obviously convinced him of his innocence.

'The Prophet said, "Don't walk with only one shoe. Either go barefoot or wear shoes on both feet." '

'Did he?' said Robert brightly. Muhammad had certainly covered the ground as far as etiquette was concerned. It was, in a way, rather restful to have a series of instructions covering almost every area of one's life.

'Long ago,' continued the headmaster, 'before the Dharjees came to Wimbledon, they shared a common history with the Ismailis. The Nizari Ismailis. Are these people familiar to you? They are an old, old sect in Islam.'

He grabbed Robert's arm and squeezed it. 'They are after Hasan!' he said. 'They won't move yet, but when they do . . . watch out! You must watch him every minute of every day! And when we come near to the time of his Occultation you must never let him out of your sight.'

'When is that?' said Robert. 'Is it in the school holidays?'

Mr Malik laughed wildly. 'My dear Wilson,' he said, 'all you need to know is that it is not yet come. But it will. There are secrets of the Nizari Ismailis that are never spoken of – never spoken of! Like the Golden Calf of the Druze, my friend, they are a real and living mystery!'

But, before Robert had the chance to ask him about the Golden Calf of the Druze, or what a Nizari Ismaili might be, or how many of either group might be lurking around Wimbledon, the bell sounded for the end of break, and, below them, in the Great Hall, he heard the sounds of the whole school assembling for nature, recreation and Islamic dancing.

Malik strode towards his study door, flung it open, and turned to Robert with a firm, manly smile. 'We will discuss this later,' he said, 'and we will think of a way to build trust between us. I like you, Wilson. I worked with you on the brochure. I want there to be trust between us. I want to feel that I have entrusted Hasan to a gentleman. You understand my meaning?'

Without waiting for an answer to this, he turned on his heel and went down to his waiting pupils.

It was not difficult to see how he had converted Maisie. After a few minutes with Mr Malik, Robert himself quite often felt like making the frighteningly short journey from doubt to belief. Islam, as the headmaster was always reminding him, meant *surrender*. Maybe he should surrender. Waggling his arms and legs in preparation for Islamic dancing, Robert started down the stairs after Rafiq and Dr Ali. *If things get too complicated*, he told himself, not for the first time in the last few months, *I can always make a run for it.*

9

Mr Malik was very fond of nature. He used it, freely, in argument. 'Look at the birds!' he would say. 'Look at the frogs! Are not they an example to us? We hang around shuffling our feet and making phone calls and they just *get on with it!*'

Whenever he had the chance he got the whole school out on to the Common. When they weren't running across it, cheered on by the headmaster, they were snipping bits off it and bringing them back to school to put in jars. Once Malik had cut down a small tree, dragged it across the grass, and cut it up in the back garden, with the help of two large boys in the third year. Flora Strachan, the ecology-conscious pensioner, had chased after him, waving a copy of her pamphlet *An Uncommon Common* and threatening to report him to the police.

'If you kill a wall gecko at a single blow, a hundred merits will be credited to your account. To kill it with two blows is less meritorious!' Malik would say, grabbing Robert's sleeve as he did so. 'Do you know who said that?' And Robert, who was by now learning the basic rule that if anybody said anything interesting it was probably Muhammad, would ask if by any chance it just happened to be a saying of the Prophet, to which the headmaster would reply, his eyes shining, 'That's it! That's it! What a man! He covers everything! Cats! Dogs! *Wall geckos!*' And, rocking with laughter, he would clasp Robert to him – something, thought Class 1's form master, as he joined the throng in the hall, the headmaster would probably not be doing a lot of in future.

'In a line, boys!' Mr Malik was calling. 'In a line! Let us show them that the Wimbledon Independent Boys' Day Islamic School is the best behaved, the best organized and the best equipped in Wimbledon!'

Mahmud and Sheikh were on the floor. Mahmud was trying to strangle Sheikh. Sheikh was trying to jab a pencil in Mahmud's eyes. Mr Malik beamed at them in a fatherly manner. 'Nature,' he beamed. 'This too is an aspect of nature. It is natural for young men to try and kill each other. Absolutely natural!' So saying, he aimed a kick at Sheikh's ribs and lifted Mahmud clear of the ground by his collar, flinging him into the stew of boys gathered around the window that overlooked the front garden.

Through the doors at the back, from the kitchen area, came Maisie. She started, very cautiously, towards the assembled school. For a moment Robert thought she might have had her feet bound, and then he realized that her problem was simply that her face-mask was now so in line with Islamic law that her field of vision was only about six inches to the left and right of her. She stopped, raised her head, and tracked it left and right, like a robot searching out its target. When she had located the headmaster she moved towards him.

Mr Malik, ignoring these manoeuvres, swept out towards the front door. Dr Ali, suddenly submissive, moved quickly in front of him and opened it. Rain and wind swirled in, scattering papers and banging the door to Class 2's room.

'I need to talk to you,' said Robert to Maisie, as the school filed out towards the Village.

'You can't,' hissed Maisie. 'I'm a woman!'

'That doesn't mean I can't talk to you, does it?'

As far as he could remember from Marwan Ibrahim Al-Kaysi, you were allowed to talk to women. There was a tricky thing called *the seminally defiled state*, and you had to make sure that when your old lady left the house she was doing so *for a specific purpose*, but on the whole even Marwan was pretty *laissez-faire* about a girl and a boy talking about subjects of mutual interest.

Maisie's conversation wasn't quite as much of a surprise as it should have been. And even her clothes, once you had got over the original shock, were part of a long tradition of home-made outfits dating back to her days at the Mother Theresa Convent, South Wimbledon. The see-through trouser suit she had designed herself had caused a sensation at Rachel Ansorge's party.

Islam was the first project they had shared since the Cranborne/ Mother Theresa joint school production of *The Tempest* all those years ago. Perhaps that was why he was beginning to find her almost unbearably attractive. He had never, before, seriously thought that she would get beyond the occasional sisterly peck on the cheek, or allowing him the privilege of listening to her troubles. But since the school term had started they had spent hour after hour in intense, ill-informed conversations about who was who in seventh-century Medina. Robert merely had to drop a few *bon mots* from Marwan Ibrahim Al-Kaysi's handbook into the conversation and Maisie's eyes widened the way they did when you offered to take her out for a meal or when she was telling you how someone had told someone that she had a beautiful mouth.

Her costume made her more, rather than less, attractive to him. '*A Muslim woman's dress consists of three items – a shift, a veil and a cloak.*' So, according to Marwan anyway, underneath that long, black cloak was a shift. And underneath the shift . . . As the school filed across the High Street and up towards the Common, Robert found he was sweating. Was there anything underneath the shift? Assuming he did, one day, manage to get her into bed, what would happen after she had shimmied off the veil, let the cloak fall around her naked ankles, and then eased her white, sweet-smelling flesh out of the shift to reveal . . . What? What was ideologically correct Islamic underwear? Presumably an item so secret that they were even keeping it from Dr Al-Kaysi of the University of Yarmouk.

She was about ten yards behind him as the party splashed its way into the swampy grass. But every time he turned round to look at the black shape labouring after him he was confirmed in the suspicion that Islamic outfits were far sexier than boring old black-leather bras, split-crotch panties or steel suspenders. What must it be like for the lads in Riyadh or Tehran, watching the women of their choice swoop around the supermarkets in twenty-five yards of black drapery? How did they cope? With each movement under the flowing garments, Robert imagined breasts, flecked with pink nipples, a pleasantly loose belly, white thighs grinding against each other. *Oh, my God*, he thought, *would that there were an Islamic garment for men, designed to conceal massive erections!* Ahead of them, a woman of about sixty in a blue tracksuit pawed the ground in the jogger's equivalent of neutral. Listing at about ten degrees off vertical, she seemed to be hoping that the grass of the Common would itself carry her forward, like a travelator. If something like that did not happen soon, Robert thought, she might well not have long to live.

'Are you all right, Yusuf?' said Dr Ali.

Robert looked down. Dr Ali was scurrying along beside him and from time to time glaring down the line of boys. Whenever he caught the eye of one of them, the boy would look away and allow his conversation to die. The maths master looked as if he was about to have another revelation.

'I'm ... er ... fine,' said Robert, desperately trying to work out how he might get close to Maisie, 'but I am ... er ... worried about the boys.'

In the distance he could see a group of dog-walkers. Dick Shakespeare, who did the gardening programme on television, was striding after his black labrador, Chesty. He was wearing green wellingtons and a flat cap, and round his neck was a huge silver whistle. 'Chesty!' he barked. 'Come away down there!'

Dick Shakespeare had a large repertoire of traditional sheepdog commands, picked up from videos of *One Man and His Dog*. He was always asking Chesty to lie down, and come away, and sometimes trying out weird commands all of his own. Chesty had been publicly ordered to 'lurk', to 'fold', to 'carry the juice' and, on one occasion, to 'walk away down there nicely'. The dog never paid any attention to any of these commands, but, like most dogs, carried on eating golf balls, smelling strangers' private parts, and looking immensely pleased with himself. When things got really bad, Mr Shakespeare used the whistle. This, too, Chesty completely ignored.

Robert wondered whether the dog-walkers might provide cover.

'Hi there!' called Dick Shakespeare. He indicated the pupils of the Wimbledon Islamic Boys' Day Independent School, put the tips of all ten fingers together, and bowed, briefly. 'Three poppadams,' he said, 'and a little piece of mango chutney!'

Behind him was Marjorie Grey, in her green anorak, surrounded by Franks the poodle, Macintyre the elderly Border collie and Stroud the unstable Staffordshire terrier. Robert waved briefly, ducked, and looked for an alternative means of escape.

He would just have to walk, openly, away from the main body of the school, get downwind of Maisie, stalk her carefully, and, when they had reached the birch-trees on the other side of Cannizaro Road, creep up on her and leap out at her when she wasn't looking. It shouldn't be difficult. With a field of vision as limited as hers it was amazing that she could see anything at all.

Just at that moment, Mahmud started to shriek. The small boy had just caught sight of his cousin, who went to Cranborne School. Mahmud's cousin, clad in a pair of white shorts, was running, with a fat boy in glasses, towards the Wimbledon Islamic School. Robert thought he recognized the fat boy. Mr Malik and he had visited Cranborne in order to organize a chess match between the two schools. The fat boy had mated him in four moves.

'Chalky!' Mahmud screamed, 'I got *Monkey Island* off Sheikh, but this is better than *Monkey Island*! It's better than *Coconut Forgery*! You're a mercenary and you kill people with laser guns! It's really good!'

Ali's nose twitched. He looked like a man who smelt un-Islamic behaviour. Either that or he was about to sneeze. But, although the headmaster turned to frown at Mahmud, Robert didn't yet feel he had any justification for leaving the neat line of boys and tracking down Maisie.

'It will be interesting to see,' said Dr Ali, 'whether, during the month of Dhu'l-Hijja, our "friend" Malik offers a sacrifice.'

'It will,' said Robert.

'Our "friend" Malik,' said Dr Ali, 'is a passport Muslim, and that is all. He is *Sahib nisab*, I presume?'

'I would have thought so,' said Robert quickly – 'a man of his age.'

He looked about him desperately. Behind him, Rafiq, as always, was walking with Hasan. The little boy had his hand in the engineer's. From time to time Rafiq would gently prise his hand free and stroke the boy's hair, murmuring some soft endearment. Hasan was almost the only person to whom he spoke. Behind him a huge, dangerous-looking jogger in bright purple shorts thundered up and then, after a brief, explosive display of sweat and breath, was off into the quaking grass.

Robert became aware that the mathematics master was talking, once again, about sacrifice. 'A camel or she-camel,' he was saying, 'if chosen, should be more than five years old.'

Robert nodded vigorously. 'We only have a rabbit,' he found himself saying, 'but we kill that usually. That or the dog.'

Mahmud had broken away from the main crocodile and was engaged in earnest conversation with the small fat boy. The fat boy was holding out a pile of thin plastic diskettes. Mahmud, as far as Robert could make out, was offering the fat boy a ten-pound note for them. It was, thought Robert, probably the same ten-pound note that had been awarded to him by Mr Malik for his prizewinning essay 'My Snake'.

'I wonder,' said Robert idly, 'what the Prophet would have thought about computer games.'

'They are,' said Dr Ali, 'the work of the Devil.'

It was amazing, really, thought Robert, that Dr Ali allowed himself to be anywhere near a place as fundamentally un-Islamic as Wimbledon. Had he fallen out of an aircraft on its way from New York to Tripoli? Had he walked out of the Lebanese embassy one night and come down with an attack of amnesia? According to the headmaster, he had a degree from the University of Surrey. Before the maths master started on what to sacrifice when you couldn't lay your hands on a goat, or how to cope with Ramadan in a modern technological society, Robert, muttering something about the need for discipline, marched off towards Mahmud.

Out of the corner of his eye he could see Maisie, who was now about a hundred yards south of the rest of the school. Whether this was Islamic modesty was hard to tell – she could have got her shift stuck in a tree-trunk. Mahmud and his cousin were haggling over the price of a game called *Willy Beamish*. 'It is write-protected,' he heard Mahmud say. 'I only got it from Lewens for fifteen!'

Robert leaned over the little boy. 'If you do not return to the line now, Mahmud,' he said, 'I am going to cut off your knackers!'

Mahmud glanced briefly up at him, considered this proposition, and went back to negotiating the price of the computer game.

Robert looked back at the school. Mr Malik seemed now to have taken on board several other members of Cranborne School who were growing tired of cross-country running. He had arranged them, with his own boys, in a circle round a plane-tree and was giving an impromptu lecture on the classificatory work of Darwin to both notionally Muslim and notionally Christian pupils. *If only*, thought Robert, *I had had teachers like that*. There was something so constantly curious about the headmaster of the Boys' Wimbledon Day Islamic Independent School that, after a while, you stopped wondering where, or indeed whether, he had acquired a degree in anything, and surrendered to that mellifluous, actorish voice.

He moved stealthily into the trees. As far as he could see, Maisie, who was now thoroughly disorientated, was headed for the pond in the centre of the Common. Occasionally she made brief, distressed movements of the head, rotated right, left and right again, but was unable to get the rest of the school in her sights. Back on the main road, Robert caught a glimpse of Aziz the janitor. He was still carrying his mop and broom and wearing his brown overalls. He looked as if he was about to start sweeping the Common.

As Robert watched, Aziz raised his mop and started a kind of semaphore in the direction of the Windmill. He raised the bucket too, and shook it rhythmically, as if it was some kind of primitive musical instrument. Looking behind him, Robert saw that he was signalling to his friend from the Frog and Ferret, who was crouched in the long grass.

Perhaps they were going to go after Hasan now. Perhaps Mr Malik had got it wrong. Perhaps the time of his Occultation – whatever that might be – was almost upon them. It was something of a shock to him to realize how fond of the little boy he had become. He didn't want him to be Occultated. Whatever it might involve, Robert felt sure that Hasan was not ready for it.

He thought about Hasan at the swimming-baths. Hasan loved to stand in the shallow end, splashing his face and chest with the warm water, his face lifted to the lights in the roof. He thought about Hasan and the television, about the way the little boy placed his olive cheek next to the loudspeaker, caressing the wooden cabinet, while the Wilson family watched the evening news. And then, without caring what the headmaster might think, he ran after Maisie as fast as he could. She was now about a hundred yards away from him, apparently on a collision course with an Irish wolfhound belonging to Jake, 'The Man You Avoid on Dog Walks'.

He finally caught up with her about thirty yards away from the pond. In order not to alarm her unduly, he moved into a space about ten yards ahead of her, and started to walk backwards and forwards on a ten-degree arc in her direct line of vision. Finally she stopped, and from deep within the black bag that enveloped her there was a kind of squeak. 'Bobkins!' she said. 'What are you doing here?'

'I need to speak to you,' said Robert.

She started to make small, whimpering noises. She sounded, thought Robert, rather like Badger shortly before one opened a can of dog-food.

'It's about Hasan . . .' he said, glancing back towards Hasan and the rest of the school. Aziz the janitor was now headed for the trees from which Robert had just come. He seemed to be focusing his attention on the group that Mr Malik was teaching. 'And what you said this morning . . . about that manuscript I gave you. With the photo of Hasan in the locket. And you said something about assassins!'

'*The* Assassins,' said Maisie, in a slightly superior way, 'were a group from the fortress of Alamut. They were the servants of Hasan I Sabah, the Old Man of the Mountains. From this sect called the Nizari Ismailis. He sent them all over the Islamic world to kill his enemies.'

'As far as . . . er . . . Wimbledon?' said Robert tentatively.

Maisie laughed scornfully. 'All this happened about a thousand years ago,' she said. 'But there's something even weirder in that manuscript you gave me. I showed it to Mr Malik, and he said it was very strange *indeed*.'

'Why show it to Mr Malik? What's going on between you and Mr Malik?'

'Nothing, Bobkins,' said Maisie. 'He's just converting me, that's all. I thought you'd be pleased!'

'Well I'm not,' said Robert, 'and I want to know what you've found out about that manuscript I gave you!'

Feeling suddenly cold and miserable, Robert moved towards a bench at the edge of the pond. Ahead of him Cranborne School presented a Christian, redbrick face to the long sky above the Common.

'Where are you?' squawked Maisie.

'I don't know why you're wearing that ridiculous outfit,' said Robert, 'and I don't know why you're telling all these things to Malik and telling him about things I gave you as a present.'

Maisie snorted and, following the sound of his voice, traced him to the wooden bench. She sat next to him. A glum-looking man in wellingtons followed his dog round the circle of iron-grey water. Above them, seagulls mewed and wheeled in the December wind.

'It's nothing to do with you who I talk to,' said Maisie. 'Why shouldn't I show it to him, anyway? He's a Muslim. He knows about these things. You're gay, anyway.'

'I am not gay,' said Robert. 'I am a normal, healthy man with normal, healthy feelings!'

This was not strictly true, but it was certainly more true than saying that he was gay. The fact was that, now that Maisie was about as closely concealed from daylight as a roll of undeveloped film, his desire for her had passed the point where it was possible to conceal it. It was somehow easier to say these things to something that looked like a top-secret weapon in transit.

'I think about you all the time,' he went on. 'I think about your body. I want your body. I want to penetrate you.'

There was a kind of squeak from deep within the black bag.

'I lied about being gay,' went on Robert. 'I lie about everything. I'm incapable of the truth. But I want you. I dream about having you. I dream about your body and its – '

'Bobkins,' said Maisie, in tones that suggested that this was a not entirely unwelcome topic, 'this isn't getting us anywhere.'

Robert rather disagreed with this. He had never before been able to be quite so frank with anyone about his innermost feelings. Was it that, at last, he was learning to face up to himself? Or was it simply that she looked like a large, mobile bag of laundry?

'You've got an erection!' she said, accusingly.

This, thought Robert, was something of an optical achievement on her part. It had been touch and go whether she would get herself anywhere near, let alone actually *on*, the bench.

'I love you,' went on Robert, 'and I want to have sex with you, and – '

'Shut up, Bobkins!' said Maisie. 'I thought you wanted to know about Hasan. And about that manuscript you gave me.'

Mr Malik and the rest of the school had now disappeared. Robert could just make out a thin line of boys struggling through the trees at the edge of the horizon. Aziz's friend seemed to have gone too.

'Where did you get it?' said Maisie. 'In an antique shop?'

If he had told her the truth, she would not have believed him. Anyway, the truth was – as usual – inelegant, implausible and hurtful. He didn't like to think he was the kind of person who took things from strangers in pubs and then passed them off as presents to girls he was supposed to love.

'That's right,' he said, trying to think of why Hasan's photograph might have been inside the locket. 'I think Hasan's parents must have sold it. Apparently they went through a very hard time recently. His father had a lot of money in BCCI.'

Maisie peered out at him suspiciously. 'You're lying, Bobkins, aren't you?' she said. 'You're telling a fib. I don't know why you tell fibs all the time. Mr Malik says he's always catching you out in fibs. I don't know why he likes you. I don't know why *I* like you. If I like you.'

There didn't seem much point in commenting on any of this.

Robert leaned his chin on his hands and looked glumly across the winter grass. 'What's in this manuscript, anyway?' he said, finally.

Maisie's voice thrilled in his ear. Muffled by thick, black cloth, it had the quality of a woman speaking of a secret assignation. As she spoke, the drab, tussocky surface of the Common, the whirling grey clouds and the unstoppable north wind were replaced by walled gardens, the scent of flowers and a crescent moon in a dark sky.

'It's a prophecy, apparently,' said Maisie. 'It dates from hundreds of years ago. And it tells how a remarkable boy is going to come and save the world. And it describes him – in great detail!' Her voice sank to a thrilling whisper. 'And, Bobkins – he sounds just like Hasan. Exactly like him in every respect. Right down to the mark on his cheek and the fact that he's blind. Hasan is the Twenty-fourth Imam!'

10

Robert was not sure whether this was good or bad news. It sounded important, anyway. He didn't know much about Islam but he was aware that being an imam was a bit like being a Vice-President for Life. People tended to make way for you in bus queues when you were an imam. They quite often leaped about on national monuments screaming, ripping apart their black pyjamas, and generally behaving as if you were all of the Grateful Dead rolled into one.

Perhaps they should have been using better cutlery, thought Robert, or calling Hasan 'sir' and making sure he had the best chair. They certainly should not have been letting him curl up on the floor next to Badger. They certainly should not have allowed Badger to lick his ear.

'I suppose you know,' went on Maisie, in the tones of someone who has recently become an expert on something, 'that there is a split in the Muslim world.'

Robert had not known this. But, then, his entire stock of knowledge about Islam was derived from *Morals and Manners in Islam* by Dr Marwan Ibrahim Al-Kaysi. He really must get back to the library and see if it had any more books on the subject. There was the Koran of course. But, so far, at any rate, he had not been able to get beyond page 12. And, in those pages anyway, the book had said nothing about a split. It had rather given the impression that splits were not the done thing.

'Don't you read *newspapers*, Bobkins?' hissed Maisie.

Robert did not read newspapers. He had looked at one, years ago, but it had taken him three days to read it, carefully, from cover to cover, by which time he realized that, if he was going to do the thing at all conscientiously, he would never be abreast of current developments. He learned about world events rather as a Trobriand

Islander might – from chance remarks and accidental contacts – and, from the little he had heard, he had not much desire to know more.

'There are Sonny and Cher Muslims, you see . . .'

She could not possibly be right about this, thought Robert.

'*Sunni* and *Shiah* – and they're sort of . . . deadly enemies.'

'How awful!'

He had got the impression, from Marwan Ibrahim Al-Kaysi and from Mr Malik, that Muslims were supposed to be nice to each other. What could they find to disagree about, anyway? Weren't they all supposed to stick together and clobber the opposition?

'The Shiah, for example, or at least the ones in Iran, believe that the Twelfth Imam – who disappeared in mysterious circumstances over a thousand years ago – is going to come back with a huge army and take over the world.'

This did not, to Robert, seem very likely. He could not, either, remember this fact being mentioned in the Koran. But, then, he had only read about twelve pages. He really *must* get on and finish it.

'What's all this got to do with Hasan?'

'The manuscript,' hissed Maisie, 'is from Iran. It dates from the twelfth century.'

Robert tried to marshal a few facts about twelfth-century Iran. They would not come.

'Mr Shah, who put up the money for the school, is a Wimbledon Dharjee. The Dharjees went from Iran to Bombay in the seventeenth century and came to Wimbledon in 1926, mainly to get away from Bombay but also, apparently, for the tennis.'

Why was she so well informed about Islamic history? Presumably Mr Malik had been giving her tutorials.

'But the Dharjees were once members of the Nizari Ismailis, who are themselves a breakaway sect of the Shiite Muslims. Like the Bombay Khojas.'

Robert wished people would not keep mentioning the Bombay Khojas. Just when you started to think you had finally got a grip on this thing they would throw in the Bombay Khojas and you were right back where you started. It was all very confusing. Just as he was beginning to adapt to the fact that there were Muslims – and that some of them were quite pleasant – it turned out that there were as many strains of Muslim as there were of the virus responsible for the common cold.

'Why did the Dharjees leave the Ismailis?' said Robert. 'Because they go around murdering people?'

'I think the Dharjees just sort of wandered off. It might have had something to do with tennis. The Ismailis are quite nice now. The Aga Khan is one of them,' said Maisie, as if this dispelled any doubts on the subject. 'He went to Harvard. He must be all right!'

Robert was not entirely sure about this. He had vaguely heard of Hasan I Sabah, the Old Man of the Mountains. And it was curiously unnerving to realize that the little boy staying in his parents' house should bear the same name. He looked over his shoulder towards where the school party had gone, but could see nothing but a flat field of windblown grass.

'Some of the Wimbledon Dharjees,' went on Maisie, 'have been waiting for the Twenty-fourth Imam. For hundreds of years. He's going to do something amazing, apparently. And this manuscript really makes it look like Hasan is the Twenty-fourth Imam! Its serious, Bobkins! It's not like us nipping down for a pint with the vicar!'

'I thought,' said Robert, grimly, 'that we were supposed to be Muslims.'

Maisie seemed surprised to recall this fact. She rocked backwards and forwards on the bench. 'Oh God,' she said – 'so we are.'

Robert did not like to remind her about the nature of her costume. She put her hand up to her veil and started to chew it through the material. He felt a stab of desire for her once again, but, this time, did not try to put it into words.

'It says, apparently,' she went on, 'that a blind boy with a mark on his face will "come out of the West". That's us, isn't it? And he'll do all sorts of terrible things. Hasan is a sort of . . . magic child!'

She turned her head and looked Robert full in the face. Neither of them spoke for several minutes. Robert thought about Hasan: about the strange, powerful stillness he carried with him, about his high, precise voice and his exquisite fingers, laced together on the desk at the back of Class 1.

It was not, Robert decided, very sporting of the headmaster to park the Twenty-fourth Imam of the Wimbledon Dharjees on him. He appreciated the headmaster's affection for all things English, even including the Wilson family, but to spring the Islamic equivalent of the Messiah on them seemed a little unfair. No wonder men had been watching the house. When the time of Hasan's Occultation came, they would, presumably, be swarming up the drainpipes waving scimitars and carrying on like a thwarted group of reporters from the *Sun*.

'I think,' said Robert, trying to stop his voice climbing any higher, 'that we should find Hasan a properly Islamic home as soon as possible. And we should hand the manuscript in. To Lost Property or something. Or put it in a left-luggage compartment somewhere.'

'Suppose it's cursed!' wailed Maisie. 'Suppose it's one of those things that follows you round – like Tutankhamun's mummy.'

He had never confided any of his suspicions about being followed to Mr Malik. He would go and see him as soon as they got back to school and tell him everything that had happened since he had come to the school. He had the irrational feeling that Mr Malik would make it all right.

'We'll be all right,' said Robert, with a confidence he did not feel. 'We're Muslims.'

'We are,' wailed Maisie – 'we are. And we should not oppress or surrender each other. We should all stick together for Christ's sake!'

Robert nodded vigorously. He must try and look on the positive side as far as Maisie's conversion was concerned. At least now they had something in common. She was a Muslim and he was pretending to be one. That was a start, wasn't it?

'Does Mr Malik give . . . er . . . classes?' he said.

'Oh no,' said Maisie, 'we just talk. And he takes me to an Italian restaurant in Mitcham. La Paesana. He does my horoscope.'

Robert did not like the idea of Maisie and Malik *tête-à-tête*. The head was not, he was fairly sure, her type. But . . .

'I feel closer to you, Bobkins,' said Maisie. 'I feel we're both struggling. Are you struggling? You seem to me to be struggling. I like that in you.'

From under her cloak, Maisie took the scroll of paper that he had given her back in August. With it was the locket. She held both out, at arm's length, to Robert. 'There you are,' she said. 'I think you'd better have them back.'

Robert touched the manuscript nervously. 'Er . . .'

He didn't take it from her.

'What exactly does the Twenty-fourth Imam *do*?' he said.

'Oh,' said Maisie, her eyes wide and shining with newly acquired faith, 'apparently he hurls thunderbolts around and sort of dries up wells and does tremendous damage to buildings.'

Robert resolved to be more respectful to Hasan. Only last week he had told him to get out of the bath and described him as 'a little rat'. It was comforting to note, however, that, so far at any rate, the little blind boy had shown not much talent for destruction. The only thing he had so far managed to wreck was the Wilson family's CD player.

'It all happens,' Maisie said, 'after his Occultation. He's fine until the Occultation, and then . . . you know . . . he's dynamite! It's all in the paper you gave me.'

Resolving to pass them on to someone else as soon as possible, Robert took hold of both locket and manuscript and put them in his jacket pocket.

'Do you think you could ever . . . you know . . .'

'What?'

But it was hopeless. It wasn't simply that he seemed incapable of telling the truth: he couldn't begin to express any thought without it sounding false or grotesque. He would go and see the headmaster as soon as they got back. He had the absurd conviction that his new boss would look after him, somehow explain things and make them right. '*A Muslim is the brother of every other Muslim. He must not oppress or surrender him.*' Except he wasn't a Muslim, was he? Or was he?

As if in answer to his doubts, from out of the birch-trees came Mr Malik, at the head of a line of boys. He raised his right arm, pirou-etted, and landed, like a ballet dancer, some yards ahead of himself, on his toes. He spun round with both arms extended, and started to shake his hands vigorously. After him, giggling furiously, came Sheikh and Mahmud. Behind them came the fat boy in glasses from Cranborne School. He too was waving his arms, then lifting a leg each in turn and shaking his feet at the leaden sky. Perhaps, thought Robert, he had been converted.

As Maisie, too, turned to watch, the whole school emerged into the vacant space of the Common, each one lifting now one arm, now the other, leaping and landing, shaking and pirouetting, and all of them, apart from Dr Ali, laughing wildly. This, to the wonder of anyone who happened to be passing, was Islamic dancing.

'Come, Wilson!' called the headmaster. 'Come! Dance! Dance!'

Stiffly, Robert got to his feet.

'My dear girl,' Malik called to Maisie, 'dance!'

This was not a possible option for Maisie. Making small noises of distress, she started to do a three-point turn, reversed – hard – into the side of the bench, and squawked loudly.

'Take off those ridiculous clothes,' called the headmaster, 'and dance!'

Maisie, from deep inside her black linen bag, was muttering about how it was all right for some people. The line of boys and masters – Hasan and Rafiq bringing up the rear – made its way through pools of water and patches of sodden black earth, across the cinder track leading up towards the Windmill, and to the chestnut-trees, now almost empty of leaves, that shadow the edge of Parkside. Hasan, holding tightly to Rafiq's hand, was laughing and thrashing his body like a swimmer in difficulties.

Robert looked beyond the line of boys, but Aziz the janitor and his friend were gone. Maybe conditions were just too bad for a man forced to operate with only one shoe. Awkwardly, moving like a much older man, he made his way after Mr Malik. Behind him, puffing and blowing, came Maisie. As he walked through the wet grass, the locket and the thick scroll of paper banged at his chest, like an urgent warning. The words of the man in the pub came back to him, crowding out his thoughts, rising up to his face like a blush of shame: *'All who serve Malik will die. And the staff and pupils of the*

Wimbledon Independent Islamic Boys' Day School will burn in hell-fire when the day comes!'

Maybe the day was coming. And sooner than he thought. With Maisie still keeping the regulation distance between the two of them, he almost ran after the headmaster, swinging his arms crazily and taking strides so long that a casual observer might have been forgiven for assuming that he, too, was practising the art of Islamic dancing.

11

Robert always had a free period after lunch. He was allowed this in return for taking detention, which usually involved sitting in an empty classroom with Mafouz and the Husayn twins. As Maisie and Mr Malik's relative were clearing away the destruction (the Huysan twins had been having a mashed-potato fight with school spoons), he made his way up to the headmaster's study.

Mr Malik usually had an hour off after lunch. No one knew quite what he did; sometimes the sounds of country-and-western music drifted out from his study, sometimes he emerged smelling strongly of alcohol, but mostly, judging from the titanic snores that shook the wall of the staffroom, he slept.

It was impossible to tell what he was doing this afternoon. No sound whatsoever came from behind the door. Robert knelt by the keyhole and fixed his eye to it. From Class 2, down below, came the noise of Dr Ali's mathematics class, twenty-five children chanting in unison:

> Eight eights are sixty-four,
> Nine eights are seventy-two,
> Ten eights are eighty,
> Eleven eights are eighty-eight,
> Twelve eights are –

There was an awful, horror-struck pause, followed by several conflicting opinions of what twelve eights might be, and, eventually, a wild scream from Dr Ali. *'Twelve eights are ninety-six! You hear me? Ninety-six!'* The mathematics master obviously intended to make up for his long silence during the earlier part of the term.

All Robert could see through the keyhole was the blur of Mr Malik's grey jacket, passing and repassing; he seemed to be running, now in one direction, now in another. After a while he went to the desk. Robert had a clear view of him there.

The headmaster pulled back the top right-hand drawer and took out a large, new-looking cricket bat. He gripped it hard with both hands and beat the air with it. Then he crouched over it and squared up to an imaginary ball. As he waited for delivery, he started to mutter to himself in what sounded like a Gloucestershire accent. 'Locke delivers it,' he said, in a slow drawl, 'Malik waiting his moment. Calm and steady as a rock, the Pakistan captain just waiting here for the ball to come . . .'

Suddenly his voice rose. '*And he plays it – smashes it through the covers straight for four! Oh, this is remarkable!*'

At the same moment he made stabbing movements, at shoulder height, with the bat. They resembled no cricket stroke that Robert could remember. The headmaster looked as if he was fighting off a large insect that was homing in on his neck.

'*Malik has done it again! It's four runs! Oh, this is remarkable! Remarkable play by the Pakistan captain!*'

He gave one last poke with the bat and, throwing it to the ground, clasped both hands and raised them above his head.

Robert knocked, quite hard, at the woodwork. The headmaster started in guilty surprise. He straighted up and, in a deep, serious voice, called, 'A moment please!' Then he scooped up the bat, swept it back into the drawer, and composed himself at his chair. From his jacket pocket he took a small vanity mirror and adjusted his hair. When he was ready, he presented a three-quarter profile towards the door and said, 'Come!'

Robert came.

Mr Malik's mood of earlier in the day seemed to have evaporated. He appeared genuinely pleased to see his reception-class teacher. He rose from his chair and held out his hand, as if this was the first time the two of them had met.

'Wilson!' he said. 'Don't tell me! You want more money!'

This, as it happened, was perfectly true. But Robert did not feel able to say so. Instead he gave a weak smile and fingered the locket, through the cloth of his lapels.

Malik clasped his hands behind his back. He moved over to the window and looked out across rain-driven Wimbledon. In the distance, a police car wailed its way towards them up Wimbledon Hill.

'It must be difficult for you,' he said, 'surrounded by all these wogs. I imagine you are deeply confused. Bowing to the East and carrying on like lunatics. I expect you say to yourself, "*Send the bastards back to where they came from!*" '

'You mean – Cheltenham?' said Robert, unable to repress a smile.

The headmaster looked suddenly serious. 'I am not a very good Muslim,' he said, 'but I do my best.'

Something in his childhood had obviously prompted this remark. Indeed, Mr Malik took on the same, sad, soulful air whenever Cheltenham was mentioned. It can't have been easy to have been a good Muslim in Cheltenham, thought Robert. There was probably not a good supply of mosques available.

'You know about my mother, of course,' went on the headmaster, 'but what can you do if your father is called Malik and your mother is called Frobisher? There is no meeting of minds.'

'I thought,' said Robert boldly, 'she was called Perkins.'

Malik shrugged with infinite resignation. 'Frobisher . . . Perkins,' he said – 'what's the difference?'

Robert decided to come to the point. He took the locket and the manuscript out of his pocket and laid them on the desk in front of the headmaster.

Mr Malik did not seem pleased to see it again. He backed away. His hand went up to his collar and started to loosen his tie. He looked from the manuscript to Robert and back again. 'I knew you had obtained this and gave it to . . . er . . . Ai'sha, Wilson,' he said. 'How did you come by it?'

'Two men gave it to me,' said Robert, 'in the pub. The day I came for the job. Do you remember?'

Malik looked at him. He looked like a man trying to do a complicated piece of mental arithmetic. 'Aziz our janitor . . . and . . . another man . . .'

'The ones with one shoe,' said Robert brightly. 'The Twenty-fourthers! You didn't seem very keen to meet them.'

The headmaster threw back his head and gave out the kind of laugh dished out by medieval jailers to boastful prisoners. 'Keen to meet them, Wilson! Keen to meet them! I hardly dare to think that such people exist! I flee from such people – and I advise you to do the same! They are dangerous lunatics! They are madmen! They are fanatics!'

'They told me to give it to you, Headmaster,' said Robert. 'But I didn't, I'm afraid.'

Malik did some more of the laugh. This time it was more the kind of mirth displayed by, say, Rommel, shortly after the battle of El Alamein. To say it was effortfully hollow would have been an understatement.

'Please don't apologize, my dear Wilson. If this should prove genuine, it is about as welcome as a High Court summons – another document I expect hourly unless the Bradford branch of the Inland Revenue adopts a more compassionate attitude to its clients.'

He looked down at the manuscript and locket and gave a little shudder. Below them, Dr Ali's boys were getting started on the ten times table. They didn't sound very convinced about it.

'Run from it, Wilson. You run as fast as you can away from it. Cower in the bowels of the earth from it, and pull the bedclothes over your head. You change your name and address and never tell a soul you saw it. You flee it, my dear boy.'

Robert looked down at the manuscript. 'And what does it do?' he said. 'Turn into a snake and slither after you?'

Malik practically ran at him and grabbed him by the lapels. 'Ha ha ha!' he said. 'Ha ha ha ha! Frightfully funny! What a laugh! Ho ho ho ho! How amusing!'

Robert did not know what to say to this. The headmaster went back to his chair and sank into it, with a groan. He put his head in his hands and rocked backwards and forward for some minutes.

'They can't be all that bad,' said Robert. 'I mean, Aziz seems OK . . . You obviously thought he was all right.'

'I wanted him where I could keep an eye on him,' said Mr Malik through his hands. 'I wanted to find out how many of these damned Twenty-fourthers there are about the place.'

Robert coughed. 'I keep thinking I'm seeing them,' he said. 'I can't take my eyes off people's footwear. They're everywhere. I'm surprised you haven't seen them. They're all over Wimbledon.'

Malik gave a shriek. 'Twenty-fourthers!' he yelled. 'All over Wimbledon! Why didn't you tell me?'

'I didn't know they were Twenty-fourthers,' said Robert. 'I just thought they were people wearing one shoe. I didn't know they were after Hasan. I haven't a clue what's going on really.'

Malik sat back in his chair and sighed. 'No,' he said, 'there is no reason why you should have a clue. We really haven't discussed these things, have we?'

He looked down at the manuscript. He picked it up with all the enthusiasm of a man finding a mail-order death-warrant on his mat.

'The Twenty-fourth Imam,' he said, 'has often been spoken of among the Wimbledon Dharjees. But there have never been writings about him. And this . . .' he tapped the manuscript and shuddered – 'points clearly to the little boy in your house. You have a great responsibility, Wilson. You must protect him. You must stand guard over him at all times.'

The headmaster did not make it clear whether this was because Hasan might, at any moment, start chucking thunderbolts around the place. Robert still felt some confusion about what Aziz and his friends might be expected to do around the time of the little boy's Occultation. Was it, he wondered, like a bar mitzvah? He had been to Martin Finkelstein's bar mitzvah and had been given a small white hat, which was still on his mantelpiece at home.

'Twenty-fourthers,' he said, 'are – '

'Are animals!' said Mr Malik. 'They are wild beasts! They are brutal, misguided thugs! And, I am afraid that, like the Mounties, they always get their man!'

Robert wondered, but did not ask aloud, who their man might be. He might have to do something more radical than simply leave this job. He might have to get some dark glasses and retire to a small island off the coast of north-west Scotland.

'This manuscript,' said the headmaster, 'must be examined carefully. We must put it in the hands of trained Islamic scholars and get them to run tests on it. They must carbon-date it and put it under the microscope, and we must examine Aziz carefully and get him to say where he found it. I assume he did not pick it up on Southfields Station!'

He looked up at Robert. 'You have indeed a grave responsibility, Wilson. I feel I do not know you. I feel I do not know all the secrets of your heart. I must look deep, deep into your soul and grow to trust you as a brother!'

Robert gulped. He tried, without much success, to look like a man who had a soul into which you could look.

The headmaster looked up from his desk and peered, searchingly, into Robert's eyes. 'Why did you become a Muslim?' he said.

This was the one question Robert had been hoping the headmaster would not ask him. He gulped again, but found he was unable to answer.

'We will fight them together,' said Malik, rising from his chair. 'You and I will fight them together. We are Muslim brothers, you and I. We have never talked of these things, Wilson. We must talk of them. The Muslim is the brother of every other Muslim. He must not oppress or surrender him.'

So saying, the headmaster flung his arms round Robert and squeezed him warmly. Robert, feeling rather like a tube of toothpaste, stood, quite passive, in Mr Malik's fierce embrace.

'I have not listened to *you*, Wilson,' went on the older man, still not slackening his embrace. 'I have talked only of my own concerns. It must have been hell for you. You are lost in a strange country, among a lot of incomprehensible wogs going on about Twenty-fourthers and God knows what, and you are probably scared stiff!'

Robert, his voice muffled by Mr Malik's right arm, said, 'I am. I'm terrified!'

Malik straightened up and broke away. 'I shall put Hasan in your trust,' he said, 'and I will inform Mr Shah that a first-class man is "on the job". We must get first-class information about what these damned Twenty-fourthers have planned. And as we approach the Occultation we must take extra care.'

Not, thought Robert, that there would be much anyone could do should the Twenty-fourth Imam decide to loon around sw19 behaving like a negative version of Superman.

'And I must hear your side of the story, Wilson. It is a basic principle of man management. You must share your feelings with us!'

At this moment the door opened and Rafiq came in. Robert could not have said why, but he had the strong impression that the engineering master, too, had been listening at the door. Rafiq did not speak but stood looking at his two colleagues, an enigmatic smile on his face.

Malik turned to him. 'Assemble the school,' said the headmaster. 'A special assembly. I think it is time we listened to our new brother. We have closed our ears to his cries and left him in the shadows while we walked in the light.'

Rafiq said nothing. Down below, Dr Ali and his class had relapsed into silence. All Robert could hear was the wind, shouldering vainly against the windows of the headmaster's study.

'Wilson is going to talk to the whole school,' said Mr Malik. 'He is going to share his feelings with us.'

Unable to resist any longer, he flung himself back at Robert. He dug his fingers into his ribs, massaged his cheeks, and patted the back of his thighs as if they were unproved bread.

Robert, gasping for breath in his arms, wondered whether Mr Malik's request for him to give an account of himself was entirely motivated by concern for his staff. *He suspects*, he found himself thinking. *He's on to me!*

'He is going to tell us,' Malik went on, 'how he became one of us. He is going to confide the secrets of his heart to us. He is going to tell us how he came to be a Muslim.'

12

Mr Malik looked round at the assembled school. They were sitting cross-legged in what he liked to call the Great Hall. There were only ninety of them, but it was a tight squeeze. Boys were jammed together like rush-hour travellers on the Underground. Saddawi, known as 'The Boy with the Pointed Head', was only just in the room. He was peering in on the proceedings from the kitchen, while his best friend, Mafouz, had retreated to the stairs and was looking down, intently, on Mr Malik's elegantly coiffeured hair. Robert was standing a little behind him. As the headmaster gave the Husayn twins what he called 'the corkscrew' – an intense stare combined with a slow quiver of the nostrils – they slackened their hold on the new recruit to Class 1 – a Bosnian refugee whose name no one could pronounce.

'Today,' he said solemnly, 'Mr Wilson, or Yusuf Khan as he likes to be sometimes known, is going to tell us how and why he became a Muslim.'

He turned to Robert and extended a welcoming hand. *He knows*, thought Robert, *he knows. He is having fun at my expense.*

'It is no easy thing for a person like Wilson, whose family has had a complex religious history – his father, for example, was a . . . er . . . Buddhist – to ally himself with a religion whose roots lie far from Wimbledon.'

The boys gazed up at him in rapture. They must, thought Robert, have seen some strange things in their lives. Their parents had travelled thousands of miles, from all parts of the globe, to make a new home in quiet England, safe among the ashes of empire, only to have their children greeted by Mr Malik, a man more exotic than any schoolboy had a right to expect a teacher to be.

'Wilson, or Yusuf Khan, or whatever you like to call him, is, as you are all aware, a man of many talents. He is a complex individual, rich in fruit, with a good long "nose" and plenty of body. In short, someone who is, as it were, drinking well now and well worth laying down for the future.'

Robert patted his hair down and tried to formulate a few opening remarks. Conversions were often the result of a journey, weren't they? Where could he have been going? *I was on my way to West Wimbledon station, when . . .* When what?

'Wilson is white. He is Anglo-Saxon. He is, although this may seem incredible, the kind of man who used to rule the world!'

Robert coughed apologetically.

'And now he is *Muslim*. He is 100 per cent pure Muslim. He reads the Koran, he attends daily prayers, and occasionally, when there is a gap in the conversation, he babbles of going to Mecca. Can you imagine him there in his sports jacket, among the thousands of pilgrims?'

The boys laughed at this sally. Robert, who found he was sweating, started to try to recall some key phrases from Marwan Ibrahim Al-Kaysi. Could a case be made for the sports jacket being an Islamic garment?

'Things are changing, gentlemen!' said Malik, clasping his hands behind his back. 'The Church of England is no longer the only game in town. And Wilson here is, we might say, the future – the first sign that British society is going to throw off the shackles of racism and colonialism and produce something genuinely multicultural, like . . . er . . . him!'

Loud applause greeted this remark. The headmaster seemed sincere enough, but his manner was so perfectly poised between gravity and teasing that Robert's discomfort increased.

'Listen to him now as he tells us how and why he became a convert. Listen to his story, and profit by it. And afterwards we will take questions from the floor.'

Here Mr Malik stepped back with a flourish, and Robert found he was walking out in front of the whole school, his heart thumping, his mind a complete blank.

'I became a Muslim,' he said, 'at four-thirty on Wednesday the twenty-third of July. On Wimbledon Station.'

This, thought Robert, had the right ring to it. It sounded concrete, authentic.

'I had never, in my life, up to that point, met a Muslim. I had never even *seen* a Muslim – apart, of course, from on the television, and the ones I had seen there – I will be absolutely frank – did not seem a particularly inspiring bunch!'

Mr Malik seemed to like this. The headmaster smirked to himself, chuckled, and drew the edge of his right hand carefully along his moustache.

'Colonel Gaddafi, for example – an obvious loony if ever I saw one. Saddam Hussein, for example, and his Ba'ath Party – a man, I will be absolutely frank, I would probably cross the street to avoid.'

Sheikh was looking at him intently. The little boy's chin was cupped in his hands. He was wearing, as were all the boys, the school uniform designed by Mr Malik himself – grey jersey, grey trousers, black shoes, and bright green tie and socks. He must get off the subject of Saddam Hussein, thought Robert.

'Ayatollah Khomeini, for example,' he heard himself saying, 'was a complete . . .' He managed to head this sentence off its track just in time. ' . . . mullah. He was in every sense a man of the cloth. Whereas Yasser Arafat . . . er . . . for example – '

Here he caught sight of Aziz the janitor, who was standing at the back of the hall with his mop and bucket. He seemed to have decided that now was the right time to clean the Great Hall floor and was poking the mop head in among the boys' legs, muttering to himself.

' . . . who bears a close resemblance to our school janitor, Aziz – although, as far as I know, Aziz does not wander around with a tea towel on his head organizing terrorist attacks – Yasser Arafat – '

How had he got on to the subject of Yasser Arafat? Why had he got on to the subject of Yasser Arafat? How could he leave the subject of Yasser Arafat?

' . . . is the leader of the Palestinian Liberation Organization.'

This was safe ground. They couldn't be expected to argue with that. Islam, as far as he was aware, had no objections to a man stating the obvious.

'The Palestinian Liberation Organization was founded, after the Second World War, with the intention of liberating Palestine. As we all know.'

This was all right as far as it went. But Dr Ali was looking restless. His head snaked forward. Over his not entirely clean white collar you could see his Adam's apple thumping. Robert tried to concentrate on a spot just above the doctor's head. He fixed his mind on a rule his father had given him for public speaking: *Get a vague plan and then say anything that comes into your head*. But no words would come. What they wanted to hear was why he had become a Muslim. And he simply could not think of anything that might have made him become a Muslim.

'I can hardly believe,' he found himself saying, 'that someone like me could have become an . . . er . . . Muslim. Because quite a lot of Islam is, frankly to me . . . er . . . well gobbledygook!'

Dr Ali, his chin in his hands, was staring at Robert. His lips seemed to be mouthing something, but Robert could not make out what it was. He looked as if he was reciting some charm to ward off evil spirits.

'Take the Koran, for example,' went on Robert. 'Take it. You know? Get it out and take a close look at it. I have to say that from my point of view – and this is only my point of view – it is *not* a page-turner. It just isn't. It is obviously a very popular book and, according to my edition, has sold millions of copies worldwide – as has Enid Blyton, for example – but . . .'

This was the wrong direction. He must get off the subject of the Koran. And why was he mentioning Enid Blyton? He must get off the subject of anything controversial. But every single thing to do with being a Muslim seemed quite incredibly controversial. Why had he become a Muslim? Why hadn't he become a Sikh or a Hasidic Jew?

'Why,' he went on, 'didn't I become a Sikh or a Hasidic Jew? I mean, it is possible that their . . . er . . . holy books are a less tough read than the . . . er . . . Koran.'

Dr Ali had put both his index fingers in his ears and was rocking backwards and forwards in his chair. He looked like an airline passenger who has just been told that all four engines on his 747 have just failed.

'Take,' went on Robert, 'the chapter called "The Bee". For the first four or five pages there is absolutely no mention of a bee. In fact it seems to talk about almost every kind of animal there is *apart* from the bee, and, for someone like myself, a total newcomer to Islam, this is, I have to say in all honesty, deeply confusing. I mean, you know, why not call it "The Ant"? Or "The Porcupine"? Or "The Frog"? You know?'

Some boys in the front row laughed. Dr Ali increased the rocking movement until the point where his forward movement was critical. Suddenly the mathematics master was on his feet. He was pointing at Robert and yelling something that sounded like Arabic but turned out to be very emotional English. 'I cannot listen to this!' yelled Dr Ali. 'I cannot allow this to continue!'

Mr Malik turned sharply to his second master. 'Wilson is simply expressing the doubts and fears of a new – '

But Dr Ali did not listen. He raised his right hand and threw a quivering index finger in Robert's direction. 'This man,' he said, 'is a blasphemer and a hypocrite! I have been watching him for some weeks, and I accuse him publicly – before the whole school!'

Robert started to shake. 'I don't think – ' he began.

'Did you or did you not read this book to the reception class?' yelled Ali. He produced from under his jacket a small paperback book which he waved in the air, furiously. 'A book, gentlemen, which will make you physically ill should you even catch sight of it in Waterstones! A book which has as its hero – as its *hero* – '

He held the book out between finger and thumb as if it contained some dangerous virus which at any moment could threaten the whole school.

' . . . a *pig!* A pig is the hero of this book! *The Sheep-Pig*, by Dick King-Smith! *And this is not all!*'

Mr Malik, too, was on his feet, waving his arms. 'My dear Ali,' he was saying, 'our religion forbids us to eat pigs. It doesn't prohibit us from talking about them. May I remind you that – '

Robert had read *The Sheep-Pig* to Class 1. He had, on rainy afternoons, read quite a lot of books about pigs to them.

'*The Tale of Pigling Bland*,' Dr Ali was yelling, 'by the woman Potter! *Horace: the Story of a Pig*, by Jane DuCane Smith. *Pigs Ahoy!*, by Hans Wilhelm. *Pig Time*, by Duncan Fowler and Norman Bates. *Don't Forget the Bacon!*, by Pat Hutchins. The man is obsessed with pigs!'

It was true that Robert had always liked pigs. But no one in Class 1 had seemed unduly disturbed by his account of them, even if the Husayn twins had said that pigs were 'boring' and had asked if they could bring in the novelization of *Terminator Two*.

Dr Ali was now incoherent with rage. He looked, thought Robert, like something out of one of his own visions. Whirling round on his toes, he kept stabbing towards his fellow member of staff with his long, bony fingers. But it wasn't until Robert thought he recognized a familiar English word that he leaned across to the headmaster to check if he had heard it correctly.

'I think,' said Mr Malik, cheerfully, 'he is sentencing you to death.' He dropped his voice to a confidential whisper. 'Apparently,' he went on, 'he does this quite a lot. I have been researching into his background, and apparently he is a member of an organizaation known as the British Mission for Islamic Purity. We must endeavour to rise above, Wilson. Rise above!'

But the mathematics master, now dribbling freely, his face contorted with hatred, continued to dance from foot to foot, watched impassively by the ninety or so young British citizens of the Wimbledon Islamic Day School (Independent Boys').

Mr Malik put his arm round Robert and continued to watch this display with apparent unconcern. He beamed again as Ali, practically choking on his own saliva, fell forward into a group of pupils.

He was practically laughing out loud as Ali reached critical mass. Foaming at the mouth, the maths master, now on his knees, raised both hands above his head and shook them violently. He was screeching, sobbing and wailing with the aplomb of a professional mourner and it wasn't always easy to understand what he was saying. But the gist of it seemed to be that there should be an early, and preferably unpleasant, end to the miserable life of the blasphemer and pig-fancier, Wilson.

PART THREE

13

Islamic time seemed to pass more quickly. Christmas had only just gone, and now the mornings were bright. On longer evenings the sound of wood against leather could be heard in the garden behind the large house.

'You'll be late, darling,' called Mrs Wilson. 'You don't want to be late, do you? It's Sports Day!'

Robert did, actually, quite want to be late. He had never found it easy to get up in the morning, and being under sentence of death did not make the prospect of a new day any more enticing.

Outside, April had come to Wimbledon. A blackbird was singing, carelessly, in the trees behind the house. A breeze stirred the curtains. On the chest of drawers in the corner of the room was Malik's newsletter: SPRING NEWS FROM THE ISLAMIC SCHOOL WIMBLEDON.

> *Admissions are up by 30 per cent and we are ahead of budget. The profit-sharing scheme is coming on line in June and we are already planning a follow-up to our successful Islamic Quiz Evening on March 12th. Well done, Mr Mafouz – we hope you enjoy the tickets for Les Miserables! Plans for the swimming-pool continue apace!*

The swimming-pool was something of a disappointment. Rafiq had dug a twelve-foot hole at the bottom of the garden, and then, in the grip of one of his periodic fits of depression, had abandoned it to the spring rain.

'You can do nothing with Rafiq during Ramadan,' Mr Malik had said. 'He just lies on his bed and thinks about having his end away!'

But, for the first time in his life, Robert felt part of a success. Every day a new parent would appear in Mr Malik's office. And, so it was rumoured, 'This is a Christian Country' Gyles, of Cranborne Junior School, had privately denounced the headmaster's operation as being 'a bucket shop'. The inspector of schools had, however, described the operation as 'offering an entirely new slant on the core curriculum'. They even had locks on the lavatory doors.

Islam had offered him a lot. Among the things it had offered him was Maisie. If it had not been for their long, soul-searching conversations about the Koran and the life of the Prophet, he would probably not, now, be sleeping with her. Next to him, she snored lightly. As he got out of bed, she moved. The top of her thigh just cleared the duvet. He gulped.

She was still convinced he was homosexual. They had been having sexual intercourse about three times a day, every day, for the last six weeks, but Maisie still maintained that Robert was faking it. His orgasms seemed to him to be perfectly genuine, but once Maisie had an idea in her head it proved difficult to shift. There were still moments when he worried about her attitude. Might Malik be something to do with it? Did Malik still suspect him of not being quite the full shilling as far as heterosexuality was concerned? Such ideas were hard to dispel.

At the mere thought of the word *shift* his penis leaped doggily to attention. *Islamic underwear!* he crooned to himself, as he groped for his grey jersey. *It takes so long to get off!* Her clothes, lying across the back of the bedroom chair, spread out in a black line towards the door. There was enough material there, thought Robert, reaching for his green tie, to shroud a fair-sized glasshouse in darkness. You could climb in there with her and still have room to conduct Beethoven's Fifth Symphony. Her garments were so large and flowing that a man could have pleasured her while she was waiting at a bus-stop and no one would have been any the wiser.

'We'll be late, darling!' he called, lightly. 'Darling!' She let him talk dirty whenever he felt like it!

She had been living with the Wilsons for nearly three months. Maisie's father had died just after Christmas. He had been briefly but sincerely mourned. Her mother had surprised everyone by dying just as they were recovering from her husband's death. She was helped into the gardens of paradise by a number 33 bus, which had reversed over her while trying to execute a three-point turn outside the Polka Theatre, but some people still claimed that her death was, in part anyway, due to a broken heart. 'If she'd been herself,' Maisie wailed to Robert, 'she'd have looked.'

Maisie had been more affected by her mother's death than most people thought possible. She had always referred to her as 'the old bat', or occasionally as 'that hard bitch'. Mr and Mrs Wilson had been very sympathetic.

Maisie had moved out of her parents' house and come to stay at the Wilsons' shortly after her mother's funeral, a multi-denominational affair dominated by the headmaster of the Wimbledon Independent Islamic Boys' School (Day). Mr Malik's speech – described by one of Maisie's mother's oldest friends as 'a masterpiece of bad taste' – had dwelt, at great length, on the sexual prospects awaiting the Faithful in heaven. Maisie was no longer on speaking terms with any of her family ever since her stepbrother's son had asked her where she had parked the camel and when she was going to be circumcised.

Robert struggled into his green socks. Mr Malik had insisted the staff also appear in uniform since early February, although Robert suspected this was only because he had a deal with the shop that supplied the ties and the socks. He had come to quite like the outfit. *I will die with my boots on! It can't be worse than Ramadan!*

He shuddered slightly as he thought about Ramadan. Dr Ali had been particularly active during Ramadan. He kept leaping into the darkroom, created for the Photographic Society on the first floor, and claiming that he had heard the sound of munching.

It was surprising, really, that the only person in the school whom Dr Ali had sentenced to death should be Robert. Close examination of the man's conversation suggested that no one in the Western world was safe. There was quite a lot of his conversation. Like the woman in the fairy story, once Ali started talking he did not stop.

There were, as far as Robert could tell, no other members of the British Mission for Islamic Purity, the organization the doctor claimed to represent. Ali had an aunt in Southfields, but, he told the headmaster, she was doomed to everlasting hell-fire. The man was, as Dr Malik had pointed out to Robert, a fundamentalist's fundamentalist. 'As far as he is concerned,' said the headmaster one evening in the Frog and Ferret, 'there is Allah, there is Muhammad, and then there is him. What can you do with such people?'

Ali, it turned out, had been sentencing people to death for years. He had sentenced the owner of a garden centre in Morden to death when the man refused to take his Access card. He had sentenced the entire General Synod of the Church of England to death. He had sentenced over fifteen hundred journalists to death, including all of the staff of *The London Programme*. He had terrifyingly conservative views on the ordination of women.

The encouraging thing was that all the people he had sentenced were, so far at any rate, in good health. Some of them, as far as Robert could tell, were completely unaware that Dr Ahmed Ali had officially decreed they were no longer worthy to share the planet with him. Some of them seemed to have positively enjoyed the experience. One of them – the owner of a mobile whelk stall in South Wimbledon – had told the doctor that he could sentence him to death until he was blue in the face and that he, personally, could not give a flying fuck. This was more or less the view of the headmaster.

'By all means sentence Wilson to death,' Mr Malik had said. 'By all means. I think we should all start sentencing each other to death. It clears the air. Let's "go for it". Sentence me to death if it makes you feel better.'

Mr Malik's tolerance was limitless. 'I may have tried to keep the loonies out,' he said, 'but once they are in, they are in!' The more eccentrically his maths master behaved, the more Malik was prepared to defend him. At half-term, Ali had offered ten pounds to any of 'the proud Muslim people of South-West London' who would be prepared to finish off Robert Wilson, but, even though he had raised this sum to twelve pounds fifty, there were, so far at any rate, no takers.

Robert's real worry was that he could not understand what it was that had caused offence. If he had been able to understand that, he might at least have been able to formulate a coherent apology. It couldn't have simply been his reading *The Sheep-Pig* to Class 1. Maybe the doctor had some inside information on him. Anyway, if he opened his mouth again, he thought glumly as he started downstairs to breakfast, he would probably get into worse trouble. He had stayed clear of the subject of religion since Christmas.

If only he could manage to finish the Koran. He had made several attempts on it. He had tried saying it out loud. He had tried reading it on trains, in bed at night, and even, on one occasion, in the bath. He had tried starting in the middle and working backwards. He had tried starting at the end and flicking to the beginning. He had tried reading isolated pages – reading three pages, skipping three, and then reading four. He had tried it drunk and he had tried it sober. He had even tried starting at page 1 and working his way through to the end. None of these methods had worked. After a page, his eyes would wander away. After two pages, he would find himself, without quite knowing why or how he got there, making a cup of tea or watching the television. After three or four pages, he found himself wandering the streets or pacing anxiously through some park he didn't even recognize, twitching and murmuring strangely to himself while mothers, at the sight of him, drew their children to them and stole softly away across the grass.

When he reached the bottom of the stairs, he turned and called up to Maisie. 'Coming!' she replied.

Hasan was sitting up at the table, eating a large slice of toast. The butter was dribbling across that huge mark on his cheek. Mrs Wilson was sitting on the sofa, smiling foolishly at him.

Immediately he heard Robert's footsteps, Hasan stopped. 'Hello, Mr Wilson,' he said, in his high, precise voice. 'I dreamed last night that Badger turned into a hedgehog. Would you see if there is a hedgehog on the lawn?'

Hasan was always having prophetic dreams. They were modest, small-scale affairs, usually about very mundane subjects. But the events described in them – the loss of some ornament, or the visit of some old family friend – quite often turned out to happen just as the little boy had predicted. There was something uncanny about him, his high forehead and his big, sightless eyes.

Robert went to the French windows and looked out to see if he could see anything. There, in the middle of the lawn, was a hedgehog. Robert whirled round on his mother, suspecting her of some collusion with the child, but, with the wistful fondness of a woman who has finished with childbearing, Mrs Wilson was still gazing at the Twenty-fourth Imam of the Wimbledon Dharjees.

'Is Badger around?' said Robert, trying to keep the panic out of his voice, 'because there's a hedgehog on – '

At this moment Badger skulked into the kitchen, loped over to the pedal bin, and stood gazing mournfully at a piece of orange peel, just visible over the edge of the plastic rim.

'Maisie!' called Mrs Wilson. '*Le petit déjeuner est servi, ma chérie!*'

There was a grunt from upstairs. Robert's father was awake.

Robert sat at a vacant space and put his head in his hands. His mother looked at him, briskly. 'What's the matter this morning?' she said, in the voice she had used when he asked her for an off-games note.

'Just the usual,' said Robert, with heavy sarcasm. 'I've been sentenced to death. Apart from that, everything is fine. Everything is a winner!'

Mrs Wilson snorted. 'I do not think, Robert,' she said, 'that anyone takes this man very seriously. All you said was that the Koran wasn't an easy read. Nobody kills anyone for saying something like that. It's fair comment. I personally think – '

Before his mother could get started on the Koran, Robert held up his hand. You never knew who might be listening. She looked, however, as if she was fairly determined to give her views on the matter, but before she could start on the *Why do they come over here if they don't like it?* speech or her *I believe in respecting people's religious feelings but would die to defend their right to disagree with me* speech, Maisie came round the door.

She ate breakfast in a kind of compromise Islamic outfit. Just after her conversion – a moment of mystical submission she insisted on replaying several times a day – she had kept the veil on even at meals, and forked meat and potatoes in under her mask like a gamekeeper baiting a trap. She also stored food in there like a hamster, and sometimes, when least expected, her head would snake back inside her covering and the crunch of crisps or the slurp of a boiled sweet could be heard. But now her outfit, although loose and flow-ing, was slightly closer to the kind of garment you might expect in sw19. It was more like a giant caftan than anything else.

It was Mr Malik who had persuaded her to soften her approach. 'Even in Libya they don't carry on like that,' he had said. 'You look like something out of a pantomime. What are you supposed to be?'

Her friendship with the headmaster remained a close one. While Mr Malik hardly ever discussed religion with Robert, he spent many evenings in the La Paesana restaurant, Mitcham, going over the finer points of Islamic doctrine with Maisie. 'We always spend a lot of time with female converts, Wilson,' he said, giving him a broad wink. 'They are a lot more work, if you take my meaning!'

Robert was not exactly jealous of the headmaster – he could not remember meeting anyone less sexually threatening. But there were moments when he almost wished that what was happening between Maisie and Mr Malik did have a sexual connotation. At least he would then have been able to understand it.

'Sports Day today!' said Maisie brightly.

No one, as usual, wanted to discuss the fact that he had been sentenced to death. They were bored with it. At first, Robert's father had got quite excited. He had even gone to the Wimbledon police, but they had not seemed very interested. They had said a Detective Constable McCabe, a community policeman, would 'look in', which, after a couple of weeks, he did. He seemed mainly interested in whether there were any locks on the windows.

Robert's father appeared. His hair was matted and uncombed, and his face, as usual in the mornings, was a rather shocking blend of inflamed pink and seasick white. He was wearing a dressing-gown.

'What do you do for Sports Day?' he said. 'Stone one of the junior ticks to death?'

A lot of Mr Wilson senior's liberal attitudes had not stood the test of having two converted Muslims living in the house. He was often to be found slumped in front of the television, muttering about nig-nogs. At Christmas he had insisted on hanging up Robert's stocking on the end of his bed, and had suggested the two of them visit the Cranborne School carol service. He peered across at Maisie now, as he groped his way to the table, his face showing the strain of his forty-eight years in Wimbledon. 'You used to have nice legs, Maisie,' he said. 'What's wrong with our getting a look at them?'

Mrs Wilson had told him he should get out of the house more. This he achieved by getting along to the Frog and Ferret at about eleven each morning, where he spent hours in conversation with George 'This is My Coronary' Parker.

Maisie giggled. Underneath the Islamic garments she was still an English convent girl. With her veil pushed back and her black hood shading her face, she looked rather like a nun.

Mrs Wilson rose and, folding her hands together, bowed in an Oriental manner. 'Thank you,' she said, 'for our meal.' It was not clear whether this remark was addressed to Allah, Jehovah or the London Muffin Company. She had taken, this spring, to a sort of generalized reverence that looked as if it was planned to accommodate any new religion to which her son or his girlfriend might have become attached.

She had also given up all her domestic routines. She cleared the table as they were eating, following, as always now, her own weird domestic schedule. Sometimes she would start laying the table for breakfast at four in the afternoon; sometimes she would pursue Maisie and Robert out into the street with plates of hot food, begging them to eat more. And sometimes she would announce that she was doing no more in the house. 'There it is!' she would yell, pointing at the fridge. 'It's all in there! It's every man for himself from now on in!'

Perhaps, thought Robert, she was worried about him. It would be nice to think that someone was. He pushed back his chair, and, after one more careful look round the garden, went to look for Class 1's homework. At the top of the pile was a beautifully typed essay from Sheikh on the causes of the English Civil War. The little bastard, or his parents, or some hired professional historian, had written three thousand closely argued words. Robert had given him beta minus (query).

'There you are, Mr Wilson,' Maisie was saying, as she twirled her skirt above her legs like a cancan dancer – 'knees!'

He had to get out of the school. But how could he do it? How could he ever admit to Maisie that the very thing that had brought them together was, like so much else in his life, a lie? He was tied to her and to Mr Malik in exactly the way he was tied to his own parents. He was also, he realized, as he went through to the hall to get Hasan's coat, tied to the little boy in a way he could not have predicted. It wasn't simply that he felt protective towards him. It was that he was beginning to understand why Aziz the janitor and his friends might be convinced he was no ordinary child.

He took Hasan's hand and went out into the clear light of April.

'Did Badger turn into a hedgehog, Mr Wilson?' said the little boy. 'I have special powers and can foresee things!'

Robert squeezed his charge's hand. 'In a way he did, Hasan,' he said. 'In a way he did.'

He was starting to believe this stuff. As he and Hasan and Maisie started out down Wimbledon Park Road, he remembered something the headmaster had said to him, quite soon after he had started teaching the reception class. 'Islam means *surrender*, my dear Wilson. And so you must surrender. You may think you stand on your own, or have your own choices, or make your own fate, but you do not do so. You submit, and let your life take its course. The course that God has designed for it.'

The trees were out in Wimbledon Park. As the three of them started to climb the hill, Maisie, who no longer walked yards behind the men in her life, took Robert's arm and started to sing. At first he did not recognize the tune, and then he caught its cadences. It wasn't English. It had the swoop and the lilt of something one might have heard blaring out of a Turkish café. It was a song Mr Malik sang, and she was singing it to what must, surely, be his words.

> Come to me,
> My beautiful girl.
> Don't be shy now.
> Leave your mother,
> Leave your father,
> Leave your people.

Don't be shy now.
Come to me,
My beautiful girl.
You are one of mine now.
You are one of ours now.
Come to me, oh come to me,
Beautiful,
Beautiful,
Girl.

14

From time to time he wondered whether he had made a mistake in sleeping with her. It was something he had been wanting to do for over ten years, but, now that he had done it, he had destroyed something that had been between them – a mysterious, almost exquisite, promise of delight. He was starting to tell the truth – that was what it was. It was hard to keep lying when you were alone in bed with someone. If this went on much longer, the real Robert Wilson might emerge – that awful, jelly-like creature that he had been hiding from the world for the last twenty-four years.

Perhaps they had taken too long to get together. If only he had moved earlier. If only he had pushed his advantage home the night the Dorking brothers gave their party ('The Night of the Hundred Cans', as it was still known in Wimbledon). If only he had made his move six years earlier, during the rehearsed reading of Martin Finkelstein's verse play *These Be Wasted Years, Brother!*

Except he hadn't. They were too like brother and sister, that was it.

If that was the case, incest had never been more fun. Sex with Maisie was about the most interesting thing Robert had ever done. It upstaged even Mr and Mrs Wilson, who had gone markedly quiet since Maisie entered the field. Maisie particularly enjoyed being spanked with a hairbrush, and liked to accompany this activity with a series of clear, confident expressions of her need to be disciplined. 'Oh my arse!' she would call in the still of the Wimbledon night. 'Oh my fat *arse*! Spank it! Spank it, you bastard!'

At the moment of climax she quite often addressed him as Derek. Robert had not yet been able to fathom why this was the case. It was possible, of course, that she was referring, for purely symbolic reasons, to a specialized form of lifting gear.

Robert wasn't sure that their sexual relations were in line with

Islamic thinking – at least as formulated by Marwan Ibrahim Al-Kaysi. They did not pray two *rak'ahs* before making love, or perform *wudu* after intercourse (perhaps because neither of them had the faintest idea what *wudu* might be), and they were woefully deficient in the sacrifice and dowry departments. Maisie was also guilty of one of Al-Kaysi's key errors, *leaving the house excessively* – a practice he quite clearly did not relish in women.

There were times when he thought Maisie was not much more of a Muslim than he was. The headmaster himself had accused her of only joining up for the uniform. But – and this was the real divide between them – she *thought* she was a Muslim. He knew he wasn't. However absurd her convictions might seem, at least they were convictions.

'Tell me,' said Robert, as they walked up the High Street, 'and I'm not going on about it, but exactly why did Ali sentence me to death?'

'Because you said Enid Blyton sold more copies than the Koran,' said Maisie, 'and said that pigs were terrific and Muslims had to learn to deal with them.'

'I did not say any of those things,' said Robert, 'and, even if I did, I don't think they merit the death penalty. I mean, this is a free country – isn't it?'

Maisie tightened her lips. 'You're not free to offend people,' she said. 'It's a very fine line!'

It was, thought Robert, a *very* fine line. You never knew these days when a casual remark was going to provide the justification for someone stalking you with an automatic rifle. He looked nervously over his shoulder, but saw nothing.

'Dr Ali said that you said bad things about Muhammad,' Maisie went on. 'Apparently he heard you.'

'When did he hear? Who was I talking to?'

'You were walking along muttering them to yourself. He said they were so shocking he couldn't even bear to repeat them.'

She seemed almost prepared to take the good doctor's part in this dispute, thought Robert. Why couldn't Ali forget the pig business? Why couldn't the guy loosen up? Robert had not even mentioned pigs in three months.

'The worse thing you can do to a Muslim is insult Muhammad.'

She was always showing off her superior knowledge these days, thought Robert. And the more she found out about Islam, the more she seemed to like it. His trouble was, he realized, that he was simply not able to grasp any religion, let alone a faith where his only spiritual mentor was a book from Wimbledon Public Library.

'I would never say anything bad about Muhammad,' said Robert. 'Even I know better than that.'

'Why would you want to?' said Maisie. 'You're a Muslim, aren't you?'

She had probably rumbled him. Even when he was being particularly careful not to offend, he seemed to manage to say the wrong thing. He had noticed, for example, that Dr Ali always accompanied the Prophet's name with the formula *'may God bless him and grant him peace!'* and, often, in the doctor's presence, Robert would work Muhammad's name into the conversation precisely so that he, too, could repeat the traditional blessing. He often went one better. 'Muhammad – *may God bless him and grant him peace* – who was, I don't need to remind you, *quite a guy* – once said – *and what he said was, on the whole earth, listening to* – on several occasions – *not that he was a man given to repeating himself* – once, anyway, said – *and he had a beautiful speaking voice . . .'* etc. etc. This cut no ice with the doctor. He watched Robert from under his hooded eyes, a slight smile playing around his lips.

'I have to get the bread for lunch,' said Maisie. 'Do you want to come in? You'll probably be safer in the shop. You could hide under the counter.'

'I don't see what's so funny,' said Robert, who was looking nervously down the street. 'There are some funny things going on around here.'

As he said this, he caught sight of Mr Malik, who was walking towards the school. Robert held Hasan's hand tightly. The little boy showed no sign of rising vertically into the air or of summoning seven hundred fiery horsemen from out of the sky.

Robert was sweating. He wiped his brow. From the other side of the road, Aziz the janitor, on his way to school, a sinister smile on his face, started to wave his mop in greeting. For some reason Aziz always took his mop home with him. 'How is the boy?' he said, in his cracked voice.

'He's fine!' said Robert.

'I would like a cake please,' said Hasan, 'with some jam on it!'

Eager to get him away from Aziz, Robert handed him over to Maisie and peered, once more, carefully around him. He was seeing men with one shoe in his sleep these days. He had been sure one was following him round Sainsbury's the other day.

Apart from the headmaster, who had now gone into the school, the place seemed clear. Robert stayed on the pavement while Maisie went in to buy the school's bread. Suddenly a heavy hand whacked him in the shoulder blades. Robert wheeled round to see the beaming face of Mr Mafouz. Next to him, his round face straining towards the cakes in the shop window, was his favourite son.

'That's enough cakes, Anwar!' said Mr Mafouz, and, placing his broad hand on his son's backside, he propelled the boy towards the school.

'How's things?' said Mr Mafouz.

'Not too bad,' said Robert.

The sun picked up the colours of a girl's dress. It sparkled in her hair as she swayed past the grocer's opposite. Clasped into themselves like baby's fists, new shoots were hung along the branches of each tree in the High Street. It was spring. Spring and Wimbledon were still here, even if at times he felt he had landed in a foreign country. As he made the conventional response, Robert felt a curious exaltation, as if the phrase had made such unpleasant things as Dr Ali melt away. He liked Mr Mafouz.

Perhaps, as Mr Malik had suggested, he was slowly learning to surrender, and, by surrendering, to enjoy the sun, the blue sky and the sweetness of having, at long last, a girl to share his bed.

'In fact,' said Robert, 'I feel great.'

'Malik declared the cricket season three months early,' said Mr Mafouz. 'Did you know one is not supposed to play cricket in April? We have been playing since February. He wishes us to get into training for thrashing Cranborne.'

On the other side of the road, Anwar was playing cricket strokes. Robert tried to remember whether the Egyptians had a cricket team and, if so, whether they were any good. Inside the baker's, Maisie had got involved in a complicated negotiation with the shopkeeper. Hasan had pressed his face to the glass in front of the cakes and was sniffing the fresh bread, a look of ecstasy on his face. Mr Mafouz and Robert idled along the pavement.

'How is Anwar's schoolwork?' said Mr Mafouz.

'He is a genius,' said Robert swiftly.

Mr Mafouz grinned. He put his right hand in his jacket pocket and produced a bulky envelope. Robert did not have to ask what it contained. Over the last months Mr Mafouz had given him two free tickets to Paris, a pineapple, six copies of the *Illutrated Tourist Guide to London* and a pair of bright green trousers. Recently, as the summer exams grew closer, he had started to offer money.

'I really couldn't, Mr Mafouz,' said Robert.

'Listen,' said Mr Mafouz, clapping Robert on the back, hard, 'there's more where that came from. If he passes his GCSEs, who knows what I might come up with?'

He leaned his face into Robert's. 'How does a week in Luxor grab you?' he said.

'Sounds fun!' said Robert.

Last week the ever amiable travel agent had asked him 'how much' the Oxford entrance exam was 'compared with what they're asking in Sussex or Cambridge.'

The two men came level with the school gates. From the bakery, Maisie emerged with Hasan, carrying a pile of loaves, and walked into the road, narrowly avoiding an oncoming lorry.

'Tell me,' said Mr Mafouz, 'about "A" levels. Are those people reachable?'

It was impossible to refuse Mr Mafouz's gifts. Robert had done the decent thing and given Anwar alpha double plus for an essay entitled 'My Cat'. He shuddered now, as he recalled the essay: '*I have a cat. It was hit on the head with a spade by my brother. It was in agony . . .*'

From the Common came more parents. Mr Sheikh and Mr Akhtar

walked slowly and seriously towards the gates. Mr Mafouz's face darkened. 'The Sheikh boy,' he said, 'is not up to much, I think.'

Robert thought of Sheikh's seventy-page project on 'Irrigation in the Third World,' his groundbreaking work in chemistry and physics, and the long short story, in French, he had recently submitted, successfully, to an avant-garde magazine. 'He is thin on the ground,' said Robert. 'There is something . . . shifty about the boy!'

Mr Mafouz grinned.

Mr and Mrs Mahmud joined the rest of the crowd at the gates. An elegant BMW drew up over the road and Fatimah Bankhead, the chain-smoking Islamic feminist, stepped out. She gave the assembled group of men a contemptuous sweep of her fine, grey eyes, and marched up the path. Another expensive car pulled in behind her, and Robert recognized Mr Shah, the man from whom they had collected Hasan last summer. He was still wearing the elegantly tailored suit he had worn on that occasion. His name was now inscribed above the door in the Great Hall, with the words OUR BENEFACTOR next to it.

'We'd better go through to the sports field,' said Robert.

He could hear the whoops of small boys from the garden. Up at the first-floor window, the curtains parted and Mr Malik peered out. Robert looked back at Maisie and Hasan. As they came up to the gates, Aziz sidled up to the little boy with his mop, an ingratiating smile on his face.

'Well, well, Hasan!' he began.

But before he could get any further, Mr Malik thrust his head out of the window. 'Clean!' he barked. 'This is Sports Day! I want everything sparkling clean!'

With a resentful grunt, Aziz shambled off into the school.

Mr Malik was wearing cricket whites and a large floppy hat; a dirty white jersey was folded about his neck. If what Robert had seen, to date, of the school's cricket was anything to go by, today was going to be an exhausting experience.

There was an Islamic doctrine, of which the headmaster had often spoken to Robert, known as *ijma*. It meant, as far as Robert could tell, a kind of consensus. It was rather like that strange spirit that hovered

over the Wilson family when they were contemplating an evening
out and told them where they ought to eat, and it had something in
common with whatever it was that told the entire Liverpool football
stadium to sing 'You'll Never Walk Alone' at the same moment. It
was absent, however, during inter-house matches at the Islamic
Boys' School (Day Independent Wimbledon). Every man was his
own umpire. During the last match, the Husayn twins had nearly
beaten the Bosnian refugee to death with the stumps after he had
refused to accept a boundary decision. (In the absence of white lines,
boundaries were hotly disputed.) As Robert rounded the school
building, with Mr Mafouz by his side, he could hear Anwar Mafouz
war-whooping his way round the lawn.

In the narrow passage that led through to the garden, they came
upon Rafiq. He was standing with Dr Ali. When he saw Robert, he
made what looked like a little, stunted bow and moved back towards
the boys on the lawn. There was something decidedly odd about the
engineering master; his manner was always friendly, but, in the six
months he had been at the school, Robert had not exchanged more
than a few words with the man.

Dr Ali smirked at Robert as Mr Mafouz went through to join the
other parents. 'Well, Wilson,' said the maths master, 'I see you are
still with us.'

'Indeed,' said Robert. 'I'm still about the place.'

Robert looked at Dr Ali. There was nothing the matter with his
features. The nose was roughly in the right place. The moustache was
well groomed. The shape of the cheeks – if slightly too reminiscent of
a cadaver – had a certain elegance. His eyes – full, black and watch-
ful – were almost attractive. His hair was oiled, and arranged with
obsessive neatness across his scalp, and his ears, the colour of raw
tuna-fish, were big, intricate and well balanced. And yet about him
there hung the indefinable air of ugliness.

The doctor smirked again. 'I wonder for how long!' he said, in a
somewhat arch tone.

'It is,' said Robert, 'in the hands of Allah.'

The trouble was, of course, it might by now be in the hands of
some high-spirited Islamic youth movement.

His earlier good spirits fading, Robert followed Dr Ali through to the back lawn, as, from a side entrance to the school, the headmaster emerged carrying a large white box. He held it aloft. 'New balls!' he said, and, swinging his arms like a sergeant-major, led his masters out towards the field of battle, in the bright April sunlight.

15

Robert took up a position on the boundary, fairly near to the maths master. As usual, he attempted to strike the correct tone with the man. You couldn't simply ignore the fact that he had sentenced you to death, but it was important to let him know that you weren't rattled. Except, of course, you were rattled. It was dangerous, too, to appear too over-confident, or to do anything that might provoke him into making his unofficial fatwa slightly more public than it was already. Ali was so mean that he was unlikely to buy advertising space, even for a religious edict, and, anyway, he had clearly found Robert's words so offensive that he had, so far, been incapable of repeating them to anyone. But you never knew . . .

Robert clasped his hands behind his back and tried for a light, bantering tone. 'Should I take out life insurance, Dr Ali?'

Ali looked at him. His expression did not alter. 'I do not think,' he said with some conviction, 'that you will find a company prepared to take the risk.'

Presumably the man expected him to add, in the section of the proposal form where you were supposed to talk about your passion for hang-gliding or free-fall parachute jumping, a brief paragraph along the lines of I HAVE ALSO BEEN SENTENCED TO DEATH BY AN ISLAMIC FUNDAMENTALIST.

'What I mean to say,' replied Robert, 'is that I feel I need to know where I stand.'

Mr Malik was fixing in the stumps. Rafiq was choosing the two teams. The Husayn twins wanted to be together. Nobody wanted the Bosnian refugee. Mafouz wanted to be captain. While all this went on, the parents sat around on the school's battered garden furniture, the mothers watching each other warily, the fathers armoured in a remote mildness that Robert recognized from his own parent. *We're the same really,* he thought. *What's the big difference?* Then he looked down at Dr Ali.

'You know where you stand, Yusuf,' said the doctor – 'you stand on slippery ground. *There are some who declare "We believe in Allah and the last day" yet they are not true believers. They seek to deceive Allah and those who believe in him. There is a sickness in their hearts which Allah has increased, and they shall be sternly punished for their hypocrisy.*'

Robert gulped. The man was on to him.

'That's the Koran, isn't it?' he guessed.

Dr Ali did not respond. Robert tried to compose his face into an expression of humble trust.

'It's an extraordinary book,' he went on. 'I'm going to take it away on holiday.'

'Are you a fool or are you pretending to be a fool?' said the maths master.

'A bit of both,' said Robert, trying to keep the tone light.

Dr Ali moved a few paces away from him. This approach was clearly not working. Perhaps, thought Robert, I should sentence *him* to death. Perhaps the gently gently approach only served to bolster Ali's confidence. He wandered over to the far wall.

As he did so, he saw Hasan walk out from the back kitchen. The little boy was wearing the same neat grey flannels that he had worn on the first day Robert had seen him, and, when the sun struck his face, he smiled up at it as if in gratitude. In his right hand was a large cake with jam on it. Robert wanted to go over to him, but judged it best to stay where he was.

Mafouz was bowling, urged on by his father. 'Smash them, Anwar!' Mr Mafouz yelled. 'Go for the bastards!'

Fatimah Bankhead gave him a mean look. Mafouz shuffled up to the bowling crease and started to wind his right arm backwards at high speed. 'I am good at cricket!' he yelled.

Sheikh, who was batting, stood crouched over his bat, patiently waiting for the moment when Mafouz would decide to let go of the ball. It was hard to tell, at the moment, whether it would be moving at or away from him, but Sheikh, a patient and methodical child, looked ready to run after it and beat it to death on the boundary should this prove necessary.

'Quiet, please!' called Mr Malik, crouching low over the stumps at the bowler's end. 'Please continue to bowl, Mafouz!'

Mafouz responded by altering the direction of his arm movement to a forward thrust. He also increased the speed. His face, red with the effort, wore a glazed, far-away expression. He started to bite his lip. 'Watch out, Sheikh!' he called – 'this is going to be a fast one!'

Mahmud, unable to restrain himself any longer, moved from his position in the slips to face Sheikh directly. 'Yeah, Sheikh,' he called – 'this will be punishment!'

Mr Malik lowered his nose until it almost touched the bails. 'You are directly in the flight path, Mahmud,' he said. 'Return to base!'

Mahmud stayed where he was. Eventually his father moved on to the pitch and, seizing his son by the right ear, dragged him back into a fielding position.

Still young Mafouz showed no sign of letting go of the ball. 'This is going to be an amazing one!' he yelled.

'Go, Anwar, go!' yelled his father.

Mr Malik did not seem anxious that Mafouz should let go of the ball until he was absolutely ready to do so. Perhaps, thought Robert, Mr Mafouz had bought his son into an unassailable position on the cricket team.

Anwar's arm revolved faster and faster, until it was no more than a blur above his shoulders. It looked very probable that the ball was not going to be the only thing to rise in the air – Mafouz himself, Robert felt, was about to climb up like a helicopter, clear of the grass, and hover over Wimbledon.

'You are dead meat, Sheikh!' Mafouz yelled.

Sheikh did not flinch. Holding his bat with the precision of a monk wielding a quill pen, he waited patiently for whatever Mafouz should deliver.

Finally the travel agent's son let go of the ball. It went neither forwards nor backwards but straight up in the air. Everyone, parents and boys, craned their necks back and stared into the cerulean blue above the Village. For what seemed an age, the dark speck hung above them, a piece of grit in the sky, and then, with languid slowness, started its descent.

'It's coming for you, Sheikh!' shouted Mafouz. 'It's on it's way, boy! Run and hide!'

For a moment, Robert thought that this was what Sheikh was going to do. He let the bat dangle from his fingers as he searched the horizon for the ball, like a fighter pilot seeking out his enemy above the clouds. The ball was headed for a spot almost equidistant between the two wickets. Suddenly Sheikh shouldered his bat and, letting out a kind of howl, set out for the middle of the pitch, elbowing a fielder out of the way. He looked like a man prepared to do battle.

When the ball finally reached him, the normally placid boy bared his teeth and, whirling the bat round his head, whacked the offending object back up to where it had just come from. It climbed vertically above the field, retracing its earlier journey, until it seemed to hang suspended at the precise point where it had rested a moment ago.

No one ran to catch it. It was more or less understood that this was something between Mafouz and Sheikh. Mafouz was flexing his hands and making crouching movements as the ball started its slow descent.

'It will destroy you utterly, Mafouz,' yelled Sheikh, brandishing his bat at him. 'You have minutes left to live.'

'Kill him,' yelled Mr Mafouz. 'Get it straight back at him!'

Indeed, Mafouz looked as if he was about to do something far more dramatic than simply catch the thing. He had made his right hand into a fist and was jabbing it up at the sky, feinting in the direction of the falling missile. Perhaps he was going to punch it straight back at the batsman.

The ball seemed to have acquired a life of its own. As Mafouz tacked one way, it would move in the other, and when he swerved round to get it once more in his sights it would sidle left or right until it was sure it was once again in his blind spot. It seemed to show a complete disregard for the laws of Galileo, Newton and Einstein, moving through the atmosphere like an otter in pursuit of a fish.

When it got within spitting distance of Mafouz, who was now standing, arms loosely apart, mouth open, as if hypnotized by the thing's movements, it did a sharp turn to the left, bounced along horizontally for a few yards, and then snarled up and down to land on the unfortunate boy's head.

Mafouz fell heavily to earth amidst sudden, devastating silence.

Robert was the only one among staff, parents and boys who was not looking at Mafouz. His eyes were on Hasan. The little boy was standing in the passage that led out towards the front garden. He was talking to Aziz the janitor. Aziz had lost his brown overalls. He was wearing the crumpled suit he had been wearing on the day Robert first saw him in the pub. He had his arms round Hasan. Robert started to make his way across the garden towards the two of them. Aziz, who had his back to the garden, did not see him.

Mr Malik was in the middle of a group crowded round Mafouz. Among them, Robert noticed, was Mr Shah. Mafouz's father was cradling the boy in his arms and saying, in a deep voice, 'Speak to me, Anwar! Speak to me!'

Robert kept his eyes on Hasan and Aziz from about ten yards away. It was only when Maisie emerged from the back kitchen, wearing her third headscarf of the morning (this one was in Liberty print and made her look as if she was about to go out to watch titled men shooting grouse), that he felt emboldened to get close enough to hear what they were saying.

'It is time!' Aziz was whispering.

'This morning,' said Hasan in conversational tones, 'a dog turned into a hedgehog!'

Aziz did not seem surprised by this information. He nodded gravely. 'I think so,' he said. 'It is time!'

Time for what?

'After my Occultation,' said Hasan, 'will I be able to see?'

'You will see with the inner eye!' said Aziz.

Mafouz was coming round in his father's arms. 'It is coming for you, Sheikh,' he murmured. 'You are dead meat!'

Mr Mafouz kissed his boy, first on the lips, then on the forehead, then on the whole of the upper body. 'We cannot afford to lose such a boy,' Robert heard Mr Malik say. 'He is a genius!' The travel agent was almost definitely slipping him something, thought Robert. Mind you, Mr Malik needed all the finance he could get. *'Spend generously and do not keep an account,'* ran his favourite *hadith* of the Prophet. *'God will keep an account for you. Put nothing to one side – God will put to one side for you!'* This was not a principle calculated to endear him to the Inland Revenue or the men from Customs & Excise. But, as he was fond of reminding Robert, one of the many good things about life in the Medina area in the seventh century after Christ was the complete absence of Customs & Excise men.

Maisie approached Robert. She too seemed uncomfortably aware of Hasan and Aziz. 'What's the matter?' she whispered.

'I think,' said Robert, 'it's Hasan's Occultation!'

Maisie put her hand to her mouth. 'My God!' she said. 'His Occultation!'

'What do you suppose he'll do?' said Robert.

Maisie seemed peeved by this question. *'I* don't know,' she said, 'what they do at the actual ceremony.'

Robert could not answer this question. Whatever it was, he felt it must be pretty nasty. It was not going to be a few bridge rolls and the odd glass of lemonade. These Twenty-fourthers were serious people. They wore weird slippers, they quoted the heavier bits of the Koran at you. What more did you want?

'I think Hasan sort of *turns into* the Twenty-fourth Imam,' said Robert. 'It's a bit like a presidential inauguration. But I imagine more basic. They probably sacrifice something. And, after it, he gets special powers.'

Hasan giggled. Aziz started to stroke his hair.

'He's probably a reincarnation of someone,' Robert went on – 'some Islamic character from the twelfth century. Didn't you say there was a Hasan in the Middle Ages?'

'Maybe they want his autograph,' said Maisie, with heavy sarcasm. She was watching the couple very carefully, and, when they started out together down the passage towards the High Street, she followed them.

'What do you think you're doing?' hissed Robert.

'I'm following them!' said Maisie.

'They're dangerous!' whispered Robert.

'That's why you have to come too,' said Maisie. 'I'm only a woman. I need your strong Muslim arms.'

Robert did not try to contest the authenticity of either of these adjectives. Since her conversion, Maisie had been very assertive about her need to submit. 'I am low,' she would sometimes say, especially before breakfast. 'I am low, low on the ground next to you, Yusuf!' In these moods, she reminded Robert of his mother. She was particularly fond, especially when asked her opinion on some current controversy, of quoting the words of Muhammad to Abu Said al-Khudri: '*Isn't the testimony of a woman worth only half the testimony of a man? That is because of her inferior intelligence.*'

'These guys,' said Robert, 'are not messing about!'

They were now halfway down the passage. Rafiq stood in their way. His face wore that same enigmatic smile, but he did not speak. Maisie pushed past him, and, with a little sigh, the older man moved back against the wall.

'Mr Shah,' said the engineering master, 'is not such a nice man as you think!'

'No?'

Robert didn't want to talk to the engineering master, but neither did he want to go out after Aziz the janitor, who, in their first conversation in the Frog and Ferret, had made pretty clear not only his low opinion of infidels but also his readiness to use cutlery on other human beings with whom he disagreed.

Perhaps, he thought to himself, this was all part of a plot worked up by Dr Ali. Perhaps Twenty-fourthers hired themselves out on a contract basis to anyone wanting to lean heavily on un-Islamic behaviour.

Maisie had gone before him into the front garden. She turned to Robert and called. 'I need your strong arms!' she said. 'If Hasan is in danger . . .'

As Robert moved forward after her, Rafiq grabbed him, hard, round the waist. 'Do not do this,' growled the engineering master, 'or you will burn in everlasting fire, and hell shall be your couch! The ground will yawn open before you, and the trees will bend to strike at your face.' He had obviously not allowed his degree course to affect his view of what was and was not possible in the physical world. It was also depressing to realize that yet another member of the staffroom of the Islamic Boys' Independent Wimbledon Day School was barking mad.

Robert broke free of him.

'You do not know what goes on at this school,' said Rafiq. 'Who do you think watches you day and night? Is not this school damned? Who knows where the little boy is? Who knows what he is?'

'You tell me,' said Robert, as he moved after Maisie.

'His name is Thunder,' said Rafiq, 'and he brings curses. What do you know of any of this? What do you know of our secrets?'

The honest answer would have been to say *Fuck all*, but Robert did not feel inclined to do so. Pulling himself away from the older man, he ran after Maisie, who was now somewhere out in the road. Rafiq followed him, and for a moment Robert thought he was going to hit him, but, instead, he ran across the road and over towards the far side of the Common.

Maisie was screaming something, but he could not hear what it was. He ran, faster and faster, towards the sound of her voice, until the noise of the cricket game faded and the familiar world of traffic and aeroplanes and reassuring English faces crowded out the thought that had been started by Rafiq.

You're out of your depth, Wilson. You're in deep, deep trouble. Get out while there's still time!

16

When he got to the High Street, he saw Hasan and Aziz walking up to the Common. The janitor was still holding the little boy's hand.

Maisie rounded on Robert. She seemed to have decided that he was responsible for all this. 'Mr Malik put him in your care!' she hissed. 'Do something! Call him back!'

Robert started after the little boy. 'Hasan!' he called. 'I think you should come with me!'

Hasan turned to him, slowly. He reached out his hands towards the sound of Robert's voice. 'I must go, Mr Wilson,' he said. 'It is the time!'

With which he turned and trotted off beside the janitor.

When they got to the edge of the grass, Aziz turned and leered at Maisie and Robert. He looked, thought Robert, more than usually unappetising. 'Leave us!' he said. 'Go back to the blasphemer Malik! Crawl on your belly to the hypocrites! You are the vomit of the devil, Wilson!'

He was always saying things like this. Robert did not like to think of himself as a snob, but, had he been in charge of the Independent Wimbledon Day Islamic Boys' School, he would have expected a higher standard of civility from the cleaning staff.

'Listen – ' he began. But, before he had the chance to complete the sentence, a swarm of people came from out of the birch-trees and Aziz and Hasan disappeared into them. Most of them were wearing wellingtons. Many of the women had headscarves and, among the men, walking-sticks of the folksier kind were popular. Every single one of them – and there were upwards of seventy or eighty in the group – seemed to have brought at least one dog.

Robert recognized faces he had been trying to avoid for weeks. There was Ron 'Rescue Dog' Hitchens, with his three Rottweilers, one of which had recently eaten a Scotch terrier. 'He's only being friendly!' Ron had screamed as Mrs Coates's dog was consumed. There was the mad Irishman with Fang, his Alsatian, accompanied by Myrtle 'It's the Best Exercise' Freeman and her Dobermann. 'It's the Best Exercise!' was what she yelled at Robert every time the Dobermann came for Badger at about thirty miles an hour with the clearly expressed intention of biting his head off. There was 'Pooper Scooper' Watkins, a young woman who insisted not only on picking up her dog's faeces with a see-through plastic glove, but also on waving it in the faces of passers-by in order to emphasize her ecological soundness. There was Vera 'How Old is He?' Jackson, a woman who had told Robert the story of her dog's operation no less than seventeen times. There was the man from Maple Drive known as 'Is the Mitsubishi Scratched Yet?', dragging his Rhodesian ridge-back, known locally as 'He Just Wants to Play'. There was Mrs Quigley of the South Wimbledon Neighbourhood Church, with her pug, Martha. There was the German from Maple Drive known as 'The Nazi who Escaped Justice from Nuremberg', who, although he did not own any kind of pet, bared his teeth like an Alsatian . . . They were all there.

All of the people he had stopped and engaged in conversation over the last four years. People who had at first seemed so friendly and decent and open and neighbourly, but who, after two or three encounters, had turned into ravingly obsessive lunatics. People who had driven him further and further into the woods that slope down from the Common towards the main road to the south-west. People who had made him skulk behind trees until they had passed. People who had persuaded him that the only safe time to take out the dog was after the hours of darkness, when you were only likely to meet George 'Let's Get Rabbits' Grover.

They were carrying placards and posters. KEEP THE COMMON FREE FOR DOGS! said one. OUR DOGS MUST NOT LIVE IN FEAR! said another. A third read I AM A DOG. I HAVE THE SAME RIGHTS AS YOU!

'It's the dog-murdering thing!' said Maisie. The Wimbledon Dog Murderer – already featured in several national newspapers – had already claimed the lives of six Labradors, eight poodles, a Border collie and fourteen Dobermanns. Although some claimed that his methods – shooting through the head at close range – were 'humane', most dog-lovers had lobbied their MP and campaigned vigorously in the local press under headlines such as STOP THIS DOG SERIAL KILLER.

There had been profiles of him that suggested that he was a jogger who had been bitten by one of Alex 'Down Sir' Snell's pit-bulls. There were some who said he was a man whose children had been savaged by a local hound. And there were some heartless people who maintained that he was a public-spirited individual who should be given as much help as possible in his self-appointed mission.

The dog lobby had clearly felt it was time to take action. Aziz and Hasan were caught up in a maze of stout shoes, Sherley's extendable dog-leads and sniffing, quivering red setters, corgis, Jack Russells, Old English Sheepdogs and pugs. Robert thought he saw Gwendolen 'Good for the Gardens' Mintoff trying to feed a Dogchoc to the Twenty-fourth Imam. And, when Maisie and he got into the crowd, he was, of course, stopped by almost every individual in it. 'I didn't recognize you without the dog!' some of them said. 'You're the chap with the Staffordshire terrier bitch, aren't you? How are the pups?' Some, with clearer memories, had long, detailed questions to ask. They remembered things about Badger that Robert had forgotten long ago. They asked about his speed and his fondness for Pedigree Chum Select Cuts, and all expressed interest in his bowel movements.

By the time Maisie and he got clear of the crowd, Aziz and Hasan were almost at the other side of the Common. Robert waved and shouted, but the little boy did not turn his head. He trotted obediently along beside Aziz. Even at this distance you could see that huge red mark across his cheek.

The two stopped outside a large house not unlike Mr Shah's. Aziz looked round, as if to check whether he was being followed. When he saw Robert, he picked up the little boy and ran towards the house. There was a high stone wall, a pair of wrought-iron gates and the kind of silence that suggested the sort of owners who could enforce their privacy.

The sky had darkened suddenly. Robert felt a drop of rain on his face. An April shower. 'What do we do now?' he said.

'We ring the doorbell,' said Maisie, 'and ask them what the hell they think they're doing with Hasan.'

'This isn't that easy, Maisie,' said Robert. 'We are talking about the Occultation of the Twenty-fourth Imam of the Wimbledon Dharjees! This is major-league stuff!'

'You talk as if you believe that rubbish!' said Maisie.

The two of them sat together on the damp grass. What had Mr Malik said the manuscript contained? A prophecy of some kind. And if Hasan was just an ordinary little boy, why did he have such an alarmingly high success rate in the prophetic-dreams department?

From behind, he heard a cough. Robert turned to see his mother and father peering down at him anxiously. What were they doing out here? Why didn't they have jobs like other people?

'Well, Yusuf,' said his mother, brightly, 'this is nice for you!'

Robert felt his mouth tighten. 'What's nice?'

Mrs Wilson flushed. 'Being out here,' she said – 'in the fresh air. With Ai'sha!'

She was almost the only person who regularly used their Islamic names. It wouldn't be long, thought Robert grimly, before she, too, was climbing into a large, black linen bag.

She tapped him, playfully, on the shoulder. 'Couple of lovebirds!' she said.

Mr Wilson, anxious not to be left out of things, slapped Robert heartily on the back. 'I wish I had your faith,' he said – 'I really do!'

Maisie looked up at him, skilled, as ever, in the ways of dutiful daughters. 'You will believe, Mr Wilson,' she said. 'I know it. It must be!' She was always saying things like that these days.

Robert drew into himself and waited for his parents to go away. His mother was making small, agitated noises, while Mr Wilson senior was beginning to edge away across the grass. They were probably on their way to the pub.

'Don't you like me using your Islamic name?' said Mrs Wilson.

'It's not that,' said Robert. 'I think I don't like the Islamic name. I think I'm going to change it. I think I'm going to call myself Omar.'

Mrs Wilson kissed him, lightly, on the top of the head. 'Omar Bobkins Wilson,' she said – 'I like that!' And, with a nod and a wink to Maisie, she followed her husband.

When they had gone, Maisie started to pick at the grass with her fingers. She pulled out a stalk and wound it round her hand, watching it cut into her flesh.

'I sometimes wonder,' she went on, 'whether you're sincere about being a Muslim.'

Robert looked over his shoulder. There was, as far as he could see, no one else on the Common. 'I'm completely sincere about it,' he said.

Of course, the only way out of his troubles would be to confess to someone that he was passing himself off as a Muslim for the purposes of financial gain. That would be the sincere thing to do. Would they shake hands and agree to forget the whole thing were he to do so? He did not think so.

'I think,' Maisie said, 'you have to ask yourself some hard questions. Otherwise there's no future for us. What do you really hold dear, Robert? Are you Robert or are you Yusuf or are you Omar? What drives you forward?'

The desire to stay alive was what Robert wanted to say, but didn't. Staying alive seemed to be pretty low on the average Muslim's list of priorities.

He got to his feet. 'Let's go, then,' he said. 'We'll just bang on the door and see what happens.'

Maisie got up too. 'I'm changing, you see,' she said. 'Becoming a Muslim was a tremendous step for me. It's altered me in ways I can't even describe.'

'It's altered me too,' said Robert. 'Things have really sort of speeded up since I became a Muslim. It's very exciting.'

If you like being condemned to death and followed around by loonies with slippers on and becoming involved with weird prophecies from the dawn of time, it's a lot of fun!

Maisie pecked him on the cheek. 'I don't want us to lose each other,' she said. 'Mr Malik says that a harmonious relationship between man and woman is terribly important. At school, all I learned was that sex was wicked. In Islam it's different.'

Perhaps, thought Robert, as he trudged after her towards the iron gates, this was a signal for their lovemaking to become more decorous. Guilt was, after all, one of the things that made sex really interesting. One of the most positive things the Catholic Church had done for screwing was trying to stamp it out. She was living the part, he said to himself, and then: no, *it's me that's living the part. She actually believes this stuff.*

Maisie put her shoulder to the gates. They creaked open – one swinging wildly over to the left, while the other ground to a halt on the gravel after a few yards. He stopped, waiting for armed Twentyfourthers to swarm out of every window, demanding to know why Robert was proposing to barge in on their most secret and important ceremony.

'Suppose he is an imam!' said Robert. 'Oughtn't we to at least consider whether these people have a right to *think* he is. I don't see what harm they're doing!'

'They're evil!' said Maisie. 'They are the scum of the earth! They're – ' her face reddened with fury – 'intolerant! Do you know why they wear one shoe? It's to shame the rest of the Dharjees, because they say that Dharjees flout Islamic law!'

She looked like Ronnie Gallagher, the pacifist organizer of the Wimbledon Peace Council, shortly before he put Derek 'Small Publisher With Big Problems' Elletson in hospital for suggesting that, under certain circumstances, war might be necessary.

'They have to be crushed, Bobkins!'

So saying, she marched off down the gravel path, making the kind of crunching noise Robert had thought could only be produced by the BBC sound-effects department.

As they rounded the edge of the building, he could see that behind the house was a vast garden. There was a brick patio over on the left, studded with dwarf cypresses in terracotta tubs. Stretching up to and away from the patio was a vast lawn, smothered with spring flowers – yellow daffodils and a parade of brilliant hyacinths. In the middle of the lawn was a cedar-tree, and, attached to one of its branches by a knotted rope, was a child's swing, idling above the flowers as the rain guttered out and another squall of sunlight came in from the west. There was a terrible quiet about the place.

'I think,' said Robert, 'we should go and get reinforcements. We should go and ask Mr Malik.'

Maisie gave him a contemptuous look and marched up towards the patio. With a heavy heart, Robert followed her towards the smooth, mysterious features of the house, whose windows, on this side, he could now see, were blacked out from the inside.

17

When they got to the windows, Maisie put her ear to the glass. Robert, who was still looking nervously up and down the garden, stood a little away from the rear wall. But after a while it was clear that she could hear something, and he was unable to resist following her example.

The cloth inside muffled the noise, but when he got close to the window he could make out a human voice. At first he thought it was unfamiliar to him, but then, with a shock, he realized it was Rafiq's. But there was a quality to it he would not have expected. It was deep and assured.

'Say,' said the voice: 'Who is the Lord of the Heaven and the Earth? Say: Allah. Say: Why have you chosen other gods beside him, who, even to themselves, can do neither harm nor good? Say: Are the blind and seeing alike? Does darkness resemble the light?'

Other voices joined in, in a low growl, but Robert could not hear whether they were repeating what Rafiq had said, or, indeed, whether they were speaking English at all.

He pulled his ear away from the glass. 'I think we should ring on the doorbell,' he said, 'and just ask them, politely, what they're doing with Hasan. If they're worshipping him, could they guarantee to us that he . . . you know . . . enjoys being worshipped. Otherwise it may well be a form of child abuse. Worshipping someone without their permission . . .'

Maisie still had her ear pressed to the glass. From inside, the noise of the voices was getting louder. Someone was beating what sounded like a tambourine, and, high above all this, Robert thought he heard a flute. Then, slowly at first, but building to an almost military rhythm, the stamp of feet on wooden boards. Rafiq's voice was calling something, like a chant, and was answered by the other voices. Robert could not understand it at first, but, after he put his ear back to the window, it resolved itself into two syllables:

'Ha-san . . . Ha-san . . . Ha-san . . .'

Over and over again:

'Ha-san . . . Ha-san . . . Ha-san . . .'

And then, when the shouting had reached a climax, there was a ghastly scream from inside the room. At first Robert thought someone must have been hurt, but, a second later, the scream came again and he realized, with horror, that this was a cry of joy.

Maisie was waving at him wildly. She had found a gap in the blackout material and had fixed her eye to it. He wasn't at all sure that he wanted a good view of whatever was going on inside the house. It sounded a good deal more basic than, say, Holy Communion at Cranborne School. And that was bad enough. Were they committing human sacrifice? And if they were, shouldn't they get the police? Or might this be regarded as an intrusion on people's right to worship as they saw fit?

'You must look,' whispered Maisie, 'it's weird. You must look.'

Eventually, Robert looked.

The room was in almost total darkness. The only light came from a group of candles high in one corner. It smeared the faces of the men in the room, fighting a losing, fitful battle with the shadows. There might have been twenty or thirty figures in there, but it was too dark to distinguish anything more than their vague shapes. There didn't seem to be any furniture. All the figures, some of them cloaked like witches, were facing in the same direction – away from Maisie and Robert. But they were not looking at one point, as the worshippers did at the Wimbledon Islamic Boys' School (Day Independent): they were moving up and down, backwards and forwards, bumping into each other and generally carrying on like people at Victoria Station during the rush hour.

The only figure that stood out was Rafiq. He was standing on a kind of pedestal a little above the others, thrusting both arms up into the air. He seemed to be focused on the black space beyond the candlelight. The room, Robert felt, might go on for yards and yards. But, as he watched, even the sense that it was a room vanished. It was as if he was looking into a pinhole camera, as if the scene before him was a mirage.

'For nine hundred years!' called Rafiq.

'For nine hundred years!' answered the crowd.

'He was hidden!' called Rafiq.

'He was hidden!' answered the crowd.

'He is coming!' called Rafiq suddenly.

'He is coming!' called the crowd around him.

'What will he do,' yelled Rafiq, as if he had a good answer to this question, 'when he comes?'

'What will he do?' yelled the crowd in return. They seemed keen to find out.

'What will he do?' riposted Rafiq. He was not letting them get away with this easily.

'What will he do?' yelled the crowd.

Robert's eyes were starting to ache. But Rafiq was still not keen to put over the punch-line. He changed the topic, rather neatly, by howling, 'He is the Twenty-fourth Imam!'

The crowd liked this. They came back with, 'He is the Twenty-fourth Imam!'

'He has been hidden!' yelled Rafiq.

'He has been hidden!' yelled the crowd.

Robert wondered how this particular breakaway section of a breakaway section of the Nizari Ismailis had managed to carry on like this in Wimbledon for the last seventy years. Presumably, behind many of the net curtains in Wimbledon Park Road things as strange, or even stranger, were always going on. It was handy, anyway, that they celebrated their religion in English.

Back inside, Rafiq had gone back to the thousand-dollar question. 'What will he do when he returns?' he shouted.

Perhaps, thought Robert, he had simply been playing for time and had now come up with a credible answer.

'What will he do when he returns?' yelled the crowd.

It had better be good, thought Robert. *After a build-up like this, you can't afford to let them down.*

'He will destroy!' yelled Rafiq.

'He will destroy!' yelled the crowd.

'What will he destroy?' shouted Rafiq.

'What will he destroy?' answered the crowd.

The answer to this one was usually simple. *Everything apart from us, guys!* seemed to be the stock religious response. Imams or Christs, Mahdis or Messiahs were there to cancel all debts, atone for all insults. But, if this was the answer, Rafiq was not giving it all away at once. He clearly had something tasty up his sleeve.

Robert heard a cough behind him. He pulled his eye away from the pinhole and, turning, saw a near neighbour who had last year changed her name, by deed poll, to Cruella Baines. She was the lead singer in an all-girl rock group. She weighed fifteen stone.

'What's going on in there?' she said. 'Is it a party?'

Robert put his eye back to the pinhole. They had started dancing now. It was a fairly individualistic affair. Some of them were whirling round like dervishes. Others crouched on their haunches and kicked out their back legs behind them, like men carrying out a complex fitness programme. One man was lying on his back and cycling with his legs, rather like Badger, while a figure that Robert recognized as Aziz's friend from the Frog and Ferret was doing a lot of semaphore work with both arms.

Robert turned back to Cruella. 'There are naked people in there,' said Robert, 'having sex! Find a hole and have a look!'

Cruella Baines grunted and waddled off along the line of windows, her steel bangles rattling against her gigantic thighs. Eventually she seemed to find a gap in the blackout and, her enormous behind reared aloft, she glued her eye to the glass.

Inside, the lads were all enjoying themselves immensely. When the dancing had reached its climax, the whole crowd flung themselves on to the floor and further worked themselves up into what looked like a communal epileptic fit. *If this is Islam*, thought Robert, *give me more!* He hadn't seen anyone carry on like this since going to watch the World Wrestling Federation with Gilbert Lewis, the man next door's nephew, who had had a major seizure at the sight of a man called Hulk Hogan and had written to Robert afterwards to say that he 'had never expected to see anything like that in real life'. Perhaps Islam had developed differently in Wimbledon than in other parts of the world. Perhaps long exposure to tennis, bad public transport, English weather and the sight of miserable middle-aged people walking their dogs had driven this particular breakaway section of a breakaway section of the Nizari Ismailis right round the bend.

After a while they seemed to get bored with kicking their legs in the air. They wanted more. One by one they struggled to their feet. A man Robert recognized as the second man from the Frog and Ferret started to hop in circles, beating himself on the head and shouting something. Rafiq was doing a lot of waving into the darkness, as if he expected something to appear – a deputation from the Noise Abatement Society, thought Robert, if they all carried on like this for much longer.

'Oh!' he heard Maisie gasp, over to his left. 'Oh!'

Being a Twenty-fourther obviously called for high physical stamina, for the group showed no signs of slacking. They were now all waving in the direction indicated by Rafiq. But, although Robert strained his eyes against the glass, he could see nothing but impenetrable blackness beyond the hectic yellows and reds cast by the candles.

Rafiq started again. 'He is coming!' he shouted.

'He is coming!' shouted the lads in reply.

Suddenly the candles went out. Someone must have blown them or snuffed them, because the darkness was sudden and almost complete. Robert did not shift his eyes, waiting for another image to swarm out of the chamber in front of him, but all he could hear, now, was groaning.

'He was killed!' moaned Rafiq.

'He was killed!' wailed the support group.

'He was sent to hell-fire!' moaned Rafiq.

'He was sent to hell-fire!' his congregation replied. Some of them seemed to be actually sobbing.

Robert thought he could hear grinding teeth. With a start he realized they were his teeth and he was grinding them. Even looking at this stuff from behind a black screen was punishing. It wasn't surprising that some of them were cracking under the strain.

'He was the son of Hasan b. Namawar!' said Rafiq.

There was a slight pause. This was obviously not a name that tripped off the tongue, but the lads rose to it manfully, while managing to weep, groan and, from the sound of it, pull out lumps of each other's hair at the same time. 'He was the son of Hasan b. Namawar!' they yelled in the darkness.

'Of the Daylamis!' yelled Rafiq.

This was easier. 'Of the Daylamis!' they yelled back.

However long they had been in Wimbledon, the suburb had not yet managed to curb their enthusiasm. The sound from the room made your average Pentecostal church sound like a tea party given for a group of Radio 3 announcers. They were starting to thump the floor now, and the chorus that had played low, while they gave out the stuff of how he was the son of Hasan b. Namawar and had been sent to hell-fire, came back in loud and strong.

'He is coming to destroy!' yelled Rafiq, once more.

'He is coming to destroy!' they yelled back.

'What is he going to destroy?' yelled Rafiq.

'What is he going to destroy?' they answered.

If he doesn't give the answer to this one soon, thought Robert, he is in danger of losing his audience. But their patience seemed endless.

Instead of answering his own question, Rafiq let out a high-pitched wail, which was taken up by the rest of the men. The wail started high and went higher, until they were shrieking off the register. It was almost painful to listen to, and Robert was about to pull his face away from the window when, suddenly, high up in the far darkness, a tiny figure in white robes jumped into vision. He did not seem to be standing on anything. He seemed to hang suspended above the worshippers, his two tiny arms held out in front of him, and he was as still and quiet and calm as he had been when sitting at the Wilsons' table or resting, alone, at the back of Class 1.

'Oh, my God!' squawked Maisie. 'Oh, my *God*!' It was Hasan.

Robert took in the neatly combed hair, the frail shoulders, the exquisite cheekbones with the red blemish on one side, and the huge, sightless eyes that roamed the blackness below him like inverted searchlights, as if to soak up the shadows. He took in the way the little boy's hands stretched out over the crowd of distressed men as if to soothe them, and, for the first time in his life, he felt something that was not quite fear and not quite joy – an emptiness that longed to be filled. He heard Maisie's voice once more: *What* do *you believe in?* And, in spite of himself, he heard he was groaning quietly, like the men in the darkened room.

Next to him he heard Maisie gasp. He became aware that she was breaking away from the window. He hoped she wasn't proposing to make her presence known to the Twenty-fourthers. Robert had the strong impression that they viewed unwanted spectators in the same spirit in which the ancient Greeks received people barging in on the Eleusinian mysteries.

'I am Hasan!' said Hasan.

'You are Hasan!' shouted the crowd.

Behind him, Maisie had moved away from the window. Perhaps she had simply had enough. Hasan's voice had a chilling quietness to it. Robert had to put his ear closer to the glass to hear it. The crowd, too, had lowered their voices, but this had the effect of making the exchanges even more momentous.

'I am coming!' said the little boy.

'You are coming!' said the crowd.

How was he staying up there? thought Robert. And why was his presence so disturbing? Even Maisie, who was now standing a few yards from the window, breathing heavily, seemed to have been paralysed by the sight of him.

'I am coming to destroy!' hissed Hasan.

'You are coming to destroy!' they whispered back.

'And what am I going to destroy?' murmured Hasan.

'What are you going to destroy?' muttered the crowd in answer.

Robert half-expected the whole cycle to start again, so long had he waited for an answer to this question. But this time the answer was forthcoming. The little boy leaned his face to one side as if he was listening to some signal inaudible to mere mortals, and he whispered, 'I am going to destroy Malik. I am going to destroy the seducer Malik and his friend Wilson,' hissed Hasan. 'They will both go to hell-fire!'

Robert felt something more than the natural peevishness of a betrayed parent or guardian. There was something so vivid and authentic about the little boy's face and voice that he had to look away. He lifted his face from the peephole, and in the glass in front of him he saw a face he thought he recognized. A round, plump, jolly, brown face that he remembered from back last summer, when all this business started. But, before he was able to put a name to it, something hit him on the back of the head, and for a long time he knew no more.

PART FOUR

18

'Stick close to me,' said Robert, 'and do not talk to strange men!'

'Can we talk to you, sir?' said Mafouz.

'Ha bloody ha!' said Robert.

His charges followed him. From time to time he would look back with a certain pride at them. Mafouz, Sheikh, Mahmud, Akhtar, and, at the back, their ears jutting out like radio antennae, the Husayn twins with Khan – or Famine, Pestilence and War, as Mr Malik called them.

He hoped the Museum had not left any priceless bits of Islamic art lying around the place. If it had, they were liable to end up in the Husayn twins' pockets.

He liked his class, though. In fact he liked the school. When it had beaten Cranborne Junior School by three hundred runs, two Saturdays ago, he had linked arms with the headmaster and sung three verses of 'We Are the Champions'. He had also, after five pints in the Frog and Ferret, referred to Malik as 'his Muslim brother' and said, publicly, that any lousy Christian cricket team could not, in his view, fart their way out of a swimming-pool.

The school was getting even bigger and even more successful. They had taken on extra teaching staff. There was a rather pleasant man, called Chaudhry, who showed worrying signs of having actually gone to Oxford. He was always saying to Robert, 'Do you remember old Jennings from Univ?' or 'Tell me, Wilson, did you use the Radcliffe Camera?' To which Robert replied that he had never been interested in photography. They had also hired a French teacher, whose name Robert was unable to remember from one day to the next.

A man from the local education authority, after being taken over to the pub by Mr Malik, had announced his intention of sending his own son to the school. 'Let them all come!' said the headmaster to Robert. 'We send our little bastards to Cranborne – why shouldn't we take *their* money?' The school was, he had told Robert, officially in profit. Mr Shah, he said, had a return on his investment.

The more he enjoyed teaching, and the more Mr Malik's school seemed to prosper, the worse he felt about his original act of deception. As this summer, even hotter and drier than the last, worked its way up to August, Robert found he had developed a rich repertoire of twitches and guilty tics. He blinked. He snorted. He jerked his head backwards and forwards. He had even developed the beginnings of a stammer.

Maisie had told him he was 'getting more and more like a spaceman'. Now he was not only unable to remember the names of politicians, sportsmen and television personalities, he also found his memory was unable to supply the personal details of people he had known since he was a child. It was probably that blow on the head he had received at the end of the spring term. He had, Maisie had told him, been unconscious for nearly two minutes. She herself had had a bag placed over her head and had been left, trussed like a chicken, under the windows of the mysterious house on the Common. When they had recovered, the Dharjees had gone.

Had the shock affected Maisie too? Was that why she had moved out of the Wilson family home?

She had said she couldn't stand living in such close proximity to quite so many facial quirks, but there was something deeper in her decision to take a small flat near the school. He simply couldn't respond to the person she had become. He would only be able to find his way back to her when he managed, for once in his life, to be honest about what he really felt and believed.

He would be dead soon, anyway, he reflected, as he made his way up the Museum stairs. If some friend of Ali's didn't get him, then the Twenty-fourth Imam would probably grind him into little pieces. Hasan was waiting for him at the top of the stairs, and, as soon as he heard his guardian's tread, the little boy sat up, sniffed the air and stretched out his hands like a cat, waking after sleep.

Hasan had been unbearable ever since his Occultation. It can't, thought Robert, be good for the personality to have a load of middle-aged men prostrating themselves in front of you and sobbing every time you open your mouth. He wasn't yet quite in the Michael Jackson class, but for the last few months the little boy had been difficult in the extreme. He had refused to go to bed on time, insisted on watching *The Late Show* on television, and claimed that Badger was 'not worthy' to lick him. He had had a few more prophetic dreams. And one of them, Robert was almost sure, had foretold that something ghastly was going to happen in what sounded like the British Museum.

'I am not really me,' he had confided to Robert a few months ago, as the two were on a bus, on their way to the Megabowl in Kingston. 'I am a reincarnation of the true Twenty-fourth Imam of the Nizari Ismailis! My father was sent to hell-fire on the sixth of Rabi!'

'Is that right?' Robert had said, with a nervous glance around at the other passengers. 'Well, I hope it improves your bowling!'

Hasan giggled and put his hand in Robert's. On their last visit to the Megabowl he had hurled his projectile directly at the fruit machines. 'Sometimes you are so nice I do not want to kill you, Mr Wilson!' he said. 'And I know you do not really believe me. But you may look me up. I am in all the history books. I feature in *The Assassins*, by Bernard Lewis, a respectable work of scholarship.'

Robert had made the mistake of looking Hasan up in the work in question, at the end of which he had almost decided to call in an exorcist with some experience in the Islamic field.

'I will come into my kingdom on the Day of False Resurrection,' Hasan used to say, when Robert was trying to get him to brush his teeth, 'which is the eighth of August. The day when Hasan the Second betrayed The Law!'

As Bernard Lewis had put it:

On the 17th day of the month of Ramadan, the anniversary of the murder of Ali, in the year 559 (8th August 1164) under the ascendancy of Virgo and when the sun was in Cancer, Hasan 2nd ordered the erection of a pulpit in the courtyard of Alamut, facing towards the west, with four great banners of four colours, white, red, yellow

and green, at the four corners. As the pulpit faced west, the congre-
gation had their backs towards Mecca.

He wished he didn't know these things. He wished he'd stuck to
Marwan Ibrahim Al-Kaysi. You knew where you were with Marwan.
'When putting on shoes they should be checked to make sure no harmful
insect has hidden in them during the night.' That was fair enough. But
the true history of the Lord Hasan – Hasan the Second, on his name
be peace – was mind-boggling stuff.

If he had had any decency he would have talked to Mr Malik
about what was going to happen. He would have warned him. He
was the only one to know that today was the day when Hasan was
going to wreak his revenge. He was the only one to know the whole
story. But neither he nor Maisie, as far as he knew, had spoken of
what had happened at Hasan's Occultation.

'Come along, Wilson!' boomed Mr Malik's voice from the next
gallery – 'you'll miss the fun! Bring young Hasan along!'

The headmaster stepped out of the gallery with a couple of the
older boys. Beyond him, Robert could see Maisie and Rafiq. Rafiq!
The man Malik trusted! The man he thought of as his oldest friend!
Malik was simply too trusting. You simply could not afford to trust
anyone – especially where religion was concerned.

Robert had tried to open up the subject of Hasan several times, but
Mr Malik seemed far less concerned about him than he had been.
'What people believe,' he had told Robert, 'is their own affair. But I
have ways of dealing with unbrotherly conduct!'

He was whistling to keep up his spirits, that was all, Robert said to
himself as the boys clattered after him. He had been nervous enough
when the name of the Twenty-fourthers was first mentioned. Down
below, in the gallery below him and Hasan, the Husayn twins and
Khan were dancing round a case stuffed with priceless porcelain.
'Shake de belly!' called Khan in a mock African accent. *'Break de glass*
and shake de belly!' A man in a blue uniform was walking over
towards them. Robert waved them on, and they scampered after the
rest of the class.

'Do you know why we destroyed Hasan the Second?' said Hasan, in a conversational tone, as the two of them followed the headmaster and the rest of the school. Robert knew, but he wasn't going to give Hasan the satisfaction of knowing that he knew. The trouble with this Islamic history was that, like the Western version, you got involved in it.

'We destroyed him because he betrayed The Law!' said Hasan, in the kind of voice that suggested Hasan the Second, the Twenty-third Imam of the Nizari Ismailis, had only just popped out of the room for a cup of coffee instead of being stabbed nearly a thousand years ago.

The Twenty-fourther beliefs were not simply rumours from the dawn of time: they came, like the Dharjees themselves, out of real history. That was the frightening thing about them.

> *Towards noon, the Lord Hasan 2nd, on whose name be peace, wearing a white garment and a white turban, came down from the castle, approached the pulpit from the right side and in the most perfect manner ascended it. Addressing himself to the inhabitants of the world, jinn, men and angels, he said, 'The Imam of our time has sent you his blessing and his compassion and has called you to be his special, chosen servants. He has freed you from the burden of the rules of Holy Law.'*

They had had a banquet in the middle of the fast. In the middle of Ramadan. And they had drunk wine on the very steps of the pulpit and its precincts. They had flouted the *shariah*, the fundamental law of Islam. That was what this argument was about, even now in the 1990s in Wimbledon. How closely should one follow The Law?

'Come and look at this!' shouted Malik. 'There's a bloke in here with nine arms! Can you beat that?' He indicated a large Hindu carving, and the boys swarmed round it. The headmaster was clearly about to give one of his informal talks.

He had to get out, Robert thought. There was nothing else for it. He had to make a dignified and orderly retreat. Put himself out of the reach of Dr Ali, the Twenty-fourthers and everything else in the school. He was simply going to have to leave Islam, the way his father had left the Rotary club. You were allowed to leave, weren't you? It wasn't the British Army. He was going to ask nicely.

'And so,' Mr Malik was saying, 'we observe the *accumulation of gods*, very much as one saw in pre-Islamic Medina. The process of monotheistic religions can be seen as the beginning of the rational approach to the world!'

It wasn't going to be easy. He had already offered his resignation, twice, and Mr Malik had simply ignored it. When he had tried a third time, the headmaster had made some slightly menacing remarks about brotherhood and commitment.

'And yet,' went on Malik, 'the holistic nature of the Hindu world-picture still has much to teach us. Religions, like arts and sciences, must learn from each other, and toleration, which is an essential part of Islam, must be *studied*, *worked at*, not simply mentioned as a piety.'

This was well over the heads of his audience. Khan and the Husayn twins were making offensive gargling noises while dancing round a statue that looked to Robert as if it might be the Lord Vishnu; behind them, Mahmud did his Native American impression.

To his relief, the headmaster walked on. Maisie walked ahead, a little behind Rafiq. There was now almost nothing flagrantly alien about her, apart from her headscarf. And yet, paradoxically, she was, to Robert, more and more remote, more and more genuinely Islamic. Mr Malik had got to her in her most vulnerable area – the brain.

'I have a problem, Headmaster!' Robert said, as they walked through the gallery.

Malik clapped him on the back. Rafiq took Hasan by the hand, and, with a sly look at Robert, joined Maisie.

'You want money, my dear Wilson?' Malik said.

'It's not that,' said Robert. 'I don't think I . . . belong at the school any more.'

The headmaster stopped. He seemed distressed.

'Why on earth not?'

'I'm having . . . doubts!' said Robert.

Boys flowed past them and on into the next gallery. Malik seemed puzzled now, rather than distressed.

'Doubts about what, Wilson?'

'Doubts about . . . you know . . . Allah.'

Mr Malik chewed reflectively.

'What kind of doubts?'

'Well,' said Robert, 'I'm not sure if he's there.'

The headmaster started to move again. They were some way behind the rest of the school, but he did not seem in any hurry to catch them up. 'I think, Wilson,' he said at last, 'that you may rest assured that he is there. I don't think there is any doubt about that.'

'For you perhaps, headmaster,' said Robert, 'but, you see, while I'm sure he *may* be there, I'm not absolutely sure he is, if you see what I mean.'

They had somehow come into a gallery full of erotic Indian sculptures. In the far corner, the Husayn twins appeared to be trying to lift one of them off its pedestal. Mr Malik walked swiftly over to them and aimed a shrewd blow at their ears. They scuttled off after the other boys.

'You must simply ignore these doubts, Wilson!' said Malik.

'But I'm getting doubts about more and more things,' replied his junior master. 'I'm having doubts about Muhammad, for example.'

Mr Malik's eyes narrowed.

'What kind of doubts?'

'You know,' said Robert – 'did *he* exist?'

This seemed to puzzle the headmaster. 'I don't think there's much doubt about that,' said Mr Malik – 'the man conquered half the Near East!'

'Did he?' said Robert.

If the headmaster was surprised by Robert's vagueness on the most basic details of Islamic history, he did not show it.

'I mean,' went on Robert, 'we can't be *sure*, can we? I mean, we only have his word for it, don't we? And other people who were all friends of his. It could be a sort of . . . conspiracy.'

Mr Malik was giving him some very odd looks. He clasped both hands behind his back and wandered over to a bench. In the next gallery, Maisie was gathering the boys around her. Rafiq was nowhere to be seen. Robert was fairly sure he was making headway.

'And even if he *did* exist,' he went on, 'I'm not sure he was a terribly nice person.'

'What,' said Malik, 'has being nice got to do with anything? Who said Jesus was a nice person?'

'I'm not sure,' said Robert, deciding to get to the point, 'that I am a Muslim. I may be a Catholic.'

Mr Malik put his arm round Robert, as the two sat together on the bench. Was this the treatment he gave Maisie in the La Paesana restaurant, Mitcham?

'You cannot be a Muslim and a Catholic at the same time,' said the headmaster. 'It is just not possible. Although the principle of *taqiyah* – dissimulation – does make it perfectly possible for a Muslim to pretend to assume a religion to which he does not really belong. When faced by a Mongol horde, for example.'

This sounded promising. Was the converse also possible? Did it apply to agnostics faced by Islamic hordes? Robert was almost on the edge of confessing everything, when the headmaster gave him a brotherly squeeze.

'Hasan the Second,' said Robert, 'was a strange leader of the Nizari Ismailis in the twelfth century. And he was stabbed by his brother-in-law, Hasan b. Namawar, because he had said the Ismailis were no longer bound by Islamic law!'

Mr Malik grinned. 'And the Twenty-fourthers believe,' he said, 'that Hasan b. Namawar's son was hidden and is the true Twenty-fourth Imam of the Nizari Ismailis. And that he will return with hell-fire on the appointed day.'

'Which is,' said Robert, 'as it happens, today!'

'Indeed!' said Mr Malik, grinning.

He seemed positively cheerful about this. Perhaps the school was not the financial success that everyone seemed to think. It seemed impossible to convince him that anyone was in any danger. Robert would have to hit him with something a bit more serious than doubts. This situation called for a full-scale nervous breakdown.

'Actually, Headmaster,' he said, 'it's not just about Allah and Muhammad. I'm having doubts about everything. I'm having doubts about you.'

Malik grinned. 'I'm afraid I do exist,' he said, clapping Robert on the back. 'I am too, too solid flesh, my friend. There is a whole department of the Inland Revenue dedicated to proving that I exist.'

'What I mean,' said Robert, feeling a direct approach was required, 'is that I think I am having a nervous breakdown.'

The headmaster got up and started towards the next gallery. He did not seem very worried by this. 'I know,' he said, waving his arms expansively. 'I get nervous breakdowns. I get them all the time. All the damn time! I have nervous breakdowns every time I see the Husayn twins!'

They had come into a gallery at the centre of which was a large glass case, round which the boys – apart from Khan and the Husayns – were crowded. The Husayns seemed to have got hold of a piece of pottery and were trying to stuff it under Khan's coat. Malik ignored them.

'I mean,' said Robert, feeling he was not making the impression required, 'I think I may be Napoleon!'

19

Maisie overheard this remark. 'What do you mean,' she said, 'you think you're Napoleon?'

'I mean,' said Robert, 'I may be Napoleon.'

Rafiq grinned. He was standing a little away from the rest of the group, holding Hasan's hand in his. 'As opposed to Yusuf Khan!' he said. He was always being satirical about Robert's name.

'I don't know who I am,' said Robert – 'that's the point I'm making. Am I Robert Wilson? Am I Yusuf Khan? Am I Seamus O'Reilly? Am I Napoleon? You know?'

Rafiq folded his arms. He turned to Malik with a satisfied expression, as if to say *this is what comes of hiring infidels – even reformed ones.* 'And who are you now, Yusuf?' he said.

Robert looked him straight in the eyes. 'I really don't know who I am or what I'm doing here,' he said.

He managed to put a lot of conviction into this. It was probably the truest thing he had said so far that morning. Now might be the time to follow it up with a few troop directions in fluent French. He could dribble a bit. Even roll around on the floor. There was, he found, a tremendous sense of relief in being able to talk like this. Perhaps he could give them a bit of something Shakespearian. *'Faith my lords – how many crows may nest in a grocer's jerkin?'* And then, soon, an ambulance would come. It would take him away to a nice, warm mental hospital, where nice men would inject large quantities of Largactil up his bum. That was absolutely what he needed.

'Take it from me, Wilson,' said the headmaster, 'you are nothing like Napoleon. I have never met anyone less like Napoleon. You are Robert Wilson, a.k.a. Yusuf Khan, and you are a vital part of the creative team helming the Wimbledon Boys' Day Independent Islamic School.'

It was hopeless. The man would simply not take no for an answer. He was clearly prepared to continue employing Robert under almost any circumstances. What did he have to do to escape?

Malik walked over to the glass case. The boys parted, and Robert saw that it contained a villainous-looking man of about four foot in height. He was preserved in some kind of fluid, like an olive or a pickled onion, and had a baffled look about him. He looked more like an ape than a human.

'He was preserved in a bog, sir,' Sheikh was saying. 'Apparently he's a Druid!'

'He can't help that,' said Malik. 'We shall take lunch now. If an official representative of the Museum approaches, stuff your lunch under your jumper!'

Mahmud could be heard wondering whether they were going to have the Druid instead of packed lunch. Then, as one man, the boys produced plastic boxes, tinfoil and greaseproof paper, and the sound of small teeth munching bread, meat and fruit could be heard.

'This Druid,' said Malik, 'was ceremonially strangled many many years ago – which is what will happen to you, Husayn, unless you let go of Akhtar's ear.'

Robert wondered whether he should stage a more spectacular form of nervous breakdown. Thinking you were Napoleon was clearly not enough to get you out of the Wimbledon Islamic Boys' Independent Day School. Perhaps he could run back into the Romano-British Collection, gibbering.

'What does it all mean?' he said, in a loud, theatrical voice. 'What is it all for?'

Malik gave him a rapid glance, and then continued his lecture. 'He was strangled,' he said, 'because the Druids believed his death might avert a Roman victory. But the Romans, too, sacrificed. And irrationality is, I would argue, more firmly at the centre of Western, Christian, culture than it is at the centre of Islam. Consensus is at the heart of the social contract the Faith makes.'

This, thought Robert, sounded like his cue. 'I am not a good Muslim, Headmaster!' he said. 'You must cast me out!'

Maisie grabbed his arm and steered him towards the next gallery.

711

Behind him he could hear one of the boys mutter that Mr Wilson had gone mad, and another reply that he always had been. 'You are being *embarrassing*!' she hissed.

She was very big on Islamic *esprit de corps* these days. She talked of entering the Birmingham Islamic Women's Games. She had almost given up drink. Her manner had changed. She cultivated the kind of aloofness that Robert had observed in certain classes of minor official – he had the constant impression she was about to refuse him a visa. Her face had changed too. She had lost weight, giving her nose an alert, intelligent quality. She spent a lot of time looking at the floor, but her shoulders had become demonstrably assertive. She was a fully fledged Islamic woman.

She turned back to Mr Malik. 'I'll take him back to the school, Headmaster,' she said. 'He'll be all right for the pageant, I promise you.'

At the beginning of the summer term, shortly after the Koran Study Week at Lower Slaughter Manor, Gloucestershire, she had been made school secretary. She was now to be seen in a small cubby-hole next to Mr Malik's office, typing furiously, or on the phone to an organization called the Islamic World Unity Fund, which was said to be about to offer Mr Malik and Mr Shah a large sum in US dollars.

Malik grinned at her. Maisie pushed Robert towards the stairs, and the two of them moved down towards the crowded entrance hall. Outside, unbelievably, it was high summer.

Halfway down the steps, Robert sat down and put his head in his hands. Maisie sat next to him.

'Are you any closer to it?' she said.

'To what?'

'To whatever it is you want.'

'I don't know what I want,' said Robert. 'Do you?'

Another crowd of schoolchildren climbed the stairs towards them. Robert could see the brilliant light flooding the Bloomsbury street outside. Maisie put her hand on his.

'Are you having an affair with Malik?' he said.

'How do you mean "an affair"?' said Maisie.

'You know,' said Robert – 'you go out to the cinema, and he sticks his tongue down your throat, and then – '

Maisie sniffed. 'Please don't, Bobkins,' she said. 'Please don't. Don't be crude – I can't bear it.'

She patted his hand absently. 'We have slept together a few times,' she said, 'but we've never done it during school hours. You mustn't be jealous, darling. We're Muslims.'

Robert found he was snarling. 'What difference does that make?'

Maisie looked at him pityingly. 'The Prophet made it clear that you can have up to four wives,' she said.

'But I don't think,' said Robert, with heavy sarcasm, 'that he said anything about women having four husbands. I thought you were supposed to be low and submissive and made out of Adam's rib, and you weren't supposed to leave the house excessively. Marwan Ibrahim Al-Kaysi says – '

'Shut up about Marwan Ibrahim Al-Kaysi,' said Maisie crossly. 'He is a pedant from the University of Yarmouk. I *am* low and submissive, Bobkins. I'm a weak, silly creature at the mercy of my emotions and feelings. And I have rather strong feelings about the headmaster.'

So, to his surprise, did Robert. He had a strong feeling that he wanted to dash back to the Romano-British section and break a piece of statuary over the bastard's head.

Wearily, Robert got up and walked towards the street. Maisie followed him. 'We've all got to share,' she said, as they passed through the swing doors and found themselves looking down at the courtyard of the Museum. 'We've got to learn to live together and share and be at peace with the world. That's what Mr Malik says Islam is all about.'

Robert was aware of this. Mr Malik used those very words about three times every day.

'I think,' said Robert, 'that Islam is all about whatever Mr Malik wants it to be about on any particular day.'

'Well, in a way,' said Maisie, 'it is. He says once you've said these *suras* of the Koran and observed the obligations you *are* a Muslim.

It's as simple as riding a bicycle. Once you've submitted, that's it. It's very simple.'

They walked across the courtyard towards a waiting line of taxis.

'What's he like in bed?' said Robert.

Maisie sighed. 'Why do men always want to know that?' she said. Then she grinned. 'He's better on the carpet.' She linked her arm through his. 'I'm so glad I told you,' she continued – 'I've been feeling terribly guilty while it's been going on.'

'How long has it been going on?'

'For about nine months,' said Maisie – 'apart from Ramadan, of course.'

The bastard, thought Robert. The snake! The lousy, double-crossing, deceitful . . . *Muslim!* There was nothing to tie him to the place now. He could go. He could walk away, down the street, go back home and try to start his life. Try to do something that was nothing to do with the ridiculous lie he had told the headmaster almost a year ago today.

Except he couldn't. This news, he realized, tied him to Malik and the school almost more than before. While he still had a chance of being near Maisie, he would take it. Submission! Surrender! They had come to the right guy! He was on his knees, begging to stay.

Maisie approached a taxi. As they got in, she said, 'I'm so glad we've got rid of that Christian guilt rubbish. I don't think this would be nearly so easy if we weren't Muslims.'

The taxi-driver did not seem keen on going to Wimbledon. Maisie took a ten-pound note from Robert's pocket and waved it at him through the glass.

'What does he think about me?' said Robert. He was curiously keen to know the answer to this question. Had Maisie said what a stud he was?

'He doesn't know we had an affair,' said Maisie. 'He thinks it's just brother and sister. It is really brother and sister, isn't it, Bobkins?'

'Not to me it isn't,' said Robert mournfully.

She patted his hand and looked out at the sunlight glittering on London's rubbish. 'I'm sure we can manage it occasionally,' she said.

'I'd rather you didn't tell him about us! We don't really want trouble at the school, do we?'

From his jacket pocket Robert took out a grubby sheet of paper – the translation of the mysterious manuscript that had been given to him in the pub nearly a year ago today. He waved it at Maisie in a threatening manner. 'Do you realize,' he said, 'that the whole school is about to go up in flames today?'

Maisie smirked. She seemed as unworried as the headmaster at the fact that the place was due to be consumed in hell-fire. 'I know,' she said, 'that today is the day when the Twenty-fourthers believe Hasan will come into his own . . .'

'It's *serious*!' said Robert, 'and Rafiq and his boys won't stop at a few groans this time. They were prepared to hit me on the head, weren't they?'

'Quite a lot of people,' said Maisie acidly, 'are prepared to hit you on the head.'

Since she didn't seem willing to read the translation, Robert took on the job himself. Leaning forward in the seat, he started to intone, in a deep voice:

> Bow down,
> Bow down and listen to my words.
> On the sixth of Rabi
> I stabbed the seducer Hasan
> And was sent to hell-fire.
> But my son lived,
> My son Hasan.
> He is the Twenty-fourth Imam.
> He lives.
> He will return.

The taxi-driver turned his head slightly. 'I'm with you there,' he said.

This surprised Robert. Were there more Twenty-fourthers around than he had thought possible? Had they even penetrated the licensed taxicabs of London? He read on. Maisie turned her face away from him towards Green Park.

He will come as a boy.
As a little blind boy.
From the West he will come.
His face will be marked.
His eyes will have no sight.
And he will bear my name.
Hasan—
Hasan b. Namawar.
He will destroy.
He will destroy with fire.
And you will show loyalty to me—
You will show loyalty to The Law—
And you will know my name,
Which means companion,
There is fire in my fingers.
Bow down!'

The taxi-driver nodded. 'Sale or return,' he said, 'is a very good basis for a business deal. And business *has* gone down, no question about it!'

Maisie was still looking out of the window. If the prophecy worried her, she was managing to conceal the fact. Perhaps the head-master had been able to reassure her in ways that were not open to Robert. As he thought of them actually screwing – of Maisie winding her arms round him, hitching her legs over his, pumping up and down, up and down – the blood rose to his face. Awful, racist thoughts and words rose in his throat like nausea, and then, moments later, a strange image of Mr Malik embracing him. '*You are my Muslim brother, Wilson!*'

He liked Mr Malik. That ought to make this situation easier to bear. But it didn't. He could not stop the clear physical image of their bodies together. He knew what Malik would say, how he would look when they were making love, how he would smile, beatifically, like a baby, when he was satisfied.

He wiped the sweat from his forehead. This wasn't getting him anywhere. He put down the paper. 'There's something weird going on,' he said. 'This man really *did* stab Hasan the Second. Because he broke The Law. And pushed Islam close to Christianity. And this manuscript describes our Hasan *to the letter*!'

She turned to him. 'So you really think,' she said, 'that that poor little chap is going to zoom in from the clouds and wipe us all out?'

'Is that any more barmy than believing that Muhammad went up a mountain and God spoke to him? Or that there'll be wine in heaven? Or that you're a duffer if you can't polish off a wall gecko in under two minutes?'

The taxi-driver nodded vigorously. 'This is it,' he said – 'two minutes! And we're given no warning, are we? We're just told to get on with it and hope the recession will go away!'

Maisie grabbed his hand. She looked suddenly nervous. 'You do believe that, though, don't you?' she said. 'Because you're a Muslim, aren't you? If you don't believe that, you aren't a Muslim. You're an impostor!'

'I don't know what I am,' said Robert. 'There are times when I think I'm a Twenty-fourther. They seem to have a lot of fun.'

'They do,' said the taxi-driver. 'They go to Spain twice a year. They have country cottages. They send their children to private schools. They pay no tax. They have it easy!'

They were crossing the river now. Even the summer sun could not take the grey away from the thick band of the Thames, sluggishly curving towards Wandsworth. As they sped back towards Wimbledon, Robert wondered why he still couldn't own up to the lie that had started all this. Why had it trapped him as neatly as she had done?

What did he believe? That was what she was always asking him. If he could say it, out loud, he might know what it was. It might even win him what he knew, in his heart, he wanted. Maisie. The spoilt, black-haired girl sitting beside him, staring out at the river. As they climbed West Hill, he started to sing, to Mr Malik's tune, words of his own.

> Beautiful girl,
> Beautiful girl,

You don't go with them.
You belong to your people.
You are one of my people.
You will stay mine.
You are one of my people.
Beautiful,
Beautiful,
Beautiful, beautiful girl.

20

The Great Hall of the school was hung with green drapery. A make-shift stage had been erected at the staircase end and, above it, Class 1 had hung a large, hand-painted Islamic crescent moon and star. Samples of their work were laid out on trestle-tables at the side. Mafouz's record-breaking account of the school journey to the Natural History Museum, for which he had been awarded alpha double plus, was in pride of place. *'My Cat'*, it began, *'was in agony due to being hung upside down from our bedroom window by my brother, when I set off in the luxurious coach provided for us. I thought only about my beautiful cat as the huge engines purred and the round wheels revolved enabling us two-legged people to journey in comparative comfort through the streets of London town!'* It had been extensively rewritten by Robert, who was now so good at doing Mafouz's handwriting that it had affected his ability to reproduce his own signature convincingly. In the garden at the back, Sheikh had organised a chemistry exhibition. There was, he had told Mr Malik, a huge explosion planned for 16.00 hours.

It was the school's first Open Day. It was a shame, really, thought Robert as he lugged a crate of lemonade in through the front door, that it was also the day the whole place was due to be consumed in hell-fire. Would Mr and Mrs Husayn get a chance to study MY HOLIDAYS by M. and N. Husayn, a hundred-word masterpiece that it had taken three months to squeeze out of them? Would Mr Mafouz be able to glory in his son's seventeen straight alphas, or to admire his leading part in the headmaster's *The Bowl of Night*, a musical based on *The Rubáiyát of Omar Khayyám*? Would anyone be able to enjoy the first public performance of a pageant, devised and directed by Mr Malik, with the working title of *Islamic Wimbledon*?

'Put the buns on the far tables!' called Maisie. Robert picked up a large cellophane bag, and, with a resentful glance in her direction, pulled it across the polished floor. Outside he could hear the coach bringing Class 1 back from the Museum. There was a squeal of brakes, the sound of Mr Malik ('One at a time, please, gentlemen!') and then a noise as of wild horses galloping across a parquet floor.

Mahmud was the first through the door. He looked with interest and sympathy at Robert, who was setting out paper cups next to the pile of buns. 'Are you mentally ill, sir?' he said, in a small, polite voice.

'Yes!' said Robert.

This seemed to satisfy the boy's curiosity. Behind him came the Husayn twins. They were carrying the Bosnian refugee, feet first.

From the kitchens came the new master, carrying an armful of cardboard chain-mail. Nobody had wanted to play the Crusader, and so it was almost inevitable that the job should go to the Bosnian refugee. He had cheered up when told he was going to have a plastic sword, a cardboard helmet and the chance to run around the stage hitting the Husayn twins.

Mr Malik came into the hall. He gave Robert a brief, concerned glance and clapped his hands together. Next to him, his hand grasping the head's trouser leg, was Hasan.

'Keep an eye on Hasan, Wilson!' said Mr Malik. 'We want to avoid a major incident if we can possibly help it!' Then he turned to the other children and clapped his hands once more. 'Gymnastic boys,' he said, 'out to the garden!'

Behind him came Rafiq. He, too, gave Robert a glance. Then he went up the stairs towards Mr Malik's study. The headmaster caught his eye, and Rafiq turned, shiftily, towards him. 'I have to get some scripts, Headmaster!' he said.

Malik nodded and went to the back of the hall. He opened the door to the garden, and from Classes 2 and 3 a small group of boys in white running-shorts and T-shirts ran silently for the open air. As Rafiq disappeared out of sight at the top of the stairs, Maisie staggered in with a step-ladder and started to put up black drapes at the windows. They looked, from a distance, as if they might well be the remains of her first attempt at Islamic dress.

Mr Chaudhry started to dress the Bosnian refugee. He grinned at Robert. 'Doesn't it remind you of Cuppers?' he said.

Robert put on his Oxford face. 'Dear old Cuppers!' he said. 'How is he?'

Mr Chaudhry chuckled. 'Wilson,' he said, 'you are a joker! All Pembroke men are jokers!'

As Robert was trying to remember whether that was the college he had said he had attended, Mr Malik went over to the far wall and began to pin up the league table of exam results. Every boy in the school was placed, and next to his marks was a small graph illustrating his performance throughout the year. The x-axis was attitude and the y-axis achievement. Most of the graphs were set on a steep, ascending curve, apart from the Husayn twins'; they started in the top left hand corner and were headed, inexorably, for the far right end of the bottom line. Next to each graph was a Polaroid photograph of the boy concerned and his own brief reaction to his assessment. Mafouz had written, 'I have done brilliant. There is no stopping me in the Sports Department. We went on a skiing holiday.'

The Open Day, Robert thought to himself, was physical evidence of how far the school had come during the year. There was a running video of the television documentary about Sheikh, who had, at the beginning of June, gained entrance to Oxford and Cambridge and had published an article in an American scientific journal that an eminent German physicist had described as 'revelatory'. That had generated quite a bit of business.

Robert held on to Hasan's hand as Mr and Mrs Brown, the new parents, came through the now open front door of the school. 'Welcome, Brown!' called Mr Malik.

'The blessings of Allah upon you!' said Mr Brown, an assistant manager at the National Westminster Bank, Mitcham. He was a small, weaselly man of little charisma. It was a puzzle, really, how he had ever risen as high as assistant bank manager, although there were rumours that his immediate superior, Mr Quigley, had been confined to a lunatic asylum after claiming that aliens were about to take over South-West London. 'If he is a Muslim,' Mr Malik had confided to Robert, shortly after the Brown child joined the school, 'then I am the Duke of Edinburgh. He likes our record of academic achievement, that is all.'

Sheikh was not the school's only triumph. Mr Malik had a winning way with the press release. His coup in the *Wimbledon Guardian* was the headline ISLAMIC BOYS SCHOOL HEADS ACADEMIC LEAGUE TABLE. The story mentioned only in passing that the league table was one devised by Mr Malik for assessing Independent Islamic Schools in Wimbledon. A rather hard-line establishment in Southfields – the Islamic Academy of Learning – had been excluded as not being of 'sufficient weight'. He had also stolen Cranborne School's prize physicist, Khan, and had offered a free place to Simon Britton, a boy whose mother had had to take him away from Cranborne because of her financial circumstances.

The Browns started to browse along the wall, and, in ones and twos, other parents made their entrances. Mr Mafouz came in wearing his best blue suit, and dragging his six daughters behind him. Mr Husayn, wearing, as always, a bright floral shirt and smoking a large cigar, came in with a woman who was quite clearly not his wife.

Robert put Hasan on a chair in the corner. The little boy showed no sign of Messianic behaviour. He sat quite still, his delicate hands folded in his lap. Robert looked from Maisie to the headmaster. How had he been so stupid? That was easy to understand. Malik had such a generalized air of gravity that his manner to individuals never conveyed anything of what he might really be thinking. He was standing, now, with Fatimah Bankhead and Mr and Mrs Akhtar, talking of the school's future plans. 'The whole of the west wing,' he was saying, 'will be turned into an art and design complex, while we are starting an appeal for the boat-house! The rowing-team need somewhere to relax and "get their wind" after a damn good session on the river. And we also, obviously, need somewhere to keep the boats. I am fed up with having them in my kitchen!'

The boat-house was news to Robert. As was the fact that they had a west wing. Why did they need a boat-house? Was he planning to restage the battle of Lepanto? They did not even have a rowing-team, as far as he was aware. The man was a swindler. Robert could not stop these thoughts. Ever since he had heard about Maisie and the headmaster they had risen in swarms, like rats leaving a sewer.

There were quite a lot of parents that Robert did not recognize. Over in the corner, by the window, was an elderly man with a white beard, wearing what looked like a cut-down fez. Next to him was a middle-aged character in a suit. As he watched, the two men wandered over to the door that led through to the garden. One thing about them surprised him. Although they were both wearing neatly polished leather footwear, the laces on both of their right shoes were undone, trailing behind them as they walked.

'In ten minutes,' called Mr Malik, 'the pageant will begin!'

Robert crossed to Maisie. She was walking backwards and forwards over the makeshift stage shaking sand on to the boards from a small bucket, trying to evoke the desert sands of Saudi Arabia. In the opening section of the pageant, Mahmud, lying underneath the stage, was due to poke a flag decorated with a crescent moon up through a crack in the stage. The flag was tightly furled, but, at a signal from Mr Malik, three hair-dryers, manned by boys from Dr Ali's class, would be trained on it and, in the headmaster's words, it would 'symbolically flutter across the stage'.

'You're right,' said Robert, 'I am a mess. I need to stop lying. I need to face up to what I am.'

'I shouldn't be too quick to do that,' said Maisie – 'you might not like what you are. I might not like what you are.'

'You can't go on lying to yourself,' said Robert. 'How can you expect people to take you seriously, if you don't have any convictions about anything?'

'Why do you want people to take you seriously?' said Maisie. 'One of the things I like about you is that you're so ridiculous.'

This was not quite how Robert had planned the conversation. Conversations with Maisie had a habit of going astray like this. You would go in there planning to discuss, say, her habit of ogling men in restaurants or her inability to repay money she had borrowed, or her ability to disseminate confidences throughout the whole of Wimbledon about five minutes after they had been imparted to her, and you would end up discussing the state of affairs in Europe, the merits of Beethoven, or, more usually, your own deficiencies.

'What I mean is,' said Robert, 'if I could be . . . you know . . . *me* . . . do you think you could, you . . . sort of . . .'

Maisie kissed him lightly on the cheek. 'I don't think there is a real you, Bobkins,' she said. 'I think you're just wonderfully insubstantial. That's why I love you.'

As opposed to the Islamic loony now prancing around on the other side of the room, thought Robert bitterly. Maybe he could report Malik to some high-up official in the Islamic world. During the summer term the man had consumed about twenty pints of Young's Special a week. Did he ever give to the poor? Not really. He seemed far more concerned to take money off the rich – especially if they happened to be Muslim. Did he believe any more than Robert did? Wasn't religion simply a pose with him, as it was for so many so-called Christians?

And yet – and yet . . . there was something glorious about him. Watching him now, as he shepherded parents in from the garden for the start of the pageant, listening to his deep, authoritative voice, he seemed, to Robert, more English than he himself could ever be. He seemed to summon up an England of green lawns, elegant teas and beautiful women in long dresses, trailing parasols. An England that, these days, existed only in Merchant–Ivory films. There was nothing squalidly European about him. He was imperial in scope.

'Ladies and gentlemen,' called the headmaster, 'we are ready to begin our pageant, to which we have given the lighthearted title *Islamic Wimbledon!*'

There was laughter, and a smattering of applause.

From the stairs came Rafiq, with the two strangers Robert had noticed earlier. If Mr Malik noticed them, he showed no sign of it. They kept to the back of the crowd, hugging the wall in an almost furtive way. Opposite them were two or three other characters Robert could not remember seeing before at the school. One – a round, jolly, brown man of about fifty – was vaguely familiar. He kept shifting from foot to foot, as if in pain. Mr Malik was guiding parents to their chairs.

There had been much discussion about the music. Mr Malik had been keen for it to 'bridge the gap between the musical traditions of East and West', and the result was something that sounded suspiciously like the soundtrack from a commercial advertising Singapore Airlines.

As the lights started to fade, Mr Malik gave the signal to the school's new music master, Mr Kureishi – a small, fat, serious man – who started to belabour an upright piano at the edge of the stage. Class 1 started to sing the opening chorus.

> A few hundred years ago
> In Saudi Arabia
> A man was born—
> A remarkable man,
> With remarkable behaviour!

Mr Malik had tried a number of rhymes for the opening number. He had been unable to find one for 'Mecca', and had rejected a stanza that rhymed 'keener' with 'Medina'. He himself was still not sure about 'Arabia' and 'behaviour', and he coughed loudly when the chorus reached this point in the song.

> He was the seal of the prophets—
> He really was an incredible guy.
> He still has a great deal to teach us,
> And if you listen I'll tell you why.
> Muhammad went up the mountain—
> He was up there for more than an hour –
> But when he came down he was different,
> He had been through the Night of Power.
> He received a Divine Revelation,
> Which we still read to this day.
> And if you read it regularly,
> you'll probably be OK.

At this point, Mahmud started to poke up the flag through the floorboards, and the offstage chorus went into the big number – the words of which were, mercifully, inaudible, but of a general philosophical nature.

As the flag waved around, to tentative applause, Mr Malik stepped into a spotlight and began. 'People have come to Britain from many lands,' he boomed, 'and today the country is a melting-pot! We are an integral ingredient of that pot!'

The audience were no surer of this than they had been of the song. The Islamic world, even in Wimbledon, thought Robert, was not quite ready for the fusion of styles unleashed on it by Mr Malik.

'We must adapt,' he went on, 'and become one with the UK while remaining ourselves. This is the message conveyed to you by the Independent Islamic Wimbledon Day Boys' School!'

As he spoke, various boys in various kinds of national costume trooped from the left and right of the stage; at the same moment, from beneath the stage, Mahmud started to poke a second flag up through the floorboards. It was, Robert noted with a mixture of horror and relief, the Union Jack. Some members of the audience applauded it.

Mr Malik raised his right arm. 'The conflict between Islam and Christianity,' he said, 'is an old battle. And one that no longer needs fighting!'

At this point the Bosnian refugee leaped on to the stage on a small wooden horse, designed and built for him by his mother. From the other side of the acting-space came the Husayn twins, tied together with a cardboard chain. 'Confess your sins, Muslim dogs,' said the Bosnian refugee, in slightly cautious tones, 'and become Christians, or we slash you up!' With these words he ran at the Husayn twins and started to belabour them with his plastic sword.

The boys stood this for as long as was decent, and then, after a particularly heavy blow to the head, the brothers grabbed the Bosnian refugee by both feet and up-ended him over the sand. 'Die, Christian!' said the fatter of the two twins.

This was not, as far as Robert remembered, in the script, but it seemed to be going down rather well with the audience. Mr Mafouz was clapping loudly.

But Robert's eye was no longer seriously drawn to the stage. The fat man over to his right had leaned down to the floor. When he straightened up again, Robert saw that he was carrying something. It was impossible, from this distance, to see what he was wearing on his feet, but it seemed likely that he was one short of a full complement of shoes, because in his right hand he was holding a large, brown, elastic-sided boot. Robert recognized him now: it was the restaurant-owner he had met on the day he had brought home Hasan – Mr Khan. Not only that: his was the round, jolly face he had seen in the window the day he had been hit on the head outside the room where he had been watching the Occultation of the Twenty-fourth Imam of the Wimbledon Dharjees.

21

Now, as he looked around the hall, Robert could see that the whole place was full of single men wearing one shoe. When had they come in? Presumably during the opening sequence of Mr Malik's pageant. It would not have been difficult to have removed the chairs from under the parents watching the curtain-raiser of Mr Malik's production – their attention was concentrated on the stage with what looked like some degree of permanence. Macbeth spotting a character he had recently bumped off could not have showed more interest.

Dr Ali, over by the kitchen door, in the darkness, was rocking backwards and forwards on his haunches, muttering something to himself. It was possible, thought Robert with some satisfaction, that he had finally got around to sentencing his employer to death. Serve the bastard right.

Robert looked around for Hasan. The little boy was no longer on his chair. Nor, as far as Robert could see, was he anywhere in the room. How had he managed to get out on his own?

Mr Malik, apparently unaware that his school was full of Twenty-fourthers, or that the Twenty-fourth Imam himself had started to display some of the talents referred to in Aziz's manuscript ('He shall come and go as he chooses, shall vanish and appear again'), was warming to his theme. 'This,' he said, indicating the Husayn twins, who were now beating the Crusader with his own sword, 'is what happens when religious bigotry rules a nation. We see it in Northern Ireland. We see it in Tehran. We see it in Wimbledon!'

The audience did not like the direction this was taking. Mr Husayn started to mutter something to his neighbour. Two or three of the ladies present clicked their tongues loudly.

Mr Malik went for safe ground. *'Those who believe and do good,'* he went on – *'the merciful will endow them with loving kindness!'*

Fatimah Bankhead was nodding in the gloom, and Mr Mafouz, too, was looking appreciative. Something told Robert that the headmaster had managed to find another line in the Koran that wasn't about chucking people into hell-fire and making them chew dust for the foreseeable future. Malik had got them on his side once again.

'If this school is to survive,' he went on, 'and if the things it stands for are to survive, then it must adapt! We must learn to live in peace with our neighbours!'

The Husayns had now got the Bosnian refugee up against the far wall and were thwacking him in the kidneys with a piece of wood. Malik turned towards them, managing to give the impression that all this was part of a carefully arranged plan, and said, 'Look! Look where hatred and bigotry leads!'

Robert could still not see where Hasan had gone, but he did see the janitor. Aziz was leering, wickedly. In his right hand he held a rather grubby trainer, and he was shaking it at the oblivious headmaster as Malik continued his speech. He looked pleased to have got it off, thought Robert. It must be torment for these guys to have to lace up a whole pair of feet every time they wished to pass themselves off as normal people.

'We are making our own rules,' went on Malik, 'and we must not allow others to dictate them to us. Our prosperity, and the prosperity of our children, depends on it!'

The Bosnian refugee was having trouble breathing. He had collapsed on the ground, and the Husayn twins, having appropriated his horse, were busy riding it round the stage, waving at the audience.

'Let us see them!' called Malik. 'Let us see the children of many lands!'

At this point the plan was for the entire school to process across the stage, carrying flags of many nations and waving their exam certificates. They were then to turn to the audience, waving lengths of green silk and go into a non-representational routine, devised by Mr Malik, entitled *The Dawn of Islam in Wimbledon*. But, as the first wave of boys hit the side of the stage, the Twenty-fourther over to Robert's right – the fat man, restaurant-owning Mr Khan – raised his elastic-sided boot and yelled, 'The Prophet said, "Do not go with only one shoe!" '

Heads in the audience turned. They wore the polite expression of people who assumed that this was part of the show.

The Twenty-fourther was answered from across the hall and all along the stairs – quite a few more of the sect seemed to have crept in during the blackout that had preceded Mr Malik's speech. 'We go with one shoe to show the shame of breaking Islamic law!' they yelled.

Mr Mafouz, who was obviously still convinced that this was part of the pageant, started to applaud vigorously. The boys, who were supposed to file off the stage in order, stopped to peer out past the lights at this interruption, with the result that the next wave of boys collided with those milling around on the sand.

At this moment, Mr Khan the restaurant-owner yelled, 'Down with Malik! Down with Shah! Down with the Wimbledon Independent Boys' Islamic Day School!'

The other Twenty-fourthers, waving their right shoes above their heads, answered with the skill born of long practice, 'Down with Malik! Down with Shah! Down with the Independent Boys' Islamic Day School (Wimbledon)!'

The audience were now definitely convinced this was part of the headmaster's grand design. Mr Mahmud could be heard telling his wife that these people represented narrowness and intolerance in the Islamic world, and that they would shortly be vanquished by the rightly guided headmaster.

Before this happened, however, Rafiq, who had up to this point been seated with the staff and parents, leaped to his feet and, in full sight of the assembly, yanked off his right shoe. He seemed to be wearing wellington boots, and he had clearly not changed his socks for some days, because the people near him started to scrape their chairs across the floor in an effort to escape. 'Mr Khan here has been betrayed by the man who bears the name of Shah!' he yelled. 'That Shah is a hypocrite Muslim! He has not given his promised support to The Taste of Empire tandoori restaurant. Especially on Wednesdays!'

He pointed at the school's principal benefactor, the tall man in the elegantly cut suit who still bore an uncanny resemblance to the Duke of Edinburgh. This Mr Shah was looking at Mr Khan in a hurt and puzzled manner. 'My dear man,' he began to say – 'if this is part of our business disagreement – '

But, before he could finish, Rafiq heaved his wellington boot at the members of the school now threshing around on the stage under the lights. His example was followed by many of his companions. A hail of plimsolls, trainers, leather shoes, mountain boots and sandals rose up in the air and rained down on boys, parents and teachers.

Robert could see that Mr Malik, who still seemed remarkably unworried by all this, was signalling to someone at the back of the hall, behind him. And then the lights went out.

For a moment everything was quiet. *This is it*, thought Robert, *Molotov cocktails!* Next to him a woman was whispering something, although he could not hear what it was or what language she was speaking. Suddenly, high up above the stage, as high as that afternoon on the other side of the Common, a light flicked on and Hasan stood before them. At first Robert thought he was hovering above the blacked-out room; then he saw that he had been slipped over the banisters of the stairs and was perched, perilously, on the edge of one of the steps.

He was dressed all in white, in a long, flowing garment of bright silk. On his left foot was a golden sandal. His right foot was naked. He stretched out his hands over the faces of the crowd and began to speak. 'Bow down,' he began:

> Bow down and listen to my words!
> You are led by the wicked!
> You are led by transgressors!
> We wear one shoe
> To show your leaders have lied to you.
> Bow down.
> Bow down and listen to my words!

Quite a few people actually did start to bow down. Robert himself, now fairly well trained in the act of Islamic prayer, felt a strong urge to make, head first, for the parquet floor. The little boy's voice was so eerily still! His face so withdrawn and delicate! His shoulders seemed to beg some invisible presence for mercy!

> My father stabbed the seducer Hasan.
> I am the son of Hasan b. Namawar.
> I am the rightful Twenty-fourth Imam,
> And I return to punish.
> Bow down.
> There is fire in my fingers.
> Bow down!

Rafiq, observing the early success of this performance, joined in well. 'Bow down!' he yelled. 'Bow down! Do not serve the hypocrites! Bow down!'

Behind Robert a woman started to hiss. Whether it was fear or anger or pleasure that made her do so was impossible to tell. All over the hall, people were murmuring and hissing and breathing in sharply. This, thought Robert, was entirely reasonable. As apparitions go, Hasan was certainly in the Angel Gabriel class. At a school Open Day he was a guaranteed sensation.

Hasan's fingers quivered as he stretched out his hands over the audience, but whether it was in a blessing or a curse was impossible to tell. His sightless eyes sought the light as he went on:

> Do not listen to the seducer.
> Do not listen to those who would lead you.
> Do not listen to those who betray the Law.
> I am the Twenty-fourth Imam.
> I come to destroy all this.
> I come to destroy this school!

People were getting quite emotional. Apart from Mr Mafouz, who was heard to announce that this was the best damn show he had seen since *The Bodyguard*, most of the parents seemed entirely convinced by Hasan's performance. One or two were openly crying. As the little boy's voice rose to a shriek the Twenty-fourthers came in, like Elvis Presley's backing group, perfectly on cue.

Destroy this school!
Bow down!
Destroy this man!
Destroy the seducer Malik!
Bow down!
There is fire in his fingers!
Bow down!

In the gloom, Robert could see that Rafiq was fumbling with something underneath his jacket. Aziz the janitor, now up on the stairs, seemed to be holding something, and, with a shock, Robert realized it was a lighted match. *They really are*, he thought – *they really are going to burn the place to the ground.*

It was then that the lights came on – not just a single lamp, but a whole battery of arc lights ranged along the stage. It seemed, at first, like a deliberate theatrical effect, which indeed it probably was. And, if the Twenty-fourthers had a developed sense of theatre, they were mere amateurs compared to the man who now strode to the centre of the stage – Mr Malik, the one and only headmaster of the Boys' Independent Day Islamic Wimbledon School. His voice rose over Hasan's as he stretched his huge hands up towards the boy. 'Who has done this evil thing to you?' he said.

It was fairly obvious, to Robert anyway, who had done this evil thing to the little boy, but that didn't deprive the headmaster's rhetorical question of any of its power.

'Who has filled your head with lies?' went on Malik. 'Who is the real seducer here? Who are the real seducers?'

The audience were now thoroughly enjoying this. They had not been sure about the song; the flags of many nations had left them decidedly cold; but this, their faces seemed to say, was worth leaving the shop to see.

'I will tell you,' went on Malik. 'This man Rafiq, who has claimed to be my friend, has sought to get his hands on a profitable enterprise. As has this fat swine Khan – a man who has the business ethics of a stoat!'

Hasan knew when he was outclassed. Anyway, in the rehearsal

process to which he had been undoubtedly subjected by Rafiq and his friends, presumably no allowance had been made for an Oscar-award-winning interruption from the headmaster.

Malik was now waving something above his head, and the Twenty-fourthers were looking at it with some interest. Robert recognized it as the manuscript that had been given him, along with the locket, last summer.

'This,' Malik shrieked, 'is the "document" that tells the story of the Twenty-fourth Imam. This is the "document" that gave substance to what, in previous times, were only whispers and rumours – a secret as closely guarded as the Golden Calf of the Druze. This is the "prophecy" with which my so-called friend has deceived you and deceived this child!'

Here he rounded on Rafiq, who, Robert now saw, was busy stuffing what looked like an oiled rag into a milk bottle.

'It is a forgery!' shouted Malik. 'I can prove it is a forgery! This gentleman here – this Khan – is the manager of The Taste of Empire restaurant, Balham, and owes our benefactor a considerable sum of money. He has exploited the credulity of a section of the Wimbledon Dharjees in an attempt to wreck a business rival!'

Rafiq, the bottle in one hand, was now snarling at his employer. But his one-shoed companions, like the rest of the audience, were giving signs of enjoying the show.

Robert was more confused than ever. What was this religion, where what looked like theology turned out to be politics? Where loyalties and friendships seemed to acquire the force of a mystical belief? Where God was not a remote, almost human presence but a chord struck in the communal mind, echoing into every corner of life, facing you when you argued or made love or fought for money or power? He had no place here. He did not – could not – belong.

'The Twenty-third Imam – ' began Rafiq.

'There is no hidden imam among the Nizari Ismailis,' said Mr Malik. 'The Twenty-third Imam was, as you quite rightly say, stabbed by Hasan b. Namawar, but there is no record of the assassin having issue. You have taken a piece of true history and doctored it, gentlemen!'

The parents and staff gave this a round of well-deserved applause. Mr Akhtar was heard to say that the opening part of the pageant had been a total let-down, but this was 'world class' and gave evidence of 'money well spent'. People could be heard muttering that Malik was a man to watch.

And then the headmaster reached down, pulled off one of his expensive brown brogues, and waved it above his head. 'See!' he yelled. 'See! I go with one shoe!'

Everyone leaned forward in their seats. Robert, wondering whether he was about to witness a spectacular conversion, held his breath.

'I go with one shoe, my people,' went on Mr Malik, 'as my so-called "friend" asks you to do! And do you know what will happen if I go with one shoe?'

'What will happen?' asked a Twenty-fourther, who was clearly expert at this kind of dialogue. 'Tell us – what will happen?'

22

By way of reply, Mr Malik ran around the stage gobbling like a chicken for some seconds. He not only gobbled, he brandished the shoe and twitched, and did a fair impression of a man who has taken complete leave of his senses. Then he stopped and rounded on Rafiq. 'I will get my feet wet!' he yelled. 'I will carry on like a lunatic and be of no use to anyone!'

Then he turned to face the audience. He drew himself up to his full height and said, 'We must learn to fight for what is rightfully ours and also *to live in peace with our neighbours*. Do we wish our sons to go to war?'

There were shouts of 'No No!' and 'We do not wish this!' Robert was not aware of any immediate plans for conscription in the Wimbledon area, but the assembled crowd, who were showing as much volatility as the Roman plebeians after the death of Caesar, pressed in on the stage, shouting, crying, and waving their hands in the air.

'I put on my shoe!' screamed the headmaster. 'And I advise you to do the same!'

All over the darkened hall, men started to struggle back into their footwear – those, that is, who had not hurled it on to the stage. Those who had done so were openly weeping and grabbing hold of their neighbours' laces. Even Aziz the janitor was, in a highly emotional manner, trying to get his right toe into a canvas boot, although where he had got this from was unclear.

'Put on your shoes,' yelled the headmaster, 'and keep them on your feet always!'

Several people were trying to persuade Rafiq to put on his shoe, though whether this was for religious or hygienic reasons was not obvious. He did not seem keen to do so. Mr Mafouz had got hold of him and was beating his head against the back wall.

'Put on your shoes,' cried Malik again, 'I beg you! I beseech you! I implore you to do so! In the words of the Prophet to Abu Hurayra, *"Don't walk with only one shoe. Either go barefoot or wear shoes on both feet!"* '

This seemed to decide matters once and for all. Quite a few people took off both shoes, and those who didn't borrowed other people's until almost everyone in the room, apart from the engineering master, was equipped with a pair of properly Islamic feet. This generated a welcome and often jolly spirit of conviviality about the place. People were laughing and joking, clapping each other on the back and helping each other find some way of getting properly attired below the ankles.

Truth, Robert's old history master was fond of saying, *is whatever is confidently asserted and plausibly maintained.* The world of Islam seemed more purely about society than he had ever supposed possible. Islam, he saw clearly as if for the first time, was a nation, a nation on the march. It was only now that he finally understood a favourite phrase of the headmaster's: *Belief, my dear Wilson, is for us an intimate part of the social contract. It was Ayatollah Khomeini who pointed out that 'Islam is politics!'*

And Mr Malik was no ordinary politician. No one even seemed bothered about testing his claim that the document was a forgery. He was a strong man, and his word – like the Prophet's – was law.

Robert thought, bitterly, about Malik. Why should the man find everything so easy when Robert found it so hard? Why could *he* sway a room with a few well-chosen sentences, when on one of the few occasions when Robert had opened his mouth to express his real feelings he had been sentenced to death by a deranged mathematics master? Why was life so unfair? Was the reason the man was so complacent to do with the fact that his religion was *right*? That fate, destiny, whatever you liked to call it, was now on his side and the world was slowly turning his way, so that soon the power and the glory would all come from a long way east of Wimbledon?

Whatever the reason, something in Robert Wilson snapped. 'Who gives a toss how many shoes you wear?' he heard himself shout into a sudden silence. 'Who gives a toss? And who gives a monkeys how many blows it takes you to polish off a wall gecko, frankly? I mean, why is it that *all* you people construct your lives around the not very reliably reported table talk of a man whose chief claim to fame would seem to be his talent for carving up his immediate neighbours in some God-forsaken chunk of desert?'

The silence that had preceded his remarks seemed to lengthen miraculously.

'All I'm saying,' said Robert, 'is that when I joined this school I knew absolutely nothing about the Muslim faith, and that, after teaching here for a year, I really feel that ignorance is bliss, frankly!'

Up on the stage the colour was draining from the headmaster's face. He moved towards Robert, and his voice had the throaty intensity of a cello in the slow movement of the Elgar concerto. 'Wilson,' he said, reaching out towards his first recruit. 'Wilson! Do you know what you are saying? You are a Muslim, Wilson, are you not?'

'No,' said Robert, with some satisfaction – 'I am not. I have never been a Muslim. I do not wish to be a Muslim. I have no plans to be a Muslim. I would, frankly, rather swim the Hellespont in November than be a Muslim.'

This did not go down well with the punters. Many of them looked as if they might well be breaking into tears in the near future.

Mr Malik held out his arms to Robert. 'Wilson – ' he began.

'Oh, stop calling me "Wilson", can't you?' said Robert – 'as if we were both at some non-existent public school. You live in a fantasy world. And you don't know anything about me. You don't know who I am, or what I think, or what I feel about anything.'

Mr Malik looked utterly devastated. 'Wilson,' he began, in a trembling voice. 'You are a Muslim. And, as a Muslim – '

'I am not a Muslim,' said Robert. 'I only said I was because I needed a job. I am not – repeat, not – Muslim. Do I look like a Muslim?'

The crowd fastened on this new act with enthusiasm. Mr Akhtar could be heard to say that Robert did not look like a Muslim. Indeed, he had always thought there was something funny about Wilson. Mr Mafouz, his thick, black eyebrows well down in his face, was fighting his way through the crowd towards his son's form master.

Robert started to walk up to the stage, and, like the Red Sea, parents, staff and pupils parted to let him pass.

Mr Malik had recovered well. He was managing some kind of transition, from deeply wounded to sad but hopeful. 'I suppose,' he said, 'someone who lies out of fear of or respect for the truth is to be helped and not scorned. I liked you, Wilson, because I saw your weakness. Like you, I feel, I am not a very good Muslim!'

The house was divided on this. Some people thought the head-master was an absolutely first-class Muslim, while Dr Ali declared him to be a blasphemer, a hypocrite and no better than the vomit of a dog.

'It's not a question of not being a *good* Muslim,' yelled Robert, as he climbed up on to the stage – 'I just am not a Muslim at all. I am an imitation Muslim, ladies and gentlemen. How many times do I have to say this to get it into your head?'

Fatimah Bankhead told her immediate neighbour that she viewed this as an encouraging sign. Imitation, she said, was the sincerest form of flattery.

Up on the stage, Mr Malik spread his hands in a gesture of endless tolerance. 'Perhaps,' he said, 'you will come to understand that – '

'I will never come to understand,' said Robert, 'because your religion is, to me, completely and utterly incomprehensible. I believe – '

Malik brightened a little at this remark. 'What do you believe, Wilson?'

Robert looked down from the stage at the faces of the crowd. He saw Mahmud, his eyes wide with horror at what was happening. He saw Dr Ali, his nose quivering with excitement, tensing himself like a man about to burst into song. And he saw Maisie. She was by the door to the front garden. Her big, black eyes looked reproach-fully up at him from the white oval of her face. What did he believe? The question she was always asking him.

'Oh,' he said, 'I believe in something really sensible. Of course. I believe that Jesus Christ came down from heaven and was born of a Virgin, turned water into wine, walked on the water, and then was crucified and whizzed back up to heaven!'

Mr Malik stretched out his arms to him. 'There is no need to caricature your beliefs, Wilson,' he said. 'If you have lied to us, you have lied for a reason. The great religions of the world have more in common than you might think. And if we worship one God – '

'Oh, then that's fine, isn't it?' said Robert. 'I'll swap you the Garden of Gethsemane for the Night of Power, you know? You'll let us believe something clearly insane, and we can allow you to do the same.'

Mr Malik's brow wrinkled. He seemed upset again. 'What are you saying, Wilson? I do not understand. You are a Christian? You are a Muslim? What are you?'

Robert strode across the sand towards his headmaster. Between them lay the cardboard chain-mail and the plastic sword that had belonged to the Bosnian refugee, who was now being given mouth-to-mouth resuscitation by Mr Husayn. Robert picked up the imitation Crusader armour and held it aloft, facing out to the audience. 'I'm nothing,' he said. 'Don't you understand? England is full of people who are nothing. You're living in a country that doesn't exist. A country where people go to church, and try and help their neighbours, and bicycle to work down country lanes, and believe in . . .' Here he brandished the armour and its painted cross in the faces of the crowd. ' . . . all this!'

The Bosnian refugee, coming round in the arms of Mr Husayn, was heard to order his men to slay the Saracen dogs.

Robert rounded on Mr Malik. He had always thought, somehow, that Malik had seen through him. That the headmaster was keeping him on for his own private amusement. And it was this knowledge that allowed him to suspect that, at last, someone had really understood quite how empty he was inside. What finally broke him was the realization that here was yet another person who, like his parents, thought him a stronger, nobler person than he actually was. Why did the world assume that you must be interested in any kind of truth, let alone the fundamental variety? Why did people always want you to have aspirations?

'England,' went on Robert, 'is no longer anything to *do* with the country that carved up India or shipped out whole generations of

Africans as slaves. It's a squalid little place, full of people who don't believe in anything. Am I making that clear? I don't believe in *any-thing*. I think it's all a load of toss really. That is my considered opinion.'

Mr Malik looked at his first member of staff. There was infinite sadness in his eyes. 'You believe in something, Wilson,' he said. 'You must believe in something. Everyone must believe in something.'

Robert looked across at Maisie. He felt suddenly tired. As if all these people were a dream. As if he had been asleep for a whole year. He would say what he had to say, and then he would leave. He would get out – not only of the school, but of the suburb. He would find somewhere a long way away from Mr Malik, from his parents, and from everyone else who wished him well.

'Maybe I do,' he said eventually. 'Maybe I do.'

Then, with the cardboard armour in one hand and the plastic sword in the other, he stepped slowly down from the stage and walked through the assembly to where Maisie was waiting.

'Look,' he said, 'you're the only person who understands. We're . . . well, we're . . . Wimbledon, aren't we? What are you doing here? You know you don't belong here, don't you?'

Maisie looked back at him steadily.

'I'm going!' he said. 'Will you come with me?'

Maisie looked at him. She sighed. Then she looked up at the head-master, standing on the shabby stage in his crumpled green suit. Malik mopped his forehead, glowing under the lights.

'No,' she said – 'I won't!'

23

Robert had not expected her to say this.

'Why not?' he said.

She looked impatient. 'Because, Bobkins,' she said, 'I love him.'

'Love who?' said Robert.

'Mr Malik!' said Maisie.

This created a sensation in the audience. If they had ever had doubts about their headmaster, they were dispelled instantly. The general feeling seemed to be that not only was Mr Malik a good public speaker and a man of learning and conviction, he had also performed well in the Islamic virility stakes.

Up on the platform, Mr Malik was positively preening himself. He smoothed his hair back over his ears and gave a little smile at a mother in the front row.

'You *love* him?'

'I'm afraid I do, Bobkins!' said Maisie, with a sigh. 'I'm afraid he means more to me than anything else.' She shook her head, and her thick, black hair trembled under her scarf. One of the spotlights caught her face.

'Why?' said Robert.

'I don't know,' replied Maisie. 'Maybe it's Muslim men. They have something you just don't have!'

Robert did not like the way this conversation was going, but there seemed no easy way to get control either over it or over its alarmingly public nature.

'What,' said Robert with heavy irony, 'do Muslim men have that I don't?'

He recalled, with some bitterness, that it was only after he had publicly announced his conversion that she had become interested in him. Was she just kinky for Muslims, the way some people were

kinky for football-players or trombonists? Perhaps he should recon-
sider his position.

'They're virile,' said Maisie. 'They're strong! They're decisive!
They're proud and certain and noble!'

This went down incredibly well with the male members of the
audience. Even Rafiq could be heard to say that this was fair comment. Mr Mafouz, who had been looking deeply depressed during
Robert's altercation with the headmaster, straightened himself up
and threw out his chest. Mr Akhtar was seen to stroke his
moustache.

'They're gentle, too,' went on Maisie, 'and loyal and straightforward and kind and clever and respectful and good with children
and God-fearing!'

This brought a smattering of applause. Robert looked up at the
headmaster, who was stretching out his hands to Maisie. 'Come to
me, my daughter!' said Malik, in deep, resonant tones. Maisie
squared her shoulders and, with a toss of her head, prepared to come
to him. She looked, thought Robert grimly, as if she was prepared to
get on the floor and kiss his feet should this prove necessary.

'I wonder why this should be!' shrieked Robert. 'What is it makes
them so amazingly wonderful? Is it that they don't drink except
behind closed doors? Is it halal meat – is that it? Is it that they have
devised an unusually energetic form of prayer?'

Mr Malik, his eyes big with grief, was still holding out his hands to
Maisie. 'Maisie,' he said, 'come to me! And, Wilson, go! Go in peace.
Without curses or recrimination.' He put his head to one side. 'If you
have been foolish,' he said, 'God will forgive you. He forgives the
ignorant.'

Maisie started towards the stage. As she walked, women touched
her dress, murmuring words of encouragement, and men, with wistful smiles on their faces, stepped back to let her pass.

'I suppose,' yelled Robert, 'it's their role model! I suppose it's
because Muhammad was such a terrific guy! Is that it?'

No one answered this question, but there was suddenly a dangerous silence in the room.

'I mean,' went on Robert, shaking his long, lank, blond hair across his face, 'it may just be that I'm an ignorant Brit and don't know anything about anything, but the thing that really puzzles me about your religion is the endless respect you're supposed to pay to this guy. What is it all in aid of, may I ask? I mean, who was he? What makes him such a big cheese?'

Mr Malik glanced down at the audience. He looked worried. 'Please, Wilson,' he said, 'go now. Go back into Wimbledon, and we will forget that we ever met. Do not – '

'I'm only asking,' said Robert, 'because I have picked up a little gen about Islam over the course of the last year and I have formulated my view of your top man which, if you like, I will be happy to give to you!'

Mr Malik, and several others in the audience, winced visibly. 'I really would not do that if I was you, Wilson!' said the headmaster.

But Robert did it.

He went on to give detailed, and not always accurate, criticisms of the *hadiths* of the Prophet. He questioned their relevance to modern society, their internal logic, and their implications for women, infidels and anyone not prepared to accept the central tenets of Islam. He quoted several at length, and laughed, mockingly, during his rendition of them.

After he had questioned the Prophet's reported views, he went on to denigrate his character in sometimes offensive terms. He went on to criticize, in an uninformed way, the Prophet's skill as a military tactician, and made several spectacularly ill-informed remarks about the history of Islam.

At this point, Mr Malik, who like almost everyone else in the room had his hands over his ears, begged him to stop. He explained that one of the missions of the Wimbledon Islamic Independent Boys' Day School was to make peace between religions and communities, and that he, personally, along with the Wimbledon Dharjee businessman Mr Shah, had worked hard over the last year to create an institution that would 'build bridges' between Muslims and Christians and, indeed, any other decent, civilized individuals who were prepared to let others live with their faith without insult or abuse. He wept at this point.

He explained how Mr Shah's rival, the restaurant-owning Mr Khan, had been trying to destroy the unity of the Muslim community, and said that their unity was only an aspect of the wider union that peace-loving and civilized Muslim men and women sought with the country to which they had come.

He went on to beg Robert not to say any more. He said that, unlike certain people he could mention in the hall – here he looked narrowly at Rafiq and Dr Ali – he was a reasonable man, and that some in his community had said he was 'a hypocrite' because he went too far in accommodating others' beliefs and opinions. He said he was not a hypocrite. He repeated that he was a sincere, if not always scrupulous, Muslim, and he repeated several *hadiths* of the Prophet – to whom, in this context, he gave the traditional blessing – to support his view that Islam was a tolerant, generous and beautifully constructed faith.

But, he said, there was a limit. Many people in the hall agreed, and said, loudly, that Robert Wilson had already passed it. Dr Ali made reference to his earlier sentence on the reception-class teacher, and several parents said that this was 'too good' for the young man who was now standing by the door, open to the summer day, waving a plastic sword and cardboard armour decorated with a crucifix at pupils, teachers and parents associated with the Wimbledon Islamic Independent Boys' Day School.

'Why do you all think you're *right*?' Robert was yelling. 'What makes you so *certain*?'

Mr Malik begged for silence, and got it. He appealed to Robert Wilson as an English gentleman. He appealed to his sense of honour and fair play. He mentioned the British royal family and the ancient universities of Oxford and Cambridge, to which, he reminded him, he belonged, and he spoke, movingly, of the game of cricket. 'Try and play a straight bat, Wilson!' he said.

Robert said he was not an English gentleman and he was incapable of playing a straight bat. He said that he had only played cricket once or twice, and that throughout his schooldays he had persuaded his mother to 'write him a note'. He said he had lied about a great deal more than being or not being a Muslim. He told

Mr Chaudhry, whom he referred to as 'the Nabob', that he had never been to Oxford or Cambridge, that he had no academic qualifications whatsoever apart from a GCE in woodwork, and that if Mr Malik had not been such a 'gullible idiot' he would never have employed someone so obviously fraudulent as he, Robert Wilson. He maintained, also, that he felt no loyalty to his family, describing his father as 'the kind of guy you would not want to get stuck in a lift with' and his mother as 'Wimbledon's answer to Jackie Onassis'.

He went on to talk about Wimbledon. He put forward the view that almost everyone in Wimbledon was, like him, completely lacking in convictions, principles or indeed anything that makes human beings tolerable. He said Wimbledon was 'an armpit'. 'Why did the Bhajjis, or whatever they call themselves, bother to cross the world to *Wimbledon*?' he asked. He foamed at the mouth at this point, and started to bang his plastic sword on the front door.

He then went on to make several spectacularly insulting, ill-thought-out remarks about the Koran. He added that *Morals and Manners in Islam* by Marwan Ibrahim Al-Kaysi was the most boring book he had ever read.

At this point he returned, once again, to the subject of Muhammad, saying that he had 'one or two home truths to put across'. He began, once again, to make wildly inaccurate and distorted remarks about the Prophet. It was at this point – and it is not necessary here to mention even the general drift of his remarks, except to say that they were offensive in the extreme – that several members of the school, both parents and staff, started towards him in an urgent and often openly angry manner. They pulled at his clothes, and he responded by beating them around the head with his plastic sword.

The headmaster appealed for calm. He did not get it. Robert ran for the street.

He was followed by Mr Mafouz, Mr and Mrs Akhtar, Mr and Mrs Mahmud, Mr Sheikh, Mr Shah, running side by side with the restaurant-owning Mr Khan, Mr and Mrs Husayn, Fatimah Bankhead, the parents of the Bosnian refugee (whose name no one could pronounce), Mr and Mrs Khan, Mr Malik, Dr Ali, Rafiq (who was now wearing two left-footed wellington boots) and Maisie. Behind them came other parents and every single child in the school – people united not only by a common faith and a common confidence and belief in their school but also by a deep desire to beat Robert Wilson to a pulp.

He ran fast. People who saw him pass – and there were people in the High Street on that summer afternoon who had known him since he was a boy – agreed that he had never run so fast in his life. His lank, blond hair bounced off his temples, and his long, thin legs pounded the pavement as, behind him, over a hundred very angry British Muslims screamed, shook their fists, and spat at his heels.

They did not catch him. Robert ran down the High Street towards Wimbledon Hill. By the time he reached the roundabout at the top of the hill and swerved right along the Ridgeway, they were spread out in a long line behind him. But none of them gave up the pursuit. Several women, who joined in enthusiastically, were in tears. The men at the head of the chase – Mr Mafouz and Mr Sheikh – were starting to gain on him as he panted his way past trim suburban houses, his face purple with effort, his neck damp with sweat.

Only one person did not seek to follow Robert Wilson, 'the fraudulent Muslim, the apostate and the blasphemer', as he later became known inside the community. He was left behind on the stairs above the makeshift stage in the Great Hall. Hasan tilted his fragile little face up at the lights as the crowd screamed and jostled out of the school, but he made no sound himself. He put his big, ungainly head to one side, like a bird listening for worms.

He gave no sign of hearing the commotion. Or of the lorry that roared past the school, turned right at the roundabout, and thundered down the Ridgeway. Or of the wild squeal of its brakes as Robert, too frightened and exhausted to look, darted out into its path. Or of the noise of the ambulance siren, wailing like a call to prayer, as it sped up the hill to take Robert away. The only thing to which Hasan seemed to be listening was silence. The silence that had been there before all these little, local noises. The silence that he had seemed to hear behind the cries and shouts in the hall and that was there, once more, stretching endlessly away, after they, like the ambulance, had departed.

24

The Wimbledon Islamic Independent Day School for Boys is still there. And, in case there should be any doubt about the word order of the title, Mr Malik has erected a large, handsome notice-board in the front garden. You may see the buildings as you pass down the High Street going south. The school has now bought two buildings on either side and is negotiating for a large playing-field in Raynes Park.

Maisie and Mr Malik were married in the autumn term that followed Robert's accident. They started to have children almost immediately. Maisie gave the headmaster two boys – Yusuf and Ahmed – causing several people to remark, openly, that he 'had very strong seed' – and, subsequently, a girl whom Maisie insisted on calling Roberta. The children are all polite, hard-working and well-behaved Muslims.

The school has prospered too. It now has a total staff of twelve, including Dr Ali, who has not sentenced anyone to death for years, and Rafiq, who has sworn eternal allegiance to Mr Malik and frequently describes him as 'a genius'. Mr Malik himself has not touched alcohol for four years, and, while observing his duties as a Muslim most carefully, is still fond of quoting *hadiths* that emphasize the Prophet's tolerance and good sense.

The pupils, too, are doing well (although Anwar Mafouz failed all his GCSEs and now works with his father in the travel agency). Sheikh took up his Oxford place at the age of fifteen, and one of the Husayn twins, to the surprise of his father, gained a place at Exeter University (although his brother is now serving a short sentence at an open prison near Winchester). The school is often spoken of as a model for others in the neighbourhood, and last year it defeated Cranborne at cricket, rugby, cross-country running and chess. There is even talk of admitting some non-Muslim children and for them to be allowed to form a Christian Circle when the others are at daily prayers.

Hasan was sent back to live with Mr Shah. He is a big boy now and helps out at the school. Mr Malik has taught him Braille, and he compiles mailing-lists of prospective parents. He never mentions his Occultation, although once or twice he has been heard telling the school cat that he is someone rather important.

Aziz, too, is a reformed character. He cleans the whole school, from top to bottom, three times a week. 'Say what you like,' he can be heard to say with a grin – 'Dharjee, Ismaili, we are all Muslim and we all must be brothers and not surrender or oppress!'

Robert Wilson recovered from his encounter with the lorry; it was generally agreed he got off more lightly than he would have done had he fallen into the hands of the local Muslim population. He has never really been the same since, although his mother told a neighbour recently that 'he was always as hopeless as this really'. He has a set of symptoms – listlessness, lack of interest in the world, and a tendency to sleep more than twelve to fifteen hours out of the twenty-four – that make him unfit for any kind of regular employment, but at least now he has a doctor's note to explain the fact to the authorities.

He still lives at home. He spends most of his days walking Badger across the Common. He always takes the same route. He follows the golf course, past Caesar's Camp, up to the Windmill and then returns to Wimbledon Park Road via one of the streets that slope down from Parkside, past quiet, ordered suburban houses, protected by English trees and English lawns. He never walks on the same side of the road as the Wimbledon Islamic Independent Day School for Boys, and if he happens to pass the place he turns his eyes away.

As he walks, he mutters to himself, though no one has ever heard what he is saying or understood why he sometimes gets angry or agitated. If a passer-by stops to talk to him – which few do, since his moods can be unpredictable – he will stand and chat for hours. Sometimes he is to be found in the Frog and Ferret, with the dog by his side, and there he usually spends hours talking to Mr Purkiss of the Wimbledon Interplanetary Society. People keep away from them. Unlike Mr Shah, who has opened two new shops in the High Street, or plump Mr Kureishi, who gives recitals in the public library, they are not really part of the community of Wimbledon.

AUTHOR'S NOTE

The Wimbledon Dharjees are, of course, an entirely fictitious Islamic sect, but the group from which they are alleged to come, the Nizari Ismailis, are a real and well-documented group of Shiite Muslims. A full account of the true, and incredible, story of Hasan the Second, the Twenty-third Imam of the Nizari Ismailis, is to be found in Bernard Lewis's *The Assassins* (Weidenfeld & Nicolson, 1967). Robert's one guide to his assumed religion, *Morals and Manners in Islam, a Guide to Islamic Adab*, by Marwan Ibrahim Al-Kaysi, was published by the Islamic Foundation in 1986.